Skara

SKARA

The First Wave

New life for Neolithic Orkney, vol. I

Andrew Appleby

Burgess Publishing

Published in Britain in 2015 by Burgess Publishing

4 Burgess Road, Southampton UK, SO16 7NX

www.burgessprep.com

A CIP record is available from the British Library.

ISBN Print: 978-0-9932812-4-2 (paperback, rev. & illustrated edn)

Printed in UK by CPI Antony Rowe.

www.skarabook.com

Contact: admin@skarabook.com

Dedication

Dedicated to my wonderful wife, Sigrid.

Contents

Why I Wrote Skara

Since the late 1970s I have yearned to write a Neolithic epic set in Orkney. I began it after a Christmas Eve walk on Birsay Beach with my wife, Sigrid. We watched the redshanks running in the ebb and across the wet sands. I said, 'At last I have the beginning and end of my book. It starts with a tsunami and ends with one'. I began *Skara* that evening, introducing Shala, her family and fellow villagers. By then I had decided that the first great wave would be described as a race memory in later storytelling. This is where the powerful character of Wrasse appears. Two days later, the huge tsunami hit Indonesia.

Skara, with Shala and Oiwa, is the first novel in this series. It sets the scene for momentous movements in knowledge and political power in Orkney. But first, the Isles were suffering from inbreeding. These dangers had to be countered, hence the spiritual insights of Shala and Wrasse – I firmly support race memory and the predictive force of dreams, having experienced these in quite abrupt and physical ways. From Skara Brae or Birsay, gazing west across the Atlantic, the next stop is unimaginably distant. This is from where I chose the hero, Oiwa, to travel. He had his reasons, as you will discover, and underwent terrible yet wondrous adventures.

My inspiration for the series has been my lifelong interest in archaeology. I have always earnestly believed that Orkney was a great centre of knowledge and culture, influencing world thinking at a time when early civilisations were about to burgeon, but there is virtually no material evidence to back this up. Only when you think deeply about the sites, the dates in world history and how the islanders were modern people in their time, at the forefront of technical advances and natural wisdom, does the notion become plausible.

The skills of people who use early technologies also fill me with inspiration. Their efficiency of movement, style and concentration bring spectacular results and the simple, yet effective 'struggle for mere existence' becomes a rich, rewarding lifestyle. I always tend to look at evidence with an alternative view and my experiments in ancient pottery, cooking and material culture have given me skills and knowledge of the past. I enjoy putting flesh on ancient bones, brains in their skulls, hunger and satisfaction in their bodies and, of course, love and lust in their hearts. I feel that many archaeologists tend to de-personalise the lives of people from the past and misinterpret perfectly ordinary discoveries as ritual. My characters are intensely practical in the way they live. Cult is there, but takes second place to real life.

There is an old Orkney expression, 'If it's hard work, you're doing it wrong'. We look back assuming everything in the distant past was difficult and survival was tortuous. Yet, as the great explorer John Rae discovered, if you take your example from the locals, there is always a right way, and a time and place to work miracles.

Andrew

PS I read Homer after finishing writing *Skara,* then I went back to my draft and put in the parts about the burning of caribou and ox femurs, etc. I feel this actually has relevance to Neolithic Orkney, looking at the lack of femurs from certain sites.

Foreword by Ari Berk

The first time I stepped foot on Orkney, I felt as though I was walking into a song, a sort of chorus of stone, sea, wind, and time. Reading Andrew Appleby's *Skara*, I can hear a continuation, a new verse, of that same song.

It is perhaps Andrew's familiarity with the earth of Orkney that gives *Skara* its honesty and its characters their believability. It is always a challenge to create a world from far-distant ancient cultures, especially from those that have no written epics to carry their feelings and fears to us directly. Nevertheless, Neolithic people's lives can be read, subtly, in the fragments and clues they've left behind. We can see archeology and a strong imagination at work in *Skara*. Both are required to make the past of Orkney speak, and Andrew is that rare writer able to read the palimpsest of stones and summon with them.

The well-limned folk of *Skara* bring the past once again into the circle of the sun. Though their world exists across a considerable chasm of time, they feel as sure and real as the land beneath our feet, even now. *Skara* is an inviting world, a world much smaller than our modern one, yet far vaster in its vision. It is a place where the elemental gods walk close beside the people of place; where word and spell give name to innumerable aspects of sacredness and make thin the boundary between human and animal; it is a world where ancestors are not lost in death, but honored in tabernacles of stone that render family and clan eternal. In its sacred honoring of family and memory, and of the sea, *Skara* presents a world that has much to teach our own.

Foreword by Ari Berk

It is no accident that *Skara* was written by a potter. Indeed, Andrew's novel and his ceramics share a considerable frontier. In both, he gives form to what Ovid called 'scumbled elements,' working ancient clay into new vision; layers of earth and archaeological strata are both given elegant and enduring expression. In *Skara*, truly, we find an extraordinary tale, thousands of years in the making, shaped by a master's hands.

Professor of Folklore and Mythology

Central Michigan University

None of the characters in this book represent living people.

Acknowledgements

I should like to thank my wife, Sigrid. Without her constant encouragement, *Skara* would not have been completed. It was while we were looking at Grooved Ware pottery from Skara Brae in Orkney that she spotted the head of a great auk on a large shard. This unique discovery gave so much inspiration for the story. Much gratitude to my daughter Ruth Colston and her husband Mark for their encouragement from the first pages to the last, also my son, Nicky, for his constant enthusiasm.

Thanks are due to the following:

John Adams, pilot, who flew us over the Isles. From his plane I could see the old landscape beneath the ripples and could photograph much of it. He allowed me to fly the plane over the Hoy Hills!

Mr Aitkin, Custodian of Skara Brae, who allowed my brother Malcolm and me free range to explore the wonderful Neolithic houses on my first trip to Orkney in 1963.

Professor Ari Berk, for his support, friendship and literary encouragement. He kindly wrote the foreword. We have spent many happy hours visiting Skara and other Orkney sites.

Meriel Best, for being my constant friend.

Joanna Buik, who helped so much in formatting my work.

My grateful thanks to Nick Card and ORCA (Orkney Research Centre for Archaeology) for allowing me access to the excavations and finds at the Ness of Brodgar.

I thank my cousins, Jennifer Copley-Mey and Emma Boden, for their huge encouragement, help and understanding.

JF: For the canoeing tips!

Acknowledgements

Trevor Cowie of the National Museum of Scotland, for encouraging Sigrid and my research into Skara Brae's ceramics.

Merryn Dinely, for sharing her knowledge of Neolithic beer brewing. Her excitement is infectious!

Dr Steve Dockrill and Dr Julie Bond, who allowed me total access to their Shetland excavations at Scatness Broch. Although Iron Age, it gave me great insights into human lives of the distant past.

Kerrianne Flett, my workshop manager, for listening.

Errol Fuller, who wrote the definitive book *The Great Auk*. He explained that the oldest representation of the bird was from a Spanish cave dated to 40,000BC. Sigrid's discovery is the second oldest, at around 3,000BC.

Christopher Gee, discoverer of Smerquoy's early Neolithic houses.

Julie Gibson, Orkney's County Archaeologist, for her lively spirit and fresh approach to archaeology that is so rewarding.

Dr Stephen Harrison, for his collaboration in OPPRA's Neolithic Grooved Ware experiments (OPPRA: Orkney Prehistoric Pottery Research Associates). I studied in detail the pottery from the Tomb of the Eagles with him. This gave me the scenes of the Ancestor Tales and the visit of Shala and Wrasse to the tomb.

John Hedges, archaeologist at Tomb of the Eagles. I have walked over many sites with John and made remarkable discoveries with him. We observed and interpreted the landscape around Tomb of the Eagles. I'm fairly sure I have spotted where 'Lee Holme' could still lie.

Keith Hobbs, who constantly asks how the next book is coming on.

Martha Johnson, whose geological knowledge was so valuable.

Christopher Jones, my dear friend, who tragically died in an archaeological accident.

Daphne Lorimer, who discussed bones and burials with me.

Willie and Sandy MacEwan, for allowing me thinking space at West Manse on Westray.

Ronald (Bingo) Mavor, writer and my wife's first husband, who advised me in the early chapters. He wanted to kill Wrasse off, because nobody would expect that, but I reprieved her.

Erik Meek, RSPB, for his liberal sharing of knowledge and

confirmation of the great auk on the Skara Brae shard, also the dunter, or eider duck, which accompanies the auk.

Dr Tim Palmer, Chief Pathologist for Inverness Shire (retired). He helped me with positioning the arrows for the death of Rush and the paralyzing of the Bald Head's victims.

Victor and Henrietta Poirier encouraged me to think hard about life in the past when we designed a television series.

Professor Colin Richards, for our important dialogues on Neolithic Orkney.

Professor David Sanderson, for his expertise on blown sand, storms and tsunamis.

John Ross Scott, Editor of *Orkney Today*, for constant encouragement and for publishing Sigrid and my earlier stories (*Now and Then Notes and Letters*).

Alison Sheridan of the National Museum of Scotland, for her time and assistance.

Ben Short, who was my English teacher and mentor.

Farmer, Ronnie Simison: Discoverer, protector and excavator of Tomb of the Eagles, South Ronaldsay, Orkney. This site is the inspiration for Shala's 'Lee Holme'. Ronnie's intuition into stone artefacts and their uses threw so much light into the dark past. Sadly, he did not live to see *Skara* published. In his honour I slipped a broken stone axe into his grave. It rests by his left hand.

Shayla Spenser, visitor to Orkney, who has amazing theories on the spiritual past.

Antonia Thomas and Dan Lee for allowing me to dig at their Neolithic 'town' on the Island of Wyre, Braes of Ha'breck. This is the inspiration for the House of Croo. I was so fortunate as to be allowed to excavate in the midden. I found several beautiful stones and artefacts. My personal belief is that these items actually dropped from a collapsing roof. It also provided the scene for the brewery fire.

Peter Urpeth of Hi-Arts, for his invaluable literary help and encouragement.

Caroline Wickham-Jones, for her information on rising sea levels and her confidence in my staggering discoveries under the waters of Harray and Stenness Lochs.

Phil and Lynn Wilkinson, for storing copies of my writings.

My friend Peter Williams, aka St Peter, needs a wee mention. He's helped me computer-wise through so much of Skara.

Acknowledgements

A major thank you to Alison Williamson of Burgess Publishing for patiently, expertly and enthusiastically copy editing *Skara*.

List of illustrations

Shala's Orkney

Shala's Story

Shala watched from high on the Skara Dune, searching through the misty spume blown from the barrage of tidal waves. Was that a speck of humanity far off on the raging sea? Was this faint vision the core of her quest, approaching from that vast, dangerous distance?

Momentarily, the flashing sandpipers' flights, searching the churning beach at the foot of the great sand bar, distracted her. She was taken inexorably back to her earliest memories.

* * * * *

Shala was late. She always was, even though there was the excitement of the Ancestor Tales. Her northern world had short winter days. When you are a four-year-old girl on a bright afternoon with the sea gently lapping on that vast expanse of sand, you just want to stand and watch. Her bird friends, the redshanks, dibbled in the tiny advancing waves, searching for wee crustaceans, casting long shadows in the low Orcadian sunlight. Her footprints were about the same size as those of her favourite birds. They had a similar redness of leg, which she now sported, her little limbs chilling in the sea's zephyr.

Her village was at the head of the bay; she turned to the wispy trails of smoke drifting inland. The main house was closer to the shore than the others. It was big and strong, the stonework sturdy and tight. The wonderful reed thatched roof pointed up to the very skies. A shimmer of warm air venting from its high pitch told her that her home was warm. Shala waved to her redshanks and ran back. At high tide mark she caught her mother's watching eye, making her even more aware of those midwinter stories. Shala's keen eyes flashed over the lines of flotsam. To her right she spotted an amber nugget. Stepping sideways, she garnered it; its yellow and brown rough-hewn shades matched her finely plaited hair perfectly.

She was dressed for the storytelling for seemingly ages. 'Why is it that everyone else takes such a long time?' Shala thought. Her mother beckoned to her, not going down the stone steps to meet her, for she might scuff her new shoes. Shala skipped over the pebbly foreshore to nip up the treads to her mum. She held out a small pair of newly braided booties for her. Shala gripped them with her left hand as she opened her right, exposing the amber.

Gull picked her up. 'Amber,' she said kindly. 'It will take on your character. It will polish in your hands. If you are rough, it will scratch. If gentle, it'll glint. All its colours, nature and hue will grow as you do. But hurry, dear. We're off to the storytelling.'

Her older brother, Flint, and middle sister, Juniper, were waiting at home. Gull put Shala down on the slab threshold as she called for Jasper, her man. From their door, many neighbours appeared. They stooped slightly as they came from the great house into the flagstone courtyard.

Everybody was so well turned out. Shala was amazed. Gull said, 'This happens every year. So if you fall asleep during the tales, it won't matter, you can catch up next time.' Gull lifted Shala and carried her to the raft on the loch, far up behind the village. Shala watched as her mum's shell earrings glinted blue and pink as they swung on a beaded loop from her pierced lobes.

The raft journey was lovely. So many villagers were on it. The short midwinter day soon turned to evening. The sun dipped as the lochan they crossed began to take on a pinkish shimmer with gilded frills. The poles-men guided it to the stone-paved slope at the far end as they sung their Solstice Songs. The raft nudged the flags, being roped to two stubby standing stones marking the way to the Ancestors' Hall.

Shala was put down on the paving. Everyone leapt to dry land, not wetting their shoes or hems. The women made adjustments to their hair as Gull straightened Jasper's feathered headband and wiped Flint's face. He had chewed a messy drake's wing on the voyage. Juniper, always neat, smoothed her reddened hair back smartly. It was a warm hustle and friendly bustle as they circled left along the cold, shaded path beside the tall mansion. They veered further as the walls lowered to an adult's waist height. The neat masonry stopped abruptly, ending on a standing stone even taller than Shala's father.

Their procession rounded that monolith. A breeze ruffled Shala's feather band. In front of them was a vast hide awning. Inside were neat piles of smouldering ox bones. Resting on the glowing femurs were the largest pots Shala had ever seen. The huge, round-bottomed vessels steamed appetizingly.

The light faded; behind, low cliffs, then the lapping sea; in front, the cauldrons of simmering meat and fish. Past them, a great arching wall with an imposing central doorway. 'It's like ours, but under a tent roof,' Shala thought. Reflecting the glowing fires, the lintel's polished surface shimmered brilliantly. Through the dark opening was the portal to their past. Within that shadow, Shala's ancestors dwelt.

This was her first time there, though she had heard of it from Flint and Juniper. 'All you could ever wish to scoff,' Flint would say, with dreamy eyes.

'Everyone looks so bonny and happy,' Juniper said, as she twiddled with her blouse.

'It's all true. Everybody in their best paints and splendid hair. A wonderful spread, too,' Shala thought. Folk mingled happily until it was time to start. They dipped strips of fish on sharp sticks into savoury, simmering water, then pulled them out moments later. 'Here you are, Shala. Yours is in a scallop shell. I'll blow gently to cool it,' Gull said. Juniper and Flint dipped theirs.

'Have some steamed oysters, Gull. They're your favourites,' Jasper said. 'And I think little Shala is ready for some mussels, now.'

'Thank you, Daddy... I love them,' she responded.

The fish pot had limpets in as flavouring, with wild chives; samphire gave body to the bree. A crab or three were seething, and had seethed long enough. They were shared round and others popped in to take their place. The meat was for later. Its wafting steams filled the air, giving a richness that only well-hung auroch produced.

The party evolved. The children played. Little hot drop scones were handed round as the first part of the Solstice celebrations entered the second. The chatter of adults subsided. A small glimmer of light showed from the dark of the ancestors' portal. A huge horn-blast echoed from within. As this subsided, another resounded, then a third. In quicker succession, a fourth and a fifth. Shala jumped, clasping her ears. The trumpet sounded again, even louder, as others from that darkness accompanied it. Auroch, mountain goat, and rams horns were all blown from the innards of that house. Suddenly the blasts stopped; only the reverberating stones retained the frequency of the diminishing blasts. The arching wall echoed, enhancing the effect, enshrouding the partygoers in acoustic thrill.

The crowd hushed; mouths opened in wonder. All stared toward that entrance. As the inner silence of the dark tomb grew, so did theirs. Moments elapsed like aeons as the company began to relax. The flutter of an eyelid, that unconscious movement of someone just thinking of another drop scone, was the signal for an uproarious clatter. Deer antlers, auroch shins and hammerstones were invisibly striking the erect stone slabs in the sepulchre. The resting stalls for those past souls were uttering their annual hammered shriek, calling the New Year forward. The woman who was intent on the drop scone stood stock-still, mouth agape, shaking.

'Nobody told me it would be like this,' Shala whispered.

'No, dear,' came Gull's answer. 'If anyone had, you'd have been too scared to come.'

'Oh. Mum, no. It's wonderful. Will they do it again?' Shala asked, beaming into her mother's eyes.

'Not that, but there will be many more things. We're going to listen to our stories, there are many and they remind us who we are.'

'Who are we then, Ma?' the tot replied.

'You'll find out,' assured Gull.

In the shadows Quernstone, Reaper's wife, reached again for that tempting scone. Quernstone's brave decision to finally take the pastry calmed all the tensions that Shala had totally missed.

Although that clamour from within the ancestors' abode was part of the ancient ceremonies, the drama of it never lessened.

Someone from within the antechamber signalled the best moment to crack the first auroch shin against the polished upright for dramatic effect. A large leather barrel was brought to the throng. The secure lid was eased off. It fizzed as it loosened. Rounded pottery cups appeared, warmed beside the main fire. The contents of the barrel smelt delicious. Malt, honey, autumn aromas of juniper, blackberry and a hint of apple were ladled into each cup. The warm cups matured the brew to a soothing mixture, making it a delight to imbibe. There were parent-sized cups, youthful measures and small tots for the wee ones. Some of the elders disappeared into the darkness under the lintel.

The flaps at the back of the leather awning were lowered, cutting out the world of sea, cliffs and the gathering dark. A nearly full moon hid behind a clouded sky. It broke out occasionally to change the translucent roof into lighter, then dimmer, shades of parchment. The air warmed. Jasper took his precious heron leg-bone flute from his quiver. Placing it to his lips, he played gently. The variation of notes, highs and lows, shrill and soft, were calling on the Ancestors to emerge from their domicile; to yawn and wake, to stir, to remember and tell.... A muffled belch came from far within the tomb.

Vertical framed parchment panels were lowered a couple of feet in front of the great facade, leaving just the portal in view. Behind these frames a line of small, stone grease lamps were lit at the slate base of the edifice's found. Gradually, as people were enjoying a second or third cupful of ambrose, the glow of the lamps increased, lighting up the hides to a warm yellow.

The heron bone obeyed the lips and breath of its master, issuing tunes of joy. Dale, a dark-haired lad of nearly ten years, knelt beside Jasper. He had a large pottery cauldron tightly skinned with a stretched seal hide, the centre painted with a black, birch-pitch roundel. Suspended from the braided belt of his hare-hide tunic was his drumbeater, a shank of springy, dried kelp. He took it in his right hand. In his left he held a mallard's wing. Kneeling at the bowl he struck the tight skin with the kelp root. The drum boomed. Striking again and whisking the feathered limb over the surface, the sound of waves and the crashing sea were summoned. The music began rousing the ancestor spirits from slumber.

From within the black void Longo leaped. He was thin, ancient, naked and dark brown. This aged figure gyrated outside the tomb door, white bones painted on one leg and the opposite arm. The flesh arm sported a skeletal hand, and the opposite side of Longo's face a divided skull. Only one side of his pelvis was human flesh, the other, white pigment. Alternate vertebrae were shown stemming up from it. Alternate ribs moved free of the disjointed vertebrae. They flowed around his chest. They had a life and death of their own. This ancient being leaped in the light and the music.

Shala gripped Gull's hand. Between them, they pressed on the warm lump of amber. It had never left her grip for a moment. It was becoming hers, part of her. She watched intently as Longo performed his dance of Twixt Life and Spirit. He leaped behind the screen and cast vast, sharp shadows on it. The assembly drew a sudden breath as his silhouette was projected forward at them. Jagged movements darted as a startling, spiky-haired figure took the opposite screen.

Other drums came into play. A skinned pot, with tight strings across, was twanged rapidly. As the dervish dancers leaped on, lads and lasses rhythmically rattled smaller drums with shells and nuts inside.

Suddenly, complete silence reigned. The music stopped with a single bang at the pitch on Dale's drum. The figures vanished, the heron bone silent, rattle drums quiet. Silhouettes gone. Nobody moved. Only the gentle glow of the empty screens glimmered. Tiny wisps of lamp smoke rose behind them. A deep chant in women's voices came from the dark ends of each screen. Their figures crouched like sheltering hares. They arose slowly, arms outstretching, every finger showing jet black, inching towards each other slowly as their chants became like the crying of seals. They eventually reached the door and lay like basking selkies.

From high above, Longo dropped to the floor twixt the silenced seals, signalling hush. From behind the doorjamb he reached backwards for a long, ornate stick. He leant on it.

Nothing stirred. Longo stood gazing at his congregation. He boomed, 'This is Longo's Story. Listen and learn.' Those words had not altered for centuries, neither the rest that he would recite. They had been told and retold by generations of Longos.

'Before there was anything, there was NOTHING!' he began piercingly. 'Then there was a Presence.' He pointed to all in his audience with his staff. 'Guman came down from the Stars.' His skeleton hand reached up, waving heavenwards. 'Tuman came from the Deep.' The half-skull peered far down as his bony foot scraped the solid stone. His look described a place many leagues below. 'Guman and Tuman met in a cavern.' The staff, clenched in a bone hand, arched to show the enormity of that cave. His voice boomed on every utterance. After each statement he paused. After every movement he waited. His flesh and bone remained stock-still.

'Guman and Tuman fashioned a clay Man,' he yelled out mystically. Longo's bony, agile, frame walked round an imaginary figure and admired its many features. The congregation murmured appreciatively. Shala watched Longo's foot lift. His heel bone shifted, showing Longo's skeleton arch and toes.

He spun on this deceased foot. 'Guman and Tuman dried Clay Man by their fire until he was hard,' he sang loudly, miming tapping gestures on the imaginary figure with his staff.

The audience repeated, 'Hard. Very hard.'

'Guman and Tuman drank ambrose in delight.' The onlookers sipped, nodding appreciation.

'Guman and Tuman slept thirty days.' Longo made exaggerated snoring sounds.

'Guman and Tuman woke from their dreams.' The old man rubbed his eyes; a bone knuckle sank into the flesh eye, a flesh knuckle into skull.

'Guman and Tuman pissed onto their clay Man.' Longo peed on the ground where the imaginary figure stood. A yellow stream twinkled in the dim light. An arched shadow was cast briefly across a screen.

'The clay image of Man parted and softened.' Leaning on his staff, Longo gazed at the stone floor.

'One side was Man.... The other, Woman.'

Longo chanted, 'The Man fell near the warm fire and felt desire stir in him.' He stroked his own skin and pulled his curly red pubic hair.

'The Clay Woman fell away from the fire and stayed cold.' Longo shivered in sympathy.

'Man went Hard, and Woman stayed Soft.' The ancient actor twirled on his heel.

'Hard Man felt Soft Woman. Man felt sad for Cold Woman. Hard Man lay next to her and mated inside Soft Woman, warming her.'

Longo paused. He looked at his riveted audience.

'Soft Woman woke. She felt life inside. She spoke to Man and called him Husband. Man's first word was, "Wife". They danced by the fire.'

Behind the shadow screen two naked figures salsa'd as Longo chanted. 'Guman and Tuman were pleased. Guman and Tuman drank ambrose in delight. Guman and Tuman slumbered for two hundred and seventy-seven days and nights,' recited Longo.

'Husband and Wife loved life. Husband and Wife embraced. Husband and Wife mated oft. Husband and Wife felt good,' Longo sang out.

'Guman and Tuman woke from their slumber. Guman and Tuman heard Baby cry. Guman and Tuman shared ambrose with Husband and Wife. Husband and Wife sang to Guman and Tuman of their loving for each other and for Baby.'

Longo's listeners sang, 'Aaaa Aaaaah Baby.'

At Longo's bony-fingered signal, they ceased. 'Husband and Wife named baby LONGO!'

A chorus climaxed, 'Aaaaa Aaaaah Longo. Aaaaa Aaaaah Longo'.

'Guman and Tuman went to other places. They made more images with different clays. They drank ambrose. They pissed on the figures. They liked what they did and saw.' Longo danced a dance of joy and creation on his drying sandstone flag. 'Guman went back to the Stars. Tuman returned to the Deep.'

He then screeched, 'I am Longo. Son of Man and Woman.' A brightly painted wooden screen dropped in front of him with a loud crack. He vanished abruptly.

Dale drummed briskly with his fingers to shrill blasts from the heron flute.

An echoing shout of, 'That was Longo's tale,' was yelled from deep within the Ancestors' House.

The remains of the fish stew were shared. The reddened crabs were broken up and enjoyed.

Flint confided to Shala, 'I want to learn drumming. It's brilliant.' He wandered off and spoke to Dale, his older cousin. Dale happily showed him many tricks. They tapped away together as the chatter and feasting continued.

Quernstone and Gull removed the large empty bowl. Quernstone lifted the last cold scone, thinking, 'Reaper might like it. If no, it'll do for something.' Jasper held Shala and Juniper's hands. They wandered in the crowd, chatting. Juniper fiddled with the heron flute, wiping a glob of spit from it. Reaper and his mate Quartz put wood on the fire to smoulder gently. They adjusted the bones, then placed a flagstone on three scorched rocks over the fuel.

That thick slab of level stone warmed and steamed gently. The fine blue smoke from the embers contrasted with the steamy vapours, creating what resembled rising gossamer. More ambrose arrived, to disappear behind this veil through the Ancestors' portal.

The footlights behind the screens glowed. The air became expectant. Flint raised his tangle root. Bang! It went. He swept the gull's wing over the selky hide. Jasper placed his lips on the flute, breathing shrill music into it. Their playing was soon accompanied by a rhythmic hum from the womenfolk; then a sonorous male dirge. Shala was wide eyed, taking in every sound, every note. The amber in her fist warmed. The duo fell silent, the voices ceased. The steam cleared, leaving only pale blue smoky wisps.

Auroch horns resounded with a clatter of bones from within the hall of the Departed Ones. In one leap from the entrance, out shot a younger, tall, red-painted man. No bones were depicted on him. Instead his internal organs were shown in shades of grey and white with pale limestone yellows. He, fuller in the body, was stronger looking: a dramatic sight. His right hand gripped a long polished leather tube. He stepped forward. In the glow of the fire Shala noticed his red hair. 'Mum. That's Partan,' she blurted.

'Shhhhh,' came Gull's reply.

'But Mum, it is Granddad.'

Gull looked down saying, 'Yes, we know. Rub your amber and watch.' Partan's role demanded fast heel spins and high splits. Shala saw the black entrance loom from beneath him. The leather tube remained gripped fast in his hand. He repeated the acrobatics many times. He juggled the tube from hand to hand, sometimes in front, then behind, between his legs and over his shoulders. To Shala, he wasn't Granddad Partan anymore. He became spirit, like Longo.

Partan ceased his whirling abruptly. His scrotum swung still. He gazed with his wide eyes, whites glistening. They contrasted against that hematite grease paint. His deep blue irises fixed those gathered before him. He knelt to reach Longo's staff from the paved stage, his gaze keeping his audience anchored.

Partan began Karnal's story in deep, powerful tones. His agile feet spun as he gyrated. Each word projected to the audience, in his time-honoured dance.

'Longo lived for two hundred and forty-seven years and became dead.' He boomed and spun again. Karnal removed the cap from the tube. He pulled out a long bone. It shone in the goose-fat lamplight. He leaped back onto the heated stone, dancing on his toes and heels.

From behind the screens, Longo's silhouette walked to and fro. At the word 'dead,' Longo's shadow fell writhing to the floor and lay still. A final twitch and deep death rattle indicated his end. The audience bowed their heads in respect.

Karnal stood still on the slab, 'This is Longo's leg.' He waved the femur around for all to see. He tapped it with the staff. Clack, clack, it went. 'Vulture took this sacred bone from him.'

A dark, swooping bird crossed the screens. The shadow-vulture ate Longo's thigh. It dragged his leg bone away and flew off with it. Squawking came from deep within the Ancestor House; Longo's venerated bone dropped loudly deep within.

'Longo was ninety-four years old. Guman and Tuman saw him in his cavern,' Karnal recited.

Longo's shadow arose and stood behind the parchment. Karnal leaped off the stone. Reaper's hand cast a dish of water on the heated slab. Steam rushed upwards. Two hazy figures emerged from the door to eternity. One hailed, 'I am Guman,' the other, 'I am Tuman.' They became shadow figures beside Longo.

Karnal continued the history, 'Guman and Tuman said to Longo, "We made Man–Woman from clay. Man mated inside Woman. It was good."' The female Guman and the male Tuman silhouettes mimed the words. A shadow figure of Longo nodded at the images of his visitors. The yellow light accentuated his spiked hair. The congregation nodded.

Karnal jumped onto the steaming stone. The air was refreshing and different. Vapour hung mistily over his head. He smiled widely at his gathering. His teeth gleamed white; his tongue, red. On his forehead, a pattern of vivid grey spirals... his brains. His red hair, bright as a cooked crab, gave him his name, Partan, also meaning crab. This mat thinned in the middle. When he bowed, the same grey spirals could be seen painted on his crown. The red of Karnal's ochre blended beautifully with that tousled crop. His smile closed. Behind him, the shadows continued their discourse.

Karnal spoke, 'Guman returned from the stars. Tuman rose from below the Earth. Together they made many clay images and pissed on them. They liked this.... It was good.... The figures split.... Making Man and Woman... Man mated in Woman. Guman and Tuman were truly happy.... Many Babes breathed.'

To Karnal's right, shadow images raised themselves behind the screens. Karnal peed into the fire. Steam ash and sparks rose in another cloud, obscuring him in mist. The risen images behind him split in two and tumbled to the ground. Karnal stepped down in front of the glowing embers. He, too, became a silhouette against the firelight. He held Longo's femur and the staff up high. He lowered his arms, leaning towards his rapt onlookers. He bowed, pointing those totems closer to the folk. Some reached out to touch as they swayed past. Karnal's brain was clear for all to see.

In one elegant move he straightened, reversed onto his hot platform and said, 'Guman and Tuman told Longo that there were many beings they had made from different clays.'

The audience repeated, 'Many beings made from different clays.'

'Guman and Tuman instructed Longo that he, the firstborn from Man and Woman, must wander and mate with the daughters of those from other clay beings.' Karnal said this slowly, deeply and deliberately. 'You, Longo! Leave your home and mate within Daughters of Clay.'

That was Guman and Tuman's command. Partan had acted this role for some years. His understanding of the History was immense. In time he would become Longo, when Longo's present actor entered the Mansion of the Spirits.

Karnal stood again on the hot dais, forcing strange muscular movements on his left breast. There, his painted heart beat. His great toes gripped the edges of the stone. An ember glowed.

'Guman and Tuman,' he sang in a high tone, 'told all the first sons of Clay Man and Woman to go and mix their clay blood. They must mate and multiply with the Daughters of other Clay Women.'

Karnal's feet twitched, changing position. His movement seemed like dance, but the film of heat protective ash and fat under his soles was virtually gone. He shifted to the cooler back of the stone. Karnal moistened his lips. His white teeth gleamed. Below his navel were twists of white, greys, yellows, creams and greens; all depicted his guts. A darker brown, outlined in black, described his liver.

Just above his neatly groomed pelvic beard, his bladder showed pale yellow.

Karnal chanted on, 'Guman and Tuman say it is right for Men and Women to mix blood. It is bad if they do not. It is therefore forbidden that more than two generations shall pass without this happening.... This is Guman and Tuman's command and mating law.

Karnal rested on his heels. The shadow pictures mimed every word and action, from left stage and to right. The lamps glowed ever brighter. Karnal's last lines were delivered. 'Longo told Guman that he understood and would obey. Guman and Tuman returned to their domains. Longo left to make his first Babe. His name was Karnal. That is I. I am he. I am Karnal,' he shouted, placing the bone of his 'father' on his leg.

Partan, completing his role, released the remains of his bladder contents into ash and ember. Through the reek and steam he took a final bow.

Shala fell asleep. Gull put her into a reed-woven hammock. The acts continued, illustrating endless history. Each generation represented aeons. Race memories were being passed down by means of theatre, poetry, mime and music, along with song and chorus. The character of Jurt was still to perform and tell of Karnal's life.

The screens darkened. No light shone from behind them. Only a bright yellow glow, beaming from the tomb's entrance, faced the clan. Flint and Dale watched a twisted straw carpet come down over the doorway. It blocked the light. Just tiny chinks of brightness escaped through its thick layers. This blind was ancient. Straw strands fell as it was raised to show the silhouette of Jurt.

Jurt's high voice screamed out, 'I am Jurt, daughter of Karnal. I will tell you his story and then mine.' Her voice rose to a high, enveloping pitch from the tunnel mouth. The space behind her echoed, enhancing the shrill tune her larynx played.

'I tell you of my father, Karnal. My mother was Nistor. My father travelled to mate as Guman and Tuman told him. He mixed his blood among many. Karnal found the great cavern. There my mother and her sisters greeted him like others who passed among us. He shared ambrose.

'Guman and Tuman came to Karnal and Nistor. They shared ambrose, too.

'Guman and Tuman announced, "We drank ambrose with you. It is now for Man and Woman, Woman and Man. All the bloods, waters and clays of human have been mixed by the sperm of Man and the grace of Woman."

'They turned to Nistor, saying, "Men have done Men's work." They anointed Nistor with honey. They put feathers in her hair. They told Nistor, "All knowledge of life is for you to hold. Your Daughters will inherit that Knowledge to guard forever."

'Guman and Tuman said, "We depart now. We shall remain only in your memory and not return."'

Jurt moved forward. Her silhouette met the light. She was adorned in feathers from many breeds of birds. They lay close, as though preened perfectly. Candles shimmered. When she moved, that glow was reflected. The colours of many species took their place and part on her; sea eagle, sandpiper, gannet, chaffinch and razorbill. Puffin beaks ringed her neck; duck feet hung from her wrists, goose feet covered her toes, shining and glistening.

Jurt's voice fell on her listeners, 'Guman and Tuman were seen no more.' She repeated over and over, 'Guman and Tuman were seen no more.' Jurt recited on, 'Nistor, my mother, took the knowledge and became bird. She flew with Guman and Tuman as they parted from this world. "Mothers will see all", was the last ever heard from Guman and Tuman. Mother returned to the depths of her cavern. She mated with Karnal. I was born of that tryst.'

Jurt raised her winged arms. They shone with the dark shade of raven, the grey of goose, the black of auk. 'I, Jurt, grew and became Aiva: the Bird who knows of land, sky and the depths of the waters. Our flocks soar and remember.'

Aiva turned, vanishing into the tomb. The straw mat descended.

Silence reigned. The ancestor house was quiet. The entrance went pitch dark as the screen lifted. Quernstone swallowed and choked on a scone crumb. Another fell and lodged between her breasts. The tales were at an end for that night. Reaper handed her a draft of ambrose. Her choking ceased.

The throng of Lee Holme sang on, as Shala slept in the comfy hammock.

2

The Spring Tide Bounty

Shala had grown. Partan stood tall in his finery. He had hardly aged. The Telling Stone cast its shadow again at his feet. He began importantly. 'The size of the moon and the shadows from our Telling Stone tell us we will have an extra low tide this spring.' Everyone applauded the chief as his mace tapped the sacred monolith. 'This will be a great bonus for us.'

'I love low spring tides,' Shala thought, 'we always gather shellfish and catch spoots.' She put her arm round her mother's waist. 'How are you feeling?' she asked.

'Much better now, thanks dear. It was such a blow for me, losing the twins. You have all been so good.'

Shala felt the lump in her throat as she recalled the sickness that took her little brothers.

'The first spoots of the year, though, always make me feel good. And I'm looking forward to oysters, too. They lift the spirits,' Gull said quietly.

'Come on,' called Flint, grabbing a basket of smoothed rib-bones in one arm then gripping Juniper's hand. 'The tide's going out. Let's go and glean, everyone.'

'I'll get oysters, dear,' Jasper said, smiling at Gull and caressing her cheek with his short red beard.

'There you are, sandpipers,' Shala thought, feeling comforted. Walking backwards, she spotted a small fountain of water spurt from the sands. 'A spoot,' she shouted, jabbing her rib-bone deep into the sand. 'Got you! That's stopped you diving.' She pushed her hand down the rib, grabbing the razor shell. 'A slow heave and out you come. Here, Mum, in your basket.'

'We're doing well, aren't we,' Gull commented later, jabbing down. 'Got one,' she exclaimed. Triumphal cries were everywhere. Gull stood and watched her youngest for a moment, grateful how she had grown. Shala threw in another spoot. The sandpipers flew over, calling out shrilly, 'Teeeeeeeoooooo. Teeeeeeeeooooooo.' They landed by the receding water's edge, searching out crustaceans. Shala watched them feeding as they coursed their zigzag search.

Partan, with Flint, Dale and Jasper, called Tangle's family, 'Quick, there's dozens here.' Tangle's brood skipped over. Heads down, creeping backwards, they hunted, stabbing their ribs deep into the giving sand.

Juniper sprinted to the west side of the bay for velvet crabs in the rocks and seaweed. She joined other girls gathering winkles. Cullen, the eldest, knocked limpets off the stones by swinging an old walking stick. Clack, it went, striking a limpet. 'You've got to surprise them,' Cullen said, 'or they stick like ticks in your armpits.'

The Ancestor House looked down and watched over the bay. The sea eagles perched on top, drying their wings. Cormorants did the same on the cliffs.

As the tide receded to its lowest, Jasper and Partan went to the east side. There, large oyster rocks protruded from the seabed.

Shala's basket quickly filled. Her amber amulet dangled on a thong from her neck. The murky, translucent nodule had taken on a hue. 'I'm so weary,' Gull moaned, 'let's carry this weighty burden back and rest.'

'Okay,' Shala agreed.

Reaching the boulder bank, Shala caressed her amber pendant then finally confided, 'Mum, I'm always dreaming of the sea. Each night I wake up when everyone's snoring. It's like I'm coming from the edge of the sand with the Redshanks. They speak to me in their shrill Teee-oooh tones.'

They put down the basket and sat on a huge pebble. Gull asked, 'What do they tell you?'

'I don't know. They fly around me, or run ahead just as they do when I'm on my own down here. But in my after dreams, as I wake, I know they were talking to me.'

'Well. Do you just hear them, or do you actually listen?'

'Not exactly, but next time I will.' They watched as the tide began turning, the redshanks still combing the waterline, the beach harvesters returning with their laden baskets. Halfway up the sands were lines tied with baited hooks and flapping flounders. Flint harpooned other flatfish in the shallows and it was time for home.

It was one of those memorable spring tides. A low ebb indeed!

Partan caught a lobster beyond Oyster Rock. Juniper and the girls found large scallops, letting their smaller ones free.

Later, fires were lit on the beach and charcoals were fanned in the houses. The spoots slid from their shells in the heat, winkles simmered and Gull had her oysters steamed. There was a lot of eating to do. Most evenings there was singing and music in their house, but this night Tide Tales were the essence. Folk turned up to listen. The fire glowed as limpets were cooked on their backs in the embers. A quick slurp from the shell, a wee chew and they were gone.

Jasper began: 'One of my old grandfather's tales was of Farn. He told how he went to the distant rim of the sands. The tide was further out than anyone had ever seen. There he found a giant lobster, five times bigger than Partan's. It lived in a chasm in the weird black rocks. Its huge claws lunged out at him, trying to crush his ankle and trap him. But he escaped. He prised the rocks apart with his massive staff. He smashed at them with a boulder, too, until he finally got the beast loose. Farn bent low and hauled the heavy old bugger out from its wrecked crevice. Its tail slashed and flailed, but Farn held on tight. Then he noticed the stones where it hid were different. They were light. They smelt of old pines. Aged Farn carried the angry lobster home. He dragged some of those weird stones back in his bag. He dried them by the hearth and, blow me down! They caught fire! Burning so hot that he cooked the mighty lobster over them. How's that for a story?'

Everyone remembered it, and different versions, too. Cullen's version was that it was a monumentally huge crab. Quartz claimed it was a vast squid.

Reaper added, 'My grandmother brought some of that rock back, too. She polished it and made beads. She got buried with plenty of them. I've still got a hunk packed away somewhere.' 'That's crap,' remarked Jasper, 'because Farn lived a long, long way from here.' Reaper assured him, 'Well, she had some.'

With that, Quernstone thought it time for bread and cockles. Gull and Juniper served beer.

Dale stood, cup in hand, 'I sailed to one of the Far Islands with the Selky Stalkers. We went way out on the sands, further than most ordinary men tread. There, basking on a blackened, waterlogged tree trunk sticking out of the sand, was King Selky. He stared at us all, barking menacingly like an angry dog. His wives swam a little beyond the ebb. Other dead tree stumps stuck out. Selkies sat on them, singing their shanty songs. The huge King barked violently again as the tide changed. It turned towards us, as if commanded by that hulk of a seal. As we hurriedly left we saw a huge heap of great, blackened bones reaching up to his front flippers. He growled threats from the depths of his throat. The water rushed in. His treasure was hidden again.'

Dale cleared his throat for a long draft of beer. Licking his lips slowly, he continued. 'We ran. The sea returned, filling deep gullies in front of us. We were cut off! This was the king's doing. Finally an old woman, Sea Guard, emerged from her hut by the dunes. She guided us shoreward. She knew the ways of the water, the seals and their king. 'When we reached higher sand, Sea Guard yelled, "Have any of you killed a seal?"

'"No", we answered. We'd heard of their greatness and wanted to test ourselves by getting as close as we could.

'"So, you didn't hurt one? I need to know." She yelled, "Come with me." We followed her to her house. It was stone, like ours, smaller but very tall. There were three floors. She took us up to the first floor with a clay hearth. She warmed cheese over a charcoal pot and dribbled honey on it for us seal men. There was only just room for us, up there. As we ate from scallop shells and licked the warm honey, she went to her shelves to pull out something dark. Light streamed in from a lookout onto her old hands. She gripped a black bone and displayed it. "This is part of Kelp's treasure. He's the selkies' king, the Great Kelp. He watches his ancestors' bones when the tide takes the ocean away. My man took one. This one. He shouldn't have." She put the knuckle in our midst. "He never reached the tidemark. I wrested it from his dead, cold hand. The female seals sang, and King Kelp barked."

'Gill, the leader of our Seal Stalkers, sniffed hard. The others shifted awkwardly. "You will pull your boats in and sleep here?" Sea Guard suggested.

'We stayed a day and another night, learning the lore of the seals. "There are greater, even more ferocious ones with huge tusks. They dwell in the far north, where ice stays all year", Sea Guard told us. "Only the very strongest and bravest of hunters can kill them. They are the giants who are made of ice themselves," she said.'

Dale took a final drink from his beer bowl. All eyes were on him. He burped and lowered his head for applause. As it came, he pushed his dark hair back. His contrasting white stripe in the long braids flopped to one side. The shell ring that pierced the top of his ear shone in the lamplight.

Gull asked Juniper to pass round more beer and Quernstone's famous scones. Shala helped. Dale tapped his drum, the sealskin reverberating. Jasper warmed oysters on a hot stone. The shells parted. Gull enjoyed what she craved.

Wrasse sat in a darkened corner. She listened with the crowd to the long sequence of stories. She lived on the edge of the village. Her house backed into the dunes, sheltered from the ocean. She had been there for decades. Wrasse arrived when she married Gravel, one Midsummer Solstice. Their first son was returned to her old home when he was twelve. Over the marshes to Tarmin he went. It was arranged that he would later share his bloodline with a lass from further north. They had to raise their family there. This had been chosen for them. New blood could then spread in Tarmin.

Gravel's effigy was in the Ancestor House. His spirit awaited its next passage. Wrasse was old, but as tough as the fish she was named after. Her low voice eventually crept from her throat, powered by that heaving breast of hers.

Her Tide Tale, the climactic one, was always heard with great attention. The words never changed. When the time came she boomed out, 'The Fore Folk once lived and bred in a beautiful place.' Wrasse looked around, making certain she had all the attention. 'They had sea, sand, fresh water and bountiful hunting.' Her voice smashed the leisurely atmosphere: everyone became intent on her fixing gaze. 'They were like us, but we never knew them,' she hailed out. 'For so many, many turns of the Sun their hearts had huge happiness at Skara.' Her voice then became soft and as gentle as a sigh. All could hear her in their own silence. 'The land, the sky, the sea, the ebb and the flow brought them all their needs, they sang each day of their joy.'

Wrasse cleared her throat. In a vast voice, propelled from her depths, she declared, as always, 'Then, from the Ocean, came the Winter Auk. Winter Auk mustered his kind. Winter Auk strode past the Fore Folk up. UP. UP.' Wrasse drew fresh breath. 'The Auroch beat their path, too.'

Everyone in the house of Partan, Jasper and Gull chanted in chorus, 'And the Auroch beat their path, too. And the Auroch beat their path.'

Wrasse's wet eyes glistened in the weaving lamplight. 'The Fore Folk looked to the waters from where the Auks so unseasonably arrived. The redshanks flew from the shore as high tide was urged to low, then drawn to lower, and even lower.'

The old woman shifted her heavy thighs and untucked a sweaty pleat of her skin skirt. Silent wind came from her arse. Comfortable again, she continued. 'The Fore Folk wondered at the expanse of the rich sea bed. A hidden larder afore them and one escaping behind.' She mopped an eye on a dry knuckle. 'The Fore Folk were caught by a seaward tempest as they chose baskets to gather sea fruit. Beasts of the depths appeared stranded. A luckless bounty.'

Wrasse's eyes glanced above to a horizon unseen. 'Gurnard was Auk Shaman. Vacar, Auroch Shaman. They took the bird and beast's path high up to the Sight Stone on Harrar's Top. There, Gurnard and Vacar stayed. They watched their totem animals and birds pass further inland. They looked down, low-wards, to the sea as Auk and Auroch passed. The sucking breeze closed and whispered on their backs. 'Doom and despair to your people will be wrought this day,' that wind, called Kull, whispered.'

The old dame's perspiring hand tugged a long, white lock in her dark hair as her voice rose like a tempest. 'As the wind sucks, so it blows. As waters fall, so they rise. As men harvest, so they are reaped!'

Wrasse stood like a vast, black cliff, her arms white like surf as she beckoned her audience. She became Waret of the Water. Those in that room, watching, glanced behind themselves for salvation. Wrasse's powerful hands summoned the great wave in all their minds. It came crashing forward at them, as from a distant but terrible dream.

'The stricken Fore Folk,' Wrasse wailed, 'peered past the rocks and sands to a tumultuous cliff of tide. The billow raged. The sucking wind rose and grew. The men, women and children were pulled to that mountainous wave by the vile moods of the changing air. Their bounty baskets emptied as they were dragged ever seawards. That rush of wind changed. Spray turned on them. Their baskets flew back at them. The rushing mountain screamed! A green and white firmament rose; its feet swirling rocks; its shins shingle; its thighs sand; its torso a turbulence of wrenched water: its shoulders solid retribution – its head, wild, white, rage – its breath, cold anger. Its pity, none,' she screamed once more, 'NONE!'

Wrasse drank deeply from a brose bowl. Her throat restored, her eyes bulging, she continued amongst the silence of the clan. Profoundly, she said, 'Only Gurnard and Vacar were left as witnesses to the waste. Only they remained as Fore Folk. Their grief was bitter. Nothing was to be as it had been. The land before them became sodden ocean.

'Gurnard and Vacar called to the distant Auks and Aurochs. Their reply was "When there's an ebb at Skara, there'll be skate on the Harrar Hill. Run, follow us!"

'They looked down from the Sight Stone to a swirling pool of tormented sea. Skara was no more.'

Not silence, but a still, cold quiet cocooned the throng.

3

Teee-Ooos' Tales

'I must go up to my bed. The eaves call me. I love my warm nook with sounds of the sea and the breezes. I know the rest of the legend; how Gurnard and Vacar left, searching for a new place far, far away, each year returning as a pair of geese to graze on the auroch-clipped grass to sleep on the safety of the lochs and marshes,' Shala thought.

'I usually lower the hide flap to shut the world out. Tonight I'll leave it up and listen. The muted music's so atmospheric, a lovely backdrop to the other tales. I know I will slumber soon.'

Deep from within her head came a dream, slowly, first, then more clearly. The redshanks' legs were like criss-crossing sticks, running, reflecting on the wet surface, their splayed feet leaving marks of their dance in the rippled sand. Red-scaled flashes splashed in the foam, their beaks feeding in frenzy as the birds gossiped.

'Teee-ooo, teee ooo. Tee tee teeoo oo,' Shala heard in her slumber. They flew in darts around her hair, then skipped up the beach and back. They glided to her feet for an instant. They circled her in a dance, teee-oooing.

Within her dream she heard Gull's words: 'Listen, don't just hear. Listen.'

'I'm listening,' she dreamt. 'Your high-pitched notes are softening slowly. Are you humming? But you're growing, or am I shrinking? Now you jump to flight, but glide gracefully round me. Your shining eyes meet mine as I turn with you. I'm in your world. I hear you. Your clear voices are in my head. You're speaking from the inner depths to me, "Shala, Shala, Shala", you are saying, 'we, the Redshanks, are leaving this shore. We, the Redshanks, have news. We, the Redshanks, know of the great forest.'

'What forest?' Shala asked. 'Listen, listen, listen and dream on.' Gull's words assured her, as the Teee-ooos swooped, saying in turn, 'The great forest of trees comes closer. We can eat the barnacles on them. We can suck the worms from their holes. We can ride the sea on their trunks. We can seek the shrimps delving in their cracks. We can ride the waves. We can meet our friends. We can gossip as the forest floats. It will come here. You will see.'

'The dream's fading. Just sounds of water lapping and a distant trill of the birds chattering far out to sea. Oh, do come back,' Shala pleaded as she drifted into a deeper sleep.

It was a dull day when Shala finally woke. Grey clouds obscured the sun. She washed her face in the cool water from the large bowl down at the door. The dipping of her hands rippled her mirror image in that still liquid. Outside there were no shadows; none either from the Telling Stone at the end of their courtyard. The tide was midway down. It was not a pleasant day for gathering sea fruit. The boys who had set lines the evening before were bringing home strings of plaice and dabs. The Sea Eagles were digesting an early catch while the cormorants sat tightly on rocky clefts. Some swallows flew back to Lee Holme, the first of the spring. They circled the houses, approving nests of earlier years.

Shala took herself over the stony foreshore to the damp sand. Puffins flew in flashing darts from the cliffs. There were no sounds, nor sight of her Teee-ooos. Not one forked footprint. No running patterns of little birds to amuse her and keep her company on that dreich midday. She only heard their words and voices in her head, 'We are going to the floating forest.'

Shala, bereft, sprinted back up the beach. She clutched her amber, making it hot. She ran up the stairway. Gull was reaching for dry reeds stored under their wide eaves. 'Mum, Mum,' she shouted. 'My dream. My Teee-ooos. My Redshanks. My friends. They've all gone!'

Gull took the reeds and squatted by the door. 'Sit dear. Help me to split and plait these into thatch cord. What's all this about your redshanks, then, Shala?'

'I listened to my dream, as you suggested. They told me they were flying to the Floating Forest far out to sea. They are going to eat the barnacles, worms and shrimps that live on them. Where are they going to nest, Mum? What's a floating forest? Why have they gone?'

'These questions I can't answer, Shala. I didn't dream the dream, did I?'

'No, Mum.'

'But, Shala, you listened. When you dream again, you may hear more.'

'Okay,' she replied, thinking of what Gull had said. They spent much of that damp day together plaiting. Wrasse called by on a rare visit and chewed the leather she was softening. Her teeth were worn from working hide that way.

Shala told Wrasse her dream. It reminded her how she had dreamt of things that came only too true in Tarmin. 'That was all such a long time ago, now. The geese arriving in the autumn, not in the usual arrowhead pattern, but in the shape of a man. I worked that one out,' she thought to herself privately.

Three days later Shala was on the beach again. She walked backwards and watched her footprints form from her heels to her toes. The lapping tide washed some away, leaving others clear and complete. The breeze came from behind. Her red hair fluttered in strands past her face. 'TEEeee-oooo. TEEeee-oooo,' she heard all around her suddenly, 'Tee tee ooooooo.'

'You're back,' she said out loud as they criss-crossed her footprints with theirs.

The 'tee-ooos' of the redshanks became distinct and ordered. Their sounds beat a tune in her head as the birds flitted close. The notes intensified as they whirled around her. They ran about her toes and piped their tunes up to her. The rhythm of their song sent pictures and patterns into her thoughts. Her mind listened. The birdsong changed into words that vibrated within her. 'We've come back to nest. We've come home to brood,' Shala heard. 'The Forest is coming, bringing food.' The redshanks whirled away and returned. 'The Forest is coming, so lots of wood,' the little birds shrieked together, vanishing seawards.

Shala walked to the west shore and climbed up the low cliff to the grassy top. Tiny bracken shoots showed through. Birch saplings had swelling buds. The cliff rose up to its highest point further out towards the great sea. The land was quite narrow there, and the cliff edge swept back to show a rocky bay stretching further west. She saw boats from her village of Lee Holme hugging the shore. She could make out Dale, creeling. Seals lay on the rocks, others bobbed about in the waters, two of them close to Dale. His white flash in his dark hair showed him up. Partan's red crop was busy at the prow of the closest craft.

The High Hills, tall and dark, peered at her from across the distance. Their sombre-looking shapes, like a sleeping giantess, dominated the view. Smoke drifted from houses and villages far into the distance. This was the scene for Shala as she thought about the Teee-ooos' words that ran in her head. 'We've come back to nest. We've come home to brood.' She looked to sea and saw their dark, darting shapes speeding to her beach. They landed above high-water line and searched the dunes. Their words, 'The Forest is coming, bringing food. The Forest is coming with lots of wood, to rebuild your nests, too, maybe,' became lodged in Shala's head.

She walked back to Lee Holme. The bracken shoots gave way to primrose clumps. An early bee buried itself in pollen-laden stamens. Another flew low on its route to its queen. The cliff edge lowered until it met the dunes that edged Shala's village. The grass growing there was perfect for basket making. She took her blade from her belt pouch and cut some. All the time the redshanks' words were revolving in her head. 'I'll tell Mum when I get back. I'll let her know they are home to nest and their year is beginning.'

4

Redshank Revelations

Shala found Gull by the stone tank set in the floor of the women's chamber. She had given birth to her family there. It was screened from the living space by large upright flags. There was a narrow entrance that led to a store at the far end. There, the Ancestor House awnings and ceremonial tackle was kept. The room had a sacred atmosphere. It was built long before Partan's great-grandparents were born, and was the oldest part of the house. She found this a good meditative place.

Scented auk oil lamps and a pot of glowing charcoal lit the aromatic space. The polished uprights glimmered, reflecting the clear, smokeless flames. 'Mum,' interrupted Shala gently, 'my Redshanks have spoken again, but not in a dream.'

'What have they said?' she asked seriously, while removing herself from thoughts of her lost twins.

'They say a floating forest's coming. There will be lots of trees, bringing them food, and wood for us, too. They've gone to nest in the shelter of the dunes. I'm so excited. I've never seen a floating forest.'

'Neither have I. None of us have. It could be so useful: new boats, firewood, rafters and beams. Are you sure it's coming?'

'Yes, Mum. I have to believe my friends.' Then she asked, 'Mum, are you all right?'

'I am really, dear. I was just remembering having the twins, over our birthing tank. How Wrasse helped and cut the cords with her white knife. Do you remember Quernstone and her constant offers of baking? It all seems such a long time ago now, but when I am here I remember them so well.'

'Yes, Mum. We all do, especially Dad, who kept the water warm. You were so happy that they were perfect. Quernstone pointed to her hare lip and then to the twins, and said they were good babies, didn't she,' Shala consoled, wiping her tears away.

'That's right, Shala. It smelled so wonderful in here, with Juniper's steeped herbs making it smell good. I don't think I'll have more children now. It will be up to you younger ones to find the right fathers for yours. That's where Wrasse is important. She knows all the bloodlines.'

Shala considered as Gull continued, 'Juniper will be going to the Learning Cott. She will understand more of Women's Law then. You will go later.'

'Would you like a drink, Mum?' Shala asked.

'Yes, please. But can you get it fresh from the spring, please? I'd love to rinse my face, too.'

Shala went to their source behind the house. It welled up gently in a stone tank just before the shingle bank. There was only a whisper of a ripple on the surface. It barely marred the reflection of the high sky. She knelt on the worn turf and edging stones to fill her sheepskin flask. Her Teee-ooos called, 'Look down to the surface.' They flitted and vanished. Shala dipped the skin towards the pool, reflections of clouds and blue sky dispersing in tight ripples. 'There's a skein of geese reflected on the water. They're changing formation. The images swirl above the fissure in the base of the cistern, where the rising water eddies. The geese reflections are turning either way. The shapes of the skeins are clear. One is a man flying in the air, the other, the usual arrow. I wonder if the geese will pour out into Mum's cup.'

They did not. Not even into Gull's wide bowl for rinsing her face. Only the sound of the Teee-ooos came to Shala as the liquid gushed.

Juniper ran in. 'That Wrasse woman is coming over. What does she want?'

'Well, just be polite, Juniper. Ask her in. You don't have to stay.'

'Good, because I don't like her. She's...'

'Juniper... don't.'

Wrasse made her way past the great hearth to the chamber. She edged through the upright entrance stones, paying no attention to Juniper's attitude.

'We are just having springwater, Wrasse. Will that do you?'

'Thank you, Gull, that's perfect,' she replied, sitting on a whale backbone.

'I'll get you the shiny black bowl. Here, Wrasse,' Shala said, handing her the cup. 'Ah, still no geese,' she commented as he watched it fill from the flask.

'What geese?' Wrasse asked.

'The ones reflected in the cistern.'

'But this is not their time,' Wrasse stated.

'But,' Shala replied, 'I saw their reflections in the wellspring. I just wondered if they'd pour out into your cup. But no.'

Wrasse fell silent, peering into her drink, then asked carefully, 'How many geese?'

'Oh, lots. They divided either way from the crack in the bottom slate. They weren't the same though. Although they seemed high up, it was as if one skein looked like a man, a hunter. In the other, all the geese looked like wee men.'

'Are you certain?' Wrasse demanded.

'Absolutely. Just as sure as how the Teec-ooos tell me that there's a floating forest coming here from across the wide sea.'

Gull nodded to Wrasse. 'She told me that just a few moments ago, but never mentioned geese.'

'Well, Mum, you told me to listen to the Teee-ooos in my dreams. Now I hear them even when I'm awake. And I see geese in the well, too. I can't help it.'

Wrasse again insisted, 'Men as flying geese? That was just like my dream from years gone.' Her face tightened. There were questions yet, but for another time.

* * * * *

As spring became warmer and the days longer, Shala asked, 'Mum, shall we go and get sea grass in the Dune?'

'Why not?' Gull replied. 'I'd like to go over to Lille Sands, too.'

'I'll get the sharp shells to cut the grass,' Shala said.

They walked past the Dune's foot towards the point. The sandy path was a favourite way for folk and sheep. The two paced pleasantly onward. Nesting birds warning shrilly, 'Don't tread on our nests.'

'Steer clear, Shala, or they'll mob us,' Gull warned, as the sand slipped between their toes. The dune ended above the west beach where the track became earthy. Sheep dung spattered the cropped grass above the low cliff. On they ambled, towards the point where the High Hills and open sea to the south and east could be seen. To the west were the lowlands and waterways. They clambered to the spine of the promontory and looked over its shoulder. Rocks stuck out from scattered gorse bushes. Sheep trails led them further along to a view over Lille Sands, the small sandy bay. 'Look, Mum! There, stranded on the beach, two trees. And look there to the southwest. See in the distance? It's a line of dark spars snaking towards us, weaving their way from the distant horizon. Are the Teee-ooos' words coming true?'

They ran down to the beach through willow bushes and birch saplings. Huge pig-sized pebbles were strewn at high tide mark. 'The roots look vast,' Shala exclaimed as their toes dug into the sands. 'The bark's almost scraped off; the upper branches are gone. Only busted, worn joints jut from the trunks. There're the barnacles and tiny mussels my Teee-ooos want. Look, Mum,' she sang as she touched them first.

She stroked the upturned roots and fondled their abraded ends. She traced those worn anchors back to the bole of the tree, where they joined the great mass like twisted limbs. 'There are still stones gripped in the roots. See, a lump of pink granite and a rounded quartz pebble. The redshanks fly past, scudding low across the water. They are landing on the larger tree.'

'Wood for **your** nests, Shala,' they twittered clearly in her head.

'It's wonderful, Shala. It's just as you said. There's another trunk washing in. Listen to it grinding into the sand.'

'Yes, Mum. More and more trees appear. Thud! Another. There's others crunching together over there. It's miraculous!'

'Quick, let's run back to Lee Holme and tell,' Gull urged. They sprinted to the dune path. There, the soft sand slowed them. Gull needed rest, but Shala ran on shouting, 'Floating forest! Trees, trees, trees.' She arrived back at the village. Wrasse was in her doorway. She heard the news. Others gathered round. Shala's dad listened keenly. Dale, Flint and Partan appeared, too. Gull turned up shouting; confirming, 'Wood! Wood! Wood! On Lille Sands,' she panted.

'Follow me,' Shala called. Everyone ran after her. 'There's one passing the point,' Shala yelled as folk charged up the dune path and others belted along the shore. Lille Sands was filling up with trunks as yet more glided past and into Lee Holme's bay. All knew what a bounty this was. 'I'm so thrilled,' Shala thought as she spurted on. Then she remembered their ancestral saying, 'Rising tides deliver, as lowering ones take.' 'Keeping those trees here could be the real challenge,' she thought.

All down the coast, trees were arriving. Other villagers watched with wonder as they heard the grinding and thudding of wooden treasure on their shores. Stone axes were sharpened, and other tools begun. In Lee Holme the flurry of preparation began as soon as the wonder had been absorbed. Tree upon tree grounded. High tide would be in little more than two hours.

Partan took control. 'Juniper, you and your friends go back to the village. Get all the ropes you can muster. There's plenty for thatching and net hauling. Get help. I want those ropes at the high tide mark.' Shala stood next to him as the bay filled with tide, while more trees drifted towards the beach. 'Word's gone round that you predicted this, Shala. Is that true?' Partan asked.

'Yes, Granddad. Well, actually it was my friends, the redshanks. They told me.'

'Well done, Redshanks,' he chirped.

Folk launched their boats and rowed out to the incoming fortune. Partan explained, 'We must get as many trunks as we can as far up the shore as possible. We can use the ropes to lash them, stopping them floating away as the tide lowers.'

'That won't be easy,' Shala added. 'Those lodged at Lille Sands are more likely to stay put. They can be strung to the huge boulders. It's the ones entering Lee Holme that could escape.'

The prevailing currents drove the floating forest round the point as Lille Sands filled. The sounds of waves and grinding wood were powerful indeed. The excitement for everybody was real and intense, especially for Shala. Her redshanks flitted past. To and fro from the wooden harvest they went, intent on finding shellfish as the logs rolled in the surf. The first trees began to nudge their shore as they floated over the flat sands. The roots began grounding them. Partan yelled out, 'Tie the ropes to the treetops. Pull them round parallel to the shore. Be careful. Don't get crushed.' Men and boys went in up to their waists in the rising water. This tactic worked. The rolling trees were unpredictable, but plenty were stranded higher than they would have been as the tide rose. Further trees floated in, battering into the earlier arrivals. These newcomers pushed their leaders further in. Their rough, worn roots dug into the beach, lodging them tight until the rising water floated them up even more, to be grounded again in a higher, safer place. Nobody then worried if trees floated past Lee Holme. They might well land at a neighbour's, providing for new houses there, too.

The tide rose to its full. 'The power of water is immense,' Partan told Shala.

'We must get organized, then,' she answered. The weight of wood in the sea broke the rhythm of the waves. Shala lunged forward into the briny, and Partan followed. 'Everyone,' she shouted at the top of her voice, 'wade in. Tie them together.'

'Follow me,' Flint screamed excitedly. His mates did so, skipping over the stranded trunks, helping pass ties through and under them. Partan urged on, 'We need as much wood up the beach as possible. Before the tide slackens.' The weather was thankfully calm and bright. Afternoon wore on, and the evening loomed.

The redshanks circled around Shala. Wrasse watched the growing girl intently as she waded and clambered onto the stranding trees. Her bare feet felt the sharpness of the clumps of strange barnacles growing in fronds from the salt-soaked wood. Her Teee-ooos tickled her toes as they pecked around them, filling their crops with the sea bounty. 'Eat before the waves rise,' she heard them say. 'Dine before destiny dashes them.' She saw them tease out the fleshy insides with their deft red beaks as the tree they were on swung, bumping others before ploughing the fertile sandy beneath. She leaped to another. It slewed. She ran along it as it turned, rolling with the inexorable force of moon-dragged water. Screaming gulls descended on the tide-drawn forest, seeking nourishment. Their noise drowned the voices of Shala's avian friends who piped, 'Tonight we must huddle. Tonight we must nestle. We lay our eggs in the raging dark.'

The wooden mass became firmly stuck on the shingle. The trunks still floating and tied were perhaps safe. 'The trees in the ripples of the returning waters might drift off,' Partan shouted. 'All hands. Catch the ones that still float free. Lift the lighter ends over the stranded ones and lash them. This'll push their roots deep into the sand beneath, anchoring them fast.' His red hair bobbed about like a beacon. His tall, elderly shape took him onto the logs. 'Get the levers here,' he shouted up the beach, 'Hurry!' Shala repeated his commands. The mighty stone-shifting poles worked on their stranded brethren. 'Lever one floating trunk over a stranded one, tie it and pull it up. Let the water work with you.' He and Shala went round encouraging everyone alike. 'Pile them up and they'll stick fast in the sand.'

Sea and man do not always agree, however.

The tide sagged. Everyone was weary. 'I've bruised my knees and blistered my fingers,' Shala realized as she Flint, Juniper and Dale headed to the smoky wisps issuing from the houses. A halt to garnering began.

Quernstone had been busy. Her baking rocks were warm. Scones, flatbread and suet cakes browned. Life's food was a continuous procedure. Cured salmon and trout were taken from the high rafters, riested mutton and ham, too. Thick tranches were cut and beaten into thin wafers, then rolled round soft cheeses. The salmon and trout were set on boards. Folk relaxed in the courtyard. From doorways, baskets of steaming morsels appeared. A warm breeze picked up and stirred the ashes in their communal outdoor fireplace. There fuel glowed, offering warmth in the shelter of Lee Holme's dwellings.

Wearied folk sat on stones or crouched around the fire. Juniper and Flint fetched heavy flasks of beer. The sunset sky shone down as they all arrived from the toil. Streaks of white cloud, like flights of swans broke, unnoticed, from the eastern horizon. Shala's Teee-ooos in the Dune huddled in their sandy nests. Talk and tales was the order of the encroaching evening. Jasper and Partan discussed how to save the timber: weighing the pros and cons of ways to raise that heavy, sodden wood up the beach. Reaper joined in with his young nephew, Rod. They hatched a plan. Shala listened. Her heart beat proudly as all around her took on the responsibility of her predicted harvest.

A natural pause in the eating and drinking arrived. Dusk gave way to moon and starlight. Partan sent Juniper for his otter-skin cloak from its hanger by his stone box-bed. The fur was smooth and firm. It shone in the house lamplight. The two mounted heads showed their bared teeth. Black polished pebbles with painted

31

circles replaced the stifled eyes that once observed fish in dark waters: eels reaching from their muddy lairs and, finally, the glint of a swiftly advancing spear.

Juniper draped the trophy over his shoulders, and Gull stroked the tails. Together they arranged the feet around his arms and hips. The fire was raked. The embers reflected on shiny claws. Partan maintained his position as Jasper handed him his lance. He cleared his throat audibly, beginning, 'I want you all to know that we have had a memorable day,' allowing a dramatic pause to enhance the villagers' awe. 'Shala foresaw a Forest on the Sea. She, bless her spirit, was right. Never before, even since the Fore Folk, have we seen such a miracle. These trees have been sent to us. We must keep hold of them. Just as the geese arrive and the mackerel, sillocks and courthes... these timbers have come. But they only come once, unlike our fish and game. We can build better, safer houses, make more boats and store fuel. We can split trunks for planks, hue troughs, make levers, bridges and roads into the marshes.'

Partan poked his lance butt into the embers. Rising sparks spiralled upwards, to be caught by a higher draught. They wafted to the west then died, ashen in the night air. Partan used his long spear to explain, 'We should use our luck. We can lever trees as the tide rises again. We can roll other logs up and over them.' A cool zephyr flicked the tails of his otter cloak as he spoke on. 'We will chop off some of the root stubs. We can align the beams parallel to each other and lever more up the shore. It will be hard, but not impossible.' His remarks met with loud applause and were toasted with ambrose.

Shala heard only the cheer. She had slipped away to the beach. 'I think I'll go to my Teee-ooo friends. They'll be flitting on the trees in the moonlight for barnacles.'

As she arrived, their beaks were twisting them off. They spoke to her. 'See. We told you. See, we told you.'

Shala sang out, 'Thank you, thank you, Teee-ooos.'

'You're welcome. You're special,' they said in Shala's head. 'We will nestle again before the fast air flows.'

'Look, Teee-ooos, the moonlight reflections from the sea sets my amber glowing,' she said, straddling a trunk. 'Its soft warmth makes my heart leap with joy, too. Okay, Teee-ooos, fly off to your eggs and chatter away there.

'I can just see the wee shrimps hiding in the roughly worn

splinters. Here, too, where the branches have snapped. The wood glimmers as if it's a salty skin. I can feel it all the way down to its torn roots. I wonder where they all came from. It seems so solid in its stillness, stuck in the sand.' A seal crooned as Shala clambered to the bole of the straight pine. 'The clefts between the roots are darkened in shadow. There's still worn bark clinging between them. I can feel how the water has scoured around. I wonder what flowers grew round you? What birds nested in you? Where have you come from? How long have you been in the ocean? What put you there with all your family?

'Your crevices smell so strongly of resin. I can just see glints of it shining in the moonlight's shadow. What's this I see, lodged and hiding there, glinting in the moon? It's a pearly white lozenge, like a shining teardrop. It's hard, crystalline and scratchy, no longer than a thumb joint. It's so tightly embedded, I'll use my bone knife.' She took it from her belt pouch and dug. 'The softened bark gives way. I see it better now. Just few more scrapes and I can wiggle it out. Wow! It's a broken arrow point. It sparkles like mistletoe in my palm. It's not even flaked like ours,' Shala realized, 'It's not our stone, either. As I stroke it, I hear distant wind in high trees, strange birds calling and the quiet tread of a large beast.

'I'll wrap this precious thing in suede carefully, and stow it in my pouch.'

5

Double Hazards

Shala returned. The menfolk joked by the courtyard fire. 'It's been a great day. Did you hear what Granddad said about you?' Gull asked by their door.

'No. I went and stroked the trees in thanks of them coming.'

'Here's a hug, Shala,' Jasper said embracing her. 'Congratulations on bringing the trees. I'm just fetching a skin of my special brew for the men'

'Thanks, Dad. I'm so tired, though. I'm going up steps to bed. Goodnight, each.'

Her head touched her bed end. She was deep asleep in moments. Much later, the men doused the fire with their pee, pulled the logs apart and drifted off to their homes. Steam and exploding ash rose into the night to be caught in a finger of wind. Similar steam rose from other villages and those tiny fingers joined, forming a waving hand. The hand began to close, slowly clenching to a fist. Those fingers of swan-skein clouds, a portent of storm, sent their messengers ahead. Wisps of steam beckoned the easterly wrist that came closer over the sea. The birds in the dunes huddled, protecting their eggs. Seals sought sanctuary in the sea lochs. Lobsters marched on the seabed to deeper water.

The windy arms reached out to the Islands. Their knuckles banged on the portals of Lee Holme with mighty blasts. Ashes blew clear away. The embers unperturbed by urine rekindled. They churned skywards like a million stars. Some settled in thatch to smoulder. The moon had descended. Only stars gave light. Dune sand lifted into the night in a whistling cloud.

Partan woke, running from his curtained bed to the door. The gale's fist punched another hefty blow. The otter skin's teeth bared themselves on his shoulders. He ventured into the courtyard, only to be thrown aside. The force blew a great clart of seaweed at him. The windy fists struck again as Partan fell back. Jasper caught him. 'There's nothing we can do.... The tempest is too strong,' he shouted, feeling the force push down his throat.

Jasper charged through the house, urging 'Juniper. Flint. Shala. Wake up! Into the Women's Room.'

In Dale's home terror struck, in Quernstone and Reaper's, too, as a fifth volley of punches hit. The pair of logs on the courtyard fire rolled together. Like drunken brothers they glowed in their own company, the wind their wine, the gusts their glory, the embers their story. Reaper saw the glaring glow. He held his lintel, waiting for the rising hurricane to abate. It did not. Sparks flew high and dark. Others, somewhat heavier, took a lower trajectory, lodging in Wrasse's reed roof.

Reaper retreated into his home. Taking two deerskins, he ran into the blasts. He was knocked sideways onto the fireplace. There he wrapped a log in a skin. The other blew away. The remaining glowing brand blazed. He wrenched his jacket off, wrapped its arms round his hands and grabbed that last log. He ran with it through the tempest to his own door, putting it safely on their fire inside. He shook ash and scorching charcoal from his torso.

The log in the deerskin burned. Jasper dashed out, meeting Dale with similar thoughts. Dale bounced in the gusts, getting there first. He struggled with the rekindling log. Jasper helped smother it. The tempest rose again. They dragged the brand inside, where the draught was less. On their hearth it behaved.

The windy fingers clenched to fists, guided by powerful arms. Kull's shoulders and torso followed from far below the dark horizon. The tide was turning. The wind quickened. Faster, stronger, Kull blew. Seaweed and sand flew. The vile ember in Wrasse's roof kindled, sinking its fiery fangs deeply into her thatch.

Fingers of wind teased, giving it flaming children to hold hands, rejoicing in wicked flame. The coal caught just below Wrasse's gable. Her pride was the magnificent reed goose wrought by Gravel, her long-dead husband. It was his finishing touch to the thatch. The faded golden fronds were strung round a core of birch twigs, pegged firmly to the pitch of her roof. The goose's feet reached down the angles of the gable. Between these webbed toes, the bright spark sunk itself.

Fresh, famished flames plied at the figurehead's plumage, encircling the bird's neck. The head drooped, ignited. The gale tossed it aside to roll down and back across the thatch. The scorched head and blazing beak fell below the eaves. Above, those hot, angry teeth bit deeper. Flame tongues greedily licked the goose's breast. The roof was soon fully ablaze. The wind-beat tongues bit deeper into the thick, dry thatch.

The body of the storm joined together out at sea. It gave extra strength to those pointing fingers. The feet of the tempest were dipped in the ocean, kicking, splashing. The moon made its circle in the heavens and began her tidal pull again.

Lee Holme knelt at the merciless fury of Kull, the storm phantom. His corpse was rising after a sombre sleep. Sometimes Kull yawned, stretched, farted and scratched. At times Kull sighed. He could also roll over and shout in his slumber. This time, he had been cursed in a dream and woke in rage. He had endured that vile nightmare before. It left him fitful and angry. His powerful left arm pointed, punching in sinister tantrums.

Kull became fearful. Wrasse smelt smoke driving into her upper floor, where she slept among memories and a wealth of old objects, things that she just could not bear to pass on or clear out. Clothes, shoes, hair ornaments, boxes of wool, Gravel's tools and all the bric à brac of a long life. Her children's toys, their first booties and drawings on beach stones. It was all there. Below were masses of slowly perishing nets, a store of old leather that she and Gravel had tanned together in the old, long forgotten, deep tank sunk into their floor at the back end of the house.

Wrasse, fearful of the fire, charged down her ladder. She ran to her door, but the wind was far too fierce. Bushes and reeds blew past. A coracle spun, crashing onto her doorway. Her neighbours were stuck in their dwellings. There was little chance of rescue as more debris blew against her door. She turned and fell over her wicker trunk of special shells, cursing at her grazed shin.

Gull and Jasper levered up their huge threshold slab, blocking their door. So did those in other households. They just had to sit it out and hope to the strength of their tight masonry and reed roofs. Wrasse's house was dark, but she knew every inch. The sound of the fire increased and the first small glowing hole appeared. 'Doomed,' Wrasse thought, sure the house would be ablaze imminently, and she with it. She ran to the far end where she would have a little time to dwell and pray. She could just see from the light of the glowing roof. She trod on the dried leather from her and Gravel's final tanning. She stamped her foot in anger and grief. Her big toe stubbed itself on the stone slab over the tanning trough. It wobbled as she felt the pain of her toe and temper. A dank smell rose from within the pit.

Wrasse decided on clear thinking, amid her panic, 'I'll somehow get down in our old cist and close the lid on myself. I'll either be broiled like a pig and make a fine supper, or survive.' She swept the mess of skins aside. Gravel's stone-shifting levers were still on top of the slab, exactly where they were left long before with their smoothing stones and hammers. She prised up the covering slab and propped it. The horrid stink in the tanning pit rose. The liquids had not quite dried up and stank powerfully. Flames entered her house. The draughts they created sent them searching, suckling for food. Her rafters were licked and tasted good. Grool, the spirit of fire, was sating himself on Wrasse's home.

Wrasse stuffed mouldy pelts into her coffer. She slipped in as the first sparks fell to the floor. She arranged the skins under herself in swift, deft movements and gazed into her burning house. The roar of flames and crackle of her possessions was deafening. Taking a final look, she pulled in a last skin and a hammer, over the edge of the cist. She knocked the strong leg bone prop away. The slab fell into place. She forced the hammer handle under the stone, raising it slightly for air. A blazing beam crashed down. She was entombed.

In Shala's home, fear reigned. 'In all my years I've never known such wind. I implore you, Kull: stop this tirade,' Partan cried out, knowing the futility.

Jasper, taking control, shouted 'Rescue our precious things from above: the hurricane's increasing. If our roof blows away, we can at least save them. This means clothes—'

He stopped under the tempest's roar. Juniper and Flint climbed the stairpost. Shala shinned up another. Flint was back up there in a second, Juniper followed. Partan took the ladder. Fishing poles, nets, paddles, clothes and pots were shifted down. The lamps flickered, giving a glimmer to see by. 'Something heavy has hit our roof. The beams shudder. My screen's collapsed,' Shala yelled. Juniper's bag of combs and collection of shiny shoes scattered in the turmoil. Flint's drum and Jasper's flutes descended rapidly. A heavy hide box of ochre paints was carefully lowered. Piles of belongings lay in confused heaps on the flagstone floor. Gull tried to order them, but it was noisy and difficult. Juniper was scared, Flint and Shala too. They escaped to the room past the birthing chamber where the great Ancestor House awning was stored. Beams above creaked, but this was still the strongest part of the building. Partan wrapped his otter-skin cloak around himself tight, quaking at Kull's rage.

Flint took his little perforated pebble from his pouch. He blew across it, making sounds of whistling wind. Juniper tapped shells on her necklace. The music helped remove some of the fear. For a few moments the wind dropped. They played on until they heard the conflagration of Wrasse's house. Jasper went to the back wall, sniffing. Their reeds were tight on top of it. No light came through. 'Burning, burning,' he uttered, trembling should their house catch. Then came the rumbling, roaring vibrations through their stone floor.

Kull had risen, flailing his arms in mighty rage, hurling the sea violently. Lee Holme Bay filled with cruel billows. The trees resting on the shore smashed together. Their thuds, deep rumbles, crashing and splintering were heard in every house.

Wrasse lay in her tomb. The earth and stone encasing her told her the story: the crashing of the seas; the huge rolling boulders of Lille Sands; the tumbling trunks from a distant land. She felt them all tossing like toys. Each thud vibrated through her. 'I'm glad I don't have animals in the blaze just above. The smell of burning sheep isn't sweet.' The glowing beam above her heated the stone cap. Wrasse sensed it through the tiny gap she had left. Scorching ash blew in, seeking refuge in the still of her catacomb.

In her constricted space she waggled her body to one side. Squashing up the side-slab, she dragged a skin from beneath her. By pulling her knees and her arse up, another was freed. She twisted again in utter darkness. Her thighs pressed onto the warming cover. Heat penetrated her garments: not hot enough to raise dough, but that could change. It did. A great swathe of burning thatch fell. The soft thud told Wrasse just what had happened. Fine threads of light, like minute red stars floated in her cocoon. Some stung her sweaty nose and face. She jerked, bashing her forehead hard on the heating capstone. A curse, hotter than the smouldering beam, passed her drying lips.

Reaper saw the raging inferno. Quernstone was devastated. Rod and Dale knew there was nothing they could do for Wrasse. Her blazing roof was collapsing, wrenched by Kull's temper. Burning thatch carried to the hills. Gorse ignited, then scrub. Pine trees sported flaming crowns. The Ancestor House high on the hill was silhouetted black and orange in the reflected flame of Grool's wicked light. Quernstone prayed for Wrasse's spirit, pleading to Kull's mercy. A futile act, but it helped her. The crashing of wood was heard over the roar of Kull's sport. His feet kicked deep in the sea. His splashing made clouds. His wet, windy hands washed waves under Lee Holme's garnered forest. With sand and seaweed the far-travelled flotsam lifted, only to be hurled at the threshold of Jasper's door. Along the face of Lee Holme, a tree barricade crashed.

Like twigs, Kull delivered his heap. Water spewed through trunks, surging in as frothy spume. It ran through the courtyard and their doors. White foam flew as horizontal welts of rain pelted their dwellings. Dale's peering face, blasted with heavy drops, looked at Quernstone in silent pity. Another battering breaker swelled over the high-water line, forcing the piled trees smack into the centre of the village. Their drenched progression ground them past the dwellings' walls, distorting their expert stone coursing. Eaves shifted and drooped. Long rafters lost their anchorage, sinking to the floor on their seaward ends. The hurricane peeled Jasper's and Reaper's roofs away in slow, suspended minutes.

Wrasse covered her sides with the deerskins against the scorching cinders, her sweaty nose inhaling hot fumes. She buried her face in the damp sludge over her tanning tank floor, only leaving her nostrils scope to inhale. The invading smoke rose to her crypt's ceiling. The only breathable air was at the very base. Wrasse took control. 'Inhale slowly, sparingly, counting five. Then to twenty-two as I exhale,' she told herself. 'The cool of the tanning sludge is a comfort, but the stench intolerable.' She summed up angrily, 'To soften the leather we tipped in piss, ash and dogshit. That's my sodden mattress now!

'My ear's hot. Bung cold sludge on it,' she thought. 'I'll cook like a slimy fish in here, and that stink's terrible.' Her guts rumbled. She blew off gruffly, recalling the ancient saying, 'Every young man loves the smell of his own farts.' Well? What about an old woman's?' she argued, giving her fleeting triumph as her stink countered the pit's pong. She giggled momentarily, like a little girl. Crash! Another beam hit the floor.

'Wind eases as rains begin.' Like tears over a mournful night, the persistent downpour began. Rod peered past Reaper's doorjambs. He saw the glowing remains of Wrasse's home. The walls below the eaves stood. Within them was a bed of fire. Towards Jasper and Gull's house he could see invading piles of trees, dumped like butchered bones. Paving, ripped up and strewn in disorder: sea foam, dirtied with mud spray, blowing into corners.

'That flag lid is heating up. I'll lay flatter to keep away from it. My air hole is blocking. I'll have to breathe slower,' Wrasse thought in dread. 'I'll do my old mantra I used to hum. I've no breath for humming, I'll have to think it.' She imagined the low notes, getting longer and deeper as it relaxed her mind. She felt herself drifting into a black space, far inside her body. She dreamed of a dark yawning chasm, then oblivion.

Morning dawned, cold and grey. Lee Holme's scars showed. Huddled in sheltered corners, folk consoled themselves. Partan climbed over the smashed end of his house. Grim light streamed where it had not shone before. He took his rescued goat's horn and shakily placed it to his whitened lips. He blew a pathetic note. Anger at what he saw gave him second wind. The next note erupted; violent as Kull's screaming tempest. Waret, the rain spirit, whose deluge turned to heavy drizzle, slept. Steam rose from the ashes of Wrasse's dead dwelling.

'I must look for Wrasse!' Shala urged. She picked her way through the tilting walls and sagging remains of their home. She climbed the piles of trees heaped in the courtyard to Wrasse's ruin. She heard blasts from Partan's goat horn, summoning everyone. Slowly, the young, the old, the tired and shivering clambered over the Kull-strewn trunks to his dwelling. The far end of his house was still stable and sheltered. A small fire glowed in the damp air.

Partan spoke. 'Some must search for Wrasse's bones. Others of us will begin stabilizing our roof remains here.' Quernstone burst into tears.

'I'll go,' Reaper consoled. Gull joined him. They went over to the hissing timbers where Shala searched. Blackened thatch, smouldering and wet, covered the far end. 'She'll be here,' suggested Reaper. They pulled at a charred beam. Sparks glowed. Drizzle spat. Shala's arm got scorched. Sooty sludge streaked her ankles. 'We have to clear this,' Shala said. 'The seaward end of her home is burned out. Only charred and creaking beams remain.' Through dunes of blown ash, shrunken by rain, they searched. Nothing resembled Wrasse's skeleton. Near the hearth Reaper spotted two whitened shins and scorched ribs. 'That's not Wrasse. It's her bacon bones that hung in the rafters,' Shala told them. 'She's not dead. She must have escaped. She can't have died like that.'

Reaper cleared scorched thatch with a hayfork. The reeds rekindled, exposing collapsed rafters. Youthful Rod joined them, saying, 'I'll look for the old hag with you.' They levered beams from the mat of thatch. New fires ignited, even in the rain. 'If we shift these sheaves they'll burn out harmlessly over there. We might find her underneath.'

'Right,' Rod agreed.

'I'm sure we'll find her,' Shala stressed.

In that blackness below her floor, Wrasse dreamed. Through her deep sleep she ached. Her spirit felt trapped, bound in a cocoon. Her coffer, which had saved her from the fire, became her trap. Through dreams she heard voices above. She smelled fresh fire: 'They're searching: For my bones?' Wrasse could have laughed, but alarm took hold in her stupor. It was like one of those terrible past dreams: the nightmare of being chased by an auroch. That dream where she could not move or run, or call for help, always tormented her. The mighty beast thundered down on her until its bovine breath blew onto the nape of her neck. This was when she woke, terrified, never facing the beast.

The dragging of beams above pierced her dream-state. Shala's 'Ouch!', when she was burned, muffled its way through the stone lid. Grunts of Reaper and that silly loon, Rod, drifted down. 'Like that terrible Auroch Dream,' Wrasse thought, 'I can't move a muscle or even call help.' She drifted into a state of conscious catalepsy. The fire was burning out. Her protruding leather and lever had crushed. The roof of her living tomb settled, leaving only the finest of fissures for breath. Face down she remained, stuck and forlorn. Her bladder emptied. The hot pee stung her legs, adding to the slime beneath her. She coughed involuntarily. None above heard.

'There's no sign of Wrasse,' Gull sobbed to Partan. 'She must have been burned to ashes and blown away.' Partan sounded his horn. Work ceased.

Wrasse heard it from below her cinder-covered coffin, 'That's his bloody trumpet. He'll be telling everyone I'm dead now. Ignorant fool!'

'Together,' she heard, 'we shall make an effigy of Wrasse and place it in the Ancestor House along with Gravel's'.

6

Rebuilding Lee Holme

Shala's home had lost half its roof. Waret sent clouds from the rim of the vast sea. Cold air seeped around Lee Holme as the Rain Spirit's new tears shed. Kull was tired and slept. Clouds gathered, casting their sodden baggage.

Partan blew his horn, summoning all to their house. He began: 'We in Lee Holme have suffered disaster. Only yesterday we rejoiced in fortune. Shala predicted a floating forest. It arrived. It's sad she hadn't foretold the wickedness of Kull's harsh breath.' Shala felt devastated by her grandfather's sentence.

'What?' she thought. 'I wasn't told of the storm.' She left immediately to wander aimlessly in the wreckage of Lee Holme.

'We've lost one of our elders, Wrasse.' He wrung his hands dramatically in the beating rain. 'Look at our broken houses, the blocked courtyard. Our village has never seen such wreckage.' All edged in under Partan's roof for what shelter they could get.

Shala reached the far side of the courtyard by climbing over the heaped, tumbled trees. Some rocked, frighteningly. For consolation she fondled her amber and gripped the broken quartzite arrowhead. She couldn't hear Partan's words of solace.

'We can't blame Shala,' he was continuing. 'Maybe her bird

friends didn't know the storm was coming. Even, if she was told, would we have listened?' The gathering nodded at Partan's theatrical address.

Shala splashed through the downpour in her sodden reed shoes. For an instant she glanced downwards. Suddenly, she saw the image she had seen in the wellspring, but coming from a wet courtyard stone. Geese flew high in a forked skein, then more, in the formation of a man. They passed. She blinked and stared, amazed at the black, shiny flag. The vision vanished. Only rain fell, gliding away from the surface in minute wavelets.

Partan's speech became a rallying call. 'Lee Holme has to change. In the past we were many folk. We had large houses to hold our families. Look at us now.' All knew what he was getting at. 'Our blood lines are too close. Guman and Tuman warn of this, in our Legends. We cannot much longer have families without our children being affected by inbreeding.' Shoulders slumped in the crowd, knowing what had to be said.

'It's time to decide.... Do we rebuild Lee Holme? Or do we abandon and move to where we can find fresh lifeblood for our children's veins?' He mopped his brow. 'I'm not speaking for myself. I'm old. My wife, Beeswax, is long dead. My son, Jasper, remains here. My other young left for different towns and villages. But even there, bloodlines are close. Too close for another generation of healthy humans.' Partan looked at Quernstone's face. He said nothing. Her enlarged eyes and strange lips attested to her family's inbreeding. Reaper's awkward gait and twist in his spine signified this, too. All their children had failed.

Driving rain pooled on Wrasse's capstone. Water, cold as fish pee, seeped down the edges of her lidded grave. Wrasse's catalepsy persisted, her breath low, rasping. Tiny bubbles bobbed from the sides, removing her vital air supply. The aged woman's mouth was forced shut by the pressure of her head, one nostril blocked with mire. The first runnels of water entered her ear, then her clear nostril, her lungs working weakly.

Shala's grass cape was sopping. Each raindrop dripped in turn from her hem to the paving. She stood spellbound at the rectangular flag. The splashes cleared. She gazed through the film of water. 'There's a shimmering face slowly appearing. It's a young man. Was this the vision I felt I'd seen in a forgotten dream? He's looking up at me. No! A wicked gust has punched the apparition away in violent ripples. Now the wind's stopped. The slab's cleared.'

'We live now,' Partan stressed, 'dwelling in modern times, but you must all ponder our plight. Think about yourselves, and what you want for your future.' He paused, leaning meaningfully on his ornate staff. 'The one we've lost is the one we need. Wrasse knew all the blood secrets of Lee Holme and around. Her young went wandering, taking her wisdom abroad,' Partan sighed, 'we don't know where.' After a silence he continued, 'She and Gravel came here long ago, to bring new blood. It hasn't been shared. Their children have families elsewhere. Where, we will probably never know.'

Wrasse felt flooding in her enclosed space. Rainwater mixed with ash. It entered her right nostril. The pull of her weary lungs drew a drowning breath of ancient tanning residues and recent pee. She sneezed, then choked. The tank's fumes stirred the bile of her stomach's pit. Windpipe and lungs convulsing, her bowels retched. Wrasse's eyes opened wide in the pitch dark of her cell. Water gushed in a torrent around her. Her life and death flashed before her.

Shala peered deeper at the watery stone. 'A new image has appeared. Long, dark hair with a white streak. Those pebbly eyes rivet me. 'I'm drowning! Get me out now!" she heard from the fierce, aged lips of Wrasse's spirit, through the flag. 'She's in a tanning pit. I can smell it,' Shala immediately realized, bolting straight to Wrasse's home. In the grey light she found the coffer. 'Are you in there?' she shouted.

Wrasse spluttered back, choking on sludge, demanding, 'Yes! Get me out.'

'I'm trying desperately to lever up the cover,' she called down, wrestling up an old hammer.

'Help!' Wrasse yelled again.

'I'm running home for it! I can't do it myself.'

All silently pondered the future. Reaper wanted to speak, but could not. Dale tapped his damp, tuneless drum skin. Its dull thud echoed Lee Holme's thoughts. The girls who had knocked off the limpets mused long about their place in the world. Flint glanced towards Rod. He was wringing out his straw hat, wondering if there were any honey cakes in Quernstone's larder. Quiet reigned.

'Wrasse! Wrasse! Wrasse!' screamed Shala, skating over the timbers. 'She is alive! I have found her.'

Gull leapt up, shouting, 'Where, Shala?'

'In her tanning pit. Drowning,' she gasped, clambering back over the trees straight to Wrasse's soaking sepulchre. Her struggling fingers tried desperately to release the solid slab. It was sucked in with the soaking leather. She clouted it with a wet, charred log. It bounced back, sealing the stone tighter.

The men arrived. 'Get her out,' screamed Shala. Wrasse heard her amongst the clamour above.

'I can't get a grip. Smash the thing, somebody,' Jasper demanded.

Time, to Wrasse, as in the auroch dream, seemed endless. She faced that repeated nightmare, but could not finish it. She heard again the thundering hooves of that violent beast vibrate through the stone and clay of Orkney. It forced the young Wrasse to the cliff edge. The enraged beast panted and snorted. 'This time I'll finish this cursed dream,' she told herself. The bull's arching horns encompassed her. 'I see myself in its piercing eyes, looking deeply into mine. He's inching forward. I'll step back. The turf's giving way. Heeeeeeeeelp!' she cried out in terror.

That shrill yell traversed the slate lid.

'I'm falling, so slowly. There's nesting gannets, guillemots and puffins. A juniper bush, hawthorn, lichen, spume, the rocks!'

That is when Jasper gave the slab an almighty clout with a smoking rafter. Dale grabbed a pitchfork.

'I've hit bottom. But I'm alive, swimming under the surf.'

Jasper's hefty swipe forced a web of fissures into the cap. Still dreaming, Wrasse watched a gigantic whale breach. 'I'll follow,' she told herself. With the power of the bull and the rising whale, she threw her back upwards. Another crashing blow from Jasper smashed the stone. Wrasse rose. Her wide bum arched. Her heavy spine burst through. A rocky shard blackened Dale's big toe.

The crowd watched astonished. She raised her head through rubble, growling furiously then collapsed suddenly to sink back into the quagmire.

Reaper and Quernstone, as did everyone, stood shocked, silent. 'Help her,' Shala demanded. Eventually, Quernstone and white-streaked Reaper knelt. They gently manoeuvred the dead weight of Wrasse's torso. The stones subsided around her. She was cold, heavy and still. Jasper and Partan heaved her by the armpits. She emerged. Her filthy head lolled. Her lips had turned blue. Her tongue hung limp. Shala lurched forward. Rod stepped sideways, accidentally tripping her. She landed on Wrasse's back.

Wrasse coughed, farting simultaneously. Wrasse's head moved, her eyes opened, she glimpsed the ruination around her. Breathing in, she laughed hysterically. 'I can't move,' Wrasse eventually commented.

'Careful now, as we lift,' Jasper said.

Rod used his brain. 'Dale, let's get poles and leather from the Ancestor Awning for a stretcher.'

"First sensible thing that loon has ever said,' remarked Wrasse shakily.

'I'll come, too,' Flint put in.

They scrambled over the litter of trees. Dale limped.

'I'll clean you up,' Shala said while mopping Wrasse's face with her own cape.

'Here we are,' Flint said moments later, 'We'll wind the hides round the poles. It'll work fine.'

'Lie still. We'll lift,' Gull said.

Quernstone, Reaper and Jasper moved Wrasse. Partan watched, as though he was in charge. 'Hold the poles tight. Don't let them twist,' he said to the bearers.

'Juniper, help me cover her,' Shala asked. She agreed, even if she despised her.

'Up, gently,' Partan instructed when they reached the log pile. 'Over now. Mind your feet,' he said. The rain pelted again. 'Don't slip,' he advised as he clambered over the trees. 'Take her down sideways, or else she could slip out,' their chief added hastily.

Wrasse's breathing eased while being carried to Partan's hall. 'Get her under the roof remains. Fuel the fire.'

'I'll heat a bowl of water on the embers. Where's that flask? And how did Wrasse become like she is, over the years?' Shala wondered.

7

The Cleaning of Wrasse

'I'm soaked to the skin,' Wrasse stated from the whalebone stool in the Women's Room.

'I'll put wood on the fire. We can certainly spare it,' Gull said. 'Shala, take that busted bowl and put embers in it to warm her back. Top up the brazier with charcoal. There's some on the ox shoulder shovel.'

'I don't take easily to pampering,' Wrasse complained.

'Well,' Shala stated, 'you'll just have to put up with it now,' not knowing how those words tumbled from her, but they did. Wrasse could be fearsome, indeed. Juniper looked askance.

'We'll have to take all your clothes off,' Gull explained. 'Your tunic's sopping and the suede shirt under it is drenched... never mind the smells.' Wrasse grunted a grudging approval.

The men were at Reaper's house, assessing the damage. The roof posts were in place, but badly split. That house, as others, sagged dangerously.

'Juniper, fetch Grandma's clothes coffer, the reed one you rescued last night.' Juniper complied. 'These will do fine,' Gull thought proudly. 'Here's her knotted grass blouse, a long skin skirt with a stripped reed petticoat and flaxen socks. Hang them up, Juniper dear.'

Wrasse's garments loosened. Her sagging body revealed distorted tattoos of bright red, blue, yellow and green. Juniper giggled. Wrasse glanced at her. She froze. Shala soaked bog cotton pads in warm water and began to clean up.

Gull found her flask of beer vinegar and egg white hair wash. 'Juniper, would you do Wrasse's hair?'

'Yes, Mum. But please, don't let her look at me like I'm some turd.'

Wrasse grunted, amused still at the power of her glance. Shala began at her neck. The old woman's naked form, broad, gross and sagging, responded to the warm water. Small rivulets eroded the grime of months to reveal pale skin and her wrinkled tattoos.

Juniper rinsed Wrasse's matted hair from the crown down, washing away the vile muck from the tanning pit. Wrasse's head nodded weakly in approval.

Partan addressed their neighbours. 'We must make this home safe and cover the damaged end with the Ancestor House awning. All of us can then bide there whilst our other buildings are repaired. We can discuss our future, too.'

Quernstone arrived with a bowl of oxtail stew and dumplings for Wrasse. She put her hand up in polite refusal, 'I'll eat when I am cleansed.' Quernstone put the bowl by the fire. The aroma wafted in the room, partially covering the stink of Wrasse's entombment.

Shala washed her tough, fat arms. 'Can I do her back, now?'

Juniper whispered, 'Okay, I'll move round.' Wrasse sat stock-still.

Shala doused her wide back with warm, scented water. The grime moved downwards, revealing a tattoo of a goose in flight. Each feather was picked out in black ochre. Behind the bird's beak a bearded human face looked upwards, to her neck. Shala showed Juniper in silence.

'So, you've seen my goose?' Wrasse said. 'You watch. He'll fly.' She rolled her shoulders up and down, whistling hollowly through her stumpy teeth like the wind in its feathers. The great bird's wings flapped as Wrasse's flesh heaved.

Gull swabbed Wrasse's wide face. Her broad, wrinkled forehead revealed a tiny yellow ochre star, tattooed just below her hairline.

'Her hair's so matted and tangled, I'll have to do it from the ends up,' Juniper complained. After patient effort Wrasse's long streak of pure white hair emerged. Juniper combed it from her brow to the bottom of her neck. Wrasse closed her eyes. Gull dabbed her wrinkled cheeks.

The room warmed. Shala scraped more embers into the broken pot.

'I'll do your feet,' Quernstone said kindly, kneeling on a thin leather pillow. Wrasse stuck out her grubby left foot with its huge, horny toenails and eased it into the bowl of warm, fragrant water, sighing appreciatively.

'Excuse me, Wrasse, may I do your, er... front?' Gull asked. She then rinsed those once huge breasts that dangled like wrinkled kippers. From beneath them an old skin smell mingled in the atmosphere. With fresh bog cotton pads, Gull began the fronts of Wrasse's tits. The moisture revealed faded colours in the lamplight: the left breast, pale yellow to white, the right yellow and red.

Wrasse commented with eyes closed, 'My left showed the full Moon, my right the Sun. They were done before they grew. It was painful: torture, in fact. That is when I learned my mantra to take my mind away from pain.' Wrasse sucked the aromatic air over her worn incisors and made the sound, 'TSssssssseeeeeee.' She held it in her vast chest then let it out, gradually, 'Hhrrmm,' she hummed. It vibrated through the stonework and creaking timbers. The bowl of warming water rippled. The onlookers' spines tingled.

Her long note faded and Wrasse said, 'When these breasts were young, the Sun and Moon looked wonderful.' Her grooms were impressed. Gull began on Wrasse's portly belly, Quernstone her other foot. Later Gull asked, 'Will you lean back?' she did, exposing her nethers, the old pubic hairs, thinning and grey. Gull washed as Shala hummed tunelessly, the sort of embarrassed hum someone knapping a stone tool might make when they are not sure where to strike.

On the inner sides of her legs, tattooed fish looked upwards. They were her namesakes, the wrasse, searching for a cleft, seeking a rocky haven in the cliff face; blue, green and red scales sparkled from her wobbling skin.

The granite pebble for the flag-lined birthing tank had been heated. The sisters rolled it onto a wet reed mat with an ox rib. They dragged it to the brink. Steam shot into the chamber as the boulder rolled in. Whale oil lamps issued a misty glow.

Quernstone said, 'We'll help you to the seat over it, Wrasse.' She and Gull hoisted her by her sweat-free armpits. 'There you are,' Quernstone comforted her, 'we can wash your bum now.' The heat and steam engulfed her. Her old pores opened. Fresh sweat oozed from her skin. The salty liquid, like meltwaters from deep snow, cascaded from her shoulders.

Quernstone rubbed auk oil over her skin. Another hot, pink granite pebble was rolled from a mat. The steam obscured Wrasse. She sat, eyes closed, the briny rivers running from her scalp over her eyelids.

* * * * *

Jasper spoke. 'Partan, we must round up the cattle and goats. The sheep will look after themselves and the pigs are safe in their pens.' The ducks waddled back and inspected the new puddles. 'Flint, come with me. Call Mutt to bring in the strays.' Their clever dog coursed the hills and herded scattered groups. Their heels were nipped if they did not go just where she intended.

'Reaper, Dale, come with me. We'll get the awning out,' called Partan. They arrived eagerly outside Wrasse's washroom to face Gull.

'Partan?' she said. 'You can't come in here, we're bathing Wrasse. It will have to wait.'

'We need the Ancestors' House awnings,' he said, grinding his teeth. Reaper added, 'We're setting it up over the ruined end of your house.'

'Well,' Gull said, 'you'll have to be patient.' She glanced behind her into the sanctum, then looked back at the men. 'The awning rolls are way past the chamber. Wrasse is recovering. I don't want her disturbed.'

'Who's that? What do they want?' asked Wrasse wearily. Gull explained.

'I don't give an urchin's anus. If they can put up with me, I can with them,' she replied.

Gull turned to Partan. 'It's okay. Make a chain and pass the stuff.'

'Right, I'll get a team together. Thank you, Wrasse,' he said respectfully. He heard no answer. Outside, the rain ceased, the sun shone, and only a gentle drying breeze wafted by.

Wrasse asked, 'What is going to happen in Lee Holme, now?' Quernstone braced herself.

'Partan says that because our bloodlines are too close we must decide if we stay here or move,' she replied, 'I'm afflicted. I understand. So does Reaper.'

Wrasse groaned. Her shoulders rose and dropped. Shala saw the gander flap again. 'I shall speak, when it is time,' she growled.

Partan ducked past Wrasse to the store behind the steam room. His team nervously entered. He passed scrolls of hide to Crane, she handed them to Fallow, who in turn sent hers to Tangle. Quartz reached through the mist and Tangle passed her load to him.

Flint and Jasper returned with the goats. The kye were safely grazing, so they joined in the chain.

Another stone slid into the tank. Mutt sniffed at the doorjambs. She saw two great feet reaching towards her. Wrasse looked directly into the dog's eyes, transfixing the dog's eyes. Wrasse stared at her toes. Mutt followed that gaze. As though she was sheep stalking, she crept across the floor, pinned with the glance. She inched forward to lick a wrinkled foot. The hard skin of ages softened, peeling away on Mutt's rough tongue. Wrasse smiled appreciatively. The bitch's agility found every crevice. It tickled terribly, but Wrasse became accustomed. As Mutt slavered at her feet, the four nursemaids scraped her down with sheep-rib strigils. Her tattoos shone.

'Now the rumpus with the awnings is over and the dog's finished, can I have that stew, Quernstone?'

'Of course,' she replied eagerly.

'I knew you weren't dead,' Shala told Wrasse. 'I heard you and almost saw you commanding me to save you through a wet flag in the courtyard.' Wrasse stared at Shala as she explained, 'You broke into another vision: A strange male from far off. His face formed in the ripples after the geese vanished.'

Wrasse's stare turned into a glare. Shala stopped.

Flint and Dale clambered in the damaged rafters. 'Tie the awning sheets over them,' Partan instructed. 'Tight, I say, and tighten them again.'

'It's all right, Partan. We know what to do,' Flint responded.

'Jasper, Quartz: organize the men to anchor them over the eaves. Weight them, wedge and tie them,' Partan stressed. 'That'll keep the weather off while rebuilding. After all, we've had the whole village in here for festivals and events. We'll cope.'

Evening came. Everyone brought food. 'I've got bannocks and matured cheeses from my underfloor cist,' Quernstone announced.

Flint sucked a goat's rib when Partan stood up by a flickering reed lamp. 'People of Lee Holme,' he began. 'Have you considered our options? Do we rebuild our village, or do we move to where we can mix with new blood?'

Wrasse stood, banging a staff on the stone floor. Her new clothes shone in the shell lamplight. Her eye-whites contrasted with her basalt irises. She drew breath. 'It is no use us moving.' She looked around. 'Where to?' She asked. 'How? Yes, our bloodlines here are far too close for safety. Shala and Juniper will not be able to have good children from anybody in this village now, nor the towns. The other girls, too.' She paused allowing this to register. There was plenty more to come.

'I came with Gravel to bring up our children here in Lee Holme.' She looked around her audience. 'See my white streak of hair?'

'Look at Dale, he has one, too. His father, Quartz, is of my bloodline. You look all round our lands.' She turned her head as if peering into the distance. 'All of us are too close. In some way we are related. So I secretly sent my own children far away. There is only one other answer.' The folk of Lee Holme winced uncomfortably as she spelled it out, 'We need new men to mate with our women. Even if those women are already wed.'

The men looked shocked, the wives surprised.

'Shala,' Wrasse called, 'Stand up and tell of your visions.'

Shala felt embarrassed and worried.

'Go on,' Wrasse urged her kindly, giving a supportive glance. She held her amber amulet tight and stepped forward into the light. It shone onto her face; her lengthening reddened hair, in thin, tight plaits, swung around her. She looked about the room, into the darkening places, catching folk's eyes. She had watched Partan doing that.

'Someone is coming,' she announced. Everyone concentrated on Shala. Even Rod stopped scratching his scrotum.

'I have seen the signs. Twice now,' she added.

Partan looked straight into Shala's amber eyes. She turned, speaking to him, but still addressed everyone. 'I saw it in our well-spring. A skein of geese and then others, flying in the shape of a man.' She paused. 'I have told only Wrasse and Mother of that vision.' Shala waited dramatically. Wrasse looked into her aura. 'I saw it again in a black slate in the courtyard. The geese flew in a skein and then in a man formation.' Shala allowed this to penetrate. 'Then, I saw *his* face in the slab.'

Everybody looked stunned.

'He has fair, yellow, like bere straw. He's got hazel eyes. He has a strong, kind look.'

'What happened then?' Partan demanded as Shala paused.

'He vanished. Wrasse blew him away. She appeared in the stone in his place.' All drew breath. She clutched the sharp quartz point, 'Wrasse shouted to me through the rain over that slab, "I'm drowning. Get me out!" she yelled. That's when I ran to the old tanning pit where she was. That's how I knew where to take you.'

Shala waited for calm. 'I know he will come here, the one who I've seen. Others too, perhaps. The number of geese suggests it.'

Shala looked back to Wrasse, and her glance was returned.

* * * * *

'Good, you're back, Oiwa,' said his mother, Quill.

'Yes. Here's fish from the traps... and,' he added with distinct pride, 'the beaver.' It flashed through his mind how he had watched the dark waters of its pool, the flight of his first arrow slipping below the water. Then the second one he had sent from his bow to intercept its underwater path. He visualized again how the flights slowly surfaced from the impenetrable dark of the deep. The final attempt the beaver made to reach its castle as it gave up its feelings for life. 'I've gutted it. Is North Star home yet?'

'No, Oiwa. Your father and brothers aren't back. Honey and Petal are getting cook-pits ready.' His two younger sisters arrived from behind the wigwam.

'Hello, Oiwa. Successful hunt?' little Petal asked.

'Great, thanks. And I got a brace of partridges for Ripple.' He pointed to her tent on the other side of the circle, closer to their river. 'She's promised to cut me arrow flights with the wing feathers,' Oiwa added.

Returning geese flew in forks high overhead. 'Winter is ending,' Quill observed as those high fliers spotted a vast distant lake to descend upon. The evening air revealed its chilly fingers as North Star arrived back leading Mica, Bark and Tine, Oiwa's three older brothers. They carried stretchers of caribou meat between them, their tightly stitched leather clothing straining with the weight. The feathers arranged in their sleeves and headbands broke the line of their features, blending them with the undergrowth of the pine and mixed forests.

'Oiwa,' North Star greeted his young son with a hug, 'I see you've been hunting, too.'

'Yes. Fish from the traps in the Dun – and your favourite, Dad: a beaver from Mirror Ponds.'

'Splendid. We can eat by the glow of the rising moon and listen to geese fly past.'

'Help us unload the meat and share it round the Clan,' Mica said. Bark and Tine unrolled the fresh skins. 'You can add your beaver pelt to this lot,' Bark suggested.

'Okay. I'm just going to skin it and remove the thigh bones.' With that, Oiwa knelt with his grey flint knife and eased the skin off his beaver. The bare body from within bore none of the grace of the former animal: Just an elongated red corpse. He cut the bat of a tail free then tackled the legs. His deft, practised movements of the knife stripped the flesh from thighs. 'Here, Honey,' he called to his sister, 'burn these two bones.'

'I will,' she answered, catching them from Oiwa's pitching hands. A blue Jay gave its evening call.

'Here's a hunk of caribou,' Tine said to Honey, 'cook that too.' She knew just what to do. Into the hot pit it went. She covered it with wet pine needles and stones. There it sizzled and poached.

Oiwa spitted his beaver and placed it over the hearth where its femurs were already blazing. Their acrid smell wafted up over the tall pines. Oiwa uttered the old prayer in his mind, 'May your legs burn so your spirit can't chase me. May their smell strike fear in my animal foes. May your ashes blow and blind my pursuers. And may you nourish me so I'll hunt forever.' He pictured his brothers doing the same after their hunt, longing to join them one day. 'Honey, would you turn it for me? I'm going inside.'

Oiwa entered their wigwam, leaning his bow by his sleeping place amongst floor furs.

'That bow of yours is very short, Oiwa,' said North Star.

'Aye, Dad. It works fine, though. I got you that lovely beaver with it; Honey's turning it on the spit now,' he replied.

'Ah,' Mica put in, doffing his feathered cap. 'You've grown. Before you come with us, you'll need a bow that fits, and longer arrows.'

Oiwa's eyes grew in amazement. 'I thought it would be ages

before I could,' he replied to his tall brother. 'Can I borrow your axe to cut the wood, tomorrow?'

'Yes, Oiwa, you can, but choose it carefully. It might take some while to find the right piece. It usually does, especially when you look too hard. And,' he suggested, 'we can knap some new arrow points when you return.'

The geese gaggled high above as another skein flew over.

'Let's go out and look,' Bark suggested.

Tine agreed, 'We can think of our forefathers,' he said, leaning on the frames stretching the last winter furs and gazed up saying, 'How they followed them, I just don't know.'

'Oiwa, where's the North Star?'

'Up there, behind our tent. Dad always pitches ours in line with it when we return.'

'Yes, just testing,' said Tine.

'I'm going for a pee,' announced Oiwa. He wandered towards the North Star. The half-moon was rising as he found their place. A small tributary of the Dun weaved through the new reed shoots. Oiwa stood on a rock and looked down to the dark pool. He fiddled awkwardly with his penis while getting it out from his suede leggings. 'Ouch!' he squeaked, catching his recent hairs. 'The urge has gone,' he acknowledged as he gazed down at the moon's reflection. The skeins flew in the darkness of the pool. They separated and went in different directions. 'There's Father's star,' he noticed, leaning forward, 'now me, reflected back,' as he glanced directly down. 'That's better, pee's coming. But my face has gone. Someone else's, someone I feel I know, is there. Who is it?' he called to behind. 'Odd, I'm quite alone. All gone, now I'm pissing froth,' he remarked to himself.

* * * * *

'So, we rebuild,' Partan concluded. He went over to Shala, 'I'm so proud of you, dear. I so hope this is true. I do believe I can trust your vision. We can now wait, sure that someone is arriving, and others, perhaps. It gives us hope and purpose.' He leaned closer in the smoky light. 'I am so glad we don't have to move.' He paused thoughtfully, adding, 'I hope I'm still living when this man arrives.'

Gull heard and looked at Jasper's ageing father. 'You will be,' she assured.

Shala gripped her broken arrow point while she spoke, then

opened her palm. 'Can I see that?' Wrasse asked urgently, as she was stuffing it back into her pouch.

'I dug it out of one of the tree roots,' she said, passing it to her. Wrasse's dark eyes stared. She felt and stroked it. She put it to her lips, kissed it then handed it back.

'Keep it safe. It might be useful one day,' Wrasse commented seriously, then asked lightly, 'Would you bring Gull to me? She's with Quernstone, genuinely excited about the future.'

'Mum, Wrasse wants you.'

'I'll be right over.'

Wrasse sat on a leather bolster, Gull perched next to her and Shala stood. She felt taller and quite different. 'Gull?' Wrasse asked. 'If I'm staying here – and thank you, by the way – I want Shala to be my attendant.' Shala's eyebrows raised, as she stared at Wrasse.

'Juniper's older,' Gull suggested.

'No, Shala's fine,' Wrasse almost demanded.

'Very well. Yes. We can give you the room above the Women's Chamber. But can you manage the ladder?'

Wrasse held her hand up. 'That ladder's fine. My only request is for you to make a hatch in the roof so I can look out.'

'We can see to that, Wrasse,' Gull agreed happily.

'I'm grateful,' she said, relaxing a little. 'It's been such a long day. I'm weary,' Wrasse admitted as she rose to go outside. The sky was clear and the stars reflected in the damp stones of the littered courtyard. Her old house still smouldered. She uncovered the huge pottery vat under the eaves and peed, then replaced the reed mat over the toilet. She adjusted her clothes, returned inside to the foot of the ladder, then climbed slowly to her new room.

Everyone chatted on. Beer and ambrose were shared. Wrasse snored deeply. The eventful day ended. New bed places in cramped spaces would be shared. There were no thoughts of mating that night, or for some time after.

* * * * *

'Now it is a new day,' Partan importantly addressed his general council, consisting mostly of those who would listen and agree. 'We have to redesign and rebuild. We have had problems with rainwater from the roofs. We must make better drains to cope with that. Our eaves seem to be too low. We need higher walls to prevent this. Then we can pile extra firewood beneath them, have better outside workplaces and store drying pots and the like.'

'That sounds worth working for,' put in Quartz, encouragingly. 'After all, we have a new future to look forward to.'

'As Chief of the Council, I will make myself responsible for the overall organization. For example, all the old, damaged thatch has to be stored carefully. We can use it to fire pots. We have new reeds stacked, but we have to allocate our growing reed beds to certain uses. It was Hornfisk, Gurnard's father, who built the last house here. Now we have to think about the whole village. Hornfisk's walls were measured up from his heels to the fingertip of his right hand. The footings of the walls were from his left shoulder to his other arm's forefinger. The thickness of the tops of his walls was from his thumb tip to his armpit. His house was very well measured. The heights of his roof he calculated using the staffs he had made to keep the measurements. If you all agree, we can make new rods and staffs from my arms, legs, feet and thumbs. With these we can modify all our houses to the same scale. Then, when we do have a growing population, we can forever plan houses with the same proportions. We have those huge trees for posts, and I am the tallest in Lee Holme.'

Shala heard all this from her new place beside Wrasse, who slept deeply. The toilet pots had been emptied onto the ash heap by the dunes and covered with sand. The daily round of work had to be done, despite all the damage.

Later that afternoon Sable, from Char, walked down the brae to Lee Holme. She brought her four-year-old son, Sprig. She wanted to see Wrasse. Gull met her instead. Sable asked, 'How are you all?'

'Okay,' replied Gull, 'but damaged. And you at Char?'

'Much the same,' Sable replied.

'Come to Quernstone's, she's got refreshing warm rowanberry juice from last autumn.' Sable admired the litter of tree trunks. Gull said, 'Shala foretold the arrival of the wood, but she didn't know about the storm.'

'Ahhhhhch well!' Sable said, 'It's an ill wind....'

They nodded in agreement at the old saying.

'How are you all coping?'

'We discussed the future and decided to rebuild here. We talked frankly about breeding. There may be an answer, but it's too early to say. Come in, I'll tell you what happened to Wrasse.' They sipped the cordial thoughtfully. Gull added, 'I think Wrasse will change and become closer to us, now.'

'It's time for that, indeed. She has great wisdom.'

Wrasse opened an eye and saw the inside of the awning gently flapping. She lay on a split birch bed. On that was a thick straw mattress in a reedwork casing. 'I hate comfort and fuss,' Wrasse acknowledged to herself, 'and folk with inane chatter.' Immediately reflecting, 'Of course, now I've been dragged from peril into plenty, I'll maybe have to learn to put up with it.'

Shala had been up long before, cutting strips of cold smoked mutton and warming them with sorrel over a pot in a sieve. 'Maybe this and a cup of well-water will be a fine late breakfast for Wrasse; sharp and tough,' she thought.

Wrasse rose and scratched. Shala passed her a string-handled pot to pee in. She lowered the contents below to be taken away later. Wrasse chewed her breakfast, dwelling momentarily on her now burnt mutton in her old home. 'All I had is now ashes, apart from memories. They are clear as the water I'm sipping. Shala, come here.'

She sat on a small suede cushion next to her. Wrasse lay in bed on her side. It creaked as she moved. 'I want you to be with me because I can tell you things. First, Shala, I want to change your name.'

'What!' Shala exclaimed in surprise.

'Shala is a child's name,' Wrasse said quietly. 'You do not have a child's head on you.' Shala looked away. 'Look at me,' Wrasse demanded. She glanced unsteadily back. '"Shala" is what you are used to, but your real name should be Aiva. The "Bird's Spirit".' Shala continued looking into Wrasse's hypnotic eyes. 'You, my girl, have a bird's affinity. You can hear what they say, can't you?' Shala nodded very slightly in agreement. 'Can you speak back to them?'

'I don't know. I've never tried.'

'Well, never mind that for the moment,' Wrasse stated.

'Wrasse? Would you leave my name as it is, please? I'm not ready yet.'

'Well. For the time being.'

'Thank you,' she said, relaxing slightly.

'Tell me all about your geese visions.'

Shala did with passion.

'Have geese ever spoken to you?'

'No.'

'Did the man in the stone speak?'

'No. But, he was just about to move his lips when you looked at me from the pit and pushed him away in the ripples.'

'Oh, pardon me,' Wrasse returned. 'I was only trying to save myself. Well, my spirit was.' She thought momentarily. 'He may look at you again. Possibly within a dream, Shala,' Wrasse said respectfully.

'You have a lot of questions, don't you, Wrasse.'

'Yes, I do. Important ones and there could be more.'

Shala drank warm honey water. She took a hard-boiled duck egg from the steam pot, shelled it, mashed it up in her bowl with her stone knife, mixed salted butter with it then rolled it in a cold pancake. 'Do you want some, Wrasse?' she asked.

'No thanks, the mutton's fine,' she answered whilst sucking her teeth.

'I have a question for you, Wrasse.'

'Go on?'

Shala paused, gathering courage. 'Why have you got a goose tattoo?'

Wrasse shifted, blinking uncomfortably. 'The whole story?' Shala nodded, noting Wrasse's gravity. 'Then I shall tell you, but whole stories are not always pleasant. Let me sip my water first.... When I was a little older than you I became aware that someone was travelling over the sea to Orkney. How that happened, I didn't initially know. It was when the geese were flying that it became clearer. Come closer, Shala,'

She obeyed, leaning against her bed; sniffing the sharpness of the sorrel and scented ewe meat.

'Every day I went to the shore, waiting as the geese returned. Sometimes they flew past strangely low. Their skeins became fewer and fewer: one day, none. I waited all that day. As evening began descending, I saw a final skein flying low over the cliff at the edge of our bay. This skein behaved oddly. It came near to our shore then circled, returning to sea. I called to my sisters who came to look. As the geese returned, rounding the cliff, a flight of swans joined them. We had never seen the like. The birds made an enormous noise. Then, slewing sideways round the cliff, a small boat appeared. It was nothing like one of ours.'

'I'll have to stop.' She gulped, drawing breath at the memory, then went on. 'The tide swung the craft past the cliff's foaming teeth. I have to stop, Shala. Forgive me a moment,' she said, interrupting herself.

'It righted and the clifftop birds swooped down over it. I shouted to my sisters to run up to our nousts and haul down a boat. The clamour brought the whole village out. More boats went scuttling down the stony slope and into the surf. My father waded in, pushing his dinghy. I paddled out with my sisters. We were the first to reach the strange canoe washing in. We saw slime from the sea and barnacles clustering astern. A wave brought the craft closer. A terrible stench hit us. Mire, my oldest sister, cast our weighted rope to the boat; the stone on its end caught. We pulled it close. That rotting stink intensified.'

Wrasse relived that whole experience, remembering her breasts were fuller then. The Sun and Moon stretched widely behind her blouse; the wrasse between her legs searched for their noust, never quite reaching that sacred cleft.

Shala shifted and handed her the black cup of water. 'Thank you,' Wrasse nodded, heaving her flat bosom and drawing a long breath. 'The birds glided around us as though they were in frenzy. The geese flew higher, circling. I was the first to look into the boat. A hide covered most of the craft. I expected to see a rotting body beneath. Instead... Instead, I was looking into the face of a hooded man. He stared at me over his tangled beard, past the sagging trim. Our boats bumped. He winced painfully. His straw hair lay over his forehead. His hazel eyes fixed mine in a look of waking agony. His jaw clenched and that fearful smell rose.'

Shala looked long at Wrasse, whose voice softened. Only Shala heard. This story was for her alone. Wrasse, who had dwelt in Lee Holme seemingly forever, talked at last. Everyone knew about Gravel, Shala remembered. Wrasse's children, her life. How Gravel died, long before she was born, lost in a seal hunt. A bull seal, hiding in a cleft, charged him. The men with him fled. He slipped, falling backwards, cracking his head open on sharp, limpet-covered rocks. A wave taking his body, floating it past his comrades, where it was caught in a tidal current and drifted to sea. Pink foam washing the rocks: Brain sliding from the points of limpet shells.

'We towed his hide canoe ashore,' Wrasse suddenly continued. 'We carried it with him inside to our house. It was extremely slippery from being afloat for a very long time. Many hands helped.

The geese landed noisily on the loch behind our hill. We pulled the canoe through our door. We tilted it very slightly as his craft entered our hall. We got lamps and looked into the boat, and the rotting stench rose.' Wrasse wheezed and heaved.

'I saw his right arm. He was just conscious; he glanced at it, too. The bone on his forearm showed through the skin and flesh. Yellow pus oozed from the fetid limb. It was horrible, Shala. Mire threw up. I held myself together. Mother, horror-struck, ran for Coutou. She had been helping with a difficult birth up at Crest and had only just returned; they ran back to our house. Coutou looked closely at the boatman, "He's not dead yet, but then again, not far off. My knives are still hot from slitting that girl, to deliver her boy. Get a bed ready by the fire where I can see."' Wrasse coughed nervously, then spoke on. 'Coutou told us to grab a foot and a leg each. Dad held his head and I slid my hands under his good shoulder. Coutou supported his right injured arm and shoulder. "Hold the canoe still and lift," Coutou said. We lifted as if we were one. He gritted his teeth as we lowered him on to a firm leather mattress. He moaned and fell into unconsciousness.'

Wrasse began to pant. She felt the memory of her young body fill her old sagging one as she relived those moments. Shala waited for Wrasse to continue. Her breath eased. 'Coutou raised his withered hand. At his elbow there were several cuts. "The sinews are severed", she exclaimed out loud.'

Wrasse paused for several long breaths. Shala remained silent. Slowly she began her story again. 'Coutou sighed and shook her head. The smell worsened, pus ran from his forearm – well, what was left of it. Coutou looked round at us all, saying in slow amazement, "He's tried to cut his own arm off." Our looks were all so confused and shocked.' Wrasse closed her eyes, seeing it all just as it was decades ago.

'"Right," Coutou commanded.' Shala jumped at the sudden change in Wrasse's voice. '"I will need hot water. I want the clay room-heater loaded with the best charcoal. Get me as much dried meadowsweet as possible, and fresh moss. I want gut cord to stop his blood. I want apple vinegar in my water to wash the knives. Find me a flint blade core. I have one somewhere in my bag, but it's nearly done"', Wrasse reported, adding, 'We were totally in her command. *He*, even, seemed to relax.

'Coutou put her hand on his forehead; it came away shining with sticky sweat. She washed her hands and told my Mum to carefully cut his coat and vests off. She did. As she cut, my father eased his skins away. Mother trimmed along the seams with her special jasper blade. I remember the sinews popping as she cut. There was a big bruise in his ribs under his right arm. This had yellowed, with time, and the broken ribs beneath had grown back together. He'd been injured for weeks, Shala.'

Wrasse put her hand out for a sip of water. Shala, shaking, handed her a brimming cup. Some spilt as it passed from hand to hand. Wrasse drank.

'"First," Coutou said, "we'll finish the job he began." She took her grey flint knife. Its blade was polished, for a cleaner cut. Coutou raised his arm gently. She asked for some rosemary fronds. Someone ran outside to pick a bunch. She told me to slowly push his hand down. I could barely look, but I did it. The smell was horrid, Shala, but I had to put it to the back of me. Coutou placed the knife at the bare bones of his elbow and cut the sinew. She pulled his arm towards her and, with a sharper tawny flint blade, parted his blackened flesh. Fetid, clotted blood oozed from his veins. My father tightened the loop of gut round his upper arm.'

Wrasse sighed, and sipped her water. 'Coutou pressed some long blades from the flint core and put the razors on a broken potshard. She placed it over the charcoal brazier and blew. Sparks appeared, and slowly the broken bit of pot heated dull red. The black flint flakes gradually turned grey then, just as they were becoming white, she took the crock off. They cooled slowly. She took the first fresh blade. It slid through his flesh easily. With only a few expert movements and twists, the man's forearm lifted free.' Shala wiped her own brow with the back of her hand.

'Coutou said to him, although he couldn't hear, "That is done, Sea Angel. Now for the rest." She gently placed his limb on the fire. It hissed as it burned. The terrible stench eased. "He won't have felt a thing during that", Coutou said, "it's the next bit I'm bothered about". He slept. She went to her house. She told me to watch him and sing softly. We all hummed and crooned. Dad played his flute so softly. The 'Sea Angel's' face relaxed into a deep slumber.

'Coutou returned with her medicine cup and spoon. She had so many different things in her house. She brought a soft skin pouch full of dried leaves and flower heads. She crushed them in her mortar with a pebble and mixed in a little hot honey. She stirred and poured this into her medicine cup. It smelt pungent, yet sweet. She washed the mortar with hot water and rinsed that in, too. She stirred with her mussel shell spoon. "Wrasse," she asked, "lift his head. I will open his jaw; that is, if it will still open," she commented. She sighed with relief as she eased his teeth apart. I saw his tongue, Shala. It was white, blotchy and ulcerated. His lips were scabby and his teeth seemed loose. I stroked his hair back from his forehead and saw his star tattoo, just at his hairline.'

Shala could see how much all this meant to Wrasse. 'Go on,' she urged quietly.

Wrasse sipped again. 'My sisters made up verses which started:
Sleep, sleep, sleep.
Sleep deeply our Sea Angel.
Sleep deeply and rise for us.
Rise when you are well.

'It was a very soft song. I can hear it now. Coutou spooned her brew slowly into his mouth. He choked a little and his eyes opened. He looked at mine. I smiled at him. He tried to smile, too. *Later,* I thought and hoped. Coutou slowly administered the draft. The Sea Angel swallowed gradually. Coutou kept on spooning from the shell until he fell deeply asleep.

'"We must wait. Now," Coutou said, "I know you won't really want to do this, but you have to cut the rest of his clothes off." My sisters giggled. I shivered. "You must gently wash whilst my draught takes effect. The washing will soothe him. Build the fires up and bring another brazier and more charcoal. He must keep warm while I cut his arm further. I also want to see if he has more injuries." Coutou looked under his upper arm at the wound. "He's been stabbed; looks like an antler tip. Never mind, it is healing and not oozing."

'I watched as his leather seafarer's breeks were cut down the seams to his feet. The front side was peeled away to show his navel, then penis, crotch and legs. The sisters concentrated their gaze on his manhood. Extremely disappointed they were, too. His stomach was hollow and wasted, his pelvis stuck out and his little tool was shrunken into his faint, tangled hairs. My sisters lifted his bum and withdrew his breeks. The fur linings were strange to us. Although they were matted like felt, they were different from anything we'd seen. Those garments came off like a lobster shell. I held his head so the last of his draught would go down. I watched my sisters clean him. I was jealous of them, but I had my part to do. As his legs were bared, we saw his tattoos. They were like fine fish netting, all down to his ankles.

'Coutou arranged a headrest for our Sea Angel, then she asked me to wash and comb his beard. "Wrasse," she said to me, "this is very important. You must bathe his cheeks and make his whiskers soft with warm water. Use moss. Then rub ewe's milk onto his cheeks. Then, with this blade," she handed me one of whitened ones, "shave his cheeks; do not shave his chin or top lip." She went on, "I have to cut more of his arm off and I do not want dirty whiskers getting in my way if he struggles. So you will have to untangle his beard meticulously and wrap it in a binding of soft goatskin. When you have done that, he should be in a very deep sleep. I will then shave his oxters off." All this I did. I noticed that even in his deepening sleep his hazel eyes were searching under his eyelids. I held up the rest of his arm. I had moss in my hand to rest it on whilst Coutou shaved his armpits. A covey of strange lice failed to escape her notice. They burned on the fire with his shaven straw hair.

'His armpit was not blighted. Coutou was very relieved. "I thought I was going to have to cut the rest of his arm off at the shoulder. Instead, I can leave a stump of bone. That's better." The Sea Angel's eyes stopped their search. Coutou saw that. She took the second whitened blade and carefully cut just above that rotting flesh over his elbow. She exposed his big veins, but never severed one. Coutou sweated. She steeped her long, grey serrated knife in the vinegar-water with a frond of her rosemary. She cut to his bone. I watched while my sisters washed his legs. The fragrance of the water filled the warm room.

'Blood dripped from his arm, but we kept the gut tight. Coutou raised it high. His face winced once. She cut a flap of skin and left it dangling from his underarm. She teased his flesh away from the bone and still left the big veins uncut. She pulled that sickening stub of meat away. It fell limp, like rotting liver on to the floor. Coutou signalled to Mum to burn it. Ashes and embers were heaped over it, stopping the smell. So, Shala,' Wrasse went on, 'do you want me to finish this, or shall I stop there?'

'I think you should finish. I believe I need to know what happened, whether I like it or not.'

'So you do. So you do, young lady, so you do.' Wrasse sat up.

The sounds of builders, chopping wood, grunting as the trees were being shifted, was their background. The smells of cooking, grain being milled. All this masked their conversation. What Shala shared was not hers to share with others. She was to keep it safe, locked away, hidden.

Wrasse sipped, beginning again. 'Coutou had sent him into an unconscious sleep. She removed her great flint knife from the heating water. The blade steamed and dried. She placed it on the bone and began to saw. Progress was not fast. She picked one of the hardened white flakes. With the back of her big knife she pressed out little notches along its sharpest edges. Between her forefinger and thumb she held the ends of her tiny saw. She wedged it in the bottom of the cut in his bone and sawed. Alternating with the knife, she cut all the way round the bone. Its end joint still shone with pus.

'Coutou stopped and pointed to the whale backbone they used for butchery. My father fetched it. Coutou placed it under his shoulder so the arm bone was sticking up. "Hold his shoulder down tight," she said. "Keep a grip on his body," she told us girls.' Wrasse wiped her brow; her eyes were wide open, as if she were there. 'Coutou jerked smartly down and the Sea Angel's bone broke clean. Marrow slipped out and rested on his flesh. Coutou wiped it away. His limp arteries and veins dangled on the slab. She tied a knot in each one, just like the baby's cord she'd done earlier. She took the blade with the sharpest point and dug holes through the Angel's flap of skin. Coutou then threaded the tied blood vessels through the fleshy side of the flap. She fumbled in her bag for her needlecase and took her slimmest needle, fashioned from a gull's wingbone, and stitched his skin flap up to his shoulder with bog cotton threads.

'Coutou looked silently round at all of us, then she gazed at our Sea Angel and said, "That's all I can do. Time will see if it works." Shortly after, she said, "You will watch over him, Wrasse. You found him. He's more yours than anyone's."

'Shala,' Wrasse admitted. 'This has tired me greatly. I need a rest. Will you get me some fruit-bread and honey?'

'Certainly, Wrasse.' She went down the ladder and asked Quernstone.

Gull enquired, 'How is Wrasse?'

'She's telling me things, but she is very tired now.'

'What things?' Quernstone said with her ears flapping,

'Things,' Shala answered.

That was enough. Quernstone knew not to ask again. She handed over raspberry bread, honey and warm milk in a bowl.

'She didn't ask for warm milk, Quernstone.'

'No,' Quernstone answered, 'that's for you.'

'Thank you,' Shala replied with a smile, and scaled the ladder with their snacks.

When Shala returned, Wrasse was sound asleep. She sipped her milk, dipping the honeyed fruit bread, and sat silently thinking.

* * * * *

Outside, where all the work was going on, Sable arrived on foot from Char. 'Play where you want, Sprig, but come the moment I call,' Sable told her son. 'Leave Mutt in peace. That bone's hers,' she warned. 'Now, Gull, the purpose of my visit... Is there anything you need from us, over in Char? If there is, then do ask. We have come off better than you. We are sheltered by the hill. I pity those over on Netland Head. They will have got the full force of Kull.'

Partan, assuming complete charge, directed operations. He ordered, 'That whole roof must come off,' as they began on Quernstone's house. 'We will have to take any loose walling down then rebuild higher. Leave the door jambs, they are fine.' Then he asked Reaper, 'Can I have your old hazel poles from up there? You know, the ones that supported the earlier awning. They will make good measures.'

'Fine,' came the reply.

'Dale, climb up and fetch them. Run them round to my wreck of a house.'

'I'm glad to see you hard at work, Flint,' Partan commented.

'I'm chopping the roots off this pine. Then we can split it into planks.'

'Rod, you be more careful with that axe. Go gently or you'll bust it,' Partan advised.

'I'll select the uprights. Jasper, can you mark off the ones for spars?' Partan asked, taking his jacket off. 'The sun's come out. It's going to be nice,' he commented. Jasper marked a tree with his axe.

Wrasse wakened slowly and looked at Shala. She thought to herself, 'She is Aiva, actually, but only she will know when to be called that.' She glanced to her tray of bread and honey. 'May I have a chunk, please?'

'Certainly,' Shala said, 'with milk or without?'

'With, please, and make sure it's creamy, not like ewe's piss.'

When Shala came back up with a cup, Wrasse asked, 'Do you want me to go on, Ai... Shala?' stopping herself from using that name.

'Yes, please, Wrasse. I only asked you about the goose tattoo and I haven't heard anything of it yet.'

'Shala, some things have much behind them. Answers to short questions aren't always simple or, indeed, easy.' Wrasse cleared her throat and mopped her chin with a swab of moss. 'I will go on,' she said. 'Sea Angel lay on his sick bed. It was a like this one, slatted so the sweat runs through. He slept long and deeply. Us sisters had to get the birthing room ready, much like the one you have. We did that and made it fragrant and warm. Coutou told us to take him through when it was done. Only dim lights could be lit. We took a corner each of his litter and carried him in. He never stirred. I stayed alone with him. My sisters went to their beds and spoke of men and giggled for ages. They had been to the Women's Lodge at Farsee. I hadn't, but I knew about men.' She moved, and the bed creaked. 'I sat through the night listening to his shallow breathing. His respiration rattled sometimes in this throat and bile crept from one corner of his mouth. He looked better in the low light. His beard cast a strange shadow. Our dog came in and lay by me. In the early hours, Coutou came back. She listened to his chest and looked at the wound under where his arm was. It had healed, but she was still very concerned about it. She wiped bile from his lips, smelt it, and I took it to the fire.

'"He might live," she said. Crusts of fresh, good blood had oozed from the skin flap and had formed scabs. There was no sign of infection on his arm any more. She removed his bedclothes gently and looked at the colour of his skin. It was less pale. She was happier. She did say, "Those feet of his could do with a good dog lick, though." That's why I enjoyed mine. It brought some of it back.

'I slept and Coutou watched over him, then my mother did for a while. It was my turn again. I didn't know how long he'd been sleeping. Then I heard him stir. He coughed up bile. It stank. I wiped his mouth and leaned him forward. He coughed and vomited up more vile stuff. I called Coutou. She helped me clean him, then he choked. She leaned him out of his bed and climbed over his body and, from behind, pulled him up by his stomach. His arse rested under her chin. From his gaping mouth came streams of muck and mucus. He stopped choking and began spitting. His eyes opened. He drew in vast gulps of air. We cleaned him up. We put a pillow behind his back and he looked at us. He then closed his eyes tight and said, "Naarwaaaaaaaaaarl," in a long, low, frightening growl. He then fell into another slumber.'

Shala listened, gripped by Wrasse's story. She sat closer and Wrasse went on. 'The next day he woke for a while. Coutou and I fed him beef stew. It had cooked slowly on and off for two days and was beautifully tender. I can smell it now, the dried mushrooms, the big pieces of rib and tail. The meat was very soft and he could chew gently and swallow. We cooled it, so his ulcerated tongue didn't get burned. His scabby lips were clearing up. His eyes brightened. He seemed to be more at ease. Coutou was pleased.

'Earlier my parents had searched through his canoe. They found the white stone knife he'd tried to cut his arm off with. It must have fallen underneath him and he couldn't get it back. It was the same stone as your broken arrow, Shala. There were a few fish heads on some bone hooks and lines. He must have fed himself by fishing and drifting. There was a leather cover for the canoe, to stop the sea coming in, but it was rather rotten. It was amazing he'd remained afloat. But it had been calm after the Equinox gales.

'The only word he would say was 'narwhal'. He was getting stronger though, and ate more. I cleaned his shit for him. I didn't mind. I'd done worse things. Coutou was called to a small house away up the burn. I stayed with the Sea Angel.

'He had seen the stump of his arm and he nodded to me. I told him my name was Wrasse. He smiled. He pointed to his chest. "Weir," he told me. I was so happy. He smiled weakly again. I fed him and put my arm round his shoulder and my Sun breast touched his amputation. Wrasse," he said. "Weir," I answered.

'I lay there and held him for some while. He coughed, so I moved to wipe his lips. Then I showed him my tattoo of the fishes. It was very dim light, but my skin shone. He liked them. I took his bedclothes away from him to look again at his decorated legs and saw his penis had changed. His balls had dropped from their receded position, too.

'Whilst he had been unconscious, my sisters had washed him and combed his hairs there. They had curled prettily and shone in the glimmer of the lamp flame. I saw his little trunk roll to one side and grow. He stood firm, as his foreskin swelled. "Sea Angel" looked into my eyes, then to my breasts. His eyes veered with mine down to his groin. He smiled kindly to me and nodded. I was trembling, Shala, I was shaking. I crawled over him and my big Sun and Moon breasts touched his nipples. I felt the tip of his penis touch me somewhere moist and warm, where those fishes pointed. I pressed down on him as though it was forever and endless. He moved within me very slightly upwards. I felt an enormous pressure. I moved forward and back as he kissed the top of my head. I moved up and down gently and firmly as he responded. Weir held me down on him with his good arm and I felt a great rush of warm wetness flowing into me as he pressed upwards. It was all so wonderful.' Wrasse shifted on her bed, it creaked again as she remembered, lovingly.

'As I lay there on him, his arm moved on my back. With his sharp forefinger, he scratched deeply into my skin from my neck to my arse. He slowly scored the image of a goose. I did not resist. When he had finished, his arm relaxed and I sat up on him and gazed down onto his beautiful face with his bandaged beard. He looked at me and was forming my name with his lips when he coughed. He coughed once more and a great clart of blood hit my chest. He coughed and coughed violently; more blood and bile came gushing out of his mouth. He collapsed back on his bed and he was DEAD!'

Wrasse burst into uncontrollable tears. Her breast heaved and she wailed. She pulled her greying hair and scratched her scalp. Everyone in Lee Holme heard those desperate cries from her depths. Cries, that had never before been released, turned into a flood that could break all dams and riverbanks. Her salty tears flowed freely from her. Wrasse's wailing and screams of woe rose. 'I loved him so,' she managed through her distress.

All work stopped on the village. There was a great silence. Folk gathered around the house and gazed up. Gull ran in the door, rushi up the ladder to Wrasse's chamber. She saw her engulfed in emotion. Shala was supporting her as she shook intorment.

Gull returned below and stood at the doorway. Shala held onto Wrasse. She stroked and comforted her. The stress of years of hidden grief were released. Wrasse tried to speak, but she could not. She wept on as Shala said, 'There, there. There, there,' the comforting words her mother used: it was all she knew to do.

Gradually, the salty sobs decreased in power. Wrasse relaxed a little and began to slump backwards onto her bed. Shala reached for another pillow. Wrasse put her shaking hand out for a drink. Shala handed her the cup, saying, 'There, there.'

Wrasse sipped very slowly. The small gulps of water eased her tense throat. But she still could not speak. Shala sat silently, steadying the cup in her hand. Wrasse, as in a dream, remembering so clearly her trauma, slid into deep slumber. Shala said, 'There, now. Sleep, Wrasse, sleep.'

8

A New Sensation

Oiwa's family gathered round their outside fire, just like so many others of the Goose Clan. His father, the chief, was a respected hunter. Mica, Bark and Tine were taught well by him.

'Take what you need,' Tine said to New Moon, the first neighbour coming for meat.

'Thank you, Tine. Please come by, I have pine-nut cakes.'

'I will. You are kind,' he replied as she left for her hearth.

'I love beaver meat,' said North Star to Petal, who pulled a rear leg off for him. 'It tastes of the smell of water lilies. It has the essence of unfolding leaves of a spring birch. When I eat it, I hear honey bees and birdsong.'

'Yes. We know you love it best,' Mica said, reaching for a piece.

'Is Big Hunter not getting any?' Ripple's voice came from behind, tickling the back of his neck with partridge feathers. 'You can share a partridge if you come by my tent.' The feathers touching his nape froze him with pleasure.

'Have a front leg,' Honey offered.

'Marvellous,' he said, 'so loose and succulent.'

'Show us your bow again?' asked Mica.

Oiwa stood, turning to get it. Ripple tripped him. He sprawled.

'Oh, Big Hunter,' she uttered. 'Let me help you up?' holding out a teasing hand and a feather.

'It's so embarrassing,' Oiwa thought, back in the wigwam, listening to muffled mirth, outside. It dispersed as he returned to the fireside. 'She's gone,' Oiwa thought in relief. He sat, picking his teeth with a beaver rib while Honey and Petal sang songs of the geese.

'Oiwa, stand up with your bow against you,' Bark suggested.

'Just touching the tip of your droopy dick,' Mica joked.

'It should be nudging your navel; that bow's too short. You've grown far too much,' Tine chipped in.

'Your brothers are right, Oiwa, you need a longer one,' North Star put in. His brothers laughed enormously. 'Stop it boys,' their father ordered. 'It's not right to tease,' he added, grinning.

The clouds separated. The moon shone on Oiwa. He remembered the face in the water momentarily. 'I have to choose someone to pass my old bow on to. I'll think about that,' Oiwa answered. 'So it's still all right for me to borrow your axe, Mica?'

'Yes, Big Hunter,' he teasingly replied.

The next morning Oiwa wakened in a brotherly huddle on their wigwam floor, remembering how every year they covered the large river pebbles with new clay. Then the hides they slept upon were stretched over it. Their smouldering fire was in the centre, surrounded by scorched stones.

Oiwa went to the bushes and dug a small pit for his toilet. 'I smell beaver,' he said out loud. 'A reminder of his successful hunt.' He covered his traces with loose earth and washed in a small rivulet rising from a bubbling spring. Walking back to breakfast he met Tine en route to the undergrowth. His sisters were returning from their ablutions on another side of the village. Quill had been up for a while and, like a good mother, had cracked stored nuts to have with honey. She crouched, hammerstone in hand, going through remnants of the previous autumn's harvest. The empty shells gathered in a ring at the edge of her rock anvil. Bark scooped them for the fire.

'We'll slice the rest of the caribou and hang it to dry,' Honey said as she took out her obsidian knife. 'Pelt will guard it.' Their big brindled dog looked eager. 'Here's a bone' she called, chucking him a shin.

Oiwa crunched his last honeyed nut and licked his shallow

wooden bowl. He swilled his mouth with clear, cold water and cleaned his white teeth with a chewed stick. The sun banished the mist from the treetops and distant mountains before he gathered his bow and quiver. 'Here's my axe,' Mica said, pulling it from his belt.

'Thanks.' Oiwa touched the sharp edge of the implement, feeling proud to borrow it. He slipped it in his belt. 'I'm off, then.'

'Come back lucky, Oiwa,' his kin said.

Passing Ripple's door flap, her young twins called, 'Big Hunter, can we come?'

'No,' he said quietly, 'Play with your little sister, be good.' Oiwa walked on. The power of the River Dun was in force. Meltwaters from the mountains rushed to where Oiwa knew only from distant legends, telling of its length, strength and mystery.

Oiwa thought. 'I'll go to where I killed the beaver. There are groves of straight trees there.' He strode powerfully through thickets and grassy clearings. He stepped over narrow rivulets and leaped others feeding the Dun. He trekked uphill to a ridge overlooking Mirror Ponds. 'I don't want a sapling. A larger tree, but supple, is what I'm looking for. I see a new bow in every tree. There's a bent one. That won't do. I can see that other one breaking. My old bow is elm. I like it: springy yet tough. I'll search on.

'This isn't easy. Wherever I look there's something that's not quite right. There's one that could suit Dad. That one might be all right for Honey, but she can have this when I've made my new one,' he decided, fondling his old bow affectionately. '"Dangly dick", indeed. I'll show them,' he thought, wandering on.

Doves scattered from trees above. Squirrels slid behind trunks. Oiwa was not hunting them. He sat for a while, chewing dried venison. As his saliva softened it, the flavour expanded with each jaw clench. 'I'll have some more. I always swallow the first bit too soon,' he remembered, masticating quietly, contemplating his surroundings.

'What was that?' A twig snapped directly behind. He looked round. 'It's a huge, huge, black cat!' He yelled, leaping in alarm, spilling his arrows with a clatter. The feline sprang, fur on end, hissing and spraying disgusting scent then turned fleeing.

'Waaaaaaah!' shouted Oiwa, shaking inside, violently coughing up venison. It caused uproar in the woods. Jays screeched. Doves flapped alarmed. Startled, unseen deer rushed deeper onto the undergrowth and squirrels raced higher in the trees.

'My heart's beating so rapidly. But it's vanished, thank Gumar. I smell its spray. And, thank Tumar, not on me. It ran right past that tree. Oh, it's sturdy and straight, bark slightly wrinkled: there are no lower branches. Let me look closer. There's a beautiful bow within. I see it flexing, bending and springing perfectly in my mind. I must feel it: my new weapon's living in there. Thank the Forest Spirits for my great fortune and for my courage to scare that terrifying lynx off.

The beautiful polished axe, flaked from silver-spangled, dark green stone, had a fine cutting edge. 'Here goes,' Oiwa said to himself, 'let's chop. Only the weight of the axe, as father taught me. If I swing with force, it can shatter. "No. Not hard, Son," Dad advised, then he'd say, "Easy, easy; remember: chip, chip, finishes the log. Chop upwards into the wood: then a downward cut at knee-height to meet the first. Chop all round, like that." This is sweaty work. I'll take my jerkin off. Here, bow and arrows, you can lie on it. Have a quick look round. Make sure that cat doesn't creep back. Right, chop away. A second round will bring it closer to falling. Stand back. Look at the stem. Decide where to chop to drop. Just a few blows here will do it. It's creaking. The high branches lean. Stand aside, look up: Watch it come down. There it goes, kissing the others goodbye. That's a new space in the canopy; and I did it. Great! Just hear it bouncing in the forest litter.

'The trunk's good. I'll take a longer bit than needed. Measure three times and cut once, as Dad says. Up to my chest, I think. Lie down, Oiwa and mark it. Right. Brush this bruck off and cut through... Not another lynx?' Oiwa thought, catching a suspicious sound. 'No. Nothing: probably just an upper branch swinging back. Time to trim and cut the length. It's thick enough to split into several bows. I'll have the best one. Only a few swings: last chop: done,' he said out loud.

'More meat: I deserve it after that. I'll squat on my trophy and cut a strip. What great sport I'll have with my bow,' he mused, chewing. 'My brothers are right, though. I need a powerful weapon. Big game, not just beavers. There's that rustle again! Listen. There races my heart. Quiet... It lunges. AAAAH! I'm caught. Yes, but it is two horribly painted arms. Leave me. Get off!' he yelped, struggling.

'I'm choking again. Get your hair off my face. Who are you?' he shouted, choking up the soggy venison.

'Big Hunter,' he heard whispered hoarsely in his right ear. 'Big Hunter. It's only naked Ripple. Don't fret. I've brought you your flight feathers. Here, look in my hand.'

'Thanks, I have plenty,' he answered, looking down at them. 'You've smeared dark paint all over my stomach.'

'Oh, poor boy. Let me clean you up,' she teased, pulling his breeks out and dropping the trimmed feathers down his torso.

'Get your hot, oily body off of me!' he fiercely responded.

'No: you're mine, now. Anyway, we have to retrieve those flights, don't we? Let me delve.'

'Urrrghh,' Oiwa thought, 'It feels like a hairy spider.'

'Nice down here, isn't it?'

'Leave that alone,' he demanded as she pulled out a knot of Oiwa's new, tightly curled hairs.

'Ouch!' he protested as she tugged again.

'Oh. Sorry,' Ripple giggled, tugging a second ringlet away, 'I'll hunt somewhere else.

'Oh no, I can't stop it. I'm going stiff. She's tickling my nuts.'

'I'll just have to feel a little further. Here's one, Big Hunter. How did it get so far down?' she whispered, deftly stroking him with it as her left hand untoggled his belt. 'Down come your furry troos. We will see so much better.'

'She's pushing them off, but I'm not moving. It feels fantastic. Eeek. My pee-er is caught. She's shoved me forward. Right. I'm kicking these things away. She's still got me. I feel her greasy belly on my bum. But it's great. She's twisting me. Her round face, it's covered in green lines. Most of her is in dappled shades of brown. A great white oval is painted round her crotch, her hairs red ochre. Ripple's inside legs are reddened with haematite: bloodlike. It's her invitation to mate.'

'Aren't you going to do anything, Big Hunter?' She teased. 'Your arrow sticking out tells me you'd like to stick it in.'

'Yes,' he grinned; thoughtfully scratching his bum; making his arrow wag. 'My first time. What a surprise. This'll be great.'

'Come here,' beckoned Ripple.

'I feel her breath on my chest. Her red-nippled breasts sway. I'm even stiffer. She's got hold of it. She's dragging me down to the mossy ground with her black hand. I'm on my knees. Oh gosh!

She's waving it on her wet crotch and shoving my foreskin back further. It... It, it is so, so... good. Ooooooooh... Ripple's pulling me in. 'Let go,' he groaned, lurching forward, 'I can do the rest myself,'

'Wow,' he uttered as Ripple's hips rose. 'That amazing sensation down in my guts. It's like yesterday, when I shot the beaver, but much more intense. Now I pull back. That's what men do. Shit! Too far: I'm out. Where's that glorious place? Missed. She's grabbed me again, shoving him back inwards. "Deeper, Oiwa," she's saying, "Don't slip out again."

'I'll show her how far I can push. There, right in: into a place of red glory. Pull gently back, not so far this time. I'm shaking. My knees wobble uncontrollably: Ripple's clenching my backside down.'

'Steady, steady. Make it last,' she whispered.

'I'm not in control. She's shoving me further into her. My balls are squashing in her wet crotch's lips. Oh... Oh, I'm going to cum. Pull back? Ripple's gripped me, pressing me in more: Her nails dig in my buttocks. Too late: I'm cuming... Wonderful, oh; so, so... w o n d e r f u l. I'm jerking inside, pumping sperm far and wide.'

He lay on Ripple, trembling, her paint slippery with his perspiration as the last three weakening shots left him.

'She's patting my scrotum gently. Now she's grabbed me, pushing me up. Now dragging me back. I understand. Do it again. Here goes. Oh, but it's sore: Magnificent, a moment ago. Now it's painful pleasure. I don't think I can do this. She's moaning and moaning, revolving my hips. She's squeezing my man in her: he's going floppy. Ugh... she's stopped. I can lie still.'

'"Wow." Is that all you can say?' Ripple complained. 'This moss is cripplingly uncomfortable now. Off you get.'

'I can't move,' he responded, feeling his calf spasm.

'Yes, you can.'

'Ow! Ouch! It's cramp. I'm stuck.'

'Why get cramp now? You stupid imp,' Ripple bitterly chastised, trying to wiggle him away.

'AAAaaaaaaaaH. Stop,' Oiwa appealed, 'It's aaaaaaagony.'

'Well, I've got a fucking pinecone up my backside, mate... Off,' she shouted pushing him up.

'Ah Ah AAAaaaaaaaHhhhh,' Oiwa screamed, gasping and threshing, his left leg bent in an agonized contortion.

His erection collapsed completely as he hopped on his good,

right leg. His chest was covered in Ripple's paintwork. Smears of red from her nipples adorned his own, his flat stomach a muddy brown mess. A stressed and tangled feather was stuck to his inner thigh. Around his glistening penis, smudges of Ripple's white and red dyes mixed to a fleshy pink. A dribble of semen, like a dewy pearl, dropped to the moss as he hopped.

'AAAAAAAAAaaaaaaaaaaaaaaaaaaaCH!' he yelled, trying to straighten his rigid leg. His hips and thighs, covered in Ripple's rouge, mixed with the tan, like marble: His left cheek and ear, messy with oily make-up. Two dark handprints adorned his backside.

'At last. It's clearing. I can ease my leg,' he remarked as his penis tip receded within the protection of his foreskin. 'Better now, Ripple. I can wriggle my toes,' he reported, massaging his painful muscle. 'It's okay. My cramp's gone,' he repeated. 'It's better. Where *are* you?'

The Big Hunter stood alone, naked in the bright forest light, searching. 'She's gone. Disappeared. Not a sign: vanished.' He wondered, amazed, staring into space. 'What a mess,' he thought, looking down. 'Where are my breeks? Oh. There, upside down on that bush.' He put his good leg in first, then slowly eased the cramp-stricken one through the other leather tunnel. He hitched them up, remembering being caught when forcibly lowered.

'My bow and arrows are still on my jerkin. And Ripple's flights are scattered all over my quiver. Now to find Mica's axe. There it is, stuck in the tree stump. The stone head's deeply cold on my hip when I tuck back it in. There's my knife, next to the soggy venison. Sheath it, balance the trunk on my shoulder, and go,' he told himself, contemplating his first genuine orgasm.

'There was no sign of Ripple's tracks, nor a whiff in the air. I feel clumsy in my gait. I'm making too much noise for a Big Hunter. I'd better be ready,' Oiwa thought. 'I'll notch my last quartz-tipped arrow in my bow and pull it tight.'

Approaching the Dun, the meltwaters tumbled, 'That sounds just like new quartz pebbles rumbling along the bed. We'll get them when the river is down to make fresh heads. Another reason why we return here.'

'I reckon Ripple will appreciate another partridge,' Oiwa thought excitedly. 'Maybe I can prong one on the way back? I'll follow the sloping banks of the river to the gravelly ridge further down. They go there for gizzard grit, near dusk. There I'll wait, silent under the willows.' There, catkins touched his jerkin, leaving scented yellow pollen. He practised pulling on his bow to see which twigs moved or did not. The river tumbled by, just yards away. Wagtails and dippers worked for their living on the rapid's wet rocks. The Dun was over an arrowshot across. The river narrowed below, deepened and slowed near the Goose Clan's village. 'I wonder if the fish traps have been seen to?' he wondered, waiting. 'Bees gather nectar in the crocuses over there. Perhaps a hare might drop by to the nibbled turf. Now I've got pins and needles in my cramped leg. Wiggle my in toes to relieve it. Mustn't rustle the leaves. Ah... there's the whiff of fox. Is she waiting for a bird, too? That's the pins and needles again, feeling like ants.

'Yes. Wingbeats. Here they come. Dark shapes, speeding in the evening sky, now landing on the shingle bank: just what I want. The covey is scanning round nervously. Soon they'll peck up the sharp grains. That's when I'll shoot one. Dang, I want to pee. Can't. Now it's a fart. Clench it back. Shhhhh. Let them get confident. At last: draw your old bow, Oiwa. Quiet. Don't shift a leaf. My triangular point's touched my tense knuckles. There's a partridge scraping happily. Check the trajectory. I hear their beaks and claws scratch. Kiss the string. Let go! She's heard it. Too late, thud. She's taken it right through, trussing her nest mate too. Load another. They're off... shoot. Got it. There the rest go, squawking, beating alarmed wings. Third one down, thudding the ground: Good,' he commentated loudly as feathers floated. 'Nest mate's not dead. Grab it. Pull its neck. Don't bust the arrow. Be careful,' Oiwa minded, as a sad vixen slunk stealthily deeper into the undergrowth.

'Brilliant! I'll take the skewered brace to Ripple and just drop the third as a by-the-way, from the Big Hunter.'

He shouldered his bow-wood, crunching proudly from the rapids towards the camp. A kingfisher darted from a stump to the rushing water.

Oiwa passed the first tent in the ring. The North Star glimmered above the horizon. There were welcoming nods from his clansfolk as he displayed his double hit. Ripple's wigwam loomed. The twins were outside yelling, 'Big Hunter,' in welcome. Oiwa, smiling broadly, reached the hide opening. The door flap shifted. He displayed his offering. A head moved from behind the moose skin. Oiwa stepped forward, the partridges dangled. A long eagle feather loomed from behind the doorway. Barb, Ripple's man's head was below it. 'Good evening Big Hunter,' greeted Barb gruffly.

Oiwa dropped his prize, gasping, not realizing Barb was home from the hunt. He hurtled to his own tent in shock. He entered the darkness, his family all there. 'Welcome home, Big Hunter,' they greeted.

'I'm speechless,' he thought mouth agape, dropping his bow-wood. His untrapped wind answered them audibly.

'How has your day been, Oiwa?' Quill asked from her crouching position.

He answered nothing.

Bark stood. The black embroidered goose on his jacket moved as he breathed. 'Barb brought you these from Ripple.' Holding his hand over Oiwa's head, he released a flutter of arrow flights. Oiwa blushed his reddest, grimacing whilst awkwardly shrugging his shoulders. North Star was the first to laugh. Quill shook, followed by his sisters' outrageous giggling. Mica and Tine joined loudly. Bark waited, watching Oiwa's face as his ability to speak returned. He put his arm round his brother and said, 'Poor Oiwa. It's okay. We put her up to it. You don't even have to tell us about the cramp.'

'I thought it was all so marvellous,' he said almost cheerfully.

'Oiwa. Young brother,' Mica put in, 'You have grown and achieved much. We reckoned it would be good for you.'

Bark commented, 'That beaver was great. We enjoyed it. You did well, Big Hunter. It's our way of saying thanks.'

'So, you set me up,' Oiwa said, shaking his head with a shy grin.

'Well. It would've happened soon,' Tine said. 'Ripple was determined to get you, you know.'

Bark grasped Oiwa's shoulders and explained, 'She does it with most of the growing lads,' flicking his nose lightly, in a very friendly way.

'You get to mate with her once. She only does it when she is safely giving Moon Blood,' he concluded.

'Yes, Son,' Quill concluded, 'there has to be a first mating. Ripple enjoys her role, Barb understands. He just acts gruff.'

Honey and Petal shifted poignantly as their mother explained. 'We all love mating, but don't abuse it. If we didn't couple, there'd be no infants. You wouldn't be here, nor me.' She and North Star looked over her brood proudly. 'We know when we can mate for children, also when purely for pleasure. We understand when not to be mated with, too.' North Star nodded, twitching his long, whiskery chin.

'I gave birth to you all. I lost two of you. That is plenty of children to bear, but I wanted you. I love you all. I want you to grow, being good people. Mica will be taking his woman from the Caribou Clan soon; she will live in our band. You, Bark and Tine have women waiting somewhere.' Quill advised, 'Sons, you've all cuddled and mated. On your travels you will caress and join with the womenfolk. The clans of man are wide and broad, the way Gumar and Tumar ordered it. If it is Gumar and Tumar's wish that you give fertility honourably as you journey, then let it be so.'

A long, thoughtful silence reigned round the wigwam's glowing embers.

9

North Star's Sweat Lodge

'Good morning, Big Hunter,' Ripple called out.

'I'm so embarrassed,' Oiwa felt.

'Stripping the bark off, are we? Pussy got your tongue, too?'

'I wish she'd go away,' he thought, searching his pouch for bone wedges.

'Ignore her. Tap one in across the heartwood.'

'Big Hunter?'

'Missed. Got my thumb. Bugger! That's it. I'll go and speak.'

She stood, holding her youngest to her breast. Milk dribbled down the baby's chin.

'Oh no. I'm getting a stiff on, turn away,' he thought.

'Oiwa,' she said kindly. 'What we did in the forest won't happen again between us. Whilst I'm suckling my child here, I cannot conceive. Oiwa, Big Hunter; for a big hunter you are. You well deserved my favour. I reddened my legs to invite you. I stalked you. I even saw the big cat. It vanished, like a spirit, at your tree. I watched you fell it. You moved beautifully. You never saw me. I creep more quietly than any lynx. Ghost lynx or not.'

'I've been cross, frustrated and embarrassed by all this,' he reacted inwardly. 'I'm calming down, but it ain't easy,' he realized, 'but I can't say it yet.'

Fixing him with her glance, Ripple continued, 'You were a lad. You're greater now. You left life's moisture in me. Now you know what it's like, achieving that. The mystery, revealed for you. You will grow. You'll understand breeding is important, special. It is not just for fun. There will be times when your urge is to mate. Remember my words. Ask yourself, is this right, now?'

'Okay,' Oiwa thought, hesitantly touching the babe's cheek, then turned and left. At his fireside he tapped his wedges, lengthening the lesions. Soon he had four fine bow-lengths.

'This piece is perfect. I can dress it with my basalt scrapers, leave the handgrip thick, and whittle long, willow leaf-shaped arms. I'll whip it below the string notches with sinew and thong to prevent splitting. I can make a fine crosshatch on the grip and up the face of the bow and inlay it with that inviting haematite. Then I'll oil it with goose fat.'

'You are doing that extremely well, Oiwa,' North Star praised. 'Here, use this lynx gut. It's the best bowstring you'll ever get. Use reed seed oil for eternal suppleness. Yours will be the best hunting bow ever.'

'Thank you so much, Dad. I'm so proud now.'

'Good, Son, you should be. Can I knot the loops?'

'Yes. I'd be honoured.'

When finished, Oiwa flexed his bow, feeling its strength, remembering forever the beautiful twang. 'Was that really a lynx spirit guiding me?' he oft wondered as the gut touched his lips.

Mica came by with Bark. Tine was away, meeting folk. 'Try this heavy caribou arrow,' Bark offered.

'Thanks, Bark. I'm itching to use it. I'll shoot it at the rotted larch. I'm not pulling my bow hard, yet. It needs seasoning.'

'Right, Oiwa. Twenty paces to test.'

'To the woods, then.' Oiwa fitted his arrow and drew back his lynx gut, feeling its smooth, tense strength.

'Don't hit the bees' nest,' Mica said, to put him off.

'Thank you,' Oiwa answered awkwardly as the gut touched his lips. Time stopped, with the resounding twang. His arrow struck home. Chips of bark and rotted wood exploded as the stopped bolt vibrated.

'Well done, Oiwa. What are you going to call that amazing beast?' asked Bark.

'I don't know yet.'

'Right,' Mica said. 'Give us your weapon and we'll test it gently while you think.'

'Halloo there,' Tine hailed. 'I've brought Lichen and Rush from the Caribou Clan.'

'It's lucky Oiwa didn't pin you with his new bow, then,' Mica called back.

'We've got a fallow deer and a hare,' he said as they ran towards them.

'I think we can see that, dear brother,' Mica answered.

'That's the name,' Oiwa realized impulsively. 'Ziit. Ziit. The sound of the arrows. It's perfect.'

The two visitors caught up, puffing with their loads. 'Hello, I'm Rush, this is Lichen.' The dark-haired young men bowed, introducing themselves.

'This is Ziit. Listen,' Oiwa said, plucking his string tunefully. 'I remember you. It was when our Clans met some seasons ago as we moved camp.'

'Yes, that's right,' answered Lichen.

Oiwa silently mused, 'I remember how different they are from our Goose Clan. They've no face hair, unlike my brothers. They constantly pluck, and trim with obsidian razors. Others grow them, threading beads. Mine's only downy yet.'

'We'll carry your small burdens to the Clan Ring,' said Bark, 'There you go, Oiwa, pick them up,' he joked. 'We'll go straight to North Star's wigwam.'

'Greetings, young men,' North Star said, wearing his impressive bone and antler necklaces, his grand feathered headdress making him appear taller than ever. 'So, you have come to court our girls, I believe?'

'Thank you for your welcome,' Rush answered shyly. 'Here's a block of razor stone from our mountainside and bears' teeth from...' Rush stuttered, 'one of our bears' heads, I suppose.'

'I'm delighted to accept.'

'Lichen, what wonders have you brought?'

'Pink salt from our cliff and panther claws... from one of our panthers.... It limps now.'

'Come,' invited North Star. Honey opened the flap. 'Be seated. Petal, pass the tray around.'

'It's slices of caribou,' she explained. 'I've beaten them out thinly, then rolled them around crushed pine nuts and grassy onion leaves mixed with poached liver pate: a Goose Clan delicacy. Mother skewered kidney to the slices of tongue.'

'I love it when visitors arrive,' thought Oiwa.

'This night,' North Star announced, 'in our guests' honour, we shall enter the sweat lodge. Oiwa, tell Greyling it's his chance to heat the stones.'

'Right, Father,' he said, taking skewered kidney and tongue while gripping Ziit.

'Greyling,' Oiwa said, being invited in, 'North Star wants the sweat lodge tonight.'

'Yes. He managed my sweat, last time, so it's my turn. My sons are away hunting down the Dun, but I can cope. You could help me now, though. Come to the Clan fire.' By it, in the centre of the plaza, was a smaller area of burnt stones. From there a cobbled pathway led down to a door in a hemispherical dome of stretched skins. It led to a round clay-lined pit. 'We must heave the old stones out, Oiwa, and shift them up the gradient to the fireplace.'

'It smells of juniper in here. It feels mystic and spiritual. I love the polished log benches and the fireside elk-skin water trough. There hangs the cloven bear's skull and goose-shaped ladle, over our large, leather bucket.

'We'll fill that down at the Dun. First we collect tinder then stack it, piling the stones amongst it. You fetch a brand from my fire, shove it deeply in and set it to smoulder. We heap wet leaves over everything so it burns slowly and the cobbles won't crack with rushing heat: Now off to the Dun with the bucket. Ah,' he remarked when there, 'That must be Barb's new canoe.'

Oiwa, embarrassed, lowered his head. Narrowing his pale eyebrows, he suggested shiftily, 'Let's get this filled.'

'Done,' Greyling said after several trips. 'Now we cut juniper and pine for the pit and fill the grease lamps. You light the wicks; that'll warm the place. Then we steep some fronds in the pit.'

'Where's Ziit?' Oiwa suddenly thought, 'Good, just behind the juniper at the door,' while banging his head on a dangling stone lamp and tripping on the moose antler stone shunts.

The first bat coursed the cooling air, inviting its fellows to chase moths. Oiwa returned, hearing news from the Caribous. When it was time to enter the sweat lodge, Greyling greeted them in his feathered finery. His quill-breasted waistcoat shimmered in the dark. Smoke from the stone clamp drifted, sometimes obscuring his painted face, but two luminous white streaks constantly shone on his cheeks. His leather-clad nephew, Tuft, was his assistant. 'We've greased the cobbled path, don't slip,' warned the youngster.

'Please enter,' North Star invited. He sat at the back of his lodge 'This is all new to me,' thought Oiwa. 'Life is changing.'

'Be seated,' came his father's voice. Oiwa watched his brothers remove their clothes and sit. He did likewise. He saw their small stars at their hairlines glittering in the lamplight. His father's glowed brightly.

'It's quite cool in here, despite the lamps,' Oiwa noticed, feeling goose pimples break out. Rush and Lichen removed their neatly stitched suede clothing, folding it carefully. Everyone remained still and silent while North Star droned softly. Slowly nodding, his wispy beard occasionally touched his wrinkled chest. He wore no adornment. Mica, Bark and Tine had tooth pendants glistening on their sternums. Lichen wore a knotted cord with a small perforated stone and Rush a thin sinew holding a drilled cobnut. 'I wish I had a token to wear,' Oiwa yearned momentarily. 'I've just got this annoying flea. Got it, "pop" you go, between my nails. And that's my blood you're bleeding, dead pest.'

'North Star's drone has ceased. The door flaps open. In shoots a hot rounded pebble, followed swiftly by Tuft. He's pushing it along the slippery path with a moose antler. It's dropped onto the soaking mattress. Wow! How the steam explodes. That smell of broiling juniper and pine fills the atmosphere. My pores have opened. Everybody's have. My scalp's oozing. There's more fleas. They're on my shoulders. Get them. We are all doing it. Rush is catching Lichen's for him. Tine's squirming. Another one... Got him. They don't like this juniper much, do they!

'Mica's standing. He's got the bear's skull. He's dipping it in the water tank. The lamplight ripples over him and around the ceiling. Tuft's speeding another rock into the basin. Mica's tipped the skull. Water runs from its eye sockets. The stones hiss. The room fills with intense heat and pungent steam. My lungs are filling with damp forest essences. My nose runs. So does North Star's. He's squeezing it out and flinging it into the pit. They all are. I'd better, too.

'Rush,' Oiwa mentioned, 'You've got fleas escaping from your armpits.'

'You too, Oiwa. You catch mine, I'll get yours.'

'Sure,' he responded.

'Bark is getting the bucket. It's nearly full. Look at everyone's phlegm bubbling in the stones, Oiwa. He's washing his hands now. We all do. Then it goes on the pebbles. That'll douse the snots.'

Up sped steam. 'Everyone's standing in the new vapours. How the lamps glimmer in the mist on us all. My ears have popped. I hear so clearly now. I feel like the whole forest has encroached. The heat's intense. My skin prickles with it. Perspiration pours and I feel so cleansed inside. We're all moving. Changing places. Now I'm sitting again, but next to Tine. How the sweat gushes from his golden oxters.'

'What do you think of this, then, Brother?' Tine asked.

'It's amazing. It's like I'm becoming new inside.' Tine nodded with sweat running from his elbow onto Oiwa's thigh.

Bark rose, bellowing 'Two more?'

'Here they come,' screeched Tuft. They rattled past Rush, hurtling into the pit. Bark held the bucket above his head and quenched the stones. The door flap descended. They were invisible again in their tight capsule. Sweat poured from Oiwa's locks. He leaned his head back, breathing in the wonderful atmosphere.

In the serene heat, Oiwa's mind wandered. 'My head seems to rise far above. I see the clear stars.'

Tine laid a wet juniper branch in the pit. The sensation increased. Oiwa's dream went on. 'I hear the swishing of powerful wings flying past the distant Moon. They beat the droning rhythm of North Star's dirge. My arms stretch and I beat it, too. I sense the tight bounds of the lodge breaking. I lift through the mists. I'm on eye-level with the Great Gander's skein. My arms are wonderful wings as I fly across the night sky.'

He sensed the drag and lift of feathers as he flew within the Great Gander's skein. 'The dark world of forest below shimmers under moonlight. The rivers shine. The Moon and constellations look back up at us from the marsh below. Behind is the vast ocean we've flown over. There, silvery sparkles flash from the waves and an ermine edge beats the shore.

'I gaggle our song with my winged brethren as we return to our frosted tundra. My skein veers. We swoop downwards. Our webbed feet push at the air as we glide to our wet landing, where the Moon reflects to us. We follow him. His wings change movements and we slow. His webs spread. He breaks the mere's waters as we follow. What sheer joy it is to be back, as we float to our nesting grounds.'

Mica cast another skullful on the steaming stones. 'Where have you been, Oiwa?' North Star asked quietly from his lamplight. His misty halo shimmered as he peered through the clouds to his son's wide, gazing eyes.

Oiwa focused along his bill to his father. The beak he stared over slowly dissipated before the steam began clearing.

'I have flown with my family of geese. I crossed a wide ocean. I landed with them in icy waters. I came back through the river tunnel under the earth, to here.'

North Star droned differently. It slowed, then quickened. A low tremor from deep in his chest rattled like dry branches. He directed his glance to one of their guests.

Lichen's head turned and looked through the dark forest. 'My breath forces clouds of mist into the cold, clear night. My hinds in the clearing nibble on low branches. I move towards them. My antlers rustle the lower twigs. Ice beads, bright and hard, cascade onto my hide. My hinds turn their nostrils. They sniff my warm scent. My presence reassures them as they graze. I look up through the clearing at stars. A dark skein passes high above. I pull soft spruce spines with my strong lips and bite them off with my sharp front teeth. They grind between my molars. The clean flavour of the clinging icicles crunches refreshingly over my tongue. A frozen cone releases its aromatic essences. My hooves press the moist moss as I push into the clearing to join my herd. I rub my coat against them. The doe next to me turns her head. She nibbles my neck. I shall lead her further into the forest. They all follow. I twitch my ears, listening in the dark as my herd gathers round. The steam from their warm bodies rises in the frosty forest. Now I mount my hinds. My fertility wets their wombs.'

Greyling slid another great pebble to the pit. Mica scooped the yellowed skull. He looked at Lichen's odd form as North Star asked. 'Where have you travelled, young man?'

He shook his head, his ears flapped. A spray of ice drops flew from his shoulders. He saw North Star illuminated along his black snout. He raised his head proudly. 'I took my hinds to new pastures in the forest. I mated with them. They will drop their fawns when the Sun allows succulent new growth.' He looked at his cloven front hooves as they changed back to hands.

Mica stood. His head bent beneath the skin membrane that connected, yet separated, them and the world. He pushed his light matted hair back. His small white Star shone. He moved behind his young brother and leaned Oiwa's head back onto his stomach. Oiwa gazed up to him as Mica took a sharp bone splinter. He punctured Oiwa's forehead with tiny, deep pricks in a star pattern. He wiped the blood down his young brother's cheeks. The members of the circle watched as he jabbed the same emblem below Oiwa's navel. Mica then placed his thumb into an open nutshell where the glistening powder of his own name was kept. He plied the mica deeply in Oiwa's belly wound and then into his upper forehead. 'You have the Star now, brother,' he whispered.

Mica's voice took over from his father's drone. He stood behind him in the glow of their solitary lamp. Bark took the skull, applying water. Mica gently massaged his father's neck, then coughed to clear his throat to begin a familiar legend. 'Many, many winters before my grandfather's father's father was ever born, we lived in another land. That place, like this now, gave us all we needed. That other place was taken from us by the great water mountain. We could live there no more.' He gazed ahead with his hazel eyes, saying, 'Only a few of us remained. We followed the geese that lived in that land, for they went somewhere good. It was a long, long journey. We came here at last.' He breathed deeply, wiping perspiration from his chest.

North Star slowly raised his head, saying, 'It is tradition to send a party of young men to revere the geese's first landing. You, Oiwa, will join your brothers. You have shown great skill and are an example to others.' North Star searched the faces of Lichen and Rush. The lamp flames shifted the shadows on his as they flickered in the steam. Bark plied a cranium of water. A heat wave swirled beneath the stretched hides. From above, hot rain fell.

'Our guests here will take two of our Clan's Daughters as wives. First, they must learn more of our ways and history. You, my sons, will take them on your great journey. You will meet our sacred familiars to gain wisdom. When you return, you will be great men: leaders. Mica, Bark and Tine are already, for they've been before.'

Bark sat. North Star plied water over the hot stones with the goose ladle. Mica crouched beside Bark. He had a tiny polished bone cup that shone in the lamplight. It brimmed with a clear, thick potion that smelt of the forest's treetops. Mica sipped. The potency soaked into his tongue. His mouth felt hot. He inhaled a great lungful of sweat lodge steam. His limb, covered in thick brown and golden fur, entered the cold, starlight forest. 'My paw is growing its dark claws again and becoming swathed in hair. I stalk in the ether of the night. My claws scratch my dark, shining nose. My great teeth shine yellow, reflecting the moon. I prowl in the shadows to climb the summit of my rocky tor. There, bears before me stood and roared through time. I command the sounds of the night. My echoes return from distant mounts. My eyes shine white as I see through the deepest dark.'

Soundlessly he placed his talons back through the Lodge membrane to sit beside Bark. His claws receded beneath his clear nails. His palms throbbed. 'North Star, I have travelled as Urs, the Great Bear.'

Bark took a sip of the ambrose. He leapt like a lynx through the pelt screen. 'I'm lapping from a clear pool. I see my whiskered face and shining eyes. Other lynxes press their red tongues into the expanding ripples. The stars shake as we lap. Our strong feline aroma pervades the night.'

Tine removed the last ambrose drop. He rose. He looked past the stretched hides. 'Far below I see our circle of tents as my vast wings spread. My hooked beak and beady eyes search the dark land. The mountain's snowy peak rushes towards me, shining with the stars. I make for Black Crag where I force my wings to slow me. My mighty talons touch the eerie. I perch, observing. They spread again. My left talons close on a downy twig. I circle and glide back to where steam dreams and reality meet. These talons slide through the leather roof. I perch back on my log. My murderous beak fades. My arm plumage dissipates. There's a furry stick between my toes. Father, I have flown far this night.'

North Star looked at Rush. The goose ladle poured its clear contents in a long stream. The bubbling and hissing seared round the hothouse. Rush leaned his dark-haired head sideways. 'I walk to the great river and take a canoe and float downstream. A feather tickles my back through my clothes. My chest itches painfully. I rise from the boat and speed up to behind the Moon.'

Rush's companions looked to where he had sat. They saw a bright light rise, as though it were a star shimmering in the mists.

North Star asked, 'Where have you been, Rush?'

Rush looked to North Star, unseeing. 'There. Not back.'

10

The Long Journey's Start

'Widgeon's my favourite, Rush. It's the way she moves, sits and looks. When she offered me those huge hot wood grubs warmed in honey, then licked her fingers coyly, there was absolutely no other choice.'

'Well, I'm as much in love with Teal, Lichen. Remember? We met her ages ago. We were only knee high, but even then she struck me. I thought of her for long after their camp visit. Those stuffed linnets she roasted were *so* wonderful.'

'Yup, Rush. I agree. We've seen so many young ladies. You soon tell who's not interested in us. I think we are so lucky. That one called Sage Tip? She's odd. Did you hear what she said to the other girls?'

'No?'

'I overheard. She told them, "Those two, especially him called Rush with his round face and stubby nose, just fail to see my Inner Beauty. He's welcome to Teal! I'm going to dig clay anyway."'

'No!'

'Yes, Cousin.'

'I'm so glad we are going to be alone with them, Lichen. This is a wonderful wigwam to be in, together. Are you going to feed her those grubs from your lips again?'

'Yes. And I'm going to roll them in milled hazels, just for her.'

'Please show me your splendid fish traps, Widgeon,' Lichen asked after their sated sleeping.

* * * * *

'Of course,' she beamed. 'Let's hunt grubs, too,' she suggested, closing the tent flap behind.

'I'm leaning my spear over the door. I don't want Rush and Teal interrupted,' Lichen added.

By the hearth, Teal whispered, 'This is what I've been waiting for.'

'And me. Ever since we met at the Clan Gathering.'

'Yes, Rush. You showed me how to dredge for gudgeon in muddy backwaters then cook them on hot stones. I do that so often.'

'I love how your lips move, when you speak,' Rush heard himself say.

'Can we fish together?' Teal asked.

Rush leaned close, trying to say, 'Of course.' He faltered, trembling, looking deeply into Teal's eyes. He put his lips to her forehead in extreme desire once more.

Teal whispered, 'You leave tomorrow?'

'Yyy esss sss,' he stammered.

In their treasured privacy, they gently removed each other's clothes. It seemed so right. In the sunlight glowing through their hide cocoon, they caressed. Rush felt Teal's passion. They held tight in long embraces. Teal hummed sweetly, swaying against his skin. Rush's knees weakened. He felt Teal's breasts on his as she pulled him closer. He stiffened. They kissed. He caressed her spine. She leaned back. Rush felt her. They stood blissfully, moving like waving moonlight shadows. Rush pressed forward, feeling fathoms of emotion. Teal held his dark head to hers, sharing his bursting gift.

'Of course we'll fish together, my beautiful Teal,' Rush whispered, united in the warmth of the smouldering charcoal.

* * * * *

'Ziit flexes easily, returning well, Honey. These new arrows are really splendid,' Oiwa stated, stroking the flights gently. 'We'll need fishing lines, a long length of net and harpoons, too.'

'Okay, Oiwa, let's gather,' she said, adding, 'I'm looking forward to the great fiesta tonight before you all leave.'

'So am I. I can't wait. It will be such an adventure.

* * * * *

'We have a very long journey,' Mica said by the Clan's central fire, 'First we paddle down river. We'll eventually get to where she flows extremely rapidly through terribly deep clefts. That is Gunnal's Vulva. Deep down it, the Dun divides through rocky gorges and caverns. One chasm widens like a bowl, worn by years of tumbling currents. There's a shingle beach on the right. There we pull our boat in. Tine, Bark and I have done this before. It isn't easy. It is essential we land there,' he said, gazing into the flames. 'The Dun gets far too fast and treacherous beyond. The cliffs narrow there even more, it's called Gunnal's Gulch. It's treacherous. Nobody survives that.'

North Star repeated Gunnal's legend, chewing on a quail. 'Gunnal, the ugly Giantess, lay over rivers, tempting men. All who entered were consumed with fire. She spat them out like cinders. Once, Farrnar rowed down the Dun on his iceberg boat. Gunnal's legs opened wide for him. The rocks squealed. They were as high as he could see. He sped his iceboat, paddling ever faster. His friends, the Bears, pushed him. He hurtled between her knees, entering her great, oozing cleft. The dark tunnel shone brightly with the ice. Farrnar's iceboat stuck tight in her womb. She froze! Farrnar escaped through her innards, casting his clothes away for the stench. She retched, cursing as she turned forever to stone. Her last act was vomiting naked Farrnar out. He spilled from her mouth into a great pool. He delved deep, through the eel-filled waters. They covered him in slime, painting him gold like the Sun. On the bank he mated with a waiting she-wolf. The undersides of their tails turn golden at night because of the tryst. That was the birth of the Loup Tribe. They always help those who suffer Gunnal's anger.'

Mica continued. 'At the cliff bottom are steps, hammered out by Farrnar's children. There's a hawser to pull canoes up. It's a high climb. We carry our craft along the clifftop and look down into Gunnal's Gulch. Rivers foam into her where the Dun disappears deeply inside. At Gunnal's Navel there's a strange spy-hole. We can look right down it. Then we climb Gunnar's Paps.' Mica paused, fanning his brow. 'Then we march, carrying our boat to her shoulders. Below them is Wolf Lake. It is an easy descent. We can watch Gunnal's Falls spill into the waters far below. It's awesome.'

Steaming, pit-cooked meat was brought from the ground. Bats whirled, catching moths, fatally attracted by the fireglow. It was a great feast with dance, fire leaping, acrobatics and shrilly performed legend songs.

Oiwa woke deep in the night, listening. 'Mica,' North Star asked quietly, 'when you get to Goose Landing, please ask the Innu if they've heard more of my old cousin Weir. He was a very fine man, but at the end of our journey to the Whale Geese he changed. He was drawn away from us. He vanished. I've never understood why. If there's news, please bring it. I asked when you went before. Tales can take years to travel.' Oiwa cupped his ear to listen. Quill let out a long fart, masking some words. 'The last we heard was, he'd seen the Glowing Mountain. He followed the flights of geese past Warm Waters. We know no more. If he's alive, or found the Old Lands, we'd somehow surely get word?'

'Yes, Dad, I'll ask and bring what news I can.' With that, they entered and snuggled down. Mica rose moments later, to cross the Plaza quietly for a naked goodbye with New Moon and her cakes.

At dawn, Oiwa wakened. 'I'm going to examine Heron's Tooth again. How beautifully she's made: a double-stitched leather hull over a rigid bentwood frame. The outside shines brilliantly after Honey and Petal's polishing. She will be so fast. Five plank seats fixed between pairs of rigid spars. I'm glad they're hide-padded for comfort. Must go back, though,' he realized after a while, 'Teal's cooking gudgeon in nut flour. Rush will be delighted.'

'Right,' Mica told them, 'I will be in the prow, watching currents and keeping an eye out for obstacles. Tine, you're behind me: Bark and Oiwa together in the middle. Lichen, you go behind them. Lastly, Rush in the stern, to steer and fish. Do you like fishing?' he asked the keen, nodding, young man.

'I'm so proud for you, Rush,' Teal told him, after, 'Here's a pouch of bone and thorn hooks.'

'Thank you, Teal,' he answered, kissing her.

'And a drawstring bag of snails, too. Wonderful bait, Rush.'

'Thanks so much,' he said, kissing again.

'For you, Lichen, a bone and antler harpoon.'

Widgeon said with love, 'It's wonderful. It's murderous. I adore it. The splendidly carved and polished shaft is tremendous.'

'Right, men. Carry the Heron's Tooth to the shingle bank. Everyone will be there waving us off.'

'There's Ripple and Barb. I don't mind, now. I feel rough, tough and ready.'

Oiwa's sisters loaded the weapons. Teal and Widgeon placed the folded net at the stern with a couple of bones wound with lengths of gut. Quill carried two rolls of leather and extra clothes. These tucked neatly into the sides of the Heron's Tooth. 'Mica,' North Star said,' 'here's a pack of dried moose. You never know when you'll need it. All of you, give your mother and me a hug before taking your paddles.'

'I blow you a kiss, Widgeon.'

'A hatful from me to you, Teal,' Rush added as they pushed off for the middle of the Dun.

Mica immediately commanded, 'At the first bend, turn and wave. Listen for the cheers. As we flow out of sight, bang your paddles on the sides to bid farewell.

At last!' Mica rejoiced, slipping out of sight. 'We're off. Hoorayyye.'

'Right men,' Mica called, 'Even though we're going downstream, it's still a few days to the dreaded Gunnal's Vulva. Paddle hard, let the Heron's Tooth's bows bite water.'

The Dun wound round hills, between rocks to flow over rapids. She bent east then west, but her direction was forever northwards. They travelled through familiar woodlands first, then passed rocky shingle-bound islets. Waders watched as the Heron's Tooth sped.

Rush looked to the riverbank. Turkeys scratched there on a gravelly beach. He tapped Lichen on his shoulder, pointing. 'Later,' Lichen said, 'later.'

'Not too much later,' Rush hoped.

The Dun widened, flowing round a wooded hill: The right bank, a treeless plain. The current slowed. Rush fished. He fitted a large carved moose vertebra from his tackle bag over the wooden stern-peg. It was wound with a strong gut line and spun easily through the hole where the spinal cord had been sucked, years before. He fitted a sinew trace and took one of Teal's hooks, whipping it on tightly. He crushed a snail in his fingers and threaded it on the hook. 'That'll do,' he thought, unravelling several yards of line, tossing the bait to one side and watching it float.

Mica leaned over the prow, eyeing the water. Oiwa paddled,

contemplating his surroundings. Above, buzzards soared in thermals, watchful for prey. A falcon perched low in a tree. It leaned forward to silently glide across the river. Its talons spread, landing on a furry quarry.

The Heron's Tooth carried them effortlessly. Mica navigated round boulders and shallows. Rush fished, and was diverted by a heron throwing its head down, taking a large dace. Then something tugged his finger. He gripped the line and jerked his left hand. 'Hooked,' he shouted, gripping the taut cord in his right hand, playing the fish. 'See it leap. It's shaking its head.' He spun the backbone to wind in slack. The Heron's Tooth glided on. 'It's tiring. In you come, my fine trout: Over the side: got you!' He bent the fish's head and sensed its spine cracking. It flapped furiously on the boat's bottom and lay still. 'Dinner for one,' he shouted.

'Me, please,' Oiwa called above the sound of paddle strokes.

'Come on, Jasper,' Rush said to his sharp knife, 'Let us cut these fins off and bind them above the hook as a lure and then shove a new snail on. Good, now for a proper cast. More gut, whirl it round my head and let go. Excellent, it's gone far. There's the splash. Drift down with us, and I'll keep an eye on your snaking line.

'There's the heron flying by. Ah! That's a big swirl by my bait: a hungry fish? Ouch! The line's tightened round my fingers. Strike.... It's a big one, chaps. It needs more line. It's headed upstream. Turn the boat.'

'Aye, Rush.' Mica responded. Paddles splashed. Heron's Tooth's spun facing the oncoming water. 'Upstream. Follow that fish.'

'That's better. Lichen, help me: grab the line, too.'

'Sure thing, Rush. Shift over.'

'Ning! It's changed its mind. He's making for the bank towards the roots of that big willow. No you don't,' Rush yelled. 'Back-paddle, Mica. Pull with me, Lichen. It's going to leap. Look at it flying under the tree. It's a beauty. Strike again,' he shouted. 'Did you see those silvery sides? The water's stilled now. We've turned it away from the roots... shit!' he shouted moments later. 'Lost it: the line's slack. But did you see it flash, just then? Paddle, quick,' he yelled. 'It's running downstream. Faster. Follow it,' he screamed. 'It's decided to hide way over there. Catch up with it. Stop the boat,' Rush suddenly urged, moments later. 'Lichen. Draw line in. Tighten on its jaw. There it leaps. Haul!' he instructed expectantly.

'I'll harpoon the brute,' Lichen shouted, reaching for his new weapon. 'There it goes,' he cheered, hurling it. 'It's cut the line: bugger, It's free,' he feared for an instant. 'No! Yes. I've hit it. Gone right through. It's writhing in the air. Take the harpoon cord, Rush. You pull it in.'

'It's a whopper, Lichen. Help me haul the writhing monster in. There, over you go: into the boat, you giant. How you still protest so violently!'

'Here, Rush, take my axe,' Mica offered. 'Swipe its brains with that.'

'Thanks, Mica. Become dead... now, fish.' He cheered, swinging the implement, splitting its skull. Then he sat back, shaking. silently stunned at his catch, nursing his blue fingers. He slowly wound the tackle back on the bone reel, knotted the line and disgorged Teal's treasured hook from the monster's gullet.

Lichen cut his harpoon from the salmon, regarding his cousin's silent gaze.

Mica broke the trance. 'Paddle on. There's far to go yet.'

11

River Rendezvous

'There's an exercise we must master,' Mica said, seriously. 'We only have one chance to land Heron's Tooth in the Vulva. We must train. When I command, "Right, beach!" Jab your paddles in on the LEFT. Turn as sharp right as possible. We drive her onto the shingle shore. We leap out immediately, beaching her. Then lash our gear inside for porting her up those steps.'

Soon Mica spotted a landing place. 'Pull to the central flow,' he commanded, thinking, 'This will be excellent practice.' Suddenly he yelled, 'Right, Right. Beach!' pointing his paddle to the small strand he'd seen. 'Aye,' the cry went up. The Heron's Tooth moved sideways. They stroked forcefully, compensating for the Dun's flow. Heron's Tooth crossed it, nudging the sand. 'Ashore, sharpish,' Mica commanded. They all stepped out onto the shingle, gripping the sides of the canoe, keeping her safe.

'Well done,' Mica said. 'We'll practice and get slicker. Back in the boat.'

Down river they went. 'This is wonderful,' Oiwa said to Bark.

'Yes. It sure beats home. I love hunting in the mountains, but this tops it. Look, Oiwa. An osprey. It's swooping. Watch its talons open to meet a scaly back. There, it soars again with a wriggling fish.'

'Smoke down river from a knoll on the right bank. We'll call in,' Mica announced. 'Wait for the command.... Right, beach!' Their paddles splashed. The Heron's Tooth jutted with the effort. She bounced into the rapid stream and was crossing it. 'Fuck!' Mica shouted. 'LOG! Coming at us. Pull harder.'

'Ah! It's hit us,' Rush and Lichen warned, feeling the brunt of the crash.

'A stump's punctured the Heron's Tooth,' Oiwa moaned as she slewed.

'Paddle! Paddle. Paddle,' Mica yelled, striking the surface with terrific force. 'She's turning. The log's crunching into shallows: the tear's widening. She's taking water.'

'What's up?' they heard, shouted from the bank.

'Struck a stump. That's what's bleeding up,' Mica returned.

'The log's rolled, pushing her under. Catch the harpoons: they're floating out.

'Grab the trout,' Rush yelped, as it bobbed alarmingly close to the side.

'Get her off the log,' Mica bayed, leaping from the prow, waist deep. 'I'll lift the stern and pull her round. Keep paddling. She's pushing me under. I'm shifting,' he spluttered, righting the boat. 'I've got her. My feet are dug into the gravel, but she's still sinking.'

Two men splashed next to Mica. 'Fall, Rail, where have you come from?'

'Hunting, visiting and now rescuing,' Fall answered.

'Marsh, too,' Oiwa said, as another of Greyling's sons balanced on the stranded trunk, then in fright he bellowed, 'My bow's floating out! Grab him, Marsh!'

'Okay. And your quiver, and the harpoons. I'll hurl them to the bank.'

'Thanks,' Oiwa repeated, as he sunk with the craft.

Rush let a curdling yowl, seeing his huge salmon's chin nudging the side of the boat. 'Don't let it escape,' he screamed, jumping behind Mica, grabbing its gills and dragging it safely ashore.

'Keep hold of your paddles,' roared Mica while catching Rush's.

'Oiwa; out quickly,' Marsh told him. 'Come here. Help shift the root out.'

'Lichen. Rescue everything,' Oiwa pleaded.

'Now. We'll turn the root and push the boat away. Shove like shit,' Marsh shouted. 'Pull the root back. It's tearing. Never mind. Push. She's coming loose. Pull the hull towards the sloping bank. Her nose is tipping. The Dun's water is running out from her.'

'Stop that net,' Rush hollered from the bank.

Mica took control. 'Roll her over gently, don't let anything else escape while she empties. Then we can carry her to Fall's camp, up the track.' They followed the masses of animal footmarks to the knoll where the fire glowed. Water ran from every seam of their clothing.

'Put her by Scoula,' Marsh suggested, 'And mind our game,' he warned.

'Nice beast,' Oiwa commented, seeing a hind slumped ready for grollocking.

'First we must think about fixing our boat. Who's got resin?'

'I've a little,' Rail offered.

'Not enough. Fine crew we are: totally unprepared. Oiwa, go to those larches and tap some. Here's my axe. Take the baler to gather it.'

Oiwa nipped off to a clump in the vale. He chopped a V-shaped cleft into several trunks. By the time the last was cut, a run of thick sap flowed down the bark. He scraped with his grey knife into the scooped wooden vessel and went the rounds until he had collected an ample supply. When he returned, Rush had been busy too.

'Help me with this stone slab,' he called from the riverbank. 'I've just hauled it out.' Together they carried the heavy rock. 'I've already set three stones by the fireplace. We can aggle this on top and make a fire under it. Then I'll cook the salmon.'

'What about our deer?' Fall protested weakly.

'We'll have the liver and kidneys, you can stash the rest for later. Oiwa, help me gut the fish. Here's your trout... Catch,' Rush said. 'Hold Uncle Salmon up by the gills and I'll run my obsidian blade down its belly. We'll cast the entrails and heart into the river as thanks. It will feed an eel or three.' As they hit the Dun's flow, Rush suddenly felt that sharp itch he had experienced in the sweat lodge. He stood, momentarily chilled.

The friends ran back to the fireplace. Bark and Tine marked round the punctures in the Heron's Tooth. Their toolkit was open by them. Bark said, 'We'll make leather patches, burin holes through and do the same in the Heron's Tooth's wall. We can stitch patches each side of the rents. We've plenty of needles. We can do it together. Rush is heating up that stone. I'm going to melt Rail's resin on it and blend it with Oiwa's. We can fill the boat's patches when they are almost sewn. Stitch the last bits. Squash them together and, swift as a bison's fart... finished.'

'Do you want that stone heated quicker?' Marsh asked.

'Yes. How?'

We've rolled the thighbones in fat to burn for Tarune and Barouci, the deer sprites. We'll do it on the stone and speed things up. They'll reek enough to get shot of the midges, aaaaand... keep marauding beasts at bay: What do you think?'

'Since you put it like that, why not? But don't crack the stone.'

'We've grollocked the deer. Fall's wrapped the flesh in its skin. We're scoffing the liver and kidneys before having the salmon, anyway.

'Okay,' Marsh said, 'we can shovel ash over the stone to spread the heat with the deer's shoulderblade.' Then he remarked, 'Look, here's burnt bones from a past feast and a busted blade. I'll keep that. It might come in handy.'

Rush thought of Teal. Carefully, he took his jasper knife from its padded sheath. 'I'm going to cut my salmon's tail off. A Greyling brother can give it to Teal for me. She'll know it was her hook that caught it and she'll dry our fine trophy,' he thought, looking round apprehensively. 'I just feel we are being watched? But I can't see or hear anything.'

'By the gods, those bones don't half smoke,' Tine said.

'As usual,' Bark put in, as they worked the patches. 'That's the terrible beauty of it all. The animal's offering crackles and spits. The femurs glow and turn white. The gnats go. The scavengers leave us alone. The thighs collapse. We push the thick ends together. The gods are sated and we cook our resin.'

'Right,' Mica said impatiently. 'Fan those embers. Let's boil the glue and thicken it.'

'That's it, done,' Mica said in relief after they'd squeezed the blister-patches. 'Look, the resin's oozed out by the stitches and sealed them. It should make flexible, watertight mends. They'll be tested the morn, anyway. Maybe now we can taste that liver?'

Rush took charge of his range. 'Hand me the offal,' he said to Fall. Everyone circled the stone hungrily.

'Here it is,' Fall answered as his bloody hand passed the organs.

'Kidneys, first. Strip the fat off,' Rush said to himself. 'More fuel under the stone. That's it. Heating up nicely. Resin's dried, now for more sizzling fat. I'll halve the kidneys. Don't they smell great? Now for the liver: I'll slice it on my knee. Never mind the bloodstains. Take what you want, men,' he said shortly after, as it curled temptingly on the slab.

'Now for the salmon,' he announced, straining to hold it up high.

'Wonderful,' Oiwa cheered, as warm hind-blood ran down his cheeks, 'This is so good. How do you do it so well?'

'Watching with mother. That's how. Mind out, the fish is going on. First I must spread extra fat over the stone. There, help me on with it someone? The lower side will cook. Then we roll the fish over. Mica, Bark, will you do that with your axes, please?'

'Just tell us when,' they replied.

'About ready,' Rush instructed when he smelled well-cooked salmon. 'Axes wedged under the side: that's good, now heave it over. The skin will stick to the rock and all the cooked flesh will be revealed. Lichen and I share the cheek. Hunters' privileges, you know. Then you can all get stuck in.'

'This is wonderful, Rush,' Tine remarked as flesh slid from his slate knife into his mouth with juices trickling into his growing stubble. 'How long until the other side's done?'

'When the spine's been picked clean and peeled away, I expect,' Rush came back. 'Would you like the eye before I turn the other cheek, Tine?'

'Give it to Mica, he's the lookout.'

'Mica, an eye for you...'

'Thanks, Rush. You enjoy the other.'

'How's your expedition been?' Mica enquired of Fall.

'Great – in fact, brilliant. We lived a few days with the Stork Clan and shared lots of our kills. I've fallen in love with one of the Chief's daughters, Gale. Here's the knife she gave me. See, it's polished basalt with a bear-fang handle.'

'That's awesome, Fall.'

'Yes, Gale's lovely... too.'

'Oh, shut up,' his brothers said. 'All he can do is go on about his new love. It's sickening.'

'You stop it. I'm going back for her.'

'It'll cost you more bear's teeth than you'll ever hunt,' they jibed.

'I can...'

'Shut it!'

'You're jealous.'

'PFffffff.'

Fall changed the subject. 'So Oiwa, you have the North Star tattoo. Well done,' he remarked, brushing his light hair back and revealing his.

'Gale saw plenty of your other Star, too,' Marsh sniggered as he dumped salmon flakes into his mouth.

Fall ignored his annoying brother. 'It's healing nicely, Oiwa'.

'I'd forgotten about it,' he replied, pushing his hair back and rubbing the tiny scabs away from the glittering specks. 'It was terrific in the Lodge. We became our Spirit Familiars. I went far on my wings of the night, then flew back to where I received my Stars. I feel different now, like I've grown,' he remarked, scratching under his trousers to free the scabs there.

'Mine was like that. I'm a Heron. That's why I love fish. When you return, we'll have a big sweat. But you'll experience Buzzard's lodge. He's Gale's father.'

'Quiet,' Marsh warned.

'Has everyone had enough?' Rush asked. 'The salmon's nearly gone. Any venison, Fall?'

'Not for me.' He burped politely.

'Your trout, Oiwa?' He shook his head dreamily.

'Listen,' Bark said, pulling his damp trousers tight. Stretching a leg high, squeezing his stomach tightly, to fart musically, he commented, 'Sufficient food for me, too.' This wrought screams of laughter.

The distant northern mountain backdrop glowed in the sunset. 'Let's put the boats together on their sides and shelter between them,' Mica suggested. 'Forked stakes holding a ridge-pole will support our leathers. One end open to the fire, and it will be cosy.'

'I'm nearly dry. Let's stoke the fire and steam off before dusk,' Tine suggested.

'Let's drag a couple of small fallen larches for the fire, Rush,' Oiwa suggested. 'I'm almost dry. Funny, you get soaked so suddenly and it takes ages drying. All our other stuff's soaked. No point in changing. We'd better hang it out,' Oiwa added.

Rush sniffed the air. 'Could rain? We'll hang it, anyway. It's wet now, if it wets again, it will just be fresh wet, won't it. Still wondering about a presence?'

'Reasonable thinking,' answered Oiwa.

Another fire burned beautifully beside the cooking table. Oiwa and Rush hung the wet things on stick frames. Evening drew in. The band crouched, swapping news. 'I'll tell you all a fascinating tale about Ripple,' Bark offered.

'All eyes are on me, now,' Oiwa realized.

A cool air wafted from the Dun. The river could be heard passing, passing... passing. Stars appeared, one by one. A thin cloud cut a rising moon. Owls hooted. Distant carnivorous nostrils smelt the acridly burnt bones.

Marsh shifted on his haunches when Oiwa's epic concluded. 'It's strange,' he related when their laughter settled, 'We had a great time with Buzzard's Stork Clan, but something worrying is up,' he told them, belching rewardingly. 'Three folk are missing. Birch Skin, one of Buzzard's plentiful nephews, and his bydie-in, Snaaaaar – they assumed hunting. She hurried back for her daughter, then cleared off with his weapons. "Odd", they all thought.' Marsh, picking his nose thoughtfully, continued. 'She's a tiresome varmint. Nothing's right for her. She'd had a series of men, but only bore this one girl, Dew. You'll hear about it there anyway. But the short story is, Birch Skin was found murdered with a stinking vulture ready to scavenge him. He was bare-naked, hunting knife busted off in his breastbone, and his prick sliced clean off.'

'Horrid,' thought Oiwa, wide-eyed, wincing and furtively covering his sacred area.

'You'll hear when you stop by. They're pitched down river. Buzzard asked, if anyone sees a suspicious woman and girl about, bring them back for questioning.'

They swapped news until Rush eventually said, 'It's getting cold. The sky is filling in. Rain is coming. Let's bring the gear inside and huddle down.'

'I'll bank up the fire,' Fall offered, as the first spots arrived.

They crawled together on a groundsheet. Rush hugged his salmon tail and curled up. The raindrops hit the hides to run down over the canoes.

'So it's a hunting trip, Mica?' Marsh asked in the deep snuggle.

'More than that. We're off to Goose Landing to pay reverence. I've been before. I'm taking a wife when I return. I'll be Chief, when Dad goes dead. '

'Fall's got his nuts twisted over Gale. He'll have to take precious presents to Buzzard, then bring her home to make her into a proper Goose Clan woman.'

'Aye. This trip's for Oiwa, Lichen and Rush's initiation. Our Caribou guests will become family by taking Widgeon and Teal.'

'Those two – they're nice, I must say. What about the ugly cousin?'

'She left in a huff, talking about Inner Beauty,' Marsh laughed.

The rain poured. The fire hissed. The drops pelted onto their hide roof. They were warm and snug within. Rush let a long, silent break of deadly wind.

Tine enquired, 'Who's guilty?'

The cook kept quiet and went to sleep, grinning.

In the rain, a pair of sly ears listened. A wet, slightly bent nose sniffed the steam from the stone. Two bulging, grey eyes stared at the shelter. The bedraggled intruder slunk back into the gloom.

Day broke. Rain ceased. The Dun roared.

Mica shook drips off after his morning pee. He had clambered over his tent-mates to wee and crap, then washed in a grassy puddle. 'Rise and look stupid,' he encouraged briskly. Slowly they followed.

Their campfire was a wet mess. The ashen hearth had rivulets running through it. The embers beneath the range still lived.

'It'll be a hard paddle up river,' Rail remarked, cleaning his teeth on a chewed stick. 'The current's strong.'

'We'll have to port Scoular until slacker water,' Fall suggested.

Rush crawled out with his salmon tail. 'Fall,' he asked confidentially, 'would you take this to Teal? It's just, I lay awake much of the night thinking of her. I love her. Tell her I'm thinking of her. And say that when I return, we'll fish together,' he requested, rubbing his dark eyes.

'Of course, Rush. I hope you don't get teased like my ugly brothers do me.'

'Thanks. Thanks,' replied Rush, 'Here it is. I'll give it a kiss first. Take it.'

'Well. It's onwards and upwards,' Marsh said as they broke camp.

'Stow everything carefully in the Heron's Tooth,' Mica said. 'It's time to move.'

'No breakfast?' Rush asked.

'That's right. Nothing. We're well fed from last night.'

'Hugs all round, chaps,' Tine said.

'Don't stop any arrows,' Rail added.

'We won't, if you don't,' came the standard reply.

The Greyling sons carried the Scoular, venison inside her, over the flat river plain to meet the Dun upstream.

'Okay. Time to test our mends,' Mica stated. 'Same positions. This'll be practice for approaching Gunnal's Vulva. The Dun is running fast. She'll be doing just that when we near her gorge,' he impressed on the crew. 'Rush. Hold the stern as we embark. Jump in after. If you miss, we'll try and come back for you. If not, you swim,' he fondly added.

Rush leapt into his seat. 'Off we go,' he said.

'Paddle on. Check those patches. Watch for leaks,' Mica spelled out.

'Can't see any,' Bark reported.

'Me, neither,' confirmed Oiwa. 'We'll keep looking, though.'

'We'll do the Left Paddle manoeuvre, later. Move into midstream. It will be bumpy, but fine.'

'I'm glad of these padded seats, Mica,' Oiwa pointed out.

'Me, too. Paddler's bum's agony.'

On the left bank the light woodland continued. The right bank was still grassy plain. The Dun cut deeper, narrowing slightly. This made her faster and even bumpier. 'How are those mends?' Mica called.

'Just fine,' came reassurance from the stern.

'I can't see a practice beach yet; better speed on,' Mica assessed

'Bison scent,' said Bark urgently, looking to the banks. The river swung. Ahead was a turn. The current took them to the high right bank. The Heron's Tooth careered round as the side heightened. Eroded loam slipped from it, clouding the water.

'There,' Tine assured, 'ahead, on the bank. Grazing beasts. They're watching us.'

'We're going right beneath,' Oiwa whispered. 'Look at that huge curling tongue gripping the grass above. I can hear the bison's front teeth shearing it from the roots. See their reflections, Bark? They're like a vast, chewing hedge lining the bank.'

'Yes. Amazing. There's our reflection, too, as though we're right in the middle of them. I've never seen the like,' came Bark's reply.

'That herd's vast. The biggest I've seen,' said Lichen, looking upwards.

'Smell their breath,' Oiwa remarked. 'It stinks of rotting grass.'

'And their extraordinary flatulence,' advised Rush with authority.

'I'm desperate for a pee,' Lichen announced as soon as they'd passed the herd. 'Can we steady the boat?'

'All pee,' Mica commanded. 'Let's get it over with. Either stand up, or do it in a bailer. Anyone for anything else?' Mica queried when all had done.

'No. Not yet,' came the reply in unison.

'Paddle left: Beach,' Mica soon surprised them with.

'Excellent,' he remarked. 'Now disembark, stretch your legs. We're on a small wooded island,' he said, disturbing nesting storks.

'Where there's storks, there's fish,' Rush thought. 'I'll wander along the backwater with a harpoon. There's large river perch gliding between the roots of overhanging bushes,' he soon spotted. 'Their spiky fins radiate like fans of arrows. Come closer,' he whispered to them while crouching on spongy moss. 'Come, perch; come,' he willed, then, 'account for refraction... hurl. Hit it. The water is clouding with mud. It struggles. Come on, perch, I'll pull you out. I can mention breakfast, perhaps.'

'Right, men, we've rested up and stretched. On with our journey,' Mica said as Rush appeared.

'Could we cook this before we go?' Asked Rush.

'No. Fillet it. Eat it raw.'

'Okay. Not much, between six, anyway.'

'Embark. Same drill. You last, Rush,' Mica commanded.

The river re-joined, the storks settled awkwardly. Heron's Tooth sped as the sun climbed. Wooded hills rose on their left; to the right, grasslands spread.

'No more stops,' Mica informed. 'With good headway, we'll be with the Stork Clan by early evening.

Vultures circled, searching for a crippled animal. The scarlet irises in their balding heads noticed two landbound travellers east of the immense bison herd. They appeared too healthy for further scrutiny.

'Paddle on,' Mica decreed. Their arms powered the rhythmically dipping shafts. A pleasing white bow wave appeared at the prow. The centre of the river flowed fastest. Mica steered into it. The craft bumped, reaching the turbulent current. A breeze caught Oiwa's hair as he eagerly paddled. They gained speed with every dip and pull. The crew chanted, their voices strong above the sounds of speeding water. It stopped their hunger as they raced between the banks.

'I smell bison again, but on the other side,' Rush remarked some hours later. 'There are more vultures too. Maybe there's been a kill.'

The sun was sinking when Bark spotted a lone hunter. 'Wave our paddles to greet him. He's raising his long spear in welcome.'

'There's a column of smoke... and another. At last: signs of civilization,' Tine remarked in relief.

'Round another bend, closer to the rising hills,' Mica reminded Bark and Tine. 'See the white mountaintops peaking in the far distance? I don't want to mention it, but that's where Gunnal's Vulva delves.

'The Dun widens here, becoming shallow. Take the deeper channel by the left bank,' he told them as Heron's Tooth scraped her bottom lightly on sand before dipping into that faster water. It took them below overhanging bushes and trees. The waterway veered sharp left and their long canoe lurched round the bend. A stretching sandbank and a great pool came speedily into view. Boats were drawn up onto the bank. Children played and fished. They shouted and waved excitedly. The Heron's Tooth had taken them to the Stork Clan.

12

Buzzard's Welcome

'Hard left, beach!' Mica instructed. 'Swing round, point to the shore, glide across the slack pool and arrive gently, kiss-like, on the sands. Me out first, then Tine, I'll hold the painter for Bark to alight. Oiwa follows.'

'Me after. Hurry up, my arse is so painful, even on that cushion,' Lichen complained.

'I'll stand in the stern pushing Heron's beak higher,' Rush added. 'She'll pull further up so I can step onto dry land.'

Clamouring children surrounded them. Their mothers appeared with dry washing, gathered from the bushes. 'Lovely ladies,' Mica remarked. 'Unload Heron's Tooth,' he said, pulling in his stomach and standing tall.

'Whoop, whoop,' Buzzard greeted. 'Meet my wives. Here's my family running to greet more Goose Clansmen. Welcome. Have you come to woo our women and take them away?' he laughed broadly. 'You can, it just depends how many bear's teeth you can afford.' He took Mica's hands, shaking them. 'And two black, spiky-haired Caribous. Your fine round faces give you away. Come to my house,' Buzzard invited. 'Your things will be brought up by the youngsters. They'll want to nose in it, anyway.'

'Be careful with my bow, and those arrows,' Oiwa said to the excited children. 'I'm keeping an eye on you,' he added as they tugged his trousers while he followed Buzzard's huge footprints along the gravelly ridge. 'The Stork Clan's village is so unlike ours; it's haphazard. There's no circle, only a rough oval. It's a mix of tepees and skin covered wicker huts. There are fireplaces everywhere. There's a massive heap of wood roughly in the middle. Are we having a fiesta?'

'Meet two more of my wives,' Buzzard said, smiling broadly. 'and this is Gale, a fine daughter.' She sat by the door burnishing a pot. Others lay beside her with patterns carved through the polish. She raised her head in greeting. Her trailing black hair shimmered in the slanting sunlight, her face, long and elegant, her dark eyes shining clear and bright. She laid her pot aside and stood to receive the visitors.

'She's as lovely as Fall told us,' Bark saw, just as the speechless Tine and Mica did.

Brushing the clay dust from her tunic, she said, 'Welcome to my father's house. One of my mothers will fetch a drink.'

'How many wives does Buzzard have?' Oiwa asked.

'That you might never find out,' Gale answered smiling. 'I have many, many brothers and sisters. Stand aside. Some of them will put your gear in Buzzard's house.

'Prop their harpoons and bows against the wigwam sides by the doorway, you young,' she instructed, then offered, 'Come in, be warm by the hearth.' Buzzard's place was evident; a great leather floor cushion on the rush matting. It had a huge depression forced by his considerable weight. Around the fire, polished logs served as seating. A curtain of white stork feathers screened the way to the adjoining chamber.

Ember entered, standing tall after ducking through the flaps. 'Cool honey water?' she offered, handing one of Gale's pots to Mica. He sipped and nodded a 'thank you' over the brim. He handed it on to Bark, wiping a small petal from his top lip. Bark noticed dried rosebuds swirling in the bowl. He passed it on to Oiwa, who strained some of the fluid through clenched jaws and handed it to Rush, while pink petals stuck on his white teeth. Ember giggled. Rush raised it to his lips, feeling the incised design on his fingertips. Plover, a further wife, entered with a second crock. They felt the reviving honeyed water settling in their stomachs. Hunger pangs dissipated.

'Good. You've had something,' Buzzard said, entering with style. 'Now. Tell me about yourselves.' He grew even larger, in the confines of his home. His long dark hair, plaited with contrasting white stork feathers, rested on his shoulders. His suede jacket sported bear-tooth toggles. The slightly open neck revealed darkened skin with a hint of a red tattoo at the top of his sternum.

'I'm Mica, of North Star; these are my brothers Tine, Bark and Oiwa. These two are...'

'They can speak for themselves,' Buzzard said, delving in his pouch for birch resin. 'Well, young Caribou, enlighten me?'

'My name is Lichen, a son of Otter. He is next to our leader on the...'

'I don't want a family history,' Buzzard interrupted, turning to Rush.

'Rush. Son of Puma,' he blurted rapidly. A pink petal slid from his chin.

'Good,' Buzzard said, 'That's got the formalities done. In your honour, I have ordered a feast. It is good having visitors.' Ember and Plover nodded happily as Buzzard bit small chunks of the resin off. 'What brings you this way, a hunting trip?' He handed a piece to Mica. 'Not a hunting trip. We're travelling to Goose Landing.' The gum softened beside his tongue. Buzzard listened with interest. 'It's part of Oiwa's initiation. Rush and Lichen are taking two of our Clanswomen, they come to earn them.'

'You'll be going through Gunnal's Vulva again?'

'Aye,' Mica responded.

'You Geesefolk are brave; maybe too brave. The Dun's still high with rain and meltwater. You should bide here a couple of days and pray for sunshine and no rain. Think about it. We've plenty to keep you amused.' He smiled, passing the rest of the resin round. Mica chewed happily; the dried, minty herbs in it released their flavours. His mouth freshened.

Ember and Plover noticed Buzzard begin to rise. They helped his hefty bulk up. 'Come, see my village.' They stooped to leave, following the Chief of the Storks.

Behind Buzzard's house stood a tall meat-drying rack, surmounted with horns. Eye, their brindled dog, guarded it. He chewed a huge shoulderblade noisily. Most of the odd dwellings had meat frames. There were skins stretching: some had piles of wooden trays to be polished. The doors of the structures were set in all directions. Outside, things were being made or mended. Everyone looked busy.

'Two more of my wives live there. Not all of their young are mine. We had a rare visitor from the Innu. He's responsible for twins. Talking of offspring, Gale is spoken for by Fall, one of your Clan. He'll need to bring good gifts, when he comes for her.'

'We met him and his brothers, way up river. We camped together. You'll get excellent presents – he's smitten,' Mica replied.

'Good,' Buzzard beamed, rubbing his ivory toggles, 'I'm longing for more bear fangs.'

As they toured, Rush noticed burning. Bits of curled, singed hide, smashed pottery and remains of a central fireplace and ruined stone tools. He looked closer. 'That's all that's left of that evil bitch's hut,' Buzzard cursed, spitting venomously. 'We torched it.' His head shook gravely, saying, 'We'll speak later.' Ashes blew in a slight breeze. Burned bone beads fell to powder. They followed Buzzard, his mood more serious. Later he said, 'There's been a successful hunt this morning. Two good buffalo: there's enough for my whole village.' The sun was setting. Fires were revived. Menfolk appeared from tents and huts, wearing furs against the cooling evening. 'Follow. We'll get ready.'

A three-quarter moon rose. Oiwa pinned his hair back with heron feathers, showing his star. He rubbed grease on it from the side of his nose and it sparkled. He tugged his short, soft beard, hoping it was a little longer. His brothers' whiskers grew quicker.

Gale lent them elegant furs. 'How is Fall?' she asked.

'He's great. He spoke wonderfully of you,' Oiwa answered. 'His brothers tried to shut him up, though. May be jealousy,' he added. 'He's so proud of your knife gift.'

'I'm glad. I miss him. He's returned for bear's teeth. That'll settle any bargain with my father,' adding, 'Let me place this beaver wrap over your shoulders. You will look good in it.'

The Goose journeyers filed to the arena. Buzzard, sitting on his big log drum, said, 'Meet my brother, Catfish. Sit in the circle of seats. I'll bang mine.' It resounded loud and long. Catfish bashed his, too. The young men's eyes opened, impressed at the sound. Oiwa sat patting one. 'Nice,' he thought.

In the centre lay polished trays of rolled raw buffalo fillet stuffed with dried mushrooms that tenderized in the blood. All was covered in scorched plantain seeds, then sprinkled with rock salt and garnished with salsify. Ember cut them into round chunks with her magnificently dark carving knife.

Rush drooled.

'Dig in, men,' Ember said, taking some.

Catfish's chief wife, Stella, joined her. 'Lovely meat,' she commented. The troupe agreed with their mouths full.

Catfish turned to Mica, asking directly, 'Did you blokes see anyone on your journey?'

Mica swallowed prematurely, hurting his gullet as the hunk descended. 'Only Fall and his brothers,' he managed, reaching for a drink, adding, 'Yes, there was a hunter. We waved shortly before we arrived.'

'Nobody else other than Hoof Tracker, then?' queried Catfish. Mica shook his head. 'Did none of you notice anybody or anything strange?' They shook their heads, not knowing if Catfish was pleased, or no.

Rush pondered as he and Oiwa took more meat. Their eyes gazed heavenwards as they chewed. 'I'll note the ingredients,' Rush thought as the others dipped in. The bowlful shrank until only blood remained.

'I'll have that. Chief's rights,' Buzzard said, draining it.

A chorus of girls swayed past, singing, as Catfish asked sadly, 'Did you hear of my boy's murder?' Tine nodded while biting into another hunk.

'Yes. We we're very concerned. Do you have news?' Mica asked.

'Absolutely,' Buzzard put in. Catfish spat in the fire; an ember darkened as his phlegm bubbled. Buzzard explained, 'What we know is, it's bizarre that that woman, Snaaaaar, went hunting with Birch Skin without weapons. He'd been very tolerant of her temper and her demands for ages.' Catfish frowned, coughed and spat in the fire again.

The smell of food grew as a cooking pit was opened. A vast hunk of roasted hindquarter was speared and lifted from the charcoal onto a huge tray. Gale scraped the ash as it wobbled slightly and steamed aromatically.

Buzzard told them, 'She, vile bitch, left her daughter Dew to go in the hills with Birch Skin. She returned, collecting her; hurriedly gathered their bows and arrows, saying cheerily, 'Birch Skin's found game, back soon.' She hurried off, and hasn't been seen since.'

Catfish coughed again. Stella slapped his back. He flobbed mucus through his curled tongue into their fire. The moonlight shone brightly. Gale carved meat, passing it round on an arrow point. Catfish chewed, saying, 'There's more. Hoof Tracker, who you waved to, was suspicious. Next day, he left to follow her and the daughter. He found their traces going in a completely different direction from what he'd expected. They were easy to follow first, then they vanished.' Catfish put more meat in his mouth and sucked the blood.

Buzzard carried on. 'Hoof Tracker returned and followed his earlier hunch. Although faded, he found traces of two adults going in one direction then it looked like one person, Snaaaaar, had hurried back.' He leaned forward, belched, wiped his chin and reached for more meat. His knife slid through it. A juicy slice fell away. He continued, 'Hoof Tracker searched the wooded hills, finding a mossy clearing.' Buzzard shifted awkwardly and uttered, 'He found Birch Skin's murdered corpse.'

Catfish shook, enraged. 'Birch Skin was my son, made by my second wife,' he remonstrated emotionally. Stella soothed him.

'Hoof Tracker saw the wounds inflicted on my boy. He'd been stabbed and slashed, over and over. Hit with stones and bashed in the eyes.' Stella cuddled her grieving husband.

Buzzard continued. Catfish wiped his eyes. 'Hoof Tracker was terribly upset. He rolled the stiffened body of his friend and saw how viciously he'd been attacked from all around. Then he noticed the broken obsidian blade, its murderous end showing black between Birch Skin's ribs. His poor mouth, agape, shocked!' Buzzard paused, inhaling deeply. 'Hoof Tracker vomited. He turned aside so not to spray his dead friend. He coughed, choking at the edge of the clearing and finished throwing up. That's where he found the blooded bone dagger handle. He stooped, making sure and discovered worse.... His manhood! It had been severed; a horrid mess. Balls and all.'

The friends were shocked by this damnable story. Their meat lay cold in their hands. A tray of spit-roasted quail followed. Trembling fingers reached for the small birds.

Catfish uttered. 'She mutilated him, she did,' pausing in

revulsion, 'We know it was Snaaaaar. It's her stinking knife.' He pulled a wing off his bird, sharing it with Stella.

Buzzard took over. 'Hoof Tracker lifted his mate's corpse over his shoulder to carry him home. Slowly the body bent at the stomach, as he made his sorry trek back. We sent out hunters to find her, but she's clever. There were false trails, then a decent trace, then none at all. Hoof Tracker later found the right one.' Buzzard swallowed some quail breast, 'He followed those two to the hills. Just at the edge of the trees he found their shits.' He shoved more in his mouth, explaining as he chewed. 'The both of them squatted and crapped, concealing their mess under pine needles, then vanished into the rocky lands. The rain of the other night obliterated any signs in the open. She could have crossed the Dun way up river at the ford, where the herds go.'

Rush asked seriously, 'But can you be sure it was their shits?'

'Yes!' screeched Stella. 'They were pure white and stank of lilies.' At her brilliant sarcasm, they fell into fits of amazed laughter, breaking the gloom. Buzzard tried adding to it, but could not. He held his belly to stop it exploding. When the outburst subsided, he thought he could say what he wanted to say, but could not. Finally he whispered bits of it to Stella, whilst holding his sides.

Stella translated Buzzard's comment bit by bit. 'And they'd... wiped their... arses... with swansdown.' Her shoulders shook, her mouth opened to tumults of more laughter hitting the night air. The rest of the Stork Clan came to hear the crack. The joke was repeated many times, dispelling lurking sadness.

Oiwa picked up a beat on his drum. It circulated round their ring. The nubile chorus returned. They ate until weariness overcame them. Stifled yawns and Oiwa's chin drooping to his chest told their hosts it was time for their guests to sleep. Gale showed them through the door to their curtained room. She had lit lamps of fat-filled river mussels. Round the walls, sturdy upright frames supported horizontal poles. Over these were thick hide beds. At the far end was a huge litter where Buzzard perched. He would come through later, or sleep elsewhere with another wife.

In the centre of the oval space was a skin-lined pit. Water covered the bottom. Large, burned river stones were piled at its side. This was Buzzard's sweat lodge. A low hum came from Rush's direction.

'Salsify makes him fart, too.' Lichen remarked. This was the last any they heard until late morning.

13

Buzzard's Lodge

The travellers awoke late. Light penetrated their room. Bed frames creaked as they moved in their cosy bunks. Nature called. They left the warmth, visiting bushes.

A dish of crushed nuts, dried fruits and maple syrup awaited them. Chunks of Buzzard's violet-flavoured tooth-cleansing gum were there, too.

The Dun had quietened. Gale worked on her pots. 'What's that carved pattern mean?' Oiwa asked, pointing, quite impressed.

'The V-shape's Gunnal's Vulva, the wavy lines the Dun. The stick-stabbings show the rapids you shoot; those needle impressions are the Heron's Tooth. It will be fired by the time of your homecoming.'

'Thank you, Gale. I'd better look more closely at clay pots in future.'

They met Buzzard at the river-brink. 'Level's dropping. If no rain, it'll be okay tomorrow afternoon, perhaps. Rest now, before braving Gunnal's Rapids.'

'Great,' said Bark. 'We're itching go.'

'When you're in the ravine, watch the rock pictures,' Buzzard went on.

Amongst all this, Oiwa thought, 'Ziit needs exercising, I'll fetch him.' Entering he spotted Buzzard's weaponry. His arrow-points were sharp. He touched a tip, pricking his finger. The tent darkened with a heavy sound behind. Oiwa spun, facing Buzzard.

'You like my arms?' he challenged.

'Aye,' Oiwa nervously answered.

'Well, we'll examine.' Oiwa relaxed, realizing Buzzard teased with gruffness.

'My quiver of points,' he handed it Oiwa. 'The flights are goose. The heavy arrows slaughter buffalo. The shaft's much heavier, denser wood. This head's special.' He placed it in Oiwa's palm, 'My quartz point. It's long, the sides swing back.' Oiwa slid his finger along its sweep. 'The shaft's oily for deep killing.' He flexed his bow. 'My sons and me have lain up crags, knowing buffalo will pass. You hear and smell them a long way off. It's height that's advantageous. You loose arrows to them; the weight does it. These ones penetrate hides twixt shoulders, striking hearts.' Oiwa gazed admiringly at Buzzard. 'I once hid in a tree to get one there, he dropped, stone-like: the arrow sunk to its flights... wonderful.'

'Let's look at your bow outside, Oiwa. Give me an arrow.'

'Here's a jasper-tipped deer shaft.' Buzzard strung it, pulled, turned to the drying meat and shot. It was pierced and spun. The dog leaped bushward and retrieved Oiwa's missile.

'An excellent weapon, Oiwa. What's its name?'

'Ziit: the sound of the flights. Give me the arrow, Eye. Good dog,' Oiwa said, fitting it and shot through the same piece of dangling pemmican.

'Ziit's like you, Oiwa, young, strong and clever, but still strengthening.' Then Buzzard asked, 'Are you worried about your journey?'

'I daren't think about it.'

'You should. Danger lurks, waiting for false steps. Be wary.' Then he asked. 'Do you have children?'

'No!' Oiwa exclaimed.

'None on the way, even?'

'None. Well. Probably not.' He stammered, tugging his soft moustache.

Buzzard grinned. 'You've sexed, then?'

'Well, Sir, I was almost raped,' Oiwa confessed.

'Tell me? I promise not to laugh.' They sat by the drying meat.

Eye gnawed his bone. Oiwa luridly acted his explicit tale. Buzzard did not make fun, but they ended in excruciating laughter. Their stomachs ached like the night before, when Buzzard could not tell his swansdown joke.

Buzzard observed, 'You and Ziit have done much together.... I'm going to advise you.'

Oiwa acknowledged the huge man, noticing again the red tattoo topping his chest.

'You're a handsome young man. I've seen the daughters of my village look at you. You're shy yet; that will fade. Your brothers, too, have a presence. Your two friends, who are spoken for, are very happy. That's good.' He paused momentarily. Oiwa scratched his nose and shifted his chewing gum from the right molars to the left. 'You, Oiwa, have a great life ahead, I can see. It's your spirit. You have qualities for sharing. Women see this.' He paused for thought. Oiwa slid the gum behind his front teeth and squeezed it with his tongue. 'They'll want to mate with you. If they have a child from you, it will have advantages over other kids. Mothers like this.'

Oiwa's jaw dropped. The gum fell to his hand from the tip of his tongue while he considered his body and just what it could do.

'Oiwa. In my village our families are well mixed. It's good; we don't make jealousy. We have respect and love for each other.' He doodled in the dry ground with his heavy arrow. 'When an interesting man stays with a clan, females might want to borrow something by mating. It's fine.' Oiwa scratched his chin and leaned on his log drum. 'If you don't want to breed, polite refusal can be given.' Buzzard leaned back, too, adding, 'You should never mate with someone you aren't happy with. The outcome is usually bad. And you should certainly not mate with a woman who does not wish it, for that's worse.' He finished, saying, 'Breeding is an art. Be comfortable; be stunning. Have another chew of gum.'

Oiwa flicked his old gum into the bushes. 'Thanks, Buzzard. That's been helpful. I hope it'll be useful. I'll mind on.' They stood and walked, Oiwa mopping sweat from his brow.

Rush and Lichen wandered with Bark and Tine. Mica told squatting children adventure tales. They listened avidly with their mothers. Hoof Tracker's hunters returned with their booty, their hunting paints dried and cracked on their faces. Roasting pits were prepared to receive their haul. Mica's story finished. The youngsters ran to the river to see if their fishing lines had profited.

They gleaned from their traps. Silver fish flapped into their baskets. Then Jay screamed out from the other side of the sandbank. 'My canoe's gone! I hauled it right up last night. Who's taken it?' she yelled.

'I haven't,' whined a boy. 'I know that, stupid. You're here,' Jay's eyes flamed. 'I'm aiming to see about this.' She raged up the beach homeward: 'Dad, wake! You've been hunting. This is an emergency!' Jay's arms flew. Her tantrum was heard over the whole village.

'Jay, calm. Let's go and look, dear.'

'It's been thieved,' she screamed.

'There's my post, Dad. That's where I tied it.'

Scale knelt down amongst the other craft and examined the post. 'It's only kids' footprints in the sand. The rope's unleashed, and that's drag marks to the Dun. Well, Jay, I hope it's returned soon,' he said, rubbing his chin. Hunt paint flew dustily in the air. 'It took us a while to make, didn't it, my pretty angel?'

'Yes,' Jay moped. 'I got sore punching holes and sewing hides on its frame.' Scale ruffled her long, dark hair. 'It'll return,' he reassured.

Rush and Lichen sat amongst young women and girls, who liked their spiky hair. One asked Rush, 'Why is your face so round?'

He grinned back. 'My mother expected to give birth at New Moon. I wouldn't come. I waited for Full Moon. Mum said that's why my face is so round. She was going to call me Moon Face, but named me Rush instead, because I was so slow.' They laughed. He added, 'But she actually sat and squashed me.' They shrieked out again.

Another enquired, 'Lichen. Do you put egg in your hair, it's so spiky?'

'No. Our hair sticks out like this. It's a Clan thing. We do our hair by pushing through bushes in reverse,' they giggled.

Oiwa strolled up. 'Your hair's a mess,' someone said. 'It's light, like sand. Why's that?'

'It's a mess, because I haven't done anything to it for ages. As for colour, our Clan's mostly like that; it's our breeding. Some of us even have red hair.'

'OoooooooooHhhhh!' the girls said.

'My brothers have the same; you've seen us Goose Folk before, you know fine what we are like.'

Moss, his teasing inquisitor, said, 'Let's do his hair, girls. Jump on him, sit him on the ground, pin him down'.

Oiwa feigned struggling momentarily, then relented. 'Okay, okay, I give up.'

'Good. Sit, we will get our stuff. Sleek, make sure he doesn't move.'

Sleek obeyed. 'Here,' she said, 'Perch on this log.'

Moss returned with friends. 'We've got combs and bowls of scented water. Head back,' she demanded, pulling stork feathers from his tangles. 'Sleek, hold a bowl of water behind his neck and I'll soak his disgustingly matted head.' Oiwa grinned at the attention. 'What's that floating in the bowl, Sleek? Pour. Wash his scalp.' Sleek obeyed. 'Uuuuuuurgh. It's gone murky. Get fresh.' Moss rinsed. Sleek held a fresh bowl for her.

'Right, girls,' Moss directed. 'Comb from the ends up, don't tug his pretty locks.'

'I like your Star, Oiwa.'

'Thank you. It's Moss, isn't it?'

'Yes. Do you have any more?'

Oiwa blushed. He didn't answer, remembering his pubic one.

'Be still, there's loads of ugly knots,' Sleek warned.

Gradually Oiwa's hair untangled. It reached his shoulders in waves. He noticed something warm and smooth being rubbed into his scalp, and the combs slid through his hair even more easily. He then felt a cool, runny sensation. 'We are going to knead this all through, and massage thy scalp, too,' Sleek told him.

'What is it?' Oiwa demanded.

'Duck fat and egg, you Goose. Now sit still.' They struck a sharp flint flake each and trimmed his hair ends over their fingers. A growing circle gathered. Oiwa's hairdo was the centre of attention.

He looked down and watched the barbers' feet astride him, working in rhythm. They straddled him as Moss and Sleek attended around his ears. 'I feel their gorgeous breasts brushing my shoulders. It's lovely,' he thought. Then they combed his hair right over his face. 'That looks better,' they said.

'Were they twins?' Oiwa wondered.

'Right, you little girls, each of you gets a thin length of his hair. Start at the crown and work round and down in a spiral.'

'Are you listening, Moon Shadow?' Sleek called out.

'Yes, Sleek,' she responded, trying to stop giggling.

Moss explained, 'I want you to plait your lengths. Sleek has beads to thread in. There are little bird bones that look good too. We're watching, so get it right.'

Sleek added, 'Take it in turns. Try not to pull his hair too hard.'

Sleek whispered to Moss, 'He'd look very pretty with his other hairs taken in hand, wouldn't he?' they giggled endlessly.

Dusk descended. Fires glowed. The travellers gathered with Buzzard and some of his wives and children. He signalled his guests to be seated. All admired Oiwa's hair. He spun his head and beaded plaits flew out. 'I'm delighted with it,' he remarked. The turfs from over the cooking pits were dragged away. Great bundles of long, steaming waterweed were hauled out expectantly. The parcels were slid onto the trays, carried to Buzzard's party and placed before them. The steaming bales smelt of river and bird.

'Share it out, Mica,' Plover said. He peeled back the hot shroud, and inside was a cooked goose. 'Wonderful,' he said eyeing it delightedly. 'I'll get my axe. Legs first. They ease off nicely,' he reported as he twisted the blade, 'Wings next and then the succulent breast.' The band devoured two voraciously, goose-grease covering the brothers' stubble.

'It's an honour having goose,' Tine told Buzzard, as Hoof Tracker passed.

'Join us, please?' invited the chieftain. The sinewy man sat on a vacant drum. He observed everything and everyone as they spoke. 'The geese are excellent,' Plover said. 'You were away really early?'

'We left afore dawn for the North Marshes. 'Crept through bordering trees and silently waded towards the goose nests. If you do it right, they think you're moose. We wore antlers and masks.' Nobody interrupted this softly spoken man. They ate and swallowed silently. 'At light, we were so close you could almost touch the birds. The mist lifted.' He tossed a bone to Fang, his dog. 'We selected geese where they slept. We shot our bows. Lots woke with arrows in them, making terrible noises. Others charged, with wings open. We shot them, too. That's one, see, a hole in the breastbone.' Rush pulled out a busted bit of flaked stone.

'When we'd got enough, Fang killed any wounded ones and carried them to our base. We collected the eggs of the dead. Oiwa, you've got some in your hair.' Buzzard's children pointed and shrieked at him. Oiwa swung his plaited locks, twisting his head rapidly.

'Hoof Tracker, would you like to join us in a sweat later tonight?' Buzzard asked.

'No. I have to track early; I will need my energy.' He stood, tapped his drum seat in thanks, bowed his head in respect and quietly left.

'Absolutely great,' Oiwa thought. 'A sweat, a cleanse, and a long sleep before an afternoon's sailing. Perfect.'

A procession of youngsters carried water through the shadows to the pit in Buzzard's house. Rolls of matting were placed round the room, for seating. Lamps were lit and the first hot stones were hauled and dragged on steaming wet mats through his doorway.

Conversation lapsed; Buzzard bid them entry. 'Undress, then; go through.' Steam filled the atmosphere as they stepped into the sweat lodge to sit. Buzzard faced the ring from the far end beside Plover: a floor lamp lit him.

They sat inhaling deeply. Buzzard's legs were parted. Tattooed from his pelvis upwards, they observed an exaggerated penis. Testicles were etched into his inside legs. The organ's staff reached his chest. The red ochre dome they had spied at the summit of his sternum was the enlarged tip. Their jaws dropped as they stared at the imagery.

'You approve of my tattoo?'

Stammering 'Yes-es' with shaky nods, they assured Buzzard they had noticed it. His actual member dangled from where his pubic hairs were expertly styled.

'When I became Chief, my wives did this magnificent artwork for me. It's our custom that when I can no longer give them pleasure they will club me to death, and skin me and my tattoo for a drum skin.' Mica and his band listened incredulously. 'Long may I be fit and fruitful and not be a drum skin too soon!' he pinched Plover playfully. Stones splashed in. Steam obliterated the potent design. Oiwa and Rush shook their heads, amazed.

'I don't want to be chief,' Rush whispered. The message was passed on. Humour replaced awe.

Oiwa stood, getting steam around himself. His lower star visibly glittered for the first time. Sweat escaped him in tiny rivulets. His hair felt glorious, draped on his shoulders. Plover scraped Buzzard's perspiration with a moose rib. Oiwa swept the sweat from his body and crouched again. He took a rib to scrape Rush's back, then Rush did Oiwa's. More of Buzzard's brood entered, bringing oils and scents. They massaged Mica and scraped him down, to his great pleasure. They sat relaxed in hot mists.

Rainbow, mother of two from Buzzard, entered holding an oval tray of hot fried elvers. She passed them round. In turn, the company tasted them. Heads back, they dropped the tiny eels into their gaping mouths, enjoying the crispy sensation. Rainbow stroked Bark's pubic star.

In the mists, a drum skin was brushed in rhythmic flow. Lizard's Toe, who massaged Lichen, left to fetch dried fruits. She had two daughters and a son, only one from Buzzard. Her boy came from Innu and her daughters from the Lynx Clan. Thus the Stork Clan grew in strength and variety of bloods. She returned with her basket of dried berries and fruit. A wondrous painted bowl of thick maple syrup bound a mass of hot fried nuts. She dipped her fruits in on spiked sticks to tempt the young men.

Bruised fennel seeds and new pine needles were cast into the waterhole, creating a sensual atmosphere. Plover asked. 'Would you chaps drag the cool stones out and make room for hotter ones? There are long tongs by Buzzard.' The exertion broke more sweat as several boulders came forth, clacking as they rolled out. They stretched their limbs after the long pull. Lichen's tree tattoo on his back shone, as did Rush's full moon. They sat and tasted fruit from Lizard's Toe's skewers. She moved to Buzzard and plied his red tongue with sweet morsels. Plover produced a white crane's wing and stroked his thighs. Bark watched as Buzzard's natural organ stiffened.

Lads dragged red-hot rocks in on drenched mats, then plunged them into hissing water. A noisy smell of splitting stones filled the chamber, mixing violently with herb and pine aromas. Reeking steam obscured Bark's vista of Buzzard's swelled tool. He wondered why he actually needed that exaggerated tattoo.

Lizard's Toe placed her lithe self above Buzzard's reaching member, carefully lowering herself over him. She moaned gently. As she took him in, the mists closed.

Rush and Lichen climbed to their bunks, where the atmosphere was even hotter. They were trothed. So, too, was Mica, though he was happy to remain prone on his comfortable mat to consume the delights of the Buzzard's sweat lodge.

The grass curtain parted like Oiwa's locks. He saw two white, luminescent figures enter. They resembled long-billed storks with feathered costumes hemmed at their hips. Their elegant legs were painted with red stork-like scales.

They parted, moving in a slow dance in and around the bathers. Their arms flexed as white wings fanned the swirls of rising clouds. Bark saw Lizard's Toe moving gracefully on Buzzard's thighs. The Stork dance revolved and quickened: Oiwa watched it attentively with wild pleasure. The feet and wings maintained a rhythm of complete unison. A feeling of extreme excitement developed in his stomach's pit, where a dark heat breathed. Lichen and Rush looked down on the arena, remembering loving Teal and Widgeon. They felt blessed by their bonding.

Two voices sang as conception began with Buzzard and his next mother. That warm, intimate aroma of fertilized baby glided amongst the scents of herbs, fruit, fish and sweating bodies. It lingered and hovered to give truth to the blessed friction of mating. Buzzard would keep his skin for another year.

Oiwa wiped sticky nut honey from his groin. He licked it from his wet finger. As it touched his lips, a feathered wing brushed his perspiring back. A soft hand took his from his mouth. The bill of a stork fell over his nose and touched his chin. He saw pert breasts through the open costume. The dance continued, and the fleeting peck sought another male.

Tine's crouching form glistened in the glowing wicks. He enjoyed caresses from the plumes. His toes curled over the rim of the steaming crater. He was gently urged back from behind. He reclined. The white wings touched the soles of his feet, then caressed his ankles. The feathers stroked his calves, knees and thighs as the winged dream placed a feather beneath his scrotum, stroking exquisitely.

The Stork moved to Bark. Tine lolled his head dreamily in his brother's direction. Bark's testicles descended in the heat. They lolled between his open legs. A loving beak stroked them. His penis rapidly covered his shining star. His eyes opened smartly. Blood pumped through his arteries; his heart thumped as he lay mating.

The other winged creature alighted at Oiwa's feet. He lifted his relaxed head and pulled his plaited hair from the floor. He raised himself to where his dreamy eyes discerned Moss. She knelt over his open knees. She took off her feathered dress and placed it where Rush had lain. She crouched back on Oiwa's feet. Oiwa looked along her legs. Her eyes summoned his glance. He extended a toe.

His hard nail discovered her warm, soft haven. Moss gazed upward, his toe delved deeper. He prised himself up on the rolled mat, his tight erection concealing his star. The low light showed Moss sitting on open bended knees. 'My toe is exactly where my pen should be,' Oiwa quite naturally thought. He licked his lips as he proposed that very move.

Moss wanted the same. She moved. Oiwa's wet toe became naked, exposed and suddenly cool. Moss leaned forward and pulled his elbows away. He flopped back. His plaited hair hit the rug with a thud. His pelvis became utterly prone. They gazed at each other. Oiwa trembled. Moss moved forward. Her neat, pert breasts poised themselves over Oiwa's nipples. They touched. A shot of hot feeling welded that moment. Her dark hair encircled his brow. His Stars glittered.

Oiwa clenched his buttocks, which had been thrust up by the rolled mat. This was a purely instinctive move, apparently the right one. With extreme pleasure he protruded his extended penis further. It touched the area where his toe had caressed. Moss kissed his tip with her vaginal lips. Oiwa's eyes rolled in his skull. Swaying slowly, she gradually engulfed him. Oiwa felt every slight move. Moss pushed down, Oiwa rose. They felt their pelvis bones meeting. Moss explored the full sensation of him being inside her. She wanted to share a part of Oiwa. She had teased him just for this. Her motive was pure. She moved upwards, as Oiwa sank. His eyes looked to hers and he stretched his arms around her to stroke her spine. She moved forward, Oiwa rolled with the mat. This forced his organ deeper. Moss exerted more pressure and felt Oiwa's stem grate somewhere wonderful. This was their moment. It lasted as they mated for sheer joy. Oiwa felt his orgasm grow. It met with Mosses. He let out a great wail of climax, which welled from the depths within his nature. Moss squeezed further down. Her voice shook. They moved and rolled, joined in bliss. Hot stones were missed and languid bodies moved from their gyrating path. Oiwa pressed in and Moss responded. They kissed and smiled and hugged. Together still, Moss scratched his bum and back. His plaits ringed her forehead. He moved inside her, giving a deep kiss when the last beat of his sperm flowed.

Their total oblivion ended with Buzzard's loud handclapping.

Mica had intended to be faithful, but had just spermed, siring twins with Sleek.

Bark was barely aware of Buzzard's applause. He had been taken by one of his wives. They were standing together, prior to mating.

Plover watched Tine. He lay, extended, by the steaming pit. He felt her glance and stood. He moved over. It was soon to be full moon. She welcomed him in as a lovely man. He mated with her as a lovely woman.

14

ᵀEntering Gunnal's ᵛVulva

The sated brothers slumbered indecently long. Rush and Lichen woke early. They stowed the Heron's Tooth, carefully not disturbing their relaxed comrades. Rush thought only of Teal. It was a fine day. The Dun was lower.

Oiwa opened an eye, lying where Moss had left him. He yawned, struggled up, then yelled in anguish. 'CrAaaaaaaaaaaaaaaaaaAAMMmmmmmmmmmmPP,' he screeched, hopping. He stumbled into Tine and crashed to the floor. This explosion ruined the tranquillity. His kin rose reluctantly to help Oiwa straighten his contorted limb. He yelled, gritting his teeth until the spasm finally eased.

'Seems regular, this cramp?' Tine observed as he dressed.

'Not that regular,' Oiwa returned, searching for his clothes.

'When was your last attack?' Tine joked.

'Shut up,' Oiwa warned, shoving the afflicted leg carefully into his breeks.

'Look, young brother,' Tine sniggered, pulling his jacket on, 'I'm showing I care.'

They emerged through the feathered curtain and met Gale. 'Here's breakfast. Duck egg and kidney puffed omelette, Dad's favourite.' It rested on a warm stone. Her beautiful mixing bowl contained a willow whisk bearing traces of beaten white.

'It's marvellous,' Bark said for them all, 'The crispy outside hides this bright yellow middle flecked with verdant sorrel.'

Buzzard made his entry. He was accustomed to that sort of night. 'It's a fine day to set off. Are you glad you stayed?'

'Yes. Thanks so much, Buzzard,' Mica began. 'Last night's mating has set us up perfectly for the journey. Thank you. And for Gale's marvellous omelette, too.'

Rush and Lichen entered. 'Risen again,' Lichen exclaimed, mockingly. 'And what was that yelling about?'

'I got a touch of cramp,' Oiwa admitted.

'HhhhmM,' mused Rush. 'That breakfast was good. I'll do it one day.

'We'd better go soon,' Lichen ventured.

'Sadly, you are right,' Mica responded, turning to Buzzard. 'We thank you very much indeed for your amazing hospitality, Buzzard. Gale is splendid. You have wonderful wives. You are a great chief. May you live long and breed many more children.' They cheered wholeheartedly. Mica meant every word.

'Thanks,' Buzzard replied. 'It has been a very great pleasure for me and my people to have you. Please stay on your return.'

'Absolutely,' Mica assured, hugging Buzzard's broad shoulders.

They reluctantly walked through the village to their boat. Moss and Sleek ran up. Sleek kissed Mica, remembering fondly their embraces. Moss made for Oiwa's side. He smiled brightly at her. She clasped his hands, pulling them to her breasts. 'Your hair's a mess,' she commented, then hugged his neck and pulled his head to her shoulders. 'We must do it again when you return. And you'll need your hair done again.'

'Oh Moss. Thank you. Of course,' he said as they walked hand in hand to the Heron's Tooth.

'Stop a mo, Oiwa? I want one of your plaits.' She took from her pouch a tiny, white blade, severed one and shoved it in her belt.

Oiwa brushed his locks back and hugged her tightly. 'It's the best hairdo I have ever had, I love it, and I love you.' They ambled inevitably to the Heron's Tooth. Plover joined them, as did more of Buzzard's retinue.

The little girl, Jay tugged at Rush's jacket, asking, 'If you see my pretty canoe, will you send it back to me?'

'Of course. What's it like?'

'It's short, just room for Daddy and me. She's called Otter. She has an otter's head painted on her prow. Daddy had just finished it. I painted the whiskers. He said, 'That's beautiful. Those whiskers are so real that we could even shave them in a few days.' He thinks I am very good at painting, my Daddy does.'

Rush stooped and reassured her, 'Your Daddy is right. You must be a wonderful painter. We'll keep our eyes wide open for the Otter.'

Jay squeezed his hand. 'Thanks. I know you will.' She ran, calling, 'Daddy. Daddy. Daddy.'

Heron's Tooth was loaded with extra supplies. The long canoe slipped into the water. Moss moved close to Oiwa, saying, 'Here's a hatchet. My father says it's for you.'

He smiled again at Moss with a deep thrill as he stepped reluctantly towards the boat. Its grey, sharp head shone. The polished antler haft fitted his grip perfectly. With tight throat he croaked, 'Thank your father very much. It's so beautiful... I must step aboard and take my seat.'

Bark's weight tilted her as he boarded to sit by Oiwa. Tine and Mica assumed their positions. Lichen sat behind. Rush held the rope then hopped in and pushed off. The crew thrust the paddles, making a strong wake.

'Don't stop any arrows,' they heard from the shore as they found faster water.

'No chance,' they laughed back. 'Now lift our paddles in farewell, then beat them hard on the water,' Mica needlessly said. White storks flew from the overhanging branches. A blue heron glided to the far bank. The Dun turned and they vanished, Moss waving to the final glimpse.

The crew paddled in silence. Each had his thoughts. Mica piloted and signalled which current to take. Shingle banks appeared. Dippers scoured them for hatching flies and pupae. They steered to the deeper channels.

Rush fiddled with the long net. He tied an end to the stern-peg, where his reel had spun. 'There might just be a fishing opportunity,' he imagined. 'Teal will have my salmon tail by now,' he thought, as his toe twiddled with the other end of the net.

Lichen pondered, 'I could make a hood for Widgeon, for Clan occasions, with a feathery stork-skin.'

Oiwa considered his new hatchet. 'Perhaps Moss's family hope we become related.' Oiwa dwelt long on the prospect. 'I'll ponder until we return.'

Bark paddled in time. 'I could make shit-hot flutes from goosewing bones as gifts. Stork wings would be good, too, and there's herons'.'

Tine could not forget Buzzard's generosity. 'I mated his wife. What an experience. I'll find something special for them.'

Mica piloted and paddled with something on his mind. 'I might ask for Sleek. I'm tough: I could have two wives.'

Afternoon drew to evening. They made excellent progress.

'Right. Beach!' Mica called. The prow touched the sandy bank. Mica hopped ashore and stretched. His crew disembarked, and hauled their boat to safety. They made camp. Mica fetched his fire kit. 'This dry grass is good. I just need twigs.' Oiwa read his mind. 'Set them there, Oiwa. Wood, now?' The others put the boat on her side and fixed their lean-to shelter. Rush took a harpoon, the net and North Star's string bag to the Dun. Mica struck his flint core against his firestone. A grand spark arched, drifting into the grass. He picked it up and blew. He sheltered the fiery glow within. He blew again softly. A tiny flame kindled. Mica held the bundle up. The fire grew in his palms. He placed it quickly in the bundle of twigs and blew rapidly. 'Fire,' he shouted, 'thank Grool.'

Rush searched the river. 'There's a gigantic eel head poking from its dark lair. I'll probe my harpoon to just behind its gills and shove.' A large rising moon reflected in the ripples. 'I've got him!' he yelled in excitement. 'I can feel his slow resistance beneath. He's so powerful. Now he's struggling. I must haul. The eel is coiling up the shaft. Heave, hold tight; wait. It's trying to squirm from the deathly teeth of my weapon. He's tiring. Now, wrench the harpoon up and grip further down, between his writhing, slimy coils. Done it. Fling the harpoon up the bank and leap after it.

'Am I being watched?' he wondered momentarily. 'I see nothing: just the evening landscape. Nought moves. Ah, a covey of distraught partridges taking flight. Their Moon shadows flit over the ground in racing dots. Perhaps one of us raised them,' he considered.

'Eel, you wait here on the jagged spike while I look for a calm pool in that backwater. It's just the place,' he thought. 'I'll empty North Star's drowned bag of pemmican and wrap the rations in the netting to sink. Who knows what will be in there, later? Now, back to camp with my eel.' He pushed the harpoon through the beast's jaw and staked it to the turf.

'What a catch!' Lichen exclaimed, handing him his knife. 'Let's cut it into chunks.'

'I'll gut it first,' Rush said poking the innards from the pulsing flesh with his fingers. 'Look, the stomach had a small string of tiny mussels, some snails and sticklebacks. I'm not sorry for you,' he told the eel, ramming it on sticks to cook.

'That'll be a fine supplement to Dad's dried meat,' Mica said.

'What dried meat?' Rush asked.

'I assumed you were bringing back a partridge, Rush?' Mica asked.

'No. I thought maybe you had.'

'Not us,' Oiwa said as he twisted his eel round in the heat. 'A fox?'

'Didn't smell fox,' Lichen added.

'Marten, perhaps?' Tine suggested.

'Possibly,' Rush put in, 'it was something.' He tested his eel on his tongue. His eyes rolled back with delight.

When they had finished, Tine said, 'I could still do with some of that pemmican.'

'Oiwa, come with me,' Rush said.

'Where to?'

'Never mind, follow.' They went off in the moonlight. Rush had the bag. They found his net. 'Help me heave this out, Oiwa.'

'Wow,' Rush exclaimed, 'it's full of crayfish.'

'They mustn't escape. Stick them in the bag. Quick.' They worked fast, getting their fingers nipped at times.

'Dad's caribou meat?' Oiwa said, seeing remnants.

'Yes, it's put to better purpose. It got soaked, anyway. We can sling this net back for the morning.'

'Sshhhhhhhhh,' Oiwa said. 'I heard something.' They listened.

'What was it?' Rush whispered.

'I don't know.' He felt for his axe. 'It came from those bushes.' They stole towards them. Oiwa swiped his chopper into the shrubs. A swarm of sparrows flew out in terror. 'Can't have been in there, then,' Oiwa said.

'Let's set the net,' Rush suggested.

'Okay.'

They left. Oiwa bore in mind Buzzard's words. He looked back. The moonlight landscape revealed nothing, but he did not like it.

Rush gathered a huge armful of dry pine needles. 'Crayfish,' he announced and dumped them on the ground.

'Crayfish!' the rest exclaimed delightedly.

'I'll pile the needles and make a wide pit in them to put the darlings in.' He tipped them out and shook the bag. He turned it inside out to pull off the hangers on. The wee lobsters began to bury themselves in the bed. 'Cover them, Oiwa. I'll light the needles with a firebrand. There it goes, burning fast and hot. That's how we cook crayfish the Caribou way. Tuck in when they cool,' he said.

'I love peeling the hot shells and scoffing the tails,' Mica said then cracked claws in his teeth to get the succulent flesh.

'The heads are so good, too,' Bark remarked. They peeled and chewed through the entire haul until Bark said, reaching into his provision bag, 'Buzzard's honey and maple gumballs. Here, hand these round. They're just right for afters.'

The meal eaten, Rush thought lovingly of Teal. 'Fall will have delivered my message and the salmon's tail by now. I'm sure Teal's put it somewhere special. That comforts my yearning for her.' His mind drifted as his friends told tales of yore. He gazed at the rising moon. As if in a dream, he was back in North Star's sweat lodge, feeling that great heat within him. His pores opened. Perspiration ran under his clothes. In a trance, he flew again from his body. The feeling came violently to him: it was as though he had been punched sharply below his right shoulder. Then another blow hit him close by. It knocked his breath away. He panted and saw him and his comrades below as he streaked skywards. Briefly, his own image peered up to him. Their campfire was a mere glowing dot on a large, darkened world.

Rush's sweat cooled on his body. His dream sped him towards the shining moon. It was easier to draw breath as the silver orb grew and the stars took different perspectives. His dream flew him behind the moon's face. He looked down on a darkened world with orange light shining behind. He felt at utter peace there, in company with other spirits. The bruising pain in his back cleared. His dream took him further past the moon. He saw the path of the silvery Dun as it took him closer to his world. He felt his soul re-join him, seated by the fire. He drew a great breath as his eyes popped wide open. He felt as though his heart had ceased beating, but it began again with a great thud in his chest. The cold sweat left and he was warm again. He pushed his gum round his palate with his tongue, his round face blank and pale.

'What's up?' Lichen asked his cousin.

'Nothing,' he replied quietly. 'I remembered the dream I had in North Star's sweating house. It startled me.'

'Yes,' Lichen replied, 'I was a caribou. I made mating for new life.'

'I went to the Moon and returned. I think I have just been there again. It was strange. I'm back. Now I know I am real.'

Oiwa joined in, 'I was a goose flying by starlight over the vast ocean. I landed on a silver lake.'

Mica added, 'I was a great bear, with claws so sharp.'

'I was a yellow-eyed lynx. I would have mated again in a cave, but I had to return,' Bark reminded them.

'You are always going to mate with something,' Tine added, 'but I was a soaring eagle in the mountains.' He yawned as he spoke. The yawns caught. They felt it was time for bedding down.

Rush lay between Lichen and Oiwa. He felt cold again and slept fitfully. He listened to the night sounds as his friends snored. Bark let wind. Mica grumbled. Rush thought he heard another sound. 'Was that a sharp intake of breath? A stifled sneeze, or a muffled yelp of pain?' he asked himself. He wriggled out of the huddle and stood in the open to listen. 'The night's clear and cold. The stars shine on me, the Moon too. Nothing moves.' He walked round the Heron's Tooth, scanning the landscape. The sound of the Dun rippling and rolling was a background to the land's silence. Rush looked to the moon's face and silvery halo: it seemed to be glaring back at him. Rush turned to go back to bed. He felt a presence of something, but could not discern what.

'Cold shivers go through me now. I need to pee.' He paced away from the Heron then commenced. He admired the arching shadow of his urine in the moonshine. He pushed his bladder hard. The fount sped into a clump of frosted grass. The icy droplets crackled with the sudden heat.

Abruptly, Rush heard a violent, high-pitched scream. He leaped into the air, yelling. A petrified hare shot up from its hide in the tuft. It jerked in terrified somersaults. Rush's arms flew out in distress. His urinating continued unabated, but inside his trousers. The hot fluid stung his cold legs.

A commotion began under the awning. The hare, still snowy white from its winter coat, arched as if in anguished, slowed time. A blood vessel, deep in its brain, burst under the extreme pressure of trauma. It descended from the zenith of its plight into Rush's outstretched arms. They both landed with a thud on the frosty turf. The stricken animal lay gasping over Rush's forearms. A wet eye and steaming lashes looked up at Rush as the hare's head lolled, dropping further as its steaming breath slowed. Its flailing legs attempted running motions. Its front paws twitched as Rush felt its pulse slacken. Cooling urine ran round his ankles. The hare's mouth opened, its tongue quivering with the final beats of a stricken heart. Rush felt he had seen this before. He did not know where.

'What's up?' Rush's fellows asked, scrambling. Their hands felt for their knives. Oiwa grabbed his axe. They fell out in a tumble from their warm ambiance and struck the cold air. They spread out to face any attacker, eyes wide in the low light. They saw Rush collapsed in the moon-glow. They approached as though he had been murdered. He shook. He could not speak. He let the corpse go with a limp flop. His ear turned as he thought he heard another footfall.

Mica looked on the soaked face of the hare as Rush crawled up and looked down his sodden trousers. Mica glanced into Rush's eyes. 'I. I. I, must have k-k-killed it w-with m-m-my pppPpeeeeeeee,' Rush stammered, as Mica's jaw opened in surprise.

Oiwa remarked respectfully, 'Good shot.' Lichen picked the hare up. It stretched long and limp. He displayed its anointed head.

In wonder, Bark remarked, 'Some weapon. No wound. No blood. Just piss.'

Tine asked, 'How do you perform that feat, Rush?'

'With this,' he exclaimed, hopping, pulling his leggings off and pointing to his willie. 'I pissed on it.'

'Oh. What a dangerous arrow, Rush,' Mica remarked.

'Let me help,' Lichen offered, doubled with laughter, but could not. He tried to point. His hand merely gesticulated as he creased up again. It became toxic. Laughter tore through the group as Rush's pants came off. 'I'll hang them up, cousin, and get you dry ones,' he just managed to articulate.

'I'll gut your hare,' Oiwa put in. 'The liver is yours: the killer's honour – here.'

Rush put his shaking palm out. He took the bile duct and ate the soft delicacy in pensive silence. Lichen rekindled the fire.

'Hare for breakfast, chaps?' Mica added.

Oiwa stripped off the white pelt. 'I'll burn the thigh bones with kidney fat for Tarune,' He said. 'That'll stop the hare's spirit biting your dick off, won't it?'

They squatted for a while in the fresh glow, then to the cosiness of the awning. Rush changed and crawled in. He slept, eventually.

The morning was misty. Oiwa woke first and squeezed out from between Mica and Tine. He chewed on his old gum to clean his teeth. He drank from the Dun and gathered branches for the fire. Rush yawned and stretched his stiff legs while the others rose, remembering, 'I dreamed of Teal and don't wish to move.' Oiwa tossed his dried breeks to him. He sat up reluctantly.

Oiwa jointed the hare with his new axe.

'Come on, Rush,' called Bark. 'Get out here and pee on a buffalo, will you? We need more meat. That hare won't keep us going long.'

Tine added, 'Rush, if you drank more, we'd never go hungry.'

'You are so right, Tine. As soon as nature allows I'll piss on lovely strawberries just for you. Then I'll pee on thee. You'll make rotten eating, though.'

'Oiwa, come to the net,' asked Rush. They hauled it from the shaded water. 'There's hardly anything in it,' Rush complained. 'There were lots last night. There should be more. Something's not right,' he said as they folded it carefully. 'I don't know what, but this just isn't proper.' They returned to camp, dejected. Bark was seeing to the hare. The others stowed the Heron's Tooth. Mica checked the mends. He was satisfied.

They crouched around the fire. Bark stood, handing hunks of hare. He coughed for attention. 'Those heights over to the North East are like a slumbering body. That's Gunnal.' He chewed his foreleg as they peered. 'She's slept for scores of decades. She can only be woken by her lover, but even so her sleep is angry.' He fondled his spear, arranging the feathers below its deadly head, to let his words sink in.

'The Dun here's quiet. Soon she'll bend towards Gunnal's Ankles. There are trees at her toes; we sail between them. As we go through her Ankles, the Dun darkens and deepens.' Bark removed the protective felt sheath and tested the sharpness of his missile's point. Its flaked surface glinted. He glanced at Oiwa, Rush and

Lichen. 'You've not been before. We have,' he iterated, while having a mental flashback of climaxing with Plover. He forgot where he was. He coughed. 'Er. When we reach Gunnal's Calves, the trees vanish. The ravine rises steeply.' He looked up to illustrate. 'Rugged scrub, like torn hair, hangs over.' He shifted, swinging the lance. 'Her thighs rise and narrow. The walls are worn smooth.' He shoved his weapon up for attention. 'High on her stony skin you'll see her pictures. Her tattoos.' Rush, Oiwa and Lichen watched Bark, holding their hunks of hare and gazing in wonder. He seemed commanding and different. Mica was usually the speaker; Oiwa appreciated their equality.

Bark drew a deep breath. 'At Gunnal's Bairn the Dun divides. It's a rocky island. Gunnal gave birth when Farrnar's great ship of ice wedged itself deep inside her. She froze. Her baby waits.'

Rush fanned his face.

'We land, and give the baby honey and milk. Plover handed me a bladder of it. We pray. This gives us safe passage. After the libation we paddle on to enter the...' he trembled at the notion, 'great cleft.' He leaned his spear, 'There we are, lads,' he added. Oiwa took his axe, placed the hare's head on a branch and split it. He shared it with Rush, making sure his friend got the eye he had peed into. Oiwa's portion of brains had a blood clot. He did not notice as he sucked them from the cavity. When Rush finished, he rubbed the hare's pelt with ash and rolled it up. 'Another trophy for Teal,' he mused.

They were ready. Oiwa checked Ziit was safe. Before launching, Rush looked over the grasslands. He found partridge feathers. 'Maybe it was a lucky fox,' he hoped.

'Are you killing game, over there?' Mica called. 'No,' Rush thought as the vision of the shining moon flashed through his mind.

They boarded, Rush as coxswain. The net lay folded at his feet. He attached it to the stern-peg, just in case. Lichen took his place in front, Bark sat centre left, with Oiwa right. Tine settled in behind Mica at the prow. They pushed off into the flow and were quickly in deep waters.

Oiwa lent to Bark's shoulder as they paddled, remarking. 'I didn't know about Gunnal's Bairn.'

'No. We didn't tell you everything.' They fell silent, paddling to Mica's piloting.

'Faster. Stronger,' he called out. Oiwa glanced at his bow, feeling pride. Mica beat time on the prow with his axe's shaft, then took his paddle, pulling hard. 'We spent too long splitting hares at breakfast. We must make up time.' He panted and pulled harder. 'The Dun's slower, paddle fast.' The crew toiled as one. A tributary of the Dun joined, as did others. She widened and deepened while small streams poured in. They sang to keep rhythm.

River life went on, ignoring them. The caribou felt no fear; these men were not hunting, they sensed. A brown bear looked idly on at their passing, as did the coypu, otter, stork and eider.

The banks closed. The strata of rock, like worn toenails, had been eroded by the Dun's power. On either side quartz outcrops glowed as they sailed over worn veins. Heron's Tooth rose imperceptibly. The water quickened. This was just the beginning of their river race. They passed Gunnal's Toes. Spruce woodlands gave way to rocky scrublands, bare, exposed. The river narrowed. The Heron's Tooth leaped up another foot as the water bulged in forced waves. An outcrop of black basalt formed Gunnal's bony ankles.

Mica whistled shrilly to signal for careful paddling. He conducted their course with hand signs. His crew acknowledged each movement. Their paddles dipped accordingly.

The bright sun sent a golden sheen over the strong waters. They saw joining currents as they tumbled into one shifting flow. Small whirlpools and strong eddies tugged the Heron's Tooth. Mica paddled and signalled, skilfully guiding as Rush steered from the stern. The Dun narrowed at Gunnal's Calves. Heron's Tooth hit the turbulence of the swirling, backed-up river water. It rose in wait to descend into the Calves' Pool. Her prow left the surface and splashed down with a shudder as her stern tipped upwards, throwing Rush into the air. He landed back on his seat, paddle still in hand. His feet were caught in the coiled net. He found his balance as Lichen glanced back at him, alarmed. The Dun, constrained by the climbing and narrowing cliffs, flowed more swiftly, darker and deeper. Rush peered down into its racing depths, as did Oiwa. They sped over unseen boulders. Barbel sucked the rocks for lodged carrion and river slime.

Lichen looked up to the heightening cliffs. Scrubby trees hung, roots exposed like arteries pulsing for grim life. Veins of red granite slanted within the exposing cliff. Banded with crystalline darts, it resembled severed flesh. Mica shouted loud. The raw cliffs echoed back over the rumble of water. 'Look. Her Knees.'

'Her Knees. Knees... ees,' the cliffs replied. Mica shouted again, 'Her Knees.'

'Her Knees... knees... ees... ss,' the echo repeated as he pointed to each side. Two huge eagles flew from the towering basalt caps. The crew gazed, amazed, as they glided by. Above, in reds, whites, blues, bright greens and yellows, paintings began to appear. Tall men and women fishing, hunting, mating, climbing trees, porting boats, casting nets and diving into the deeps were all magnificently depicted. Birds, fish, bison, all manner of animals were there. On each side of the canyon, pictures looked down to them.

'Paddle left,' Mica shouted.

'Dle left. left. eft. ft.' The paintings called back. Heron's Tooth slewed away, just in time, and rounded a rocky outcrop. 'Baby's Vomit,' Mica called out over the splashing. 'Best to avoid that,' he shouted. 'Vomit. Vomit. Vomit,' the cliffs chorused.

'Paddle right,' then, 'Back-paddle left,' Mica commanded. 'Don't look up,' he yelled.

'Up. Up. Up,' Gunnal's Thighs retorted as the echo rang over the cascading torrent. 'Pull hard left. Hard left again. Hard left. Left. Left. Left!' He repeated urgently, as did the adorned rocks. Then he shouted. 'Again. Again. Once more. Another time. Do it. Do it. Paddle left.' His voice cooled, they were in slack waters in midstream and Heron's Tooth relaxed. Her hides and frame stopped straining at every jerk the Dun delivered.

'Right, men. We are in the shelter of Baby's Vomit,' Mica announced. 'Vomit, vomit, vomit,' the rocks tediously chimed.

'Now we simply paddle downstream to two short promontories coming from a small, rocky island. Those are the Baby's Legs.' 'Legs, legs, legs,' they heard again.

'Between them is a large, slowly flowing whirlpool.' Mica listened as 'Pool, pool, ool' faded. 'We paddle to the right heel and the current will carry us to a sandy bank called Baby's Bum. There we beach.' The crew ignored the echoes. 'Now, paddle to the far right of the pool.'

Heron's Tooth caught the fringe of a huge eddy and was pulled towards the left. Mica allowed her to be dragged round. A small, sandy bay lay on their right between the smooth Legs of Gunnal's Bairn. 'Beach now. Paddle fiercely,' Mica coaxed. Their craft turned from the swirling pool and nosed into the crisp sands. Mica hopped swiftly ashore. His crew followed. They pulled their boat well up to the sloping rocks.

Oiwa's toes dug into the reddened sand as he lifted Heron's Tooth with the others. Fine lines of stranded quartz and agates graced the Baby's Bum. The crews' toes and heels scattered them as they ran up the shore. Dippers fed in the waters that lapped around the Bairn's Toes. The rocky outcrop, not more than sixty paces long, rose towards its head. Oiwa wondered at the shape of this islet. He looked up to the glowering, dark cliff walls, some hundreds of feet apart. The huge paintings looked down and across at them. 'Who made them?' he asked Mica.

'Some say it was the River Spirits, others blame it on Gunnal's Lover, who does it to tease her. Buzzard says he gets his women to brush them up and paint more.'

'Look up there, Oiwa,' Rush pointed to a vast skein of geese flying in frozen formation.

Tine spoke. 'They're us: they were painted generations past, when we first came this way.'

'There, see, packs of wolves,' Oiwa said.

'They're the Loupfolk who bide below Gunnal's head. We'll meet them at Wolf Lake.' Mica answered.

Oiwa wondered at the reflections of those pictographs. 'They drift and ripple on the surface and penetrated the depths. Perhaps they live another life beneath with the barbel, salmon and trout.'

They stepped over the Baby's Belly. Oiwa glanced down and spotted a small pit graven into the low bulge. It was filled with still water and red weed. A single snail sucked its side. Oiwa nudged Tine, 'What's that?'

'It's the Baby's Navel,' Oiwa felt for his, in sympathy. 'There's more.' Tine pointed to the child's chest. 'A nipple,' Oiwa shouted. 'Nipple, nipple, ipple, ple,' came the cliff's answer. 'There's another.'

Bark made for the Baby's Head. He stood on its eroded chin. The crew gathered round. Oiwa saw scraped contours of a face, eyes, nose, ears and a gaping mouth, the lips desperate for a mother's breast. 'Who carved this?' he asked Bark.

'The locals claim Gunnal's midwife did. Look, there's a painting of her.' They all turned. 'That tall figure in white. See her red arms, crossing her belly, and her triangle breasts. The insides of her thighs are streaked red, too. But the Goose Clan has a different story. We say it was Gumar and Tumar, Gunnal's ancestor, Mother and Father of all Clans. Look again at the 'Midwife'. See there. Look hard. She's painted over two other faded figures.' They stared. Oiwa began to see, in faint ochre, two naked people, hand in hand. Gumar's rounded breasts were faintly picked out in dark manganese. Her pubic forest grew in worn shadow. Tumar's penis was accentuated. As they looked, a flight of rock doves emerged from Gumar's cleft.

The overpainted Midwife looked down with her slit eyes. She nursed a suckling baby. 'We must feed Gunnal's Bairn,' Mica remembered. Bark held the bladder. Together he and Mica squeezed it between those lips. The sticky yellow fluid dribbled into the rock as the flask was wrung. The Midwife's gaze seemed less severe when they looked back up at her. 'Now. All kneel around the kid's mouth. I'll utter the prayer. 'May this ambrose keep you until your mother awakes. She'll suckle and you'll walk from the river. You will grow strong. You shall be the Great Hunter and sire many to follow. These are the wishes of Gumar and Tumar. Now rise,' Bark said.

'Hungry kid. I hope it doesn't throw up,' Tine remarked. Rush giggled, his first happy moment since his moon dream.

'Tine, it was my turn to crack that joke,' Bark complained.

'You should've been snappier, then.'

Oiwa peered downstream. The Dun took a right turn to disappear into a deeper, darker ravine. He gazed at the precipitous cliff wall on the Dun's left. There, a gigantic, multi-coloured man was depicted clearly and crisply. The black manganese shading with ochre on the contours made him real. He, too, stood and faced the river, his hips twisted in silhouette. He wore a raptor mask. The beak protruded from above the giant's nose. Outstretched arms supported vast wings. Down his back draped a feathered cloak. His feet pointed downstream. The torso supported his stiff phallus, which disappeared round the river bend. On his wrists dangled magnificent armlets.

'Look at that!' Oiwa shouted.

'That must be Buzzard,' Mica exclaimed, 'He said to look out for him. I didn't expect that.' He trod from the Bairn's forehead. Dippers took flight and a redshank darted off. He moved carefully to the slippery left ear.

They followed. Oiwa said, 'It's Buzzard, all right! Remember his sweat lodge. How *huge* he grew,' they nodded in wonder. 'Oh. I feel those twinges in my stomach's pit again, just thinking of being with Moss.' He tugged a lock of his hair and grinned. He recalled Buzzard's advice about mating, and verses from the Gumar and Tumar legends.

The water ran fast. 'See: up there. A bloody dangerous sling.... Just hanging from the cliff-top,' Lichen pointed out. 'There's women in it, possibly Storks. They're painters.... By Gumar, I wouldn't like being up there.'

'It's lowering.... Ooops. It bumped!' Tine cringed. 'Amazing. They've swung to the tip of his prick.'

''Looks like they're about to daub it,' Mica observed. He cupped his hands to his mouth, calling. 'Is that Buzzard?'

'Who else? We've left the potent bit to last,' came a distant reply.

'Can you paint mine?'

'Come up here, then.'

'On the way back?'

'Sure thing, Mica,' they called.

'Woooo,' Tine flashed to smirking Mica. 'Your reputation's gone before you.'

From the clifftop shouting, waves and laughter grew confused in the echoes. Mica and his band waved back, blowing kisses. 'Time to press on,' Mica said. He led them past the Bairn's lips. The libation had vanished.

'Don't puke, little one,' Bark said. Rush noticed how Oiwa's traveller's beard had thickened, as his brothers' had. A great diver disappeared into the huge eddy as they manoeuvred their boat towards the slow current. Before boarding, Mica informed them, 'We follow the flow left of the Bairn, pass its lug and paddle right below its head to the main stream. There are countless paintings of snakes, birds, strange fish, the stars, the Sun and the Moon: spirits, symbols of our ancestors and other clans. The Dun's too fast and treacherous to look up at them. You might catch a glance. Don't be distracted, or we'll be ancestors quicker than we want.' He met everyone's eyes for acknowledgement. He certainly had it.

'Keep your paddles ready. Listen. Soon we'll enter Gunnal's Vulva. It is a huge fissure in the mountain. Way up, part of it is blocked by a massive rock. We go beneath. It's her lover's foreskin. The noise is tremendous there. *You will all have to watch for my signals.* At times it will get dark, even though it's midday. The Dun divides, careering into different ravines, *WE MUST KEEP RIGHT.* We will come out where the ravines reunite. It'll be turbulent.' His eyes widened as his team stared back. For Tine and Bark, it was a rueful reminder of what they achieved before. They were glad of Mica's words. 'As I said, there's a small protected beach, which will be on our right. Paddle swiftly on to it, hauling up below the hewn steps. We climb up with Heron's Tooth on our backs and our tackle strapped in.

'I will repeat.... We port our canoe over Gunnal's Belly. There's a sheltered valley between her paps where we can camp. Tomorrow we make for her shoulders, where Gunnal's ugly head is. The Dun spews there from a vast cavern as a fantastic waterfall into Wolf Lake. We can climb down the side of the falls, re-launch and meet the Wolf Clan.' Then he added, 'See. It's simple.' His crew shifted anxiously. He finished, reaffirming. 'We must *NOT* miss the beach.' He took a deep breath and warned. 'Nobody has gone past there and lived.'

'I feel sick,' Oiwa thought. 'What if we get it wrong? There will be no future! It's just here and now, then nothing if we fail. My guts feel wobbly, like they want to empty.'

White-faced, he glanced at Rush for reassurance. He and Lichen trimmed strands of jet-black hair off. 'It's a Caribou sacrifice, asking for protection from the River Gods. Oiwa took his jasper knife. He severed a lock with a red shell bead on it. He cast it on the water.

A diver bird reappeared, waving a small fish. 'A sign of good fortune,' Oiwa hoped.

'Embark,' Mica bade. In trepidation they took their positions and paddles. They dipped them in the river to move with the whirlpool of Bairn's Toes, meeting the current that would draw them into Gunnal's Vulva. The diver flew off, landing on Vomit Rock to digest its catch. They paddled from the whirlpool's gentle pull and rounded the Bairn's Toes. It took them past its chubby legs. Their speed increased as they sped by the ribs, where a rough arm seemed to slide by. An otter pulled up with a silvery dace and watched the Heron's stern vanish round Baby's Head. Two sandpipers dibbed as the captain called, 'Paddle hard right.' The boat responded, hitting the rushing flow. Her prow jutted through the tumble of water. Spray splashed their faces: a last wake-up call. 'Hard right,' Mica shouted. They plunged their paddles vigorously. She leapt to another baulk of careering water. 'Ride the waves,' Mica encouraged them. She slewed; a wave hit broadside on. Oiwa was soaked and the Heron's Tooth took water. Spears floated in their ties. She righted herself. 'Bale!' someone shouted. The women up high yelled a farewell. The crew raised their paddles, saluting, then plunged them deep to guide their craft. The artists watched their progress down into the ravine. They wondered who it was who went before.

The Heron's Tooth bounced. The Dun boiled beneath. Mica called, 'Hold her steady.' Their paddles went in. They held firm and level. The canoe veered around an awkward twist. The river suddenly widened to a great pool. The cliff painters watched the men enter. At the far side opened the enormous cleft of Gunnal's Vulva. There, the river plunged to the roots of the mountain. The pool was water in waiting, putting off being swallowed into the mountain's chasm. They saw the awesome basalt pillar that had crashed into her crevice – all that remained of her lost love.

The water in the centre of the pool dipped to a lower level. The Heron's Tooth was inexorably drawn... pulled faster. The darkened cavern narrowed frighteningly. The painters in their distant cradle peered as the tiny stick, with six good men in, was drawn to that gulch. Oiwa felt the craft's prow dip. Mica ducked his head in reverence as the Heron's Tooth commenced her plunge. Rush wondered why his life seemed to be drawn out of his control. The darkness cast by Farrnar's Foreskin was chilling. Ahead, a silvery light loomed. The tumble rocked Heron's Tooth. Oiwa bounced alarmingly. Rush pushed himself tightly in the stern. The boat lurched and listed terribly. Oiwa looked into the deep current as water flowed into their skin craft. Mica signalled urgently to right the boat. Paddles dipped the other side and the Heron's Tooth righted. She sat lower in the water. Ziit floated. 'Bale!' came the command again. Tine did what he could: chasm walls flashed by. They suddenly appeared in a blinding, silvery light. Sunbeams shone in a watery arena. Spume and foam flew. There, the Dun divided.

'HARD RIGHT!' Mica screamed. Instantly, the crew worked as one. Heron's Tooth's prow looked to its course and entered the tossing torrents. She bounced towards her destined ravine, hitting the side as she entered. Mica was cast forward. Tine leaped and caught his leather belt. He hauled him from certain ruin. The

Heron's Tooth's stern washed across the current. She listed seriously. Oiwa back-paddled hard, Rush followed, as did Bark. The scraped prow looked down the Dun and slid over the waters as if naught had occurred.

They rounded an angle where the sun barely reached. Huge icicles, like ogre's hands, clung to the slimy walls. Oiwa felt the chill batter his face. His nose froze. The ravine widened. Gunnal's rocky flesh appeared redder. She closed in through dark veins of cruel igneous rock. The Heron's Tooth jerked in the narrow strait's thundering rapids. Her mends held, though water bounced between stern and bows as she tipped fore and aft.

It seemed like a lifetime, fleeing down the tortuous canyon. Vague slits of grey light showed them the way. 'Get ready!' Mica called, 'Soon. Soon.' Then, 'Very soon, now!' The Dun veered left and daylight streamed down as they shot from their course to enter a splendid, golden pool. The canyon came back together again. 'Paddle RIGHT. BEACH!' Mica finally commanded.

Heron's Tooth grounded. Mica prepared to leap to the shingle. 'Look,' said Rush. 'Under the steps. There's Jay's canoe. That's smudged whiskers on an otter head.'

Tine moved forward, wiping his brow after that fearsome escapade.

Snaaaaar hushed her child from a dark cleft overlooking the beach. She pulled hard on her bowstring. Her buffalo arrow aimed at Mica's spine. Rush stood to cast the rope to him as she uncurled her fingers. Her missile sped. 'Here, catch, Mica!' Rush called. Mica had one foot on the shore when Rush leaned forward. Lichen reached for a handhold to disembark when the arrowhead struck Rush just below his right shoulderblade. He only felt a dull punch. He sat heavily down in his seat. This caused the Heron's prow to rise. Water ran to the end. The Heron's beak shifted and lifted from the shingle. She refloated.

Snaaaaar angrily took another missile and pulled again, saying. 'Shit! Missed the fucking bastard. He'll have this one, instead.' Mica heard the arrow flight. He leapt backwards in alarm onto the shingle. She let her next projectile loose. Mica looked in her direction and saw the woman's raging eyes. He arched backwards and fell. The arrow passed his throat, a flight feather nicking his windpipe.

'Back! Back!' he yelled. The arrow splintered behind him. He jumped into the escaping prow. 'Paddle fast! Down the Dun, Now!' he yelled. Rush reached for his paddle. The arrow-shaft stopped the movement. He tried again, feeling awkward discomfort.

'Fucking bastards!' Snaaaaar screeched, fumbling for another murderous point. 'I have to kill *him*, not that Hare Pisser!' She strained her string, seeing Mica's face, and aimed for his nipple. Rush, deaf to the commotion, stood to get his paddle. His suede shirt tightened. He glanced to his chest and saw the shiny black point sticking through. He was horrified. His fingers went to touch it, but his scapula denied the movement.

Mica heard the searing of the third arrow. He saw Rush stricken by the first as he stood again. Rush looked past Lichen, who paddled furiously. Tine grappled with his paddle in confusion. Mica saw the deadly point sticking through him. He blinked as Heron's Tooth shifted in the current. Their eyes met as another punch struck Rush's right ribs. He coughed and looked at his first wound. A second lethal stone erupted through his jacket. He sat with a thump and rasping breath.

'That little shitty bastard!' Snaaaaar screamed. 'Ruining my shots, the weasel. I'll kill that fucker yet!'

'Dew! Follow me.' She sent another arrow to shatter on the cavern ceiling. Gunnal's Gulch swallowed the Heron's Tooth. Dew stood in shock. 'Come, Dew, my flower. Follow Mummy.' Dew did what she always did, through fear and loyalty: she followed.

'Leave the kid's boat. Run. We'll see their stinking corpses float on Wolf Lake beneath the waterfalls!'

'What waterfalls, Mummy?'

'Shut up. Carry these.' She passed her quiver.

'Paddle down the middle! Use your ears. Keep heads low. Fend off the edges,' Mica yelled. 'Don't get your brains bashed out.' It became pitch dark. Reflections on the turbulent waters vanished. They used the sounds and echoes to judge where the cavern's walls were. They bent to stop the roof bashing their brains out. Mica held course in the central flow past hidden rocks. Rush felt the pain of puncturing skewers. He breathed shallowly, preserving what life remained. He wondered if the arrows could be snapped and pulled. He realized this was not the place. There was no time.

Mica commanded his crew as best he could in the dark torrent.

Rush felt with his right hand to find if his precious net was tied to its stake. It was. When he had recovered from twisting, he painfully reached to the net's other end and wound it tightly around his left ankle. He removed Teal's fishhook and threaded it in the mesh, tying its sinew trace to secure his lifeline. He sat back, careful not to scrape the arrow flights or nudge the shafts. He rationed his shallow breaths. He did not want to cough to cause more internal bleeding.

They arrived in an immense underground lake, where the current slackened. They could judge the scale of the space by the echoes. Lichen spoke first. 'What's happened to Rush? Is he hurt?' 'Yes. Badly!' replied Mica. 'He's been struck by two arrows. I don't know if he is alive or not.' Lichen reached round to his dear cousin and clutched his knee. Rush moved it to let him know he was still with them. Rush held Lichen's hand and slowly lifted it to the arrows, so his cousin and friend knew exactly how he was. Lichen wept. His cries filled the great cavern.

Mica said, calmly and rationally, 'Paddle on. Follow the flow.' With every dip of Lichen's paddle his heart felt like bursting. Oiwa turned to comfort his friend. 'Sssssshhhhhhhh! Oiwa,' Mica called back, 'paddle on, young man.' Oiwa dipped his paddle. His arms felt frozen. Bark patted his shoulder in comfort and reassurance. Their peril sunk in.

After a distance the cavern opened. A shaft of silver light shone to the black water. They sailed towards it. Rush's head arched back. He looked dimly to the glow. As he slipped into it, he saw a patchy full moon looking down on him. He remembered his dreams. It was the crew's chance to look at Rush's sad features. A great island of ice loomed in the distance. It reflected what light there was as they paddled by. Far off shafts of silver light beamed on the subterranean lake through the pierced roof. Rush bent forward, keeping focused on them.

Mica glanced to Rush. His dark form contrasted with Farrnar's isle of shining ice. He waved his arm, indicating a course to the right. 'Paddle right,' Mica uttered. Rush, unseen, nodded.

Mica headed for the furthest right-hand exit. Eroded pillars held up the cavern's opening. There, the Dun tumbled from its darkness for an instant. On either side, rocks piled the edges of their branch of the river. The Heron's Tooth bounced and tipped. Rush was in agony. He felt the netting on his feet. He breathed in, long and slow. He saw two pointed rocks, like petrified twins looming. This was his moment. Rush drew his feet up under him. The rocks closed in.

He leaped. His final force landed him between the megaliths. The arrows, snapping, wrenched his lungs.

Heron's Tooth was caught in the rapid cascade. She sloped alarmingly to another dark abyss. 'Hold on tight!' came Mica's scream over the crash of water. Spray soaked them. Tine was flung upwards, landing in the Heron's bilge among the spears. Oiwa was nearly thrown over the side. Bark caught him. Lichen bent in weeping misery as the Heron's Tooth lurched, wailing when Rush vanished. Suddenly, Heron's Tooth veered towards the bank, striking jagged boulders. She burst her prow and was stricken. Mica was thrown headlong onto wet rocks. The current took her wreckage towards the dark cave. Mica raised his grazed head, watching, knowing they were doomed. 'Great Goose of our Clan! Save us!' He shouted. No one heard.

The netting uncoiled as Rush landed between those jagged boulders. The Heron's Tooth and her precious cargo careered downstream. Rush's net paid out. The tie on the stern-stick held. Rush felt the first tug on his foot. It reassured him in his action. The net stretched taught. He felt his leg extend. A loud bang within told him of the dislocation of his hipbone from his pelvis. Heron's Tooth slowed. Rush's knee joint sprung, but held. The Heron's Tooth jolted to a stop. Rush's leg swivelled freely. His knee stretched further. So did his ankle. His hook's knot tightened. Rush's face looked down. Blood flowed from his lips. He coughed; the arrows splintered to puncture his diaphragm. He thought of Teal and mouthed her name. His tongue relaxed and hung from his mouth. The tiny ball of gum he had kept in his cheek slid from behind his canine tooth as he died.

A rising spirit looked down, seeing a twisted corpse. It hovered momentarily, then rose, spiralling, over a desolate torrent. Fraught figures struggled as another was washed deep underground. The soul slanted away. On its passage to the moon, it saw Teal's small tepee engulfed in an aura of moonlight, then two dim figures on a barren landscape.

15

Aftermath

'I'm hungry, Mother,' Dew protested, struggling behind Snaaaaar.

'Keep up, dear. We'll stop between those hillocks.'

Dew plumped down, looking at the Paps' exposed summits. In the dell between, stunted trees huddled for shelter.

'Have we any crayfish?'

'No. All gone. And you ate the meat Mummy got. You do have an appetite, don't you?' Snaaaaar answered, racing far ahead.

Dew saw smoke rising from the scrub and stumbled on. Snaaaaar warmed her hands as she approached. 'See what a lovely fire I made for you, my buttercup,' she said as Dew's bare feet crunched through the coarse undergrowth.

'Yes, Mummy. But I'm hungry,' she whined, flopping beside her.

'Tend the fire; I'll find something good to eat.'

Dew sat contemplating the flames, casting dry leaves on them. They curled, glowed and became ashen membranes, to rise and drift. Her eyes followed them to notice vultures circling high in the distance. Far further, snow-covered mountain peaks shone with the declining sun. Behind her, the moon looked over Gunnal's desolate landscape. Dew's precious moment broke. Screeching nesting birds, white, like phantoms, arched and wheeled round Snaaaaar's dipping head, angrily diving at her. Snaaaaar paid no attention as she robbed their downy craters.

'Here, dear...'

The hysterical birds plunged, mourning their lost clutches.

'I've got eggs.' She shook one at her ear, listening to the movements inside. Her sharp fingernails rent its shell. Mouth wide open, she emptied the egg in. She shut her mouth. Poking her tongue through the rich yolk, she tasted, swirled and swallowed. Her slate eyes rolled in gratification.

She shook another speckled egg by her lug, where dangled a dainty straw earring of a wee bird. It went so nicely with her hairband, she imagined. Snaaaaar listened. The swirling sound within it was not so pronounced.

'Here you are, dear. Open wide.' Dew edged to her mother's side, jaws apart. 'Put out your tongue, my little one, and I'll crack it.' The egg's contents slipped. 'Shut and swirl.' she heard her mum say. Dew closed her eyes, trying to wriggle her tongue. She found a lump and choked.

'Swallow, darling. Swallow,' Snaaaaar shouted.

'Can't!' Dew uttered through slimy lips. 'Can't. Can't!' Her teeth bit the diminished yolk and she gagged.

'Come, my bluebird: if Mummy can, you can.... Swallow.'

Dew tried with difficulty.

'Finish it!' Snaaaaar snarled.

'What, Mum? Even the beak?' she spluttered, then spewed over her mother's lap.

Snaaaaar lurched back, hissing. 'Just like that stupid Birch Skin. No bleeding guts.'

Little Dew cleaned her mother's front and curled up where it was least cold, to sleep.

The Heron's Tooth halted in the rapids, swinging immediately towards jagged rocks, the net rending disgustingly on Rush's limb. Their canoe belted its nose on the rough boulders, crashing smartly. Mica was hurled onto them, his left ear and temple smashing on the sharp edges. He lay stranded in a wet heap, motionless amongst a litter of rough boulders.

Bark was flung face forward into the wrecked prow. Tine was cast half out, legs and feet strewn over the side, feeling the force of racing waters. His torso faced rising water in the Heron's bilge, his arms flailing as he righted himself.

Oiwa, still seated as the impact reached him, saw Lichen fly, yelling, into the treacherous currents. He hit the torrent and vanished, to be hurled down a thundering cataract. Oiwa landed amongst their cargo of sodden weaponry and stores.

'Grab what you can!' Tine roared over the tumult.

'Ziit first, then his arrows,' Oiwa instantly knew. 'Grab the spears. Blast! Dropped the paddle and the pemmican satchel. There goes the rope, floating off. Snatch it. Quick before it vanishes. Got it! Hurl it ashore. It's landed on Mica's body. Bark's bent over him. He can't be dead,' Oiwa thought, bitterly concerned as he stamped hurriedly from the stricken Heron.

'He's alive!' Bark called out. 'Tine! Help me up with him. Get him on that ledge under the overhang beneath that sheer cliff. We'll drag him under those stunted ferns. It's more sheltered there. I'm clambering down to help Oiwa rescue our stuff. You stay with Mica. He's moaning. It's a good sign.

'Good man, Oiwa,' Bark said as they retrieved what they could.

'Rush leapt out!' Oiwa told him desperately, 'We've lost Lichen, too! Flung from our boat. Washed down the Dun. There's no saving him.'

Bark slapped his forehead in sudden remorse then controlled himself. 'Stack what's left against the cliff. We'll have to stop here. We can't go on until Mica's fit. It's late. We're exhausted,' he uttered, distraught. 'That's two of us we've lost. It's tragic.'

'Aaagh. This is terrible,' Mica grimaced agonizingly, feeling the bloody mess dangling from his lobe. 'Are we safe?'

'No,' Tine answered him. 'Rush flung himself out, saving us. Lichen was hurled into the deadly Dun. Heron's Tooth is fucked. It's just us, stuck here,' he spelt out over the roar of the river.

Mica lay trembling in a vast, vertical-sided collapsed cavern: the sharp rubble, strewn where it fell; the Dun, scoring channels through it. Downstream, a huge gaping chasm swallowed the powerful waters, which rapidly thundered in a vertical drop where Lichen had cruelly vanished.

The sun moved upstream. Its late-in-the-day beams rested on an obscured cliff. A vast icicle, like a gigantic hand, adorned this precipice, the temporary afternoon warmth making the wrist of ice daily minutely thinner.

Rush lay face down between his rocks, still anchoring the Heron's Tooth. His body cooled in the atmosphere under that frozen spectre. The meltwaters trickled over its thinning wrist to refreeze on the enormous spreading hand. The sun hid behind the high horizon after touching the frozen flesh. Droplets of freed water ran, solidifying on those huge knuckles. Dark closed in the crater. Only silvery reflections revealed this stricken, hanging form. The massive hand's weight became too much for its dwindling arm. Minute fissures filled with weakening, running water. The iceman's arm parted. The fist fell to shatter in bright cascading shards. The noise of its descent roared like stampeding bison.

The survivors looked around, terrified, as the hidden limb smashed on the rocks directly behind Rush's corpse. The hurtling ice careered beneath his head and stiffened arms. His extreme efforts locked him in rigor mortis at death's instant. His rigid corpse dislodged from the stone vice to be elevated high on the bright cascade, careering past his comrades. They watched Rush's crystalline bier levitate him towards the Dun. The dune of ice halted, Rush sliding gracefully off. The Heron's Tooth edged forward into the flow as Rush's net slackened.

Her stern yanked her smashed nose from the blood-stained rocks. The net tightened again on Rush's heel, to drag him into the raging river. The brothers looked on agape as the boat took her own life. She entered the fast flow, following Lichen. Her broken prow raised in salute as she vanished.

Rush was towed into the flow. His rigid body spun. His arms raised and dipped as he passed his comrades. Oiwa called out 'He's swimming.' Bark held him firmly.

'He's not swimming,' Bark said quietly. 'Just wave him goodbye.'

Oiwa lifted his hand limply, not really comprehending why. He felt a great lump rising in his throat like an immovable flint nodule.

The four of them looked around. The only shelter was the largely ruined winding grotto, eroded by millennia of water. It wound round the cliff and out of sight. Bark announced, 'We can't scale the cliff. It's too sheer.' They looked up into the sky where vultures wheeled, eyeing for fresh carrion.

'We must have fire. Oiwa, find wood,' Bark said.

He nodded, remorsefully searching. 'Here're wood splinters lodged in rocks. I'll chuck them to Bark then hunt along the old cave floor.' He rounded a corner. 'That must be Gunnal's Guts, where Rush and Lichen plummeted. It's appalling.' The cave went on. Blocking it was a great barricade of stranded tree trunks and branches, washed there by earlier spates. 'At least that's more wood. I'll tow some back. Here's a whitened bough. Pull it, Oiwa,' he told himself silently. 'It's giving. Tug... Oh no!' he gagged, as a loathsome stench erupted. The pile involuntarily shifted when a finely balanced trunk turned. Its weighty root delved into the Dun's flow and dislodged. It fell. Some of its allies followed.

'The stink's overpowering. My throat aches,' he realized, grabbing it for comfort. The dam loosened. The tangle tumbled: some Dunwards. The head of a rotting bison fell, slithering to Oiwa's feet.

'WWWWHAAAAAAAAAAAAAAAGH!' he screamed gutturally, while a volley of black, flapping bats careered past. They chafed his face as the dam of wood and rotting meat collapsed. Oiwa held his ears, screeching out in terror. Clouds more bats rushed past. 'Run.... Quick, to my brothers,' was all Oiwa could register. Dragging wood, he opened his mouth, shaking. 'My lips and tongue move, but no sound comes. Try again. Nothing!... Shout... Nothing... Just harsh breath.' He dropped his branch. Tears broke. He shook. Tine wrapped him with his arms in deep understanding. Oiwa sank, shaking, to the cavern floor; despairing; crying soundlessly; convulsing with each burst of grief and terror.

Tine gathered him up carefully, softly asking. 'Where did you get that wood?' Oiwa pointed. 'Show me. We need more.' Oiwa limply turned in his brother's arms and led, the stink of bison greeting them.

'We will drag the branches out, Oiwa. Don't you come near. That foul carcass is about to shift. You've had enough. Just haul some wood back.'

'Okay,' Oiwa nodded bravely, but with a smashed heart.

'You are rocking with pain and chanting to relieve it,' Oiwa saw when he returned to Mica, who clutched his ear.

'We'll get the fire blazing: night's closing,' Bark said as their world shrank to the fireglow. Stars shone. The silvery waning moon passing over gave Oiwa strange comfort in his severe state. 'I'll hum a tune,' he thought miserably, but nothing came. Bark heated wet moss until it steamed. He applied the poultice to Mica's swollen jaw. Mica moaned painfully.

'Can you pee?' Bark asked.

'I already have,' Mica answered through his clenched jaw.
'Can you again? It will stop infection.'
'I think so,' he replied.
'Then piss on this other moss.'
'Good,' Bark said. 'I'll bathe your lug. There's grit, slime and chunks of rock in there. Your ear's actually hanging off. I have to remove it. This might hurt.' Mica nodded. Tine took his flint blade core from his pouch and pressed a sharp flake with his axe butt. The translucent sliver fell into his palm. He sliced the swinging ear away.

'When are you going to do it?' asked Mica abruptly through the gap in his teeth.

'It's done,' answered Bark.

'Really?'

Oiwa sat, trembling, by the fireside. Tine gripped his hand to watch the amputation. 'It is so hard,' Tine said. 'Goose journeys have never been like this. It's gone so menacingly wrong.'

Oiwa nodded grimly. 'My throat aches so. I'll lean back, it might help,' He thought, 'No. Only the glimpse of the Moon soothes me. I will sing something: I just can't,' he found, burying his head in Tine's breast, shaking.

Bark nursed Mica. They watched the fire. Tine's chin dropped and Oiwa lay down. Bark shifted, allowing Mica to rest on his chest. They slept. The moon slipped by. Clouds obscured the stars.

Oiwa dreamt of someone far off. She gazed at him through a shimmering veil. He woke and rekindled the fire. Mica tried a yawn. His jaw remained locked. Grey streaks of daylight saw the last black bats flap leathery wings back to their cavern. Oiwa tried to say, 'Good morning.' His mouth moved, but silence came. Instead, he picked up a stone and flung it at the rock face. It shattered, but still he could not speak.

The crack woke Tine. He groped in their sodden supply bag for dried meat.

Oiwa shared some in silence. The food pushed against that stone stuck in his larynx. The meat sat coldly in his stomach. He moved from the fire, where his dark thoughts lurked and ventured away, looking at the speeding waters, then wandered towards the bats' retreat. Midges buzzed around the strewn bison body. Behind the collapsed barrier, a dark path wound. Oiwa held his breath and ventured into the tunnel. 'That's the bats' roost ahead. I hear their distant chatter and their dry wings fluttering. Maybe we can escape that way? I'm going to tell my brothers.

'I'll grab my bow and strike him on the rock face for attention,' he thought, pointing Ziit to where the bats went. They looked, as Oiwa acted a leader's role. Mica stood, saying painfully, 'Follow Oiwa.' As they made for the cave the sky darkened. Sheet lightning flashed, crashing behind grey clouds. The first heavy hail was forced down by quickening wind.

Oiwa took his quiver, Bark the spear, and Tine carried the rope and bags. They held their breath and climbed the slumped tangle of boughs into the unknown. 'Forward and inward,' Oiwa wanted to say. He just looked back with his hazel eyes and blinked. Mica understood Oiwa's command. 'I'm sure that's Oiwa's voice, in the depths of my brain,' he thought.

'Follow,' Oiwa signalled as he clambered over the flotsam-strewn floor. Bones, antlers and horns of drowned beasts were littered there. They picked their way until the cave turned into utter darkness.

Oiwa stuck out his arms, stopping his brothers. He ushered them back to the light. He gripped his new axe and ran to the bison. He took a huge breath and looked inside the rotting rib cage from where its offal had spilled. Dangling under the spine were the huge, fat-encased kidneys. Oiwa bent in, severed them, then ran as the bison slumped, nearly enclosing him.

He flung the fat to his brothers' feet, returning for strewn femurs and a loosened horn. Back with his kin, he chopped the bones' ends off with his precious axe, stuffing the fat inside. Tinder lay at his feet. He pushed it into the lard. Bark understood. He took his firestones and struck. Sparks flew through the gloom to the dry fuel. Oiwa blew. Small embers grew then flames melted the grease. Soon, a bright torch flared.

Mica forced his mouth open a little, spluttering, 'You're brilliant, Oiwa. Show us the way.'

'I now feel better,' Oiwa thought despite all. 'Right. Onward into the dark,' he resolved.

Their path weaved. The cave roof lowered. They stooped. Later the ceiling became so lofty that it escaped the light from Oiwa's torch. Mica carried the spares. Inexorably, their trail descended.

'A strange odour?' Oiwa sensed first. 'Underfoot, it's peculiarly soft; above, things shuffle,' Oiwa peered, clicking his tongue.

'Bats,' Tine said.

'Yes,' Oiwa nodded excitedly, signalling Tine to bend. Handing Bark his torch, he mounted Tine. Reaching high, he gently picked two bats like ripe plums. He passed them to Mica, who clubbed them with the butt of his green chopper. Oiwa harvested a dozen. He climbed down and signalled to go, tucking their next meal in their battered jackets.

'Gather wood if you can,' Mica said as though repeating Oiwa's words, as they moved on. Later, the cave opened into a vast gallery. Water dripped from above. Their torchlight shimmered from wonderful yellow and green streaks sparkling in the stone.

'Let's cook,' Mica murmured, as his jaw relaxed. They made a fire. Oiwa pushed an arrow through a bat. The smell of singeing fur filled the still air. The leathery wings crisped and he crunched. The fragrant flesh warmed beneath the fine skin and loosened from the light bones.

'I've not had bat,' Bark remarked. Oiwa gestured, 'Me neither.'

'Nor I,' Mica added, turning his.

Tine shafted another. 'My second ever bat, going down. Small but tasty.' Their fire comforted them. Smoke rose to the high roof, leaving the air crisp. Tine sang a soft, serenely echoing song before they explored the cavern.

'Look there,' Mica pointed, 'In the middle. It's a small pool of the clearest water.'

'I'm approaching it warily,' Oiwa thought, as he examined its surrounding stumpy stalagmites, their tops worn hollow and nursing polished, conical pebbles, shining in their fonts like eggs in a coot's nest. Their torchlight flickered in reflected glory. They stood at the pool's edge where the ceiling's reflection looked up. Veins of golden sparkling stone shimmered in its depths. The stillness was profound. They looked above, pointing to flashes of shining brilliance, then leaned over and saw themselves framed in the glorious light.

'This is the most beautiful thing I've ever seen,' Mica whispered reverently, while watching in wonder his brothers' reflected gazes. He glanced again round the sanctuary of beauty. Then he quietly said, 'We have to move on.'

'Let's embrace and seal this moment forever,' Bark suggested.

'Yes, and then we will drink from this wondrous pool,' Tine added.

Stooping, they drank deeply from the brilliant water. The ripples made great play of the torchlight on the glittering rock roof. Oiwa imagined glimpsing a familiar face, glancing back at him.

'Reluctantly, we must trace our sloping path where the cave narrows again,' Mica told them. 'There's a long log across it.'

'I'll climb over and light my brothers' way,' Oiwa thought. 'The path looks easy, though the tunnel twists. If I stop and listen with my mouth wide open, cupping my hands to my ears, I can hear far better. I sense distances with the minute echoes.' Mica spoke, but Oiwa hushed him. Nervously he took hold of the horn he had found and placed its open end directly on the cave wall, pressing his ear to it.

Oiwa looked to them in alarm, mouthing the word 'RUN!' and hurtled on. 'Follow Oiwa,' Mica yelled. The first of the terrified bats flew past into Oiwa's flickering torchlight.

Bark caught up, 'Light my torch, Oiwa,' he asked as more bats darted in a fearful cloud, uncaring of men.

Oiwa sprinted ahead. 'There must be a way out. Follow the bats,' he thought. 'Run, run, run, through the dark. There's a distant grey light appearing far ahead,' he panted to himself. 'Make speed. I know the peril they flee from. The light ahead is dimming. The flying creatures are careering up the beam.' Oiwa saw the opening. He turned and tried to scream, 'HURRY!'

16

Scoured

They all reached the light. Swarms more bats ascended the lum. Bark bent. Mica jumped on his back and was lifted to the rising tunnel. He shinned up. Oiwa scrambled onto Bark, too, and was pushed vertically. He crawled onto the ledge where Mica was perched. The tumultuous roar of tumbling water Oiwa had heard became deafening. Tine leaped on Bark's shoulders. Mica dropped his bone lamp. It fell past Oiwa and scorched Tine, who scraped onto the ledge. He leaned down, grabbing at Bark's outstretched fingers. They clasped. The torrent gushed at his ankles. Oiwa reached down too. The water rose enormously. Bark's face came into the light as that stranded log struck his knee. It dragged him. Tine could not hold on. In one terrible instant, Bark vanished.

'No! Not now!' Bark thundered inside, feeling the speeding trunk smashing his joints. 'Keep my head up! The cave's flooding: I can't hold on,' he gulped as he foundered, being washed away. 'Look ahead. Swim! Save myself,' was his powerful instinct. The flume curved along a quartzite curtain, which split into arches. Bark's feet and smashed knees careered through one. His head caught in the narrowing point as the water heaped.

Bark felt the base of his skull separate from his stretching neck.

In those final moments of bodily life, he felt warm breath enter his nostrils. Before his ears ceased hearing and his heart crashed to a stop, he found himself looking deeply into the eyes of a large mother cat. The lynx's stripy grey face licked his cold one. He felt long whiskers caress his temples. Bark noticed his body shrinking. The cat's teeth softly gripped his furry neck. She swam with him. They saw a familiar broken corpse slip from a rent in the quartz curtain to wash from sight. The new kitten emerged into a starry night, high on a mountain cleft. There he suckled with his new brood of brothers and sisters.

Oiwa was frantic. His torch spluttered out as he scrambled up the steep flue. The bats shat on them, panicking. Tine's spear clattered down the chute. Mica slipped as the air, pushed by the flash flood, blew his hair up in front of him. Oiwa gripped where he could and sat in a depression, splaying his legs onto the walls of their tunnel. His slight beard blew over his chin while the final escaping bats scraped past his face.

Tine felt a shunt of debris elevate him. Oiwa cast the rope to Mica, who slipped. The rising flume forced his head up to Mica. Tine's head sped between Mica's legs as the rising tide forced him up. Tine's shoulders met Mica's rear as he rose to face his navel.

The plug of water and men ascended. Mica's head crashed into Oiwa's scrotum. The water ripped over Tine's head as a hunk of rotting bison mashed under him. The power of the speeding haunch forced the trio violently upwards. They hurtled into a cavity to sprawl on a cold platform.

There they lay, hearts pounding, temples thumping. Mica moved first. Tine felt Oiwa shift. In the all-consuming darkness, Tine spluttered and sneezed. That stench of rotting bison made Oiwa take a hand from his dashed testicles to cover his nose. The intense pain made him speed it back to nurse them. His mute yell of agony was felt by Tine and Mica.

Oiwa panted savagely, curling up as the searing convulsed. Miraculously, Ziit was over his shoulder. He lay crouched when Mica spoke. 'Are we all here?' he asked, as water brimmed at his feet. Tine answered with immense difficulty, 'We lost Bark. I tried grabbing his hand, but he got swept away.' Tine's words sank in. The swirling pool reached up at them where a putrefying carcass dissipated. Its bones drifted slowly down.

'We lost Bark?' Mica questioned in alarm.

Oiwa grimaced desperately, 'I don't know how to cope with this. What is happening to us?' He so wanted to yell.

Above the tunnel curved higher. The bats had fled.

Tine looked around, spying a grey hue far above. 'There's light!' he declared urgently. 'Mica, Oiwa, don't move.' He put his hand up, covering the glimmer. He removed it. Light was still there.

Suddenly, dreadful sounds like horrid nasal snorts loomed. The column of fetid water withdrew noisily, dragging the buffalo remains like vile catarrh. The reeking mucus drew deep into Gunnal's interior. Belching and vomiting echoed in a cacophony. Despite everything, fresh air sucked down to them in a thin refreshing rush. Thus, the bison stink cleared.

'We must move. Gunnal may blow her stinking nose again,' Tine warned. 'I'll take the rope, Oiwa. I can shin up further and see.' He edged over Mica's knees. 'Sorry about your ear,' he said as he clumsily bashed it.

'It's fine,' Mica winced, 'Just get up there.' The tunnel narrowed. Tine wedged his feet on each side to scramble up. He slipped on bat excrement, but not far.

'How are you doing?' Mica called, whilst distraught about Bark.

'Okay,' Tine answered, banishing thoughts of his lost brother. 'Further yet,' he puffed through cool, sucking air. His head reached to where the grey light eked. His chin edged above a rocky shelf, and far, far above daylight shone down.

'It's LIGHT! It's LIGHT!' he called, lowering the rope.

'Are you safe?' Mica shouted.

'Yes. You grab the rope, I'll hoist,' Tine yelled over the noise.

'Okay. Oiwa's coming first,' answered Mica fumbling in the dark and putting the rope in Oiwa's hands, saying, 'Tie it round you.'

He gripped it, moving his hands from the throbbing pain, then roped himself, banishing the agony from mind and body.

'Up you go,' Mica encouraged.

'Pull,' Oiwa commanded himself as Tine tugged. 'My effort is weakening the fearsome pain in my crushed balls,' he noticed as he climbed.

'Oiwa's pelvis is bloody hard,' Mica thought, rubbing a painful swelling on his forehead.

Oiwa edged higher to find Tine's ledge, then looked up to the late afternoon light.

'Your turn,' Tine called. Oiwa cast the rope. Mica heard it drop.

As he felt for it, he found an arrow. He gripped it in his teeth then grasped the rope. He shinned up the steep flue. Dragging himself up, he squatted next to Oiwa. Fresh blood trickled from the soaked scab round his ear.

'I'm going further,' Tine announced. 'We'll do what we did just now. Oiwa, then you, Mica,' feeling wretched, not mentioning Bark.

'Oiwa, is your quiver okay? I rescued an arrow,' he nodded in the gloom. Mica found it and dropped it in the emptied container.

Tine heaved. 'Come up, Oiwa.' His pain had eased, but he was wary. The light and his heart strengthened as Tine's silhouette appeared. Ziit was scarred, but undamaged.

The rope touched Mica's shoulder. His green axe was still in his belt. His mood lifted. 'I'm on my way.'

'The next bit's easy,' Tine said when they settled. 'I'm going up. The cave's surface has rills. I can grip with my toes.' Soon he reported, 'I'm up on a wide ledge, startling nesting pigeons. Otherwise, it's quite flat. Other tunnels drop away. I'll crawl and squint down one.

'There's a cold breeze fanning me from far below. Above, fungi hang like weird ears. Beyond there's even brighter light.

'Come on,' he called excitedly. More birds took flight down the other shaft. He felt the rope tighten. Shortly, Ziit's tip appeared above Oiwa's shoulders. He rose, blinking, into the light. His matted hair had few beads left. He coughed. It sounded so different, just a rattle from his chest.

Mica pulled up next. The rumbling of Gunnal's innards threatened. A surprisingly warm draught rose, the fungi vibrated. Squabs in their nests instinctively drew back.

'I think we're safe,' said Mica as he sat by Oiwa.

Tine stooped to peer down the dropping cave. Silvery reflections waved up and down its walls. He craned his neck and looked through a narrow, level cave. Golden light of sunset beamed back.

'Safe. Yes. For the moment,' he added urgently. 'Look down there and listen.' Mica stepped forward, his head brushed the fungi; giant slugs within withdrew their stalked eyes, shrinking alarmed into the crevices. Mica leaned forward and looked down to the silvery flickering light. 'Gunnal's Falls,' he said to Tine.

'Yes. We saw them last time, but from the cliff above.' He inhaled deeply through his nose 'We're up Gunnal's Snout!' They all looked at each other. 'We can't go down,' Tine warned. 'It's a sheer drop to her gaping jaws and the waterfall,' he added gravely. 'We would just follow Rush, Lichen and Bark. We must explore.'

'Okay, Tine, but the light's fading fast, and we're exhausted. We can actually rest here.' A draught of warm air rose greeting them, their only comfort. 'Look, we've got grub. My bats were washed away, but in these ledges there's pigeon squabs. We can cook on a fire of old nests and dry fungus.'

'Cook,' Tine said, 'I've got two drowned bats in my jacket.'

Oiwa nodded almost eagerly. 'Here,' he wanted to say, and pulled another bat from his. There was enough fuel for a warming glow. One arrow for a spit, one spark from Mica's stones to catch the fungus. Then the old nests glowed. The aroma of bat and fledglings followed.

Oiwa dreamed the moon was looking on a craggy mountain. In the mouth of a cave a lynx lay suckling a man baby. It slowly turned into a kitten. 'I will call you Purrrrer,' the mother cat said lovingly, as her new incarnation reached a soft, pink nipple.

* * * * *

Dew slumped, crying. 'Can we stop? My feet are sore. My knees shake. I can't go on.'

'Just over the brow, dear,' her mother called back to her. 'Not far now.'

'But it's getting dark, Mummy!'

'Yes, my bluebird. The stars will shine and you'll see your way. Come on now.'

The bare, rising expanse seemed endless as Dew followed Snaaaaar's angry quest. She stopped to wait for her Little Treasure, but went on directly Dew caught up.

Eventually, Snaaaaar stopped. Her form, darker than black sky, stood out against her starry background. Her straw hairband shone. The tiny knotted earrings dangled.

Dew met her at the summit of the smooth rock slope. She gazed down the precipitous edge. Far below, an immense black pool was held back in a cavernous mouth, dammed by Gunnal's Teeth. The silver cascade roared over her jutting chin, falling thunderously into Wolf Lake. It swirled deeply down into the darkness of a spectacular pit, eroded out over aeons. In those terrible depths barbel sucked foul bison meat. A fresher corpse was spat out and forced into those depths to be tossed in the heavy, golden dust that settled at the bottom.

'We are here, Dew,' Snaaaaar softly informed her awestruck child. 'In the morning we shall see them floating like spit on a puddle.'

Dew drew back, exhausted. 'I hate this,' she whined.

'You curl up and sleep, dear. You didn't drop any arrows now, did you?'

'No.'

'There's a good girl.' She extracted a morsel of pemmican from her hidden store, 'Here, my little summer fruit, have this to help you sleep.'

Her mother then ranted secretly by the precipice.

'Why didn't my Dad come back, all that time ago?' Dew asked.

'Don't start asking silly questions now, dear,' she hissed. 'He probably fell over a stupid cliff on his crazy expedition. How should I know, anyway?' Her voice changed from a chilling tone to that of sweetness and love. 'Now you curl right up and go to sleep. I'll light a little fire. Have sweet dreams and stop asking... awk—' she stopped herself, 'silly questions, my tulip.'

Dew's head fell forward in slumber. She dreamed of her father waving to her as he disappeared into the forest.

Muttering to herself, Snaaaaar remembered Birch Skin's last, surprised moments when she hacked the deadly knife into him, snapping it. 'And those other bastards,' she recalled. 'Carrying their stupid boat of meat. An arrow in the first one's kidney sorted him. How the second one turned. Smack, right into the bridge of his nose and deep in his dull brain. And the third one who carried that fish tail. Got him in the nipple, didn't I? How they writhed in their unexpected deaths. Then I carried the meat back to my sweet little poppy, who waited so patiently.

* * * * *

The mountain cold penetrated the brothers' bones. Eventually, dawn broke. It reflected light up Gunnal's Nostrils, then rays shone along their escape tunnel. They wakened and stretched. Pigeons fluttered. 'Watch out for those terrible sheer drops,' Mica managed to say. His ear wound hurt. 'And the one behind into Gunnal's Gullet.'

Oiwa wanted to say, 'I need a pee,' but couldn't. Tine said it for him. They lined up and pissed down the Nostrils.

'Eggs for breakfast?' Mica suggested. 'I'll get some.' They cracked them, sucked them out and dropped the shells down the shaft. Alarmed, the pigeons took flight.

The passage was dry. Mica edged along as the noise of the falls from outside amplified. A nesting raven flew from a ledge. He made for there. Two grey chicks waited helplessly. Tine put them aside and rested. He listened to Mica and Oiwa scraping through behind.

Tine moved, squinting, into the full morning light. Mist from the falls below wet his cheeks as he emerged behind a flattened boulder. He sat; the wind flicked his matted hair. He peered down to Wolf Lake. Oiwa appeared with Ziit's string flicking his ear. Mica followed shortly.

'Look at Gunnal's Falls,' Mica blurted as he emerged, 'that huge cascade, the foam, the swirling, black water.' Oiwa gasped, shaking soundlessly. He pointed below and touched Tine's shoulder. A tiny, bright, splayed form floated on Wolf Lake. Tine covered his eyes, stricken, then looked again as Oiwa gripped Mica's hand.

'It's Rush,' Tine said. The situation hit immediately.

'Or it could be Lichen,' Mica added sadly.

'No. There's net tied to his ankle,' Tine observed.

'Why does he look so bright?' Mica asked. 'He seems like he's lit with rays of golden sunshine.'

An osprey clasped a shining fish and rose with it, wriggling, to its eerie.

Oiwa pointed. Another body emerged. Mica shook. 'Bark,' he stated mournfully. They watched in still remorse as their brother's corpse spun gently in an eddy. It, too, shone as it turned on the black depths.

'We must leave,' Mica said quietly, sadly and respectfully, forcing back his tears. Oiwa tugged him, pointing as a third body bobbed up from the dark fathoms.

'It's Lichen!' Tine said. 'He glitters too. Why?'

'He's drifting towards Rush,' Mica added. 'They're going to touch.'

They crouched and gazed down, shocked, over the expanse of water. Their cave hung below a great overhanging black rock. 'A ledge!' Tine shouted amidst the roar. 'It leads down, then round the cliff face.

Tine stood slowly and moved ahead along the ledge. Oiwa smoothed the flights on his arrow and flexed Ziit. Ziit responded to Oiwa's tired muscles. Mica followed Tine, signalling for Oiwa to wait. He did. He prayed silently for the spirits of a lost brother and two friends.

Oiwa watched Mica round the corner. He waited.

'Come. Oiwa,' he heard Mica call. 'It's quite safe.'

* * * * *

Snaaaaar looked down from the cliff-top in cruel satisfaction. 'That's three of those bastards dead! What about the rest of them? Look, Dew.'

From above the roar of Gunnal's Falls, Snaaaaar heard voices. Mica's call rang in her ears. 'Bastards! Shits! Fucking useless, idiotic men,' she hissed. She removed her curved bow from her shoulder and lodged an arrow shaft at the string. Dew stirred, distressed at her mother's anger.

Snaaaaar leaned over the sheer drop and looked towards the falls. A movement below caught her eye as Tine edged unknowingly into sight. Instantly, she fully bent her bow. Tine passed behind an outcrop and was lost to her. She maintained the strain while she heard small stones drop, as Mica's shoulder edged into view.

'Stop!' she heard Tine call back. 'It's no use, we can't go on. The ledge has fallen away.'

'Just like her stupid father,' Dew heard Snaaaaar hiss. 'Fucking around on a mad, crazy journey. 'Should have stayed with me!'

Mica's head appeared. 'Do you need any help?' he called.

She tightened the string. 'Straight into his fucking, ignorant cranium,' she thought, as Mica's head turned back, telling Oiwa to wait. That move exposed his shoulder. A piece of the ledge dropped from beneath Mica's toe. He pressed himself back as Snaaaaar loosed her missile. It streaked by Mica's stomach, grazed his left shin, and smashed into the rock shelf. Another large flake fell to the distant water.

Mica yelled in alarm, pressing further into the rock face. Tine then heard Snaaaaar move above. Scree slipped from her toes to dribble over the edge.

Oiwa pricked up his ears. He felt his body redden inside with blooded anger. He picked his way along the high path. Far above he saw Snaaaaar's head disappear. He pulled the only arrow from his quiver and fitted it to Ziit's string. She vanished, but he heard the scree move.

He stole along the ledge. Looking up, he spied her slightly

bulging stomach protrude through a deeply cut cleft. From her position she saw Tine. Tine saw her. 'There's no escape. The ledge has gone! I can't backtrack. I'll be in full view. Diving's my only chance.' He hurled the rope behind him.

Tine sprang into thin air. Snaaaaar loosed her bolt. He did not feel any terrible piercing of an arrow; instead, just the rush of breeze as he plummeted.

Snaaaaar's bolt entered the nape of Tine's neck. The point exited, sticking through the Star on his forehead. The bitter red darkness of death covered the insides of his eyes. His body dived to the water, hundreds of feet below.

'Got him!' Snaaaaar cheered. 'Now for that other turd!' She swivelled, ready with another arrow. Mica was still a viable target. 'I can see his ribs and hip. I'll kill him through his kidney, like that other one.'

Oiwa, unseen, pulled hard on Ziit's string as she pointed her missile at Mica's midriff. He had edged back, but was still fatally vulnerable. She adjusted her aim. Her belly protruded just a fraction further.

Oiwa pulled Ziit back to its fullest. He only had a light arrow, and its delicate jasper tip was designed for small game. His upward shot was long and high. He strained back a little further as Ziit creaked. Ziit's string twanged in song. His arrow flew in its near-vertical trajectory. Almost at the end of its range, the small point cut into Snaaaaar's suede jerkin, which hung lightly round her hips. His tiny barb pinned that loose flap tightly to her belly. It hurt her, burning like a flying ember. Her bow arm involuntarily tilted as her arrow left her string.

Oiwa's shot was not fatal, by any means. It could not have been, at that range, but his jasper head lodged just at her pelvis. Its small, fiery point scored the fringe of her pubic curls as it snagged her stomach lining. This caused her to step back slightly, but her left knee weakened. It bent very slightly. This pushed Oiwa's arrow into her as its butt pressed firmly on the cliff's rocky top.

Dew understood her mother's last tirade of violent venom. The rounded stone she had been fondling sped from her hand to Snaaaaar's back. Her mother's right knee wilted. Oiwa's feeble projectile slid perilously deeper, puncturing Snaaaaar's bladder. She looked down and saw what pained her. Oiwa's arrow bore more weight, so was forced up through her intestines to her liver.

Snaaaaar watched with absolute horror, disgusted at the searing pain. She felt the shaft's relentless progress. It punctured her diaphragm, then squeaked through the spongy tissue of her lungs as she involuntarily squatted.

Before her arse touched her heels, Dew's stone struck the back of her head. Oiwa's long flight feathers scraped her blooded pubic hairs. The arrow-tip forced its way out behind her collarbone. She did not scream much. She coughed, bloodily, and spiralled over the precipice.

Tine's spirit looked up from the depths. It saw a long trail of bubbles rise from where he had broken the surface. Just to one side of it, a distorted form crashed on the water. He swam up through the currents. His new eagle wings broke the surface. He looked into the bulging, unseeing eyes of his deathly assailant as his spirit soared high above Gunnal's Falls.

17

Wolf Lake

'I'm sorry, I'm sorry. I didn't mean to kill you. But I couldn't let you do it again,' Dew sobbed, looking down at her mother's twisted body by her murderous floating bow.

Oiwa stood, staggered at his arrow's effect, hearing Dew above.

A flock of doves flew past. Oiwa whistled, the first sound he had made since his voice left him.

'You saved us,' Mica shouted from around the cliff. Oiwa whistled in answer. The doves flew back, vanishing above.

'I'm going to edge along. Stay there, Oiwa. Keep your back pressed to the cliff face, like me,' he called. 'I feel sick,' he thought. 'The sight of those minute corpses below accentuates the height.' He composed himself to say, 'Oiwa. It's you and me now. Keep still. I'll come to you. Don't move. The ledge is crumbling. That's another bit gone from under my heel. There you are. Okay?'

Oiwa nodded, gazing blankly down to the bodies. 'That's my kin and my friends. How placid they look in their shining garb.' Snaaaaar floated in crumpled contrast. 'Come forward,' he whistled to Mica.

'Phew. The ledge widened. I can turn and step smartly to Oiwa and hold him tight. He's terribly shaken.'

'Tine had the rope. Was it with him when he fell?' Oiwa shrugged in Mica's arms. 'I'll go and look. Stay right where you are,' Oiwa nodded, tears dribbling over his cheeks. 'I've got it,' he shouted back from round the jagged crag.

'Throw it up to me,' they heard Dew's sad voice call. 'I'll help. I didn't do it. It was my mother. She killed your friends. I had to stop her. I had to!' she cried out.

'Are you all right?' Mica called back.

'No... But I'll help you. Trust me.'

'I'll tie a stone to the rope and hurl it up. Watch out.'

Oiwa edged round the crag, holding a rock. Mica took it. Flaky stone dropped alarmingly from their ledge as he tied the rope around and around the weight. He swung it below, gaining momentum. 'Stand back. It's coming up,' Bark called to Dew.

She stepped away, looking for a good anchorage. There was only a criss-cross of worn fissures, eroded by driving rain and wind.

The stone landed heavily on the cliff-top. Dew ran to grab it. It bounced, skidded back and tumbled.

Oiwa heard her warning. 'The rope's snaking back. Grab it!' he thought, as the knotted rock hurtled below.

'I'll hold you,' Mica said, gripping Oiwa and leaning into the cliff face.

'It's tearing through my hands, burning my palms. Hold all the harder!' he realized. 'The rock's stopped. Pull it back. Swing the block again. Cast it higher.'

'Watch out!' Mica called.

Dew moved then leapt forward, catching the stone. 'Got it,' she yelled, jamming her foot on the rope. 'I'll wedge it into a crack. I'll tell when it's safe,' she shouted. 'I'm securing a boulder over the rope, too. You'll be all right now,' Dew shouted.

'You go first, Oiwa. You're lightest.' He looked at his sore hands and tugged the rope again.

'I'm holding the boulder down, to stop it shifting. The rope's tightening.'

Mica looked up at Oiwa's heels. 'That rock is so crumbly. Bits fall in my eyes. Thank the Spirits he's made it. He's safe. Now me.'

'Here comes the first one,' Dew saw. Ziit's tip emerged before Oiwa's head appeared. He flung himself over the edge. She noticed his empty quiver.

Oiwa gazed at Dew. She put her hand out to him, but would

not leave the rock. Mica began his ascent. Oiwa leaned over the edge, 'He's coming up: that stone under his foot's dislodged! He's swinging freely on the rope! It's twisting at the top. Hold it steady! Thank Tumar he's climbing again. He's not looking down. You can do it, Mica,' he urged inside. 'Give me your hand,' he wanted to say as finally his fingers felt the top. 'I'll grasp Mica's wrist to help him over. Oh! What relief. He's scrambling away from the drop and squatting on the bare rock, sobbing in relief and anguish.'

Dew watched him from her stone, not daring to move.

Oiwa soothed his brother's heaving shoulders, then went to Dew. She looked up to him. 'My mother did it. I hate her. I killed her. My stone hit. She fell.' Oiwa shook his head. He held her trembling hand, mouthing 'No,' touching Ziit's string. She stared again at the empty quiver.

The doves landed on the clifftop, then flew away to the cave. A skein of geese honked high in the sky.

Mica scraped himself onto all fours then knelt, watching Oiwa with Dew. He controlled his heaving chest and slowly got to his feet. Unsteadily, he went to Oiwa's side. 'Let's get the rope,' he said softly, unable to utter consolation.

'It was the stone I slung. It hit her head and knocked her over.'

Oiwa mouthed 'No,' again.

Mica stepped in. 'Oiwa's right. He wounded your mother. She sank on his last arrow. You probably didn't even see it. Your stone dropped with her, but you certainly didn't kill her.'

'Well, I'm glad she's dead. She murdered my Dad. I know she got rid of Birch Skin, too. He was lovely,' Dew said, as though dazed.

'Take my hand. We must leave this place.' Dew gripped Mica's fingers. He shifted the rock, retrieving the rope.

'We will go down Gunnal's Arm. Look below,' Mica said. 'Large hide boats are sailing across Wolf Lake.'

At the closest prow, Musk stood tall, a wolfskin over his shoulders, its head making a fine cap. He guided his craft to the Heron's Tooth's wreckage. Rush's net was still tied. The knotted strands were dotted with bright golden specks. Musk leaned over to pull it. The net tightened. Rush's body followed, turning in the water. His face gazed up. His tattered garments, floating hair and disjointed leg reflected the sunshine in a gilded sheen.

Musk drew Rush's remains to the side. 'Some of you lean away, the others of you pull this good man out.' The stiffened corpse drained. A stream of glittering specks sank gracefully to the lake bed. They laid Rush carefully on a central plank, where a shimmering pool gathered. Their hands glistened.

Claw, at the helm, drew alongside Bark. He touched Bark's shining yellow back. His crew drew the rigid body into the boat and watched golden waters leave him to drift, glittering, to the bed of Wolf Lake.

'There are more craft moving towards Lichen and Tine. Another slows at the side of Snaaaaar's body,' Mica said, as her limp carcass was dragged from the lake and dumped in a shapeless heap. Her bird earrings were wrecked, her hairband gone. Oiwa's fatal arrow jagged up into her jutting jaw, keeping it firmly shut as she was heaped in. Thin blood dribbled from a pulseless artery. Bristle's barge began its return to the Loup Tribe's camp.

Eyewhite's women rowers retrieved Tine. 'Look at that terrible buffalo bolt sticking through his forehead,' she remarked. 'How his beard glitters golden, though, from his sad face. When I saw that wrecked boat plummet, I knew something foreboding was happening. It's far worse than I imagined,' she remarked to Pelt, her sister.

Musk looked pitifully at the smashed arrows protruding from Rush's chest. 'Paddle at once to Gunnal's Hand to meet his friends,' he commanded.

'The big craft is turning,' Mica reported. 'The shores here are quite changed. The larch woodlands are gone. That was thick forest, last time I was here,' Mica said. 'What's happened?'

Musk's boat rounded the cliff. A ram's horn trumpet blast rent the air. The oarsmen raised their paddles in salute as Zeal's prow pressed gently into the gravel. Mica and Oiwa took Dew down the back of Gunnal's hand to the shingle. They saw Rush. Musk's crew gathered round. 'We have a victim in the boat.'

Mica looked downwards. 'He, he saved us,' he stammered. 'He became a human anchor to stop Heron's Tooth, so we could escape.'

Another trumpet blasted as Claw's boat floated to draw up next to Zeal. Claw jumped ashore. 'We have one with us as well.' They looked into Long Wake. 'It's Bark,' Mica said. The crew stood in respectful silence. The brothers gazed at the golden forms. Bark's beard seemed thicker and tighter. Rush's dark head of hair was brightly streaked in gold and glittering sunlight, his face in total peace. His skin reflected the moving ripples. The bodies lay as dreamlike figures.

Eyewhite's rowers pulled the Osprey shoreward. Pelt blew a peal of reverberating blasts on a bark lur. 'Come with us,' Eyewhite said. Oiwa, Mica and Dew stepped in. The Osprey set slowly off.

The sombre flotilla began its slow progress across Wolf Lake. Mica looked at the barren hills that climbed to snow-tipped mountains. He watched the long expanse of water open to a vista of level calmness. Oiwa saw the Loup Tribe's encampment on the far treeless bank. Huts, wigwams and turf shelters spread themselves over a grassy rise where an arm of land pointed into the lake. Smoke rose from many fires. Piles of fallen trees were heaped around the village.

Musk guided his boat back. He peered deep into the dark, clear waters. Sunken roots from upturned trees poked about nearer their shore. Fish hid in their waterlogged remains. Herons hunted patiently.

Bristle's craft reached the shore first. Its dark cargo was lifted out as Zeal approached. 'Should we pull that arrow out of her?' Heng asked as the wet corpse unfolded on the bank. 'No,' said Bristle, 'cover it.'

The Osprey made headway over the lake towards Wolven Den. Dew wondered what would happen to her mother's body. Oiwa and Mica sat silently. The women paddled.

Zeal felt sand under her prow. Musk hopped out. His Wolf's head dangled askew. Long Wake's prow, decorated with eagle feathers, touched the sand. The rowers lifted Bark on his wooden litter and carried him up the shore towards the Resting House. Rush was aloft on Musk's men's shoulders. Tine and Lichen were being carried, too. Oiwa and Mica watched, tragically stunned.

'Come with us,' Eyewhite said to Dew. 'You will be cold and hungry.'

The brothers followed their dead remorsefully to an avenue of smooth quartz pebbles. The biers continued up the slight gradient to the raised oblong building. It had a hide roof with open walls down to waist height. It was a quiet sanctuary for the dead to relax before burial. Mica and Oiwa followed the grim procession. The four bodies were placed on the floor while a vast central pile of quartz rocks was arranged to take them. The smell and sounds of the stones scraping together was like that of life and death meeting.

Musk said. 'Lift your lost ones on their boards and lay them on the stones. They will rest there while we make a proper burial place. My people will prepare and guard them. You shall come and relate what happened.'

Mica and Oiwa shifted the planks. Their fingertips smudged the golden residue. They felt lonely.

Musk led them to his splendid wigwam. It stood amongst a family of others. Huts and stretched skin shelters were scattered over the shoulder of land. 'Come in. Sit round my glowing fire in the ring of leather bolsters.'

Eyewhite entered. 'We have been listening to Dew's sorrowful story. She's suffered. She sleeps now. You two have also had terrible experiences.' They nodded to Musk's wife.

Pelt came in. 'Here's food for you. Maybe you don't feel like eating, but it is here. Oiwa reached for the steamed bream, but pulled back. 'Not yet,' Mica replied. The wooden dish was laid on the rush floor.

Mica began their story. Bristle and Claw listened. Slowly, the tent filled. Mica's voice related all. Oiwa confirmed sequences with gestures. His throat ached. Sounds of horror at Snaaaaar's venom broke the silent intent of the listeners. Oiwa held his head in his hands during those vile episodes. The people of the Loup Clan understood their plight and their quest.

When Mica finished, Musk said, 'We will prepare a place for your honourable dead up with ours. I must explain. Our graves were ruined two years ago. Late rains filled the soil just before the great freeze. During early spring an immense amount of snow fell on the frozen ground. The thaw commenced, the mountains and hills shook. The ground rumbled and the soil shifted. I ordered my Clan to cross Wolf Lake. Its waters shook and splashed as we headed for the other side. We all watched as the whole hillside slid down onto our village. The trees piled up and filled Wolf Lake. Our place was scraped away by roots and shifting mud. Wolf Lake became jammed. It took a year for it to clear. The river that runs into Wolf Lake was dammed. The Dun's meltwaters flooded the whole valley. The forest swirled on its surface. Eventually the dam unclogged. It all gushed along with the raging flood and broke free towards the ocean. Our ancestors were washed into the lake. We moved back when it was safe. We remade our homes and respected our ancestors' new resting place.'

'That's why this place has changed so much,' Mica realized.

'Our first newly dead inherited the old place to begin their afterlife. Yours will go there, too,' Musk stated.

Mica scratched the scabs around his ear. They cracked and bled. He had forgotten the injury. Eyewhite whistled. Her wolf-like dog bounded in. 'Lick that man's ear,' she commanded. Mica shied away. 'It's all right. He will be gentle. He'll clean it, sooth it, stopping inflammation.'

Pelt spoke to Oiwa. 'You've been struck dumb, Oiwa,' he nodded, clicking his tongue. 'Can I feel your throat?'

'Yes,' he clicked solemnly.

'Open wide.' Oiwa's jaw slumped. 'Say AAAAaaaaaarrrrhhhhh.' Only warm breath rasped. 'Let's leave it now.' He nodded, fiddling with his hair, deep in thought. Absent-mindedly, Mica reached to the wooden tray with his sore hands. Warm flakes of clean tasting fish caressed his tongue. It was their signal to eat.

Snaaaaar's corpse was dragged up the valley and hidden in an obscure cave. They dumped ashes over her so no animals would eat her, lest her poison would send them mad. Musk's men stopped the entrance with boulders. He instructed, 'Do not pull Oiwa's arrow out. None should know where she is. She must never be spoken of again!'

18

Burial Rites

Musk and Eyewhite dressed ceremonially, she in a finely braided skirt and beaded blouse. Her dark-feathered shawl contrasted with her white-painted face. Black hair was piled above her head in a backcombed fan, stuck with ivory wolf-headed pins. Strands of red beads dangled from her earlobes.

Musk greeted Oiwa and Mica, his handshake rattling with shining bone bracelets. He wore his wolf cape and carried a long spear. Its great polished head glinted in the fading sunlight. 'Are you ready?' he asked through his mask of star-dotted blue paint. His family led them back to the small mortuary.

'Across the threshold we feel death,' Eyewhite said. 'Our quartz pebbles are the seeds of birth. The red stony floor, the blood of life... enter,' she whispered.

The bodies lay on their pink quartz dais. Rush's golden form rested on a low litter. Lichen, Bark and Tine lay on theirs. Over Tine's wound a new Star blazoned, glistening like sunset gold. Stone lamps, burning fragrant oils, graced their resting corpses. The bodies were unworldly, beautiful and distant. Bark's face was clear and distinct in every feature. The river gold from Gunnal's pit remained like a second skin. Their soaked clothing had finished draining onto the leather surfaces. The glittering silt seemed to weld them to their litters.

Bark and Tine's travelling beards were bound with fine leather tatting. The darkly polished strands made dramatic patterns terminating in knots under their chins. This tightened their skin, making them resemble spiritual beings. Mica leaned forward and pushed Bark's long, fair hair aside to show his Star.

Oiwa removed the broken arrows from Rush's chest. He solemnly leaned forward and compressed Rush's ribs. Stale air came up Rush's windpipe as a last sigh.

The snapped wooden projectiles stuck up like rounded splinters. He twisted at one and pulled it free. Black, clotted blood dripped on to Rush's jacket. Oiwa pulled the second lethal stick out. Rush's chest sank with a gurgling sound. His corpse relaxed, his head lolled forward.

Eyewhite and Musk's daughters chanted a slow lament. Their sons beat a rhythm with their spear butts. Eyewhite lit other pungent oil lamps, then led her family away. Mica followed into the evening starlight.

In the still of the sacred precinct they heard wolves howl and sing. The waning moon shone brilliantly as the canine chorus hit the still night air. Silence struck, then Vulpan, the Wolf Captain, growled. His voice evolved into a high-pitched solo to Luna. The moon seemed brighter, renewed with another spirit.

The morning was windy and wet. Musk and Eyewhite's people gathered at the death house wearing their finest clothes and parading their best weapons, despite the weather. They chanted their song of paradise and rebirth. Oiwa mouthed the words, feeling the emotion. Drummers played a heartbeat rhythm, symbolizing a new pulse. The breeze abated and the rain slackened as the procession began.

Oiwa and Mica lifted Rush's bier on their shoulders, and two of Musk's men took the back poles. Musk and Claw followed with Bark. Eyewhite led the procession. Dew and Day followed Lichen and Tine's bearers.

They left the rose quartz platform and proceeded from the building at the other end. An avenue of low wooden stakes took them up a slope to where the forest had stood. Their feet trod bare rock, where springy moss had been.

The chants continued until they reached a long terrace

overlooking the Loup Clan's village. The level spit of hillside widened. Five conical stone cairns stood in a close group. By them, a square platform had been prepared for a sixth. Vulpan and Scurran, his wolf harem's leader, stood boldly in the centre of the stone quadrant. They watched the approaching procession.

Musk halted the funeral train. He paced slowly to greet the two ambassadors. They came forward, circled him and sniffed his crotch and anus. They then bade him to caress their necks and sniff noses. Eyewhite joined Musk on the rammed stone surface to repeat the greeting. The wolves sat and bayed. The rain ceased, the sun shone in great streaks through the clouds and anointed the new resting place.

Vulpan and Scurran shook water from their fur. Small rainbows shone briefly through the spray.

Musk signalled the procession to advance as the great wolves slipped away up the loose scree. In the centre of the platform was a flat boulder. It had been pierced to take a carved pole decorated with feathers. 'Place the biers by the rock,' Musk said. 'Sons, bring the basket with Rush's net.'

Eyewhite added, 'Take the dead and sit them back to back on the eternal rock.' Her white face remained expressionless, yet full of calm. 'Claw, come forward with our totem stake and set it in its socket.'

Oiwa and Mica looked at their brothers and friends. They seemed distant. The gold film on them caught the brilliance of the new shafting sunlight. Their rigor mortis had weakened so Rush's leg had relaxed. Oiwa and Mica lifted the bodies one by one and sat them leaning against the feathered pole. They removed Rush's net and wound it round them, keeping them in place. Its gilded knots and dark fibres glistened.

Eyewhite said, 'Daughters, place the bowls of sacred food at their feet. Sons, give them knives, bows and arrows and firestones. Day, put the dishes of quartz pebbles on their laps to symbolize new life and rebirth. I will put their painted leather masks over their faces. Then we begin building.'

'This is like a bad dream,' Oiwa thought. 'Mica says nothing. What is going to happen?'

Many poles had been cut. They placed them like a wigwam round Rush and Lichen, Bark and Tine. They joined at the totem, which rose above prominently. Musk's team quarried stones from the hillside and began constructing the pyramid. Oiwa and Mica assisted. This custom was new to them, but it felt good. The stones were packed in neat courses. Eventually the top would be reached.

The funeral feast was lavish, lasting well into the night. For Oiwa, the worst was over. 'My brothers' spirits are in another place. So are Rush and Lichen's. It's Mica and me, now. Where do we go from here?' he thought, as he curled up beneath a pile of pelts.

In the dead of night a lynx, hunting to feed her kittens, crept over the low pyramid wall and dragged off a duck that had been placed at Bark's side.

Oiwa's sound sleep restored him. 'I want to move on to Goose Landing,' he realized, rising quietly and pulling at Ziit. 'You seem much stronger, Ziit, but you needed arrows. That's Mica stirring. Now he's stretching and sitting among his swathes of furs and grass matting. That's his morning fart erupting.'

'Nice one,' Mica commented.

'My throat pain is less, but still no speech. I will stare on Mica's brow until he feels the glance.'

'What's up, Oiwa? Your look pierces down into my head,' Mica asked, rubbing it.

'I need to talk,' Oiwa wanted to say. Instead he flashed his eyes to their hut door and left. In moments, Mica was by his side, brushing his teeth with a chewed stick. 'I have to finish our trek,' he said from within, pointing along Wolf Lake. 'I must go on, for the sakes of all of us.'

'This is hurting inside now,' Mica felt. 'I know Oiwa's speaking to me, like in the caverns. What's he saying? He's pointing to the Wolf Clan's boats, then to the watery distances of the lake. He's looking up to the rising tumulus for our brothers and friends. Now he's gripped my head in his palms and turned it to the vanishing point of the lake. He's clicking his tongue and miming moving forward,' he realized. 'I'm going back in the tent,' he told Oiwa, shaking a little.

Oiwa followed.

'Oiwa wants us to continue our quest,' Mica announced.

Musk woke, yawning. Eyewhite handed him his leggings, saying, 'Oiwa's right, of course. He feels that, after everything, it would be such failure giving up.

'I just don't know,' Mica admitted.

'We'll talk over breakfast,' Musk suggested. 'Finish your toilet, get yourselves ready and we'll discuss this round beechnut mash and boiled eggs in Claw's tepee.'

Claw and Peach Leaf sat drinking thin meat broth. 'Welcome, sit,' they said. They bowed gently and squatted. Eyewhite and Musk joined the circle.

Wooden bowls of warm beechnut mash with toasted pine kernels and dried apple were handed round. The boiled eggs steamed in a coloured grass basket. Oiwa took one of the green duck eggs, nodded and tongue-clicked, 'Thank you.'

'Take more, there's plenty,' Oiwa smiled back to Peach Leaf, taking another. He shelled it and dipped it in his nutty mix. He bit. Rich, runny yolk trickled onto his beard. He dipped again, the nuts soaked up the yolk. 'Delicious,' he indicated, shelling his other egg eagerly.

'I am glad we are met,' Musk said as he convened their breakfast meeting. 'So, Oiwa, the speechless one, told Mica he wants to continue.' He looked directly to Oiwa.

Oiwa answered with a nod and a click.

'That's natural for a spirit like Oiwa's,' Musk observed. 'How do you feel, Mica?'

'I do not know what's best,' Mica began. 'I led and we've lost our brothers. Our parents will be devastated. Those who they mated with will be stricken, too.' He rubbed his eyes, gulping, 'Rush, as well; he saved us with his wit and brave resourcefulness, and Lichen drowned horribly.' Mica dropped his egg on the beaver skin at his feet. Its white held as it wobbled, picking up loose hairs. Eyewhite wiped it.

'For myself, I just can't think what's best. I need time.'

Musk looked at Oiwa, asking, 'Can you explain how you feel, somehow?'

Oiwa made little balls of yolk and nut granules, arranging them thoughtfully in a neat circle round his bowl.

Peach Leaf quietly passed fine, ivory coloured pottery cups of Claw's soup. Oiwa set one by him. 'I'll stand,' he thought, 'the effect will be better.' He opened his mouth, closed it and shook his head. Mica gazed up to him. 'Compose yourself, Oiwa,' he told himself, clasping his hands where his heart rattled. He stared past the tepee skins, miming distance with paddling motions. He stepped forward, pointing to illustrate the immense range. He spoke loudly and shrilly in his own head. Oiwa shaded his eyes and squinted to an imaginary, far place. He turned behind to indicate his lost brothers and friends. He mimed shaping the construction of their pyramid. The words inside him said, 'I have to go on! I have to complete my destiny. I must find out why, who we are and who I am. My feet are set on this trail. I cannot stop.' He sat and reached down for his soup. It tasted of the full essence of life.

Musk breathed deeply, blowing on his broth. 'Mica. Do you have anything to add?'

Oiwa stared at his brother's brow. Mica's head ached with confusion.

Mica began, 'From what Oiwa demonstrated, he obviously needs to...' His own words ended abruptly. In their confused place Oiwa's thoughts, lodged in his head, came tumbling forth. In Oiwa's voice, he repeated exactly what Oiwa had said in his own mind. 'What... did... I.. just say?...' Mica asked his listeners slowly and blankly, directly he had finished.

'You spoke Oiwa's thoughts most eloquently,' Eyewhite observed. 'He might have lost his powers of speech, but when it's vital, he summons another power, which we modern folk have begun losing.'

'I've given this great thought,' Musk began, 'You and Mica should honour the Whale Geese.' He popped a dove's egg into his mouth after rolling it in his nut mix. 'My reasoning is that Oiwa is positive what he should do. Mica is not.' Musk swallowed and drank broth. 'Mica's leadership and his feelings of responsibility have been shaken. What happened to you was not accidental, it was brutal MURDER!' He sipped again. 'You could not stop that, so you are not blameful, Mica.... It was not your fault.'

Peach Leaf handed beakers of rosehip tea as Musk gathered his thoughts. 'Mica, it would do you good to accompany Oiwa to his journey's end,' and paused thoughtfully. 'Oiwa, what do you think?'

Oiwa stood tall, his face unburdened. He smiled, gripping his axe, wiggling his toes and feeling good.

'That's decided,' Musk concluded. 'Here's the plan. We'll kit you out with new arrows, clothes and supplies. Claw's going to the end of Wolf Lake in his log canoe, Evergreen. He can set off tomorrow and take you. His boat's heavy, but once she gathers speed she's unstoppable.' He sipped hot tea and swirled it round his teeth.

'Thank the starry spirits,' Oiwa felt inside, tingling with emotion.

19

Onward

'It's strange walking past the empty burial house they've left here. Now we are making them a new home on the mountainside. Building their tomb helps free them. I can travel my trail and remember,' Oiwa thought, as he and Mica strode to the cemetery. 'Their bodies haven't been disturbed.' Vulpan and Scurran had guarded, but condoned the theft of the dried duck by the mother lynx, knowing she was nurturing Bark's new life in one of her kittens.

Marten, Claw's nephew, greeted them. 'I've been quarrying,' Oiwa regarded his contemporary as he spoke. His bare feet sucked tightly to the rocks. 'I've cracked the stone with fire. It makes it easier. We have put more supports inside the chamber as well.'

Oiwa looked at the banded strata of pink granite. 'The flesh and bones of the mountain to house our dead,' Oiwa thought.

'I am so sorry about your terrible ordeal. The best I can do is crack stones and help build with you,' Marten said.

'Thank you,' Mica replied as he looked at the fresh courses of stonework being laid by Musk's clan.

'Their masks are good,' Oiwa thought. 'I can remember them as they were instead of in death's changes.' He lifted a stone, placing it looking to Wolf Lake. 'I'll scratch eyes on it so they can see where I'm bound,' he decided.

As the mists rose and dissipated over the lake below, their building rose. The space within became separate from Oiwa's world, as each new block added to the pyramid. He looked down into the sepulchre and saw Rush's feet in shadow while other hands packed the granite chunks together.

Mica and Oiwa worked with the team until they finally placed a capstone on top of the monument. 'Time to leave,' Mica said. They walked downhill. Marten followed. His slim, light build belied his strength, borne out of natural knowledge and wisdom. His suede clothing flopped easily about. His necklace of bone beads rattled harmoniously as he moved.

The mists over Wolf Lake cleared. The tranquil waters reflected the mountains and blue, cloudless sky. Dark trunks from the landslide trees poked out in places. Occasionally one dislodged to float with the slow flow. Dippers and flycatchers fed on the muddy carcasses.

Musk said, 'We've packed for tomorrow's voyage. If there's anything you fancy, let us know.' Oiwa mimed chewing, and ran his tongue round his teeth. 'Yes, there's gum?'

'Here's some.'

Oiwa nodded thanks, enjoying the caraway flavour. Musk imagined hearing Oiwa's words deep inside.

'Would you come with me to set my sun-sticks, Oiwa?' Marten asked.

Oiwa nodded, wondering what was up.

'I'll fetch them,' he said with eagerness, returning with a bunch of thin, short stakes bound with cord. He also carried Ziit.

Oiwa clicked 'Thank you' and strung it deftly, mouthing Ziit's name affectionately. He pulled on the tight gut. Ziit responded as he let the tension go, springing back to his original faint arc. 'That's better,' Oiwa thought contentedly.

Marten said, 'I'm going to set my sticks in the stone. The sun is nearly over Rut Mountain. Oiwa looked across the lake to a black, pointed summit where the sun approached. It was a stunning sight, framed by a golden aura.

Marten loped down to a grassy plain by the shore, stopping at a black stone slab. Oiwa followed. In the centre of its level surface Marten stuck a single stick into a water-filled hole. 'I drilled this with my stick and bow, Oiwa. It took ages. I used really coarse sand to grind it out.' Oiwa looked over the surface. There was a ring of holes round the central one. Each was filled with water, reflecting the sun as golden discs on that flat, black rock.

He inserted a stick in each of his thirty-two other holes. Rivulets of shiny water trickled from Marten's wells as he shoved them in.

'The shadows form an ellipse,' Oiwa realized. 'They also touch opposite sticks at different heights. There are tiny golden sunlit lines of shining water radiating from Marten's circle, too.'

'Lovely, isn't it?' Marten commented.

'Yes, like the shadows from our village I saw whilst gathering honey from the tall pines. My wigwam's shadow became part of an ellipse too.

'See all my engraved lines, Oiwa. They've filled with water and reflect the sun.'

Oiwa looked into Marten's face. 'His slightly scarred cheeks are sucked inwards in concentration. Those scars resemble the spirals of a whirlpool. They've got a faint blue dye in them, the colour of compressed arteries.'

'My main line is scored directly towards the mountain peak. It crosses my circle and continues on either side. All these other lines go to fixed points, like the North Star and Gunnal's Falls. With the Sun being above Rut Mountain now, I know its position for late spring. It will be there earlier and earlier and higher until midsummer, then begin to come back and go down as the year goes on.' He leaned back and looked at Oiwa. 'I can check the Sun's rising and setting positions, and as for the Moon, well, that's something else entirely.'

Oiwa understood. But Marten had not finished. 'There's so much more! I've discovered—' Eyewhite rang her stone chimes and called them. Marten left his sticks. They walked towards Eyewhite as Marten began again. Oiwa chewed, trying to understand.

Musk's family sat round a clay brazier. On its raised points rested a shallow pottery dish with a painted zigzag design. Duck fat sizzled within. Hundreds of plump white grubs wriggled in a hide bucket. Eyewhite poured whipped eggs over them and stirred. Oiwa and Mica licked their lips in anticipation. She spooned some out and fried them rapidly, saying, 'The dead trees are full of larvae. It's wonderful,' adding, 'When they stop wriggling, they're ready.'

'Marvellous,' Mica exclaimed as the first ones popped warmly in his mouth. Oiwa agreed.

'There's plenty of fish hiding amongst the roots, too,' Marten explained as he fetched a large perch. 'Lots to be thankful for.' He placed the fish over another fire. Its fins burned off slowly and the aroma of deep, dark waters wafted past.

There was little for Oiwa to do. The sun was high and warm. With a full stomach and a feeling of ease, he lay down and snoozed. Marten returned to his sticks. Oiwa's sleep became profound and deep.

In a faraway dream, Oiwa looked over the side of a canoe into dark water. His reflection stared back from the ripples. Under the chin was an egg. He saw himself curled inside it. In his sleep he reached for his throat.

It rained heavily in the night. Gunnal's Falls spoke loudly, as the spout grew in power. In the early morning Claw's head appeared where the brothers slept. 'Time to go,' he said.

The waning silver moon dipped as the night sky lightened towards the East. The night shift of the wolves and owls finished. A blue jay hopped about the muddle of huts and tepees as Marten joined them. 'I'm coming too,' he said.

The Evergreen lay in a cutting that dipped into Wolf Lake. Her smooth, pointed nose touched the water. Oiwa saw her heavy load of skins, bags of moss-green stones, bundles of furs and baskets of grub chrysalises. Marten told Oiwa, 'The Baldheads of Lake End love our chrysalises. They don't have the green jadeite there, so we can trade.' Oiwa listened as he placed Ziit and a quiver of new arrows into Evergreen.

Mica pushed the stern. Claw guided Evergreen's prow into the black water. He and Oiwa hopped in, then Marten and Mica. Musk and his family waved them off in their dugout canoe. She rolled slightly as the crew got used to their positions. Short planks seats were wedged into side slits. Leaning on them were strong wooden paddles; they dipped them into the lake. 'Pull hard,' Claw called, and Evergreen's nose cut the sun-drenched ripples. 'Paddle steadily. Increase power as she speeds up,' Claw called. 'Soon we just dip paddles to keep the momentum. It will seem effortless. My boat cruises well. We're avoiding the shores. Keep to the deeper waters. I'll watch out for floating or submerged trees, but there won't be so many out there,' he stressed, pointing to the middle distance.

Marten and Oiwa paddled in the stern. Marten began, 'I've got thirty-two sticks in the ring, but it really doesn't matter how many you have, it just means that you can make different observations. If you have an even number it is easier to divide the areas up into squares or oblongs with fine twine.'

Oiwa's ears seemed to close over as Marten went on. 'There are so many applications I can create,' he continued energetically as his paddle dipped into the dark lake in time with Oiwa's. 'You see, I can actually peg them out on flat ground with the aid of a string tied to the centre one.' Oiwa's mind drifted, as he feigned interest. He thought briefly of his dream, recalling his reflection. 'And then,' Marten energetically explained, 'by knowing when it is midday, I can tell you exactly which peg is my North,' Marten exclaimed, pausing for Oiwa's reaction. There was not one. Marten nudged him with his paddle butt.

Wakened abruptly from his daydream, Oiwa nodded. Marten began again. 'When I have North, I can plot East, West and South then, with some thought I can tell...' Oiwa's head began to ache slightly as Marten rattled on about his sticks and all he could do with them. Oiwa nodded wildly to clear the dull pain in his forehead, but it just moved to the back of his cranium. Marten's lecture flowed. 'Oiwa,' he confided, 'I can also put on two centres some way apart and, with the aid of cords, arrange my sticks in a perfect ellipse!'

Oiwa shook his head. Marten took this for Oiwa's sheer amazement. He leaned forward, saying into Oiwa's ear confidentially. 'That means that I can—'

'LOG!' Claw shouted, 'Hard on the prow! Paddle left,' he commanded. Evergreen turned and rolled slightly as they passed a nearly submerged trunk. 'That was close,' Claw uttered to Mica.

'Yup,' if it weren't for those dippers landing on the tiny knot sticking up, we may not have seen it.'

'I wanted to travel at night, but if there's no Moon it's dangerous,' Claw commented. 'Gather speed,' he called. Their paddles dipped as Claw and Mica looked out for flotsam.

'There won't be a Moon, tonight,' Marten assured them.

'Claw?' Mica asked. 'I forgot to enquire earlier, but is there any news of Weir?'

'That was a long time ago, a very long time,' Claw thought as he paddled. He said, 'All we heard is that he went to the Lands of

Steam and as far as Fire Mountain. He left there in a boat, and that's all we know.'

'Thanks, Claw. It is just that our father still wants to hear if there is anything new.'

'He sired two children with us: a boy, Cedar, and a lovely girl, Hazel. They have wedded children now,' he answered guiding Evergreen along. 'Is that any help?'

'Well, we knew, but thanks,' Mica instantly remembered the stay in Buzzard's village and wondered if he'd sired, too. 'Thanks, Claw, I'll tell Pa when we get back that there's nought new.'

No more log alerts interrupted Marten's endless stream. Oiwa could not answer, nor change the subject. He tried making the best of it when Marten did wild calculations in his head and explained his theorem of time and distance. Oiwa thought of starting a paddling song, but that was not possible. He beat a rhythm with his paddle on Evergreen's side as he dipped it in and out, but it did not catch on.

Evening moved closer. The dipping sun sent the waters golden. Evergreen eventually bumped the lakeshore. Oiwa took gum to chew while they erected a small leather tent along Evergreen's length. She was bone dry inside and was a fine place to sleep. Claw pulled out dried venison and there were hard-boiled pigeon's eggs in a grass box. It was enough.

20

The Bald Heads

Morning mists hung over Wolf Lake, the water dark as ever. Oiwa stirred in the hollowed trunk. Mica breathed slowly. Marten slept, flopped over the rolled hides. Claw slept sitting at Evergreen's prow. Oiwa lifted their skin cover. Light crept over the canoe's sides. He slipped out onto the moist shore over the stony beach, feeling sharp grit scrape his soles. Soon the softness of saxifrage soothed his toes as he meandered up the bank.

A hare dashed from behind a boulder as Oiwa poised to pee. He jerked inside, remembering Rush's hare. The purple flowered saxifrage wiggled as his torrent dashed among them. The crew gradually rose and flung the cover aside. Oiwa found a hollowed stone filled with clear water and washed sleep from his face. The crew made for the springy verge where a waterspout charged down the slope. From this they drank. 'Hurry,' Claw called. 'The sun is creeping through the mist. We can be there for evening if we shift.' Oiwa went to the boat in the refreshing cold mist, chewing his tooth-cleaning gum.

The day sped by. Mercifully for Oiwa, Marten paddled deep in thought. Claw chanted in time with his paddling; duck rose from the water. Geese gaggled on island nests. Evergreen's wake spread behind. The lake widened and the far side was out of sight.

Evergreen slipped easily through the rippled surface as she headed for a bank of fog. The murk glided gently before them. Gradually, the mists burned away. A backing breeze urged them forward. Wolf Lake roughened. Evergreen rode the waves. The crew paddled strongly and evenly, keeping her steady. A spit of land poked out into the lake. Claw signalled to make for the lee of it. The sheltered waters were easier and safer. The signs of wrecked spruce, larch and pine had diminished, but the banks were bare of forest. Ferns, buckthorn, knotgrasses and flowering saxifrage had begun reclaiming the land.

Keeping time to Claw's voice, they became as one with the Evergreen. They felt a glow in their muscles as the water sped beneath. Marten worked out his mental puzzle with a satisfied expression. He moved his arms gracefully in an effortless flow of paddling.

'Mother of Gods!' Mica shouted, pointing forward and to his left. 'It's Heron's Tooth,'

Oiwa tried to say, 'She's just drifting skin and busted spars. Look. Air has caught under the leather; there's the mends we made.'

Mica poked one with his paddle as the Evergreen took them slowly past. 'The bubble's moving and wobbling along under the hides,' he said. It reached a great tear and burst out like rumbling flatulence. Evergreen turned and glided steadily on as the Heron's Tooth's flabby remains finally sank into the depths.

Mica shook his head, bewildered, and looked to Oiwa. The memories returned like an evil flood.

Claw noticed and took up his tune loudly. Oiwa gripped his paddle. The rock in his throat hardened as he bent to his task.

After some hours, Evergreen felt a slight current. It drew her into a flow in the lake. The bank turned, ahead, creating a distant barrier.

'Lake End,' were the first words Oiwa was aware of after his trance-like paddling. He had been remembering their ordeal in a dreamlike state. Marten was aware and kept his silence. He could feel the darkness of Oiwa's inner soul. Mica repeated 'Lake End,' as he pointed to the black line of land rising at each end to meet the hills.

Beyond the water's edge were more distant mountains. The sun shone warmly on the paddlers' backs. Glaciers dripped far away, sending their tears down to an unseen ocean. Geese gaggled on marshy islands. Mica and Oiwa's Whale Geese were some distance, yet.

Claw heard the welcoming rattle of paddles from ahead as a long, hide craft appeared. Oiwa came suddenly to his senses. He stepped over their valued green jadeite cargo to Mica and gave him a brotherly kiss on his neck and hugged his shoulders tightly. Mica heard Oiwa's voice deeply inside him saying, 'It will pass as we go forward.' Mica noticed Oiwa's beard's matted tangle. He nodded, returning the affection.

'Claw,' a voice called, 'It's Char. Have you got our rocks?'

'Yes, Char, and your grubs. How's your father?'

'Well dead!' Char answered from his painted prow. Their crafts closed in, bumping gently. Char leaped into Evergreen. He wore the scantiest of clothing. Around his thick waist he sported leather shorts with beaded string tassels. He had a plaited belt of dyed hide tied at his left. Hanging from his muscular shoulders was a flapping red-lined waistcoat of rattling quills.

The friends banged foreheads loudly in greeting. Claw's shiny black hair contrasted utterly with Char's polished, bald head. His cranial dome had swathes of colour enhancing his skull's contours. Thick stubble jutted from his temples and a long, tight plait whipped in the momentum of his leap. His tight leather clothing emboldened his muscular frame.

His crew of five braves stood in the Salmon's Fin. Their toes mingled among their silvery catch. Each wore similar garb. Their muscles shone in the reflected light from the lake.

'What happened?' Claw demanded, shocked.

'Fucking murdered by those shit-eyed bastards up at Warty Hands,' he returned. His forehead smacked against Mica's, who had forgotten the painful greeting. 'Mica!' he exclaimed, 'About three or four springs since we met. And who buggered up your ear? Some pup of a lobe-sucking bitch?' he suggested rudely. He looked towards Oiwa and hurtled to greet him.

'Good. Jadeite, lovely,' he laughed as his brow clashed Oiwa's white Star. 'I need some to carve the old man's bleedin' death mask for when we stuff him underground.' He looked directly at Oiwa, 'You're new. Quiet bastard, aren't you?' He cracked Oiwa's brow again before he could shift.

'Ouch!' Oiwa thought, withdrawing, feeling if his skin was split.

Char lurched past Oiwa and grabbed a green pebble by Marten, who held his paddle behind, slowing Evergreen. 'I've been here before,' Marten thought, 'I'm not getting brow-beaten. I'm moving back as Char lurches and raising my paddle to where my forehead would have been.'

'Shit!' Char yelled, tumbling on his knees. 'What a wanker's way to say hello.' His crew looked round at the unexpected spectacle. Char aimed to punch Marten's testicles. He placed the paddle deftly in the way. 'Bugger him!' Char shouted and nursed his bruised knuckles.

Char's mates in the Salmon's Fin screeched with laughter. 'What a perfect twat,' Cod's Eye called from the stern. Char composed himself rapidly as the Evergreen rocked.

'For fuck's sake, where did you learn that stinking trick?' Char moaned as Marten placed his paddle back.

'Mother's advice,' he replied.

'Well, you get first chew of smoked eel when we get back,' Char announced, regaining his dignity. 'It's a reward for remembering vile tricks.'

'What happen to Smolt?' Claw asked, as Char recovered.

Char shook with rage. His back plait swung violently from the nape of his neck.

'My dad was ill. He'd scoffed something that was off. He had the shits for days. Well, he decided to go out. He was feeling better. He sorted his tidal creels. That's when he got caught short. Limpet saw it all. She was going down from Salt Slap to help. That's when she saw those two young fuckers from Warty Hands.' Char sighed seriously as the Evergreen began drifting towards the town. 'Pa stooped for a crap behind the rocks. When he stood after wiping his arse, one of those smelly turds pulled back his bow and sprang his shitty little arrow into Dad's throat!

'Smolt was fucking raging. He didn't need that filthy arrowhead through his windpipe. He was a fighter. Those two virgin wimps stabbed him in the guts, all deliriously laughing. Limpet snuck back to us. We crept over the boulders to the ebb. Yeah, they'd gutted him, the mean bastards. The shits took his liver for a trophy and humped off with it, if you please.' Char spat yellow phlegm over the side in disgust. 'But we followed.'

Claw remembered the shocking hostility between the Bald

Heads and the Mouflons of Warty Hand Hills. Char ranted on in his tribe's abusive manner, Oiwa staggering at the strings of expletives exploding from his lips. It was all returning to Mica.

The sun dipped behind them as Salt Slap came into view. An incongruous copse of tall pines stood uphill above the stone-walled huts, wattle houses and wigwams. People came to the shore in greeting and fires began glowing.

Oiwa saw that Salt Slap was sited on a broad bank separating Wolf Lake from the sea. To their right, the current ran through a breach in the bank where it spilled to a tumble of rocks and gravel banks. Then it ran through a deep trough to the hidden sea.

Char finished his tirade. Evergreen's helm bumped the gravel bank. 'We followed those two Mountain Farts and spotted them climbing the small cliff back to their home. Me and my brother, Sether, fitted our arrows. We shot them just below their fucking shoulderblades into their spines. Our arrows hissed like piss from a rutting wolf. They thud through those crappy swines' shirts. Their bleeding poky little black eyes must have fairly popped out, shocked, when they felt our arrow-tips. They fell, dropping Pop's liver.'

'I don't know about these Bald Heads,' Oiwa thought when he helped tie Evergreen to a fish-shaped post. He sighed and rubbed his rump to ease the discomfort of his hard seat. The soft aromas of pine wafted in evening mists. The babble of the Salt Slappers' welcome surrounded him. Oiwa stood and looked. 'I'm getting used to being mute,' He thought. 'I'll just have to walk tall and be mysteriously silent.' Mica strode ahead with Claw. Char greeted Sether with a smart tap on the skull. Marten followed, with his bundle of sticks.

Sether put a curling ram's horn to his mouth and blew across its pointed end. The note began with a tremble, growing to a tremendous blast. The sound exploded into a shrill and alarming firmament. He wrenched the horn from his quivering lips when the note was at its height. The roar of it rang around the echoing mountains and across the silent water.

'Fucking show-off,' Char called back.

'These are very challenging people,' Oiwa thought, 'I had better rise to the occasion and come out from this depression.' He looked back to Evergreen, 'I will leave my feelings there on that hard seat.'

Oiwa swaggered up the shingle to the scrubby turf where more carved posts stuck out. Some represented strange distorted humans, others birds and animals. One had a vast eel writhing round it with garish yellow eyes, another a dismembered human body. Chilling, dark eye sockets stared from the severed head, each sculpture a remarkable feat. Oiwa looked back for an instant to the cavernous eyes, then turned to meet Salt Slap's welcome.

Mica chatted with folk like long-lost friends as Char took them to his building. It was dug into the rising bank with a low masonry wall at the front. This held a wooden framework covered with thick hides. Outside in the evening glow, Limpet crouched over a steaming pit. She greeted Char, her man, as a crowd gathered. She hauled out a thick bundle of dark, slippery, broad-leaved vegetation. It smelt salty and had an essence Oiwa had never sniffed before. In the chilling air too, there was a different aroma and a huge sense of space and distance.

Limpet signalled to the visitors to sit. She yodelled and her three daughters appeared from the house. Her two sons followed with skins of fragrant water. Gneiss, the older, poured this into a bowl for the girls to offer. Oiwa accepted his from Thrift. It was strange; like bone, with a smoothed edge. She smiled.

'Thrift,' Char shouted, 'Get Marten the smoked eel. He deserves it. Won by the depth of respect he showed me.' His mates screeched with laughter.

'Thank you,' Marten said, accepting the compliment meekly. Thrift returned quickly with a yard of eel. The smokiness wafted into Oiwa's nostrils as Thrift nudged him in passing.

Limpet opened a long parcel from the cooking pit. 'That's an amazing aroma of cooked meat, like the sweetest pig,' Oiwa thought, as voices behind began an excited chorus and Limpet handed the first steaming pieces to Char. The girls passed hunks round. The brothers served more drinks. 'Have some eel,' Marten said to Oiwa. 'Thanks,' he signalled, as he was handed a tempting joint. He held the tender meat by its protruding bone. As it cooled he bit some off and rolled it on his tongue. 'It's just like tender young boar. Cooking in the wet leaves makes it even more succulent.' Forgetting his woes, he soon found he had finished, except for the butchered bone on which he greedily gnawed. Other hunks of meat rose from the pit in swathes of steaming weed.

'Was that good?' Gneiss asked Oiwa.

'Yes,' he eagerly nodded.

'More?' Gneiss asked politely.

'Yes,' he wildly clicked, as meat slid from a rack of ribs onto his lap. Oiwa looked to Mica and smiled delightedly.

'I'm so pleased to see you happy,' Mica said.

Thrift sat between them to share water from her shining bowl. 'The stars are appearing brightly,' Oiwa noticed as he gazed upwards. 'What's that dog growling at, in Char's house? Something's shuffling about, too?' he questioned with a furrowed brow.

'Don't pay any heed,' Thrift remarked, 'That's just Shit Eye, our bitch, she always gets excited when there's folk about,' Oiwa remembered their dog, as he watched Thrift disappear into the house. 'Stay and guard,' she told Shit Eye. 'Here's a bone.'

'Thrift,' Limpet called. 'Bring that nice shoulder out. We can put it in for later.' She arrived with another bundle for the pit and sat next to Oiwa again.

'The feet are a real treat, but they take a lot of baking,' Oiwa nodded knowingly, remembering the trotters he had chewed with his family. Drumming and singing took his mind away, as a spectacle of acrobatic dancing and leaping the fire pit commenced.

'Where would you ugly sods like to sleep tonight?' Char asked his guests. 'It's either in our place, by the fire, or one of the wigwams.'

'I prefer the sound of your hearth,' Claw answered. Mica signalled approval while sucking a vertebra. 'Delicious, I love the spine marrow,' he remarked reaching for his toothpick. They continued supping as the other daughters prepared bedding. Thrift, a hefty individual, served strips of smoked fish and ice-cold aromatic herb tea. Her shaven head shone. Small shells dangling from her ear piercings sparkled in the light of the rising moon. Oiwa heard distant water tumbling from Wolf Lake. There was another rhythmic flow, too, but further away. Oiwa could not understand it. He stood in the fireglow, listening.

Thrift rose, putting her broad face close to Oiwa's. He looked round. She made a welcoming gesture of rubbing noses. Oiwa responded. She pulled her head back slightly then swiftly struck his forehead with hers. 'Welcome!' she screeched with a wail of infectious laughter. Oiwa's head reeled. His silver Star swelled. The inside of his head thumped. Everyone laughed, clapped and sang. During the clamour, he felt Thrift's hand take his. She pointed to the sound of the water. He looked down to her leathery cuffs and the tiny jadeite discs, sewn in a line up to her powerful shoulders. A dark leather choker with a finely carved stone roundel glinted as she moved. She pointed again to the running water and tugged Oiwa's fingers, saying, 'I'll take you... there, Oiwa,'

Before he knew, they were far from their firelight. 'Just follow me,' Thrift urged. He looked down her strong, broad back. Three tight plaits swing to her ample waist, which was drawn in by an elaborate woven belt. It caught the light of the distant galaxies in its brilliant polish. Her skirt moved over her powerful muscles. From her high hem, a curtain of soft grass tassels swung to her knees. The small black shells that weighted them clacked as she moved.

'We're going to the viewpoint.' Their path seemed warm under his bare running feet. The tiny shells on its surface prickled his dry soles. Oiwa's virtually beadless matted hair bounced around his ears. The path took them higher on the undulating terrain. They saw the moonlit silver of Wolf Lake spreading. It reminded him of the dream when he had landed as a goose onto shining water. They stopped. He went to speak about it to Thrift, but not a sound came forth. He looked to her and she responded. Oiwa immediately struck her a violent blow on her forehead and mouthed the word, 'Welcome,' Thrift laughed, and it was the first moment for seemingly black years that Oiwa laughed himself. Even without sound, the humour engulfed him.

21

Salt Slap

'Take my hand,' Thrift said warmly. 'We'll go along the ridge.'

To Oiwa's right, Wolf Lake spread. On the other side, far off, he saw for the first time the ocean. The moon shone on the incoming tide to a vast arm of the sea. Waves broke like swan's wings.

Thrift pointed to still, green pools, shining in the night air, the same green as her choker charm, the hue of her eyes and the emerald flash of the dipping sun. 'Our salt ponds,' she said, taking a tiny birch capsule from her belt bag and unscrewing the tight lid. 'Taste,' she said proudly.

Oiwa licked his finger and fitted it in. He touched his tongue with the rough grey crystals. They slowly dissolved as he cracked one with his white teeth. 'How highly salt's valued at home,' he mused. 'Our scarce pink rock salt is so different.'

'Come to the outflow where white waters roar. Listen. The wolves howl to the moon from the slopes. This is a place of change,' Thrift explained, pointing lakewards, 'From there, everything is landward. This outflow is land's gate to the ocean, where it all changes.

'This is amazing,' Oiwa thought, 'It's nothing like the Dun or the lakes. It's powerful, living water.'

Thrift continued, 'When all the trees slid from the hillsides, they backed up here like a mountain and jammed up this entire bank. They froze solid. Ice built behind, until finally the lake exploded with underwater pressure. Wolf Lake spat the trapped trees to the sea, taking them to who knows where.'

Oiwa gripped Thrift's meaty hand. She grasped his with undulating fingers, flowing with tidal rhythm. Oiwa gazed, pondering. He heard in his head gaggling geese. His toes curled and clawed the gritty soil; they spread, web-like, under him. His skin turned bumpy. His neck grew. His eyes pierced the dark of the hillsides. The gaggle amplified, filling his ears with the call. He saw waves below as he flew. 'That's where I'm going,' he said in an avian voice.

On the rim of his brain he felt the guidance of a power attached to all things. He saw under the moonlight the nests of his goose familiars, then a vastness beyond comparison. Oiwa looked down over the endless sea.

A voice rang in the plumage of his ears, stately, powerful and prophetic. 'Your earth spirit's destiny, Oiwa, is almost boundless. You will venture to far places, revealing what life will bring you and those whom you travel with, and those you leave behind.'

Oiwa's wings faltered momentarily at the words in his head. He then turned in the night air and saw himself talking with someone far below by water's edge and water's beginning. He flew back over the icy ocean and down to re-join his human host, becoming absorbed again within its skin and bones.

Oiwa blinked as the sun rose. Time had played tricks on him. Thrift took his hand carefully, leading him back to Salt Slap while morning duties began. Mica wakened as Oiwa came to the hearthside and lay down by the ash grey embers. He dreamed of distance and time. He dreamed of faces reflected in pools. He saw crowds of people, then vast fields of beings from different ages, past, present and future in multiple ranks, like terraces up a hill, each level a generation, like great wing feathers working in unison. In front was his figure, clear and distinctive. But behind those levels of humanity, his own face looked straight back. He gazed deeply into his eyes and saw... With that, his dream ended, but the images remained clear. He slept, utterly undisturbed, until the following day.

Oiwa woke to Sether's horn. 'I feel different, taller. My body moves freshly, like I've shed cumbersome skins.' Shit Eye growled again at that muffled rustle as Oiwa took Ziit and made for Char's doorway. Sether stood in the sunlight with his wife.

'Good day, Oiwa,' Sether said, enjoying the shattering effect of his horn. 'Sound sleep is good for youths. Here's Birch Twig, my youngest wife.' Oiwa bowed and looked into her eyes. 'Birch Twig is a granddaughter of Weir. Hug thy distant cousin.'

'Astonishing!' Oiwa registered, opening his arms to embrace and rub noses with her.

'Sether and I have children. Weir's blood runs within them,' she said.

Oiwa looked deep into her face, 'Yes I recognize familiar features. Her plaits are lighter, with a reddish tinge. Quite unlike Sether's black ones, springing from above his forehead, with thick jadeite rings at the knotted ends.

'Oiwa,' Mica shouted, 'you've wakened? I hope you had sweet dreams.' They came immediately back. He stood, slowly taking them in. He noticed that urgent rustle again. Shit Eye barked angrily.

'Hallo, Oiwa,' Thrift called and thumped on his back. 'I'm taking you sightseeing, lazy bones. Look lively, drag your ugly feet.' Still winded, he gripped Ziit and waved to Birch Twig. They walked off round Char's house, which was cut into a grassy mound of clipped herbs and juniper. To one side was a heap of old refuse that birds pecked.

'We're going to the Last Pines, where we perform certain rites,' Thrift said, taking Oiwa's hand. From Char's midden they climbed a buckthorn slope. The shadow of the Last Pines met their toes as Thrift led to the quiet space. The tall copse felt different from the rest of the hillside: still and timeless. 'Here we do our dead ones,' she said, pointing high into the branches.

Oiwa looked up high. 'That's a tall, dangling body suspended under its shoulders by taut leathers. Stones droop from the ankles.'

'That's Smolt. My Granddad,' she grumbled. 'Killed: arrowed dead by those sneaking, greasy turds.'

'I'm not accustomed to foul language. I used much gentler phrases when I spoke. But, I suppose it's the Bald Heads' way,' he thought, staring at the pendulous corpse. 'How the breeze dries her grandfather as he twists, creaking, on his plaited leather cords. That spear up his spine holds his shrinking head high. How the skin glistens. And those amazing precious beads hanging from the stitches up his grollocking wound.'

'We salted him after those cockless shits gutted him. The rocks stretch him.'

'There are more corpses, old and young, hanging in different states of preservation.' He stepped forward. His foot found something in the pine needles. He kicked casually. 'Ah!' he choked, as a desiccated hand flew up.

Thrift grabbed him, saying, 'This is how we do it. Don't be shocked. We face death like life. It's all one for us. It's how and when dying happens that's horrid.'

Oiwa stared at the withered fingers. They landed by a fine stone axe with a wonderful haft, nearby, a scatter of beads and broken pots. Clothing hung like bats in the branches. Deceased remains of tight skin on bony frames cast fleeting shadows.

'Follow me,' Thrift urged, pointing to the edge of the clump.

'I'm very glad to be leaving,' Oiwa thought. 'I'm not glancing back.'

They emerged overlooking the sea and ran down a grassy slope towards the shore. The couple came to a low cliff. 'What are those?' Oiwa shouted in his mind in amazement.

'Seals. Silly,' Thrift replied.

'But I can't speak,' Oiwa tried to say.

'You can, Oiwa. I saw you become a goose by Land Gate. You spoke; as a goose you flew away, but your image remained. We stood until dawn. You told me all. Not with words, but I understood. You endured terrible events, but you had good times with fine matings. Your Goose Spirit returned and filled you, and I still hear what you think.

Yes,' she continued, 'they are seals. Their skins make good clothes, their fat wonderful lamps and their meat's gorgeous. Watch them lollop into the water.'

'They are amazing,' Oiwa thought.

'Now, Oiwa, follow me along the cliff and round that bluff. There's a tall cleft up in a crag.' As they ran, more seals vanished into the surf.

A small oval hovel stood at the crag's base. Strings of drying fish swung under the eaves. Old Skellig crouched at the doorway. 'She's older than the rocks,' Oiwa thought.

'Be quiet,' Thrift told him.

'Announce yer bleedin' selves,' the crone screeched as she tried to get up.

'Thrift and Oiwa.'

'Too soon to bring Smolt here,' she moaned. 'And who's this fucking imp, Oiwa?' she asked.

He noticed her shiny head, 'Maybe her hair fell out naturally,' he thought. Then he saw a bedraggled grey plait sticking out from behind a waxy ear.

'He is a traveller and deserves respect,' Thrift put in.

'Respect? My arse,' she sneered. 'Want a lamp?'

'Please. You twisted old bitch,' Thrift answered.

'Got something for one?' Skellig demanded.

'Here,' Thrift pulled a seaweed parcel from her skirt pocket, 'Stuff that down your shrivelled gullet.'

Skellig sniffed, smiling a nearly toothless grin. 'Smells nice: very, very nice. Here're two whelk shell lamps, fatted and wicked.'

Skellig crouched by her door, undoing the package as Thrift led Oiwa towards the cavern. A narrow path led up to the jagged cleft. Stunted bushes and spiky shrubs suffered poor lives in the fissures. The sides of the ravine narrowed. Buzzards screeched, circling above. Their pathway was worn and smooth. Small offerings lay on stones. Odd empty bowls leaned among the rocks. 'Was it the buzzard or Skellig who emptied them?' Oiwa pondered. They turned a corner. The pathway delved between polished, living rock. Thrift's hips rubbed the smooth sides as Oiwa followed, watching her contours change as she pushed through.

A high cliff appeared in front. Below it, the path widened into an open precinct where pots and baskets lay strewn. Stone tools, wooden mallets and stakes lay scattered. Drums hewn from tree trunks waited to be played. A skull lay on its cranium, its eyes staring emptily upwards. Oiwa picked up a mallet and struck a drum. The sound boomed and echoed round the courtyard. Starlings flew out of a narrow cave at the base of the cliff. Thrift led Oiwa there.

They stooped to enter. 'Our shadows blank out any light, but ahead a flame flickers. Thrift's now standing, showing the height of the space. Sleeping bats shuffle,' Oiwa thought, stretching tall himself, watching the glow ahead.

They picked their way through more votive litter. The cavern echoed as fragile objects snapped underfoot. Oiwa reached the torch. Thrift handed her lamp to him. He touched her wick to his flame. They walked on under their lights. 'That's paintings of people. They seem to move in the weaving glow. Some wear horns, some, masks, others... nothing. Now, further in, pictures of those strange seals appear with an image of man with huge tusks in a seal's skin. On the gallery roof there's a dance circle, under the moon and the stars. A central triad holds spears and a bow.' Oiwa felt for Ziit. He was there.

Thrift led him further into the hill. Another entrance opened to their right. The rocks shimmered in the flame of Oiwa's lamp. It warmed in his grip. They bent and crept through the smooth rock passage of worn painted images to stand again in a wide hall. Oiwa held his lamp high. He pulled his breath in sharply. A leaning skull with dry, flaking skin suddenly returned his glance. He turned. His elbow struck something hard, yet brittle. 'Be careful!' Thrift shouted. Oiwa turned and Ziit caught in an open rib cage. A body began tumbling from its shelf.

'Stand still,' Thrift warned urgently. Oiwa froze. She unhooked Ziit from the jutting bones. 'Calm down, Oiwa,' she said almost gently. 'This is one of our sacred places. Only special visitors come here. Follow me slowly and put Ziit down before he does further damage.' Thrift's hand held Oiwa's as she took him forward. They arrived at a rounded entrance to a further chamber. An aroma of pine cones and juniper emanated from it. They edged through. Thrift took her lamp and lit others in the gallery. Slowly, the glow penetrated the domed chamber of pale pink rock. Standing on a low shelf all the way around the wall leaned stiffened bodies. Each had a jadeite claw hanging from under its chin.

'I'm not startled any more. I'm getting used to these surprises in this death hall,' Oiwa realized.

'My ancestors, Oiwa. We care for them. Over there is a son of Weir. He's an ancestor of yours called Elder. He had many children here. He travelled, too.' Oiwa looked up at the strange, shrivelled face. Elder's lips had stretched and thinned. His teeth jutted. A salty sheen shone on his body. A seal's skin hung down his back. At his feet were hammerstones, an antler and an obsidian blade. Oiwa tugged his beard and gazed at his dead relative. 'He never knew Weir, but his mother, over there, always spoke beautifully of him. Weir journeyed on, never returning.'

'This is tremendous,' Oiwa thought, gazing round the tomb. He listened to Thrift's tales of the departed and how their spirits lived there and came out into the world.

'There's one last place I must take you,' Thrift said. 'Come.'

She led to a tall slit in the rock face. They squeezed through a translucent hide that divided from the floor up. Thrift led Oiwa in, holding her lamp out. 'These are our chiefs: men and women. This is their place. Smolt will dwell here when he's dried.'

Oiwa ogled the huge death-claws. Ornate spears leaned beside their owners. Shields, masks, carved staffs, huge shells, headdresses and baskets of clothes lay at their feet. Their totemic jadeite jewellery hung profusely. The ancestors' eye sockets had shells in, helping them to observe. Their plaits hung over their shoulders proudly. The salty crust on the flesh glittered. Oiwa turned to Thrift. 'It's wonderful,' he wanted to say. She nodded and looked back at him mysteriously in the lamp glow.

'I have to ask something of you, Oiwa. I am to breed soon for my first baby. My mother and Birch Twig suggest I take one from you.' Oiwa's eyes opened widely. 'You're smart and good looking. They know you'll be something big in the world, but you're passing through like Weir. They say we should mate together.'

Oiwa's eyes bulged; his jaws parted. He looked at Thrift. 'She's strong and interesting. The very thought's making me hard.'

'I don't want one off Marten. He's clever, but I couldn't cope with a child that went on about sticks and time, forever. If I pull one from you, I would be really happy. Even if I never saw you again.'

Oiwa mopped his brow, 'That hot breeding pit in my gut's growing. I must mate.'

'Just think, Oiwa, if you make a baby in me, it might become a leader and then be in here forever.'

Oiwa realized. 'I haven't had a mating thought since Rush was hit by the arrows.' He inhaled the pine scented air, 'Not a single urge... till now.'

Thrift glowed in the lamplight. A rich tingle shot from deep inside Oiwa's belly to his throat. She undid her salmon skin belt and felt Oiwa's passion. Her skirt slipped to the cave floor. Her jacket's toggles loosened from their leather nooses with silent ease. Oiwa moved, taking it from her shoulders, casting it on a heap of ancestral gear. He looked up to shell eyes then kissed Thrift's neck as his clothes rubbed against her.

She fumbled for his belt-fastener, deftly slackening it. Oiwa helped. He shook off his trousers with a couple of kicks and felt his penis touching her navel. He stepped back to doff his suede jacket and felt liner, then returned for a naked embrace. He tugged at her plaits, pulling her head back. They kissed, passionately sucking tongues. Thrift's breasts rose; his slim form sank between them. Oiwa felt her moist hairs against his shaft. Thrift rose gently on her toes. His tip flicked to her warm, wet vagina.

Thrift felt his potent point touch a spot just within, making her glow deeply. A simultaneous thrill streamed back to the pit of Oiwa's stomach. They stayed there, joined, hardly moving, while those mollusc eyes watched. Thrift's toes relaxed. She felt Oiwa's penis slant directly in. She pressed down and Oiwa's hips pushed up. Thrift's heels raised themselves as Oiwa gently dipped, careful not to lose his place while he enjoyed his arrow being caressed by those inner lips. They moved thus. Oiwa counted the gentle strokes. He felt Thrift's thrill and grip on his stem as she moved. He knew he could come at any time, but wanted to preserve that moment for Thrift. Her movements became wilder as she clenched him. He held her close with his strong arms as she cried out in pleasure. Her warmth ran like hot liquid down his crotch as a great space opened up within her. Oiwa pressed his hips, thrusting deeper. This was the moment he came. He shook. He felt life spring from him in that place of the dead. A new being beginning, as the long beats of sperm flew out from his engendering nib.

The two stood together, hugging, feeling the wondrous warmth of each other. Oiwa's erection remained and he played with Thrift's plaits. It was such pleasure. Whilst he fondled her hair, he moved out a little. Thrift moaned deeply. Oiwa pushed in and the sound continued. He partly withdrew again. Thrift pulled him back in. That deep feeling within Oiwa began again. His head swam as he moved back and fore repeatedly in ecstasy. Thrift's passion climaxed, as did Oiwa's, once more. His male thrill deepened for his second coming. After, they stood motionless together, holding each other, feeling as one, as the hard part of Oiwa began to slowly soften. They felt they could begin to move apart. There was a new smell developing in that ancestor cave: the smell of Thrift, Oiwa and infant.

The flickering lamplights bathed them in a warm glow. Their deep breathing gently subsided as they looked into each other's eyes. Thrift moved first. Oiwa experienced the cooling of his member as she came off him.

Oiwa swung round to look into the eyes of the dead watchers. Shadows and glimmering reflections came from them as though they blinked. He turned, looking away. That muscle in his left thigh tightened. The sudden contraction gripped down his calf. If he could have screamed, he would have. All he could do was hop and try to straighten his cramped, contorting leg. He fell, writhing, onto his jacket. Objects crushed beneath him. His head struck ancestral feet during his collapse. The perished cord that held those remains to the wall snapped. Oiwa looked up in agony as the stretched mummy drooped. It tilted, tottered, turned on hardened heels to tumble directly over him.

The sound was new to him: breaking bones rattling in dry skin. His spasm intensified. This did nothing for the condition of the corpse. Oiwa inhaled mummy dust from the bouncing body. He choked and coughed, tasting the preserving salts. His leg was shackled in pain as Thrift came to rescue him.

'The damage! The damage,' she shouted in shock. Crushed pottery jabbed into Oiwa's ribs as he rolled. 'Fire!' Thrift yelled, as Oiwa's lamp caught fragments of fabric. 'Put it out!' she demanded. Oiwa rolled again in panic under the ancestor. Thrift picked up her skirt and flailed at the sparks by Oiwa's side, stamping flames out. Bone and skin crushed underfoot.

Slowly, the terrible muscular grip in his thigh eased. He lay there and gradually extended his leg. Thrift pulled smashed a body from his chest. His head poked up between the corpse's legs and he blinked. Dust covered his face as he looked over the busted spine. The dead head lay, eyes down, between his feet.

Oiwa tried sitting. The ancestor's legs lifted on his shoulders as a trickle of bone beads fell from above.

Thrift looked deeply into the eyes of the father of her first child, and laughed and laughed and laughed. Oiwa chuckled inside. His tight stomach jerked. To their sheer mirth, the dead spine slid gently from his navel onto the stone floor.

It took time to dress before emerging from the sepulchre, where slanting light dazzled. They looked in Skellig's croft on the way back to hand in the shells. They enjoyed a romantic feeling between them as Skellig screeched out knowingly, 'It's a girl. She will live for ninety-two years. Watch that cramp, boy. You can do a lot of damage like that.'

'Oh no,' Oiwa thought. 'I feel so embarrassed.'

'Pretty prick you got, though. I seen it through my special spy-hole,' she added with a lurid cackle, as her wrinkles spread.

Oiwa automatically covered his genitals.

''Too late for that, but I told you, you're fucking special, Oiwa,' Thrift added to the hag's comment.

The couple went on towards Salt Slap. 'See the salt ponds? Well, we let the seawater in. Then block them off and it dries up. When that grey salt sticks to the edges, we trade it. It's good for cramp. You should have some. It would stop you buggering up our bodies. It's right good for preserving fish and healing wounds, too. And I hope Skellig's right that you made me pregnant.'

'I'd rather not go back through the copse of corpses,' Oiwa thought.

'We'll return along the shore,' Thrift said. 'The sea goes everywhere. There's no bounds to it, once you get up the inlet.'

'Where's Everywhere,' Oiwa wondered.

In the town, folk heaved salmon from an ice pit. They sliced it with long flint blades.

Limpet was laying out swathes of broad kelp for wrapping meat. Shit Eye snarled in his guardroom as Oiwa and Thrift arrived. Mica was drinking warm honey water with Marten, who had his sticks out. Claw was telling Sether and his young brood exaggerated adventures.

'I'll put Ziit away,' Oiwa decided. Shit Eye grumbled while Oiwa passed. 'I'll make myself presentable. It looks like we are having a feast. Where's my gum?' He brushed his hair with his hands and took the chew from his pouch, then heard a terrified yell and a violent struggle. He ran to the cell where the commotion was. Round the narrow door he saw Char in front of a writhing man, hanging upside down from the rafters. Shit Eye stared obediently upwards. The victim's head dangled at Char's chest, his arms roped behind. Oiwa advanced. 'Stop, Oiwa!' Char said. 'Watch.' He took a long serrated blade from a shelf and put it on the throat of the struggling man. He grabbed his hair, to stop him swinging, and bent his head back. Shit Eye bristled expectantly. Before Oiwa could blink, Char slit that exposed throat. The man's torso convulsed wildly. His blood sprayed around the slaughter room. The rope tying his feet twisted as the naked man spun.

Like Oiwa's cramp, the spasms slowly decreased as the blood rhythmically pumped out. It drained down the dying chin into the gaping mouth, then over his horrific face and hair. When all was still, Shit Eye licked the blood off the dripping head. On the man's final twist, Oiwa spotted a snapped arrow surrounded by swollen bruising just above his twitching shoulderblades.

'I feel disgustingly cold, with jellied guts,' Oiwa thought, quaking inside.

Char opened his victim's stomach with one swift gash. Guts tumbled. Char reached in, severing the intestines. His sons carried the flopping body outside to Limpet for butchering. 'Good carcass, well bled,' she said as she wrapped joints in the seaweed.

'I can't take it! Run. I'm being sick,' Oiwa realized, retching into the salmon pit.

There he felt Thrift's breath. She put her arms on his shaking shoulders. 'We do this,' she whispered. 'We eat our enemies when they harm us,' Oiwa heard while looking down at his bile seeping into the crushed ice. 'Them fucking bastards murdered my grandfather.' She waited while Oiwa stopped vomiting. 'It's justice.' Oiwa shook his head between his knees. 'If those stinking Mouflons had a chance, they'd have dragged Smolt off. Instead, all they could get was his sodding liver for their cunt of a leader up at Warty Hands.'

Oiwa stood glaring at Thrift. For a split moment she saw a huge gander standing in front of her. It vanished, as Oiwa cut himself off from her. 'Oiwa. Wait. You don't understand. If we get an arrow in the backbone below their shoulders, they get paralyzed from hips down.' Oiwa strode off in front of her. 'They live longer, keeping their meat fresh! If it goes bad, it can send you blind,' she shouted as he stormed away. She ran and grabbed his wrist. 'Another thing. When we've scoffed them, we shit them out. Then they can't do more harm. You shat some out today.'

Oiwa spun and looked at her. Her stance was much less bold. He sent one thought to her. 'I don't do your shitting for you. Neither does my daughter.' He turned and walked back to Salt Slap to squat by the fire pits. He signalled for dug-up fish.

Thrift squatted near, but not too close. 'Dug-up fish too, please.'

22

Goose Landing

Thrift confessed guiltily to Limpet and Birch Twig about the smashed ancestor. Word spread like wildfire. A seething mob arrived at Char's house, filling his precinct. 'Oh no!' Oiwa thought, suffering that jellied feeling, tinged with acute fear. His hackles rose. Sweat poured down his spine.

'Oiwa,' Mica warned, 'you could end up cooked in kelp if this goes badly.'

'Thrift, tell this story publicly,' Char ordered.

Bravely, she stood with Oiwa and repeated it. Oiwa faced the crowd, trembling in the night air. Their jury's faces flickered unnervingly in the torchlight.

Finally Thrift finished. Silence prevailed. Two hands clapped.

'A terrible portent,' Oiwa judged. Ominously, a drum struck. Further hands clapped and Thrift's sister, Spark, choked then laughed simultaneously. Sether attempted to blow his horn, but failed. He burst out laughing, too. The Bald Heads' funny bone was struck a mighty blow. It was so hilarious they could barely make a sound. They slapped their sides and pointed at the couple. Others collapsed, weeping in mirth.

Oiwa and Thrift stood in bewilderment as the racket grew.

Marten dropped his precious sticks and clutched his stomach, hopping.

The more surprised the pair looked, the more the cackling chorus grew. They gripped hands and gazed at themselves. Oiwa kissed Thrift tenderly on her neck. This made the crowd gather in momentum. Oiwa and Thrift grinned and shamelessly giggled. Oiwa's silent mirth made it all the funnier.

Folk mimicked mating and cramp attacks. Others tumbled like mummies on the stricken pair. Then Skellig appeared, thanking Thrift for the baked Mouflon foot. It all became funnier. The old woman related the lurid spectacle she had spied from her secret viewpoint in the upper cleft. Her ribald commentary on the mating received resounding applause.

When Char was finally able, he banged his drum. 'Thank you for the best tale in years. I pronounce you Heroes of Salt Slap. I name Thrift's baby Skellig.'

The feast commenced at the confession's aftermath. It was a magnificent affair. Oiwa and Thrift stuck to fish. Mica sucked a gristly kneecap knowingly. 'Any feet left?' he heard Skellig ask.

'You'll be off soon, Oiwa, won't you?' Thrift asked. He nodded back with wide, moist eyes. 'If that's so, will you come again, to make sure of this little girl inside me?' she implored. Oiwa grinned. Thrift led him to the gate where the land ends and the ocean begins. The moonshine witnessed their deep tryst.

'It's only a couple of days by sea canoe to the Whale Geese,' Mica told Oiwa the next morning, while he massaged his thigh by the fire.

'Okay, I'm ready to leave,' Oiwa thought, looking up and nodding.

'We can, soon. Claw and Marten will wait.'

'Here's gum,' Oiwa wanted to say. He passed Mica a lump, indicating agreement.

'Char has salt and a vole-skin hat for Ugruk, the Innu chief. He's lent us clothing for colder conditions and a boat.'

Oiwa wondered why the Bald Heads did not wear much. 'But then, Thrift felt so naturally warm,' he realized.

She came bustling in with a birch-bark box of salted meat with honeyed fruit and nuts. 'Here you are,' she said. 'It'll keep you going. The meat's mountain goat, not mountain man, Oiwa.'

'We will escort you,' Char said. He and Mica walked ahead by the salt ponds.

Oiwa and Thrift followed, talking privately together, then slipped aside. 'One more time? Let's make really sure?' Thrift suggested. 'I know you should be coming back, but I feel you won't.' Oiwa looked to her, but his face gave nothing away. He held her gently as he entered. They heard Mica calling. It made no difference.

They emerged later, dressed, from the reeds. Oiwa felt his axe from Moss wedged in his belt. His index finger tested its sharpness as they meandered past pools. 'We take our dead ones to soak in brine here, before we hang them,' Thrift informed her stud. He glanced over the thick solution and wondered if there was anyone in there. 'I expect Old Skellig will pickle soon, but she's salty enough already,' Thrift joked, weakly. 'Oiwa, I'm sorry you're moving on. Maybe that old crone was right. If so, I'll have something of you with me forever.' Their palms met with passion. 'A strong child's attractive to other men, too,' she admitted.

Oiwa suddenly stopped. The pain seared up his thigh. 'If mating does this every time, I'd better stop,' he thought, as he hobbled along.

The sea breeze caught Oiwa's hair at the nousts by the shore. 'Here's your canoe, Burbot: it's walrus hide,' Char said.

'What's walrus?' Oiwa thought, as the muscle tension subsided. Mica recognized the musk ox rib and bentwood frame. 'Your other clothes are in that,' Limpet told them, pointing to a sealskin case, with walrus tusk toggles. 'You'll find good parkas in there.' Char added, 'Ugruk's stuff is inside too. If you find him, split his forehead for me, please?'

''Certainly will,' Mica joked.

Marten watched them from where Oiwa and Thrift mated the night before. He had noted how the days were lengthening and the moon waning. The sun rose further around the rim of the world and set further along it. His mind considered a concept. He sucked in his spiral-tattooed cheeks thoughtfully.

The brothers settled on the Burbot's seats.

Marten observed seals lolloping across the stony beaches into the gently breaking waves. He watched gannets diving like darts. Cormorants flew parallel above the ripples. Eider duck and ducklings swam in flotillas. They braved lines of surf, always appearing behind them further out to sea. Marten watched the Burbot's first paddle strokes, taking them north east, where the ocean's arm bent. The water darkened in the deepener channel. He was jealous.

'Hug the north shore,' Mica called. 'See that snow-capped mountain? We're heading the other side of it,' Oiwa nodded. The Burbot rose to the waves.

'Those legless seals look so weird, lolloping down the shore,' Oiwa thought to himself. 'But they swim wonderfully.' He nudged Mica to watch them, watching them. Mica smiled and paddled harder. Disturbingly, though, Oiwa found that the Burbot's rising with the swell affected him. The unsettling motion increased. 'Oh no. I feel sick,' he wanted to say, gripping his paddle and looking to Mica. 'There are two Micas glancing back! It's worse! I must stand. Oh. I'm so giddy.' He burped noisily. The taste of his last meal burned in his throat. 'I'm going to throw up.' Bile shot to his mouth from deep below. He hurled himself to the Burbot's side. The dark sea took the hot contents of his retching stomach. The stench ran through his nostrils. His nose gushed. A stream of stinging mucus linked him to the yellow bile passing beneath. Oiwa's belly spasms continued uncontrollably. His head reeled. He looked into the depths. 'I wish I could just sink into them,' he thought, as he collapsed against the sealskin baggage. He glared up to the shifting clouds. 'Oh. I feel so wretched,' was all he could think and shut his aching eyes. There he languished long until Mica eventually beached, much later.

'Wake up, Oiwa!' he heard Mica bawl.

'My guts feel terrible.' He burped again. 'But my head's not spinning. I'll try moving.' The boat tipped as he lurched to his knees. Oiwa sprawled on the wet, weedy shore. He shook himself as a flight of white terns swooped screeching towards them.

'We'll stay until the tide can take us further,' Mica said, looking at the mountain. Its paps were covered in cloud, but he could see the snowline and the ravines cutting darkly into its side. Geese honked, but not their geese, yet.

'Gather driftwood,' Mica suggested.

Oiwa searched fuel for Mica's blaze, then returned to the water's edge, watching the surf coming up the flow. He heard the seals singing on an islet. 'This is all new to me,' he thought. Seaweed waved in the currents. Small snails sucked the stones. He grabbed a handful. 'I'll take them to Mica.'

'Buckies,' he said. 'Here, watch this.' Mica pulled some fire away and said, 'Get some of that kelp. It's what Limpet wrapped that Warty Hands man in.' Oiwa dragged a great swathe of it to the fire. 'We lay some out, put the winkles on then fold it, shoving embers over,' he informed Oiwa. The smell of ocean wafted in the breeze. Later, he swept the fire off and revealed the steaming shells. 'This is how you eat them. Get your toothpick, shove it under the cap, there, and twist them out. They're great,' Mica exclaimed.

Oiwa copied him repeatedly.

'I'll show you what else we can eat,' Mica said. 'Look, over there, clumps of mussels. Bring them to the fireside. We can cover them with seaweed, then heap fire over them. They cook in moments.' Steam rose, the weed spat, crackled and shrank in the scorching heat. 'Ready,' Mica said. 'See them opening? Watch me... delicious,' he said as he sucked the body from a bivalve. Oiwa joined in. 'Use your empty mussel as a pair of pincers, grip another, part its shell and down it.'

Oiwa learned. 'My guts feel better after that,' he thought. 'The stomach's accepting this shore food.'

'Let's have that fruit and nut mix,' Mica suggested.

Oiwa took the boxes from the case. They sat and enjoyed the fire, beach and food, but Oiwa suddenly realized, 'I'm getting cold, despite the hot food. I want to try those clothes.' The breeze quickened as he untoggled the case. 'There're two pairs of tall leather boots lined with fine plaited grass. I've never seen the like. I'm used to bare feet, except in the coldest weather.' He slipped a pair on and fitted his trousers inside.

Mica went over and pulled his on. 'Here's a pair of salmon skins. Tie the sinew loops round your knees and over the tops of your boots, like this.' Oiwa copied him. 'That will keep water out if we get into choppy seas,' he said. 'Here are the parkas, made from split seals' guts. They're watertight and windproof,' Mica told Oiwa as he pulled one over his head.

'I've never seen clothing like it before. I can see Mica through the stitched translucent membrane. His voice is all muffled. Now his head has popped up into the fur-lined hood. My turn,' thought Oiwa. He pulled his parka over his head, then down to his shins.

The mounting breeze had no further effect. 'Wonderful,' he thought.

They hauled the Burbot up before the tide rose. 'I'm going to sleep in the boat, Oiwa. We set off when the tide's come right in. Hopefully you'll get your sea-stomach and stop puking.'

Oiwa pondered as he stamped about the beach, watching the rhythm of the ebbing waves. 'I can't believe why I was so ill. I went through the Dun's rapids and down Gunnal's Vulva. I never felt the least bit sick.' He then wondered, 'What's this tide, anyway?'

Misty clouds obscured the other side of the inlet. He lifted rocks to catch elvers in his hands. They tried slithering away, so he strung their heads on twine with his bone needle. They wriggled into a writhing knot as he hunted more. The breeze never affected him. The boots felt strange, but warm. He built up the fire and waited, watching the water amazingly return slowly over where they had gathered shore food. 'Strange,' he thought.

It was mid-afternoon when Mica stirred. Oiwa anticipated it and broiled the young eels in seaweed for a snack. As soon as the tide slackened, they paddled off. The outgoing waters sped them on. The breeze felt cold on their faces, but they kept snug in their new clothes.

'Those Bald Heads,' Mica stressed, 'are quite amazing. They never feel cold. It must be their blood,' Oiwa nodded. 'And the way they dish up their neighbours. Last time, I had heart and kidneys. Maybe that's what keeps them so hot.' Oiwa blinked, feeling ill again. 'How they keep their victims fresh is cruel. But at least the Mouflons have nothing against us. Just don't let them know we've eaten any, if we should meet.' Oiwa got queasier. 'Lovely girl for a Bald Head, Thrift is. North Star's Clan will enjoy that story. It's even better than the Wood Sprite epic.'

Oiwa nodded, holding vomit back as he looked ahead, wondering what lay beyond.

Back at the Bald Heads' village, Marten made a decision. 'Claw, I have something I have to do,' he said. 'I know exactly where Oiwa and Mica are going. I'll catch up and come back with them.' Claw knew there was no stopping him. His eagerness was formidable. 'I'm borrowing Gneiss's kayak.'

Thrift overheard and approached Marten. 'Take this to Oiwa, please.' She handed him a small, flattish green pebble. 'He can burnish his leather with it,' she said coyly.

Marten set off that afternoon on a falling tide, well equipped with dried food and his astronomy sticks.

Ahead, Mica knew the way. The Grey Mountain changed colour as they came closer. The bottom of the snowline undulated around her lower contours. Deep crevices still contained shining snow. The honks of the Whale Geese sounded as though they came from the mountain's spirit.

Inexhaustibly, the brothers paddled as the evening light stretched. The backing breeze sped them as the southern mists cleared. Oiwa discovered an energy he had never experienced. His arms gained power to paddle with the surf. The sea was like wind; it carried them. The cold of the air sliced like a cutting edge that seemed to pare the skin from his face, making it feel new. His soft beard enjoyed the salty spray as they crashed through waves they overtook.

The first stars and moonlight shone as day slipped into twilight. The sun slanted below the western edge with dignity. Her last rays pinkly lit the undersides of thin cloud. The sun finally blinked from view. The jade flash sparkled fleetingly. It struck Oiwa in wonder. The days were lengthening.

A leg and toe extended from the Grey Mountain into the open ocean. Mica and Oiwa paddled into the sheltered ankle, where they made camp. 'Early in the morning, Oiwa, we will sail round that promontory to meet our familiars,' Mica told him.

A cold breeze blew all night. The sea drenched the Grey Mountain's toes. Starlight glittered in the shortening northern nights.

Marten, a tide-flow behind, watched the starry hunter in the sky and the progress of the waning moon. His camp and fire was in the leeward of a low hill of old shells and ashen dumps. As he watched the galaxies, he ate pickled char and smoked eel with sliced seaweed. He, too, would arise at first light.

Oiwa woke uncomfortably, with a stone boring into his hip. 'I wondered when you'd wake,' Mica said quietly. Oiwa yawned, shaking in the bitterly cold shadow of the Grey Mountain. He sprang up and leapt about for warmth. They chewed dried goat, launched the Burbot and paddled to the pointed toes of Grey Mountain. Seals sang on the rocky end as Oiwa heard a great roar.

'Walrus,' Mica said. 'They're gigantic seals. They make wonderful boats, like this, and their tusks are solid ivory; great for harpoons. You should never get between them and their pups: very dangerous indeed,' Mica added.

Oiwa took it all in. They rounded the rocky toes. The walrus roars were amplified, along with the high-pitched shrieks of terns. The dark waters turned suddenly golden as they rounded the first toe to the screech of gulls. The light of the low, rising sun was blinding. 'Hug the toes,' Mica told Oiwa. 'The current will take us into the open sea if we don't paddle hard and keep close to the shore.' Oiwa nodded and looked away from the bright sun. As they rounded the toes, seals slid into the glittering water, their backs gleaming golden in morning glow. The walrus roared, rearing aggressively at the intruders.

'Paddle harder,' Mica shouted. Oiwa, though distracted by the wonders, dipped his paddle and pulled forcibly. The swirling currents eased as they entered waters more still. Oiwa looked behind, seeing sea heaped up where it rushed round the foot. Mica spied the long bay, the beach broad and sloping gradually to the sea, the white sands tinged with pink gravel and grey shingle. Above, a ragged edge of grasses spilled over the dune. Mica pointed to the middle of the bay, where the sands joined a rocky shore covered in seaweed. 'That is where we land.'

They paddled across the lapping wavelets. The gathering breeze blew them shoreward. The Burbot's bows kissed the soft slope. Cormorants lifted their wings and flew just above the sea to rocky vantage points. The seals watched. Walruses settled their mounds of blubber on rocky slabs.

'Pull the boat up,' Mica whispered as they touched the shore. They stepped silently from her bow and carried the Burbot over the sand to the tattered edge of the dunes. The light brightened into full day. The final star vanished, as the sky donned her morning mantle.

'Take Ziit, Oiwa. I will bring my weapons, this isn't a hunt – it's security.' The two climbed the slipping slope of blown sand, grabbing tough grasses that rooted in the fragile terrain. As they rose, the wind blew harder. They pulled on tussocks and gained height with the force on their backs

This land was so different. The gale and the sound of the tide filled Oiwa's ears. Gradually, they reached the crest of the long dune. As they peered over, a deafening roar of gaggling geese erupted. They looked down over the vista to a wide plain of pools and grassy marshlands. A winding river cut through it.

Dotting the estuarine landscape were hummocks of grass, like a million warts on a rough hide. On each one a goose sat. Oiwa glanced to the base of the dune where dark heads of goslings poked out from under their parents' wings. He edged forward; a rivulet of sand ran down. The guardian geese raised their black heads in alarm. Oiwa and Mica were spotted. The goose chorus rose to a trumpeting tumult. They all stood facing the intruders with wings raised and outstretched necks. The look of the plain changed. Geese rose, their black webbed feet and claws dug into the matted roots. The goslings' heads disappeared behind their parents' wings. They trumpeted in a violent racket, alarming Oiwa to his liver.

'There they are,' Mica said. 'The young have hatched. We were delayed, but that is okay.' Oiwa could not hear him above the tumult, but felt it. 'These are spirits of our past and future souls.'

Oiwa stared back as the hullabaloo rocketed.

'Now we go down there.' Oiwa looked back in blank disbelief as Mica squeezed his hand and urged him forward. They crawled over. Geese from the distant river joined in the rallying call, drowning all sound of sea and wind.

The vanguard of angry birds spread their wings, violently hissing as they descended the slope. The reek of digested grass hit like a hot blast as they neared the fierce phalanx. Maddened terns buzzed.

'Put your bow up, Oiwa, or they will peck your head. Keep your hood on. Go slowly forward.' The front line of Whale Geese advanced, leaving their young to scatter. 'Put your arm out. Point at the nearest birds. They'll think it's an outstretched head. Now look into their eyes and walk towards them. Hiss, if you can, but make no aggressive moves.'

Oiwa stood tall. He stared, pointed and breathed in deeply, exhaling through his teeth with a loud, HHSSSsssssSSSSS. He stooped to become level with his adversaries. Ziit jutted forward like an outstretched beak over his hood. His short, pointed beard wagged from his chin. His steamy breath jetted another hiss. The geese widened their wingspans and ran directly at him, to stop suddenly short, jostling his bow-point. Oiwa hissed as he fixed the closest protruding head with his glance.

The birds stopped. Oiwa felt the heated breath of a mother goose on his brow. He blew gently onto the protruding black, beak. She moved her head back and clacked her bill. Oiwa saw her wet tongue. Shining spittle rimmed her sharp, jagged jaw.

The racket subsided. Oiwa looked to his brother. Mica's feet had changed. He could see him, but he was different. He had become two figures, one rising from the other. A large, feathered bird stood within Mica's skin, then stepped forward.

Oiwa became aware of himself as a beak clacked against his. His beak rubbed down the neck of his erstwhile foe and preened its wing. He received a similar greeting across his tight feathers. Oiwa stepped with the goose to a shining pool, where he settled and floated. His webbed feet paddled. He followed his guide, watching her tail wiggle. Tiny whirlpools from her feet welled up behind her as Oiwa kept up the pace.

They swam past tranquil nests and waddled over beak-clipped hummocks, then followed narrow rivulets in a maze of tangled waterways. Oiwa saw dark goslings nibbling at the shortened grass. Others went with their parents towards the river. He turned his long neck and thought he could see Mica in his plumage amongst another huddle of Whale Geese.

Oiwa followed, squeezing through a narrow gulley that divided around a distinct mound surmounted by a great, downy nest. On top stood the mighty Solan.

'So. Oiwa. You have come to see me?' Solan said clearly in Oiwa's head. 'You've had a very hard journey,' said the Great Goose. 'You have travelled far from your nest.' Solan's voice was loud and clear, each word perfectly formed and distinct. 'It seems a very long time ago when you flew with me and my brood from your father's sweat lodge. Is it not?'

Oiwa turned and looked into Solan's deep red eyes. 'Yes. A very long time,' Oiwa answered.

'Come on to my island and squat with me.' Solan moved sideways, making room.

Oiwa's clawed toes touched the submerged, matted roots of Solan's nest. As he began to mount the turf hummock, Solan's mate, Mere, raised her head from behind him. 'Welcome, Oiwa,' she said.

Oiwa dipped his beak in acceptance. Five goslings poked their heads up from their warm den. Oiwa felt his plumage drain as his breast rose from the water.

'I am going to take our young to the beach to feed,' Mere told

Oiwa. 'You can keep my place warm.' They slipped into the gulley and made their way to the ocean's shore.

When his brood had left, Solan said. 'You have far to go yet, Oiwa, and much to accomplish.' He gazed at Oiwa and enforced, 'Yours will not be an ordinary life. Your destiny will touch and affect more of your human kind that you could possibly imagine.'

Oiwa listened in silence as he tried to absorb what his familiar was telling him.

'Weir was like you, only he perished.'

'How?' Oiwa asked.

'You will find out in time, Oiwa. Now, Goose, look into my eyes and gain from me what you can.'

Oiwa swallowed spittle down his long neck. He fixed his glance into those shiny irises. Within them he saw the night sky, just as he had from his father's sweat lodge. He and Solan were high above the world, which curved at its edges. He blinked. As his eyes shut, a star and moon map set hard in his skull. He moved his head, but the image did not turn. It remained like the heavens do as you walk, sail or fly.

'Now you have our chart, Oiwa. My goslings have it from my milt.'

'Solan, thank you,' Oiwa's responded. 'I can see a dark space in my head. There's a skein of us, far ahead in the night sky. We are guided by the stars. Now I see daylight, but I can feel the heavens and the Moon. They guide me, Solan.'

'That's correct,' the Goose King replied, 'This is how we travel our vast distances. As you journey onwards, you'll have to do it as a man does. With man's impediments and man's skills.'

'So I am going on, not back?' Oiwa asked.

'Oh. Yes, Oiwa. For you, a very long distance, and further after.' Solan ruffled his plumage then nibbled short blades of grass. Oiwa did the same. They tasted succulent. 'We geese mate for life. Our families are strong. We travel from here to where your ancestors came. We live in harmony there and feed to return here to nest and hatch.' Solan looked towards the river and the sea. 'Here we have everything to bring up our young. We cannot fly during much of this time. We've shed many of our feathers to make our nests. We watch our goslings feed on the fast-growing plants and grasses. We take them to the shore, where they dive for seaweed that sways in the depths. Their small wings are like the flippers of seals, and their feet propel them down to snatch the succulent algae from the rocks.'

Oiwa's head filled with goose-lore as Solan continued. 'Our young rapidly grow big and strong, as we ourselves replenish our migration fat and flight feathers. Then we fly back to that wonderful land for the winter, where there is little snow and plenty to sustain us.' Solan paused as Oiwa took it all in.

'Now for you, my man-goose. Your human voice is gone, but your inner one remains. Some menfolk may hear it. You will find ways of hearing others' inner voices. This will show you the truth,' Oiwa listened, saying nought. 'Your journey is necessary, but it's for you to discover what it will bring. There will be many risks and much to overcome. I hope you achieve. I hope you will fare better than Weir.'

'Thank you, Solan. I knew there was more for me than just returning to my clan. I will think deeply on all you have told me,' Oiwa said in his own clear voice.

Solan acknowledged him and suggested, 'Then let's spend some time with you being a goose. Then we will go to the shore.'

23

Ugruk's Advice

Later, Mica joined Solan and Oiwa. Solan led them to the river. Oiwa felt comfortable as they bobbed down its last few yards to cascade to the sea. Other geese and goslings fed in the salty water. Oiwa dipped his head below the surf, seeing goslings flying underwater and tugging the masses of nutritious plants. He tasted the swaying fronds, feeling, 'I know that flavour.'

He paddled, feeling at home amongst his huge family; each goose an individual, as with humans. He drifted, watching Mica floating up the shore. He paddled to meet his brother. He turned his head and looked. He was distanced from his flock. His scaly claws touched the shingle beneath as he watched Mica waddle, then stand as a man. Oiwa trod from his fading Goose reflection to walk the incline, his wings, transparent; his arms, solid in his seal-gut parka. His booted feet crunched shingle. Mica's hand reached. They embraced. Oiwa heard his soft words. 'Now you know what and who we are.'

'Yes, Mica. We're different from other people. We're part of something else. There's so much to understand. I've grown. I'm fuller. My head has new wisdom. I must discover all that's locked in it. I'm tugging my beard, ensuring this real. I know you can hear me, Mica.'

'I hear you, Oiwa. You are new and changed. This is why we come here.'

They looked along the shore. Gravel crunched under their boots. The dune rose beside them. By the Burbot, smoke from a small fire crept skywards. A thin figure waved. 'It's Marten standing by a circle of sticks. He's coming to meet us.'

'Here, Oiwa. A gift from Thrift.' His outstretched hand opened, revealing the green pebble.

'Thanks,' Oiwa nodded remembering their togetherness. 'It's so smooth; lovely to touch. I'll cherish it.'

Marten spoke of sticks, 'The further north I bring them, the more the shadows change. I could draw you a diagram in the sand...' But he noticed a difference in the brothers and stopped. They sat by Marten's fire. He said, 'My calculations demonstrate it will be light all the time in seventeen days!'

The three sat in silence. Mica listened to the waves and birdcalls. Oiwa removed his polished stone from his pouch to warm it in his hands. 'There's a flaw on its edge. Slight silvery specks, like cold moonlight, shine from within it. I'll get my axe and place its sharp edge gently into the crack and set the pebble on a beach stone.' Mica watched as Oiwa pressed his axe blade into the fault. He raised them slightly then brought his chopper down. The pebble split neatly in half.

Oiwa spent the rest of the long day meditating while rubbing the two halves of his stone until they shone. He rummaged in his pouch for a ruined quartz arrowhead. With its jagged edge he drew a flying goose on the smoothed surfaces. He skilfully scored the sparing lines of his emblem until it was powerfully emboldened.

Oiwa thought of his future during carving. 'I remember all that has happened and how changed I am: my gains, my losses, my loves, my hates. I know the sweetness of mating now. But that great rock is still in my throat. Turning back with Mica is wrong, no matter how it hurts to leave him. All I see is my journey to the unknown. I hear voices of geese telling me how to follow. I curl my toes in my boots to feel if they are goose. They aren't now'.

He looked to Mica, who spoke with Marten of theories. The fog of words wafted past as he spied Gneiss's kayak. 'I need time to gather physical and mental courage,' he realized.

His own words rang as he listened to Marten's final conclusions, 'If you travel far enough, you will arrive back at the place where you began.'

'That's completely crazy,' Oiwa thought as he stood and looked out to the horizon, imagining the utter impossibility of Marten's words.

As Oiwa's eyes strained, he spotted a flotilla of craft approaching. Oiwa nudged Mica and pointed to the canoes. 'It's Ugruk and his clan,' Mica explained. 'Build the fire up.'

Their skin craft nudged the shore. Ugruk's fleet made for their smoke. Mica walked down as the Chief advanced, greeting him. Ugruk shoved back his parka hood and hugged Mica. He had scrubby, dark hair and a thin, black moustache. He was quite short. Ugruk's power was not in his size, but in his intellect, serenity and knowledge. They crunched their way up the beach to Marten's blaze.

'Ugruk. Here's the vole hat from the Bald Heads, and salt.' The hat made Ugruk laugh at a private joke between him and Char. 'This too,' Mica added. Crack! Went his brow onto Ugruk's forehead.

'I let you do that!' Ugruk blurted, rubbing his bruise.

'Bring the seal meat, Sgeir,' he asked his wife. Her young fetched rolls of flesh, dumped them on a skin and cut it up with sharp ulus. Ugruk passed some to Mica. They ate. Mica admired Ugruk's garb as he chewed. His jacket was seal suede trimmed with arctic fox, the chest fasteners tiny carved ivory selkies. His hood lining was of white hare's fur pulled in by wolf-bone toggles. He sported a necklace of engraved bear's teeth over his inner vest. The red trim of his caribou calf trousers was stretched tightly on his legs.

They swapped news. Oiwa listened. Marten explained about his sticks to the young.

'We are hunting walrus. Will you come?' he suggested.

Oiwa looked the other way, pretending interest in Marten, desperately feeling his calling. 'I can't stop myself. I'm standing to walk shoreward. I'll turn to wave. But he's deep in plans of walrus hunts and what they'll do with the tusks. "A fine gift for Buzzard," I hear him say. They discus killing; weapons. How they'll stalk and have hides for boats, feasting on flesh, mating after, lamp blubber, bones for tools and whiskers to string beads. "Oiwa could make Moss a fine bracelet from polished flipper bones," says Mica. My heart sinks, I would love to mate with Moss again, and Thrift, but no!'

Mica heard Oiwa's voice scream in his head. He stood, facing him, shocked. 'I am not going back!' he heard Oiwa yell. 'I'm following the geese. I am going to discover what happened to Weir.' He ground his feet into the shingle. He thrust his hand into his pouch. 'Here's my talisman. Take it from my open hand.' Staggered, Mica gripped Oiwa's palm. Oiwa squeezed the intaglio deep into Mica's until the bones separated. Mica had never seen his brother so troubled, yet so empowered. He leaned back, looking into his face. He saw the change, the resolution set firmly there.

Oiwa galloped to Gneiss's kayak. He lifted it, sprinting to the ocean. He laid Ziit in it, his arrows and what belongings he had. Mica looked bewildered at the stone, the goose carving swelling on his palm. The gem was beautiful. He ran to Oiwa as he climbed in the boat. 'Don't go,' he bitterly prayed.

Oiwa looked at Mica powerfully.

'I will come with you then,' Mica implored.

'No!' he heard.

'Our parents? Our clan?' Mica shouted as Ugruk's people gathered round.

Oiwa's voice hit home in Mica's head as he heard the words. 'My life! My destiny! My future!'

Ugruk clenched Mica's arm as he tried to pull Oiwa from the kayak. 'Let him go. Don't hold this young man back.'

Oiwa stood, hugged Mica firmly and pushed off.

Ugruk held Mica as Oiwa paddled across the flow of Goose Landing's river. Geese called, honking tumultuously. Dense mist descended over the ocean. Oiwa vanished.

24

Wrasse's Recovery

Quernstone creaked up the log ladder with a trug of bakes: it was her excuse to see what was happening in Wrasse's new chamber. Her rounded head met Shala's downward gaze.

'I've brought some—'. She was cut off by Shala's hushing finger. She slid the basket silently onto the planked floor and descended. She waited downstairs, then tripped through the door into the courtyard, assuming the air of being privy to something confidential.

Wrasse slept. Her lined, elderly face smoothed. Frowns surrounding her forehead's Star eased. It was hours before she stirred.

The carpentry and masonry outside continued unabated. Walls were demolished, rubble graded and stacked. Partan's plan developed. He and Quartz visited the lichen-covered Telling Stone. 'Quartz. I want the measurements of me carved on the monolith.' He looked up at its colourful, slender mass. It was not their usual flagstone. It had been moved, generations before, from Stark Hill. It had lain there forever, an object of veneration from before memory. Some said it was a giant's tooth knocked out in a fight with his aged mother. Others pronounced it Vacar's spear, lost whilst fleeing the great wave. Whatever the truth, Partan's ancestors had shifted its mass to Lee Holme, giving it new importance. Its shadow told the time and seasons. Its colour foretold the weather. The granite dish at its feet dictated when to harvest. Now Vacar's spear would keep the measurements.

Partan stood at the monolith's toes and reached up his right arm. 'Wait a moment,' Quartz said. 'We'd better lay a slab for you to stand on.'

'Quite right, Quartz,' Partan remarked. 'I'll get Jasper's team to set one; then we can do it right. It should be a level bench, to mark my feet and pace. What do you think, Quartz?'

'Excellent plan: and a celebration to cheer folk up. We can mark all the poles from Vacar's Lance forever.'

'Right. That's a plan, Quartz.'

Shala fanned glowing charcoal on the small clay hearth with a gull's wing. The light breeze stirred Wrasse from her dreams. Gradually, she opened her eyes under the dim eaves. She yawned, rolling on her side. She lay in silence. Shala waited.

'Give me a drink, Ai... please, Shala.'

Shala filled a burnished cup of cool, scented water. Wrasse drank, leaning on her elbow. Her dry, tattooed breasts sagged from her body. Wrasse coughed. They wagged like empty bladders beneath her flax tunic.

'Shala,' she said quietly, 'I'd best finish what I began telling. I need to do it for me, too.' Shala sat on the cushion again. They shared a buttered fennel scone.

'Have I told you how Weir died?' Wrasse asked.

Shala nodded gravely.

'I knew he was gone. The stink from his clotting blood reeked of death. I couldn't move. His man was still inside. I felt him there. I yearned so not to shift, but I had to. I couldn't make a sound. I wanted to scream, but my breath was lost. I was paralyzed from within.' Wrasse held her breath, remembering. She sat up under the inclined rush roof. She shook, thinking of his blood on her breasts.

'That is when Coutou returned. She stood stock still for an eternity. Then I felt her heavy hand swing on my back. The shock made me gasp. I drew breath and babbled senselessly. I pointed to Weir's blooded face.' Wrasse looked past Shala, almost through her. Shala waited, knowing Wrasse was seeing it all again.

'Coutou put her arms under my shoulders, lifting me gently.

She knew he was inside me. My horrified family arrived, seeing. I felt him leave me while my sisters screamed at me.' Wrasse heaved herself up, gazing at the glowing charcoal.

'Coutou scolded them. "Don't you know you are not wanted here?" she barked. Mother ushered them out, returning angrily. "That goes for you too!" Coutou exploded.

'When she'd gone, Coutou said, "Now Wrasse, I will clean you up. Then I will tell your sisters to return. They will apologize. I will make them clean your Sea Angel. That would be too much for you to bear." I nodded. I felt torn into ragged tatters.'

Shala moved closer. Wrasse rested her weighty head on her shoulder. She gulped down spittle, beginning again. 'My sisters cursed the smell. They couldn't look at me, even when they'd said sorry. They wept for Sea Angel. *They* wanted him. They blamed me, but I wouldn't speak.' She locked her mouth tight like an oyster, showing disdain for her sisters.

'Coutou took me aside. "I want to speak to you Wrasse, but tomorrow," she said.' Wrasse raised herself from the bed and shifted forward under the heightening roof. She tugged at loose strands of thatch, twisting them twixt her wry fingers. To Shala she seemed taller and moved with a flow that was absent before. The floor creaked as she made for a low stool. She took bannock from Quernstone's trug. 'Useful woman, Quernstone is,' Wrasse remarked. 'Always there with a bit of baking.' Like the oyster, she closed her lips over the crumbs, ruminating.

'Coutou returned. She'd seen the scratches on my back and described them. "Your wounds are a sign," she told me. "I have thought long about them." "What do they mean?" I asked. "It's a totem, like the Star on his forehead and the one under his navel." I wanted to cry, but nothing came. My throat was dry, my eyes stung.' Wrasse sniffed; her eyes moistened; tears welled; she wiped them away.

Wrasse rested her head on Shala's shoulder, remembering, imagining Weir's arm round her for the first time, since then having always shrugged her feelings off. 'I never forgot Weir, though. Gravel knew. He understood. He knew he was not my true love. We said nothing. We got on with our lives when we moved to Lee Holme from Tarmin all those years ago.'

Wrasse suddenly shook herself. 'Coutou said, "Can I make you a goose tattoo there, from the marks?" I agreed, even if I couldn't see them. "I'll make a slate sketch in case the scratches fade, so l can start tomorrow." Then Coutou asked me something else. "I want to cut into the Sea Angel's chest. Can I?" she asked. "Why ask me?" I responded. She said the loveliest words I ever heard. "He was yours, dear to you, even though you did not know who he was, or where he was from." I lost my breath again in sheer emotion. All I could do was nod agreement. Then I tugged her sleeve hard. She waited until I could tell her. I *did* know who he was! And where he came from. He told me his name. It was Weir. I told him mine. "You know where he was from?" she asked, amazed. I told her, from Naaarwaaarl. I wept again inside, shaking. Please don't tell my sisters! He was mine! But only for an instant. It was private: just between him and me. Coutou agreed. "Wrasse," she said, "it will be absolutely secret. Not even a sparrow will ken."

'She prayed for me. She fondled her necklace, which had a small phallus amulet dangling. She stroked it as she prayed. "It could help your baby, if you took one from him. Here, kiss it." I did. Then I told her, "Cut into his chest. It's like saying goodbye."'

'Why did Coutou want to open Weir's chest?' Shala asked.

'Because she was a real healer. She knew how people worked inside.'

'Did she find out what had happened?'

'Yes, Shala.' Wrasse fell silent, pulling herself together, saying, 'Coutou told me he'd been stabbed through his arm and into his ribs. The weapon pierced his ribcage, damaging his lung. Weir must have pulled it out, but the tip splintered off and lodged. He might have recovered but for that.' Wrasse waited. 'Shala, I think of this so often. If only things had been slightly different.' Wrasse's shoulders shook. 'Coutou showed me the tiny, cruel barb. Why should such a little thing cause so much damage? "Weir's ribcage inside was poisoned,"Coutou told me. "If I had known," she went on, "I'd have tried to do something else for him. His wound outside had healed, but within he was terribly ill. I just did not know," she told me.'

Shala realized, 'That's why this woman I've known all my life has been awkward; distant. Abrupt and rough is her nature. All know her to be wise. If we dare, we ask Wrasse's advice. Sometimes she won't answer for weeks, then call round and give a few moments of her time. If she's feeling good-natured, which is seldom, she can be pleasant. But that's rare.'

Wrasse continued, 'Coutou explained that Weir probably knew he was dying, even in our embrace. "It was a good final act, wasn't it?" Coutou told me. I felt comforted. We had to make him ready for our tomb. My sisters did most of it. I was tattooed. I got to rebind his beautiful beard. It was very long and fair. I wrapped it in thin strips of red and green kidskin with a criss-cross pattern. It looked beautiful. It pulled his face tight. He looked handsome: strong. Coutou removed his stomach. She returned it to the sea. Weir, my Sea Angel, looked contented.'

Shala stood, allowing the blood to flow past her knees to her toes. She was stiff after being so still. Wrasse was more relaxed and human in Shala's company. 'When did you get the white Star put on your forehead, Wrasse?'

'I did it myself, the day he went into our Ancestor House. He had dried by then. Special people had special treatment. He was one. Coutou saw to that. I was very proud. My tattoo on my back was painful, but I knew I would carry part of him with me forever. I punctured my forehead with a needle and rubbed powdered shell in. There you are. That's it Ai-Shala. Question time is over.' Wrasse's lips shut like an ormer: an improvement on an oyster.

Wrasse stood and went to the centre of their room. In the high rafters, dowels held hams and hanging baskets of stores. They caught the gathering smoke high above their heads. The awning leathers were pegged temporarily onto the rising rafters. Further back, in the dimness of their mezzanine, a wicker wall separated them from further rooms, accessible from other steps rising from below.

'This great house is to be shared by many whilst the initial rebuilding of Lee Holme lasts,' Wrasse pondered aloud. 'It will be the centre of organization and communal living. I need privacy, but with a place of vantage, too. This is an ideal point, but it is not private. For the moment we've been left alone, but life for the village will go forward. Soon the house will be full.

'Shala, I want you to ask for a partition to be erected at the edge of our floor, with a door at the head of our ladder. The screens from the shadow theatre will do. They will let in light. Behind them, I will feel secure from public gaze.'

'I will ask Dad now.' She tripped down their log steps to her family in the bright outside. Partan returned from the menhir and watched the progress of the stone sorting.

'Dad, can I speak to you?'

'Shortly,' he replied. The busy noises of scraping stone and creaking timbers were all around. Jasper pulled at a long rafter from Quernstone's dwelling. Dale was up there, easing it down. The whole end needed rebuilding. Other parts of the house were weakened by the storm and slumped with age. Kull's temper had exposed much that was symptomatic of Lee Holme's predicament.

'It's okay, Dad. It can wait,' realizing he was too busy. So was everyone else. Juniper was under the dusty eaves further along Quernstone's home, bundling up the thatch staves. Some would be useful, others firewood. Flint shifted armfuls of reed to the rear of the house and built a stack: 'Good for animal bedding, compost or firing pots,' he thought.

Shala stepped over the piles of timbers. They were slowly being organized. She passed the doorway and spoke to Juniper. 'Wrasse is getting much better, but she would like a screen for privacy. Would you help?'

Juniper stood back from her work, glaring. She cast her staves on the ground. 'That old witch? Why should I do anything for her? She's got you right where she wants you. Companion, eh?' Shala knelt to pick the wood up; Juniper kicked it away. 'She will have you running around like a worker bee. Not me. I'll sort wood, just like anyone, but don't ask me to lift a finger for the old sow. I washed her and cleaned her, combed her wretched hair. What thanks did I get?' she uttered, flinging her fists in the air and stamping off.

Shala stood shocked. She felt like running to her mother. She looked around for her. She was at Quartz's home talking earnestly with Quernstone and Tangle. 'I will leave it be.'

Flint sprinted round from the stack, noticing Shala's hurt expression. 'What's up, Sha?' he chirped as he climbed to loosen thatch from its pegs.

'Up there, I see how tall he's become. It's strange not to have noticed before. It's the way he stands on the sagging stonework stretching, pulling at the twine,' she realized, before saying, 'I asked Juniper's help with something for Wrasse. She lashed her tongue at me as though I was some vile whelp. What have I done to upset her?'

'Jealousy. Jealousy,' he jibed. 'She's furious that you are looking after her and not she. She's done nothing but stamp about being hard done by, all day.'

'Oh,' Shala said.

'And she's mad about your visions and the fuss folk are making of them.' A couple of stones slid from the wall under him. He shifted, 'She can't say it to them, but I've had to listen to her going on and on.' He adjusted his foothold, 'Here, catch these,' he pulled out a series of thatch pegs, allowing a sheaf to come away. 'The wall looks pretty sound past the doorway. This end of the house took the most damage.' He bent to look along the line of the walling. 'I reckon it would only need packing here and there to keep it right. No need to take it all down. But I reckon the whole roof has shifted. It needs a new one.' He sniffed and whipped the back of his hand under his nose, running it down his tight breeks. 'What did Wrasse want, anyway?'

'She just wants a screen at the edge of her apartment for privacy.'

'What kind of screen?'

'The shadow show ones would do.'

'Where are they?' he asked, as he looked again at the roof.

'Probably in the back, where the awning was.'

'Okay, Shala. Grab a bundle of the thatch pegs and I will see what we can do.' He heard Rod's voice singing away whilst he was hammering a wedge to split a trunk. Flint called him. Rod came loping over the debris.

'Hello, Shala. Off duty for a moment?' he asked cheerily, wiping his sweaty brow.

Shala smiled at the friendly reaction. 'Yes and no. I need help, Flint will explain.'

'Rod. Grab an armful of those pegs and follow me.'

They entered the house and looked up. Wrasse peered down imposingly, but Shala knew her enough not to be perturbed. She ran up the steps and began clearing where the screen was to be. Flint and Rod went to the back store, carrying a lamp. Bundles of wool and baskets of grain along with piles of dried cow manure fuel were stored there, some of it years old. Mice scurried at the sight of the flickering wick.

The tight screens hung on hazel pegs in the rafters. They took them down, the stretched skin drum-like under their fingertips. They carried several through and up. Flint nodded his respects as he proceeded to bang in a line of pegs into a convenient split in the beam. Others, he poked into the thatch. Using grass twine, he and Rod secured the skin frames in a line, up to the centre post. 'There, Wrasse, he said. Flimsy, but adequate.'

'Flimsy enough and adequate. Thank you.' She looked at the youths without a smile, but her face showed gratitude.

Shala rearranged the room so they could see down from one side. Gull returned. 'Okay, up there?' she called.

'Fine,' Shala replied. 'Do you want help?'

'Please, Shala. I need the fire made up. Quernstone and I have organized the feeding of us lot over the next weeks. I have plenty to do.'

Shala ran down and arranged wood. Juniper returned, scowling, but said nothing. Quernstone arrived with rising dough in flat baskets. Tangle had dried fish to soak. Slowly, the house filled up as the sounds of work outside diminished. The warmth of people below was pleasing to Wrasse, though strange to her. She sat on her bed, thinking.

25

Partan's Rule

Partan donned his finery. He took his black-banded stone mace from his polished auroch-hide chest. It had a splendid ash handle inlaid with mother of pearl lozenges. He clicked open the side-catches on its seductively shiny birchwood presentation case. He smelt its glistening protective oil in the padded box. It was the new egg-shaped style, slightly waisted along its length. It had never been used in anger. Its most violent use was for sacrificing. With it, he would clout a wooden stake smartly into the victim's skull. This spike was affectionately called the Third Horn. This was such a day.

Gull was on his left as they entered the courtyard. The timbers were now ordered into neat stacks. Extra trunks were piled where Wrasse's home had stood. Quernstone and Reaper's house was just a heap of rubble. Only the doorjambs remained. Four postholes had been dug to receive the much taller uprights.

The day was bright but chilly. Gull's hair was swept tightly up in a bun and stuck with vast bone pins. Long, spiralling earrings of silver birch bark swung at every move. Juniper looked her best. Her long red hair glinted like dark amber to hang over her dyed suede waistcoat.

Jasper stood behind Partan, holding two measuring poles. The top feathered tassels flicked in the slight breeze. Flint followed with a polished mallet. Its head swung just at the hem of his knotted grass trousers. He enjoyed his wood-soled sandals clacking importantly on the paving.

Shala proudly held a cow horn of ceremonial springwater.

Moving forward, Dale drummed a dramatic march. Sable followed with Wrasse along the courtyard to Rod's searing goat-horn trumpeting.

The crowd cheered as Partan formally led his procession to the newly marked obelisk. It passed the central fireplace where meat roasted. Flint's heels clicked on. Juniper looked round, delighted at her admirers. Shala held her horn up high.

They arrived at the monolith. At its foot, a laden offering dish lay on the new level stone. Partan's feet and pace were clearly marked in it. His other statistics had been deeply carved in the upright: ankle height, knee, hip, shoulder, arm height above head and armpit to fingertip. The top joint of his thumb became the inch; elbow to fingertip, the cubit; and hand, a span.

The immaculately groomed goat bleated. It leapt onto the great level slab. The horny, cloven hooves made soft clicks as it skidded at the end of its tether.

Partan mounted the block and caught the animal's halter. He pulled it towards him and caressed its head, calming the beast. It stood nobly beside him during his worthy speech.

Rod blew a fanfare. The goat jumped. 'We are about to rebuild Lee Holme,' Partan boomed. 'A new future is before us.' Quartz initiated wild applause. 'It will be hard labour, made easier by the knowledge that we will have improved, modern dwellings. Our new standard measures are taken from me, your leader. The plans we've drawn up are good. We can get on, house by house, knowing exactly what we intend to have as finished structures. We have new ideas of construction. Different designs too, which are adaptable to our new conditions and requirements,' he paused for applause. The goat bleated, the crowd cheered. 'As we have the gift from the great wide ocean of the many tall trees, as Shala predicted, we can build far higher. Our new postholes will hold the trees' tops. The root stubs above will spread out high up. Our locking timbers can spring from there. Our walls will be taller. We will have more living space and extra floor levels.'

All applauded, largely because beer skins had emerged from Tangle's surviving malting room.

'Our eaves will reach further out. The paths beneath will be raised slightly. Drains can be laid under the eaves drip. This will keep outside stores dryer; our houses, too. Conforming to our new measures, we'll know exactly where the eaves come to. Headroom and wall heights will be standard.' He yearned to continue, but the cheering grew so loud he finished on this high note.

Partan called on Shala. She mounted the slab to pour her libation into the lines of Partan's feet and splash the monolith.

Partan gripped the pointed Third Horn. The goat looked up to him as he removed his magnificent mace from his belt. It gazed trustingly into his eyes. Its lips parted in a bleat. It reached to lick water from Partan's footmarks.

Flint drew close and raised its head. Partan held the stake between its eyes. With one smart blow the animal collapsed, writhing. The clatter of its flaying hooves echoed from the stone. They hobbled it and hung him from Vacar's Spear. Partan slit its throat with a swipe from his axe. Blood gushed.

Shala and Partan left the dais, leading the procession to the building site. They stood at the brightly painted doorjambs. Between was a spread of clay slurry. For luck, Quernstone placed five scones there. Jasper and Quartz edged a huge slab, laying the new threshold. The scones flattened. Flint proudly handed the mallet to Partan. He knelt in his finery and tapped the flagstone into position. After he held the mallet high above, shouting, 'We have begun!' The assembly roared. It was time for the pork feast.

Wrasse retired. She listened to the revelry from her eerie. The hubbub of drumming, hornpipes, singing, laughter, joking and storytelling gave her a feeling of wellbeing.

Gull saw to Partan's comfort, ensuring his bed was ready. She tossed his straw mattress, placing it back on the hip-height planks that were wedged between stone uprights. She fluffed his linen eiderdown. She closed his regalia kist. His ornate fire-making set, ceremonial sickle and sculpted stones saw the light of dark under his bed.

Partan celebrated, leading the singing and praising their new plans. At last, Shala climbed the log ladder to join Wrasse. Juniper came in later to take warmer clothes from hangers by her inset, stalled bunk bed. Above her, Flint had his bed. His wooden platform lay across the tops of the uprights. From it hung a curtain to shut out the light from Juniper's bed.

Shala's looked across to Wrasse. The parchment panels glowed yellow in the light from the fire below.

Much later, Partan staggered in with Quartz, trying to be quiet. 'I've got something for us in my chest.' He fumbled for his shiny leather flask. 'Mead,' he said, 'For SsssssPessssscialllll occassssionsssss.' Quartz turned a log on the fire. The flask glinted. 'HEEEEeeeeer Tiss. SSSSShhhhhhhh.' He pulled the stopper. They sat on his bedside sharing it. After some sage, slurred conversation, their shoulders touched drunkenly. They slowly leaned back, slumping onto Partan's downy.

Wrasse gazed into the rafters. She imagined pigeon nests and beehives in the roofs of the new buildings, thinking, 'How convenient to have honey and eggs at hand.' She poked Shala with her stick to tell her, before forgetting. Shala watched the panels. A shadow passed across the screens. Another streaked by. She looked to Wrasse and pointed. They saw the silhouette of a goose glide over the parchment. Then another, and another. More followed.

They watched, transfixed, at the black skein arcing to land. They saw their shadows grazing and heard them gaggling. It sounded like stifled words. They gazed at each other then back to the shadow pictures. Other geese arrived. They landed, forming the shape of a man. He stood, then slowly stooped to spring into the air as a winged being. He flew off the frame, vanishing into the dark of their loft.

'SsssSHhhhh,' Wrasse said. 'We shall speak later.' With that, she drifted into a dreamful sleep. Shala lay watching as the fire glow dwindled.

'I think we will go to Char,' Wrasse decided as they woke, 'I haven't been away for years. It's time to travel.' Shala was amazed. 'Tell your mother.'

'All right,' Shala answered, and climbed down. Quartz groaned and turned over, grunting.

'Good morning,' Juniper said haughtily. 'Doing someone's bidding, are we?' she sneered.

Shala said nothing.

Gull came from her toilet. Partan groaned, making for the doorway. 'Good day, everyone,' he said blearily as he brushed by into the courtyard. 'We will have to sow soon,' he remarked abruptly.

Jasper commented, 'He's got a headache. He's always sharp when he's hung over. Then he says something obvious, to show he's in charge.' Quartz pushed by, following Partan to the dunes. Shala, too.

When she returned, Wrasse was by the fire with Gull. 'So dear, it's all arranged,' Gull said. 'You and Wrasse are going on your travels. I must say I'm envious.'

Wrasse stood, looking as though new energy came from within. 'Well. Girl, that's it. We're off soon. We'll get ready, but we're travelling light.' With that, Wrasse scaled the stair. Gull said, 'Take your bow, a fish line, fire drill and a sling.'

'I'm so delighted,' Shala thought.

Wrasse called down. 'Before we go, I must tell Partan about the beehives in the roof and the pigeon nests.' She whistled a vibrant tune over her stubby teeth, combed her hair and cleaned her gnarled nails.

26

The Travellers

'Say goodbye to Shala.'

'Okay, Mother,' Juniper whinged.

'What's up with you, girl?' Gull admonished.

'Sore throat,' she lied.

'Give her a hug, like Flint did.'

She embraced loosely. Shala responded fondly. 'Look after Grandpa, won't you, Juni?'

'And you look after our Wrasse for us. Won't you, Sister,' she replied coolly.

Shala ignored her hurtful rebuffs.

Wrasse waited outside, leaning on her stick. 'Ah. My bow and quiver; my backpack's nicely loaded. Let's go, Wrasse,' Shala said.

Jasper put his hammerstone down from tightening masonry. 'Here's a hug from my dusty hands.' He kissed Shala, saying, 'Be careful; look after yourselves.'

Partan sat on the newly scored slab, drinking cool water. 'An egg for the offering bowl,' Wrasse said.

'I wish you the happiest of tripssss,' Partan answered in an overhung slur.

'Rewarding, possibly,' Wrasse answered, 'As for happy, we'll see.'

Partan tried to make sense, then stopped. 'Give your Granddad a hug. Have a lovely time. Ignore the crone's miserable comments. Off you go. Bring me back something nice,' he whispered, smelling of stale mead.

They took the track up towards the Ancestor House on the hill. 'The onion sets survived the gale, Shala. The leeks and chives look good,' Wrasse commented, passing the neat beds.

'It'll be time to plant the beans and peas,' Shala mentioned. 'I like it when the autumn nasturtiums trail over dykes, too.'

'Yes, everything seems good when it all grows. We'll need loads of barley and bere for beer. It's coming up. All will be fine, let's hope.'

They reached the lochan. 'I was so small when I first rafted across. It looked huge! I know the Ancestor Tales by heart now. I'll punt; you lean on the rail, Wrasse.'

'Look, Shala, mallards feigning injury to draw us from their nests. We're not fooled,' Wrasse called out to them.

'Watch the landing slip, Wrasse. It's slimy. Careful; I'll follow in your footmarks.'

'That spring's like our boxed-in one at home,' Wrasse explained. 'The slate leat takes the water to the lochan from the back of the tomb. I'll tell you more, later.' They followed the mossy pathway to their monolith. Meadowsweet grew at its foot. Small ornamental irises showed their spikes. A swathe of blooming primroses faced the sun. To their left, high islands looked back at Lee Holme across the blue grey ocean.

'It pongs of fish, here.'

'Yes, that's the sea eagles. There's one taking off: his partner's on the nest. It's a good omen if they brood up in our resting shelves.'

'That was an ear-piercing squawk!'

'The males do that warning when leaving the nest.'

The brooding eagle watched them cross the natural arena in front of the tomb. It sloped gradually down then swooped upwards, cutting out the sounds of the sea. They felt the breakers crashing onto the cliffs below. The strange fissures in the rocks reached down like sinews, carrying the vibrations to their feet.

Seabirds wheeled noisily from the rise at the high cliff face. An oily smell of gull manure wafted. Sea pinks bloomed. Bees were busy. 'We are where the screens stood under the awning,' Shala remarked. 'It all looks so different: the great cooking hearth is just cold, reddened earth and stones. Large broken bowls lay strewn and a cloven cup's become a beetle's nest. Rain-washed bones and shells lay scattered. I remember the nights we spent here,' she said, observing the stone sockets for the awning poles protruding above the packed gravel and paving of the forecourt. Stuck in one was Dale's tangle drumbeater. The whole scene came alive.

Wrasse prised at the door slab with her stick. 'I'll help, Wrasse. Wait,' Shala called.

'Too late. No need.' The flagstone slid smoothly on its pork-fat greased edge. It stopped by a stone lamp, the solidified fuel pecked away by birds.

'I'll go first,' Wrasse bent stiffly. Ahead was a skin curtain, like a divided membrane. She probed her way through. It closed behind her. Shala noticed her own shadow cast upon its dotted design of flying eagles in manganese and ochre.

Shala pushed through, sensing the bird's talons. Deep inside, she stood. 'It's surprisingly warm,' she remarked.

'I'll brighten up the brazier,' Wrasse said. 'Hand me that bone blower. Watch.' She placed the hollow femur at a tiny hole in a rough clay bowl. The smouldering charcoal sparked in the darkness, then flamed. 'Light this big whelk shell lamp from it, Shala.' She held the spiralled end and the wick caught.

'It's amazing, Wrasse,' Shala said as the light brightened. 'The stonework's beautiful, so tightly laid. This rush mat has our zigzag pattern. Those digger sticks are gigantic. They're wonderfully painted. There's so much in here: bows and arrows. Oh, what lovely antler points! Look, a huge sickle with scallop shell blades to reap eternal barley. There's the laden grain basket. I'll light this candle. See the marvellous corbelling?'

Shadowy figures appeared in the flickering light. Even the warmth from the charcoal burner did not stop a shivering chill run down Shala's spine.

'My toe's touched something,' she said in trepidation. She peered down to a withered foot and followed it to drooping clothing. Staring back were the sunken eye sockets of a shrivelled face. A withered headband of braided leather stretched around the protruding bone forehead. One eagle feather leaned from the rigid, upright corpse. A crispy ear held a dangling hooped ring of shell. Shala turned abruptly, facing Wrasse.

'It's all right, young lady,' Wrasse said softly. 'These are our ancestors. There are many here. This is Flounder. Do you remember him? He was the Tomb Warden. He kept the charcoal smouldering. Every day he'd come here. Now it's Wheat Germ's task, until it's her time to push Flounder aside.'

Shala fell silent. 'I've oft wondered what it's like inside the Ancestor House.' She moved further in, conscious of more figures leaning against the other side of the tomb in eternal stillness. The tallow melted, the light swelled around her. The smell of roasting pork filled the still air.

'There's another. She's a redhead. Look at her old straw hat. Her eyes are so deep and her nose has gone beaky. But she seems familiar.'

'She's your grandmother. She died before you were born. She has your features. Partan misses her still. He comes here, asking her advice. Look, there's fresh oyster shells. There's her bone amulet. You can touch it, Shala.'

She stroked the decorated plaque. Pierced shells hung above it on her linen shroud. 'I remember now: Mum told me how she'd played with it when she was little. Her reed shoes could do with mending. See how her toes stick out. What long nails!'

'Yes, Shala, nails and hair grow after death. I don't know why. Look at her crossed wrists bound with meadowsweet. You can see how hard she worked.'

'Why's that dark, figure-like plank leaning between those folk? The forehead's painted with red dashes?'

'That's Gravel,' Wrasse said quietly. 'We never found his body. I made this effigy with my last son before he left to find a mate. We placed him here on Lost Souls' Day.'

'Oh, look at the children,' Shala said sadly. 'They're squatting at the feet of the adults. Some have gone to skeletons. She's still got skin on her legs. Look, Wrasse, there's their dolls and perishing farm animals. It's so sad. I remember Stag. He died of fever. I can't see him; I don't want to look.'

'I'm sorry, too, Shala. It's sad, but the others look after them and their spirits.' Shala stood on their felt carpet to pray quietly for them. 'Behind Gravel's statue, Shala, is a chamber. I'll light a candle stub. Can you lean Gravel to one side? Mind those bones on the floor. Inside you'll see a huge heap of very, very old bones.' They knelt together.

'Gosh, Wrasse, how they glow. Look at all those skulls on top.'

'These are the Past Ones. You see, we are all on a journey. In worldly life we live. In worldly life we die. Life is a journey and, when our mortal flesh dies, we begin another life.' She paused while Shala took her words in. 'That journey begins when we leave these lives we are living now. Our bodies alter and our spirits begin to dissipate. When it is time, some of us are taken here. In this building we slowly fall apart. That is all part of the journey.' Wrasse hid her feelings at seeing Gravel again, particularly when remembering their sons. 'Later these bodies will be jumbled in here. Then, there will be space for others to begin their journey. When the bones are piled in, they mingle as one spirit to leave together gently over the years, becoming new again as they seep out. They will flow from the spring behind the Ancestor House and trickle into the Lochan of Spirits, then begin again. We do not know when that will be. It's for them to decide.'

Wrasse stood and put her candle by a body propped in a corner. 'Look, Bristle's leg's fallen across this recess. Have you heard of him, Shala?'

'He was my great, great grandfather. A chief, like Partan.'

'That's right. And on the other side is your great grandfather, Skerry.'

'I like Bristle's limpet eyes. But his head's about to drop off, like his poor leg.'

'He was a wonderful singer; see his tiny throat bones. I'll hold the candle.'

'His hair's just like Partan's, Wrasse: thick and ginger round the sides and quite bald on top. His otter cloak's the same, too, but for the eagle talons down the side. Hello, Bristle,' Shala said softly. 'I'm your great, great granddaughter. You must have been very fond of fish, judging by all those bones over your toes. And fruit. Look at the wrinkled apples, and prunes stuck with honeycomb.'

'See below, Shala.' Wrasse bent her stiff knees. Shala crouched at her forebears' feet. 'I'll shift Bristle's leg to peer in the chamber. Put your lamp closer, Shala.'

The waxy flame lit the low space. Eight polished skulls looked back wryly from a heap of ancient bones. In the sudden light, a vole scampered back into an eye socket to protect its nest of naked young within.

'They, Shala, are other past leaders and their consorts. You wouldn't think those dead bones had children who are dead now, would you?' Wrasse's flame flickered on the ossuary as she explained, 'It was the wives who really ruled. You will find that out. We do still govern things, though. Men can be manipulated; it suits us that way. Bristle will go in there when Partan enters through the portal. But before then, Partan will come here for guidance when he does not know what to do. That is when he decides to do what us females have hinted to him. That's the way.'

Bristle's wife crumbled on the opposite wall and Skerry's first and second spouses, who had limpet shell necklaces, were propped up on her. At their feet was a sealskin rug.

'It is getting very full, isn't it, Wrasse?' Shala remarked. 'There's the leather tube holding Longo's femur. Next to it's the staff, an auroch leg and a long horn.

'Indeed it is, Shala. I expect when Lee Holme is finished we will need to tidy it all up and extend the other way. It has been spoken about. We may even build an additional sepulchre.

'Before we go, let's stand holding hands, feeling the still of the inner world. It's so different from outside; it's as if it doesn't exist. There's a sacred security within. It's part of us and we are part of it.'

Wrasse then surprised Shala, asking, 'Would you blow the horn? I'm sure the ancestors would love it.'

'Is that all right?' Shala asked.

'Perfectly.'

She lifted it, blowing sideways into the mouthpiece. A long, clear, vibrating note rang.

'Strike the uprights with the leg bone. It makes a wonderful sound, enough to wake the dead, as they say.'

'May I?' Shala asked swinging the dented tibia against an upright, which was chipped with eternal percussion. A huge resounding crack rang through the mummy house. But the vast shin splintered in Shala's hands. 'Oh no! That's done it,' she remarked, shocked.

Wrasse, surprised, picked a shard from her hair. 'I think it was ready to fall apart. After all, it *was* very old.'

They crawled back into daylight. Shala swung her backpack over her shoulder, strapping it across her chest, enhancing her breasts. The eagle's mate swooped in with a flapping fish as they left.

'I'm going to the smokehouse,' Shala said, 'I've never been in it yet.' The cliff walk took them to the tall, round building. Its pointed thatched roof was storm damaged. The smell of old, tarry smoke hung in the air. They looked through the narrow doorway into the wattle structure. The central fire was cold. Up in the rafters, a wide smoke-blackened lattice platform spread. 'Up there is where the dead lie for curing, isn't it?'

'Yes, but no one's at home presently,' Wrasse observed. 'Let's go, Shala, lest we get morbid.'

'I'm not morbid, I'm interested. Sorry about breaking the bone clapper, though.'

'Never mind, we'll get another.'

27

Walking

They walked along the old clifftop sheep path. The crossing byways of red deer went up to wooded slopes. They grazed in the distance, one with a watchful eye. Below, goat clappers clacked as they scaled a crag of bramble and scrub, following their goatherd, Cullen. She was their deity in flesh. Folk said she could become one. Whatever the truth, goats always did her bidding, never straying into crops until after harvest.

They reached a higher, deserted plain. The sheep path was dry underfoot, but either side changed to marsh grass and bog cotton. A harrier swooped, catching a vole for its brood.

Across the marsh were islands of dogwood, willow and elder. Mixed woodlands of pine and birch grew on dryer ground with hornbeam and rowan. There, the hinds dropped their fawns.

The ridge of land widened. They walked side by side again. Shala had been thinking of Wrasse and how it must have felt not to be with the one she loved. She had a burning question.

'Wrasse, I need to ask something.'

'Go on.'

'It's difficult, but did you get a baby from Weir?'

'I wondered when you'd ask, Ai... Shala,' covering her mistake with a snort. 'I'll tell you.' Shala watched Wrasse's staff swing with their pace. It was something to focus on whilst the tale unfolded.

'Yes, I did begin a child. I felt so lucky. I kept it secret from my jealous sisters. I wanted privacy. Only Coutou knew. I stayed with Coutou; her excuse, doing extra tattoos. She fed me special things and explained her lore. That time with her was the best I can remember. I'd had a terrible loss. She helped me grieve. I had my baby to look forward to. That was a huge solace for me.

'Eventually I told my family. My sisters chided me. My mother wouldn't speak to me. I heard her say, "She stole the child from him". My older sister, Fernfold, should have bred with Sea Angel when he was better.' She lost her pace in agitation. Shala held her elbow.

'Fernfold was to be married, but fresh blood was essential. Her future man was willing to be a father in name and have others with her. Such was the way. My father tried to sort everything out. Nobody listened. I was mourning for Weir's death. I could not bear that. So I went back to Coutou. They were happy to be rid of me... and I happy to be rid of them.' The ridge widened, the sheep paths diverged. The tooth-clipped grass either side broadened into a low berm. Skylarks rose, singing their shrill choruses.

'I was fine, fit and happy. Then I got sick; my head ached terribly. Coutou gave me her birch bark drink to ease my pain, and potions for sickness. Then others in Tarmin fell ill. I weakened. Some died. Coutou rushed around, doing what she could. I was recovering when I felt the terrible pains. I screamed out. Not for me, but for my little child.'

'Let's sit on those rocks,' Shala suggested.

'Not yet. Walking, swinging my stick helps,' she said, 'I don't want to blubber again. This moss underfoot sooths, too.

'I was losing my baby. I tried preventing the contractions. I cried out. When someone came it was all too late. They ran for Coutou, but I knew it was over. I held my little girl and her warmth still touches me. I felt her tiny, wet body on mine and I just hugged her and wept.' Wrasse stopped and wiped her eyes.

'Please? Let's sit on that boulder,' Shala insisted.

'I can feel it all again so vividly,' Wrasse confessed, and broke down on the whale-like rock. 'When Coutou came and saw me squatting, holding my lost daughter, she was distraught. She cleaned me and washed my baby. I was frozen in shock, Shala.'

Wrasse looked at the hills sloping into the centre of their land. An observant stag peered back from across the marsh.

'I called her Dilly. Only you know that.' The stag raised its head and sauntered towards a distant stand of trees. Wrasse stood. They strolled on. The wanderers said nothing, just walking in understanding.

The slight incline took them to high pastures. Old sheep droppings lined the route. Moss gave to grasses and spring flowers. Larks sang on high. From there they could see the broad sea and small islands, diminishing into the distance. 'Look,' Shala whispered, 'mushrooms.'

'Good,' Wrasse thought silently.

'They smell so fresh. I love the touch of the skin. That yellow tinge of the big ones. The buttons are like great, white eggs. Wrasse, can you look in my caisie for the leather bag? It's probably at the bottom.'

'You've got a lot of stuff in here, girl,' Wrasse was able to say, picking through the varied contents.

'Porters go best loaded.'

'Here it is. Let's pick. These spring beauties are scarce, but wonderful,' Wrasse managed. 'We can take what's left to Char.'

'I'll clean the soil off the stems. You pick, I'll pack, Wrasse.'

'I'm leaving the tiny ones to grow and multiply,' Wrasse said, allowing her feelings to abate. 'I'll carry them too, Shala. Old hags go even better loaded.'

The pair giggled for the first time.

'The horizon gets further and further away,' Shala complained as another ridge came into view.

'Patience,' Wrasse puffed, pointing out old auroch dung. 'There it is,' she announced later, 'Shelter, and none too soon. Rain clouds are creeping over. Put a step in it,' Wrasse urged.

'Good,' Shala thought. 'She can walk fast when she wants. That staff of hers is really banging along.' Then Shala saw the garriot; the sheep path fanned out before the door.

'What's she doing?' Shala wondered, 'She's stooping oddly at the entrance to the corbelled hut.'

'I'll just bend and squeeze through,' Wrasse thought.

Shala watched. 'She's left the mushroom bag outside. Her backside's blocked the little door. Now it's jerking wildly. What's she up to? What's that cracking sound? She's yelling!' Shala dropped her caisie and ran, bow at the ready.

'Gotcha!' Wrasse shouted as her stick whacked the wall.

'What are you doing?' Shala shrieked as she backed out.

'Tonight's dinner,' Wrasse proudly announced, 'Blast. Missed that one,' she cursed as a petrified pigeon escaped above her head. 'Catch. Pluck that. Freshly killed pigeons are easy. It's a good place to stop, too. Over there is marsh with a rickety duckboard pathway. There's a handrail to help old folk like me across. I hope it's intact. It's years since I was up here. Let's go inside.'

'It's dark, but we'll get used it. There's a little fireplace. It's like ours. Look, crooks against the wall. There's a sheep-fat candle by the door. Would you light it?' asked Wrasse.

'I'll dig out my fire-bow and anvil. There's tinder and dried dung piled at the back.'

'I'm unrolling these sheepskins onto the mossy bed ledge. They'll cover most of the pigeon shit.'

'The tinder's smoking,' Shala reported as her arm whirled her bow.

'Two more,' Wrasse shouted. 'They've been hiding. Watch this.' She clobbered one with a hunk of firewood as they flew off. 'Two each,' she chuckled triumphantly.

The fire blazed. The interior gained a comforting glow. 'I'll clean out those mouldy old bowls in that niche,' Shala offered.

'Yes, Shala, they could do with a good burning,' Wrasse said as she left to pluck the birds.

The mould in the bowls wilted from powdery blue to a pale crust as Shala watched them heat. 'The fat from sheep stews is melting and pooling in the rounded bottoms. Hmmmmmm... The smell of the last meal's wonderful,' she thought, watching fat sizzle. 'Meat remnants slide from the sides, collecting in the fat. It won't be long. That aroma is wonderful. I'll mop them out with moss. Now the bowls smoke, I'll get embers in them. There's a ram's shoulder bone. Two loads of that and we'll be fine. A handful sticks, a quick blow, and that will fire them out nicely.'

'Shala, outside there is a spring covered by a flagstone to keep the sheep out. Would you fill a bowl from it?' Wrasse called whilst pulling wing feathers.

'They're too hot. I'm burning them out. I'm coming for the mushroom bag. Wrasse, you're smothered in feathers! They're everywhere. I'll empty the bag,' she said laughing loudly. She shifted the stone. Two coupling toads floated on the surface. 'Excuse me,' Shala whispered whilst carefully dipping the bag into the water. The toad beneath flexed its hind legs. They glided slowly away.

'First it's mushrooms, poached with sorrel. I picked it while you staunched the pots. Then seared pigeon breasts. The carcasses can simmer overnight for breakfast, Shala. How's that?'

'The gods have provided, haven't they. I'll search the caisie... there's Quernstone's oatmeal to thicken our broth; she's wonderful.'

'Looks like we have all anyone can desire, Shala.'

'I'll tip the ashes out and we can get cooking. I love the smell of young mushrooms as they simmer.'

The clouds moved by and the late afternoon became pleasant. The old friend and the young stood outside, leaning against neatly coursed walling. 'This sunshine is delightfully unexpected. I was sure it would rain. Listen, dear, the visions we saw on the panels: what do you think?'

'Wrasse. I'm *so* glad that we saw them together. The way the skeins gathered, making a person, must symbolize something. Could it be a goose shaman?'

'It may be. It may be,' she repeated thoughtfully. 'The point is, Shala, it's only us. Others see wolves, whales, sea serpents or deer in visions, but not something as ordinary, or perhaps as special, as geese.'

'I'm certain we are brought together by this. I speak to the redshanks, or rather them to me. I'm sure they are telling me someone is coming. I've had dreams, too, with someone's face that I've never seen, except for when he appeared in the slab when you were trapped.'

'Yes, Shala. I know only too well. I had visions before Weir arrived. I think you're going to be She who beckons this new one with your mind and will. I've been obsessed by this. That's why I asked you to be my attendant and then travel with me. Walls have lugs, you know. Even with all the noise of work at Lee Holme, we would never have proper time to ourselves to talk. That's why we haven't, yet.' Wrasse scratched her itchy back against the stonework. Tiny fragments of frosted rock trickled to the ground. 'The thing with visions is, sometimes you remember clearly, and others not. Often, when you suddenly recall, the clarity returns and you have a chance to interpret them.'

'Yes. It's as though they reappear. You can hold them. I keep coming back to the first one in the spring, then a distant dream from long before. Then the night of the storm and other dreams and sudden flashes. I'm convinced someone is coming over the ocean. A new Sea Angel. I feel it. I'm sure of it. As I look over the land to the distant sea horizon, I know it's all connected to geese. That's why we are here together. I know it. I know it, Wrasse.'

'Shala. I'll guide and help you. I will advise you, knowing what I know. I will speak to others for you when required. I will teach you to be strong. How to deal with situations that you will *have* to go through.'

Shala looked into her old eyes, accepting the words. 'I feel my future is unfolding: I need you. I have to learn to cope with this destiny. I believe someone else is doing just that in a faraway place. I have to make this happen, even though it seems to have begun. Weir was lost, Wrasse. I must not allow *my* Sea Angel to be. He's precious to me, and invaluable to our people.'

In Wrasse's eyes, Shala thought she saw a minute goose flying deep in her pupils. Wrasse saw similar in Shala's. She knew that the young woman before her had taken in and understood what her future was. What the importance of her life would be. That she was prepared to take on the huge responsibilities before her. That she would need immense strength and dignity: that there was no other way.

Shala nodded very gently, slowly resting her forehead on Wrasse's breast. Tears welled from Wrasse's eyes. She held Shala's head tight, where Dilly had been all those decades before. She caressed Shala's hair, feeling fulfilment. Her throat ached with emotions she had never imagined feeling.

Swifts wheeled above them, a grouse called, plover picked around on the pasture. In the distance a long lowing could be heard. Shala and Wrasse were aware of none of these. They stood together, not wishing to break their moment of understanding.

'I smell the mushrooms, Shala. We had better eat,' Wrasse said, gently breaking the spell. Shala nodded against her breast. They moved apart, but still emotionally together.

Wrasse turned to the door. They ate in silence, but the rich flavours of the fungi and sorrel remained with them the rest of their lives.

'I'm glad I told you about my life, Shala,' Wrasse confessed, biting into a pigeon's breast. 'It's made everything so much easier. I can remember now without that sense of loss. What I had was actually a gift. I didn't realize it until now. This is why I can help and guide you. You may well have people against you, Shala. Jealous ones, cheats.'

'Like Juniper?'

'Is that so, Shala?'

'Well, she's jealous. She hates you.'

'How do you know?'

'She's horrible about you. Flint says she's jealous because I was chosen and not her to be with you.'

'Well. Well. Silly young lady she is. What did you say to her?"

'Nothing. I never rise to her when she gets like that. It is not wise.'

'That's quite right, Shala, there is nothing better to put someone in their place than that. Just treat her with the respect you would expect for yourself.'

'What if she continues?'

'Ask her to share doing something important, whether you need to or not. Then see.'

'That sounds good. I'll ask her to wash between your toes.'

'No you will not!' Wrasse laughed.

'Let's cook more breasts, Wrasse. It's lovely up here: just us, in the shepherds' hut, cooking with the evening drawing in.

'Yes. But it's about to rain. Light another lamp. I'll shut down the hide curtain from the lintel.'

Directly, the hailing downpour beat a rattling tune on the skin.

28

Auroch Escapade

'I slept so well. And you, Wrasse?' Shala whispered.

'Yes,' she yawned, 'Not even a dream.'

'After yesterday I understand so much more. I feel prepared.'

'Good. That's the way. It's very dark in here: just the beam from the capstone up there.'

'I don't want to move.'

'The fire will need seeing to, if we want breakfast.'

'Why are we whispering?'

'You started it, Shala.'

'We could have it cold and suck the bones?'

'I'm going back to sleep.'

'Me, too. But why's it so dark? There's not even a blink coming from the door.' Wrasse drifted off and dreamt of that frightening auroch chasing her from the sunken tank. 'I need a pee,' she thought as she reawakened. 'My old bones ache. It's still pitch dark. Why? What's that sound? Shala,' she whispered, 'Are you awake?'

'Just... What's up?'

'Can you hear that?'

'It sounds like hefty breathing.'

'Sssssssshhhhhhhh, Shala, I have a terrible feeling. Where's my staff? Don't move.' She got onto her knees and crawled to the leather hanging.

'Be careful,' Shala warned.

'Fuck it!.. Fuck, fuck, and fuck it!' she swore under her breath. 'It's a bloody great auroch.'

Shala shook. 'How are we going to get out?'

'Not bloody easily. It's not good. We will just have to wait until it moves.'

'How long?' Shala whispered.

'As long as piece of fucking rope, is all I can say.' Wrasse swore uncouthly, feeling at her age it did not matter. 'I'm notorious for frankness and shortness of tongue,' she remembered. 'We will just have to wait. There's nothing else for it. Keep bloody calm. Aurochs can go absolutely crazy if roused. They may look bulky and slow, but they are quick and agile. So keep still and quiet.'

'But I need to pee, Wrasse.'

'Me, too. We had better do it in the back, far from the door.'

'I need to poo, too.'

'So do bloody I.'

'But what about the stink?' Shala asked.

'That's the problem. If it smells us, it could get upset.'

'What if we do it quickly and cover it with ashes?'

'Good thinking. Get some ready. That will stop the stink. We can wipe with this moss.'

'Okay, let's get it over with. You go first, Wrasse. I'll get the ash ready.'

Wrasse pulled up her twisted flax skirt and squatted, saying, 'AAhhhhhhh. That's better.' Then the farts began.

'SssssssssHhhhhh,' Shala urged.

'Can't help it,' Wrasse whispered in relief.

'Here's a wad of moss.'

'Quick. Cover it, before the reek rises.' Shala rapidly tipped a bowlful over the steaming stools.

'Your turn, Shala.'

'I've lost the urge,' she whispered, then, 'Oh no I haven't. Fill the bowl, Wrasse.' She pulled her plaited grass skirt up over her back and crouched too. Her pee soaked into Wrasse's ash pile. 'I can't do anything else,' she said. 'It can wait.'

The auroch's breathing changed. She lifted her head, sniffing the air. She moved a leg. Her glistening tawny and snow-white fur shone. Light then penetrated the dark cell. The occupants froze. Shala's armpits drenched. She closed them by her sides, stopping her scent.

The huge beast let out a long, loud bellow. Inside, the noise was enormous. She arched her head back. Her long, curved horns scraped the drystone wall alarmingly. Then she dropped her head onto the churned ground. The thud vibrated through the stone floor. Her great horns lifted wearily again as she moved her front hoof from the door. She eased her shoulders forward, allowing light to pass through the drape. The great cow knelt on her knees. Her hips rolled forward. Her rear rose as her front legs straightened. She shook, bellowing violently. Her eyes boggled, her cheek muscles undulated as she readied herself for another huge roar.

Wrasse and Shala shivered in silence. The beast scraped the earth at the doorway. Then light streamed in below her as the curtain slipped. They smelt her strong bovine breath.

The animal moved, scanning the land for hunters. Her suspicions were roused. Her wet muzzle dribbled a great candle of mucus. It stank of ruminated grass. She moved from the door. Her tail swished at the hide hanging, beating like thunder at the doorjamb.

'I'm scared,' Wrasse's whispered. Her eyes bulging like those of the great cow.

'I'm terrified!' Shala answered, clenching her arms down tighter, stopping sweat erupting.

The auroch's vast tail swished, dragging their flimsy drape from its frail fastening. Light flooded in.

They froze against the back of their stone prison. All thoughts of a future fled. They knew the beast was powerful enough to demolish their hideaway, if crazed.

From between its hind legs they glimpsed its full udder. Runnels of blood and dribbling slime issued from her behind. It daubed their doorjambs in red and pink splotches.

'She's about to drop a calf,' Wrasse whispered. 'She will be at her most dangerous directly she has. We can't escape through her legs. It would be suicide.'

The pregnant auroch scrutinized the pasture. The sun broke on a slight rise. The grass looked inviting there. She moved slowly towards it for a better view, looking out for any threat. She liked that high plain, close to the hills. She had dropped her calves there before. She knew the terrain and the people who lived down by the sea. She had lost sisters, a brother and mother to them. She was wary for her child and as anxious as any parent.

Her calf moved inside. Shala and Wrasse watched with bated breath. She made ungainly progress from their door. 'Where would she stop?' Shala wondered. 'A long way off, I hope.' They saw the cow pace carefully. She stopped, bellowing deafeningly, then moved directly away.

'Phew,' Shala exclaimed almost silently.

'Dare I breathe?' Wrasse thought.

She bellowed again, telling her widespread family she was about to drop her infant.

'She's not gone far enough,' Wrasse murmured. 'See the calf's feet, emerging from her behind?'

'Yes, indeed,' Shala signalled, then watched the glistening legs appear before the calf suddenly slid onto the grass.

'Wish it was as quick for us,' Wrasse stated quietly.

The mother bent round to lick her calf.

'She's spotted us, Shala!'

She lifted her head sniffing the air. Her calf struggled to its feet, urged by her long horns.

'She's done this before,' Wrasse commented under her breath. Shala stared in wonder at the scene.

'When the calf takes its first suckle, we move, Shala. Pull your caisie on quietly, be ready to creep away.'

'Good: the calf's going along its mother's flank. She's licking afterbirth off. Look, Shala. Its mouth's open. Its tongue's searching for a teat. I hear suckling. We'll leave stealthily. I'll lead to the planked pathway. Out we go. Don't look at her, but keep an eye open. A direct glance can attract their attention. They seem to feel it.'

Shala crept like an otter. Wrasse gripped her staff as they rounded the hut. She led Shala past the well to the marshlands. 'There's the track,' she said, 'only a few yards further.'

The mother bellowed. They stood stock-still. Wrasse turned. The auroch glared, her head twisting threateningly. Her calf drew in close.

It was not the cow that froze Wrasse to the spot, but her bull, rising from directly behind the garriot.

'Run! Shala. Run!' Wrasse screamed with all her energy. 'It's my dream, but real.'

Shala fleetingly watched the bull rise to its terrifying height. 'It's scraping the ground threateningly. I must run!'

'My old legs feel they're sucked into the turf, but I must fly.' Wrasse shoved her staff to the ground, forcing hers forward. 'Shala's on the planking, thank Tuman.' Behind she heard the enraged, thundering bull. Wrasse's staff spurred her on. She drew it forward, plunged it ahead and vaulted. 'I'll get there,' she yelled.

'I must do something,' Shala knew, 'Shoot my bow. Anything!' She grabbed it; fitted an arrow. Wrasse fled towards her, stumbling. 'Pull. Shoot,' she told herself.

Wrasse scrambled up, the planking was almost within reach. The charging bull closed behind her. She got leverage on her staff to jerk along. Shala loosed her arrow. It seemed to move so slowly. Wrasse rose with the power from her pole. Shala's arrow zipped past her ear. The bone point continued towards the bull's brow. The frantic beast raised its head. The arrowhead sunk into the flaring right nostril. This did not improve its temper, but delayed his thundering long enough for Wrasse to sprawl onto the split birch boarding, hurting her ribs.

The narrow path was a mere foot and a half wide, with handrails each side. Wrasse was wedged face down between them. An arm stretched towards Shala. 'I'll save you. Hold on.' Shala gripped her hand and yanked hard, dragging Wrasse's feet from beneath the bull's flaring nostrils. The arrow snapped between Wrasse's heels.

The bull smashed into the rails, halting its angry progress. Shala pulled Wrasse to her feet. The auroch waded into the morass. They edged backwards. The beast rocked the fragile track. With a splintering crack, the planks buckled. Wrasse grabbed the wobbling hand support and they retreated. The bull spread its feet, advancing menacingly. 'I've had enough!' Wrasse screamed out. 'Taste my staff.' She stepped forward on the sinking beams. She glared into the bull's eyes. Wrasse's growl displayed her ugly mood. 'Take that!' She swung her hefty staff. The bull stopped, clouted. Their eyes met. Wrasse's plank sank into the mire. They drew even closer. The animal's vast horns swept around her. The enemies were head-to-head, feeling each other's breath. The bull backed off as Wrasse's staff rapped his horn-tips. He turned, pulled his feet from the sucking mud. He lowed to his mate, bellowed at Wrasse and stamped away.

Shala edged forward, 'Here, Wrasse, take my hand again. You are incredible.'

'Thank you, young lady. I shall. Are the mushrooms safe? If so, let's go.' She turned looking back at the nuzzling aurochs.

They stepped shakily along the elevated way towards the rising ground half a mile away. They went over young reeds, thick tussocks of bog grasses, occasional clear pools and through willow groves. The path bent, others joined. The track widened at passing places. Nobody was on the marsh way. Birdsong, amphibious croaks and the cheeps of yellow ducklings greeted their ears. 'I need that poo now,' Shala said suddenly.

Wrasse pulled a swathe of hanging moss from a leaning willow, 'Here you are, Shala,' she said.

'Thanks.'

They reached rising ground at the marsh way's end. They stepped on terra firma, flung their arms in the air and hugged. 'Mind my ribs, Shala. I think I've cracked some.' That started them giggling, which only hurt Wrasse more. But it did not matter. 'I'm still alive and kicking,' she thought gratefully.

They looked back along the narrow track then spotted the terminals of the handrails. Each had a leather warning sign with a scorched design of an auroch and suckling calf. 'Beware. Aurochs!' it indicated.

29

The Village of Char

At the height of the rugged slope their sea view was impressive. 'That sandy bay down there set between those rocky peninsulas resembles Lee Holme, doesn't it, Shala?'

'Yes. The houses are behind the high-banked shore. They are rebuilding some'.

'That's Char Loch, Shala. Char Burn winds from it to the sea between the dwellings. It looks like a new bridge is being wrought from Kull's timbers.'

'Their tethered cattle have cut circular swathes in the new pasture. Pigs, sheep and goats are at their business far below.' On the slopes was a wood going around the bay like a halo. A group of impressive pines slanted from the ground where Kull had wounded them.

'Have you been here before, Shala?'

'Oh yes. Several times, but by boat.'

'I think that's very wise. Onwards and downwards to civilization, then.'

'Are your ribs okay, Wrasse?'

'They'll heal. A bit of pain won't hurt,' she winced.

'I'll help you.'

'Go ahead, Shala, I've got my staff.'

They reached the woodland, where the path separated. 'We take the zigzag route down. There's a rail for the frail in places, and posts to swing around.'

'I see a bench further down. You can rest. It's a lovely view.' That is when they heard a child call: 'I can see you. I can see you. And you can't see me.'

Shala called back, 'Oh, I do, because I see everything.'

'What colour hair have I got, then?'

'It isn't green, I can see that. And it's not blue.'

'No! But what colour is it?' the boy answered impatiently.

'Well,' Shala said, 'it's not white and it's not grey, is it?'

'No, it is not!' He shouted from high up.

'You haven't any hair at all,' Shala remarked.

'Yes I have!' he yelled down from his tree house. 'Look.' He poked his head out tugging his locks.

'I knew it. Reddish, like mine, because you are Minnow. And you haven't grown an inch since I last saw you.'

'I have,' he shouted as he ran down his ladder. 'I'm really big now.'

'Well, if you're that big, you can run and tell Sable that Wrasse is on her way to see her.'

'All right. And who are you?' he said impudently.

'Just run along, will you?'

Minnow ran downhill, calling Phantom, his sow. She waddled out of the undergrowth and leisurely took the path down.

They reached the lower part of the woodland. It faded on gently sloping ground. Char Loch was still below to their left. Dugout canoes were pulled up on its beach where yellow flags poked through the muddy edge. A raft lay marooned on a stony bank.

Minnow ran to one of the houses on their side of the burn.

'Excuse me,' Minnow said, poking his head through the string curtain, 'Some woman called Worse is coming to see you, with Shala from Lee Holme.'

'Where are they?' she asked Minnow hurriedly.

'Coming down from the wood.'

'Thank the souls for that. I've got time to clean up. Knotwood, shake out two mattresses. Timber, tidy your bed. Sprig, little one, shift your farm away from the fireplace, your haystacks might get trodden on.'

'I'm off home, and Phantom's here,' Minnow said as he ran away, bumping into Copse and his dog, Gum.

'What's the rush?' he asked.

'Your wife's in a cleaning frenzy. An old woman's visiting. I'm off before she needs my help.'

'Okay, Minnow, thanks for the warning. Gum and I will go hare coursing.'

Phantom led slowly, grunting at each step, her hairy tail whirling behind, then she waddled off to Minnow's house. The hikers continued.

'Can we come in?' Shala called.

'Of course,' Sable answered casually, 'I'm making rose tea.'

'Here are some spring beauties. An auroch damaged them, but they'll make soup.'

'Thanks very much. Timber got some from above Charwood. How long are you staying?'

'Not long. A couple of days, if that's all right. My ribs got bruised by an angry bull.'

'Oh no! Here, sit, Wrasse. It's lovely to see you again, Shala. Knotwood, hand Wrasse the tea bowl, then we can pass it around. Timber, fetch firewood from the eaves and put on some dried bones.'

'Well, this is nice. You still keep a neat house,' Wrasse remarked, feeling the exquisite reed mat as she crouched by the fire. 'Rosehip tea, too. Refreshing: a touch of chopped kelp in it?'

'Yes, Wrasse. I think it gives it a little body.'

'Just what we need, after our auroch experience,' Shala added.

'Oh. Do tell us,' Timber asked as he edged up to her.

'That was amazing,' he remarked when the tale ended.

'Have I missed something?' Copse said as he and Gum returned with a swinging hare.

'Yes. A tremendous story about escaping a raging bull up on High Marsh, Dad,' Knotwood replied.

'Tell it again later, would you? We'll ask everyone round.'

Timber edged closer, unable to keep his eyes off Shala. 'Here's my new knife,' he said to her.

She looked down to his lap where a long, sharpened bone lay. 'It's beautiful,' she answered.

'It's brilliant for filleting and spooting,' he assured. He was a year younger than Shala, and quite in awe of her. 'We could fish for char tomorrow, if you want.'

'I'll think about it,' she answered, as Wrasse was in full swing with other news.

It was after the repeated auroch tale, when the neighbours had gone, when Sable asked, 'What's the real reason you came?'

'Where can we talk tomorrow?'

'We'll take the raft out on Char Loch and set eel traps, if that suits?'

'Perfect, Sable, but I'm not punting with my ribs like this,' Wrasse commented wryly.

'There's fresh mattresses for you in the spare bed neuks. Sleep well. We'll chat the morn.'

The two woke late after deep, refreshing sleep.

'Hot porridge, honey and cream?' Sable asked as they stirred.

'I haven't slept so well for years,' Wrasse remarked sitting up in bed. 'Not even an auroch dream.'

Shala yawned, 'Yes, but I did.'

'Shala, Sable and I are going eeling on Char Loch to talk. Do you want to come?'

'Not especially, I was fancying going fishing with Timber. Do you need me?'

'No. You enjoy yourself. I can tell you about it.'

Shala surprised Timber with his digging stick under the eaves. 'Can we fish?'

'I was just off to plant, but I'll get a net instead. Follow me – they're hanging under the thatch. We can carry one between us. Mind the dangling weights. Gum, come on,' he called eagerly.

'Knotwood, look after Sprig', Sable asked before she and Wrasse set off. 'I've packed lunch. I got creel bait, hare's guts and a chopped up seagull in the bucket.' It swung between them as they walked past herb bushes and turf-walled kale plots. 'There's our new bridge. Kull delivered the trunks. We split them to span Charburn. Copse, how are you and Carve doing?' she called.

'Just hammering in the last stones of the abutments,' Carve replied above the sound of the burn. 'Good luck with the eels. We can have an official bridge opening, if you get enough,' he teased from their shadowy workplace.

'They will be planning something, those two. Eel fishing indeed,' said Copse.

Sable's sandy tresses drifted over her shoulders onto her goatskin jacket. The threaded shells clicked together as she walked. She had made a special effort. Wrasse had made none. They passed other buildings, one newly roofless. Kull's footprint was in its midst. Folk worked there, as in Lee Holme.

'The raft's through the dogwood bushes,' Sable said.

'I know,' Wrasse thought, 'we saw it from the ridge.'

Nesting birds protested while they pushed through to the stony jetty. The Shifting Isle was roped there to an upright stone. They stepped onto its planking, strapped to three upside-down dugout canoes.

'I'll punt to that pig's bladder creel marker.'

Wrasse sat on a low bench over the middle canoe and began, 'We came over the hill because Shala and I needed time alone. You can't have that with eager boatmen, can you?'

'That's right, Wrasse. They listen for gossip.'

'In any case,' Wrasse added, 'I wanted to show Shala inside our Ancestor House, and that is not by a convenient jetty, is it?'

'Oh no. It's precipitous up there.'

'I don't speak to just anyone,' Wrasse began seriously. 'That girl's different, with unique qualities. I can trust you, that's why we came here first.' Sable punted to the bobbing float. Wrasse moved so she was more comfortable. 'She might need you when I'm dead and gone.'

'So you're going further, then?'

'Yes, when I'm ready.'

'Where?'

'Tarmin, where it all started. I don't want to go. They probably imagine I'm dead, or they've forgotten all about me. I haven't told Shala yet. I will choose my moment.'

'They wouldn't forget, Wrasse.'

'Maybe not, but I feel Shala should come with me. It will be part of her training. She has visions, as you know. They are foretelling. I used to have them, and now I do again. This is very important, Sable, and not a word to anyone.'

Sable hauled on the creel rope. The first wicker trap pointed its way above the surface. Wrasse continued, 'Stories will spread of her prediction that someone is coming from way across the sea. Well, all the indications are that others will follow. We don't know when. We need this man to breed among us.' Wrasse paused and took the plunge of explaining herself. 'I have to tell you here and now that I have had deep and bitter experience of this before.'

'Yes,' Sable acknowledged as she pulled the weed-covered creel on board. 'I'd heard hints.'

'Shala knows everything. I can tell you the full tale later. I would like Shala to be named Aiva, eventually. She must be helped through the difficult time she will have after his arrival. I am going to explain to her fully what she will have to do, and I am going to tell you now.'

Sable turned to Wrasse as she tipped the bait from the leather bucket. 'I need my salt,' she said and poured some from her birchwood cubbie into the bucket. The creel held a knot of eels round its central bait locket. Together they untangled the writhing creatures and let them drop into the bait container. 'That salt sure sees to them. They will be dead and ready for smoking by the time we get back. I'll re-bait and the creel can go back behind the raft. But I am listening, Wrasse,' Sable said as she sat next to her.

'As you know, we had a big conference at Lee Holme just after Kull's wicked temper.' Sable nodded, as they watched Shala and Timber launching their dugout at the other end of Char Loch. 'Well, I had to explain that our population is now at the point where it isn't sustainable, because of inbreeding. This has always been a problem. You know we have taken strict measures to avert just that.' Sable went to speak, but held back. 'Before the storm I had spoken with Shala about her visions and her conversations with birds. Her visions, though, of the Geesemen brought it home to me. It was just what I had experienced, when I was young like her.'

Sable said nothing, but she had heard old rumours of Wrasse's past before arriving at Lee Holme.

'You see, Sable, I'm terribly worried for Shala. If this all comes true she will have immense responsibilities. He, whoever he is, is meant for her. She would not have had the dreams, the visions of Geese People and even him, if they were not going to be bound together. I know very well indeed – it so nearly happened to me.' She paused, rubbing her sore ribs. 'Look at those two now, stretching a net across the narrow mouth of that bay. That is normal. Shala will never have a normal life. Not now. I don't want to see her hurt, but she is going to be. This is why she may need your support and strength. I am looking to the future. She will love him, but she will have to share him.'

'Yes, I see, Wrasse. Of course she will. If he's going to solve our bloodline problems, she's got to give of his fertility.'

'There will be factions; jealousies will surface. Sadly, this is part of human nature. Men will be men. There will be fights, discord in families, troubles we haven't even considered. This is why we have to plan,' Wrasse stressed. 'If we get an influx of people from abroad, then they will have to be settled peaceably with us. We will need to be able to get on and learn from each other.' Wrasse clutched her ribs again, and Sable dragged up another creel. 'They will have different customs, other ways, other beliefs. There will be foreign attitudes to absorb. This is why we must begin to prepare now. Us women will need to guide the process. The menfolk will react differently: we know that, but we also have to convince them of how important this is for our survival. We will have to perform together, stick together and be STRONG.'

They emptied the latest haul of eels among those already suffering salt. Wrasse spoke on, 'When my house burned, I lost all my bloodline records. They were kept as groups of shells. A big whelk for family heads, then small for their children; I could match whom they could marry. Their grandchildren would be winkles and others were coloured sea snails. With all this and further codes thread on my strings, I had a history of the families. I knew them without looking, but this was for handing down. It's all gone now.' She wiped her brow as though she was still under that fire.

Sable pulled a creel aboard. The water drained through the slits in the raft's planking as she listened. 'If I'm alive when he arrives, I'll help Shala with a new system. You see, Sable, the old way became useless anyway, because within one, or in a few cases two, generations it will all be too late. Already we've had too many strange births. It is terribly sad when we have to place a babe underwater because of deformities. It happens, and we hate it.'

'Yes, Wrasse. My sister Cornflower had ugly twins. She had to drown them. It upset her so much that she left her own life behind, too. Her house became overgrown with brambles. Her man, Stook, left. He wandered away one wintery night. There it is, just a mound of bushes. Yes, Wrasse,' Sable said at last, 'there will be difficult times for Shala, or Aiva, if all this becomes true.'

'We must have this Goose Man escorted to all the villages to breed with chosen women,' Wrasse stressed. 'I said this at the meeting, but it hasn't sunk in. Someone has to make a record of who he breeds with, who actually gives birth, what sex, colour of hair and phase of the Moon. These single young ladies, or even wedded women, have to be selected by someone.' Wrasse rubbed her ribs again, 'Shala will have problems with this. I will, if I'm spared, help her through it. There will be squabbles between the ones he must mate with, as well. But Shala is the most important of them all. She has been chosen by who knows what spirit to receive him. At all costs she has to be protected, given strength.'

Sable dumped more eels in the bucket. 'So you want me to do the choosing?'

'Yes, Sable.' She stood watching the two fishers across the still loch. A red-throated diver took flight from behind their boat as they laughed with each other. Sable went back to her seat and listened. 'I am old, Sable. This is my last journey. I haven't been away for years. When we return, there will be much to prepare in Lee Holme.' She stared at Sable. 'Later I want you to go on the selection tour. You must prepare everywhere, as I will in our township,' Wrasse added. 'But you should have a pretext for your journey. Few can know what you are really about, only those of our trusted female circle.'

'I understand,' she said seriously. 'I've been preparing myself from when Minnow poked his head through the curtain saying, 'An old woman called Worse is coming to visit.' I knew life was about to change. For the sakes of all of us, I will take this on. It's for our children and their children's future.' She fingered the shells in her hair, considering the impact of Knotwood being selected. She stood and shook the last pair of clinging eels into the bottom of the bucket and baited the weighted creel.

'The Goose Man will probably not arrive for some while. That's my guess. He has a long journey; so has Shala. There is time for you to think.'

Wrasse watched the dark wooden canoe with its two occupants. One of them whistled to Gum, who was splashing around in the shallows at the head of the netted bay. The dog knew his business. The net began to shake in front of Timber and Shala as char and trout entangled themselves in the mesh.

They finished the eel round. The bottom of the bucket was

obscured by their slimy catch. 'Their skins will make a fine skirt,' Sable commented

Shala and Timber gathered the netting. Gum swam to their craft, lurched over the side and shook himself, surprised at Shala and Timber's vexed cries.

Their catches would be a fine start for the Char Bridge inauguration.

30

Seaforth

'The ceremony for blessing Char Bridge is important, Shala. Sable wants you to tell of Kull's Rage at Lee Holme. Don't mention the predictions, but please praise Partan's measurements.'

During the lengthening twilight by Sable's outdoor hearth, Shala told the dramatic story with the sounds of Char Burn, the cries of plover and piping from Timber's reed flute as her backdrop. As evening cooled, her audience sat under the wide, spreading eaves of Sable's house. Broken potsherds held smouldering embers for warmth beneath the thatch. Gum lay across their threshold, gnawing a knuckle. Sprig's toys were everywhere. 'Look at our bridge,' Timber said.

Theatrically, Shala related all: the strength of the wind, the searing rain; the burning of Wrasse's home, the trees thumping, tumbling past. Timber instinctively created the sounds through his music.

Finally, Shala spoke of Partan's Measures. Copse and Carve understood their value.

'We should go and make copies,' Copse suggested under his breath.

'Yes, next time we're there. It would fun to get away.

'We could take Wrasse and Shala back in Seaforth, tomorrow.'

'As soon as that?' Carve whispered.

'Yup! No time like as soon as possible. We can drag lines for mackerel going, and long line for cod coming back.'

'Excellent. And we'll enjoy Lee Holme, too,' Carve answered furtively.

'Copse, what are you up to?' Sable asked. 'Go and open the stone jar of pickled fish. I've warmed cheesy oatcakes. We can wash it down with juniper and plum ambrose.'

'That drink was good,' Shala thought after, her head reeling slightly. 'I feel so warm inside. Timber's piping is perfect.'

'I'm going to bed, if I can get past that dog in the door,' Wrasse said finally. She stepped over Gum and pushed her way through the strand curtain as Timber played on in the starlight. Shala followed Wrasse a little later.

The sun slept beneath the horizon, waking as morning slowly turned into day.

Wrasse was talking to Sable when Shala woke.

'I'm going to do your hair,' Knotwood said to Sprig as she tugged his tousled mop. 'You will look really bonny.'

'I'm bonny enough,' he protested.

'Not for me. Keep still,' she told him and dug her bone comb into his matted mess.

'Do as your sister says, Sprig. When she's finished I want to look at your bridge,' Sable promised.

'Oh, all right,' he complained.

'It's misty and wet outside,' Copse said. His short ginger beard glistened with dew. He removed his dripping skin cap and sailor's cape and stood by the fire. His leather dungarees hung on short hide braces, keeping his legs dry. 'I've got Seaforth ready to sail to Lee Holme. Is there anything you want taking there, apart from Wrasse and Shala?' he asked.

'I beg your pardon?' Wrasse said as Sable looked surprise at her husband.

'I'm going round to Lee Holme with Carve. We want to copy Partan's poles,' he reported, looking mystified at the opposition.

'Have you asked Wrasse and Shala?'

'Are we ready?' Copse added expectantly as he stepped inside.

'Can I go too, Mummy?' Sprig enquired eagerly.

'No, you can't. Nobody is going anywhere until we discuss this.'

The men leaned against a roof post. Carve fingered his weighted long line, expectations diminishing by the moment.

'Do you two want to go back yet?' Sable asked.

'Actually, no,' Wrasse answered.

Shala looked up from by the fire asking, 'What's the fuss about?'

'I'm wondering what we are going to do.' Wrasse said easily. 'I have just decided that we are going to go on.'

Shala stood. Gum shifted.

Timber came in eagerly. 'Everybody ready?' he asked with an expectant air. It collapsed at Sable's glance. He removed his hood, shifting uneasily on his bare feet, wiping dew from his youthful ginger moustache.

'Look, men,' Wrasse said kindly, 'your offer's very thoughtful. Ordinarily, we would have been delighted to be sailed back. However, I am taking Shala further. I'm not exactly sure where. We are just on a journey.'

Timber hung his head, whilst keeping his eyes fixed on Shala. She looked at him and he shrugged his shoulders and hung up his feathered mackerel line.

'May I ask you a favour, though?'

'Of course,' Copse responded. 'Delighted. What?'

'Would you sail us in the other direction, please?'

Shala looked surprised.

'Certainly. Yes, with pleasure,' Carve said, reaching for his hood.

'Not right now. We are staying a little yet. '

'All right. We will work in the fields until you want to go. Come on Timber, get your digging stick.'

Sable kneaded crushed hazelnuts and dried damsons into her dough. A flat stone warmed over embers in the corner of her fireplace. A big, round pot was ready to upturn over the slab.

Knotwood knelt and ground oats in the quern. Sable put the dough on a whale's shoulder bone to rise by the fire. She reached up for smoked black sausage in the rafters and chopped it up with her pebble knife. Shala watched her push the hunks into the rising breads.

'So, where are we going?' Shala asked.

Wrasse squatted on a huge whale's vertebra. 'Tarmin, Shala. I never meant to. But I want to take you there. I have reasons for myself, as well.' She shifted, pushing a dried cattle bone further into the fire. It burned with a hot, blue flame. 'I have been facing demons lately. There are more I need to meet before the ancestors have me.'

'Gosh... Tarmin,' Shala repeated quietly.

'Have you got anyone left there?' Sable enquired knowingly, over the sound of Knotwood's rhythmic grinding.

'I don't know. Perhaps,' she said distantly. 'You need a kneepad, Knotwood,' Wrasse said, loudly changing the subject.

'Yes, or I'll get knobbles, just like Mum.'

Sable felt her joints, regretting not looking after them.

The big stone slab heated. Sable broke her dough into four, patted the pieces round and placed one on the oiled stone with the pot over it.

Knotwood continued milling.

Shala took out her sewing kit for mending. 'Do you need anything done, Wrasse?'

'You can stitch up my ribs, if you like.'

Sable sat on a vertebra next to Wrasse to peel small onions. The loaf baked on. The fruity, meaty aroma wafted by as she imagined something totally different for baking her bread in. It was a structure in her house, made of clay, but hollow. It had a door like a pot-lid in its side. She envisaged a fire within, then a stone over the embers. In that contained heat, behind the door, she could cook. Under her imaginary bread cooker was a niche for her fuel. It all seemed so simple. 'I could stand up and bake and not do all this bending over hot fires. I'll get that man of mine to make me one. There's splendid clay where they dug for the Char Bridge abutments.'

She put another dough ball under the bowl and got the pot of pate and ripe cheeses from the stone coolbox set in the floor.

'Clean your feet before you come in,' Sable instructed, hearing the men returning. Wrasse broke the first loaf. The black pudding steamed temptingly within. Shala and Timber sat on his bed and ate.

The other loaves baked on for the cheese and pate.

'Can you take us tomorrow, Copse?' Wrasse asked.

'Surely we can. Seaforth is ready.'

The next morning they were prepared.

'Heave to the surf,' Copse called. 'Ladies, leap in.' He, Carve and Timber launched the Seaforth into breakers. As the foam beat around her strong hide sides they leapt aboard, paddling rapidly out. Copse took the helm and Carve the stern. Timber sat by Shala. 'Here's your paddle,' he said.

The next wave broke. 'Paddle hard,' shouted Copse as Seaforth rose in the surf. The boat's nose reared into the foam. Her stern scraped on the swirling sand beneath before shooting forward. A flight of redshanks flew past. Shala heard them whistle to her over the noise of the pounding tide. 'This is exciting,' Shala felt as a sudden inner thrill rose with the salty waves.

Above the noise of the rushing tide, though, she heard a stranger's voice. It called urgently among clear sounds of gaggling geese. She felt a cold, damp fog hit her face. The sounds faded in the moving tide to a distant murmur.

Shala shook her head, looking to Wrasse blankly. The day was bright and beautiful: there were no geese. They had long gone. She held her oar tight, feeling the water's pull. She imagined momentarily she was holding something shorter to propel a boat. Wrasse said quietly. 'Shala, where are you?'

'On a different sea, hearing different sounds,' she answered inwardly. 'I feel distant. Timber's next to me, I see everyone, but I'm apart. Even Wrasse's voice is odd, like I've water in my ears.'

Her redshanks reeled in the clear air ahead. She distinctly heard their calls as the flock swooped beside her. Her ears popped, she blinked and touched reality once more.

31

The Sea-Girt Land

'Carve, cast a mackerel line for Wrasse. See if she can't get lunch,' Copse suggested, 'then we'll row together.'

'Aye,' he responded.

'Lovely feathers,' Wrasse said as she pulled the cord. 'Got one,' she immediately yelled.

'Wind in quick,' called Carve from the helm.

The wriggling fish fell off the blackthorn hook. 'Wonderful,' Wrasse enthused, 'I'll cast again, even though my ribs ache.'

'We can take you to Cutlip Bay or Shepherd's Tongue, depending on currents and tide. We can be there in a couple of days. That is, if we get through Auk's Passage safely.'

'That's Auk Island far in the distance, Shala. See the breakers at its rocky feet? Just look at those high cliffs,' Wrasse said as they mounted a wave. Another fish tugged her line. 'That's three at once,' she exclaimed, sinking the tackle again. 'The thrill of sailing's all coming back,' she shouted as a wave splashed her hair.

The men sang a shanty as they pulled on their oars. Shala followed the rhythm, learning the words. Directly she had them they changed them, to confuse her. 'This is great,' she thought. 'I like sitting with Timber.' He smiled at her as their shoulders went back and forth in their rowing motion. Their wood-framed craft bounced over the waves, responding quickly to the oar strokes. The cool sea breeze spurred them on.

Copse shared Sable's bread and cheese from his birch box and filleted Wrasse's mackerel for lunch.

The hours of rowing and drifting were rewarded as they closed in on another boat. 'Drake! Guillemot!' Copse called through cupped hands.

'Copse, Carve. It's you. Pull alongside?'

'Backs into it. Haul ahead,' Copse commanded, piloting them to Drake's dinghy.

'Good catch?' Carve asked as Wrasse peered over the side to inspect.

'Pollack and courthes. We'd hoped for cod. Next time, maybe.'

'Pollack,' Wrasse thought as Drake wound his long-line in. 'Wonderful fish.'

Auk Island loomed a little closer. The breeze lessened in its shelter. The birdcalls clearer and the water slackened. Their voices echoed from the nearing cliffs.

'Who's your new crew?'

'Wrasse and Shala; they are going up coast.'

'I've heard about her,' Drake said quietly to his mate, then, 'Pull for shore, you can bide with us the night,' he cheerfully added.

'Fine, Drake, we'll follow your wake,' Carve answered. They paddled to a small bay set between steep cliffs on the long coastline.

'We are going to Whale Arch,' Timber informed Shala.

'That's right. I've heard of it. Isn't it a long cliff sticking out to Auk Island, and a huge whale smashed into it?'

'Yes, it was Sea Shadow. He was shooting through Auk's Passage to mate with his lover. He got stuck. Then a tremendous wave washed him back. He was so enraged he bashed into the cliff, knocking a hole through it. Then he got angrier, and chased her into that deep cave in the cove. He still snorts up there in rough weather, spouting spume through a vent under the pastures.'

'Amazing,' Shala said, recalling the legend.

She watched Auk Island slope down to low, bare rocks. 'There's masses of auks,' she remarked, 'all waiting in ranks with their white flashes and shining orange bills. They're like huge, flightless guillemots. Timber, are those their nests up in the grass?' 'Yes, it's white with their shit too, just like the cliffs where the other birds roost. And there's Whale Arch beyond Auk's Passage.'

'Yes, but the pass is too narrow for a whale.'

'Aye, but when the tide's right we can race through: it's more fun than rowing all around.' They closed in on the cliffs. Seabirds whirled above. Ranks of puffins took off in coloured flashes as long rows of guillemots leapt into the sea. 'Don't jump,' Timber shouted to them, 'don't jump!' But they jumped all the more. 'You see,' he remarked, 'they never listen.' Shala laughed happily at his silly joke, as the birds came bobbing up again from under the sea. 'See the water rush through Whale Arch, Shala?' She nodded in awe. 'Now, we row to that shingle beach. See the huge, banded, ram-sized pebbles? That's where we land, under the shelter of the high cliff.' His voice echoed.

Drake and Guilly drew up close to their bobbing creel floats. 'Haul them up,' they heard him say. 'Two lobsters and seven crabs, a welcome bounty.'

Their boats nudged the beach. Drake's family came down the cliff path to carry the catch. Some hauled the boats along a grassy pathway to a sheltered terrace of nousts. 'Those pebbles are vast!' Shala remarked, as they went further up the path.

'Yes. And that's Sea Shadow's Cave,' Timber whispered.

They reached the top of the path. Several small stone houses with turf roofs appeared. They trod by a pile of shells that slipped over the narrowing cliff edge where water dripped from a spring. The smells of cooking wafted through welcoming strings of drying fish as they put down their heavy burdens.

'I'm Heather, Drake's head wife. I'll whistle for help.' Immediately folk appeared from the little dwellings with food. 'Sit, drink and eat. You'll be tired. Copse, introduce your guests please.' Wrasse's name turned several heads.

'Come on, Shala, let's go to the top of the hill,' Timber suggested later. 'It is not far.'

'Isn't it rude to go so soon?' she remarked.

'No, not a bit. Let the old ones gossip.' He sprinted up the path between the huts. Goats, herded by two youngsters, came down. 'We go up towards clumps of gorse and stunted birch then to a crest overlooking Auk's Passage. We can stop and look,' he said. They gazed down at the swirling sea. 'Over there's Whale Arch's Ancestor House. It's a splendid oval tower set into the slope. Let's go to the lower door along the paved passage. Its slate portal has a picture of a boat riding on a whale.'

'There's an old mace, baskets of dried fish and mussels,' Shala noticed when they arrived, then suggested, 'Let's climb these hewn steps, going round the back.'

'Yes. There's a planked leather door at the top. It's windy up there.'

Shala began the climb. Timber watched her move. He wanted to push her from behind, but dared not. She reached the platform at the door. Timber edged closely by. 'It's punched with designs of fish and auks. Look at the windbeaten feathers hanging from the lintel.'

'Shall we go in?' Timber suggested.

'I don't think we should. Not without being invited,' Shala said. 'And there's footholds at the side. We can climb right to the top.' She reached up, found an even higher one and began. Timber watched again. 'The stonework's lovely up here,' Shala called back. 'It's laid like zigzagging herringbones. The courses are in different colours: red sandstone and black. It's very clever, Timber,' she remarked, feeling him push her upwards.

Shala reached the top rapidly. A raven took flight from its nest between two moss-covered whale skulls. They gazed with skeletal eyes out over Auk Island. The raven circled. Its mate joined her above, calling. Timber scaled the footholds as Shala sat on top. Two stone spearheads lay there, their shafts slowly rotting away. 'Here, Timber. My turn, I'll pull you up.' She looked down his freckled neck and saw a thong strung with small, shiny bone beads beneath his jerkin.

'You're strong,' she remarked as they stood together gazing in the breeze. 'It's an impressive sight, Timber.' Three raven fledglings hid in the skulls.

'We sail all along there,' Timber responded. 'See below, Auk's Passage. We'll fly through that tomorrow, then row on.'

'The cliffs wind and bend into the distance. They rise and drop to long beaches, inlets and bays. In the very misty distance I see low-lying lands between endless hills. Narrow waterways and shallow lochs dot the land there,' she said to Timber. Then wondered, 'Is that the way to Tarmin?'

'But see over there,' Timber said softly, 'that great spit of land way up the coast. It's an arm of sea-grass reaching far into the ocean,' Shala nodded. 'That's Shepherd's Tongue,' then sadly said,

'That is where we leave you, or else over at Cutlip Bay. That's where the Giant Farrel showed off his great power to us humans. He swam quickly from the mountains of Big Land so we could witness his great speed. Well, us clever folk pushed the land further out with the help of the ancestors in the hills. He hadn't noticed. He bumped right into it and cut his lips so badly, he swam back crying, never to return.'

'Really?' Shala remarked.

'Oh yes. It's true, ask Dad.'

They turned to go back down. Shala saw the ocean curving behind the distant hills. The view gripped her. 'This is the first time I've really appreciated the size of our sea-girt land. I knew there were places far to the north, and the Big Land south, where the mountains are. We see them often. But now I feel that it is special. It's separate, beautiful and wholesome. I'm part of it and it's part of me.' Shala gripped her piece of amber and held it tight, 'I feel as though I'm taking hold of what I see before me.' She squeezed the undulations of the smoothing nugget. She peered to the west across hills, like slumbering giants, then on to where the geese came from. Timber held her hand and laid his head gently on her shoulder. 'I hear a strange voice calling far away, or is it the ravens?' Shala imagined then turned and asked Timber, 'Can we see Tarmin from here?'

'Yes, Shala. Look, it's where you were staring. It's a great distance away towards the end of that very long hill down by the sea. It's a big town. Bigger than Lee Holme, so I'm told. I've never been there. Not many from here do, even though it's famous.'

'Thank you, Timber,' she said, surprising him with a kiss on his forehead. 'Let's go.' She turned and descended the notched steps to the thrift. Timber followed down to Whale Arch. The ravens returned as their young reappeared from within the skulls.

The morning mist cleared. From the small clifftop village the sea sparkled. Waves on the shingle called them. The company went to the beach. 'If you make for Shepherd's Tongue, Sprang might crew you back,' Drake suggested.

'Good idea,' replied Copse as Guilly and he launched Seaforth into the surf. 'Everyone comfortable?'

'Quite,' replied Wrasse as she shifted in her stern seat.

Seaforth bit waves. 'Sea Shadow's gaping arch is awe inspiring,' Shala remarked to Wrasse as she peered down to the clear depths.

'The tide gurgling in the cave is really strange,' Timber added. 'It's marvellous how the seaweed sways here in the shelter of the bay,'

'Row to the point,' Carve said. 'The water's not too high. We can see our way through Auk's Passage.'

''Best time to go,' Copse said. 'We will have to row fast and catch a wave to carry us through. When we enter, up oars. Don't drop them.'

'There's a good crest. Row for it,' Copse called.

'Wow,' Timber yelled as Seaforth rose in the rushing breaker.

Shala felt the hurtling water drive them. 'It's wonderful,' she thought excitedly.

Wrasse, in the stern, sat wide-eyed, heart pounding, 'This brings back what my father did on the wide surf.'

Shala and Timber held their oars upright. The rocky chasm funnelled the raging stream. Startled seals rolled away. 'Don't jump!' Timber called as they flopped into the torrent behind them. Auks joined the rush as they flung themselves into the turmoil, disappearing then rising, black among the white spume.

The foam lifted Seaforth in a roaring rage, moments later spewing them into another bay.

'Down oars, row right,' Copse commanded as they exited the shoot. 'Avoid the Skerry!' They sped past the mussel-laden rocks unscathed.

'Wow. That was something!' Shala exclaimed as Seaforth settled.

'Yup. Nothing like tide racing,' Timber remarked.

Wrasse looked back at the receding trough, whistling joyfully through her stumpy teeth.

They rowed in steady motion for the rest of the day. Gulls watched their slow progress across the currents and changing colours of their domain. Wrasse fished, but with little success. She was not worried. The Auks were chasing the shoals. 'My turn later,' she mused.

A large headland protruded into the sea. 'We will make for that and stop in Eagle's Noust,' Copse said over the spray. 'Just a few hours rowing, now.'

'Let's put our backs into it,' said Timber.

'Aye, we will,' Shala responded as they cut through the waves.

Reaching a new current, the flow worked against them. 'Pull hard. Harder, harder,' Copse shouted.

'This is tiresome,' Shala thought under the strain. 'The breeze is veering,' she said to Timber. He nodded and rowed on. She watched his muscles feel the strain as the oars dipped.

'The headland doesn't seem to get any closer,' Wrasse commented, watching the two from her seat.

'You can take an oar, then, Wrasse,' Timber ventured cheekily, 'Here, have mine.'

'I would gladly,' she spluttered through the spray, 'but my ribs won't stand it.'

'Harder! Harder,' Copse shouted. 'Head for the shelter of the cliffs. Row along them to that distant promontory where the waves are breaking.'

They ploughed on, singing a shanty to the sound of the sea until Copse announced, 'There's Eagle's Spear.'

'That was hurled there by the Great Shepherd when he was defending his flock. Now eagles nest there,' Timber explained. 'Look, one's flying from the top, Shala.'

'Yes, he's circling over us. Hear that shriek echoing.'

'The nousts are behind it. We will pull in for the night,' Copse explained.

'At last,' Timber thought, 'I'm knackered!'

'We've got to steer right under the Spear. There's a deep channel either side. They say the point still sticks in the giant wolf far below. Careful now,' Copse warned.

Shala nudged Wrasse, 'It's amazing. The eagle's shadow just skimmed over us. Did you see it?'

'Yes, Shala. And look at the wolf's back, all covered in seaweed and mussels.'

'There's the nousts in the cove at the end of the pebbly ayre,' Carve announced through the sound of reeling gulls. 'Pull hard: make for it.'

They saw the rising shingle below the high cliffs. 'Bump,' went Seaforth's prow as she grounded.

'Leap out,' Copse commanded. 'Port her to the ruins by that old boat.'

'There's a heap of driftwood too, Dad,' Timber said.

'Yes. Home for the night,' he replied.

'Hunger, hunger, hunger!' Timber shouted.

'Calm down, young man,' Wrasse told him, as they set their boat into an old noust.

'There's a lean-to shack under the cliff. We can kip there, tonight,' said Carve. 'The flagstone roof still looks safe, despite those rickety walls,' he added as they crunched across the shingle.

'I'm still hungry,' Timber reminded them.

'Just wait,' Wrasse told him. 'If you clear away those old creels and baskets of junk in there, we can start a fire and get comfy.'

'Okay,' he whinged. 'Shala, give us a hand, will you?'

'I'll surprise them,' Wrasse thought. 'There's two cooked lobsters, a couple of crabs, goats cheeses and a hunk of smoked pollock that Heather tucked in our mushroom bag.'

'Thank the Spirits. Food!' Timber cried out, as the first flames flickered.

'I just love partans,' Shala said crushing a claw between her teeth. 'Sucking the juices out before they run down the chin is the art of eating them.'

'Aye, and lobster hands too,' added Carve as he licked out a huge span of shell.

'The pollock and cheese were splendid. I'm well fed and all in,' Wrasse said as the fire began to die.

'Me, too,' added Copse. 'Huddle up, folks. Timber, you're next to me. Wrasse, you and Shala can be on the other side of Carve.'

'I'll play my pipes for a bit,' Timber added, wishing he could lie next to Shala.

In the morning, the low grey clouds moved towards the direction of Shepherd's Tongue.

'Right now,' Carve said with a yawn, 'we'll have a quick breakfast, then load Seaforth. You ladies jump in when she's floating. Copse and I hop in after. Timber, you shove her out to water, then leap for it. Don't get too wet.'

'When I'm aboard we can take up that shanty again,' Timber thought.

'Okay,' Carve said on the swell, 'it's tricky getting out of the cove, but there's another channel past the Spear. You'll see the deep green. We follow that to clear sea. The wind's backing us, let's hope it don't rain.'

'Look over there,' Wrasse said, 'there's orcas, chasing seals.'

'Oh no! We're in the whales' way,' Shala yelled, as the hunters headed right for them.

'Hold tight!' Copse commanded, wondering what good that would do.

'The seals have scattered,' Timber put in.

'Here they come,' called Carve in alarm, watching the orcas' sleek black and cream bulks slicing the surf.

Dark shadows of fleeing seals flashed beneath in the clear trench below.

'I can see their eyes,' Shala tried to utter as the hunters closed right at Seaforth's side.

'Grip the sides!' Carve repeated.

'Phew,' Timber exclaimed, expecting a crash, 'they've dived.'

'There they are, by the rocks. The seals have beached. They've got one! Look at them hurl it. That's awesome. See the bloody foam,' Timber reported.

'It's being torn apart,' Shala added. 'Now it's the fulmars' turn. They're diving for bits.'

'Oops. One's been guzzled by that orca. Did you see?'

'Nope,' replied Copse, 'Carve and me are rowing out of here. Put your backs into it. Start that shanty.'

Behind, fishes darted amongst the blood and blubber. Wrasse watched guillemots diving for them. 'Don't jump,' Timber called, just before taking up the sea song.

Many choruses later, Timber nudged Shala. 'There's Cutlip, where Farrel bumped his face. See the blood-red rocks? Further on it's the Low Lands and the swamps. See the distant dunes. Behind are the wetlands and lakes. The River Rouse comes out way over there, by Shepherd's Tongue.

'Keep a steady rhythm. Make for the Tongue,' Copse announced, 'Pull hard. Don't let up.'

'I wish I was fit, so I could row, too,' Wrasse thought.

'It's beginning to squall. We'll hug the shore in case the weather comes down,' Copse called.

Redshanks flew by. 'Sorry, no time to chat,' Shala shouted to them.

'What is she on about?' Timber wondered, as Shala took up the shanty.

Oystercatchers homed in on the nearby beach.

'Sandbank ahead. Veer right,' Wrasse warned.

They rowed, singing, as the rain shot down and the breeze took them along the coast.

'There's the Rouse, running wide across the sands,' Timber pointed out later. 'See the break in the dunes?'

'I can feel the tow of the river on my oars,' Shala mentioned.

'Yes, it should drift us towards Shepherd's Tongue. Look at all the waders,' Timber said.

'It's clouding over. There'll be more rain. Put your backs into it. The Tongue's drawing in,' Copse urged.

'He's just being mean, Shala. See the wooden jetty ahead? It sticks right out. We'll soon be there,' Timber announced as Seaforth rocked in the swell.

'The wind is getting up. Make for the pier,' his dad shouted above the screeching of gulls. 'Broadside on. Let the gusts take us.'

Wrasse felt the bump as their sturdy boat hit the wooden piles.

'Pull along the stakes to the beach. When we ground, Timber, you climb out, run along the boardwalk and tow us to that ladder. We can get out and pull her up. Okay.'

'Aye, aye, Pop,' Timber answered.

'Good. I'm finished,' Shala thought secretly.

'There are loads of boats here, Dad. What's up? Coracles? Reed rafts? Dinghies like ours? Dugouts and kayaks too?' Timber queried, 'But there's no one around.'

32

Shepherd's Tongue

'Watch out for the swooping terns, Shala,' Timber said as they trod on tussocks of sea grass.

'I'll wave my bow at them,' she replied.

'There's smoke coming from Sprang's lodge,' said Copse. 'You can see it's been damaged by Kull.' They crossed sheep-nibbled turf towards the boat-shaped building. 'We'll dump our stuff on the stone benches. Nice broad eaves,' he commented, fingering nets hanging beneath.

Shala placed her caisie down, avoiding bone marlin spikes and cord bobbins. Wrasse admired the huge round-based pots by the doorjambs.

Copse parted the sea grass curtain, rattling its small stone weights as he did so. 'Sprang?' he called softly. The large interior loomed dimly in front of him. He picked out all the trappings of a family home. Two big posts supported the restored roof. Long fillets of fish hung in the reek of the smouldering fire. Their dog's gnarled shinbone lay at his feet on the polished threshold. 'Nobody,' he said. 'Not a single body home. We'll try the next door. Something's up.' Sprang's irate drake suddenly quacked, flying furiously, pecking Copse's ankles as they rounded the end of his hall. His duck's brood scurried, hiding in the ruins of the next building. 'Follow me past the midden,' Copse said.

Further buildings looming in the twilight. Hooded crows flapped squawking from the midden into the evening sky. A newly driven sand dune buried the seaward end of a smashed house. 'There's no sign of my floating forest here,' Shala thought. 'It probably washed straight past. That old house must have been salvaged to mend Sprang's.'

Suddenly successions of great horn blasts broke from a larger building ahead. Through flowering rowan trees, a door faced them. They followed the shrill notes. The portal loomed beneath thickly thatched eaves.

'Let the Trial commence,' Sprang's voice boomed. The crowd within replied deafeningly, 'Aye! Let the Trial begin.'

'Compose yourselves,' Carve said.

Osprey, the dog, bared her teeth, growling from between the legs of a leather-clad man.

'Quiet now,' said Copse, stepping forward, patting her wet, brown nose. Osprey's pups wriggled inside her as she retreated. 'Enter quietly,' he turned and said.

Sprang reeled round on his central dais, 'Copse. You're late,' he shouted over the assembly's bowed heads. 'SSHhhhhhh, make room, mourners.' He continued loudly, 'Before us we have the next witness.'

'This is embarrassing,' Shala felt, shuffling in. 'Everyone's in their finest clothes, all smelling of polished leather, while we're in such rough stuff. And this is a solemn occasion. That's meadowsweet I smell, too. Who's mace is that touching my hand?' Then she saw the corpse, surrounded by the dried flowers on a raised slab.

Sprang stood beside the dead lady on the slab. A tall masked figure stood either side of him. 'He's looking at me,' Shala realized.

'Who's the old one?' came a sharp demand from a white, pointed mask.

Wrasse peered into the piercing eyeholes of the birch-bark face. 'Wrasse of Lee Holme,' she answered. Shala observed nervous shuffles.

The figure, garbed in shining fish pelts and shells screeched, 'You are NOT invited.' Sprang touched the hand of the Sea Spirit, whispering into its ear. He turned to the other deity. She held a long harpoon and was draped in dripping seaweed. Her huge seal-head mask turned. Shala felt the eyes behind it lance into her breast as the giant lobster shell shoulders rattled.

'And you?' the sharp selky voice yelled, thrusting the threatening harpoon towards Shala's amber amulet.

'I am Shala, daughter of Jasper and Gull, granddaughter of Partan and attendant to Wrasse,' she replied clearly.

Sprang's head, wreathed with rosemary and meadowsweet, moved forward over the corpse. 'Lower your weapon, Selk. They can stay for the Trial,' he said, looking to Wrasse, of whom he had only heard tell.

Sprang's costume of loose, glistening leather scales floated around him. His skin showed through as he moved on his platform. He pulled the horn from behind, gave a vast blast to shout, 'Let the Trial begin... AGAIN.' He regarded the body seriously, 'Spindrift is gone. See how beautiful she is, even in death. Her long plaited hair spreads over the black slab like the setting sun. Her lifeless face stares upwards. Three days ago those shell earrings swung prettily. The gash on her forehead, the twisted shoulder and arm, show her fatal injuries. Is she a fit person to join the Spirits in our Ancestor House?'

'No!' screamed Selk's seal mask and Orci's birch face.

Her old mother wailed from the darkness, 'She was a kind, wonderful girl. She deserves a place with our forebears.'

Her brother began, 'She adored her skills. She was a loving mother.'

Her sister began earnestly, 'She yearned for the sea. She was devoted to fishing. She knew all the ways of the weather and waves: when to trawl, where to long-line, when to haul the creels. She taught us her sea-lore: she was good, talented and clever. We miss her instincts of the deep.'

'I'm her crippled uncle,' a caring voice came, as he limped into the lamplight round her body. 'I taught her. But she gleaned from the spirits even more. She was instructing her son, who will be a great fisher for us one day. He now cries at his grandmother's breast. She, Spindrift, was not a person of the land. She could charm shrimps from the sand. ease eels from stony lairs, summon spoots, pry partans from their beds. This was she. This was the girl I became a father to when my brother was killed. I tremble as I look at her. I speak for her when I say that her aura craves the waves, as mine does. She must be with her sea spirits under the surf and the glinting ocean. She would not rest easy in our stone hall on the hill.'

Up ramped the ancient bellowing Cattle Gods, kin of the auroch. 'We Land Spirits agree. Sea bounds us, scouring the shores. It gives and takes pastures. We see the terror of the waves in the anger of the ocean. Spindrift's spirit within the waters may calm Kull and Waret. This is our statement for Spindrift's Trial. We will scrape this flag floor with our hooves and bellow loud and long as our signature.

We, Selk and Orci, desire her grace.
Demanding her spirit in our deep-sea place.
We'll nurture her Sea Haven's Dwelling.
So make a creel coffer for a fisherman's daughter.
Then sink to the depths off High Crags Water,
To gaze through eyes of Partan spies.
To lure great fish of sea hunters' wish:
Gleaning our bounty of tight nets and fine fish.'

'The evidence is clear,' Sprang summed up: 'Killed while doing land work; her life, taken by the falling beam while repairing Kull and Waret's devastation. Now Spindrift lies broken and stiffened. She should have been in her boat, guiding her son. Now her family must weave her a willow creel, to take her beneath, where her spirit will be freed in the hidden mystery of the deep. The Trial is over, the verdict clear: Spindrift's spirit returns to the wide, sparkling ocean.' Sprang raised his horn, blowing a tremendous final note.

The gathering repeated thrice his sentence in a resounding chorus. Her eleven-year-old son drew close and placed her netting bone in her hand. Slowly, all filed by with shells, nets and fishing tackle until only her face showed. Crab shell lamps were finally placed around the stone bier. Their light became the focus of the wake. The feast to rejoice in her life and her future in the mysterious depths began.

'Good evening, Copse,' Sprang said. 'What brings you here? Spindrift's service was just a local affair.'

'It is happenstance, Sprang,' Copse answered as he was handed a long razor fish shell of seafood. 'We brought Wrasse and Shala here as part of their journey. The old one wants to go to Tarmin.'

'That's where she was from, wasn't it?'

'I believe so. These pickled cockles are good,' Copse added, 'and the smoked mackerel.'

'We will miss Spindrift,' Sprang began, 'It is her sort we need. Her boy, Reel, will be special. We have to look after him. Is there a suitable mate for him growing up in Char? There's none here.'

'That is our problem, too, Sprang. It's rumoured that Wrasse and Shala may be working on just that.'

'I can't see why we don't get a band of us men and go to the Big Land and bring back some women.'

'We tried that, years ago. Half the men stayed. Those who returned had merely mated the women over there with promises of the infants later. Of course, nothing happened. We lost out. Their menfolk assumed our women weren't up to much, so there was no exchange from them either.'

'Excuse us,' said Reel and his sisters. 'Do you have a coffin gift for Mum?' Their huge, leathery turtle shell was filling with offerings. 'We've already got these beautiful thorn hooks, coloured feathers, fine lines, polished floats and shiny sinkers.'

'Here, Reel,' Sprang said, unpinning a polished shell amulet. 'For your mum, with my love.'

Copse felt in his pouch, 'Here's my special jasper blade from my fishing kit.'

'Their Granny is in charge of them now, Copse.'

'That's good. Their collection's mounting. What will Wrasse give?'

'Here's a trace made from my hair,' Wrasse said.

'Here's an amulet from my necklace,' Timber said. 'It is yew. One day it will float away and spread her spirit round the sea.'

'I'll find something,' Shala said, fumbling in her pouch. 'Here,' she was about to say, as she revealed the broken arrowhead she had found in the roots of one of the trees.

'Where did you get that?' Wrasse asked under her breath. 'Find something else!' she said abruptly.

Shala's hand returned to the secrecy of her pouch. 'Here's my haematite divining bead. The cord is plaited from my mother's hair. I am sure Spindrift will like it. I use it for seeing if duck eggs have drakes or ducks in them.'

'Thank you so much,' Reel said as they moved on.

'Follow me, Shala. Excuse us for a moment, Timber.' said Wrasse. 'Come to the lamps. Show me that stone.'

'Here it is.'

'Where did you get it?'

'I pulled it out from the roots of one of the great trees. It's just a broken arrow point.'

'It is, indeed. But it's the stone. Our quartz is different, it's coarser. This is fine. It's flaked shallower. More light comes through it, too.'

'I hadn't really thought about it,' Shala remarked.

'Shala. It's the same as Weir's knife that he tried cut his arm off with. The way it's finished is the same. It must surely have come from his land.'

'You are trembling, Wrasse. Maybe you are right.'

'Here, have crab and smoked cod,' someone offered. 'Thanks,' they said taking a filled scallop shell from the wicker tray.

'Yes. It's very sharp,' Shala observed, handing it back to Wrasse.

'I will be careful. This is precious. I'm certain it's from Weir's land,' she said, pushing it into the ball of her thumb, 'There has to be a connection. We may find out. Here, put it away safely.'

'Did you enjoy that?' a lady said as she took the shells. 'Here's fennel and rye bread, its lovely with the herring pate that's coming round. Then there's kelp pickle.'

Sprang appeared from the gloom, saying, 'Here's the ambrose cog.'

'I'd love a swig,' Wrasse asked.

'We are honoured to have you here at Spindrift's wake,' Sprang said, while Timber edged back to Shala's side. 'Copse tells me you are heading for Tarmin?'

'Yes,' Wrasse answered guardedly. 'I haven't travelled for years and I thought I would like to see the old place once more.'

'Do you still give predictions, Wrasse?'

'I have never given predictions, merely advice to those who come to seek it.'

'When you get back to Lee Holme, will you help with the breeding problem we have here?'

'My house is burned. Kull took it in his rage. All my records are gone.'

'But we had two bad births last year. We placed the poor things under water. It's very sad. A young lad slowly changed. He became gross and had fits. We had to halt his life. What can we do?'

Wrasse held his private stare. 'There is nothing I can do just now. Something is possibly developing. Have patience and will. I cannot give people hope. That is for them to hold and keep.'

'I see: as abrupt as your reputation. I won't pry, then. This is my young cousin's funeral. She chose her man. He's dead from fire and gone now herself, but they had good young.'

'For now, instil discipline in mating. That's very difficult, but better fewer fine bairns than rotten ones. That's my advice,' she concluded.

'Wrasse, you will all stay in my hall tonight.'

'Thank you. We will be pleased to accept your hospitality. The ambrose is excellent. Would you pass me more?'

'Erica, bring the elixir,' he called to his wife. 'Copse's party shall stay with us.'

Music began, with rhythmic scraping of scallop shells. Blown up bladders with winkle shells played in the background, as Timber introduced Shala to his friends. The wake took wings into the night.

'Good morning, Wrasse. I see you slept well in the bunk. Was it warm enough?' Erica prattled.

'I smell bread baking,' she thought as she stirred. 'A lovely night, thanks. Where's Shala?'

'Out with Timber, getting Seaforth ready. The sea funeral is tonight, under the moonlight.'

When alone, Timber asked his father, 'Can I go with Shala?'

'I think not, lad. That's a Women Only journey.'

'Oh,' he replied sadly.

'It's easy for them now; still waters, lakes and burns. They won't need us.'

'I won't even ask them, then?' he replied hopefully.

'No, you won't, boy!' Copse said sharply. 'Their refusal will be awkward for them.'

'I can see Shala when they get back, then?'

'That's different. Now we must get on.'

Wrasse got up. 'I'm desperate for that pee I was dreaming about,' she mumbled making for the great pots by the door.

'We're lending you a coracle,' Erica said, over the gush of urine. 'Bread's done. Come and eat,' she called to all.

'The coracle's ready. You could have used our reed boat, but it's beetle fodder now,' Sprang informed Wrasse on that dull, misty morning.

'We might not return this way, Sprang.'

'That's okay, it belongs at Tarmin. She's called the Spinner, for some reason. She's got a couple of paddles and fishing tackle.
''Sounds quite perfect,' she replied.

33

River Rouse

'I'll carry your bow and caisie,' offered Timber, awkwardly.

Sprang ported their coracle over his head to the Rouse. The paddles, strapped inside the craft, stuck downwards. 'You look like a giant beetle about to fly,' Shala remarked.

'There's swans and cygnets all over the water,' Wrasse remarked. 'They are an omen.'

'I see what you mean, Timber, about the dunes damming the lake. Look at all the mudflats, reed beds and islands, Wrasse.'

'Here's your stuff, Shala,' said Timber miserably. 'I'm in torment,' he confessed, 'I just want to be with you,' he whispered shakily. 'Come with me for a moment, please, Shala?'

She followed the few paces along the bushy shore as Sprang placed the coracle at the water's sandy edge.

'I know I can't come with you,' he said while pulling his jerkin off. Shala saw his reddish, downy chest. His ribs moved with passion. 'Here, Shala, I want you to have this.' He dragged his ornate bone necklace over his rough, carrotty hair, 'Here, it's yours.'

'I don't know what to say,' Shala thought, totally surprised.

'Here, have it,' he insisted, handing over the warm, sweaty love token.

'It's so beautiful,' she said feeling its warmth, and admiring the shining eagle bones. 'The seal tooth amulets are wonderful. Do you really want me to have it?' she asked, while fingering the dark cord stringing it.

'Yes. It's for you, I want you to think of me.'

'It's too big a gift,' she answered, pushing it back.

'I won't take it. It's yours now, whether you want it or not.'

'I don't have a choice, then?'

'No, Shala. Neither do I.'

'Thank you. Then I will,' was all Shala could say, seeing he yearned to hold her, but was too timid.

'Come on,' she heard Wrasse call from within the oval craft, 'everything's loaded.'

'Okay, coming,' she answered, a little relieved.

Her feet touched the rigid planking on the bottom of the rocking craft. Timber stooped and gripped the bentwood framework as she sat on the plank. 'I'll wade in and push you off,' he said reluctantly. Shala watched his blue, shining eyes as his toes bit into the soft sand. Behind, a flock of sheep baaa'd mournfully, reflecting his feelings as the Spinner drifted from his grip. He stood, shirtless, waving, waist deep.

'I'd better wave back,' Shala reflected, clutching her uneasy gift. 'His glance is so meaningful. I'll look away first,' she thought, pretending to mishandle her paddle and glancing to the distant inland horizon where low grey clouds mingled with wooded hills and winding shallow vales. On the spreading water, reeds and willow thickets were the rulers of the territory. Waterways wound into mazes of tangled, slow currents. Nothing moved quickly. The herons were never in a rush. The swans ahead glided effortlessly across the reflected clouds.

'We head for them, Shala,' Wrasse said quietly.

They paddled silently. The Spinner glided, pushing ripples aside, creating patterns behind them on their liquid road.

'I know where we're going, Wrasse,' Shala said at last. 'It's to that distant terraced hill, far off to the northwest. Timber and I went right up to the very top of the Whale Arch Tomb. We could just see it.'

Wrasse glared at her new necklace swinging over her breast. The multiple strands and spacing beads enhanced her grubby, antler-toggled jacket. Wrasse said nothing of the gift.

'Yes, that's right. We have a lot of paddling. Follow the swans. We head for where the lake ends at that far arm of forest. It looks far bigger than I remember, or am I just getting old? No, it definitely is larger! Well, all the more fish.'

'The sky's brightening,' Shala said, conscious of Wrasse's discomfort over the necklace. 'The lake's gone like silver moonshine.'

Their conversation ceased for a long while. They took in the passing scenery and life. Occasionally, the rising land had smoke curling from it to the brightening sky. One such place was just ahead of them. The swans dispersed, gliding to their nests on reedy islets.

'Look at the lily leaves below, Shala,' Wrasse said, breaking their silence. 'The pale leaves are growing. Soon they'll come up, darken and bloom fragrantly. Then moorhens will run across them.'

'We are doing well,' Shala remarked, as a sudden breeze rippled the surface.

'The Spinner's turning. Paddle down your side. Steady us,' Wrasse said. 'That's better. Real Ladies of the Lake, we are now.'

'We've hit a sunken log,' Shala shouted moments later, 'Whoops, the Spinner's spinning.'

'Compensate!' Wrasse yelped. 'Plunge your paddle in.'

'We're spinning the other way, Wrasse!'

'Keep her steady! Don't wobble.'

'I'll move.'

'Don't,' Wrasse screeched, as her side went down.

'I'll lean back.' Her side suddenly tilted. 'Help!' she yelled as she tipped overboard.

'What!' Wrasse gasped as her weight sunk her side rapidly. 'No!' she yelped, careering from the coracle. The Spinner shot in the air, returning with a sharp slap.

Wrasse saw sky through the rushing bubbles. She gripped the rotting tree stump. Its squidgy bark parted in her hands as she levered herself up. She pulled her feet from the muddy bed as her head emerged from the peaty morass. She opened her eyes. Mud trails ran from her drenched hair, and peaty water swirled brown around her. 'Shala! Where are you?' she spluttered. 'The boat and paddles are floating away,' she realized. 'What can I do?' Wrasse screamed to herself. 'I must look, I'll turn round. Still nothing.

'I'll go under.' Wrasse drew a deep breath and dived. 'I can't see a thing!' she realized as she groped forward.

'Where's Wrasse?' Shala thought in terror as she surfaced from deeper water. 'Just a paddle and the Spinner floating away. What can I do? I'll dive again!'

'I need air!' Wrasse knew.

From the submerged lilies, Shala looked up, 'There's her legs above, thank the Sprites.'

Wrasse was diving down again when they met. They grabbed each other and shot to the air above.

'Saved!' they both spluttered.

'I'll swim for the Spinner,' Shala coughed out. 'She's blowing away.'

'I'll save the paddles,' Wrasse thought in the mayhem.

'Good afternoon,' boomed a voice from behind.

Wrasse turned, startled.

'I'm Otterman,' the tall man explained from the prow of his long dugout canoe. 'Take my hand.'

'I don't believe this,' Wrasse responded while extending her arm.

'Relax,' was all he said as he gripped her wrist, to hoist her suddenly over the side.

'Welcome aboard the Harpoon,' two of his children chirped excitedly, as Wrasse flopped like a stranded seal.

'Shala. Shala,' Wrasse called from her prone position.

'It's okay, Lady of the Lake, I've spotted her,' Otterman said. His bare arms, tattooed with writhing eels, pushed his paddle into the water. The sleek canoe responded. Wrasse admired his elegant, muscular frame as he edged the boat skilfully around a reed bed. 'Stay there. Hang on to your boat,' he called to Shala, 'I'll pull you out'. Wrasse watched the undulating, black tattoos of salmon and trout on his back. His tight boar skin trousers stretched as he crouched. 'Grab my hand, Miss,' he said.

'Thanks. I see Wrasse is saved,' she remarked as she felt Otterman's strength lift her from the water.

'Welcome aboard, Young Lady of the Lake,' he said calmly. His two young copied him, laughing uncontrollably.

'Thank you so much,' Shala began to say.

'Shut up and get the paddles,' Otterman told his kids, then answered Shala, 'No bother. All in a day's fishing. Throw the line to their coracle, Sprat. You and Mackerel pull it in close. Caisie, staff, wet loaf? Is that all that should be in there, apart from your good selves?' he asked.

'What about my bow and arrows?' Shala replied in alarm.

'Yes, them too. Just testing, making sure you're not drowned.'

'Not drowned, just water in my ears,' remarked Wrasse. Sprat gripped her sides, weeping with laughter. Mackerel went blue in the face.

'I've lost my staff,' Wrasse said urgently. The two kids erupted. 'Forget it,' she said grumpily as watery ooze dripped off her nose.

'Shut up, you rude sods,' Otterman warned his young, as Shala kept thanking him. He dipped his paddle from his position on a solid rise of wood dividing the canoe. Sprat and Mackerel giggled by the catch, in their end.

'Enough fishing for today. We'll get this precious catch home, though. How shall we cook them, kids?' Otterman joked. 'I like your necklace, young lady.'

'Yours is very smart too. And your tusk ear-spikes,' Shala replied. 'Home's through that young reedbed – see the planking jetty?'

Shala noticed other craft reflected in the calm water. The sun broke the clouds and the encroaching evening became warmer than the day.

'Excuse me,' Otterman asked, running forward along the narrow sides of the Harpoon, 'Loop the painter rope over the post and cast on, Mackerel,' then looked to Wrasse, announcing, 'I'm Otterman. Who calls you what?'

'I am called Wrasse, by most.'

'Tough fish, the wrasse. They swim better than you, though. And you, Miss?'

'Shala, I'm called by all at Lee Holme.'

'Shala's just a baby noise,' Otterman remarked, leaping onto the jetty. 'Bag the catch, kids. Bring it ashore then bring our guests' belongings. Stop giggling and get a move off.' The pair, barely two years apart, snapped to their dad's commands. 'Good kids, those. Follow me along the rickety planks. The quay's seen better days. It was longer, but it sunk some. Those reed boats are mine, even the rotten one with ferns growing from it. It makes a good harpooning spot. That half-buried canoe was my Grandpop's. His soul still sails it, sometimes. Hello, Brill,' Otterman called to his wife, as she came to meet him.

Wearing a wide-brimmed reed hat and a long, flowing grass skirt,

Brill called, 'Here's your cape. It's getting chilly.' Her berry bead necklace snaked between her breasts to her protruding navel.

'We've got wet guests; give it to the old one.'

'Welcome, I'm Brill. Here, let me wrap this round you. Come up to our house before you get a chill.'

Their way was lined with low mounds, from which carved wooden stakes protruded. The one at the jetty was large and hollow. At their bases, small offering bowls held morsels of food. Shala could smell the pungency of the smouldering juniper fronds from within the tall, round house. Smoke eased through the pointed thatched roof, where eels and boar-meat hung. Its eaves overhung the smoothed, dried mud walls. Otterman and Brill's two older offspring leaned on the doorposts and waved in the scantiest of clothing. Morning was a year younger than Shala. Her breasts showed delightfully and Night, her older brother, was showing off his first adult tattoos, smiling brightly at their visitors.

'Come in. Get those wet clothes off. I'll bring dry. Warm up by the fire. Morning, fetch them drink. There's bread in the basket. Night, move your corpse, stop posing and get a bucket of water. Springwater, not lake water, you lazybones.'

'Right. I'm off,' he gyrated with agility, for Shala's benefit, 'Well-water it is. Do come in,' he gestured.

'Here's my knotted wool shawl. Put it over you,' Brill offered Shala.

'Thank you. I'm Shala.'

'I'm Wrasse. Can we take our soaking stuff off, first?'

Brill stuttered, startled, 'Y... yes of course. H... Help them get dry, Morning.'

From a high loft, through streams of smoky light, through an open vent croaked a voice, 'Who is it?'

'Visitors, Mother,' Brill called up.

'What, "itors"? I can't hear.'

'V I S I T O R S, Mother.'

'Oh. Shall I come down?' the old girl mumbled from the top of her ladder, 'I could be dead up here, for all they care. Fetch me my stick. Who are they?'

'Wrasse and Shala from Lee Holme, Mother,' Brill shouted clearly.

'No need to shout, dear. Just tell me who they are.'

'W r a s s e a n d S h a l a f r o m L e e H o l m e.'

'It's all right, dear, I heard you the first time,' she grunted, catching her foot on the bottom rung. 'So you're back, Wrasse!' she screeched while hobbling round. The old sisters stared at each other. "Fine mess you've got yourself into. 'Always were in trouble. What about that man you took from us? Wasn't that enough?'

'Mother. Shut up!' Brill scolded, turning to Wrasse, 'I couldn't believe it when you said your name. I should have warned you. Otterman should have, too. He just laughs and let's things happen.

'Why are you here? Come to torment us?'

'Mother. Shut up.'

'Shut up, in my own house? That'll be the day.'

'It is our house, Mother. The sooner you go in one of those mounds, the better. And don't think I'm going to put out nice offerings for you.'

'Can I interfere?' Otterman asked as he darkened their portal. 'Now then, ladies. Let's not have all this impoliteness and fuss. It's our house, Granny and I will say just who goes under what mound and who gets the nice offerings, so watch it. Now, greet your lovely sister nicely, Lintel.'

Lintel watched Morning drying Wrasse's hair through her fingers. 'Her old body's straighter than mine, and those wrinkled tattoos are still recognizable.'

'This is a total surprise,' Wrasse stated abruptly. 'I didn't know you lived here. Nobody told me.'

'Why should they? None of your business, or theirs,' Lintel snapped.

'Don't speak to my aunty like that, Mother. Act civilized, please,' Brill warned.

'She never could be nice,' Wrasse put in.

Shala stood, amazed.

'Are sisters Cran and Mire still living?' Wrasse asked.

'Dead, dead. 'Don't care, anyway. Get me a drink,' Lintel demanded, as Night returned with the bucket. 'That took you long enough,' she complained. 'No, not water. Get me and your Great Aunt, here, a proper drink. Fetch that juniper wine. That will sort us out. Bring me my whalebone stool.'

'I'll hang your clothes under the eaves,' Brill said, thinking, 'At least they are talking.' Then she admonished, 'Night, stop leaning on the ladder and posing for Shala. You'll get such a stiff on we could hang a hat on it. Sprat, Mackerel, knock out slices of ham nice and thin with your sea-stones.'

Night dodged aside and rummaged for the concoction's flask. 'Here you are,' he said as he pulled the bone stopper. 'Leave some for me.'

Otterman crouched by the fire, musing, 'Interesting to watch them women, sparring. That stuff will mellow them,' he thought. 'Funny how Lintel's hearing improves with each sip.'

'Does Gravel live?' Lintel asked.

'Long dead. Lost to a bull seal. His body never came back from the waves.'

'Simple sort, but reliable,' Lintel commented. 'I got a Marsh Man, that's why I'm here. A good breeder, so my family is well. He mated in the north, too. I never met his line there. He's got a mound with them as well. Bits of him are in it. They got his pelvis, lucky sods.'

Shala sat in her shawl. 'It's fascinating to see Wrasse and her sister. What an utter surprise,' she thought. 'I'll ignore Night's tattoo display, though. He does think he's wonderful.'

Outside, bats fed on a fresh hatch of flies. Their high-pitched squeaks swirled round the thatch as they hunted.

'Yes. That Sea Angel?' Lintel enquired. Brill's ears pricked up. Shala listened discretely. Morning lolled on a sheepskin on the clay floor. Otterman twisted his bone nose-spike. Sprat and Mackerel drew close, sensing drama. Night mooched off outside. 'How did you know he was coming?' Lintel asked.

'If you want to know, I kept seeing him in dreams. The birds told me, too. I saw other things, which I understand now. I tried to tell you.'

'I know,' Lintel admitted. 'We were so jealous when he arrived. But he was such a rotten mess, we were almost pleased you'd have him.' Lintel coughed vilely and spat dark phlegm into the fire. 'It's that fucking juniper smoke that gets me,' directing her comment at Brill.

'More likely the wine,' Brill muttered.

'When he was recovering, we made plans with Mother. She'd worked out the order we were to breed with him. She wished she could, too. You were last.'

Wrasse listened, feeling livid. 'Keep calm,' she told herself.

'We hated you,' Lintel rasped, curling her cracked tongue and spitting into the embers, 'We were delighted when you went. But

I can see you're still the same Wrasse. Your wary expression, like when you were a little girl. She's got it, too,' pointing at Shala. 'After you left, pregnant with Gravel, Coutou came to visit. She said, "Do you think that girl will ever be happy after the way you treated her?" She looked at Mother, saying, "I doubt if she will ever forgive any of you." Then she told us everything you'd been through. She said his death could not have been prevented. He knew it was his last mating chance.'

Wrasse's brow dipped into her hands. She shook, remembering the dreadful time: the loneliness, excepting Coutou's friendship. 'Why, oh why am I going back?' she thought.

'Then Coutou stunned us,' Lintel continued. 'She said you knew who he was and from where he came.'

Wrasse lifted her head. She saw wisps of white hair, like her badger stripe, coming from under Brill's hat. She recognized the family line.

Lintel went on, 'Coutou sat staring at us. Father came in and squatted next to her. He glared at us, one by one. She then opened her mouth and said, "Who he was and where he was from is Wrasse's secret. It will die with us both." She then stood and left.' Lintel's phlegm-filled throat wobbled. 'There. You have it, Wrasse. We are sorry.'

34

The House of Croo

'Birch wine!' Lintel demanded, 'She'll have some, too.' Morning found the skin flask. 'Put mine upsteps. I'm going to bed.' She hobbled to her ladder, shakily climbing, then crawling, to her mattress on the creaky wattle bed.

'Here's your wine, Granny,' Morning said as Lintel coughed, spitting into a dish.

'Good,' she answered, hawking painfully.

Below, they heard her bed heave as she finally breathed a long, rattling sigh.

'Old cow's quiet at last,' Otterman commented, poking the fire and twisting his nose-spike.

'Let me sit by you, Wrasse,' Shala said.

'I'll break the bread,' Brill suggested, 'Sprat and Mackerel hand round the ham. Morning, get cups: fill your father's with the juniper, then me. Offer our guests, too.'

'I heard that flask gurgling,' Night said as he came back in.

'An apology, Shala,' Wrasse whispered in shock. 'That's the last thing I thought she'd ever do. Let's drink to it.'

Wrasse sipped wine thoughtfully for ages, then wearily asked, 'Where do we sleep?'

'We all stay down here in the alcove beds. She's better on her own up there. Have more wine and smoked pig before you go.'

'Thank you. It's lovely. I must go out and pee first.'

Otterman said, much later, 'Brill and I will stay up to make sure the wine flask dries right out. You sleep if you want.'

Shala woke early thinking, 'I'm not used to clay houses. The sounds are so different. It's nice enough, though.'

Night went fishing on the misty Lake. Morning slumbered. Mackerel and Sprat giggled about the rescue the day before. 'Quiet you two, or I'll set your fierce old granny on you,' Otterman warned. They laughed all the more.

'At least she's stopped coughing. Where's my spike?' Otterman added rubbing his face.

'I took it out and poked you with it. You were snoring. I couldn't get you off me, or out of me, either,' came Brill's answer.

'Sorry, dear,' he replied grinning.

'Otterman, she still hasn't coughed.'

'Nor she has, dear. Perhaps she's better,' he answered, squeezing out his morning fart.

'My bones ache,' Wrasse grumbled.

'I'll take Mother her morning drink and mix her oats.'

'Okay, dear,' Otterman yawned slinking back into his warm pile of pelts.

The ladder creaked as he drifted into a delicious dream of mating again.

'AaaGGhh!' he heard Brill scream, 'She's dead. She's dead!'

'What?' Otterman shouted, 'I'm coming up.'

Mackerel and Spratt sat up alarmed, watching their naked father scale the rungs.

Morning came from her torpor. 'Dead! Dead! Dead!' was all she could hear. 'Who's dead?' she asked wearily.

'No?' Wrasse thought, 'Not her? Not now? Not when we'd just met after all this time.'

'Can't be dead,' Otterman said on the ladder, still farting. 'Gosh! Look at her. She's all crunched up, mouth wide open – as usual – but those staring eyes. Look at her skinny legs and her willow tree tattoo. Shove her dress back over her flabby stomach, Brill, she looks horrible. Never drank her drink, either. Yes, she's dead, all right,' thinking, 'about bloody time, too.'

'That means we are going to have a funeral,' Sprat and Mackerel said eagerly.

'You two keep quiet and leave your grieving mother alone. And stop sounding so thrilled.'

'What can I do?' Shala thought. 'Nothing's probably best right now,' then said, 'Oh, Wrasse, you look so shocked. I'll crawl over.'

'Oh, Otterman. Look at her. She must be frozen.' Swifts flew by the roof opening, casting shadows across the body. They dashed up Brill's arm as she gently touched her dead mother's outstretched hand. 'Frozen,' she said. 'Stiff, too. Rigid.'

'Stiff and frozen,' Otterman tried to say sympathetically. 'I'll cover her, dear.'

'Thank you,' Brill replied quietly, 'I've been expecting this pretty well every day now.'

'Have you, love?'

'Yes. Now it's happened it's taken me all by surprise. I'm going to cry. Sit next to me, darling. Give me a cuddle.'

'Of course, dear,' he replied.

'Do you think you should fetch Night, Morning?' Shala suggested.

'No. He'll be out on the lake. When I do get him, she'll still be dead, so what's the point? I'll just stay in bed.'

'Yes, I suppose so,' she answered.

'We will have to arrange a good burial,' Otterman said usefully. 'Will you two down there stay for it?'

'Yes. Of course. She was my sister, after all,' Wrasse said quietly.

'Fine. At least someone will be present from foreign parts. Brill and I will stay up here for a while,' he added feigning sympathy.

Night returned to the quiet household with a string of fish. 'What's up?' he asked.

'Granny's dead! Granny's dead. And we are having a funeral,' Mackerel shrieked excitedly.

'Dead? When?' he reacted, looking up the ladder, where his mother was busy.

'Funeral's tomorrow, we hope,' Sprat got in.

'I didn't mean the funeral, stupid. I meant when did she croak?'

'Stop this,' Otterman said, quelling a laugh. 'Have some respect. Your mother's very upset. Sprat, Mackerel, stop giggling. Out you two go. I'm coming down to get dressed. We can bang the drum this afternoon, Night.'

'Great. I'll search out my drum bones. Morning, paint my face.'

'No! Ask Shala, I'm helping mum prepare Granny when I get up.'

'Thank you, Shala,' Night eventually said after she had painted his brow.

'You can oil your own tattoos. Your checked cheeks look good. They go with the light dash in your hair.'

'Night,' Otterman called. 'We're going to the jetty drum mound.' They stood on a stone slab either side of the upright, carved, hollow trunk. The inside was burned black; the exterior had a pike's head carved over its undulating surface. 'Bang it with Longo's thigh, I'll use his other. That'll announce it to the neighbours. Them at the Kit of Otter will be here first. Keep time with me, slowly though. Change tempo as I do. Do you feel the bones resonate, Night?'

'Yes, Dad, and that's the Kit Folk answering. Their drum booms nicely, doesn't it.'

'Yup. They'll be here by evening, and more from elsewhere, too.'

'What was Granddad like, Night?' Sprat and Mackerel asked later while Otterman shifted the thick, moss-covered planks from over his cist.

'I was so young, I hardly remember. Only he was huge and covered in tattoos of boar mating and hunting.' The gathering crowd agreed.

'Will we see them?'

'There won't be much left after the slugs have been at him. Anyway, watch. Squeeze through the folk's legs.'

'That's the smell of sweet decay,' Otterman thought, as the first plank shifted. 'You kids, keep back, you're knocking the sides in.'

'We want to look.'

'Well, wait. You can get a gander later.'

'That's kids, Otterman,' a friend commented.

'I want to see his skull,' Mackerel whinged.

'You'll see your own, soon, if you don't shut up,' Otterman replied swiftly.

'Look!' Sprat exclaimed when the third thick sleeper was pulled away, 'His ribs are sticking out of his jacket. Why's he so short, Dad?'

'Because we sent his pelvis and mating gear north. There's the wooden one we carved him.'

'It's too big.'

'Shut up. He liked it like that.'

'His nose spike's dropped out. Why's he on his side?'

'It's like he's sleeping.'

'His skull's great! Can we have it?'

'No! His leather cap hasn't gone yet. You can have that, but later.'

'Can I get his ear spikes?'

'That's enough. You can stop thinking about that cup, too. That's his last drink. We'll fill it up when Granny goes in. Let's hope he doesn't fall apart too much before she does. They will need a new rush bed. His one's had it.'

'That means we have to shift him.'

'Yes, but Mother and I'll do that tomorrow. You keep your interfering hands off.'

'Can we watch?'

'Ask your mother.'

'Come on, kids,' a visitor said. 'We've got a wake to prepare. You can help.'

By daybreak Lintel's corpse was still stiff. 'Can you carry her down, Otterman?'

'Yes, I'll be right up, Brill. Her hammock's ready.'

'Careful with her, Otterman,' Brill implored.

'Her arm won't shift, dear.'

'I'm hoping she'll soften up during the day. Better take her down as she is, just now.'

'It's awkward, she won't bend.'

The crowd was still waiting at the grave when Brill finally said, 'It's time, even though she's still stiff. Night, Otterman, take the head end: Sprat, Mackerel, her back. Morning and me will be at her feet.

'We can put Erica's soggy loaf in,' Wrasse told Shala. 'It will be a fine offering.'

'Careful, Night, I'll step in, you steady her shoulders,' Otterman advised, closing his eyes guiltily as he felt the cup crush underfoot. 'Carefully now, Brill. Feet down,' he said, covering the accident.

'Ahh,' Brill remarked almost brightly, 'her outstretched arms look like she's caressing him. Otterman, would you put her bowl of unfinished wine in?'

'Yes, dear, fetch it, I'll place it between them. Now, neighbours, you can put your offerings in the grave until evening. Then we'll cover the reunited couple with blankets. Here, Mackerel, there's Grandpop's rotten old cap; I see we have a nice new straw one.'

'Let's go and play Dead People,' Sprat suggested. 'We might get nice things, too.'

'Wrasse?' Brill asked. 'Would you go through her belongings with me?'

'Well, yes. Are you sure?'

'There's not much, only shell jewellery she never wore and a few old knives and scrapers, and then there's her leather box. Can you manage the ladder?'

'Yes, easily, but it feels strange.'

Wrasse looked awkwardly round the sparse room: a small marrowbone lamp, her low bed, the imprint of her body still in the mattress and, by her pillow, the chipped dish with her drying spit. Necklaces hung from a peg in a beam.

Under her bed was what they both stared at: a familiar, yet ominous, round leather boar-skin box.

'That was our Mother's,' Wrasse broke the silence. 'Not very big, is it? Lintel kept it nicely polished, though.'

'Open it, Wrasse. It needs twisting. I've never seen inside. Just the sun emblem on the top.'

'Neither I, Brill. Open the shutters, let's get some light.'

'Okay, we can sit on her bed. Ease the lid gently.'

'I know that smell,' Wrasse said. 'It's Mother's rose powder.'

'Lintel used that on special occasions. She called this box her 'Little House of Croo.' It was private. There are secrets inside. "Potent objects", she said.'

'It's coming off. Look, Brill.'

'It's all covered by a marsh cotton doily, Wrasse. Take it out.'

'We'll do it together. There's stuff from two mothers in here. Yours and mine.'

'My hand's shaking, Wrasse.'

'Take your mum's lovely cloth. Pull it with me.' Worried, Wrasse smelt something else.

'Look,' Brill said, 'that's her antler phallus. See the red tip and the balls at the base?'

'Yes, my mother had it before. It was part of her fertility kit. Lay it on the bed.'

'There's her horn bracelet. I only saw it on her once. I loved the cowries set in it.'

'Yes, Brill, but see that white, polished knife. I think it was Coutou's, I recognize the resin handle. How did she get it?'

'Lintel used that to cut my babies' cords, Wrasse.'

'Mmmmmm,' Wrasse responded as that odour increased.

'We'd better look under next bit of lace.'

'Gosh! Look at all her amulets. What lovely pierced shells and this tiny amber man, threaded with flax through his armpits. You take him out, Wrasse.'

'Very well, Brill, but it's caught on something underneath. We'll take the other bits out first.'

'I'll arrange them on the bed. All these carved pebbles. This one looks like me when I was pregnant! Ah. See, there's a chamois pouch, our amber chap's tied to it. It's got a jet fastener. Take it out, Wrasse.'

'It's looking back at me,' Wrasse thought, shivering in a cold sweat.

'Take it,' uttered Brill.

'I feel my hand move. I can't stop it. I know what's in there. It's dangling from the amber. I can't let go,' Wrasse thought silently. 'You open it, Brill.'

'No, Wrasse. I'm sure it's for you. I'll hold it.'

The pull-string loosened. Wrasse wept as the contents spilled.

'Are you all right, Wrasse? I've just come from the grave. I saw something,' Shala called from below as she scaled the ladder.

'Come up,' Wrasse sobbed.

'What is it?' Brill demanded.

'I knew that smell,' Wrasse managed. 'Look, it's a purse. It's made from my Sea Angel's kayak. I thought it was all burned! And those strange barnacles.'

'My, my,' remarked Brill, blankly.

'That toggle fastener's from his jacket. What's inside?'

'You have to open it, Wrasse,' Shala expressed quietly. 'I'll twist it, if you like.'

'No. It is for me. Lintel or my Mother kept these things. I'll look. Ah!' she exclaimed, wincing, 'It's the deadly point of the narwhal tusk that killed him! I know the rest! It's some of Weir. It's his dried flesh. What bit? Why did they do this? There's a scrap of Sea Angel's parka where we cut his arm off; see the felt lining? I can smell him so strongly.'

'Those are exactly like the barnacles from the Trees, Wrasse.'

'Yes, Shala. They were stuck to his boat.'

'Well, Wrasse, I just had a vivid vision. I looked into Lintel's wine cup in her grave and saw him in his boat. I was coming back, I knew you needed me.'

'That's the smell of his infection. It's all so real again. Now I know why we are going to Tarmin. They kept these things for some kind of power. I wonder what else we'll find?'

'I'll tip it out,' Brill said, sneezing violently, blowing the dusty powder away. 'Look, Wrasse, there's a temple with an altar incised in the horn base.'

'Let me look, Brill,' she turned it, making out the stylized lines. 'That curve over it is sky and the zigzag line beneath, water. It must be the House of Croo. Look on the edge, too, there's the Moon's shapes.'

'What's the House of Croo?' Shala asked.

'It's the Nurture House for women's learning. I have been thinking of taking you there.'

'I'm taking Morning. Should we go together?'

'I'm not sure,' Shala thought awkwardly. 'Maybe it's like our teaching house though, where Juniper's been?'

'You look worried, Shala. It's all right; I'm from these parts. I assure you, if you don't want to participate, that's fine. It's a special precinct where us women learn, but some more than others.'

'Here's your box back. I must hold Weir's relic. Now you know our secret, Brill. I told Shala everything. I trust her. She's my heiress. She will be my equal and, one day, a great deal more. Her own story is growing even yet.'

'I know the legend of the Sea Angel,' Brill stressed. 'How he crossed the wide sea guided in by magic swans. How all the birds of the water pushed the waves, bringing him ashore. How his boat was the strangest ever seen. It had wonderful shells outside with splendid seaweed flowing behind. How he was growing another arm. How magnificent and rare his pale beard was. How he died and was brought back to life to become the most beautiful of men. We heard it many times: my children, too. Then, how a wicked young nurse made love with him and took his spirit. She was banished, her name never to be mentioned in Tarmin again. She was you!' Brill revealed. 'Here, in our garret, a new part is unfolding. These things must be powerful totems that our mothers guarded.'

'Yes, Brill. But it wasn't quite like that. There have been many changes to the story. May I keep this package? It's so important to me.'

'Certainly,' Brill exclaimed. 'It's more yours than anyone's. Is there anything else?'

'Yes, Coutou's knife, as a keepsake. But turn the lid over, please, so I can see inside.'

'Here,' she answered, 'It's just plain, but polished pitch black.'

'Yes, Brill, but see the bright specks of mica? Get me some of that birch wine!'

'It is all gone, Wrasse, Otterman and I finished it last night.'

'Do you not have more?'

'No.'

'I can get some,' Shala announced.

'Where from?' Wrasse asked.

'Lintel's grave.'

'Good idea,' Brill answered.

Shala slid down the ladder. Outside, a crowd surrounded Sprat and Mackerel, who were enacting two dead heroes killed in mortal combat. Mock prayers were being said over them. Piles of delicious offerings were being placed at their feet. 'Arise, young spirits,' Shala blessed, 'for you have an errand beyond the grave.'

Sprat's eye opened. She rose as if in a trance. 'Wooooooo,' the assembly chanted. Mackerel's eyes also miraculously opened, becoming conscious again in the Spirit World.

'Your Earthly Mother has commanded that you reach down into your Grandparents' hallowed sepulchre and retrieve the cup of sacred birch fluid. Do not spill a drop, for you will be in peril of your eternal life in the exulted places.'

Ghostlike, they made their way to the open grave. 'I will enter and lift the cup,' Sprat said, carefully stepping in and handing it to Mackerel. 'Ooops,' she uttered under her breath, feeling her grandfather's nose spike snap beneath her heel. 'Here, take the grail from my outstretched arms. Hand it to Shala for her errand of sorcery.'

'Your souls are blessed,' Shala answered as she took the cup back to Lintel's room.

'Thanks,' Wrasse said gripping the plain vessel on Shala's return. 'Watch. Sit around it,' she added filling the lid amongst the strewn contents. 'The mica shines like stars. There's the Hunter, the Sheep, the Wolf and then the Mother Star, shining brightest.'

'And our reflections,' Shala added.

'Very useful,' Brill said adjusting her hair.

'This was my sister's fertility kit. Those perforated cockleshells, you can count a menstrual month on their ridges. The ends have been grooved specially. That oblong bit of polished quartz, it's special. Why, though, was something of Weir there?

'This will all be very useful one day. Keep it safe, Brill.'

'I will, I will,' she promised.

'We should return Lintel's drink and re-join the wake?'

'Stop!' Shala said urgently, 'The geese. Look in the lid, there's two flying towards us.'

'Yes,' Wrasse answered, 'the attic's filled with their presence. I feel them all around, can't you?'

Brill shivered as the apparitions swirled, to vanish through the skylight.

'Not a word to anyone of this,' Wrasse said, when all was calm.

35

The Shrinking Island

'We must return Lintel's bowl,' Shala said at last.

'Rise again from your tomb, please,' Shala asked Sprat and Mackerel. 'Lintel must have her sacred grave grail returned.'

'Yes,' Brill added. 'Now for their meadowsweet wreaths; then replace the planks and complete the mound.'

'Let's drink and feast on,' others implored.

'Wrasse?' Brill asked during the celebration, 'When will you go to the Isle of the Nurture House?'

'It's not an island, surely, Brill?'

'It is now. Reeds grow where the causeway was.'

'Really? Well, as soon as it suits.'

'Otterman can take us, and the Spinner there in the Harpoon. Sprat and Mackerel can stay with Clart from the Kit. Night can be on his own, here.'

'Tomorrow morning?' Wrasse suggested.

'Why not? Mother can look after herself, now. We can plant herbs on their mound later.'

Morning dragged herself up. The early pillars of mist rose from still waters. Fish fed within, making invisible ripples. A kingfisher flashed unseen. An osprey perched in a tall pine.

'Will Clart let us play tombs?' the young asked.

'I expect so.'

'Goodeeee,' they yelled, jumping into the Harpoon.

'I've Lintel's House of Croo,' Brill whispered to Wrasse.

'I have Weir's parcel in my grass skirt.'

'Push us off... Night, Don't get up to anything stupid, like burning the house down,' Otterman said.

'Milk the goats and don't take any more duck eggs,' Brill added.

'Okay. Trust me,' he replied delightedly, thinking of all the things he could get up to.

The osprey glided to a different tree. An otter slid unobserved into the still depths.

Otterman punted round a reedbed to open water. 'There aren't any sunken tree stumps out here. Absolutely safe,' he assured. They drew up to the new plank pier at Otter's Kit's. 'Hop out, you two. Be good, and help with Clart's new baby.'

'Bye, Morning,' Sprat called before sprinting up the mooring to Clart's home.

Later, Otterman remarked, 'We take this arm of the lake. Notice the slight current? There'll be sunken trees, soon. Carp swim here. Sometimes their backs stick out. Tench are feeding on the bottom. Watch the bubbles come up. There's pike as well. I'll fish for them on the way back.

'See where beavers have taken saplings down, Shala? I haven't tasted one of them for a long while,' Wrasse reported, asking, 'Weren't these woodlands dry land, Otterman?'

'They were, but we had a big flood. Not all the water went. Even our island got smaller. The Otter's Kit was Kits. Some sunk and are reedbeds now. That trunk you bashed into, we used to play and dive from it when I was wee.'

Wrasse shook her head, 'Perhaps Brill's right about the Nurture House being on an island.

'We saved our neighbours' pigs and sheep,' Brill told her, 'then slaughtered lots because there wasn't room. Well, we have more fish now, so that's all right.'

The Heron's Tooth scraped past a submerged trunk as Otterman said, 'The main flow's there, where it's lighter. Be useful and paddle. Watch for other submerged wood. It's a while yet before we get to the end of this.'

'The current's stronger,' Shala remarked to Morning. 'Are you going to paddle, like us?' She shook her head and curled up in the beam.

'Soon be there,' Otterman told them. 'The water's clearer and the bed's sandy. I'll watch for boulders. Mind your scalps... Low branches ahead.' The Harpoon scraped the bottom. 'The water divides here. We go left and wade. I drag. You push.'

'It'll float better when you're out, Morning. Now roll your skirt up and join in,' Brill cajoled.'

'She's moving again,' Otterman said, 'The waterway gets narrower soon. The current increases as we go. Next time she grounds, we'll build a dam behind and wait for the water to deepen.'

'Good idea,' Shala thought.

'If it holds, it will take us a long way,' Otterman added.

'Good,' remarked Morning, 'I'm tired.

'You're always tired. What's the matter with you?' Brill commented.

'It's rough work, making dams. All those branches; the moss, the stones. Beavers do it much better.'

'I'll wade and tow,' Otterman said later, alerting a heron in the willows. 'Soon we'll be at River Head at the outflow from the loch above. We can all drag the Harpoon up the shallows and relaunch on the still waters.'

'There's the Nurture House,' Brill pointed out when they boarded again, 'right out in the middle.'

'Ssshhhh!' said Otterman, 'There's a huge pike. It's watching for prey. Pass me my harpoon. Careful, it's shifted.' He became sticklike, blending into his background as he lifted his harpoon slowly, barely seeming to move. 'It's turning,' he whispered, 'watching for roach.' It hurled itself forward with a gaping mouth as Otterman hurled too. 'Got it!' he yelled. The water exploded. The pike flew out of the loch; its jaw gaping, tail flailing. 'Stuck him good and proper,' Otterman's voice rang out, seeing his harpoon jutting between the fish's eyes.

'Right, ladies: off to your Nurture House. Grab a paddle.'

'I can just see the grove, Shala, but not the yew avenue along the ridge. It's all reeds. We walked along the causeway. It's vanished,' Wrasse said surprised. 'When I was taken, there were other girls from over the Hill. I felt punished, because of poor Weir. Mother wouldn't forget. I had to go through the ceremonies before I could be matched with Gravel.'

The loch sped beneath as they drew ever closer to the blossom-covered isle. 'Whack the boat, Otterman, announce our arrival. Look! The cherry blossom petals are blowing towards us. It's beautiful.'

'I'll nudge the Harpoon up to the wattle wharf. You climb the plank steps to the paving,' Otterman said, 'You don't need me here. It's taboo for us men, ain't it? Here, grab the fish. I'm off to Sparrow Hall. You can send for me when you're done.'

They stood on lozenge-shaped paving stones and watched Otterman paddle by the decaying yew stumps. Behind them was a low, neatly trimmed, hawthorn hedge, just in leaf. It parted and led up a flight of rectangular stone steps. At the top stood two women with white, feathered robes over soft openwork suede suits. In their hazel hair were gentle ribbons of marsh cotton. As the pair moved forward, a caressing breeze ruffled apple blossom. From behind came the gentlest of singing. There were no words, but within the midst of those melodies a sense of utter peace enveloped the landing stage.

Swans nibbled the neat grass along the shore. Ewes and lambs grazed peacefully under the flowering trees. Seven hinds looked down from the placid orchard. The sun shone warmly as swallows swooped.

'Come, I am Velvet; this is Lily, your other Priestess. Here, take these garlands of violets,' she said, gently welcoming their visitors.

Lily bade them ascend the steps. Velvet kissed each on the forehead. They said nothing. The voice from the grove sang on with the swooping swallows as Lily placed the flowered ringlets on their heads.

At the head of the steps, a long stepping-stone path wove across a verdant, daisy-dotted lawn. The hinds raised their sedate heads to peer at the newcomers, while keeping a keen eye on their fawns in the shade.

The path took them deep into the orchard towards a large, beautifully built circular house. The resplendent reed roof soared above. Pale doves flew at its apex and cooed as the singing ceased. 'That door. It's like none I've seen before,' Shala thought. 'It curves in on itself. The roof rises like an angled porch. The wonderful coursing's got random pink granite pebbles. A curtain of fine rushwork covers the entrance. Velvet and Lily are pushing gently through.'

Wrasse remembered her visit, 'Yes, my mother assisted in the ceremony. Then it was a promontory into the lake. Now it's separated. And still no male animals are kept here, apart from their young.'

'I need to duck below the carved stone lintel,' Shala realized. 'It seems far older than the building. Its worn face is hewn with interweaving circles, looking down invitingly. The walls heighten and curve back. Inside, it's lit by tall candles and there's a warm glow from those pottery braziers. Everything smells of dewberry.

'Leave your belongings behind the entrance screens,' Velvet explained quietly. 'Over there are couches to relax on.'

'They're made of moulded clay covered with flowing skins,' Shala noticed.

'When you are rested, please explore our island. Food will appear. Think of nothing. We leave now.' After Velvet added fragrant wood to the braziers, blue smoke drifted through the Nurture House.

'That's the same central altar,' Wrasse remembered. 'Clay, like the couches, but shaped like a sleeping auroch. Yes, I lay on it. Was that the cause of my dreams? I can't remember. I just know it was so special on the soft pelt coverings. How they glisten in the candleglow, even now. The rock-lined well rises yet from the sacred spring. Do trout still lie in those dark waters?'

Shala thought, 'The colourful rugs are wonderful to tread on. The aroma is so relaxing, too. I'm weary. I'll lie on the auroch. I see we're all thinking the same. There's a bark cup of fragrant water with blossom petals. My arms feel like logs. I must sleep.'

In her many dreams, one lasted. 'I am shrinking. It's so warm in this deep pink place. I'm floating among soft cushions. Gentle, pulsing heartbeats surround me. I'm a mere speck as the heartbeats grow with passion. I'm now new, moist and warm... Growing as I sleep. I travel through flowering woodlands along a winding path bordered with white anemones. Gentle fronds caress me as I move while the woodland tunnel widens. I see a bright light ahead. I'm forced forward in spasms. I see past the end of the cavern. Before is a wide valley within undulating hills. I'm bare. The path before crosses many others, I can see far, far ahead. Many strangers look towards me as I edge to the beginnings of this great road. Birds fly high in the sky singing clearly. I feel I will never pass this way again. But I see him ahead! As I look back, there is nothing, only me.'

Shala woke slowly to Velvet calling, 'Aiva, Aiva.'

'I'm different,' she thought as she shifted from her feathery pillow, propping herself on the down bolster. 'My hair's flowing around me lightly instead of a matted mess. I'll just relax in this delightful comfort. I feel so light. I don't want to move. But I'm wearing a wonderful shift, like gossamer. How come? My breasts feel fuller beneath. There's Morning, deep in slumber. Her hair looks so glossy, and there's a thin, white stripe that's been daintily plaited. That's amazing, as well! My travelling clothes are clean, folded.'

'You have slept well,' Velvet said quietly.

'Indeed,' Shala said sleepily, rubbing her eyes. 'The light's different. I seem different.'

'That's right,' said Lily softly. 'There's fishcakes and warm milk on the wicker chair beside you.'

'Every movement seems new. I must try to sit up for my milk. It's lovely, so warming,' she thought, 'but the cup remains full. I'm hungry, I'll try a fishcake. Mmm! They are wonderful, the soft oaten crust, the chive flowers and caper flavouring is divine with the succulent fish.'

'That's Otterman's pike, Aiva,' she heard Velvet say through her mist of pleasure. 'The recipe will make you feel new and fresh inside.'

'Yes, I feel wonderful changes as I swallow. But there are still two whole ones, even after I've eaten. And there's more milk, again?'

'That's a House of Croo breakfast. It goes on until you are quite replete and feel the new spirit of woman within, Aiva,' Velvet said distantly.

Shala, feeling absolutely new, stood to her full height to look down past her translucent gown to her perfect feet.

'You can take your meal outside,' Velvet told her as the singing commenced.

'Sit on the bench with us,' Wrasse said, looking resplendent.

'You have slept well,' Wrasse said. 'Nearly a day and a half.'

'Really?' Shala replied yawning.

The singer, Ebb, appeared with an air of utter peace. He seemed neither old nor young. In the female domain he was not out of place. His voice, not of man or woman, harmonized with the singing of the finches. Its richness and control transcended the most perfect of sounds.

Shala's breakfast faded, as her hunger passed.

36

Women's Rites

Velvet showed them the island. 'That's Croo Farm and College across the water. Everything is done there. Nothing is slaughtered or butchered here. No grinding of grain, no cutting of wood. This is a tranquil place. All toil and breeding is done there, keeping the Nurture House clean. Morning can go there for her second stage, this autumn.'

'Follow,' Lily said, ushering them towards the tall portal.

'I feel I have to stoop more to enter this time,' Shala imagined. 'The brazier smoulders smokeless. The air's dry, perfectly warm. There's a great bowl of simmering water. Rose petals swirl on its surface. Lily's pouring water from the sacred well. Now Velvet's going to the auroch altar. How beautifully her feather gown flows.'

'Yes,' Wrasse thought, 'it's still the same. She's lifting an otter pelt. There's the niche in the auroch's flank. Here comes the black phallus stone. How it glistens with iris oil in the candleglow.'

'Here, Morning, take it. The acorn-like lumps are testicles. Feel the shaft. The pointed tip will enter when you are ready.'

'It reminds me of my brother's stiffs he shows off,' Morning thought, 'and Dad's, too, before he and Mum cuddle.' She ran her fingers along it again, wondering. 'Here, Shala, you hold it,' she offered.

'It's much thicker than others. It's symbolic, after all. But gripping it makes me feel rich inside.'

'Let me take it, Shala,' Velvet asked, using her preferred name, 'I must bless it and warm it in the bowl. Do remove your clothes, Morning. You won't get cold. Lie on the altar. Become comfortable. This is your time. You can disrobe, too, Shala. Morning will feel better that way.'

'She's so beautiful!' Wrasse saw as Shala stood almost shadowless in the diffused candlelight, her lace undergown at her ankles.

As Velvet spoke the words, Ebb, unseen, repeated them in slow song, like an echo in a timeless space.

'A man is a vessel: a blessed vessel.'

Ebb's notes flowed like warm vapour, rising like fine gossamer to meander above, 'I will remember this forever,' Shala thought in wonder.

'He is raised to give his image: sharing desire, his blood and love of living,' were the fading words of the long hymn.

'Take alder wine,' Lily offered, handing round cups. 'This holy cordial will make you sparkle inside. Drink with us. We shall recite again, Ebb will chant.'

'We receive his potency, sharing desire: we blend his blood as he endows his manhood's milt.'

'I feel Ebb's song in my veins,' Shala thought shivering as the wine tingled within.

Three times Velvet repeated the third verse. Ebb's notes finally faded.

'Please sit on the suede cushions between Wrasse and Brill,' the priestesses said. 'This is your day when you find your power. I have told you of Man's desire. His want to mate is powerful. He oft believes it his right. Guman and Tuman told men to go and mate when the world was young, sharing their bloods. They have done as they were bidden. Women mate for our souls to divide within, delivering new lives. Since beyond time, though, it has been our power to choose. Our desire, too, is immense. We must learn how to make those choices. This helps us retain our power over men. If we are taken by man and penetrated, he assumes he has the power. If he breaks us inside and causes the blood to flow, he makes ownership his aim. This is man's nature.'

Brill drank listening, reaching for Morning, touching her shoulder.

'When we mate with man, giving our free permission and desire, it is a wondrous deed. But we have the choice and when that mating will be: even if he thinks the choosing has been his. It is our custom to take our power.' She waited in the ethereal candlelight while her words settled. 'We do not allow a man to break the seal to our womb. We are in charge. It gives us strengths of allowing man his pleasure or to deny. This is our control.'

'The warmth is correct. Smell the rose petals,' Lily announced. 'I will mount the altar. Velvet, remove the phallus stone. Bring it. I shall lie prone over the auroch's back, my head at its neck. My swan-plume robe shall part. Place it at my love opening as I listen to Ebb's song. Girls, watch, learn, as I place its tip at my vulva.'

Morning watched the flesh-warm point glide gently in. Shala saw Lily's head loll with the sensations of the sculpted rock.

Wrasse filled herself with Ebb's flow of song as the carving moved.

Lily, gripping the acorns, allowed its repeated penetration to the meter of Ebb's music. 'No man of flesh has taken me. Only Guman's stone belongs in our coven,' she remembered, her body in spasm.

Lily calmed. Shala watched as she later turned and sat, the stone still lodged within. Lily stood. Her robe gathered around her as the weighty penis slid into her cupped hands. 'I will replace it in the warming water,' she said.

'Our power is vital,' Velvet continued. 'The season will arrive when we feel our time to breed. It is our choice of father. From within us, we know how we want our child to be. The babe will take from him what we admire. This is our nature. There may be a time when we desire another father. Remember that men can be fathers with many women. We have that right, too. Your elders know the risks our society faces. The bloodlines are too close for the health of our young. The choice is hard. A man you take forever may not be he who makes good children with you. If so, he will need to understand and love you for you and your children. He could place his seed in another. But above all, these are the difficulties we face. It is hard for the men, too.'

Ebb's eunuch voice lowered.

'The laws of Guman and Tuman must be held. We pray that they will return and grant us new blood,' Velvet said as she returned to the holy bowl. 'Mount the Auroch altar of knowledge, Morning.'

Morning meekly nodded. She straddled its shoulders and sat on its great spine.

'I will oil Tuman's penis again,' Velvet said as she pulled a stopper from a carved shinbone vessel. A few sparing drips were sufficient to spread over the surface. It gleamed in her hands. 'Here. Take it.'

'Now?' Morning asked.

'Yes. But only if you feel ready.'

'I am,' she murmured.

'I will place it on your belly with the tip at your navel. Then it is up to you.'

Morning fumbled for the acorn grips and moved it downward. The oiled point slid until it reached her black hairs. She compressed her buttocks. Her hips rose. The dark point descended. Its body warmth touched her moist interior. She slowly pressed it within. She paused. The tip invisible, but the stem was there, waiting to shift forward.

'This is my moment. My decision: my action. Not a man's. I have the power to take it from him. It's my own will. I feel the change. I'll wait. It is so thrilling. I will still wait. I'll control my urge... Now I will push Tuman's testicles. He can enter with my consent. I feel the swelled basalt. It stretches something inside: it resists. Now it deepens further. The thrill engulfs me with exquisite movement. I'm filling with desire as I shake!'

Ebb hummed deeply, as Morning drooped.

'I'll help you,' Brill said. 'You've been very brave and good, dear. It's over now. Stand up and let Tuman's man come out.'

'I'll place it back in the bowl,' Morning said, shakily.

'It will be me next, no doubt,' thought Shala apprehensively, Wrasse watching her every expression. 'I had better mount the altar. The skins do look wonderful and the spreading horns quite magnificent. Yes, it's my time to accept the phallus. The rafters high above look so distant and dim. Does Ebb's voice hang there?' she wondered.

'I just wish I could call her Aiva, as Velvet does,' Wrasse thought. 'She looks so sedate there. She has a might all of her own. She's far more than just a young woman. This must be her moment.'

'I shall bring the Tuman's phallus from the bowl,' Lily said as she dipped her hands, rippling the water.

'Look at the wonderful lights reflected under the beams,' Wrasse observed, 'they are hovering over Ai... Shala, lighting her gracious body like the boreal glow of winter.'

'Here, Velvet, you place it.'

Its blood-warmth rested heavily on Shala's abdomen. She watched the spectres of light flow over it. 'I'm shaking inside,' she realized. The trout in the spring jumped for a fly. The ripples multiplied the array of spangled candleglow around her. 'As I gaze up to the heights, I feel so minute in this vast building. The weight of Tuman's stone is oppressive. I sense it pressing on my pelvis. I must move his penis to where it should enter,' she thought as she gazed at it over her amber amulet and past her growing breasts. 'I feel the stone testes as I slip it down towards my vulva. Its warm smooth end is touching me with gentle harmony. I want so to slant it and embed it deeply. I feel it needs to be there. I had not expected this. It seems so natural. I will make it wait.' The trout's fin tickled the surface of the sacred spring. The reflections began again. 'Now it's time,' she decided, as she waited in the rainbow glow. 'Is that his face I see in the rippling light above? It's as if he's gazing through a glittering pool down to me.'

I'm not doing this!' she suddenly announced clearly. 'I'm removing it. I will not have a stone token in me. I make my own decisions. It's my power. I do not need basalt emblems to do my will for me. The chosen one will be the first. No other. He will do this rock's work. Not some soulless, graven block.'

Ebb's voice rang as Shala stood away from the altar. 'I am replacing this in the ritual bowl. I am my own mistress. I rule my life and destiny. No graven object can do that for me. When I become Aiva, I will say. Meantime, I will preserve myself until I am entirely ready. I will choose my mate as he will choose me. He will be whom I will be with forever. I will have nothing else. I have my own strength, which is the same as any man's. Our power will be joint, inseparable and strong. Nothing less will suffice,' she made plain, as the graven member grated down the interior of the pot.

Ebb's refrain stopped. They all stood in silence.

Wrasse's ancient hands met in a muted clap. Lily's perspiring palms came together sharply. Velvet's eyes stared, startled, at Shala before she applauded. Brill followed. Ebb's hands rang. Morning stood cheering aloud, her arms high in the air as Shala imagined she saw a white goose drift high among the rafters.

37

The Cursed Wrasse

A huge, wooden-clappered bell sounded sunrise. Shala awoke, left her couch and greeted the morning. Outside, slanting sunbeams drenched her perfect skin.

'You will be taking different ways,' Lily said.

'We wish you well,' added Velvet, arriving with a laden breakfast tray. 'No initiate has spoken like that in the House. The future is your destiny now. It will be quite different for you, wherever you go or whatever you do.'

Slowly the visitors emerged to breakfast in the dazzle. The tray emptied as Morning took her last nibble.

'Let me take you to the raft,' Ebb at last said. 'Everything is stowed. Otterman waits.'

Ewes nibbled quietly under the blossom as Ebb guided them. He punted to the distant shore where Otterman floated under a willow. The timbers touched. The ladies changed craft. Ebb sang, drifting away.

'I'll take you to Top Loch,' Otterman offered. 'From there, the currents flow downwater to Tarmin.'

'Thank you enormously,' Wrasse replied. 'The Spinner will behave, I'm sure.'

Brill hugged her husband. 'I am so looking forward to Top Loch. We haven't been there for ages. Can we go back to Sight Hill?'

'Of course, dear,' he answered, adjusting his crotch. 'That's where you were conceived, Morning. Well probably, yes... er... almost certainly,' he added whilst twisting his nose-spike.

Morning blushed, having just experienced the fertility rites.

'It isn't too late for another, Otterman,' Brill offered.

'Welllllll, okay!' he replied hopefully as he ploughed the water. 'Grab paddles. Let's get a move on.'

'How was Sparrow Hall?' Brill asked.

'Just the usual: we had a wild feast and got steaming drunk.'

'That's lovely, dear. I'm glad you had a good time.'

'We head for reedbeds on the distant bank. There should be dredged channels through to Top Loch. It's quite a distance. Keep paddling,' Otterman said from his prow.

'I'm hungry,' Morning moaned.

'Gutsy slob,' Wrasse thought, as they entered the reed channel. 'The amount she had for breakfast would keep them all going for a day.'

'Shhhhh. Voices ahead,' Otterman called. 'Paddle quietly.'

'Dilly, that's my one,' a girl's shouted.

'No. It's mine. It landed in my net.'

'That's my net. You're just borrowing it. I want my frog,' she yelled.

'Dilly, give it to her, she chased it into the net,' Otterman heard Shearer say.

'Yes, but she used my stick to nudge it.'

'Good, then we all have another frog. Give it to her.'

'Thank you,' Dilly answered as they turned the bend into a large pool.

'Hail, Shearer,' Otterman called. 'Frog hunting?'

'It's you. Long time, no see,' he returned, 'Yes, they frog hunt while I clear reeds. Who's the company?'

'Ones from Lee Holme,' he answered as the Harpoon nudged Shearer's reed boat. 'We've got old Lintel's sister.'

The youngster's reed boat bobbed in the chase as Shearer asked softly, 'Not Wrasse?'

'Yes. And old Lintel croaked the night she arrived.'

'Keep her name quiet. It's still a curse round here,' Wrasse was shocked to hear. She bristled, about to stand.

'No. Sit,' Otterman said.

'Kids, the last one home's a hairy toad,' Shearer shouted through his grey beard. 'It's the boat race tomorrow. It'll be good practice.'

'Why's my name a curse?' Wrasse asked in ire, directly the young were gone.

'It's that old story of the Sea Angel. Nobody forgets. Your name's used whenever anything bad happens. The children get threatened with a visit from you if they misbehave. We thought you'd been dead for years.'

'She certainly isn't dead,' Shala put in, 'and she's nothing but truthful and good. Truth's hard to take, sometimes.'

'Careful. The boat's rocking,' Otterman said.

'If you don't mind, Shala, here, and I are headed for Tarmin. We'll carry straight on in the coracle, if you prefer.'

'I'm sorry if I've upset you,' Shearer began, 'but you can stay. I've got nothing against you. We just won't let on. Paddle back with me.' Shearer's channel soon opened into Top Loch. On the north-western shore a distant stone jetty jutted from a cluster of masonry and timber houses. Square set, with rounded corners, they lined an uphill track. The sunlight reed thatch glimmered.

Towards the top of Sight Hill, Scanner watched from his tower that rose above his small town. Inverted images of Otterman and Shearer's approaching craft flickered through the small spy-hole on his smoothly plastered walls. From there he could view the vast wetlands between the hills; the low-lying farms and meadows, the lochs and even as far as Shepherd's Tongue. In the other direction, he could see Tarmin's vast House of Souls and then Tarmin itself.

'I must go down to my chambers, while my wives are brewing ale with the kids.' His dark hair bounced on his shoulders as he jumped from the third rung. The planking vibrated as he landed before taking the next ladder.

He went to his bed stall. Below the thick plank supporting his wide mattress was his leather chest. His knotwork flax robe caught in his toes as he hauled the tough auroch hide box from its place between the upright flagstones.

'I'll unclip these tight antler toggles. I need more light, though. I must do it before those visitors arrive. I'll light a candle. Good, the miniature axes are here; all rolled up in their dyed chamois. They are lovely trophies, thank the ancestors,' he muttered quietly to himself. 'I must unwrap one. Oh, the yew shaft's beautiful. Its red leather binding is so exquisite. The yellow tassel at the butt's a bit gaudy. The slate head's good and sharp, and that red line on the edge looks like blood.... Just right for the trophies,' Scanner mumbled.

The doorway darkened. 'Who's there?' he said spinning round in surprise.

'Checking the winners' awards again, are we?'

'Of course not, Foxglove: I'm looking out my vestments. I thought you were malting the ale?'

'Yes. It's getting too hot in there. The vestments are hanging in the niche behind the curtain. Now stop panicking. The first part of the race isn't until tomorrow, and the results won't be drawn until the day after.'

'Mummy, can we look at the prizes again?' her toddler asked, ruining her secret.

'No, cherub, your father's too busy. Run and play.'

'Have you been showing these to the babes?'

'Certainly not – although they may have peeked when Rose and I were hanging your stuff up.'

'I thought the chest seemed a bit empty, dear,' Scanner remarked.

As Otterman and Shearer slowly paddled, Shala spotted smoke.

'Fire! Fire! On the hill near the tower, Look!'

'Oh no! It's the brewing house. Not again!' Shearer shouted. 'Paddle hard, or it'll be too late.'

When they reached the pier, everyone had run uphill.

Inside the smoke-filled building, Foxglove dragged Rose and her daughter to safety. The draught from the open door fed the ramping flames, which licked the rafters and planking of the grain store above.

'How did this happen?' she yelled at Rose.

'When you went to spy on Scanner, you left the door open. That's when the malting fire spread,' she choked out. 'I tipped wet maltings from the bowls to douse it, but smouldering chaff flew sparking into the air. It was so dusty we couldn't see. Then you opened the door again and everything went bang, and suddenly caught. We flung ourselves on the floor, which is what you should do in a fire.'

The smoke hit Scanner's nostrils. He screamed when he realized. 'Everyone! Put it out!' he yelled to the gathering body of folk.

'It's no use,' Rose snuffled as thick smoke billowed from beneath the crackling eaves in malt-smelling clouds, 'it is doomed,' she cried as she swept back her singed hair.

'That's seen to the beer for the Boat Race,' Shearer said, as he ran up the hill with Otterman.

'I'll follow with Wrasse,' Shala said as the others flew ahead.

'Chuck water on the other roofs. Use beer if you must. But save the houses near the brewery,' Scanner ordered, stubbing his toe on a quern.

'Wrasse,' Shala commented, 'I think it might be best not to mention your name, with all this going on.'

'Indeed,' she stated, drawing breath over her teeth. 'You may be quite right.'

The blaze crackled and roared through the thatch as they approached the paved courtyard. The heat was intense. 'Just like the fire in my house,' Wrasse thought.

Inside, the grain ran through the burning planks to crackle and sparkle violently as it ignited on the scorching floor. The reed thatch soon vanished, leaving the hotbed of cereal to bake the fine clay surface.

'There you are,' Brill said to Shala. 'This is a terrible mess.'

'Yes, it is,' Wrasse added, 'I think we should actually make our way, though. This is no place for us. Will you thank Otterman? We can get the Spinner ready and travel on.'

'Okay, it might be wise. We'll stay and help. It was wonderful to meet you and Shala. Good fortune in Tarmin.'

'Come, Shala, we'll leave now,' Wrasse said, leaning on her stick. They made their way back to the jetty. The noise of the commotion on the hill faded. 'It's such a shame,' Wrasse said. 'The boat race might be cancelled. All that good ale gone. What a waste of grain.'

'Yes, it's terrible indeed. I do hope nobody thinks it's because you were arriving.'

'Well, if they don't find out, they won't. Now let's get the Spinner and load up. There's Top Loch to cross. We can sleep at the head of the Tar Burn.'

The water shone golden in the dipping sun. The pattern of gentle ripples behind the Spinner reflected them. The smell of the fire drifted strongly down as they paddled over the rope starting line. The rocky islet, where Scanner would have started the event, projected proudly from the water. An evening mist hung over the still water ahead.

'There's a boathouse,' Shala remarked later as they approached the end of Top Loch. 'Maybe we could sleep in it.'

'That would be fine. Tar Burn runs from there to Tarmin. We'll be there tomorrow,' Wrasse added pensively.

'Ah, Wrasse, there's a couple of coracles in there, but it looks damp. I think we should curl up under the Spinner for the night. There's dry looking woodland up the rise. I'm really tired. I could sleep anywhere.'

'Me, too, let's camp. The Mother's Star's showing: I'm ready.'

Under the coracle, Wrasse gripped her relic of Weir. 'It will be a big day for both of us,' she said in her mind to his waiting spirit.

All night she clutched the relic, dreaming of his arrival and tragic departure from life. Another dream showed him grown old with her. She so wished for the latter. As she stirred, Shala woke, rising in the morning light. 'I'll take my bow and see if I can't catch breakfast,' she thought. As she passed the boathouse an owl flew silently out. 'Strange,' she thought, 'a coracle gone and a reed canoe in its place. I wonder who's been where?' Then a carp swam by, its back out of the water, the bow wave distinctly parting the mist. Shala drew her bow, loosened the arrow. The shocked fish leapt and fell. A heron took off from a reedbed; a kingfisher darted from a stump. 'Breakfast,' Shala thought.

The burn flowed slowly through marsh woodlands. 'We should come to a wide pool below Rouse Hill,' Wrasse informed Shala. 'The deer always gathered up there. Sometimes they'd be driven down into a big pool like this. Then the boatmen would come out from hiding in the willows and club the animals. It was easier catching them like that. We saw which ones to keep for breeding. There will be a dam soon, just wait. Yes, there are the flagstone steps up it. We can drag the Spinner over to the burn below.'

'Shhh!' Shala warned. 'Listen. Maybe a beaver or otter,' she remarked.

'I thought I noticed something earlier, Shala,' Wrasse said as they took the current.

'Yes. One of the coracles had gone from the boathouse and a reed canoe was there, instead. I didn't think much of it, now I do.'

'That's a branch swinging back. Someone's running!'

'Yes,' Wrasse answered. 'There's another pool ahead, when we're out of these willows. It's one of our old flax ponds.'

'More willows ahead,' Shala said. Startled ducks took noisy flight.

'Pull into the shore, Wrasse of Lee Holme!' a stern voice commanded.

Spar, tall and gaunt, stood on the prow of his magnificent canoe. It emerged from the parting branches ahead, its vast painted eyes at water level, staring directly at Wrasse and Shala. Spar's long spear poked skywards, the black stone point sporting dangling eagle feathers.

'Unfinger your bow, Shala. I'm no sleepy carp,' he said as his canoe glided to the threatened pair, his dyed flax clothing matching the darkness of his weapon's head. A black leather cape draped down his back was secured by a long bone pin at his neck, his red curled hair encircled by a band of feathers swept back from his forehead. Four others stood behind him in the advancing craft.

'Keep calm,' Wrasse said urgently. Two more men with bows trained on them stood either side of the slanting stone landing. 'Keep very calm,' she added under her breath.

They neared the landing point. Spar glided effortlessly behind as Wrasse and Shala maintained their cool. As the Spinner bumped the masonry, Spar's canoe rammed them, wedging them tight.

'Got you!' the bowmen said, as they grabbed the travellers.

'Don't worry. We will take care of your cargo,' Spar said sternly. His grim looking guards brandished their polished maces.

'What are you doing?' Shala blurted, being manhandled from the Spinner.

'Just welcoming you both,' said one, as his face paint flaked from his wrinkled brow.

'I smell your fear,' Wrasse said as she was hoisted ashore. 'You had better be careful,' she warned.

'Take them to Black Cott,' Spar directed, as the Spinner scraped the stonework.

'Be careful with that boat. It is not ours,' she warned as they were frog-marched away.

The men paced along a worn path through scrubby woodlands towards open fields.

'I remember this. It's all coming back,' Wrasse hurriedly thought, 'The place seems smaller. Less imposing, but this is terrible.'

'I can march on my own. I don't need your assistance,' Shala admonished.

'Let them make their own way now,' Spar instructed his men. 'No need to tire your elves unduly. They can make the gradient.'

'Where's my stick?' Wrasse asked as she looked at the lines of painted wooden idols they stepped through.

'You might get it back at if you behave, old woman,' said Spar.

Past the guards in front, Shala saw a low building on a broad terrace cut into the hill behind. the dark stonework neatly faced. The thatch had decorative ridges spreading from the pitch. In the smoke curling from the roof, two ravens flapped their wings, cawing loudly.

Wrasse watched the woman standing in the doorway, thinking. 'Is she the power around here?'

'Wrasse?' the woman wondered. 'Why's she returned? What does she want, after all these years?'

Their armed escort arrived at the threshold, banging their shining maces together. They parted. Wrasse and Garnet stared directly at each other, waiting for the first to speak.

38

Captured!

'Good day,' Wrasse said immediately. 'A fine welcome, indeed. Are we worth it?'

'Enter. I'm Garnet.' The white-robed lady turned. Her plaited leather belt of green and red accentuated her slim waist under her flowing linen drapes. Her dark hair shone in the shaded, oblong room. Fire glimmered in a corner of the square central hearth. The rest was swept clean to the baked clay. At each corner stood a stone slab, holding wax-filled candle pots. Yellow flames shone from their wicks. The paved room was sparse and neat.

Opposite the fireplace, Old Cairn sat in her high-backed wicker chair. She wore a striped robe of knotted flax and twisted wool. Hiding her fawn, dyed hair was a tall, conical parchment hat. The open top of her official garment revealed a great mussel shell pendant. Its polished pearly interior reflected the lamps' small flames.

'Sit,' she said quietly, with an air of authority. Spar pulled the other chairs from the hearth. Wrasse took her place to the left of Cairn, Shala to the right. Garnet sat with her back to the door. Cairn looked at Spar. He disappeared into a dark corner, returning with four translucent horn cups on a long wooden tray. He passed them round.

'Welcome back, Wrasse. We've been expecting you. I am Cairn. This is Garnet, my heir. I hear Shala, here, is your heir.'

Wrasse glared.

'News travels fast as a flying duck's arse o'er the Marshes, Wrasse,' Garnet said. 'Why have you come back? Not to burn down *our* brewery, we hope?'

'The reasons for my return are becoming more apparent every moment,' Wrasse parried.

Shala, composed, sipped her splendid raspberry water from the excellent horn cup, the lamplight reflecting beautifully in its polished surface.

'Why do you ask?' Wrasse questioned Garnet.

'Your presence here is awkward,' Cairn butted in sharply.

Spar passed round apple and bramble scones. Cairn dipped hers in a dish of thick cream. The dried fruit had swelled in the moist mix before cooking on the stone griddle. They tasted expensive. As Cairn inhaled, a crumb flew down her throat. She coughed violently, hurriedly putting the cake on her knee. She drank rapidly, washing it down. It did no good. Her choking ejected the cordial.

Garnet stood in alarm. Spar rushed to pat Cairn firmly on the back. Her shining pendant bounced on her chest. The coughing fit subsided, as did Cairn's pompous attitude. Her conical cap slanted backwards. Her thin hair poked out from under it over her forehead. The scone wobbled on her knee. Shala moved across, saving it.

'Thank you,' Cairn returned, recovering her composure.

'Why?' Wrasse asked blatantly. Shala took a bite, munching confidently. Spar retreated into the shadows.

'It is well known in Tarmin,' Cairn began, 'that when trouble starts, your spirit is blamed. We know your heir here induced that huge storm that nearly wrecked Tarmin! That poor girl at Shepherd's Tongue, crushed just prior to your arrival. Lintel died when you visited. Yes, Wrasse, she died to your prediction, which was, "Apologize! That's the last thing she'll do". Then, of course, there's the burning of Scanner's brewery. What trouble do you bring here, may I ask?'

'You appear to be very ill informed,' Wrasse returned. 'What oaf spread this muck?'

'Your delightful companion to the House of Croo, Morning. She took her new power and mated with Scanner's oldest just by the heat of the fire. His cock was still dripping when he arrived here with news of your return.'

'I haven't returned, Cairn. Merely visiting. You must feel so insecure, fearing a visit from me. Just let me tell you, we only offer good. I've knowledge of all the breeding lines. I am passing them to Shala. This is one of the reasons for our journey. It is to enhance that knowledge. You know how perilous our bloodlines have become. I also possess a relic, of which only I know how to implement the potency.' Spar returned with charcoal as Wrasse continued. 'You could blame anything for bad happenings; a pig, an auroch or an unfortunate person. It just shows your weakness, and Garnet's too.'

'You are a legend in Tarmin, Wrasse,' Garnet interjected. 'But you are now a living legend. We thought you were a dead one. We know all about you and the Sea Angel. How you stole his baby, only for it to die within you. How you were then initiated properly and exiled with Gravel. My aunt here has all the lore. We took your first son back, as agreed in the terms.'

'I did not steal the Sea Angel's baby. He gave it to me. It was his last chance to breed. It was my honour and I was punished,' Wrasse retorted, wondering if her first son still lived.

Garnet sipped thoughtfully. Shala watched the liquid within touch her quivering lips. She added, 'Your father made moves to bring you back to become his heir, but then bad things started.'

Wrasse's scrubby eyebrows rose almost imperceptibly.

'Children died. We lost a boat full of fishers. Our sheep started to perish and the sacred auroch fell mysteriously from the cliff,' she said, adjusting her hat in agitation then shifting closer to the reddening coals.

'It's all blamed on you,' Garnet announced. 'The geese stopped coming. A huge wave caught one of our rafts. Her crew washed far inland behind the Hill of Calling. The sea never quite went back. The violent storm we had recently bore your name. Years ago your old sister, Mire, said she'd seen you in a dream doing these things. Then the stories started again about you and your visions of things that would happen. She blamed the catastrophes on you. Then came the threats.'

'What threats?' Wrasse questioned, whilst biting into a scone.

'The ones to the children. We told them that your fearful spirit would cast spells on them if they were bad. Even if they weren't, something horrid could still happen. When anything fearsome occurs, your name's used. Even your ghost walks the shore at night, scaring the cod fishers.'

Wrasse shook. She handed her cup and confection to Spar for safety and guffawed. She leaned back. A sharp end of wicker caught her bum through her grey skirt. It pinched. She jumped, yelped and laughed the more. Spar steadied her seat. Shala retained her composure, as Wrasse's mirth became a long cackle. The guards outside shrank back from the jambs, uttering, 'The witch is returned!'

Wrasse gained control, sat back, reached to Spar for her refreshments. 'Do continue,' Wrasse said. 'Let me hear more.'

'When Mire was ending her life, she passed her stone ball to me.' Cairn held out the glistening black and white orb.

'Like Wrasse's hair,' Shala observed.

'I will hand it to Garnet, soon,' Cairn said. 'Before Mire became quite dead she told me much. To help build her power, she invented stories about you.'

'That surprises me little,' Wrasse informed their hosts. 'What do you think, Shala?'

'From what I have heard from you, Wrasse, and what I learned from Lintel, my surprise is also small. Lintel did actually apologize to you. You were quite right when you said to everyone that apologizing was the last thing you imagined she'd do. And so it was. As for the brewery fire, that had happened before. Building accidents occur, too. Wrasse is no witch. She's clever, wise and truthful.... Sometimes truth shocks,' Shala stated.

Garnet and Cairn sat awkwardly. 'To maintain our status and smooth running of Tarmin, we enhanced the myths.'

'Myths are myths,' Wrasse stated. 'Real power comes from truth, if you are strong enough to utter it. To stay in charge, you will need us dead. Don't you? You could easily do murder. But , you won't have the secrets of the breeding lines. You will not discover the power of the totem I have brought, nor how to use it. And as you say, news does fly like a drake's backside!'

Cairn stood and limped to Wrasse, 'It's not just about you, but other things,' she hissed. 'With your unexpected arrival, it jeopardizes our status, therefore everything in Tarmin.'

'So you want our help to cover up, do you?' Shala quietly put in.

Wrasse turned to Cairn, 'I have never been popular. In Lee Holme I made my home, lived and worked. I never sought power, but I have it because I speak truth. At times people find right by merely asking. They assume I have helped. I never lie. That's real power.' Then she asked, 'By the way, Spar, I'd appreciate another scone.'

'Help me to the door, Garnet,' Cairn asked.

'All of you leave, except Blunt and Lime. Keep your silence,' she ordered. 'You two, go twenty paces down the path and wait. Step quickly!' she barked. They jumped like lightning had struck, darting from earshot.

Cairn returned, muttering, ''Should have done that right at the beginning. Right, where do we go from here?'

'Are you asking me?' Wrasse put in.

'No! I'm speaking to Garnet.'

'Sorry, I misunderstood.'

'Garnet. What will you do?'

'So it's up to me, now, is it?'

'Yes, but we must have a strategy,' Cairn admitted.

'Don't you think that may take some time?' remarked Wrasse, 'Your footmen out there are hardly likely to keep our presence a secret. Then you will have questions to answer. Thank you for the nice drinks, your reception and the cakes. Shala, I think we'll leave now.'

'Spar! Call Blunt and Lime. No. Wait,' Cairn spat out.

'Us or Spar?' Shala asked, as they rose. The jagged point of wicker caught in Wrasse's cloth again. The chair swivelled and followed.

'Let me help,' Spar asked.

'Get her another seat,' Cairn ordered.

'So, you're inviting us to stay?' Wrasse enquired.

'Yes,' Garnet slung in.

'Yes... what?' Shala demanded.

'"Please would you stay and discuss this with us?" is what Garnet meant to say,' Cairn implied.

'Did you?' Wrasse queried.

Garnet nodded to Wrasse and Shala, and then to Spar.

'So you won't need Blunt and Lime?'

Cairn shook her head.

'May I have another of those excellent drinks?' Wrasse asked as she sat in the replacement seat. Spar returned for his tray. 'Thank you very much,' she said politely. 'Now, let's discuss this in a civilized manner.'

Garnet began thoughtfully, 'Now you are here, how does Cairn explain and still retain power?'

'What power?'

'Well. Our authority,' she replied.

'Authority isn't power. Truth is power. If you use that, you may get somewhere,' Wrasse told them abruptly.

Spar worked in a corner in the light of several lamps, listening in.

'That won't be easy,' Garnet admitted.

'I never said it would,' Wrasse's retorted. 'You've not got much time. So I am going to do something quite rare. I shall give unasked-for advice while I have my drink.' Shala's attention was fixed.

'The most powerful thing you can do is to explain publicly exactly what you have learned, then hand over your authority publicly, too,' Wrasse said calmly.

'What? Give up all we've worked for?' Cairn said, glaring at Garnet across the fireplace.

'Not what you've worked for, but what you've manipulated,' Wrasse offered. 'You may stress that I, the fearful Wrasse, will make offerings for your eternal wellbeing and for thy elevations within the spirit world. You will become for evermore heavenly beings. This is against my principles, but for you and Tarmin it will be best. You can name a new leader and live under that one's protection. Blunt and Lime can put down their bows. We are your help, not your enemies.'

'Who do you think should have the honour of leader?' Garnet asked expectantly.

'That's entirely up to you. Shala and I do not know anyone here apart from you, Spar and your henchmen. It's your choice. It has to be for the best for Tarmin and its people. Remember, if they discover you've lied and killed us, you're in peril anyway.'

'What are you making, Spar?' Cairn asked, giving herself time to think.

'Sliced smoked salmon rolled round pine-nut paste with ground fennel and crab, all arranged in scallop shells. It's good for the brains,' he answered, while working on a wide stone shelf lit by stone lamps. His cape draped over his deadly spear in the curved corner. The bone pin dangled from an eyelet. His feather headband hung colourfully from a peg. 'Stay seated. Relax,' he advised, 'This had to happen. I shall have the West House made ready,' Spar added knowingly.

'Please do,' Cairn answered.

'The fire needs a poke. I'll do it,' Shala suggested as the pair sat back. Sparks flew up from the scorched hazel rod as Spar brought a tray of his specialities.

'Thank you,' Wrasse said as she was served first, then Shala.

'Excuse me,' Spar said as Garnet took the fourth shell, 'I must instruct the men.'

Wrasse's acute hearing increased her confidence when she discerned the distant words: 'Blunt, Lime. Make the West House ready.'

Immediately Wrasse asked, 'Have you reliable people to do your will at the squirt of duck's turd?' she said, referring to Cairn's comment.

'Naturally,' they replied, realizing the point.

'Dismiss Lime from his West House duties. Send him to Tarmin to announce there's to be a public gathering and fiesta tomorrow evening at Tarmin's House of Souls.'

'Lime,' Spar bellowed. 'Return! Blunt, continue.'

'That will just give time to organize a feast. Your musicians can prepare, too. If you want to remain in control, then you have to act as if you are, until the passing of power and your elevation.'

'Are you on our side, then?' Garnet meekly asked.

'I am on the side of what is best.'

'Quite right,' Shala agreed, before they enjoyed the salmon fingers.

'Spar,' Cairn called. 'When will the West House be ready?'

'It actually is already,' he gently said. 'Blunt's merely setting the fire.'

'Fine,' Cairn responded, surprised.

They walked up through a wooded path to the opulent West House. Yellow butterflies rose from the flowery verges. On the sophisticated thatching another pair of ravens bathed in the smoke rising through the top vent.

Shala's belongings and Wrasse's staff lay by sleeping alcoves draped with ornate grass matting.

'You must tell us the local history and news, Cairn,' Wrasse suggested immediately.

'We can discuss all tomorrow's events,' Shala added, making herself comfortable.

Worn out, Cairn and Garnet later spent an uneasy night, unlike Wrasse and Shala.

'Blunt returned the Spinner yesterday. You will come with the ladies in my canoe,' Spar said after breakfast.

'Thank you for the changes of clothes, Spar,' Shala remarked.

He looked gentler without his feathered band as he pinned his cloak on. At the long pin's head was a large carved ring, where a fine cord of plaited grass swung. At its end, a tightly strung bale of accurately clipped hog hair dangled. He pushed the polished bone through eyelets at the collar, thrusting the point into the tight hair. His cape then draped elegantly behind. 'We are glad you approve. That yellow flax skirt suits you.'

'It feels crisp around my heels. The suede jacket is beautifully stitched. Could I get another string for my amber pendant, in red cotton, perhaps, to go with the sinew seams?'

'I'll ask Garnet.'

'May I borrow Timber's necklace, please?' Wrasse asked.

'Certainly,' Shala replied, feeling in her caisie, 'It will look excellent over your dyed bark jacket. See how the shell buttons reflect the doorway light? Let me tighten your belt over the matching skirt. I'll pin it with a boar's tusk.'

'The reed shoes Spar put out caress my feet wonderfully. They take me back, so. Will you comb my hair, Shala? I want the white stripe to shine in a wave.'

'We must all head off. Preparations have gone well and we expect a good turnout. By the looks of the sky, we are in for a fine day,' Spar said, handing Shala a splendid cotton cord.

Cairn appeared from a doorway behind a flagstone partition. Garnet followed.

'My knees aren't good today, Spar. I require the litter.'

'Certainly,' Spar said, as Cairn wondered if it was the last time she could order it.

Shala noticed they wore the same robes as before, but with beautifully shaped mantles of plaited grass over their shoulders.

They clipped together at the back with neat bird-bone toggles. Garnet's had a triangular shale plaque sewn into the front. Cairn's had an amber disc attached at her sternum, with matching amulets dangling over her flagging breasts. They held broad-brimmed straw hats for outside.

'The litter's on its chocks,' Lime announced as they pinned the elegant hats into their richly adorned hair.

'Allow me to assist, Cairn,' Spar said. 'Lime and me will carry you around the shafts onto your leather pouffe.'

'This boat trip,' Wrasse said later, 'brings back many memories. Those familiar hills, the woodlands and farms. The loch's much wider, though. See that island, Shala: the one with pines on? It's shrunk. Some of them just jut from the water. Oh! Look up on the hillside terrace. That's the House of Souls.'

'It's huge,' Shala observed.

'Yes, even bigger now. It stands so powerfully, even against the rise behind it and that arc of trees framing it.

'It's the largest building I've ever seen,' Shala said in awe. 'It's like a vast upturned boat. Look, there's a tall pavilion at its entrance. It's sticking up above the sanctuary walls.'

'Yes. And there's folk milling about on top, around the resting boxes,' Wrasse added.

'Landing stage,' Spar called. 'Blunt and your men. Help the ladies out. Shift Cairn gently onto her litter.'

A trumpeter marked their arrival with fearful blasts from his spiralling goat's horn. Cairn was elevated. Spar and Garnet walked gracefully either side of her.

'We will proceed respectfully behind, Shala,' Wrasse suggested.

'Yes, Wrasse. The path's gets steep and windey. Lots of folk are coming across the loch. Aye, and from the fields too, and there's more in the precinct above.'

'Listen to the larks, Wrasse. And the kye, speaking to each other.'

'I can smell them, and the pigs. See the youths chasing each other with that ball up the hill. There it goes, down again. I don't know how old that game is.'

'There's still neat rosemary hedges here,' Wrasse added, watching the litter negotiate the stone steps. 'And the herb gardens behind. Mint, thyme, borage, chives and fennel, lots more, too. See the meadowsweet by the damp spring. It so smells of honey. Round those tall, curving walls is the plaza in front of the great house's entrance.'

'It's full of folk,' Shala remarked as they entered.

'Yes, and there's drummers and horn players on top above the pavilion. Plug your ears!'

Music echoed vibrantly into the swept auditorium.

'I'll help you out,' Spar said to Cairn.

Suddenly there was hush. 'Take me to my position,' she responded.

'Yes, onto the dais under the canopy in front of the portal. Do you like the ornamental shrubs either side?' Spar asked. Cairn barely nodded.

'I see the thrones are in place,' she croaked as she saw the shining otter and fox pelts draped over the magnificent wicker backs. The animals' heads grinned toothily towards the gathering.

'Hold on to your ears again,' Wrasse said as log drums beat out a fast, intricate rhythm.

'Up onto the stage,' Spar urged. Cairn's retinue followed.

Cairn stood, gazing at the massed people. The drums were silenced. Not a breath was heard as she turned on the carpeted surface. The others had all taken their allotted positions. A lark sang. Cairn threw her wide hat behind her head. Her hair shone in a high, pinned-up display.

Her voice rang out. 'I have something to say!'

39

The House of Souls

The echo of Cairn's voice abated. 'I am old,' she announced dramatically. 'I have pondered long and hard. I am handing on my Orb.' The crowd shifted, unprepared for such momentous news. Shouts of 'No, no!' from prompted Hench Folk filled the crowded arena.

Cairn raised her arm. Silence reigned.

'Before I relinquish my position, I have announcements.' Every syllable was clearly succinct. The well-trained speaker's voice carried high in the air, captivating her audience.

The impressive concave headdress behind her ears projected her words and enhanced her hearing. She could detect the slightest whisper, even a thought, sometimes.

'So I have invited a Living Legend: someone who's been unjustly vilified here. For many, her very name has been taboo to utter. I hear you muttering, but hush. Though she has been blamed for misfortunes, I must show to you today the living proof of our predecessor's errors. Yes, murmur, heckle indeed, but listen! Her ghost has been reported on shores before storms, gloating at funerals after tragic deaths. I do not exaggerate the fear that has struck our children, who have grown to adulthood believing in mischief created by her unrestful spirit! Yes! Gasp, indeed.'

Wrasse coughed quietly behind her hand as she sat in a minor throne beside Shala, who stifled a giggle. Spar stood behind, ready to hand them fans to hide behind.

'Here, in the living flesh, is Wrasse! You may sound horrified, but fear her not. She has lived obscurely for a very long time. We believed her dead. We were misled by past authorities,' she announced quietly, yet utterly audibly. The curving walls vibrantly amplified every word. 'I have waited until now to assure you of this fact before I hand my responsibilities forward.'

Wrasse reached for a fan, 'She hasn't said how long she's been pondering this,' Wrasse whispered.

Shala responded, 'She certainly makes up truth when she wants. It's tumbling out like an ox farting.'

'Before I complete my solemn duties, Wrasse will speak, so you know the truth. Truth is the strength by which we live.' The populace applauded weakly until Cairn's retinue cheered vigorously. All, then, joined the accolade. Cairn signalled for it to cease as it climaxed, waiving Wrasse forward.

Wrasse stood to tumultuous drumming, stepping forward to Cairn's podium. Cairn moved back, taking her seat.

'I thank Cairn for her invitation and splendid hospitality. May I say, on her behalf, if it were not for her astuteness, your continued prosperity and peace may well have been undermined.' Wrasse accepted, with unexpected elation, the rapturous applause.

'I will not dwell on what has befallen you in my name, falsely, I concur. I, too, suffered tragedy, misfortune, loss and peril. We endured the horrors of the unprecedented storm. Lee Holme, where I dwell, seemed the worst hit. I was close to death, incarcerated in a premature tomb beneath an all-engulfing fire! I, Wrasse, never blamed a dead nor living soul.'

Her voice carried over the precinct, touching the populace. 'I prayed, having visions within that tomb. It was Shala here, who lowers her fan so you can see her face. She heard my desperate calling from the underworld. She saw me within the ground, hidden from other mortals. To her I am due my rescue. She is my heir, and I have brought her here to meet you. Stand, Shala! Be recognized. Let the drums roll again and trumpets sound.' Cairn sat, amazed at the response.

Wrasse concluded, 'I thank you for your rapture and your splendid welcome. I reiterate: neither I, nor my spirit, had any presence within Tarmin causing ill. I only pray for your good. As does my heir.'

They stood for the fervent ovation. A vast auroch horn, blown by a grand woman atop the monument, rent the air. As the blaring note faded, Wrasse concluded, 'Now back to your retiring leader. May her future advice always be respected and may you allow her peace and happiness in her life ahead.'

Wrasse's recognition was astounding. Cairn stood. Spar held the orb of accession. Cairn moved forward. She took in her outstretched palm for the final time that gleaming stone. She held it high and stepped towards Shala. She passed Garnet's bowed, expectant head, Wrasse's, too, and Spar's. Silence reigned.

'Kneel, everyone.' She faced the people and waited, extending her last moments of privilege. 'Spar. Stand.' He rose in one sleek move. 'Hold out your hands.' She paused, listened to the silence then announced dramatically, 'You, Spar, are my new heir.'

'This can't be true,' he uttered, holding his palms forward, feeling the weight of the crystalline globe.

'Take it. You will lead well,' she whispered.

'People of Tarmin, Spar is now yours. Respect his word, honour his deeds and trust him. You will be well rewarded.'

Shala watched Spar step forward as Cairn retreated behind her old throne calling out, 'Part the Portal Curtain. Bring forth our Ancestors.'

With a trumpet fanfare, three mummified bodies were carried from within.

'I must think quickly,' Spar said to himself, 'They need a speech. Garnet looks ruined. She'd expected this. Cairn's been clever. She knows I'll look after them. She thinks she will have power through me. Maybe not,' he summed up.

'I am proud to accept this orb,' he began confidently, 'I hold it high and will bear all the responsibilities it signifies. My preparation for this moment has been long, though it has never been my ambition. With my service to Cairn and to all assembled here, I feel confident to continue the notable works she and her predecessors initiated. May we continue in harmony. May our community strive for constancy in our traditions with honour in our lives and labours.'

Shala heard the choir chant their high-pitched Ascension hymn. The ceremonially garbed mummies advanced, witnessing the change of leaders, giving their eternal assent. Their light bog cotton robes, like flowing shrouds, covered their dried remains. They wore tall conical hats of shining white birch bark. The late sun shone from behind the long tomb, causing lengthy shadows. With the ancestors' appearance, the musicians above let their sounds flare. From behind the far hornwork walling, food arrived on wicker trestles. Shala sensed that this, for most folk, and the drink to follow, were the highlight of the occasion.

The ancestors' attendants put their conical headgear to their mouths to sing amplified solos of the acceptance hymn.

Spar found himself standing next to Cairn again. 'Why me?' he asked her under his breath.

'You're the right one to accede. But I want you to create a new position for me and Garnet.'

'What would that position be?' he enquired cautiously.

'I would like you to call it Eternal Upholder: I keep the West House with a retinue. When I'm dead and embalmed, you can elevate Garnet. All we do is agree your decisions, giving you peace and support. It could work well for us. Get the Ancestors there to agree it. Also, I must be deified at my death. Wrasse has agreed to offer prayers for my spirit's ascension.'

'I'll consider it. You may retain the West House and its services. That's easily organized,' he offered, thinking, 'She's worked it out, but she won't get it all.'

A page came up to Wrasse and Shala. 'Mmmmm! Sheep's cheese on crisp black bread and cups of warming ambrose,' Shala remarked, watching the hubbub in the precinct.

'I'm Cliff,' a gentle voice said from behind. Wrasse turned abruptly to a mid-aged man looking lovingly into her eyes. 'They told me you were dead. In the end I accepted that,' he said quietly.

Wrasse returned the look. The clamour stilled. There being silence in her ears.

'I am your son,' he said softly.

Wrasse gasped, feeling a sudden swell of lost motherly emotion.

'They needed me for breeding. But I'm not a big success. I only bred one. He won't pass anything on. He just loves to sing, so he's at the Nurture House. The Priestesses there know how to keep a boy's voice perfect. That is enough, for him.'

'I'm speechless,' Wrasse thought, standing in front of the quiet man. 'He seems feeble in frame, but there's strength coming from his meekness.

Shala put her arms around her as Cliff continued looking at his mother.

'I'm Tomb Keeper. I like my place. It is peaceful, mostly. I never knew all this was going to happen,' he said dreamily, rambling on quietly then asked, 'Take my hand, please, Mother?'

Wrasse nodded. 'I feel his pulse. I gave him that. It's my blood,' she thought as her finger touched his wry wrist.

'You see, I talk to all the dead ones. They only answer when I want them to,' Cliff continued softly, as if in an odd trance. 'They make no demands. I just see to them.'

'My knees are weak,' was all Wrasse could say.

'Here, sit in a throne. Let me help you,' Shala offered.

'I'll kneel next to you,' said Cliff, imagining her skeleton after feeling her hand. 'This is enough for me, you know. My boy is singing; doing what he loves. I am here. That is all.'

Wrasse stared at him, misty-eyed, observing his likeness to Gravel.

'Behind you will see your sister, Mire.' Wrasse turned slowly. The singers continued their amplified songs. 'She's nearest,' Cliff informed her gently. Wrasse blinked at the rigid corpse. The white cotton shroud caught on a singer's drape, showing her dried leg. 'The middle one is your mother. Don't tell anyone, but her arm dropped off. I had to stitch another on. I hope it was hers,' he mumbled almost to himself.

Shala listened intently. Wrasse kept silent, only hearing her son's faint, well-spoken voice. 'Then there is your grandmother on your father's side. She isn't in good condition either, but I made her ready. She's been paraded too often. I don't think we can handle her remains much longer.'

Wrasse shook her head in strange understanding. A question formed, but her voice was still mute.

'Nobody speaks to me up here. I like it that way,' he said, holding his mother's elbow, gently laying a kiss on her shoulder.

Shala knew Wrasse was about to weep.

'It's wonderful seeing you... hearing you talking to me,' Wrasse thought with swelling eyes. 'This is no dream. My relic of Weir is by my hip. This is all happening.'

'Would you like to come inside?' Cliff asked delicately.

She nodded, making to rise. Her knees still weak.

'Let's lift her, Cliff,' Shala said, taking an ornate chair arm.

'This way,' Cliff directed, 'through the coloured bark curtain. It parts easily. Just push past. It's light and warm inside. The charcoal burners glow.'

'Each vertical stall has a waxen candle melted to it,' Shala realized. 'They light the long passage as it goes into the distance. It's warm, dry, like ours, but so much larger,' she thought.

'Put Mother here,' Cliff suggested.

Wrasse at last stammered, 'I never stopped loving you. It was the rule. You had to go back to Tarmin. I couldn't. I never understood why. I just accepted it.'

Cliff held her hand, looking into the face he had felt he would never see. They stayed motionless as the sounds from outside began penetrating their peace.

'I'll close the inner fleece curtain and silence that din,' Cliff said.

Wrasse blinked as she gazed along the avenue of resting places. The ones at the entrance were vacant. A huge polished bowl, made from the root ball of a yew tree, contained fragrant offerings. This was Mire's end of the catacomb.

Calmly Wrasse asked her son, 'Is Weir here?'

'Who's Weir?' he enquired gently.

'Sorry, Cliff, I mean the Sea Angel.'

'Ah. Yes, Mother. He is,' he replied with reverence.

'Will you take me to him, please?'

'Of course.' He gripped the chair.

'I can walk now. Just let me gather myself.'

Cliff stood slowly, letting his mother's hand rest on his pelt-covered arm.

She remained in silence momentarily, absorbing all that was transpiring.

'I feel stronger now. It was a shock and a wonderful surprise meeting you. I have a special pouch. It contains relics of him.'

'Come, Mother.'

As they moved, Shala looked into the spaces on each side. A pair of figures were seated on collapsing willow seats. Between them was a clay bowl with dried fruit, shells and a salted fish; another, only mackerel bones. A rounded cup and a quern lay beside two more withered corpses.

'That's an old bark mask I've crushed,' Wrasse thought as she progressed past a pier of neatly stacked bones, momentarily forgetting where she was. 'So much has happened. My first son's at my elbow guiding me in a place I never thought I would see. My past's becoming my present as these things crumble underfoot and these ghosts from either side watch.'

'Here,' Cliff said, holding a candle, 'I'll light another.' The flame bred onto its wick. A shrunken face looked out of the growing glow. The smell of the sheep-fat candle changed the atmosphere as the closed eyes, set with strange barnacles, looked back from the past.

'It's him. It's Weir. There's his beard. I dressed it. Still bound in laces of leather. Still curled at its end,' Wrasse uttered, her heart leaping.

'That's the prow of his boat behind. It makes a wonderful frame for him,' Cliff said caringly.

'Oh, at last I'm looking at you again, Weir,' Wrasse uttered. 'Your eyes shine through those shells. I can't help it. I have to kiss you. Weir, my dearest one, your lips pulse as though you live! I'm feeling you again within me. It can't be, but it is.'

'There, there, Mother,' Cliff said, as he and Shala saw Weir looking back at her.

'His shining hair is lovely,' Shala thought, 'and his fine, red beard's moving as he smiles. Their Star tattoos touch again as they kiss. Now, as she retreats, slowly his visage gradually reverts to that desiccated face.'

'Yes,' Wrasse said at last, 'this is he. His perished shirt only has one arm. There's the stub where Coutou amputated it. Below is the stitching she did after she'd cut his chest open to discover his mortal wound. But I have a piece of him. I know where it belongs. We found it in dead Lintel's secret box. Here Cliff, you replace it.'

She handed him the string container. 'It's his manhood, isn't it, Mother?'

'Yes. Why Lintel had it I have no idea. Coutou's knife was there as well.'

'Your mother stole the knife when Coutou died. She cut Sea Angel's fertility away to keep for her daughters' magic. That is why there are those offerings at his feet. There's a false one attached to his pelvis. I'll take it off and stick his one back with molten beeswax. It will make his spirit more potent.'

'Thank you, Cliff,' Wrasse replied.

Muted sounds of reverie from the celebrations penetrated from above. There, the evening sun beat across the hill. But in the stillness of the charnel house, Wrasse looked down to Weir's feet. 'There's his quartz knife, Shala. It matches the arrow-point you found in the tree roots.'

'Yes, you're right, Wrasse. And look, all those small, carved phalluses. I thought they were toe bones at first. Remember the one in Lintel's box?'

'They are for special conception rites,' Cliff explained.

Wrasse gazed back at the figure of Weir before her as Shala listened.

'They're used by the elderwomen to help daughters conceive at the right time. The Sea Angel still has potent powers. If one of these is used right after mating, a healthy baby with new blood will be born. When he's complete again, he'll be even more potent.

'That's why Weir's was wrapped up in Lintel's Croo box under that straightened bone penis,' Shala realized.

'I'm glad I look my best for you, Weir,' Wrasse thought. 'Shala's necklace makes a beautiful crescent moon over my old breasts. My hair's shining in the candleglow for you. This place seems to have shrunk around us, as though you don't want to let me go. You still look handsome, even in your death,' she said, then looked to Cliff. 'Yes, my son's a person in his own right. He's made his life as best he could. I wish I'd known about him. I wish he were Weir's. I'm so glad he's alive. And my dear grandson too, neutered though he is. I feel immense contentment. It heals the hardship, the remorseful sadness.'

Shala noticed the distant curtains open. A rectangle of bright light shone, beaming up the aisled passage. Silhouettes of the singers with the mummified marionettes moved into the shimmer. The ancestors were returning. A deep peace re-entered the tomb as the curtains closed.

'We will go now, Weir. I will see you again,' Wrasse told him. She passed by her sister, her mother and grandmother without a glance. She pushed the curtains to, entering the evening air. The first bats flew past, hunting moths attracted by the arena's flaming torches. The stage was empty. The party was going on above.

As Cliff emerged Wrasse asked, 'Where can we go where there will be nobody to disturb us?'

'To my shack, at the other end of the tomb. No one ever visits.'

40

Tarmin Town

'Come into my hovel, Mother. It's only a rocky hollow with walls in front. Mind your head. I'll fan the embers and light my marrowbone lamp. I sleep under the overhang at the back.'

Wrasse noticed the strewn skins.

'I'll shove a tree root and a few gnawed sheep bones on. It'll warm up in a mo. Nobody will disturb us,' he said quietly.

'Shala, would you tell Spar I will see him tomorrow?'

'Certainly, Wrasse. I'll go now.'

'It's still busy up on the House of Souls,' Shala thought. 'He's likely up there. I'll climb these steps from Cliff's cave.' As evening drew in, Shala spotted the structures on top. Curving drystone walls enclosed bed-sized spaces. In the twilight she saw the slab shelves within, over a cubit apart. Two were occupied. They were faced off with pierced stonework, leaving small ventilation gaps into sealed-off chambers. Offerings of food in bowls and baskets lay on the shelf projections. 'This is where the corpses must lie until they became bones,' Shala realized. 'These souls aren't needed for parades. In their good time, Cliff will stack them neatly in his caring way, just as we do above our Ancestor House at Lee Holme,' she thought. 'Are you listening?' she addressed the corpses. 'The music has quietened now and there's singing and dancing. Can you feel the feet slapping a rhythm on the stones? It's like a heartbeat all through the building, isn't it? I'll go now to find Spar.'

'Ah. There's Garnet and Cairn. Someone's carried their thrones. They look quite pleased, watching the dancers, enjoying their new status. At least Spar's in charge now. There he is, leading the whirling dance with his cloak flying. I'll wait until it ends.'

'There you are, Shala,' he puffed when the final whoop was yelled. 'Where's Wrasse?'

She's with her son, Cliff, who takes care of this place. She would like to see you tomorrow.'

'I'll send a messenger,' he said, panting. 'He will take her to me. Will you dance with us?'

'Yes. But after I've told Wrasse.'

'Excellent,' he remarked energetically.

'I see the bats are out,' she thought as she returned to Cliff's hovel. 'Something's scurrying from the shadowy shelving. And I *can* smell a body, but the ventilation's dispersing the odours. Ah. There's the ocean ahead, past that huge black dune. The moonlight's wonderful on the water. Listen,' she said to herself, 'that's geese honking. I can make them out above the singing. There's nothing on the horizon, but I feel something distant from behind it. It's so strong. It's him. I know it. Weir knows too. I feel it powerfully. I won't tell Wrasse. I'll leave Spar's message and return to the party.

Shala awakened next day in a comfortable bed alcove in a Spar's house.

'I've sent the messenger,' he said brightly. 'My home's usually busier at this time of day, but the kids are still out cold in their bunks.' She looked across to the curtained alcove from where sleeping sounds came.

'What would you like for breakfast, Shala?' Spar's wife, Moth, asked.

'It's so comfortable,' she thought, as the chaff mattress moved beneath her.

'I've got milled oats and apple sauce, then ham after?'

'That would be lovely,' she tried to say, while yawning under her calfskin cover.

'I'll take that as a "yes".'

Shala nodded, and flopped back to the comfort of the nook bed.

'There's Tarmin's harbour,' Wrasse judged from the long canoe. 'Everything's changed. It's further out and made of upright slabs. Not the neatly coursed one I knew. The houses look smaller, too. The dune between the town and the sea has grown.'

'I'll escort you to Spar's home,' the boatman said. 'You've noticed there's been changes. My parents weren't even born when you left. They always said the Dune would cover us, one day. We're taking stone from that old, half-buried dwelling there.'

'I see you have piles of trees that washed up in the storm. Are there more on the other side of the Dune?' Wrasse asked.

'Yes, plenty,' the young man answered.

'There won't be many folk alive that I knew,' Wrasse said thinking aloud. 'Cliff's told me who's dead, what sort of trial they had and whether they went into the House of Souls. Coutou became ill and died when plague took the children. He learned that from Old Purse, who did his work before him.' She laughed to herself, remembering how he won his food from the offering bowls. 'They don't need it,' he said, 'I just return bones and crusts. The relatives think the dead have had a fine feast!'

'There's Spar's house. Through the herb gardens and vegetable plots.'

'Welcome, Wrasse. Come in.' Hearing her name, the children ogled her from their curtained bunks. 'We've made a bed for you. You can stay as long as you like.'

'This is Moth,' Shala told Wrasse. 'I have just had a wonderful breakfast. Thank you again.'

'Would you like something?' Moth asked.

'No thanks, I ate with Cliff,' remembering their carrion with bizarre pleasure.

Moth nodded knowingly.

'I want to look round Tarmin,' Wrasse explained. 'There have been many changes.'

'Yes,' Spar said, 'I can show you now. I have meetings this afternoon.'

'Congratulations, Spar,' everyone said as they walked round the houses, courtyards and gardens. 'You are the right man to lead – far better than that old hag and her cronies.'

'Our houses are built smaller than those you remember. It's partly because of the shifting sands. But also it's simpler to make sure the young mate with the right match. We shall move to higher ground, anyway. The water seems to be coming, and Tarmin is being squashed between the Dune and the Wetlands.' He pointed dunewards, 'That, I believe was your house.'

'Surely not?' Wrasse answered in shock. 'It was a massive place. Those pathetic bits of wall sticking out can't be it.'

'It was, Wrasse. Tapstone's hauling out another slab; there's his pile of old timbers for firewood.'

'Ouch!' Tapstone yelled as he scraped his thumb. 'Hi. You'll be that terrible woman come back to haunt us,' he said humorously. 'Wait, I found something you might like. I shoved it in my bag. Here it is. It was tucked in a crevice by an old bed.'

'I don't believe it! It's my wooden doll my father whittled. See the scorching for the hair, Shala, and her funny little face. I called her Owl Eyes.'

'Well, you must have her back, my dear,' Tapstone said, beaming at her.

'This brings it all back. But it's strange, we could see the sea from here. Now it's a creeping heap of sand.'

'It's like that along the coast, too. That old deserted place, Skara, has a dune that stretches right across the bay now. But I want to talk about Tarmin,' Spar said as they wandered back towards the landing stage. 'I am going to change things. I want a big public building for proper discussion, feasts and gatherings. I want that unifying us, rather than just a dwelling for the dead.' They walked slowly along a flagstone alley. In a paved courtyard someone split wood from the drifting forest into staves. He nodded a respectful hallo.

'There has been too much ceremony and influence from the mysteries of the House of Souls. I want to keep the traditions alive, but things have been manipulated through it. I saw all of that,' he said, reflecting silently on his service to Cairn. 'Whilst it kept power and tradition, I know there's a better way.' Spar rubbed his foot on a stone and drew in the blown sand. He ruffled his swept-back red hair. 'I want decisions closer to the people and not mystic edicts related to secrecy and dead people. I respect our ancestors. They are core to our existence, and their afterworld should forever be cared for. But I feel our society can only improve and progress with open discussion. That's why I want this building right here, not somewhere remote.'

'A brave concept, Spar,' Wrasse replied. 'We are close to this in

Lee Holme, and have been for a long time. We usually use your house, Shala.'

'Yes. My grandfather, Partan, is our leader, but things are always talked about, particularly the difficulties with family lines and breeding.'

'I would like to discuss this further. I'll arrange better accommodation for you.'

'What we have is fine,' Shala said. 'I like the family atmosphere.'

'I want to spend time with my son, too, so I might stay with him,' Wrasse added.

'That is excellent,' Spar agreed.

They explored Tarmin until a communal lunch of wonderful smoked squid. After, Shala asked, 'Will you take me to where Weir came ashore?'

'Certainly, Shala. I want to go there. It won't be the same though, by the looks of things.' They climbed the dune then went down past boat nousts scraped out from its face. Lines of tree trunks littered the high-tide mark. Many had been hauled up the slopes and were being split gradually with wedges, time and skill.

They came onto a sandy bay with drifts of pebbles and eroded rocks. Wrasse looked along the shore to her right. 'That's the cliff where geese and swans made all that noise. I'm very moved at being here. Take my arm. We'll walk to where he came ashore. Having seen him in the House of Souls, it feels like he could appear again.'

They looked out to sea. Wrasse's heart leapt. 'Boatmen are fishing and creeling. Youngsters wade in the ebb with their shrimp nets, each with a bulging bag at their side where the catch wriggles in crowded darkness. Nothing's really changed. This must be where we pulled his boat up,' Wrasse said as if in a dream. 'We carried it with him in it. I can almost feel the strange barnacles scratch my skin and see his emaciated body inside.'

'Let's sit,' Shala said, putting her arm around her. 'Then we can go back.'

They stayed in Tarmin some days. Wrasse met elders who knew her from long before, some from nearby villages and others from Calling Hill past the south end of the dune. There the land rose before the tidal inlet and sands.

Spar and they confided. Shala explained her visions and dreams, and their connections with Weir. 'Now I know all this,' he remarked, 'I can understand the real reasons for your journey back here, Wrasse. I look forward to new prospects of healthy bloodlines, though I'll keep it to myself for now. But what I really want is a set of Partan's measuring poles. They're just what we'll need. Before you go, my family will host a celebration for you. I will even make Cairn and Garnet feel like honoured guests. I'll put word out. But you, Wrasse, will have to tell the wee children charming stories of flowers, maidens and frogs to dispel your terrifying image.'

During the party, Shala realized how they had been so greatly honoured. 'Would this continue at home? No,' she answered herself. 'Life will return to normal,' she realized as she dipped her peeled prawns into an oily egg yolk sauce.

Time slipped by as they conversed in the throng until Spar called them aside. 'Someone awaits you. Follow me to my hearth.'

'Cliff,' Wrasse said in surprise. 'How your grey hair shines as you crouch by the fire,' she thought, saying, 'Don't get up, we'll sit next to you.'

'Here, Mother. This is something from the House of Souls for you.'

Wrasse unwrapped the strange, long package. 'It's Weir's white knife with the broken blade,' she said looking to her son in an overwhelmed way.

'Continue unwrapping, Mother,' Cliff said.

She unravelled the decorated parchment. 'It's a mummified arm,' she announced surprised. 'There's a polished jet ring on the long finger.'

'I put that on Weir's hand for you, Mother.' Wrasse shivered as Cliff continued, 'I thought that when you eventually go into your Ancestor House you might like to take some of Weir with you.'

'I never expected this,' she tried to say as she tearfully trembled. 'It's such an honour. It's so precious.'

'Nobody will know, Mum,' he said lovingly, 'I've replaced his arm from a body ready for breaking up. I got the ring from a tiny crevice. You can wear it if you like.'

'Can I?' she murmured. 'Later, later: in the Ancestor House, maybe? But black does suit me.'

Their clothes had been mended and cleaned. The long skin canoe, like the Sea Angel's, waited at the end of the dune. There, water escaped from Tarmin to the sea. Spar knew they did not want any more fuss. Nor he. 'I've plenty to do in my new role,' he thought. 'This is Cleat and Shank. They are Sea Star's crew. Stow their belongings, men,' he ordered. 'All provisions are in the watertight sternhold. I'll grip Sea Star firmly. Wrasse, Shala, embark, there's a good wave coming. Shank and Cleat, jump in. Man the paddles. Here comes the billow!' he shouted as he ran into the surf, pushing the canoe into deeper water. 'Paddle!' he yelled. 'Safe journey. Don't forget Partan's poles, Cleat.'

'On the high seas again, Shala,' Wrasse said as they mounted another wave.

'Yes. It smells fresh and different. It's deep water now. They paddle extremely well.'

'That's Calling Hill. It looks like a goat's leg sticking out to sea,' Shank announced. 'When we pass that, the current will take us round a bay, then under high cliffs to another bay, then past Skara.'

'There they are,' Cleat shouted, brandishing his paddle. 'Wave and shout to them, you two,' he said as folk standing on the rough cliff knuckle-banged drums and blew horns. 'That's their parting cheer,' he said. 'See the beacon they've lit? Watch.'

Those on the cliff heaped seaweed over the blaze. Acrid grey smoke palled from it in a voluminous farewell plume. Their horns blared, vast cheers resounded from the promontory.

'What a send-off, Wrasse,' Shala remarked.

'Yes. A lot more auspicious than my last leaving,' she answered, gripping Weir's wrapped arm.

'Next bay coming up,' Shank announced soon after. 'Smell the smoke, can you?' he asked, as they passed beneath the dispersing cloud.

41

Skara Bay

Cleat and Shank paddled hard past the next bay. Tide drew them landward between Calling Hill and the approaching High Lands. There, Burr's Head protruded. Waves broke on his ribs as the slumbering Giant lay there. When they rounded Wounded Shoulder, Burr's Neck appeared. The gash in it, called Wolf's Bight, was a deep cave.

Cleat and Shank said, 'If you enter and Burr snores, you'll be sucked so far inside you'll never come out. The old Hero lies there recovering from war with Wolf-Man. In his last battle, Burr collapsed naked into the briny sea. His tough chin crushed his lifelong enemy, drowning him. At very low tides the jagged Dead Wolf Rocks appear. They are covered in flowing seaweed. Brave youths glean the Wolvenfur. It's dried, then crumbled into sacred soups. High above the foaming waters is Burr's Brow: up there, all the birds of the sea nest. Their cries in the sky are the sounds of the warrior giant's dreams.'

'There's Burr's Beard,' Cleat pointed out, 'It's a tall basalt pillar supporting the slumbering God's chin. Only the bravest and most skilled of sailors go under it.'

'That's us,' Shank shouted eagerly. 'The water's stiller here. See the light beaming through? Turn the Sea Star, we're going under. Out of the way, seals. Don't rock the boat.'

'Quiet,' Shank warned, 'we mustn't wake the old giant. It'd be the end of us.'

'Look at all the mussels, Wrasse,' Shala whispered.

'We'd better not take any,' warned Wrasse, 'he might stir,'

'There's a wee sandy cove below the lofty cliffs. It's called Dead Man's Pillow. It's where unskilled mariners end up. Not us, though,' Shank reported as they emerged from under the chin. 'We'll sing you all the legends as we go the rest of the way.'

'Skara coming up,' they eventually announced as Sea Star rounded the low cliffs.

'That dune's massive, Wrasse. Look at the tall grasses waving. It's far bigger than Lee Holme's. Does anyone live here?'

'No, Shala.'

'We'll beach at Dune's End where the water rushes out,' Shank called over his shoulder.

'At last,' Wrasse said. 'This is a special place. After we land I'll tell you why. My father took me here, so I've heard the legends. It was lovely to hear them again. They've not changed at all.'

'Turn the boat; beach,' Cleat said. 'Don't bash any stranded logs.'

'There's the gushing outflow from the loch behind the dune, Shala.'

'Yes, and look at the tall, jagged cliffs just the other side. They make the tumble of water echo,' Shala pointed out as Sea Star's prow bit the sand just below a pile of strewn trees.

'Khul's business, again,' Wrasse remarked as they disembarked.

'There's one of those smooth quartz pebbles gripped in a twisted knot of roots, Wrasse.'

'Yes. They're from a very long way away, Shala. Past all horizons they have come. I'm certain they're from Weir's land. See, if we were to knap that stone, it would look just like his knife inside.'

'Those are the same barnacles?'

'Yes. Hear them rattle in the breeze.'

'The redshanks are coming, Wrasse. I hear them. 'The trees, the trees,' they are saying. 'Weir's trees, and someone else's, too.' Oh, my head's feeling strange. I must sit, Wrasse. I can see in my mind people on a distant shore, then one person alone in the fog. Someone's shouting. It's a name. I can't make it out. It's fading. It's gone.'

'Yes, Shala. I heard nothing, but felt strange. It is you taking over, I think. Believe in your visions. Keep them. The redshanks have settled now. See them on the sand in the ebb?'

'We'll make you ladies comfortable,' Shank announced. 'There's a tent in the hold and ground hides. We'll get a fire going between two logs. All will be comfort and joy,' Shank announced.

'The presence is still there, Wrasse. I hear the name deep inside me, but I can't make it out. He's alone. The name's faded. There's desperate paddling, but just misty images. It's him, coming here. I know it. Just him. Alone, like Weir. I've dreamed this before, but now it is clear.'

'Do you want anything to eat, ladies, or are you going to sit aloof on those logs up there?' Shank called.

'We will come, men. Don't worry. What is it, anyway?' Wrasse answered.

'Ham, smoked mackerel and a tub of that seaweed sauce you both like so much.'

'Thank you. It sounds excellent. I would like to stay here for a day. I am sure you need a rest. We want to explore.'

'As you wish, ladies. Take your time, there's no hurry.'

'This is a wonderful place. Look at the fine clouds, lit by the sinking sun. See the pinks, reds and golden tones. Shall we climb the dune, Wrasse, and take a better look?'

'Yes. The slope's gentler where the burn hurtles past. We'll see the other side from up there.'

'Oh! It's wonderful,' Shala said moments later. 'The way the burn empties from the shimmering loch, making tiny flowing whirlpools. The whole place has a magical atmosphere. How the colours of the clouds reflect themselves. Look. Trout are rising. There's an otter slinking in and a heron watching. It's beautiful, and nobody lives here.'

'Shala, watch the swans gliding to the reeds on the far bank. Their wake shimmers in golden glints. It's so still behind the dune, yet full of life.'

'Yes, Wrasse. It's the sort of place one dreams of. I feel I mustn't move. My destiny also seems wound into this place. He's going to land here, I'm certain.

'Yes. That's why we are here.' They remained silent, taking in the gentle wonder of what was before them.

'We can go up the slope,' Wrasse said quietly. 'The view's even better. Slowly, though. I'm weary.'

'I'll help you.'

'I can't make the top, Shala. I'll stay here,' Wrasse admitted after a while.

'Okay, Wrasse. You rest. I'll go on to the ridge. Listen to Cleat and Shank's songs. I won't be long.'

'It's hard going, even for me,' Shala thought pushing through the sea-grass spine of Skara's dune. 'Each side is wonderful: the sea and the setting sun, the distant crest of Big Land's mountains, burning in sunlight like wolves' teeth. Down there is the splendid loch, bathed in glory. This is truly a haven on Mother Earth.' She waved to Wrasse, pointing to the mountains, taking it all in together.

Wrasse waved back, pointing out giant auks emerging from reeds. Their young followed as the sun dipped, showing them as dark silhouettes on the gilded surface.

'I'll go back now,' Shala decided.

'I'm feeling extremely tired,' Wrasse confessed when Shala met her. 'It's all we've done, catching up on me.

'Well, we can just sit here and take it all in until you're ready to go down.'

'The Moon's rising, huge and yellow,' Wrasse remarked as an owl swooped, gripping a meaty vole. 'It's looking at you, Shala.'

'Mmmmmm. Yes. I seem to feel its glance. There it goes, down to the willows. Look, Wrasse, do you see those huge reflections going across the loch. It's flying geese! But there's none in the sky.'

'No,' Wrasse answered, 'I don't.

'A great skein is slowly curving over its surface. I can see the leader's eye. It looks at me like the owl did. Listen to their wingbeats. It's deafening. The air's moving in a rush with them,' she said as her hair blew in the total stillness.

'The swans are taking off, Shala.'

'Yes. They fly among the reflections.'

'That owl's peering at you again.'

'I feel her. Can't you see the goose shadows streaking across the sea?'

'No, Shala. This is your vision.'

'Now I see their dark shapes crossing the Moon, Wrasse. It's amazing. I just want to sit and watch. Let me hold you.'

'Yes, of course. Tomorrow we will explore Skara.'

Shala woke well before snoring Wrasse. 'I'm going to swim. My hair's needing fresh salt. Cleat, Shank, would you take the boat up to Skara Loch? We will explore when Wrasse is ready.'

'Aye, lass,' they replied.

'Cold water is just what I need,' she shouted, plunging into the welling tide. 'It is so refreshing. It's like I can feel the whole ocean and I am part of it. It makes me new inside: powerful, with will, energy... strength. My amber is stronger, too,' she thought as it bounced over her growing bosom. 'I can cope with my future. It is part of me now. I know he *is* coming. I *am* sure it will be here, now I have seen the geese ghosts and the swans. It's like a prelude to Wrasse's story. I will make certain it works for me, him, us.'

Wrasse emerged from the conical tent to see Shala dressing. 'She's changed and grown on this journey,' she summed up.

The sound of the Skara Burn tumbling from the loch to the sea filled the air.

'Cleat and Shank have taken the boat to the loch,' Shala said, shaking her hair of water.

'Good, we can explore. Look, there go the auks, Shala.'

'Yes: lots of them dashing into the rapids with their young. Their coloured beaks are magnificent.'

'Their clacking chorus is amazing, Shala. They can't fly, but they make up for it underwater. I've seen them dive deep, surfacing far away in moments.'

'There they go, Wrasse. Their flashing bills are wonderful.'

'Come, we must get on,' Wrasse urged.

'Yes. But just smell the fishy scent from their plumage as they queue up.'

'Aye, Aiv... Shala,' Wrasse corrected herself. 'They're fearless of us. Just watch them tumble down those rapids. How they love it. They will all leave together in the winter.'

'Where to?' Shala wondered aloud.

'Maybe the Land of Logs,' Wrasse mused as they walked upstream to the Sea Star.

'Do you remember the Tide Tales, Shala?'

'How could I forget: that story of the Far Folk. You were so frightening. It was the way you told it. You became that wave. We were all in sheer dread.'

'Oh. That good, was it?' she smiled as she boarded. 'It was here, Shala,' she said bluntly as she sat, 'Right here in this place. Some say it happened north, at Farsee, as well. But it was aeons ago. See how tranquil it is: The still waters, the willows and the lovely yellow flags. It was then, too, until the Skara Ebb.'

'Comfortable, ladies?' Shank asked. 'Then we'll paddle off.'

'Look past the swans, Shala. That's Harrar's Top. There's the stone sticking up amongst the pines on the summit. You can even see its reflection on the water. That's where Gurnard and Vacar watched the terrible wave. Then the Auk and Auroch passed them as they escaped inland. They were the last of the Far Folk. They saw everything washed away, with fish flying past them. Vacar hurled his spear in despair. It landed near Lee Holme. They left here, following the migrating geese, and chased the wave back to where it had come from. There they stay to this day, keeping it.

'One day you will have to tell that legend, Shala,' Wrasse added as Cleat and Shank shivered at the story. 'Your turn will come, when I'm in the Ancestor House clutching Sea Angel's arm.'

'Beach where the deer are drinking below that sharp knoll, on the far side, men. We will explore from there.'

'They've seen us, Wrasse. Look at their antlers. They're mooching off out of arrow range.'

'Yes, Shala. They will be heading for the hidden loch behind the knoll, then the nut groves and damson woods on the slopes.'

'And the flowering gorse whins, further on,' Shala added.

'Mm. And the birchwoods, where their young might be hiding.'

'Wrasse. It looks as though no man's hand has touched this place, except for the sacred stone in the pines.'

'That's right. Nobody has lived here since Gurnard and Vacar followed the tide, and the geese. We are beaching, now. You jump out first, Shala.'

'Geese flock here in vast numbers,' Cleat told Shala. 'Nobody hunts them,' he said pulling the boat up. 'Mind the clay. It's really slippy,' he added, skidding himself.

'Whoops! Careful,' Wrasse said to Shank as he slewed sideways in the sticky, hoof-marked bank.

'Watch it yourself,' he retorted as his hip dented the deposit.

'I'll help you, Wrasse,' Shala said. 'Use your staff, I'll curl my toes into the stuff. We'll make it,' she advised, as she considered the value of the clay for making pots and face packs.

'Well, our boat's nose is really lodged tight. She's not going to drift off,' Shank remarked as he rubbed his mud-clarted side. 'Shove her stake in and tie her. Then we can go up the grassy bank.'

'I want to go to that sandy knoll,' Wrasse insisted, 'and the ancient dune striking off it.'

'Okay. Mind your step, Old Maid.'

'Mind yours, Shank; and your tongue.'

'There's an otter's scrape under it, Wrasse,' Shala observed.

'Yes. Stinks like it, too. She's shifted loads of sand, making it cosy for her brood of kits.'

'See the old stones above her hole, Wrasse? 'Looks like they got burned ages ago. Let's get to the top.'

'Okay. But go steady. I'm getting old.'

'There's another huge reedy loch over there, Wrasse,' Shala called from the brow. 'It's beautiful. The waving flags are in full bloom. It smells of honey. There must be hundreds of ducks in there, not to mention eels, carp and other splendid fish.'

'Yes. I told you,' puffed Wrasse as she caught up. 'Absorb Skara. It's taboo yet, but it's pivotal to you and our race, I believe.'

'The sunshine's wonderful here. See how the flowering thistles glow in this secret place, Wrasse.'

'Let's follow the deer path along the sand ridge. There's rising ground looking over Skara's Loch.'

'Right dear,' Wrasse replied, 'you can see the sea from there, past the dune to the high cliffs at Auk Falls.'

When they arrived, Shala stated, 'The marshy loons behind are even richer here. You could have boats, protected by this promontory, to range over Skara's marshlands; ones below, too, to fish Skara Loch. We could have an ocean fishing station by the foot of the Great Dune. This is a truly magnificent place. The hills around enclose Skara. It's like being cocooned in the landscape. I want to return here and never leave. It's like being inside a vast egg with an invisible shell.'

They sat meditating, silently watching Auk Falls tumble. Wrasse broke the quiet. 'I want to speak to you about the Nurture House, Shala. I have to say how I admired your strength in not accepting the phallus. I believe, for you, it was right. You have become the master of yourself. I said before, I wished I had your strength at my time. I'm sure you know your destiny. It gives you the power you need. You will be the greater woman for it.' Wrasse paused, considering. 'Every young woman takes from the Nurture House what is right for them then. What happened within the building, and on that Sacred Island, where we heard my grandson sing, just made my belief in you stronger. If I am still living when your Sea Angel arrives, please bring him to me. I can wait for some time, but not forever,' she admitted falteringly.

'You're weeping, Wrasse,' Shala said while putting her arm around her.

Wrasse could not work out for whom her tears were fell: herself, Shala, her Sea Angel or for the next one.

42

ʟee ʜolme ʙound

'ʟook what we've found,' came Shank's excited voice. 'Wee sharp flints.'

'Far Folk tools,' exclaimed Wrasse as she came from her emotions. 'Where did you find them?'

'At the otter's den,' he said urgently.

'Let's see.'

'There, just above the sticky clay, is the otter's hole. Niff the fish,' Cleat remarked.

'Let me see,' Wrasse interrupted. 'Well. That just shows us. This must be the legendary place. The burnt hearthstones buried deep in the sand. There's the Sight Stone overlooking us. That's where the procession of the Great Auks and Aurochs went. The Old Dune must have been washed here by the wave, burying everything and everyone except Gurnard and Vacar. Now there's a new dune, vast and strong. Skara's safe again. Maybe the curse is lifted? Maybe they'll return?' she muttered to herself. 'Right, men. To Lee Holme.'

They soon ported the canoe over the sands to the waves. 'We've never been further than here,' Cleat admitted, 'but if we sail along the cliffs past the Huge Hills, you eventually get to where you live. Is that right?'

'Just about,' Wrasse confirmed.

'Righto,' Shank said, pushing the loaded craft into the waves. 'Everybody comfortable? Right. Let's paddle. Get in Auk Force's current and make for Gare Head.'

'There's the Sight Stone, Wrasse. It's peering down from the pines.'

'Yes, Shala. It beckons.'

'Look,' Shank shouted. 'Auks coming up.'

'See, Wrasse,' Shala indicated, pointing downwards, 'there's masses of them surfacing. Yes, we're in a huge huddle of them now. It's amazing. Listen to their clacking.'

'They're trying to tell us something, Wrasse. Just like my redshanks do. The din. It's so great, echoing from the sheer cliff. What is it they are saying?'

'Some are mounting the rocks in the surf and shouting at us.'

'That one's drumming on the other's bill. Now lots of them do it.'

'Well,' Shank announced, 'I've never seen a display like that. I think they're calling you back.'

'Yes,' Shala realized, 'as the stone beckons, so do they. I will return... that's for sure.'

'The tide's against us. Pull hard. Past the head there are caves: Old Finny lives in them. She tries to suck you in. Then there's the Virgin's Cock. I've seen a picture of it. It's a huge rock sticking up with another reaching out to it from the cliff top. Finny somersaults over it to attract her mates. She scoffs them whole when they've filled her womb. Sometimes she's a giant lobster and at others a huge squid. For sailors, she's a vision of wonder. Lucky it isn't full Moon!' Cleat added.

Shala thought only of the deserted Skara, as the paddlers retold the ancient legends.

A backing breeze moved them onwards. Big Land's mountains disappeared behind a veil of sea spray.

They floated past a bay sheltered by high hills. Their treed slopes gave onto a bare top where deer gathered. Low down, smoke rose from shoreside dwellings. A single craft, like a bobbing nutshell, lay close in. They sailed on.

Wrasse pointed to breaching whales in the slate grey distance. Their backs shone as they rose and dipped in the swell.

'If it weren't for you two weights, we'd be making much better progress,' Cleat called from his paddling stance.

'If it weren't for us two items of precious cargo, you wouldn't be dipping your fancy paddles anyway,' Wrasse rejoined.

'Ply your might more efficiently,' Shala added, 'and we'll get a good few leagues nearer home.'

'Show us how?'

'Glad to,' they both replied.

'There's spare paddles strapped under Wrasse's seat,' Cleat answered. 'Shank, reach down and unlash them.'

'They are quite beautiful,' Wrasse remarked as they dropped in the bilge.

'Yes, carved with twisting colourful eels up the shafts and over the wide, spear-shaped blades.'

'Come on, Shala, I want us to get to the Forest of Kaime below the Big Hills. There is fine shelter there amongst the Timeless Trees.'

'So, ladies, you paddle well,' Shank stated as they sped through rising swell.

'There'll be calm in the lee of the mounts when we round these cliffs. It looks like sheltered lowlands after. Our passage will be easier. What's this Forest of Kaime, then?'

'Another sacred place, where men don't dwell. The Great Deer ruts there and rules his domain. We can stay one night. No more.'

They passed a wide vale. Two rivers, separated by low wooded hills, cascaded over huge rounded beach stones. Cleat and Shank waved to a couple of boats, whose crew were long-lining for cod, Pollack and ling. Much later, Sea Star's prow touched the protected sands below the Kaime Forest.

'I am weary,' Wrasse admitted. 'Help me ashore.'

'Yes. I've never seen you so tired.'

'No. Indeed, Shala. Our journey has exhausted me. I forget I'm old. The grave beckons the likes of me.'

'There are none like you, Wrasse. So stop this nonsense.'

'It isn't nonsense. But I'll stop, for now.'

'Men. Go ahead and light a fire. Take no branch from the Forest. Use only driftwood. Kull will have left plenty,' Shala instructed.

'Quite right, young lady. Just what I would have said,' Wrasse added breathlessly. 'The deer-grazed grass looks comfortable. It's a fine lawn for me to rest on.'

'We will pitch your tent on it, ladies. It will be as comfy as a feather mattress,' the men said.

'I'll help you when the ground hides are laid,' Shala said. 'I'll get the men to drag a hot stone in, if you want.'

'Don't worry about hot stones. I'll sleep like one, directly.'

'Cleat, Shank. When she's snoring, roll one through the door. I'll hop over it when I go to bed.'

'Quite right, lass. But we'll give you a good feed first. There's mussels below the cliff.'

'Mussels,' Wrasse overheard as she drifted into oblivion.

Hours later, Wrasse wakened. 'I need to pee,' she thought. 'Shala's sleeping soundly; I'll crawl into the grimling.' The sunken sun's light complemented that of the arcing moon. Only the Beautiful Star showed. 'It's so wonderfully still,' Wrasse thought as she crouched and gushed at the edge of Kaime. The men snored as the sea lapped the shore. Her bowels performed, her farts agitating the sparrows. In the midnight twilight she discerned the sounds of distant geese as the surf brushed the sand. Her mind went to Weir's arm. 'Now I see a young man's earnest face. A white Star shines from his forehead. His fair beard flows forward: He's not Weir, but he's so similar. Oh. I'm losing him in a swirling fog.' The men snored on.

'I feel drawn into the woodlands. The beautiful dewy lichen shines in the gloom. How the wind has blasted these ancient, stunted trees. There's a deer path, beaten into the mould. I smell the beast's pelts where they have pushed through the twisted branches. It draws me in. Ouch! That's my hair caught. There are animals moving in here. I sense it. I'll go deeper. Deeper....

'Now I'm at the edge of a clearing. The moon shines on a glistening menhir. It stinks of stag. Yes, there's his rutting circle, beaten around the upright rock. Who's calling my name? Where's that hot breath coming from?'

'It is I, Wrasse. I'm Ven. This is my place. I swam here from the Big Land. I smelt the need here. I clashed antlers with the Hinds' Lord and beat him. I covered and mated his tribe, giving them blood anew. Man... he culls the weak. I mate only with the strong.'

Wrasse gazed, amazed, into the stag's steaming muzzle.

'Your fresh blood is coming. He will mate. He will fight. Who will cull your infirm? Time? Yes. Time culls all: you, before long: Me, when another swimmer scents his right.

'I hear your thoughts, Wrasse. We know his name. The geese know, the auk and the wolf. Go now and forget.'

At the wood's edge Wrasse smelt the salty sea. There, her steaming movement lurked, Ven's potent odour, gone.

'Such a strange dream,' Wrasse said to herself as she snuggled back in the tent.

'What dream?' Shala asked sleepily.

'I can't remember. But Shala, would you cut me a staff from in there? Something gnarled to match my nature?'

'Mmmmm,' she answered as she drifted off.

Hours later Wrasse finally rose. 'Here's your crutch,' Shala announced as she whittled flaking bark away. 'It took ages to find. There are so many. Then I saw a huge set of antlers move a branch. This is it. But even stranger... I saw someone... Him... Cutting a tall, straight tree. It all seemed so distant.'

'The Forest of Kaime, though small, is powerful. Especially the beings who dwell there,' Wrasse replied.

'Right, ladies,' Shank interrupted. 'Do you want to stay here all day chatting, or will we sail on? If we go now, we can call in at Mount Cove.'

'Shank. Cleat. I would much prefer to sail past. I'm not in the mood for swapping news. Shala can carve away at my staff while you paddle. We want to get back to Lee Holme.'

'Okay. We will put further out to sea, but we will need to stop somewhere.'

'The lonelier the place, the better for us. Thank you, men.'

'Understood perfectly. Can you trail a long line?'

'Be glad to.'

'Let's launch Sea Star, then.'

For hours they sailed below the vertical heights in the rain. Rocky stacks stood like sentinels, hip deep in the rising and falling waters. Dark caves loomed from under the staggering heights. Gannets circled above then dived deep for innocent fish. A burn, fed by the power of Waret, issued over the clifftop. It fell, breaking into a mist before touching the moving ocean. 'Pissing Pony of High Hump,' Wrasse informed everyone. They watched the white water as puffins flew past.

The sounds of the sea rising and falling in the caves came to them. A strange music, like the calling of seals and the moaning of demons, came ringing in a song of brine and rock.

'Mount Cove, ahead,' Wrasse announced. 'There's a wooden creeler. They are hauling. Don't go close. Just wave your paddles in greeting. Signal we are heading on. Looks like a good catch. See, they are holding up lobsters. The boy's got a redfish! They'll feast well tonight.'

'Aye,' Shank remarked. 'I've cut willow for weaving creels when we get home. It'll just need a soak. Paddle on, Cleat.'

'Yup, Shank. The breeze is backing us, and the rain. Do you need waterproofs, ladies? There are some in the hold.'

'A cape would do me,' Wrasse answered. 'I like spray on my hair.'

'I'll get them,' Shala said. 'Whoops!' she added, tripping, 'The swell's getting far stronger.'

'It will, here. The current rips between Big Land and High Hills. There's distant sunshine though. Is that Vaar ahead?'

'I don't know,' replied Shank, 'I've never been this way, but I've heard tell of it.'

'It's gone now. Watch out on the next crest,' Wrasse put in.

'There it is,' Shala stated later. 'Under the sunshine, out east. Breakers bash at its toes. Gone again,' she said as it vanished.

'Pull hard, men. We'll make for there. This boat responds really well in swell,' Wrasse encouraged.

'It's the skill of us sailors, Madam.'

'It will be no trouble then.'

'Quite,' they puffed.

'There's a horn blast,' Wrasse announced later.

'It's a craft. She's dropped in a trough. I'll blow my whistle,' Shank reported, placing the wing-bone to his lips.

Gallow sounded his goat horn again. Russet, his boy, steered their skin boat around, encouraging them to follow.

'That'll be the Vaar family,' Wrasse informed them. 'The boy will have seal lips. They live at the Bay of Calm.

'There's a scaring of mackerel,' Shala pointed out.

'Watch for hunting porpoises, then plunging gannets,' remarked Wrasse as the Sea Star followed.

'There they are. Listen to their clacking jaws. Here come those gannets. You were quite right, Wrasse,' Shala admitted.

'Rain again,' complained Cleat as their boat touched the sand below a long, low, turf-roofed house.

'Come up. Have minty tea,' Gallow called, 'You'll have to stoop. The lintel's low.'

'It's quite a step down, Wrasse. They need to clear midden away,' Shala observed.

'Maiden Gallow at your service. Minty goat broth?' she lisped. 'Sit, be comfy. Here's chives and parsley to sprinkle in the cups. Blow, now. It's very hot. Get your sodden feet dried. Warm yourselves by the fire. I'm malting barley, too. Lovely smell when you're brewing, isn't it?'

'Thank you so much, Maiden Gallow. I'm Wrasse, this is Shala, then Cleat and Shank, our crew. We are sailing back to Lee Holme.'

'Then we have news,' she spluttered through her hare lip. 'But first meet our children. Come on down from the loft, you lot.'

'Grace, Favour, Luck and Charm,' she said as the two daughters and their other two sons nodded a greeting.

'Grace and Favour are not exactly ugly sisters,' Shala thought silently, 'but they seem inbred. Luck and Charm look reasonable, but Favour's lip is definitely a sign. Maybe they have different fathers. Wrasse's white streak shows faintly, too. I'm sure Maiden Gallow has a cleft palate, but a lovely nature.

Maiden Gallow then came out with it: 'Partan of Lea Holme is injured and probably dead.'

'What!' exclaimed Shala.

'I heard yesterday. My man was fishing. He caught those mackerel I'm smoking. Signal's boat came alongside and he told him,' Gallow nodded.

'I don't believe it. Gallow, why didn't you tell us?' Shala asked in shock as Wrasse sat on a whalebone seat, flabbergasted.

'I didn't know who you were,' he stammered.

'He'd had the entrance to your Ancestor House altered,' Gallow told them. 'He'd been in there alone with the spirits. Eventually he emerged. He spread his arms wide and stood rapidly. He forgot the new lintel above and cracked his head open. He hasn't spoken since.'

'I don't believe it!' Shala cried out, dropping her cup. 'We must go now. If he's still alive, I have to see him. Shank, Cleat: get ready. We're going.'

'Mind the lintel,' Gallow advised ironically.

'Leap in. Keep your feet dry,' Shank said as Cleat held the boat steady.

'Lee Holme's around a headland in the misty distance,' Gallow indicated.

'Push off,' Shank shouted.

'We'll paddle too, for speed,' Wrasse put in.

'Fine,' Cleat answered. 'There's a backing breeze. The current is with us. Just watch us speed past that floating log.'

'There's my redshanks on it. I wonder what they know?' Shala thought as each swirling paddle-stroke took them nearer home. Time stood still for her, as she pondered on the future. Her muscles felt hot, wrenching the paddle deeper as they sped over the waves towards Lille Sands.

'There's boats appearing from everywhere,' Shala said at last. 'It can't mean he's dead, can it?'

'I don't know. We shall see. Be brave, Shala,' Wrasse urged quietly.

43

Partan's Parting

'Help Wrasse up the beach steps,' Shala said urgently as the Sea Star bit the sand, 'I'm running to Granddad.'

She squeezed into the packed room from the crowded courtyard. 'Excuse me. I'm Shala. I'm home. Let me pass.'

'Certainly. It's Shala: back from her travels. Make way for her.'

'Shala,' Gull said in surprise. 'Everyone, move back. Give her space.'

There lay Partan in his polished stone bed.

'Home at last,' Juniper snapped.

Flint took Shala's hand, stating, 'He's breathing better.'

'Welcome home, Shala,' said Jasper, tapping his sweating palm with his basalt mace. 'We think he's recovering.'

'He's so thin under his suede cover,' Shala answered. 'Shouldn't we sit him up so he can breathe better; he rasps so.'

'We are scared his wound will open.'

'Here's fresh hot water, Gull,' Quernstone said.

'Thanks, I'll bathe his crown.'

'Here's new moss with plum vinegar. It might sting.'

'I shall sooth his bruises, then the scabs.'

'He's winced. He can feel it,' Shala uttered with hope.

'Wrasse is here,' someone announced.

'Flint. Get her a stool,' Gull said. 'Open up that new leather one leaning against the wall.'

'He's stopped breathing!' Jasper barked in alarm. 'His head's drooped. He's gone.'

'Keep back,' Shala ordered as the crowd moved closer, 'Give him space.'

Without warning he coughed violently. 'He's sitting up. Thank the gods,' Gull exclaimed. 'He's going to sneeze.'

Shala held him in support. 'It's going to be all right, Granddad,' she soothed as he sneezed painfully.

'Shala, you're home. Who are all these people?'

Everyone sighed in absolute relief as Partan shouted, 'Well! What's all this damned fuss about?'

'You've been seriously injured. You've been unconscious for days,' Jasper told him. 'Take it easy.'

'Look Jasper. I've never felt better in my life,' he barked, then suddenly grimaced bitterly. His entire body shook. His eyes, gazing directly at Shala, filled with blood. His dry, thinning mouth opened wide as he frowned deeply. The cranial scabs split and oozed as he howled a long wail, to slump from his bed into Gull's lap.

Shock rooted all when Partan's final bowel movements broke the silence.

Gull trembled, saying, 'Help. Move him back to bed. Quernstone, please clean his behind. Give me a lift. Flint, Juniper, take his legs. Shala, help me with his shoulders. Lay him on his side so Quernstone can do her work.'

Quernstone took the sponge from Gull's shaking fingers. She began the first mourning wail: a low moan that slowly gathered height. Other womenfolk chanted in torment. Wrasse sat stoically leaning on her staff. The men shuffled uneasily.

'Bring scented water and swabs, Juniper,' Gull asked. 'Add meadowsweet, mint and crushed juniper berries. When Quernstone's finished, we'll share the washing.'

'Yes, Mum. What's Shala going to do?'

'She'll help. Please get fresh bedding, Shala,' she said tearfully. 'The old will soon smell of death.'

'I'm so glad I got here in time, Wrasse,' Shala said over the intensifying wails.

'Yes, seeing someone die helps one know life for what it is.'

Shala turned saying, 'Mother, Granddad's face looks as if the pain's gone. He's relaxed and calm.'

'Yes, dear. I'm so glad you're home. Even for this. I see the menfolk are moving outside, leaving the washing and wailing to us.'

'I've got drink ready,' Quartz announced in the fresh breeze. 'We must toast his life while he's being prepared for the next.'

'Now we've cleaned him,' put in Jasper, 'we should prop him up. Give him a cap to hide his bruises. Flint, pull out his otter skin cape. Get his mace. Find the finest furs.' The wailers continued in sorrowful rhythm.

'You're exhausted, Wrasse,' Shala said as Gull and Juniper joined the drone.

'Yes. I am,' she replied through her long, tumbling hair. 'I'll not shriek with grief like the others. I've seen too much death.'

'Somehow, I don't feel the need either,' Shala answered, immediately collapsing in tears on Wrasse's lap.

'There, there. There,' Wrasse soothed, 'It will all be all right, you'll find. Jasper is putting his mace firmly back in his belt. He's Chief, now. We all know Partan decreed it, as a right of his marriage to your mum.'

'I feel such responsibility descending on me,' Jasper thought as the weeping steadied. 'I will wait, then let them continue at Quernstone's. She will have prepared.'

Above Juniper's wailing, Jasper addressed Wrasse as she consoled Shala. 'We have a new flat for you.'

'Thank you so much. I feel old and tired. I'm very grateful.'

'We've moved Shala. You'll be next to her. I hope you can manage the new log-cut stair? Will that suit, and are you feeling all right?' adding, 'Juniper and Flint have rooms at either end.'

'Yes, thank you, Jasper. I can crawl up. I'm just weary and rocked at events.'

'I understand, Wrasse. Life goes on though. What do you know about preserving bodies? We will have to keep him as an ancestor.'

'I'll tell you tomorrow. There's plenty of time, but he hasn't had his Trial yet.'

'No, but it's understood.'

'Of course,' she replied as Shala's sobbing subsided. 'Do you want to come up, Shala?'

She nodded, following Wrasse's slow progress. She looked down at Partan, washed and clean, his grass cap back over the wound, the lamplight, warm and precious around him. Juniper led the wailing. Flint drummed a gentle tune with his thumbs.

Their restored house had a higher upper storey. Each side was divided into rooms. At one end was Juniper's space, the other Flint's. The central fire sent warmth up between the floored clerestories; the smoke went gently out through the higher pitch of the roof far above. There, meat and fish smoked slowly.

The smell of new thatch was so inviting: everything clean and fresh. The tough planked floor creaked slightly under the rush matting.

'I have a nice wee hearth,' Wrasse thought, 'and a charcoal pot.'

'The house is lovely,' Shala said sadly. 'I wish Partan was still with us. He was so clever. I expect it was his idea to put the tree roots uppermost, with the narrow tops in the postholes. It makes the whole place so much higher.'

'Yes, dear. He was ingenious. It's a sad loss. But your dad is great, too. The huge beams under the floor lock the pillars tight. What they have done in our absence is amazing.'

'Yes, Wrasse. And I see Flint's been carving faces into the salty posts,' Shala answered with a throat lump. 'I'm going to my bed now. I'm exhausted.'

'Me, too. Quite shattered.'

Wrasse listened to Shala weeping again as she curled up among her pelts and knotgrass covers.

'I can't get Granddad out of my mind,' Shala thought, crying herself to sleep.

Shala realized it was Wrasse's voice as she eventually woke.

'An incision just above his penis hairs,' she instructed.

'What's happening? I'd better look from the balcony,' she thought urgently. 'They are about to begin Partan's disembowelment. There he is, laid out on his bed. I can't look.'

'That's it, Jasper. There will be nothing in his bladder,' she heard. 'Press your polished knife beneath his skin,' she said as he gripped the smooth hawthorn handle.

'A bit like a deer,' Jasper confessed. 'But it isn't, is it. Juniper, bring the salt crock, then fetch sea grass and moss.'

'Yes, Dad, but when's Shala getting up?' she rebuked.

'When she's ready, Sister,' replied Flint as he carved scars on the forehead he was sculpting on the pillar.

'They have both matured whilst I've been away,' Shala thought.

'Then, so have I. But Juniper's still as spiteful. I'll dress and go down. This is all part of Granddad's journey to the Ancestors.'

'Here goes,' Jasper said. 'I'm slanting the serrated blade in and up his belly.'

'Cut round his navel,' Wrasse put in as Shala stepped off the stair. 'It's his sacred connection right back to Longo's first mating.'

'Okay. Up goes the blade.'

'Don't snick the gut. Be careful.'

'Yes, Wrasse, I've done pigs and all sorts before.'

'I know, but he's for preserving, animals aren't.'

'So, you've risen, Shala,' Juniper announced to the sound of her father's knife rasping towards Partan's umbilical knot.

'Can I get a drink, please?' Jasper asked. 'My throat's gone suddenly dry. It's only nerves, but—'

'Here, Dad,' Flint offered, 'have mine.'

'Thanks, Son,' he replied as his whitened blade protruded from below the belly-knot.

'Father looks so peaceful, doesn't he,' Gull said. 'Even with your knife sticking out from him. I'll take your drink when you're finished.'

'Thanks. Here goes again. Round a bit, then straight up to his ribcage.'

'Did you bring the stuffing, Juniper?' asked Gull.

'Yes, it's in bags behind Flint's pillar.'

Wrasse, leaning against the toe slab of Partan's bed said, 'We need fine ash from the ember pots. Flint, please fetch some. Make sure it's cold.'

'Sure,' he said.

'Shala, Juniper, would you mix the grass and moss together on the mat here?' Wrasse asked.

'Yes. It's time my sister did something useful,' Juniper jibed.

'No guts punctured, Wrasse. It's going well,' Jasper reported.

'Carefully up to his sternum, then.'

Quernstone arrived. She sat, chanting softly.

'Here are the ashes,' Flint announced with a bowlful.

'You're covered in it,' Juniper pointed out. 'Look at his chest and new beard. He looks like a sprite from the Nether World, doesn't he?'

'I'll sing like one, then, and join in with Quernstone.'

'Please don't, Son. This is serious. It's your grandfather we are attending to,' Gull warned.

'Sorry. I'll drum with her, instead.'

'That would be wonderful. Thank you.'

'It's done,' Jasper gasped as he removed the greasy blade, 'and he still looks relaxed. What next, Wrasse?'

'A small, leather-lidded fermenting bin.'

'I'll fetch the ambrose one.'

'Thanks, Shala,' Gull responded.

'Hold it by the side of his bed, Gull,' Wrasse instructed. 'Jasper, you and Flint roll his stiff corpse on its side. Good, there's still ambrose left. Right, jiggle him so his guts spill into it.'

Shala watched the cold, grey intestines descend.

'Good. There's sufficient ambrose to mix with them. That will stop the smell,' Wrasse commented as they dropped in like wet squid, 'Hold him right there. There's a pool of blood to drain. Put meadowsweet in and snap the lid on after.'

'I'm glad that bit's done,' Jasper said wiping his brow.

'This is very exciting. Can I have a go?' Flint asked eagerly.

'Are you sure?' his mother queried.

'Yes. He's dead anyway. Look, Partan's face is really calm. It looks like he's actually enjoying this. He knew it would happen anyway. I think he's smiling at us.'

Quernstone's lullaby for the dead went on.

'Okay, Flint. Take your dad's knife.' His ashy eyebrows peaked in surprise. 'Go on,' Gull urged. 'Listen to Wrasse.'

'His guts are linked either end.'

'Yes, I know, Wrasse. I've grollocked a pig. The anatomy is much the same. One end is behind his arse. It's quite simple. All I have to do is slice through and it all drops out. I'm glad he did a shit before he croaked. That could have been messy.'

'Respect your Granddad!' Gull snapped.

'All right, Mum, but I'm just being real about it,' he responded, giggling nervously.

'Jasper. Take the knife from him!'

'No, dear. It'll be good practice for when he does us. I'm sure he will be a lot more serious then. Get on with it, lad.'

'Cut the gut a few inches behind his bum. If there is any shit left in there, we can reamer it through with a bone dibber. Just a smear can ruin a body,' Wrasse advised.

'Here goes, then,' Flint said as he drew a deep breath and gritted his teeth. 'Arse end's done,' he informed them as more intestines tumbled into the ambrose. 'Just the gullet to slice and it's job done.'

'Not quite,' Wrasse said. 'Here's a sheep shank. Dib that through his bottom to make sure it's all clear inside. Shala, would you pull it through when it appears? Then everything can finally flop into the tub.'

'Clean as a whistle,' Shala thought silently, when the bone appeared in a sheath of tubing.

'I'm going to cut his diaphragm now. There will be blood. Can anyone pass me moss to sponge it up?'

'I hear him w-w-w-wheeze,' Gull stammered.

'That's just his wind coming out as his ribs sink, dear,' Jasper explained.

'Here you are,' Juniper said.

'Thanks. Now I'm doing the gullet end. Dad, your knife needs grinding, but it'll do. Here they come,' he announced as he sawed through the last bit of cartilage.

'Now roll him back. Give him a good swab out with Juniper's moss. Sprinkle salt in, too,' added their instructor.

'I can do that,' Juniper offered, 'and I can clean Flint's face. He's got slime and bleeding all over his brow. What are you going to do, Shala?'

'Watch, think and learn for the moment, Juni,' she replied, using her pet name.

'Flint, will you take out his kidneys?" Wrasse asked.

'Yes, if Dad will hone his knife on the bed-stone.'

'That's better,' he said moments later. 'Here goes again. One... two... Dad, you take them. Wrasse is going to ask me to remove his liver next, then heart and lungs, I expect.'

'That's correct. And don't forget to remove the gall bladder. That's poisonous.'

'I know, Wrasse.'

'Father's kidneys didn't have much fat on them,' Gull thought, watching them changing hands.

'Bring your dad the big burnished bowl, Shala,' Gull asked. 'He can drop the kidneys in.'

'Keep it ready for the rest,' Flint said proudly as he sliced away. 'His liver's nearly free. I've got the gall. Here, take it.'

'Put it in the gut bin, Gull,' Wrasse said. 'That's all for separate burial.'

'Liver out. Here it is,' Flint said, turning with it in both hands.

'It's quite pale,' Shala remarked as it slipped from Flint's reddened hands into the bowl.

'That'll be his age,' Wrasse remarked. 'Mine will be, too, I expect.'

'Look, Dad. There's his lungs; I'll cut them out now, then do his heart.'

'That's right, Son. Carry on.'

'It's not him anymore, anyway. It's just a dead body being prepared so the spirit can go in and out freely.'

'That's right, Flint. To and fro, until it's time to go elsewhere,' Wrasse added.

'The knife's certainly sharper,' he commented as the lungs separated. 'In the bowl?'

'Yes, dear,' his mum answered.

'There's loads of congealing blood. Someone will have to mop it out. Here comes his heart.'

'Well done,' Jasper praised, adding, 'As I will be the new Chief, I'll mop up. Give me the moss.'

'His organs look in rude health: this augers very well for your succession. Congratulations, Jasper,' Wrasse stated.

'Here's some moss, Father. Can I help?' Shala asked.

'You can do the final clean. I'll get the worst out.'

'Thank you, Dad. I am uneasy, but it's something that has to be done.'

'That's right.'

'Can I make him look lovely after?' Juniper asked. 'Well, when he's been stuffed and stitched?'

'Yes, dear,' Gull answered. 'You will be very good at that.'

'Just put the blooded swabs on the fire,' Wrasse suggested. 'We will stuff him with fresh. Flint, fetch Shala the bowl of ash. She can rub it all round his inside. It stops the flies and helps dry the flesh. Gull, mix moss and grass with salt and ash for stuffing. I know it's sad for you now, but it will help you later.'

'Yes,' she agreed quietly. 'I want to stuff him, too. Make him look fuller again.'

'You're doing very well,' Jasper told her encouragingly. 'He'd have liked to know you were helping with this. He's probably watching from somewhere right now.'

'Do you think so, Jasper?'

'Yes, I do. Shall we stitch him together?'

'You can,' Wrasse advised, 'but not too tight. We will need to open him up and change the stuffing several times until he's really dried. It's a good idea to puncture all the needle-holes before his skin toughens up, though. We should bury his guts today. Maybe Reaper and Quartz can make a cist outside the Ancestor's House?'

'Yes. I have his old otter cape. I'd like to put that on top. Jasper, go and find Reaper and Quartz.'

'Yes, Mum. I can help them.'

'Of course.'

'Soot and egg white for the soles of his feet,' Juniper said as she descended with her paint box. 'That shows he's been on a long journey. Powdered haematite to redden his pubes: They are looking old and withered. The same goes for his head. We can place a headdress over his scabby scalp. Beeswax to polish his toe and fingernails,' Juniper added importantly. 'We can dress him in all his finest robes. Then he'll be absolutely ready for all his friends and the whole Clan to admire in his glory: mace, spear and all. Would you like to help me, Shala?'

'This is the recipe for a chief's offal,' Wrasse informed them. 'The family must pound the liver and kidneys in a stone mortar until they're liquid. Then put it all through a hair sieve. Cut the heart up and mash it to pulp. Same with the lungs. Mix the whole lot in a greased cooking bowl with bruised barley, oats and bere, chopped chives, crumble dried seaweed in, a little ambrose, a cup of cream and finally, salt. Place the bowl into hot embers and everyone stirs regularly. When hot, add butter and keep turning until cooked right through. Pray for his eternal soul, then eat together. What is left, push into his bladder and allow it to go stone cold. This is to be cut up and shared with all who knew him. Then he lives forever within us.'

'Do we hang him in the smoke house, or suspend Granddad above our fire?' Flint asked.

'Partan will lie here for a two days, then go up for curing prior to entering the Ancestor House. Everyone can visit him first and taste his essence.'

'We can all tell tales of Partan, during this,' Gull said tearfully.

'Yes, it will do us all good,' remarked Shala.

'And you can tell us all about your travels, too,' Jasper suggested.

'Of course,' Wrasse answered, 'in time,' she added wisely, nudging Shala discretely with her new staff. 'You all have to get used to your new positions too, now Jasper's our leader.'

'Yes,' Gull thought, 'there's succession to think of. Juniper needs pairing. Flint's maturing. We have to find good blood for them. Dale's breeding with Breeze from Nether Holm hasn't worked. Their child's deformed, and another coming. They will have to find other mates somehow, or just stop.'

'We will have to decide on mates for the young,' Wrasse said, reading Gull's thoughts. 'Now Partan's parted, we have to think even more of the future. The young should be allowed to marry for love, but that isn't safe these days,' she commented, thinking of the Sea Angel's arm in her room.

'Did you meet possible mates on your travels?' Jasper enquired whilst stirring the steaming bowl.

'Dad: family; I want so to tell you how I see our future. I must wait, though, until I am certain,' Shala intimated, taking the spoon.

44

Wake's Progress

Oiwa's wake streaked white in the swirling fog. 'Mica's shouts are fading. I'm flying across the sea like a skimming goose. I know I know the way. My paddling arms are like beating wings. The wind is on my back, blowing me along.

'I'm much further out. Its misty still. Spray's leaping from the waves. I can feel the ocean's vastness and depths below while I paddle further and further from land. They'll never find me. I'm leaving no tracks.

'I'd better button down the skin covers. The spray's worsening. Yes, I can balance now. I don't feel that terrible sickness. Like a goose, I can keep this up. I must stop thinking about Mica shouting.... Paddle. Paddle. Paddle.

'Solan was right. Every time my boat turns I sense the change, then correct. Look past the waves. Mount them, speed down; go forward. They are larger. I will use their weight and power. The spray is running off my matted beard to the skegs.'

He paddled on until the evening, 'The shorter spring nights begin. Strangely, I feel the land arcing back. I know it's there, but Mica and all I knew is far behind. No it isn't. There's Father's Star, low in the sky. A wave's hidden it. I see it again. I must keep it on my left. My course is easterly. I know it. It's the goose's instinct driving me. I have its strength.

'There are more stars. A different sound too, like a huge rustle of angry leaves. I'll look from the crest of the next wave. There's a dark arm of land ahead. A snowline above. The waves break like raging river foam on its edge. Avoid it. Out to sea, Goose. Fly the waves. Don't land. Keep going. Don't tire. Keep steady. On. On. On.

'There's a wintery chill on my eyelids. Frost on my moustache, too. I'm warm in these good clothes, but it's getting colder. Ride the waves. Pass that jutting finger until it's safe,' Oiwa urged himself.

The early dawn broke silvery blue. 'There may be shelter,' Oiwa thought. 'The sea is quieter in the lee of that limb. It looks snowy and rugged. Seals sing from the black edge, like my sisters bathing in the Dun. Whoops... there's ice floating about. I must take care. Surely there's somewhere to land? The surf's calmer past the seal's rocks. I'll paddle for that. Wow. There's one at my prow. Dad's Star is reflecting in its eye. Follow it,' he told himself.

'There's the shore, dark and undulating. It's moving. It's seals. Masses of them lumbering into the water. They are coming up all round me. They're under my boat, like a wave beneath, taking me ashore, nudging me landward to the grey sand. I've made it to the shingle. Leap out, Oiwa. Keep your feet dry,' he heard himself say. 'Pull the boat up on the next surf. The seals have vanished. Not a sign. No.... Out to sea, there they are watching with their huge gazing eyes, each reflecting the Star. What do they see: me, or goose? Why am I thinking such strange thoughts? Drag the nameless boat up. I'll name you Sand Kisser. Run up the shore. It's cold in this breeze. Head for shelter. Good, there's grass and driftwood above the pebbles. I can rest.

'My legs are so stiff, though, from ages in Sand Kisser. I have to stretch. Make the blood live in my feet. Feel the tingle. Bend, pull my knees up. Twist my back; touch my numb toes. Exercise; rest.

'Dawn is breaking to an amazing chorus of birds. So loud, I can hardly think. I'm so very tired. I'll pull Sand Kisser to the swathe, turn her over, and sleep underneath with Ziit.'

For an eternity Oiwa had a kaleidoscope of dreams. Everything that had happened passed through him. Snaaaaar's evil arrows through Rush's chest. His missile closing in under her belly. He saw his parents, as though not in a dream. Solan, too. His final scream at the rotting bison: the fearful escaping bats: Bark becoming dead in Gunnal's foul intestines.

'Mica!' he yelled as he tossed under his skin craft, 'I have to go. I'm taking *my* chance. I'm leading *my* life. I'm following *my* destiny.' His dreams then ceased as he slumbered deeply within his stolen boat.

From the clear sky, the sun warmed his walrus hide kayak. 'I'm in a terrible sweat,' Oiwa said to himself as he eventually woke. 'Where's Ziit, my quiver. Where am I? Yes, under Sand Kisser. The light streaming beneath her edge is so bright. I must peek. Well, the breeze is refreshing,' he thought, crawling out, pushing his hood back. I'm drenched with sweat, though: from my boots, up my suede breeks to my oxters. Well, the light breeze is refreshing,' he thought as he crawled snail-like and slimily out to the fresh air.

Kittiwakes took flight from eroded tufts. Basking seals lazily looked up at his emerging body as he awkwardly stood. Hot perspiration ran down his spine.

The seals watched as he pulled off his boots. The odour of travel exuded richly from his toes. 'This feels great,' he thought as he wiggled them. 'I must exercise again. I feel so taut.' The seals watched. His thoughts moved while he gazed around, 'I'm totally alone. I'm here: by myself. Gannets dive for fish. Snow covers the inland hills as dark cormorants fly past them. But I don't feel lonely. I have come from that ocean past that rocky arm. I paddled through the night. I made it. I'm here.... I'm on my way,' he thought confidently as deep hunger suddenly struck. 'Where's Ziit?' he thought, as he lunged for his bow. The alarmed seal colony streaked like crazed maggots to the incoming tide.

'They are used to men,' thought Oiwa as he gathered his bow and ammunition. He went barefoot into the windblown grassland. Sea holly scratched his toes, as saxifrage freshened them. Gradually, his soggy hard skin peeled away among the sandwort.

'There's a faint track,' he observed, stringing and flexing Ziit. 'Hare shit,' he thought, peering down to the collection of rounded pellets. 'Fit an arrow, like Buzzard would. Yes, I hear his voice with me. Listen... That's running water. There's no cover, just grasses. I must move with stealth. The sound makes me thirsty. There's the river bending to the sea. Aha, a snow hare. It thinks I can't see him. Sit still, little man. I have a sharp point just for you. He's bolted! Fly arrow, fly. Oh. That lovely sound when jasper hits pelt. Relax now, Hare, whilst I pull your neck. Don't ruin my flights, please, stop kicking. That's better. I hear your bones parting now. Roll your eyes. Good, dead. Skinning time. I shall have the liver body-hot. Wow. That was good,' he thought hungrily as blood ran down his chin. 'Now for the drink. Here, gulls,' he mouthed as the guts swung from his hand, high in the sky.

'Your white fur is beautiful, Dead Hare. I'll make you into a cushion so my poor arse won't get so flattened when paddling. Thank you.'

As Oiwa knelt and drank, spirals of gnats rose from eddies. Wagtails skipped, feeding on them in the shallows. 'Now to cook,' he thought. 'Hare and I will go to the Sand Kisser. We can gather kindling on the way. You will make a fine meal.'

Each well-chewed bone was gathered on the wing by circling gulls. He loved the sport.

'This parka is too hot,' Oiwa realized, 'You are coming off. My open jerkin lets in a cooling breeze. It'll dry my sweat. That's better, though I'm still itchy with fleabites. My hair's a mess. Just feel it! Ah, there's a bead from Moss's hairdo. She was lovely, and how well we mated. It was so exciting. I haven't thought about mating since Salt Slap. Coming with Thrift in that tomb of bodies was amazing. Gosh, the very thought of it is making me stiff. Now my balls have got caught. Ouch! I will have to hop and loosen my trousers. Phew. That's better.

'Now I must sort my gear, and that in the kayak's hold. Yes, usual scraps of leather, bone needles, sinew, slate awl, an oulou, a net bag. Ah, and a water flask. I'll fill that sharpish. Next hold.... Good, fishing tackle: a nice line wound on a square whalebone plate. It's got antler hooks, feather flies and a granite sinker. There's a knuckle truncheon to bump off the catch. Excellent. Lots of spare line and rolls of mending sinew in case of disaster. And here, extra hooks and an obsidian gutting knife in a hare's ear sheath. I hope the owner isn't missing this lot too much.

'Well. I think I will sit and carve my emblem on the other half of Thrift's pebble. I need the rest and it is a perfect day. With this to do and all my gear, I'm really well off.

'Strange, I never noticed all these colours when I carved Mica's. But the state I was in, I could barely see to engrave the goose. Not knowing whether to escape or not: making up my mind. The carving helped me. Now I'll carve again, but with a different purpose. I'll polish the banded colours first. There's white, red, green, black and brown. It will be wonderful. The outside is just a dull waterworn pebble, but inside it's resplendent. That quartz I will leave as it is: dull outside, brilliant inside.'

Busy smoothing his precious rock on an even stone, he forgot time. The fire crackled on. The day passed. Eventually, when the agate sparkled, he began scratching out his goose with his hard stone knifepoint. The long, outstretched neck and wings flew across the agate. The white appeared as streaks of cloud as he polished into the grooves. His familiar crossed a sunset sky.

'I will press it into my palm. Maybe the bird will appear? Yes, there it is,' he tried to say. Instead, he watched it fade as his skin puckered back.

'I have a long way to travel yet,' Oiwa realized later. 'This rest is perfect, though. I'll sleep the night, eat shellfish the morn, keep some for bait, then go.'

That night the seals sang their blubbery songs. Oiwa curled up in the Sand Kisser with a hare-skin pillow and listened. When he slept, he dreamed of his matings. The pleasure took him by surprise: he found himself ecstatically moving as if coupled. Delightfully, his rigid organ spurt. The sperm of orgasm cooled under his belly and dried. There was little he could do about it but enjoy the sensation, wishing it might return.

'I feel so rested,' Oiwa thought the next day. 'Now it's breakfast. After, I'll stow my parka, pack Ziit and the arrows. I'll spread the hare's skin and rub ash from the fire over the inside, fold it and roll it up. That'll preserve it. The seals are watching me from the glittering sea,' he noticed as he pushed off from the mussel rocks. 'The hare skin is much more comfortable as I paddle along the rugged coastline.' Gannets watched from soaring heights as he guided his boat on his forward journey.

'I'm not running now,' he realized. 'I'm free, making my way by myself. This is my new beginning. I wish I could shout it aloud. Journeying back? Facing all those memories? No. Not back.... Forward. That's my way. The sound of my wake pushing behind adds to my determination. I'm not escaping from my life. I know what happened. I am going somewhere. Somewhere that will make it all worth it. Now I'll concentrate on the currents, tidal flows, the sky, where the seabirds are going and the hump of a distant whale. My arms work as wings, powering effortlessly.

'I won't hug the shore. Goose sense tells me there are deep bays and inlets. I see snow-covered hills and mountains. Keep them on the left, to go east. That's the direction: Weir's way, I'm sure. He must have seen all this.'

'I will head for those islands. They are my landmarks. The water's changed suddenly from blue-black to clear green. The Sand Kisser's prow cuts into it, deep and clear. There's a dark shoal of fish, like a waving spearhead, moving across my path. There's another. Now it's turned bright silver, flashing in the light, suddenly vanishing. It's a staggering sight. Paddle on, Oiwa. Make wake.

'Is that noisy white summit birdshit or snow? That hullabaloo's even louder now. Birds and shit, I think. There they go. Up in the sky, like steam from a raging geyser. Did I disturb them with my hare fart? Sorry, birds. Now they hurtle like plummeting arrows. How quickly they surface from the green depths. There they go, off to their eyries. Their stack has a very unwelcoming shadow. It darkens the cold water. That's no place for man.

'There's another stack. It's like a jutting spike sticking out from the sea. It slants north as though a giant's hurled it. There's more. It's so strange. I'll give them a wide berth.'

Oiwa paddled on, his arms working as wings, tireless, ever moving. In his waking dreams he felt the heartbeat of a goose. He smelt grass on his breath and watched his translucent beak pointing east.

The sea darkened. 'I'm in far colder waters,' he realized, waking from the goose-state. 'There are huge chunks of ice floating before me. I need to pick my way carefully. There's another spiky rock. It vanishes as the ice rises with the undulating water. Oh, no. That noise as they scrape together. It goes right through me, like sharp, painful screams. There's that terrible lance getting closer. This could crush me! Think, Oiwa, think,' his inner soul shouted. 'I am trying to cross this floe. It won't work. No! My prow's stuck... Caught under an ice sheet.'

'Paddle back! Paddle back!' he heard Bark's voice yell. 'Pull right. Do it, Oiwa. Do it. Careful. Don't rip the hide. Watch behind.'

'Okay. Okay,' he answered, pulling from sudden danger.

'I'm sweating again, even in this dread cold. My Star itches. It's like when it was first pricked on my forehead. I see all my Clan in the sweat lodge. They are watching me. Willing me on. I'll follow the ice and edge out of it if I can. Now it's time to put that parka on. Keep this cold out. Keep moving. Keep alert. Keep warm. It's dangerous. I never knew it would be like this, but here I am: in it. Nearly under it. Oh no. I'm shivering now, even with my parka on. It's not the cold... it's terror. I must keep my head. I am on my own in this desolation. I have to extract myself. I felt so good, and now this? Don't despair... No! There's an ice block rolling. I'm being sucked back to it.'

'Forward,' came an inner command. 'Stop,' came another, as the Sand Kisser rocked in the turmoil. 'Obey,' was Oiwa's instinct, plunging his paddle.

The craft escaped from the rolling ice. 'Saved again. I'm alive. I'm in control. I will survive. I will find a way out. I must. This ice seems endless. How did I get in here? I'm in a new world; one that I don't understand. Don't cry, Oiwa,' He told himself as he fought off despair, 'Keep hold. Keep strong. Keep looking for the way out.'

'What's that?' he wondered. 'There it is. It slid into the water. It's vanished. Gone. I'll look. Paddle very carefully, Oiwa,' he instructed himself as he edged between jagged icy obstructions. 'There's a clear pool. It's mirror calm. How come? Well, it's safe. There's a seal. Life exists here... and so do I. It's gone. It saw me. Its huge eyes blinked and it dived.

'Now I'm hungry. I'll eat some of my fish bait. Here's a whelk: tough, but tasty. I can drop a line here, too.

45

Ice Floe Foe

'This is a strangely calm place. Do I hear a seal? I sense something. Yes, I'm in a small bay in this huge ice block. There's the seal sound again. Now it's gone. Its ripples sparkle against the edge of the ice. If I land there, I could fish and camp, maybe. I might even shoot the seal with Ziit? Thank the stars I've got bait. I could chop steps into the ice, then pull my kayak up. Climbing out won't be easy. I'll throw the fish line up with the weight. That might help. Ah, but there's a gulley. I'll wedge Sand Kisser in it and disembark.

'My knees ache from sitting in this cockpit. Bum's okay, though. That hare pelt has a mould of it now. Pins and needles are starting. I'd better climb out, pull Sand Kisser up, then exercise. Gosh, it's slippery. Where's my axe? In my belt, stupid. Chop here, the ice's softer. Whack it in, Oiwa, and pull yourself out. Heave... That's it. Whoops! Nearly slipped back. Oh no! Sand Kisser's bobbed up. She's lurching away. Quick! Where did I throw that line? Dang! Slipped again. Crawl, Oiwa, if you can't stand. Everything's drifting off. Shit!'

'Ah; the sinker; I can haul her. Please, please, whalebone; lodge somewhere. Don't pull out. Let me tow her in. Good, here she comes. Thank the stars! Come to Oiwa, Sand Kisser, my treasure.

When you are safely up here I can stretch these aches away. Then I'll bait a line. Better string Ziit, too, just in case a seal decides to join me.

'I think that's it plopping somewhere. A bight. Yank, great. This is the life: food coming up. Safe at last on the island, floating along: nothing now to worry about. I can sleep inside Sand Kisser and maybe paddle on tomorrow.'

Snow flurried around him, then vanished. Just the lapping sea against his small berg dominated his frozen world. He breathed steamy breath in and out, feeling the brittle frost on his beard. In its fine mist he glimpsed all the colours of a rainbow whilst winding up his line. The hues changed as the steamy droplets froze to icy spangles. Again he glanced round, searching the ice floe and narrow waterways for life and means of survival.

'Fish,' he yelled inside as he hauled one over the ice. 'More, more, more,' he realized as they came slipping up. 'I can just swallow this wee one. Bite its head, kill it and gulp. Down it goes. This one's bigger. Where's that obsidian? Ah, got it. I'll club you first. Here's the shank. Smack. That's stopped you wriggling. Lie still while you get filleted. Oh, you are nice and oily. So tasty, too. How much more can I eat,' he wondered as he made sure his grip was firm. 'One slip and that's it,' he told himself. 'Kush would have loved this. How badly I miss him. Change the subject. Change the subject! I can't dwell. I must keep my wits and survive,' he commanded himself as morose thoughts impelled into his brain. 'Concentrate on now. Good. Another fish. I must re-bait and cast again. Eat these while it is sinking. Feed and fish; go forward, think forward; not back. Enough fish now. I can rest, digest, and think. Maybe even dream of Thrift?

'What's that movement? Something shifted. The water slurped slightly. It could be my seal. That would be wonderful. I'll hold Ziit. But this bitter cold will affect his spring. Be careful, in case he snaps. I'll rub oily fish on him. That will help. I mustn't break him. He's terribly precious. Something scraped? Maybe ice nudging? There's an odd hunk of snow floating in the bay. That must be it. I'll tidy my flights. Strange? That snow has sunk. I think I'll notch an arrow. Pull back very gradually. Yes, just a little springier, but care is crucial.

'I'll fillet the rest of my fish. They can freeze for the journey. I do feel good inside after eating. That roe was delicious,' he mused on quietly, thoughtless of the ripples in the still bay.

'I think I felt this ice float shift? Only very slightly, but it did move. Grip Ziit and arrows just in case. That's where it came from, in the bay. That snow's moving underwater. What is it? A huge bow wave's heading right here!

'Snow Bear, Snow Bear, Snow Bear!' he repeated in terror, pulling back on Ziit as the wave washed over his booted feet, suddenly spilling behind him to the sea, dragging his fishing tackle off.

'I'm falling backwards. My heart's racing. My arrow's slipped. Quick! Fit it again. Its horrid claws are scraping the ice. There's my seal. He's flung high over me. It's thudding, bloodily behind. It hasn't seen me, but it will. What do I do? No... No... It's spotted me. It's standing there, glaring. Pull my bow. Wait. It's straining its neck. That horrible head, it's closing in. Now it's shaking again, but with anger. I'm between it and the dead seal. It's bearing down on me,' he screamed inwardly as dreadful family legends sped by. Powerful breath from its brilliant black nose sported another rainbow as water from its shaking fur fell in a sparkling, frozen clatter.

'Pull carefully. Don't snap... Shoot,' Oiwa told himself, as he lay prostrate, listening to the weak twang. He watched the bolt fly into that hot, oily breath that stank of seal, sea, fish, beast and man flesh.

'It's getting closer. That fearful smell. Fit another arrow. Quick, before it's too late. I'm the hunted, not the hunter. I should have known. Did Weir end this way? Shoot again. It's standing like a giant and roaring angrily. Notch another shaft. It's turned its ugly head. My arrow is up its nostril! It looks pathetic, but the terrible bear detests it. It is glaring right at me again, roaring, trying to dislodge my missile with its huge paws. Help! Pull... Shoot... Crawl back. Got him! Smack in the eye. He hates that, too. Get another arrow... quickly. Bugger it, they've scattered. They're sliding to the sea! Grab the chert one. The bear is raging. It's down on all fours, mouth wide open, coming for me! Those deadly teeth in those gaping jaws: NO! NO!... NO. Ziit's creaking: he'll break. Let go.'

The sharp chert grazed the animal's flashing red tongue as it sped through its flaring epiglottis.

'I've got it in the mouth. It's screaming in agony. Blinded in one eye, but it's still coming for me. It's crunched my arrow. Blood's bubbling through its fangs: that harsh breath is propelling spurting, red saliva. You're not getting me,' he yelled from deep within. 'My axe. My axe. Where is it? Belt... Belt... Belt!' he though as he fumbled under his back.

'It's closer. My arrow in its nose is going to stab me. Hit! Hit, hit,' he screamed inside, as he clouted the flights with his grey axe butt. 'Up your face. Whack it in deeper. Scream, you ugly brute. Die,' he threatened as the shaft splintered.

'Now for the one in your eye. Whack! Yell at that! Bleed... Wail,' he mimed, as the bear quaked fearfully. 'Into your skull,' he threatened as he hacked at the beast's forehead. It reversed with a bloody brow and a splintered shaft skewering its eye socket.

'Last arrow,' Oiwa realized, as he frantically scrambled up the slippery ice.

'It's standing, crazed, watching me. I can hear its hind claws cut deep in the shiny ice. That gargling roar is summoning its attack. There's no time,' Oiwa cried inside as he fumbled with the bone-tipped projectile. 'Fit it... Fit it. No! I'm slipping. I've dropped Ziit. Hold the arrow. Hold it up.'

The bear looked down on Oiwa as its knee buckled, to crush him.

The great shadow engulfed him as Oiwa thrust. 'Here's another bone for your stinking flesh,' Oiwa threatened as his assailant collapsed on it. A feeling of final pressure entered its chest as the tine tortured its heart. Gravity drove it home into the beating, bursting muscle. It died, regretting ever seeing its unexpected, dumb enemy.

'Quick! Roll out before I'm suffocated,' he thought instantly, as the animal wilted. The pressure on its chest caused a final wheeze. Mucus and blood mixed in a lagoon under its nose.

Oiwa scrambled backwards, pulling himself along on his elbows. His heels scraped past the huge head. 'It's over for you, but not for me, you disgusting hulk. Whack! Have that,' he gestured as he clouted his blooded axe into his foe's cranium.

A trail of dark yellow urine trickled down the ice from the conquered creature's bladder. Melting its very own canyon to the salt sea, it blended and faded as the bear's nerve endings twitched.

Seabirds screeched in the air, excited to witness the great battle below.

Oiwa sat and panted wildly, watching the piss trail. 'I need an urgent shit,' he realized suddenly. He slithered backwards and undid himself, watching circling birds above as he heaved. 'Aaaaaagh; that's better,' he felt, as the long turd curled beneath him. 'Snow's a good arse-wipe. Refreshing, after that battle,' he mused. Then his jaw dropped when he saw what he had actually done, as his own bladder emptied. Standing still, he watched his pee run and mix with the dead bear's rivulet. The fading steam wafted colourfully and vanished.

'I must take this in,' he thought and sat on the Sand Kisser's prow. 'You birds are just waiting for bit of bear, aren't you,' he imagined as he trembled. 'Yes, eat the enemy. But first it's my turn. Where's that obsidian gutter? It's far sharper than my knife. It will be good for bear. Yes, it's in the tackle hold. Right, Bear, show me your guts. I'll roll you over, nicely, so we can begin. Your fur is so tightly matted, it's hard to get through. Lovely to keep you warm, though, wasn't it? Let's cut through now. This dark green obsidian is so sharp. It's see-through at the edge: very fine indeed, just the job. Yes, there's your skin. Look, it's all pink with little grey spots. Who'd have thought that? Right, we will give you a bit of a shave so I can slit through to your fat. I'll cut a line up your belly as well, then my grey knife can slit you from inside when I poke it in and draw it along. Then your stinking guts, the ones that you wanted to digest me in, can fucking well spill out, can't they,' he thought in justified temper.

'Phew. They are so hot and steamy,' he noticed as they began to droop out. 'The heart! The heart! I want the heart,' he realized suddenly. 'Never eat a bear's liver, was mother's warning. It's deadly poisonous. There it is, hanging down and dripping. There's the gallbladder: nasty green thing, like a monster slug. That's real poison. The birds can have it. I'll get that heart, first, though. Yes, there's my bone tip. I'll kick the guts away, crawl in and push it out.'

The entrails tumbled out ungracefully to untangle and loop into the sea. Screaming gulls swooped to wrench at them below Oiwa's heels. Fish sensed food and gathered.

'There my arrow goes. Oooo, the blood it's let jets out; I'm covered. Never mind. Let's sever the heart, now. I'm eating it while it's hot. It just twitched! Last nerves, I expect. The birds can have the liver after I've eaten. It's champions first. Well, for a terrifying animal, it certainly cuts up easily,' he noted as he sliced it on his knee. 'It is enormously tasty: much stronger than a caribou's: it's got the essence of wild killing, fury and power. I can take that on. I can have a bear's heart pass through me. Shitting it out, along with all that fish, will be an absolute pleasure. Now I will sever the gut ends. The birds and fish can have them, then the liver. They will remember this feast, when they see another bear.'

Oiwa sat watching the feeding frenzy in the warmth of the open carcass. 'I'm proud. I don't mind not having witnesses. The bird spirits will know. I can tell my Geese later. They will believe me. But would men, even if I could tell them? I think it's trophy time. Open your mouth, you monster. 'Need help, do you? Right, here goes. Oh, your poor bloody tongue. Look at my mashed arrow. Say "Aaaah". That's it, keep your mouth wide for Oiwa. Now, where's my axe? I'm just going to pull your lips back and gently smash your teeth out.'

Oiwa hacked mercilessly at the gums. 'Moss' father makes good choppers,' he thought as he swung the tool. 'That's them loosening. Fangs first. They are so sharp. Imagine them in me. No, it's too cruel. Here come the others. They don't like being pulled out. I will scrub them up later. Right, Bear, let's roll your head over and knock the other side out. There's some of my arrow stuck in here,' he observed as bang went his axe. 'A fine set of teeth. Thank you, Bear,' he said to the wrecked face. 'Right, your wicked tongue's coming out now: chopper or knife? Knife, I think. Here, birds,' he indicated as he tossed it sky high. 'Good, I can retrieve my arrowhead.'

'Now for your claws. Give me your paw,' he thought mockingly. 'I think I'll just cut the whole thing off. Only one, though: those huge pads are quite heavy. I have to travel light, but I can rip your other claws out from you, can't I? If I slip my blade up under thy skin and cut round the talons, they should loosen from the joints. Yes. Excellent. That didn't hurt a bit, now, did it? I'd skin you, too, if I had room. But you can't have it all. I'll just take your ears, then rip off your testicles for bait. I've got enough pee left for a last insult, so here it is,' he thought wildly as he slashed his final foaming act of contempt into the bleeding crotch.

'Right, I must stow all this stuff evenly so we don't list. That poor seal: it looks so sad,' he thought as suddenly a berg tipped and rolled ahead of him. 'I'd better be off; leave the seal. That could happen to this berg. I felt it shift earlier. There are spaces appearing in the sea too. I must pack and get off immediately. Ziit, axe, last arrows, and what little tackle that's left.

'We are off again, Sand Kisser,' he informed his craft by telepathy. 'We can slide down this ice slope and launch. Here goes! That poor Bear is glaring at us with its good eye: shame about his teeth, aye, Sand Kisser. His open belly's full of birds now. They will be enjoying his kidneys and lungs. Lucky things. Right. Let's be off. Bye bye, Bear.

'Oh shit!' he thought, shuddering, 'That's killer whales moving in. I'm surrounded! Wolves of the sea, I was told. They'll be here to feed off the frenzy. I'd better paddle. There's one! It's too close. That vast pied back is nudging Sand Kisser. I'm scraping along its skin. Steady her, paddle gently; don't splash. Keep calm. They are diving. Phew. NO! Here they are again. Calm, Oiwa; calm: you killed the Bear, you can get out of this. The seal's slipped in. They've got it. Paddle; paddle; paddle, but make no ripples. Glide, Sand Kisser... glide. Take me away from all of this. I am not whale food, nor bear's food. There's more coming. My penis has shrunk to nothing. I can feel it gone. It's the tension. I must keep calm. Sand Kisser's gliding away. The killers are behind me, now. Good, my mating man's coming back. That's better.

46

Solitude on the Sea

'What a terrible noise there is out here. It was so quiet, before the bear fight. The orcas make such a racket with all their snorting. There's more arriving. They are incredibly graceful, though. I'm so glad I'm not among them now. The icebergs are separating, too. Watch out for the dangerous little ones, Oiwa. They can easily jag Sand Kisser.

'It's getting colder, though. I'll sing old clan songs in my head for warmth. Here's one:

Warming hands beside the blaze,
Watching stars through the smoky haze,
Cooking young frogs that hopped in the dawn,
Chewing their bones and praying for spawn.
That's the way we enjoy our nights,
Then there's wrestling and sparring fights...

'This is good,' he thought, 'I know where I'm heading in this swell. My Star Map tells me. I can sense the stars' positions. I almost see them. They draw me. The sun hugs the horizon. The Moon can be magnificently big. There's little difference between night and day. It's even lighter than at home during summer nights.

'I think I'll slice the bear's balls to bits and bait up: a last supper to die for? I'm so happy, out here. That's more killer whales in the distance. They won't bother me. Neither will those huge ones further on, I hope. Ah! Here comes a hungry fish.

Catching trout in the Dun for us...
Cooking on skewers once they've been trussed.
Crunch their fins and taste that skin,
Pick your teeth with the jawbone thin...

'That is a good song. Now I've got porpoises leading me. They look like good company.' Hours later he realized, 'They are heading for that icy shore. Those cliffs are vast. The hills reach high, like mountains behind, with huge sea caves below. I might peek in, now the swell has gone. The echo is amazing in here. How the water laps on the glistening edge? I think I'll give Sand Kisser's side a paddle-bang and test that echo. Whack. Oh no! Hunks of ice are sliding in. Quick, duck. Don't get smashed up in the waves. Paddle out. Paddle out. The swell is ejecting me. Phew, that's better. Just keep a safe distance, Oiwa,' he chastised himself briskly.

'Paddle to that icy headland. I'll see my way better when I round it. Good grief. The end has just collapsed! It's sunk. Now it's surfacing. It's rolling. More is falling off. Get out to sea, Oiwa. That looks dangerous. Ooops! The waves from those enormous splashes are heading here. Here they come. Ride them, Sand Kisser... Ride them. That's it; up, over and down. Here comes another. Wahaaaaay! This is good.

Finish Dad's beaver and lick its skull,
Suck out the eyes now they've gone dull.

'There's a log over the next wave. Skirt round it, Oiwa. Watch out for more. We don't want to collide. There's a porpoise leading again. Follow.

Bake that quail in a ball of clay,
We all love a birdie cooked that way.

'Oh, I'm getting so tired. The food song makes me sleepy and homesick. I'm in open sea now: past those tumbling ice blocks. I think I can shut an eye and nod my head. Don't lose grip of the paddle. Stow it. I'd just love to walk on dry land,' he thought as he drifted off dreamily. He walked and spoke Goose with Solan in his dreams, then dreamed of someone he thought he knew. She was nearly his age. He woke as their intimacy was about to be fulfilled. 'I wish I could start that dream again,' he thought, adjusting his crotch. 'Finishing it would have been even better.

Snuggling down by the heat of the glow,
Hearing drums beating very slow.
'That makes me even sleepier. But awaken, Oiwa. Paddle on.'

For days he progressed like this, driven by his instinct and power through rafts of bill-clacking auks that would suddenly disappear to fly and hunt deep below.

'*Burning my toes on an ember hot,*' went through his mind as he woke.

'An albatross soars. Its vast wingspan is crossing the Moon, and now the Sun. Follow it, Oiwa. Take me to land, Albatross,' he thought as he swigged from his water flask. 'I'm tired and stiff. It's cold. I want rest. The ice cliffs curve off out of sight to the north east. Salmon skin clouds are in the sky, now. Mother always says they bring bad weather. I'll exercise my aching muscles and paddle for shelter. I'll go along the ice cliffs,' he urged himself, singing more verses.

'The ice veers north. It's even colder and foreboding. The wind is behind me. The sky's darkening. It will either hail or snow. The swell is taking me. Here comes that hail. Wow, it hurts. Ouch! The noise! Paddle. Keep control. I can't see the cliffs now. But I know where they are. Hug them. Not too close. Watch for ice. Be wary,' he heard Buzzard's voice say through the crash of hailstones pounding on boat and sea.

'I can't sing to this. Fight the billows. Ride them. Force yourself, Oiwa. Keep it up. It's been so long now. I'm worn out, but I must go on. Ride this billow. Climb it. Get to the crest then swoop down it. Up, up to the top. Is that a log past the next trough? No. It's a boat. There's another. Follow them, Oiwa. Make speed. Catch them up. They've gone. I'm surfing down, climb the next and look again. There's more craft. I'm racing... They aren't. Here comes that painful hail again. Fly the waves like a goose, Oiwa. Use your wing power.

'It seems to take forever, catching up. Another trough. Here we go. The ice, or is it the land, has turned. Up, up again. There are three kayaks ahead now. They've dipped down the next valley of water. Catch them, Oiwa. Dang! Another tree. Slew round it, Oiwa. Where's it going, I wonder?

'My muscles are burning. Keep going. There they are again. I'm closer. They are big boats full of folk. Life, ahoy! People, people: make them aware. I'll beat my paddle on Sand Kisser. I must join them, whoever they are. I'm gaining. They've heard me. They've seen my wake as I shoot down. I can hear them shouting. They are waving their paddles as I bang mine. They're whooping in welcome. The boats are parting to let me in. I'm safe. They are pointing in a new direction. The wind has risen, but these hunters are taking me between their laden kayaks.

'They babble excitedly at having me here. I can see it in their faces. This is wonderful: they see me smile, too. He's pointing around the cliff. There's a bay. More hunters are arriving from the sea to join us. They are talking about me. I hope it's nice.

'The wind is blustering on the black, sandy shore. A river crosses it. There's houses and summer pasture reaching into a dark valley.'

Quickly, all the kayaks beached. 'I'm being helped ashore,' Oiwa realized. 'So many of these folk resemble Rush. 'Hello,' he wanted to say, as the women greeted the men with nose rubbing. Oiwa stepped out. The folk fell silent. 'A round-faced woman's coming forward. I'll pull my hood back so we can snout rub. Why are they all gasping, so?

'Weir's mark!' she shouted, hugging him.

Oiwa nodded and pointed to his own brow feverishly. 'Yes,' he thought, amazed.

'Weir returns to the Albatross Clan,' he could just make out.

'No,' Oiwa gestured by shaking his head. He reached into his pouch. 'Yes. I am Goose Clan,' he indicated with his agate emblem. Mouthing the name 'Weir', he pointed to his crotch and then his right elbow, 'Weir's my father's uncle,' he signed.

'I can't understand what they babble,' he thought as they crowded round, pulling his beard and tugging his fairer hair. 'They are obviously intrigued.' He pointed to his chest and snaked his arm forward, signing, 'I follow him.'

'Come with us. Welcome, welcome.'

'I understand what they mean, but not the words,' he felt. 'Up the beach we go. Those excited kids are porting Sand Kisser. I think they are asking for stories. How I do that, I don't know. Ah, that's a parent explaining I'm mute. They understand. Good.

'It looks like they have walrus meat, tusks and skins. That's birds they've caught. I expect they will dry them. Seal flesh, too, and bags of fish. There may be a feast. That's great. Oh. Here come the giggling girls to tug my hair.'

'He's blushing,' one said as she poked him in the ribs.

'I wish I knew what that meant,' Oiwa thought, feeling his eyebrows being stroked.

'I'm Ice Crystal,' a woman said to Oiwa, as he was led to the low door of the main house. The walls were of rough, dark stone; just like the hillside. The door jambs were two large upright rocks with a huge lintel of driftwood. The vast roof was of tightly sewn skins in a patchwork of many colours and shades. Smoke rose from a hole in the peak of the roof.

'Come in. Mind your head. You are taller than us.'

'It seems even bigger inside. Yes, the floor dips down. It's dug into the slope. That makes it much higher. There is the central fire with elders seated behind. Some of the roof skins let light over them. 'Must be seal gut, like my parka. There are skin drapes over doorways to rooms at the edge as well. Hmmmm. Work goes on. People sit chewing leather. Others pound it with bones, softening it. What beautiful clothing they make. It's strewn all around.'

'Wait here,' Ice Crystal said.

'Those giggling girls are still fiddling with my hood,' he thought, smiling and clicking his tongue in answer. 'Now I'm being shoved forward. I'll lean back just for fun. Ice Crystal has gone behind a pelt curtain. Now she's back beckoning me. I'll lean back even more. Right; jerk forward. Ha, ha, ha. You've all tumbled down,' he thought, as the girls sprawled in a giggling heap.

'It certainly smells of fish smoking in here. The shell and bone lamps reek. There's a dried guillemot standing on its feet by the door with a flickering wick in its upright beak. What a terrific candle it makes. Now Ice Crystal's reappeared from the dark cell with an ancient looking couple. She's changed quickly into that fine eel-skin skirt. How her hair now tumbles over her naked shoulders.'

The girls watched as Oiwa stepped back into the firelight. Its gentle flames were reflected in his blood-stained anorak. His blooded axe hung from his waist and its polished haft glinted. The long boots he had been given bent limply below his knees. He shook his tangled hair. The old couple stared across the fireplace to him. 'What a mess,' they mumbled to each other.

'Foaming Wave,' Ice Crystal announced to Oiwa.

'I had better bow in respect,' he assumed, even though he could not understand the name. 'Mouth the sounds to remember,' he told himself. The white-haired Foaming Wave looked at him. He had a plaited leather band round his head with small ivory amulets dangling from it. 'That's an amazingly large nose-spike he's got. And his colossal ear-pins, too. What a strange thin beard he has, just spindly hairs hanging over his wrinkly chest. Those thonged arms have seen stronger days. His wrinkled, sweating stomach must have been muscular once. His suede shorts hanging with shells and teeth rattle when he moves his scarred, spindly legs.

'Moon Sky,' Ice Crystal introduced in her language.

'Mouth the sounds again, Oiwa,' he told himself. 'Now bow to the aged, dark-haired woman. She's impressive, though: those long hairpins in a fan of spikes. That pierced hide robe flows as she moves. Its knotted grass trim tickles the floor at her feet and perspiration glistens down her open crinkly neck. No wonder. It's hot in here. I'm sweating, now. Off with this parka,' he thought, as the house filled with hunting folk. 'They are hanging their stuff up around the pillars. Where's Ziit?' he wondered, as a lad handed him his bow. 'Thank you,' he tried to say as everyone watched him.

'Take him and make him decent,' Moon Sky commanded.

'Careful,' he wanted to express as he was girl-handled up to a cell and pulled through a tasselled drape. Three whalebone lamps lit a pelt-strewn couch. 'I'm at their mercy,' he thought. 'What's happening? They are telling each other what to do. Oh. They're stripping me! This is embarrassing. I wish I could understand what they say. Look. They are examining how my clothes are made. It's even hotter in here, now. I'm running in sweat. Oh, I stink. They don't mind. Oh gosh, here comes an erection. Why are they laughing? She's coming at me with a long rib bone. Ah, it's for scraping me down. How sharp it feels on my back. Oooh. That's good, now my arms, bum and legs. This is very nice. Another girl is doing my chest. Ah, my stomach now. Careful down there. I wish you'd stop giggling. That tickles. Ahh, ha ha haaar,' he responded inside as they flicked his manhood with the bone.

'Was that Weir's name I heard from outside? There it is again, again, again.'

The girls watched his stiffness slacken as he listened. 'That's nice,' he thought as they draped a grey leather shawl around him. Finely cut strips dangled loosely below his waist, where bright shells jingled. Clipped to the neckline, a band of quills radiated downwards. 'I feel really good in this. It's so fine and light. I'm now going out to meet these people, I suppose. Through the curtain I go.

'There they all are, around the fire of bones. This is a very hot haven in an icy land. Ice Crystal's leading me by the hand to Moon Sky, Foaming Wave and what could be their family.'

Moon Sky said to Oiwa loudly, 'Meet Weir's descendants.'

'I don't understand,' he wanted to say. 'She's handing me an engraved bone plate. It has a star motif and a goose.'

'Weir's,' Foaming Wave explained.

'Amazing!' Oiwa thought in a flash. 'There are two lines drawn from the goose and star. One ends in a great seal, the other a fine boat. From them, other emblems spur off. This shows with whom he mated and who was born. These folk before me are my kin. I must hug them.' He rapidly clicked his tongue, pointing to the plaque then to himself and flung his arms wide open, embracing his cousins.

Everyone cheered loudly. Sharpened Tooth came forward grinning. 'He seems taller,' thought Oiwa, 'and more muscular. Through that grin shine his pointed canines. I am sure he's filed them like that. He's got the same patterned scars on his legs as old Foaming Wave. I can see them through his tasselled kilt. His bone nose-spike shimmers in the firelight, and so do the carved wolf-tooth toggles in his lobes. What's that bundle of mine doing in his hands? He's unwrapping it for all to see. He's holding up my bear's paw.'

'This is from this young man's kayak,' Sharpened Tooth announced to a stunned audience. 'Here are the deadly beast's lugs,' he proclaimed to huge adulation. When that quietened, Sharpened Tooth displayed the glinting claws. 'What a brave hero we have in our midst! There's more. Watch me unravel this bundle of bloody fangs. Now the rest of the talons,' he announced to the stunned crowd, who began a slow handclap of honour.

'This place is packed with folk,' Oiwa observed. 'Where have they all come from? Those glowing, dark-haired girls look lovely. Their breasts are so tempting.' He drew a long breath over his teeth and hissed it out in delight.

'Bear Killer, Bear Killer,' he heard them all chant in their tongue. 'The maidens are singing my new name and pointing at me. This is wonderful.'

Ice Crystal bade Oiwa to squat by the fire with the elders. They signalled to Falling Star to bring food. She moved from the group of groomers and picked her way through the crowd to a walrus-hide bowl.

'Here's soft roe and cured char fillets, Bear Killer,' she offered, holding the roe out temptingly.

'I love roe,' he thought, sucking it from her long fingers to squeeze it between his tongue and the roof of his mouth. 'Wonderful,' he repeated inwardly.

Falling Star rubbed Oiwa's nose and laughed cheerily, signalling all to begin. Oiwa was handed a dish of warm scented water. A small white floating flower stuck to his lip. Falling Star removed it with her fingertip and put it on her tongue. She pressed it to Oiwa's mouth. He took it with his. 'You smell lovely,' he thought as excitement welled in the pit of his stomach.

'Scorched seal meat?' she offered. Oiwa nodded, grinning as blood from the rare flesh ran into his beard.

Sharpened Tooth sat next to Oiwa, asking about the bear. 'I can hardly understand what you say,' Oiwa indicated. Sharpened Tooth gestured at length. Finally, he understood, 'He wants me to mime the adventure. Right, here goes. Where's Ziit?' he signed. 'Axe, pouch and dagger are in the changing room. I'll fetch them.' He returned to a circle of shell footlights where he began to perform. 'Paddle my canoe,' he thought, 'then act climbing onto the ice. Slip a bit, for laughs, and sit catching fish. Be watchfully suspicious, then relax. Show horror at the seal flying past, then the terrible fear of seeing the bear.'

The crowd winced audibly at his fright.

'Be the bear, now,' Oiwa thought, changing stance and swimming stealthily underwater, to rise huge and frighteningly onto the ice.

His audience hissed long and loud.

'Become me again,' he thought, grabbing Ziit to loud cheering of 'It's behind you!' 'Aim, twang Ziit's string and be the angry bear again, with an arrow painfully wounding his nose.'

Oiwa loved the applause and did it again.

'Now, skid and spill my arrows.' His onlookers drew breath dramatically as he played the scene again. 'Now, get him in the throat. Draw Ziit; stumble... shoot. Be the Ice Bear again. Clasp my mouth, then nose and mime the roar.' The gathering hurled terrible abuse at the animal.

'Grab my missile for his eye. Hammer the arrows in with my axe.

Act him again standing tall and going for the kill. Hold my little bone-tipped arrow. Let him fall; roll away quickly: chop into his forehead in rage. Don't forget to perform the shitting. Piss in its pee. Gut the bastard. Be the gulls. Eat his heart. Cast out the liver, then piss on his balls.'

Oiwa danced a wild finale to tumultuous clapping, roaring and hooting.

'Brave deeds. Brave deeds,' they yelled. 'Do it again. Do it again.'

'I'm so excited, being with my cousins. I can even begin to understand them. Mouthing their words helps, too. This new water they are passing round is lovely. It tastes different. I think there are fine slices of little red fungi in it. It makes me glow inside. Phew, things look different too. Everyone seems to have pink rainbows around them: don't they look beautiful. This is so wonderful.

'Their songs are marvellous,' he thought after a while. 'Oh, that was a great love song. This is such a happy day.'

'This new one is especially for you,' Sharpened Tooth indicated.

'It's about me. I'm fighting the bear,' he realized. 'It's marvellous.' As choruses continued he felt Falling Star's fingernail scratch his sweating palm.

'More dream water?' she asked, holding out a carved ivory cup.

'Perfect,' Oiwa thought, as she held it to his lips. The water glinted like stars in the blackened interior. The crimson fungus swirled within as he sipped. In verse and song, his last arrow greeted the bear's heart. 'I feel so tall and strong,' he imagined as a fleck of mushroom stuck to his tooth. 'I'll offer it to Falling Star,' he thought, putting it to his tongue-tip with his finger. She gazed into his hazel eyes, held the vessel with him and took the soft morsel with hers.

'I'm going to kiss you. I can't help it,' Oiwa knew, realizing the thrill as their tongues touched and twined.

Foaming Wave clapped his wrinkled hands approvingly.

'She's leading me back to the chamber. We are kissing again. She is so beautiful,' he thought as they stood trembling by the scented bone lamp. 'The furs have been arranged,' Oiwa noticed as Falling Star allowed her seal pup skirt to drop. 'My robe is in the way. Oh. That's nice, she's un-toggling it,' he realized, feeling his scrotum tighten. They stood together, hugging.

'His tip is touching my navel. I do so want him to feel deeply behind it,' Falling Star knew.

'She smells so thrilling. I'm going to stoop and kiss her breasts.' Bone flutes played outside the pelt drapes as his penis stroked past her moist crotch. His lips caressed her pert points in turn. Then on his knees, his nose bridge nuzzled where his man would delve.

'I'll bend over him and caress his back. I'll trace his spine downwards,' Falling Star thought, feeling Oiwa's nose caress her, moistening her. 'He is moving. He is licking from my hairs up to my navel, now over my nipples again. His beard tickles. It's lovely. He's wonderful. I am so happy that the Elders sanction my mating with this hero.'

'I'm standing with her now. She is wet around my top. It is beautiful. It is time... In I go... So, so deep.'

'There he is,' she felt. 'How beautifully and firmly he slid in. The way he sways, and I with he. The flutes know our rhythm. Let him move. Allow his passion. He has conquered the Bear. Now he has me.'

'Oh gosh,' Oiwa thought in ecstasy. 'Maybe only two strokes before I come. One... Two... Oh! Oh! Wonderful. Three, four, fi... i... ve. I'm shaking. She's holding me as I beat inside her. Now taking me down to the furs. We roll together as I still throb within her. I am in a wonderful place. I must not move. Just be and lie here with her here, mated and sated.'

Dreams and dreams later he woke. 'I feel strange. Have I lost something? No. Here's Falling Star. Next to me. Waiting. She needs a good kissing,' he thought, inhaling the scented air deeply. 'She's rubbing my nose with hers,' he realized with passion as his deep urges returned. 'I must mount and mate.'

As his last spasm of orgasm depleted, an unwelcome pain returned. 'Cramp!' he wanted to yell. He jumped free of Falling Star's vulva to hobble and jerk his agonizing sequel to sex. Falling Star calmed him with gentle, loving massage until sleep took Oiwa again.

'Am I awake, or still dreaming?' he thought, hours later. 'There's my robe, and new shoes, too. Oh, and outdoor clothes. They must be for me. I am being very well looked after. What wonderful mating. I feel so good. Where's Falling Star? I'll dress and seek her. She's not with the leather workers. What's that they are saying?'

'We'd better make baby clothes,' they muttered in their tongue.

'There's Ice Crystal with breakfast. How lovely. Smoked seal, hard roe and walrus fat. Ah, there's Falling Star with a sister, perhaps?'

'Here,' Falling Star ventured. 'Your Bear trophy.'

Oiwa understood the words as he gaped. 'My Bear's fangs and claws! All made into a beautiful necklace. I can't believe it.'

'Here, our hero,' she said, as she and dark-eyed Sprig Leaf placed it over his bowing head.

'I'm so proud,' Oiwa thought as it rattled powerfully over his quill collar. 'It fills me with strength. I love it. Let me find my goose gem for this lovely maiden. She can drill it and mount it between the great fangs.'

Sprig Leaf bowed in understanding as he handed her his emblem.

47

Initiation

'You've slept ages,' Sharpened Tooth said, nudging Oiwa. 'The young are itching to kill that bear again. Get up, can you?'

'Falling Star's gone,' Oiwa thought, blinking his heavy eyelids. 'What's he on about?'

'Okay,' he signalled, then dressed. Emerging from the bed-nook, a great cheer rose. 'That's me,' he thought suddenly, spying an older child, named Span, dressed as the Bear Killer.

Dramatic piping, drumming and stone clacking shook him as the drama commenced.

'They are singing it in verse. Every bowshot, lunge and axe-blow, done to music.

'Again. Again. Again,' they all shouted as Span cut the heart out. 'More. More,' they screeched.

'I can't shout, but I'll clap and stamp. They're doing it again: this time faster. It's amazing. There's Falling Star and Spring Leaf. I think they are discussing me. Maybe I don't mate well enough? Or maybe I do? My old life seems so far away in this great house with all these folk. It's wonderful. Here comes that play again. Poor Bear,' Oiwa summed up.

Later, rain poured. Warmer conditions prevailed. Snow and ice melted. The river tumbled even faster. 'I'll smooth my arrow flights and grease Ziit,' Oiwa thought. 'There's no wood here for new ones,' he deduced. 'The sea's heavy. It's horrible out. The warmth and company inside's good. Everyone's making things. Ice Crystal's carving bone toggles. Moon Sky's working a cormorant skin into a fine hat: Sharpened Tooth's honing a shale knife keenly. It is all very fine. The kids are even acting another legend as the old ones watch, plucking little birds they've trapped.'

'Your bow's beautiful,' Sharpened Tooth said.

'What?' Oiwa thought, beginning to understand as his new friend stroked Ziit's smooth wood.

'No trees here. We make other weapons.'

'Visitors! It's Ugruk and his band,' came a cry from the flapping door.

'Oh no,' Oiwa thought. 'Is Mica with them? There's Ugruk, standing solid and strong at the edge of the sloping floor. He's dripping wet. That's his seal gut parka coming off. The water's running from his salmon-skin leggings. Now his duck skin hat's away. The others have entered behind him. There's no sign of Mica. Whooooooo. Good,' he thought as Ugruk told his men to pile their shining harpoons at the portal.

Foaming Wave and Moon Sky stood in respect. 'Welcome to my house. Come closer to the fire. Hang up your clothes. Sit and be warm.'

Ugruk stepped forward and caught Oiwa's eye as his comrades greeted old friends. He untied his leggings, taking in the warmth.

'This is awkward. He's looking at me. Has he come to take me back to Mica? I'm forging a new life. I don't want to return,' Oiwa thought, alarmed. 'What's that he's pulling from behind his leggings? Stop looking at me like that, Ugruk,' he wished. 'It's a busted arrow-shaft. Those are my flights, like the ones from my breeks in the forest.'

'Is this yours?' he asked directly.

'Yes,' Oiwa nodded with shy surprise.

'Then this will be yours, too? Musk Bone, hand me the bundle.'

'What is all this?' he nervously wanted to say.

Ugruk paced to him, staring, the skin package in his rugged outstretched hands. The crowd expectantly watched the confrontation. Oiwa clicked his tongue and rang his toes into the musk-hide mat he stood on.

Ugruk slipped loose the intricately knotted laces. 'Here. Look,' he shouted, flinging it towards Oiwa's curling feet. A small girl from the group of children nuzzled between Ugruk's legs. The parcel unravelled as it rolled towards him.

'It's my Snow Bear's skin,' Oiwa realized in total surprise. 'Look, no ears and a paw missing and with a horribly bashed-up nose.' Oiwa moved forward and stood over the ear holes. He looked at Ugruk, clicked his tongue and smiled confidently.

Ugruk stepped onto the tail. 'Undo this bag. These will be yours, too.'

'What are those nodules in the bladder? Wow! It's the Bear's back teeth. Wonderful,' he thought, surprised again, as Ugruk cuddled his wee daughter.

'Take them out,' Ugruk said clearly.

'The knot's tight. Here it comes. Out they pour. This is real hunters' treasure,' he thought as the sixteenth tooth spilt around his toes on the yellowy white fur.

'Here, Bear Killer, put this on,' Spring Leaf said.

'Ah. My necklace of fangs and claws. Good. How it seems to sing as I fasten it,' Oiwa remarked silently. 'It rattles comfortingly over my quill collar. The agate jingles with the fangs while the claws play a tune on the bare feathers.'

'You look marvellous,' Spring Leaf said in his ear. 'So powerful and brave.'

Oiwa gripped her hand.

Falling Star appeared, saying, 'Here's the broken arrow from your quiver by our bed.' Oiwa signalled, with a look. Falling Star handed it to Ugruk.

'The bits fit, Oiwa,' he remarked, as he joined them.

'Oiwa, Oiwa, Oiwa,' everybody shouted, hearing his name at last.

'Mica wishes you well on your travels. Here's a nose rub from him.'

Oiwa moved forward for the tender greeting, relieved Mica was not present.

'You're a brave hero,' Ugruk announced.

Oiwa, smiling benignly, moved to return the greeting with Ugruk's oily nose. But crack went his forehead forcibly on Ugruk's brow, knocking him backwards.

'That was a vicious Bald Head welcome,' Ugruk remarked painfully,

'Yes,' Oiwa nodded, pondering, 'and maybe from the father of one, soon?'

The whole company erupted laughing, while Foaming Wave summoned Ugruk and his little daughter. 'Fox Tail is growing well. You'll be proud of her, Ugruk. We are; and you have one to be born soon from your last visit. It's good to have your courageous blood within us. This new man, Oiwa the Bear Killer, we want him to leave souls too, as Weir did.'

'I'm sure he will, so Mica tells me. But I have something special for you, Foaming Wave. Musk Bone, fetch me the package,' he asked his brother.

Foaming Wave smiled as he unwrapped it on his knee. 'Snow Bear thighs,' He cried out excitedly, 'Perfect for playing my singing stones. I'll hit one now. How it rings the hollow pebble. And that's the signal for food and drink. It will appear soon.'

'We have bear meat left from Oiwa's kill, and some birds who were guzzling it.'

'Wonderful,' Moon Sky put in. 'It's time for feasting, brave tales and songs.'

'Hmmm,' Oiwa thought happily, 'listening to Ugruk speaking my language, then talking in theirs, helps me understand it better.'

'Stories, stories, stories,' the kids shouted to Ugruk.

'Later. When we've eaten.'

'Greedy dog,' they yelled, 'Stories now. Now.'

'All right. Shut up, be quiet, listen,' he said. 'It's one you've never heard before. It's of brave, heroic deeds. Of tragedy and joy, love, longing and wonder.' Silence fell. Faces glowed with wondrous anticipation. 'It's the history of Oiwa,' Ugruk resoundingly announced, pointing proudly to the Bear Killer.

'What's this? I'm shocked,' Oiwa modestly thought.

'I learned it from Mica,' Ugruk explained while leaning against a roof post. He began with Oiwa's beaver kill and his forest seduction and his lineage. He dramatized everything in the telling, like all the best legends.

'This is embarrassing, yet exciting,' Oiwa thought, as Ugruk told of their river exploits: their stay with the Stork Clan and Buzzard's hospitality. All listened eagerly to Oiwa's mating with Moss in embellished prose. 'That's how legends grow, with a slick tongue,' he saw, as Heron's Tooth became a vast craft and the Dun a heavenly waterway: Snaaaaar, assuming even more vile powers for Oiwa to conquer.

Their speeding journey beneath the majestic paintings before entering Gunnal's Vulva impressed the audience. Ugruk's descriptions inspired the crowd: the terrible tale of their entry into the underground torrents. They had never heard the like of it. They gazed at Oiwa as though he were a hero, adorned with honours.

Bitter anguish and contemptuous hisses erupted when Rush was struck by Snaaaaar's arrows. Folk spat venomously in the fire, careful, though, to miss the sizzling meat of the Snow Bear, white foxes, lemmings and musk ox.

The tense tale of woe in the bowels of Gunnal followed. Silence framed the dramatic adventure. The imaginations of the listeners flew with suspense at the giant, blood-sucking vampire bats: the wondrous dry cavern, the visions that came from it, then the terrible force of water about to overtake them. Their narrow escape: the tragedy of Bark. All shook their heads. Folk cried and wailed at his end. Next came the gripping moments as they emerged from the eye of the cave, overridden by the appearance of the murderous Snaaaaar. Her attack: Oiwa's accuracy with Ziit! At that, he held his famous bow up high amid huge applause. Inside him great sadness gripped his throat at his missing friends and brothers. Speech seemed even further away from his grasp.

His whole tale and history was related: the golden bodies of Rush, Bark and Tine: the burials. Later, the Baldheads and more of Oiwa's mating. They applauded wildly at the exploits in the cavern of salted dead.

'So I do have an amazing tale,' Oiwa realized. 'I'm being treated with honour. But I was only doing what was necessary. It didn't seem exceptional. My necklace and intaglio mean something very special. I know now.'

'Oiwa. Act it all from when you left Mica,' the crowd insisted.

'I will,' he nodded, taking the invisible paddle in Marten's boat, knowing he would have to kill the bear yet again.

The feast of land and sky meat followed. Rain beat on the tight roof. Rivulets gushed down to the tideline over the dark pebbles to the salty sea.

'Whilst we eat, Oiwa, I'll tell you the rest of Weir's tale.'

'Oh, please,' Oiwa gestured.

'Well, Oiwa, Weir managed to go through Gunnal's Vulva

unscathed and went with his band to Wolf Lake. His matings there left two young. At the Bald Heads, more. One will have watched you as a salted body when you mated in the cave. After Goose Landing and meeting Solan, he vanished from the company of your Clan; much like you, Oiwa. Here, have a roast lemming,' Ugruk offered as he threw the burned skull and teeth from his back into the fire. 'Your Snow Bear's good. Maybe you'd prefer that. You've earned it.... It was after he left here with a hunting party that trouble started.' Ugruk swallowed a hunk of bear leg. Oiwa bit into another fillet as he listened, the juices running into his beard. 'These folk, the Albatross Clan, are very helpful. They decided to hunt along the east shore. That way they could take Weir in the direction that the autumn geese fly. It was his quest to follow them. They said that sometimes he could change into one.'

'I know exactly how that feels,' Oiwa remembered.

'They hunted seal. They filled their skins with little fish. They caught young gulls, fat and rich. They ate well. Some of the group loaded their kayaks, taking their supplies home to dry and store. Others continued. Between two towering islands they were caught in a whirlpool. Weir followed with two of the Albatross. The first boat was pulled in suddenly. The screams for help died rapidly. Some followed to assist. They were lost in an instant. Weir and his crew back-paddled as fast as they could before being dragged down.'

'Horrid,' thought Oiwa nervously.

'A stink, like rotten eggs, filled the ocean where other currents rose from the depths. The water smoked. A disgusting fog descended, like a giant's vile fart. They crossed a great inlet, where the sea flowed and weaved in weird colours. Greens, grey, silt brown and dark blue. Each colour was driven by a different current from deep under the sea. There, the bodies of the drowned hunters and their twisted kayaks slowly bobbed to the surface like floating turds. Two of Weir's crew went mad at seeing their friends' and brothers' faces. They looked as though they'd been boiled.'

'I can't listen,' Oiwa felt, holding his ears. But Ugruk went on.

'Weir led, forcing the crew to paddle like they had never done before. They entered another thick cloud of horrid fog. Weir knew the way. It was the Goose Spirit. Stinking bubbles burst on the surface, breaking more disgusting wind. Weir forced them onwards until they heard waves hitting a shore. The men were yelling in fear as he made them paddle, but paddle they did. The choking fog slid away as they reached a rocky beach below steep grey cliffs. They were in a small cove echoing with the dead hunters' screams.

Have a drink, Oiwa, here,' Ugruk offered holding out his walrus skull cup.

'Thank you,' Oiwa's face responded.

Ugruk cleaned a lemming rib between his teeth and went on. 'The men wailed in sorrow. Weir took command again. He swore at them. He slapped them with his paddle. He knew it was no place to stay. It was filled with evil. He got them back into their boat and set out to sea again. He shouted the words of a terrible dirge in demonic rhythm. This drove the crew onwards and around Skullar's point, where the air was clearer. He didn't let up until they reached a sloping beach far away from the disaster, where they camped many, many leagues further on.'

Folk huddled round to listen, even though it was in Oiwa's tongue. 'They were exhausted. They slept and slept. When Weir woke, Orca Fin was sitting next to him. The other two were utterly dead. Their faces showed terror, as though they'd seen a horrific vision.' More Albatrosses gathered in to listen. 'Weir and Orca Fin sailed along the coast to the safety of the Hot Rocks Clan. They lived by Reeking Mountain. There, Weir rested. Later, he left alone to journey on. He reached the Echoing Caves of Black Island. There's mystery still how he came to leave that evil place, or where he went. Maybe, Oiwa, you'll discover?'

'I need another drink,' Oiwa signalled as he sat pensively.

'I told Mica. He will tell North Star,' Ugruk said, nudging Oiwa from his trance.

Oiwa rested his head between his knees, thinking of his journey forward. Spring Leaf and Falling Star massaged his back, soothing his taut muscles.

The sound of Sharpened Tooth honing his array of sacred shale knives ceased. Their moon-shaped blades shone in the lamplight. Their hasps glistened, carved as human forms prostrate over a whale's back.

'That's good,' Oiwa wanted to say, as Falling Star rubbed his shoulders and neck. 'She's unclipped my quill collar. Those oils feel so warm, almost hot. It's so good on my tired back. She's sitting me up. Spring Leaf's holding a leather bowl of pungent, steaming water. Little dried yellow mushrooms are swelling up. They get brighter too, and the water's changing colour. That's a tiny red fungus expanding as well.'

'Drink, Oiwa,' he understood Spring Leaf. He felt his fine leather robe being lifted from him.

'Sip,' said Falling Star.

'Quaff,' urged Sharpened Tooth.

'It's sweet, yet bitter,' Oiwa thought as he swilled it around his teeth. 'Strange how it makes my tongue feel numb. The smell's beautiful, though. I can't feel my lips now, but my insides are glowing. Strange, some is dribbling down to my legs.'

'A little more,' Spring Leaf suggested as she held the bowl in Oiwa's weakening grip.

'My nose is running; my forehead sweats; I feel my Star swelling. Was it the bump with Ugruk? Why is my head spinning?'

'I'll wipe his nose,' Sharpened Tooth seemed to distantly say.

'I'm dropping the bowl. There's lots of lovely colours. I think I'm flying.'

'The potion's working,' Falling Star assured them. 'It won't be long. Inhale the fumes, Oiwa the Bear Killer.'

'My head's heavy. I can't think. I can't move. I'm falling,' were his last notions as he completely relaxed.

'I'll stick my nose spike under his thumbnail. If he flinches, he's not ready. Good, not a flicker. Now into his armpit to make sure.... There, he's senseless,' said Sharpened Tooth looking at the blooded point.

'I can hear you, though,' Oiwa knew, 'and the pretty colours follow the beautiful women.'

'Lie him out on his Bear pelt, then carry him to the fire. Lay him prone on the upturned kayak,' he heard Sharpened Tooth say. The ceiling swirled above him in spangles as he was moved. 'I see your faces looking down at me, I feel the fur under me. The kayak stretching me. I can't move, and I don't want to. This is bliss.'

'It's right we do this on his Snow Bear pelt,' Falling Star said.

'All the Albatross Clan will see. Remove the rest of his clothes, Sharpened Tooth. We will swab him with the potion to numb his skin further,' Spring Leaf added.

'I don't know what they're about to do to me, but I don't care,' Oiwa dreamed as his arms flopped down the kayak's sides and his shoulders stretched back.

'I'll do his ears, now,' Sharpened Tooth said as he shoved his nose spike deftly through Oiwa's lobe.

'Out cold,' an old woman shouted from the audience. 'His mating tool didn't even shudder.'

'Give me a toggle. I'll plug his lug with it.'

'Here's my walrus ivory ones. He's earned them,' Foaming Wave said, pushing his agile way through the gathering.

'That's stopped the blood, now the other one. These are your Albatross-headed ones. Are you sure?'

'Yes, my son and heir. Don't worry, I've plenty other. I'll go back to playing my stones. We can all chant with them whilst the initiation rites continue.'

'I didn't feel a thing. But I hear the stones and Bear bones making music for the chant. I'm flying again. Drifting. It's wonderful.'

'I'll begin at his ankles. Where's my knife? First cut here. That's it. Very fine, like a hair. Another across it and slowly up. Pull the skin so the lacerations open. Slice the lattice up his shin and cut a crosshatch over the man's knee. Now I shall make a matching pattern on his other leg.

'Falling Star, whilst I sharpen my blade would you and Spring Leaf stretch the pattern and rub the black dye in? It will show up his new Albatross scales nicely. Above his knees, I will incise the feathers. After, if he's still in a stupor, I'll shave his curling hairs away and prick in an Albatross head, so whenever he mates our God will see. I am sure Solan will approve.'

'I heard that,' Oiwa addressed himself. 'But I feel so good, I couldn't care. I don't mind the bird watching. Just get on with it, Sharpened Tooth.'

'That's good, you two. The design is coming out well. This brave will be one of us wherever he roams.'

'Here,' Moon Sky said in her ancient voice, 'Take this palate of bloodstone paste. I mined it many ages past from the chasm in Upper Hill where Sange, our God of Eternal Blood dwells. Use it for the Albatross, too. It will symbolize our blood and his.'

'My legs are beginning to sting,' Oiwa noticed as he felt the razor shaving. 'I can't move. That's the needle. He's working. I can't see for his head of black hair. Ah! That smarted,' he thought as Sharpened Tooth became aware of Oiwa's deeper breaths.

'Won't be long, Oiwa the Bear Killer,' he responded.

'That's his nose spike sticking in my navel. Good, he's removed it. I think he's using it to puncture the eyes. That smarts.'

'All done. Now for the bloodstone and the soot dye for the eyes. Then we can all relax. Oiwa, I'm going to give you another dose. You can rest as your tattoos heal. Dream away. Sleep. Enjoy the colours. Spring Leaf will watch over you.'

'I'm drifting again,' he knew after the horn spoon poured the draft over his tongue. 'I'm gliding like an Albatross over the Dun. There's my Goose Clan looking up. They wave as I pass to another life. There's Buzzard now. He's become greater than before. His spirit encompasses his Clan. There's a dark space. It follows us like an evil wrap to hunt and kill. I have to conquer it. Bark's face vanishes. It becomes a cat's. Rush floats on a golden shimmer and drifts to the Moon: the smack of the arrow through Tine's head as he plummets. He sprouts Eagle's wings to fly o'er woodlands. I kill Snaaaaar. Dark becomes light in the far distance. The stone in my throat shifts and returns. Now peace, as I feel myself sinking into the fur beneath me. I fly with Solan to that distant place set in the ocean. The dune below: sleeping hills, towns, pastures, strange animals living among people. And Her... Looking to the waves.'

Oiwa eventually woke. Foaming Wave's gentle stone music caressed his mind. The warmth of the fire enveloped his skin. 'My tattoos tingle. I will lie and listen. That's Sharpened Tooth singing now like a bird on high. The others join in as I blink. Yes, I flew from here. I saw and returned. I must take my own human flesh to that place.'

48

Towards Reeking Mountain

Oiwa wakened, blinking, to peer round the dim cell. 'The walls are hung with Snow Bear skins. There are harpoons, spears and long, bone clubs. Coils of sinew rest on the floor. Light from the translucent roof touches my sore skin. But the rain's stopped.'

'Don't move,' said Ice Crystal. 'Ugruk teach me Goose. Be still.'

'My ankle's raw,' he wanted to say. 'My shins smart, too.'

'You will have sore, Oiwa. Be still on nice bed. We heal you. Falling Star and Spring Leaf come. You in our sacred Bear-Hunt Lodge.'

'That explains all the fine equipment. Ah, the naked girls are pushing a hide dish of grease under the lintel. It pongs of fish. Now they're behind gripping my armpits. Don't twist my oxters,' he silently prayed, as they hoisted him upright.

'Huguk!' they exclaimed to lift him.

'Ouch!' he wanted to yelp as the sweaty hairs tugged. 'But their lovely skin feels gorgeous next to mine.'

'We oil you now,' Ice Crystal translated.

'That feels so good. How their hands ripple over my skin. I feel the oil in the cuts as the soreness vanishes. The tiny scabs seem to come away. This is lovely. Oh. Now they are doing my Albatross.

Well, Falling Star watched me stiffen before. Be careful,' he wanted to add.

'I'll take him in next,' Spring Leaf volunteered in Albatross, 'Moon Sky and Foaming Wave agree. Ice Crystal will breed too. We'll share his blood-seed.'

'My skin's absorbed the oil. I'm getting more, now. Oh. If you stroke my man like that any longer, I'll spurt. Aaaaah. Aaaah. Aaaaaaaah! Oooooo. I did try not to come. Now they are laughing. And I'm getting cramp!'

'See how his dickie-bird spat,' Spring Leaf admired, 'He can do that in me next time.'

'Yes, you deserve him. How well you plaited his beard and threaded his moustache beads, then combed his hair and nursed his ears as he slept,' Falling Star said kindly. 'You deserve a wean from him. He's now half Albatross.'

'Ears? Oh, I remember. They feel stretched. Sharpened Tooth jabbed me with his spike,' Oiwa recalled, calming from orgasm. 'My beads feel good. They remind me of Moss. What's happening now, I wonder? Oh, there's a wee louse. Quick, I'll pop it between my fingernails. Got it. Good.'

'Stand there, Oiwa,' Ice Crystal asked. 'We finished the oil. Now it Skring's turn. He lick. His tongue heal wound.'

'Sounds like a dog,' Oiwa thought. 'Yes, here he bounds. Eeeeek! He's licking the oil off. His tongue tickles, rasping simultaneously. It's quite good. Well... very good. Most stimulating, just don't do my Albatross, Skring: he's had enough treatment. Yes, Skring knows his work. He's licking each cut carefully then going to the next. No, not my nuts,' Oiwa willed. 'You'll know how sensitive they get. Good dog, good dog. Ah, you seem to have finished now. I'm all clean, skin tingling.'

'Doesn't he look beautiful, girls,' Ice Crystal commented in Albatross.

'Yes, it's the way he stands, looks and moves. We want that in our Clan. Let's sit him on the whalebone among the furs. We can feed and pamper him until he can mate again.'

'Breeding is great,' Oiwa thought as he came with Spring Leaf later on. 'I wonder what my Albatross saw?' he mused before she moved off him.

'That is thrice now with Oiwa. It will be Ice Crystal's time next. She should still be fertile this moon,' Spring Leaf thought. 'I hope it will be as lovely for her. I'm sure it will be. I'd love to mate with him again, but he must travel on. It's funny how he always gets that pain in his leg after.'

Oiwa finally emerged through the low exit to stretch in the great space. 'Well, I feel great in this pelt with my tooth and claw necklace. Did Weir feel like this? I hope so, proud, strong well bred with, and full of life.

'There's Sharpened Tooth. His polished fangs really shine as he grins.'

'You feel good?' he asked awkwardly. 'Ugruk teach me Goose words.'

Oiwa nodded assertively, thinking, 'Brilliant, wonderful, marvellous and utterly great.'

'Yes, Oiwa. You look... very good. You make good babies? We see. Sometimes it not work... you have to come back,' he laughed in the light from the clear overhead panel. 'We have new clothes for you down by fire. Cross the pelts with me,' he indicated, 'and throw off the one you have. Them better for travel.

Oiwa saw long trousers with stitched panels of soft sealskin. White silver fox tails trimmed the waist. There were thick walrus hide boots. They fitted over his trouser legs and tied with laced cords. A jacket, which knotted down his left, clipped together with bone hooks over his ribs. An albatross motif was stitched across the chest. 'I'm honoured with the clothes,' Oiwa knew as he found a bird skin hood folded in a pocket.

'Here's your pouch,' Spring Leaf said, bringing it in, 'Still strung on your belt.'

Sharpened Tooth continued in broken Goose, 'Ugruk come with me... You come with me... We go Reeking Mountain way. Ugruk's people go back. Just we take you.'

'Sharpened Tooth. That's wonderful,' Oiwa wanted to express.

He could see it in Oiwa's face, 'You happy of that?'

Oiwa's embrace told him, 'We go after next feast. We take the Ormer. Everything fit? Leave you there. We come back. Okay.'

'I'm so happy. I'm getting closer to Weir. I'm being helped on my way. The dangers ahead seem less perilous. My companions are strong and experienced. This is splendid.'

'Follow me, Oiwa. We go to walled sun shelter.'

'Little Moth,' Ugruk said to his daughters, 'you are growing well. So are you, Shingle. I'll bring fox furs. Maybe you have a new brother or sister by then?' Oiwa heard him say from the sheltered terrace by the fire of dry bones.

'It's so still in here,' Oiwa thought. 'This crescent dug into the slope is great. These high stone hunks round the edge still the breeze. It's nice. Huge pebbles for seats and working on. I'll build one, some time.'

'Come in, Bear Killer, sit; be warm. Meet Ugruk's Albatross family: Skua, granddaughter of Weir and mother of Shingle. Myrtle is still growing a baby.'

'So it seems,' Oiwa thought in silent greeting.

'Foaming Wave and his household come,' Sharpened Tooth informed him. 'He bless my beautiful kayak, the Ormer. Great day: calm sea, only tiny clouds. Maybe good for going?'

'Yes,' Oiwa thought as he took in the blossoming slope. Behind, snow-covered foothills of jagged mountains glared. Up there, dark, frozen clefts and shining rock faces peered down to the Albatross haven. Within those cold chasms the Winter Gods hid from the summer light, only to creep out when the dipping sun slept.

'Little Moth, Shingle. We go now and hunt those foxes,' Ugruk said, rubbing their noses.

'Spring Leaf has Ziit, his arrows and my small bundle of trophies. The pelt stays in the Bear Spirit's chamber,' Oiwa added.

'I'll return the Sand Kisser to the Baldheads.'

'Thanks, Ugruk,' Oiwa nodded, glad his theft would be made good.

'Two days, Sharpened Tooth and I will paddle. Your scars need healing. Skring will not be there to lick them,' Ugruk confirmed as Falling Star and Spring Leaf sat either side of Oiwa.

'Here's chewed porpoise fin,' Spring Leaf managed to say, passing it into Oiwa's mouth, 'Part of our farewell feast.' Falling Star, hoping to grow his child, tongued her mouthful to him.

'Let's carry the Ormer to the black sands by the river,' Sharpened Tooth said later in clear Albatross.

'I go,' Oiwa signalled with energetic nose rubbing, 'Be well. Remember me. The horizon beckons.'

The trio silently carried the kayak to the lapping ripples, a light breeze taking them to the wide rising ocean.

'Weir travelled so very far,' Oiwa assessed. 'Then roamed further. What drove him drives me. He saw those pink, shimmering mountains, the ice floes and the whales. He bred and left lives, loved and lived. That's for me. Gumar and Tumar said to do that. I do,' he pondered as his paddlers worked.

After two days Oiwa pointed far to the north east. A ridge of cloud drifted southerly from a dark, distant, mount.

'Reeking Mountain,' Ugruk said. 'Ice ahead, beware. Go steady.'

'I can paddle now,' Oiwa indicated, admiring the far-off plume.

'That's where we head: a warm place in the midst of frozen land. It looks black from out here against the snow,' he replied, handing Oiwa a paddle.

'That's better,' Oiwa felt, stroking the water.

'Oiwa, see those two ominous stacks sticking up? The ones covered in guano?'

He nodded, pointing his paddle as cascades of kittiwakes hurled themselves from the pinnacles. 'They look like the ominous waving hands of a drowning victim,' Oiwa thought in fearful awe.

'Between them Weir's whirlpools whip,' Ugruk turned, explaining. 'We veer well away from them. The temptation is to look closer.'

'I'm beginning to hear the sucking sound. There's a dead gannet being dragged to it, and a log,' Oiwa observed. 'There's more diving birds, but we're steering well clear.'

'I need to look,' confessed Sharpened Tooth.

'No!' Ugruk shouted. 'Oiwa, pull away, with me. He's caught by the spell. I'll slap his lugs to bring him round.'

Oiwa clasped his ears, feeling his Albatross earplugs jag, as a whirling flight of whitemaas screamed at them.

'Paddle with me, or be dragged in,' urged Ugruk. 'The whirlpool senses folk and widens its spread... Paddle!'

'Just a little way, I want to see Ungrinn,' Sharpened Tooth said dreamily.

'No we don't,' yelled Ugruk, slapping him again as Sharpened Tooth stroked his paddle harder.

'I'll take his paddle. Oiwa, you strike away; quick!'

Oiwa clicked his tongue urgently. Hearing the gull screams over the swooshing of the rapidly spreading pool, Oiwa plied his might, turning the Ormer away.

'You are not visiting Ungrinn,' Ugruk told the stricken mate, confiscating Sharpened Tooth's paddle.

'Oiwa, keep going. Anywhere, as long as it's away,' Ugruk commanded, dipping his paddle back. 'Ungrinn's a monster: a huge foul Man-Fish with masses of swirling arms to drag his prey in. One dark winter he fought against the Ice Giantess. He won, turning her to stone. Those jutting towers are her reaching hands, warning us. Ungrinn's beaky mouth, deep below, still sucks the sea in search of food. Sharpened Tooth's grandfather vanished with others of his ancestors on Weir's quest. Paddle,' he yelled again as Sharpened Tooth came slowly from his trance. He pulled his nose spike out, drawing blood as he traced the whirlpool's helix on his cheeks.

'This is Stinking Water. Paddle, Oiwa. See the bubbling eddies on the smooth surface. It's Ungrinn's farts erupting like rotten eggs.'

'More like that terrible bison in Gunnal's Vulva,' Oiwa remembered.

'It's as if the sea rises higher, here, too,' Ugruk stated.

'I heard my Grandfather call. He waved at me,' Sharpened Tooth eventually said as he came around.

'That was just Ungrinn's Lure,' Ugruk answered. 'Now... Paddle.'

Gannets whirled angrily, feeling cheated at no scraps.

'Log!' realized Oiwa, suddenly veering away as it hurled itself up in front of the Ormer.

'How did you know?' called Ugruk.

Oiwa tapped his forehead. 'Just did,' he signalled. The log's cleaned surface had been sucked of all slime and sea life.

'But there it goes again.' he wanted to yell. 'Another whirlpool! Ungrinn's trick! Paddle.' Instead he punched Ugruk, pointing. Ugruk lurched forward. Sharpened Tooth's spike pierced his cheek, hitting a molar, fully awakening him.

'Paddle right,' came Ugruk's alarm call. 'I don't know how, but we've been dragged back on this weird water.'

'My tattoo's split,' Oiwa thought as he strained.

'Go with the flow. Speed up, we are heading round to the Hand, watch out,' he commanded as they reached the ominously dark shadow. 'Paddle left... Now! Turn. Don't hit the Hand or it's doom,' he screeched over the renewed sucking.

'That's the trunk going again. Roots and all,' Oiwa saw as he pushed his paddle on the rising stack, avoiding crashing.

'Yes, push off,' Sharpened Tooth rejoined, shoving the Ormer from the sheer pinnacle.

'The water is dragging us. Keep pushing,' commanded Ugruk, thinking of Ungrinn's deep, gnashing fangs below.

'Get round the other side,' Oiwa knew as he thrust at the basalt height. 'On, on,' he urged as the water began to drop away.

'We are getting past it,' the Albatross Heir announced in triumph, choking on the foul air.

'Paddle straight on. Fast as we can. Don't look back. Make speed,' Ugruk spat out, matching Oiwa's thoughts. 'There's choppy water ahead, then swell. It looks safer.'

'Okay,' panted Sharpened Tooth, as they slowly began to pull free of Ungrinn's vortex.

'Log beneath!' Oiwa wanted to shout, but too late.

'Thud,' it went at the Ormer's prow, hurling Sharpened Tooth aloft.

'I'm tipping out!' Oiwa felt, as he watched Ugruk lurch over the side.

'Same trunk,' Oiwa realized, 'Ungrinn's foul weapon,' he thought in panic.

Sharpened Tooth swam in the ice-cold water, holding onto his paddle.

'Don't look back,' Oiwa thought, seeing his friend in peril. 'Manoeuvre the craft. Get closer. 'Here,' he indicated, 'grab my paddle. I'll pull you in.'

'Thanks, Oiwa,' he spluttered in the reeking air.

'Boat's tipping. Lean back,' Oiwa told himself, as his mate dragged his body up to slither, seal-like into his cockpit.

'Your spike's gone. Blood's running down your cheek and you're dazed,' Oiwa assessed. 'Turn the Ormer. Find Ugruk. There he is. Oh no! Don't grab the trunk!' Oiwa wanted to shout. 'It's Ungrinn's harpoon. He's going to drag you. Let go! I'll save you.'

'That's Oiwa's voice in my head, I know it,' Ugruk thought. 'He's right, I can't let go. I'm being dragged back.'

'I'll paddle alongside. Sharpened Tooth, grab him,' Oiwa urgently signalled, as he saw Ugruk trying to push away. 'His feet. His feet: grab them whilst we swing past. Let go, Ugruk, let go,' was all Oiwa could think.

'Thank Guman and Tuman; you've got him. Pull him free. Don't touch the log. I'll paddle on. We are being drawn back again. That stink's worse. Drag Ugruk aboard. The spell is getting him. Good. Up, over and in. Now paddle too, Sharpened Tooth. We are not out of this yet. Paddle, and you, Ugruk, if you can, we are being swept back to the basalt hand. PADDLE!' he yelled within.

Sharpened Tooth responded as if driven. 'That's Oiwa compelling me into action. I'm out of my terrible trance now. Ugruk, here you come. Now we can escape.'

'There's small whirls yet,' Oiwa noticed as the gulls swooped down again. 'Paddle away. Now. Fast!' his mind urged as the black pile receded. 'The log's following us. Go. Go, go,' his mind flashed.

'Yes indeed, Oiwa,' Sharpened Tooth responded at the clamour in his head.

'That must be the inlet Weir made for after his battle with Ungrinn. We have to make for it,' Ugruk said, still dazed. 'We are soaked. We will freeze to death if we don't get shelter.'

'The Ormer's listing badly,' Oiwa noticed. 'He's right. These two must get dry. The current is still strange. Ungrinn might try again. The shore's closer now. What vast pebbles line the beach! Some higher than me.'

'Ungrinn's juggling stones,' Sharpened Tooth remarked as the Ormer's prow lodged between a pair. 'We'll pull the Ormer through. You keep dry, Oiwa.'

'On land at last,' Oiwa remarked to himself, as water poured from the Ormer's side onto the stony beach. 'Strange?' he mused, 'There was no water inside. Wow. It's a double skin. No wonder she dragged. How clever. That stopped us sinking.'

'Good, Ziit's safe, but these men are chilled. They shiver. They could die if I don't act. Fine. They are jumping about, keeping warm. I'll find driftwood. Excellent, there's a dried cormorant up a cleft: brilliant kindling, once I get it going. There's wood and tangled bark. Great. They're rummaging, too. Quick, beneath the cliff overhang. Here's my pouch. Flint out, strike the firestone: spark in the bark and onto my tree fungus. Here's the tinder. Blow gently, glowing now. Good, fire. Catch the bark and show flames please? Greill, Fire God, work for me. Save them.'

'Cave,' Oiwa heard Ugruk shout. 'Bring the fire.'

'Okay,' he thought, 'I can run with the sparks.'

'Here, Oiwa. Light that pile we got. Good, an oilbird, that'll help. We must get our clothes off before we perish,' he said with chattering teeth.

'At least it's dry in here. The smoke's being drawn up the fissure. It's warming. Wood now,' he told himself, as the seabird crackled.

'Th th th that g g good,' Sharpened Tooth stuttered as he pulled his jacket off to reveal wet fur.

'I'll hunt for more fuel,' Oiwa decided, 'They need heat. Their clothing must dry: so, so lucky about the cave.'

'Pull up the Ormer,' Ugruk asked when Oiwa returned. 'There are emergency provisions in the holds.'

'Hmmm. Dried seal. We can chew that right now by the fire,' Oiwa gratefully realized.

'No more risks,' said Sharpened Tooth. 'We sit here in warm and sing songs. Ugruk know good sagas. We share more seal. Clothes dry, too. Thank you, Oiwa. You save us. And make fire.'

'I'm going to explore,' Oiwa decided soon after. 'The cliff's rugged, but not that high. I can grab those gnarled willows growing from the crevices. It smells distinctly fishy up here. Plenty of footholds, though. Oh no! That's a nesting fulmar retching. Aaaaaaaagh!' he yelled inwardly, 'For shit's sake! She's covered me in stinking gull puke!' Another volley of fulmar vomit hurled itself from the nesting birds' gullets. 'Fuck! That bile stinks. It's in my ear; over my hands. It's so slippy. I could lose my grip. They're screaming at me now. I should have worn my hood. There'll be more coming. I'm off. Missed, you bitch of a bird,' he screamed in his head. 'Fuck again! Straight in my face. I'm covered. I'm slipping. Can't grip: too greasy. Ah. Trod on one. She's wild, and her two fat chicks. Don't look up,' he thought, squinting aloft. 'Oh. Fuck and fuck; shit lot! That's rows of them aiming at me. I'm off the way I came. There are ranks of them below, too.

'Thank Tumar. I'm down. I'm watching,' he told them, 'I'll keep out of range of your foul beaks. There's more. Duck!' He shouted inside as a volley streaked overhead. 'I'll have you,' he warned, shaking his bile-covered fist as he crunched across the foreshore. 'Your babes look tasty. You just wait. We'll be hungry yet,' he threatened, grabbing dried moss to wipe his face. 'My ear-studs are thick with it; there's a rock pool. I'll squat and wash.

'That's better,' he thought later, 'I'll just sit here and gaze. Those Giantess hands look terrible from here. Poor woman. I expect she has to watch Ungrinn work his foul deeds. How many victims has he dragged down? Yes, sometimes that water's calm. Then it rages, swirls and drags you in. We were lucky. What is Ungrinn? A magical sea spider: a bunch of foul snake devils? She knows. I don't want to,' he thought, shivering. Then he remembered Falling Wave and Moon Sky, then Buzzard's hospitality and Moss. 'Before I left home, I'd only mated once. Now I've mated with four more. Luck,

I suppose? Will I have caused a child? Surely no? Not me? What if I did? Where am I going? Will I ever find out? This is so confusing. But Buzzard told me; some men are breeders, just as Gumar and Tumar want. I think I'll return to the cave.

'Good, they are sleeping. And it's warm. They won't smell the bird reek for a bit. Their clothes are drying nicely in the fireglow: my turn to sleep too. I'm knackered.'

'We've got a long way to go, Oiwa,' Ugruk stated, nudging him conscious. 'Phewk! You stink of puke. Been bird-nesting?'

'I've got three fat plucked fledglings,' Sharpened Tooth stated, returning to the cave. 'Stir the embers. We can cook. There's more for the journey.'

'That makes up for all their vomit,' Oiwa thought. 'I'll poo in your feathers and wipe my bum with your heads right now.'

'I love gull babes: their bones are so tender,' Sharpened Tooth remarked to Ugruk as they roasted, dripping from a harpoon spit.

'Better fix the Ormer,' Ugruk said after breakfast. 'They were good, though. I particularly enjoy their crunchy feet.'

'Aye, but I ain't eating their severed heads today,' Sharpened Tooth commented, grinning at Oiwa.

'I've saved some clean ones for you,' Oiwa eagerly indicated.

'This is thrilling,' Oiwa realized soon after. 'Off shortly. The Ormer's tight. That's my direction. It seems so easy now once Ungrinn's behind us. We paddle along the coast passing the grey, snowy mounts. That must be Smoking Mountain's plume again in the far, far distance.'

'Musk herd,' Ugruk announced, pointing to the low pastures, 'Fearsome to kill, but wonderful meat. Have you seen them afore, Oiwa?'

'No,' he gestured, then drew in his hand indicating, 'Just a bone engraving.'

'Paddle on,' Ugruk said. 'We are in the Green Waters, Oiwa. Look down. They are so clear. You can see to the deep, sandy bottom. They go black later. The colours guide us.'

'Yes,' Oiwa thought, 'When I flew with Solan, I saw them far below. I know the way, too. It makes me feel full and strong. My arms are like wings again: powerful and tireless. It's as though I can hear my skein's wing beats carrying me onward. My Star Map shines in my head. There's my skein, reflected deep below. Now I look up, there's nothing: only the low sun ringing the horizon. But their wing beats are taking me to a dream. I see my companions, but they are separate. They paddle silently as I fly behind them, pushing us on.

'I'm in the bright, deep reflection. Yes, Solan, I'll follow you and Solange. Who is that lone boatman on the high seas, riding huge waves?'

'You; later,' came the King Goose's answer.

'I'm back,' Oiwa knew suddenly. 'But we've travelled far. The land's changed. How?'

'There's Echoing Caves,' Ugruk pointed out.

'I just hear my Geese calling, calling. I hear me shouting out my own name too, over and over: Oiwa, Oiwa, Oiwa, repeatedly. Just like a goose call urging me on and on and on.'

'Skullar's Point ahead,' Ugruk said, turning back to Oiwa. 'What!' he exclaimed as Sharpened Tooth turned in shock, watching Oiwa change from an immense bird back into himself.

'Did you see that?' Sharpened Tooth spluttered.

'Yes: he must be a shape changer,' he answered as Oiwa paddled with renewed power. 'I wanted to tell him the legends here, but that amazing light from his eyes prevents me. We'll paddle on to Orca Fin Bay, land there and rest,' Ugruk whispered.

49

Lava's Kiss

'That strange protrusion from the cliff is called Hot Rock,' Ugruk told Oiwa, passing it in the Ormer next day, while Sharpened Tooth wondered if he had become a goose again as they had slept.

'Reeking Mountain,' Ugruk went on, 'You will see it as we round the ugly lump. It was flung there by the Fire Giant, who even scorched his own flaming fingers on it.' There's the smoke plume. See its distant dark shadow?'

'Yes,' thought Oiwa. 'From far above once, in a dream.'

'The swell's moving faster,' Sharpened Tooth added. 'There's a breeze getting up. We'll see the volcano soon.'

'There it is,' Oiwa saw finally. 'It looks huge: the top glows. With the sun behind, it stands out black from the icy land. The dark reek pales as it moves across the bright sky. The air's warmer on my face, too. The water's changed colour again as we paddle in this great inlet.'

'Not much longer now,' Ugruk encouraged.

'That's one of their musk horns sounding. Is it a warning?' Sharpened Tooth asked.

'What a high-pitched blast. I hope it's friendly,' Oiwa wondered, as the motion of the sea slackened under the echoes.

'Two canoes coming from that crag,' Ugruk announced warily, 'They're heading our way. Turn the Ormer to meet them. Paddle-beat her sides in friendship, then hold them high.'

'They good friends, most time,' Sharpened Tooth told Oiwa.

He nodded, sucking his moustache thoughtfully. 'More strange rocks along the shore,' he observed. 'Jutting angular ridges, then gentle slopes into the sea. They look like stone rivers. That's steam spurting up on the rise. How it roars. Those boatmen take no notice. Now the steam's pink. This is a bizarre place.'

'They're paddle-beating too. It's okay. They are in a good mood,' Ugruk said as another blast split Oiwa's ears.

'How did we get so close, so quickly?' he wondered. I must have been dreaming again. That mountain looks bigger and darker, even at this distance. This water smells pungent. It's gone red, like thinned blood. The air's heavy. That's another blast. I was nearly ready for that one. There's more canoes now.'

'They've raised their paddles. You two, get ready to rub the Ormer's nose with their canoes,' Ugruk advised. 'They'll circle us first to check.'

'I'm coming aboard,' Long Spoot shouted, straddling the Ormer's prow. 'Where's your nose-spike, Sharpened Tooth?' he asked as he gripped his shoulders.

'Swallowed by Ungrinn,' he replied. 'It choked him to death.'

'What's that scar on your cheek?'

'Ungrinn's loving kiss.'

'Then we'll take you to Lava's Kiss,' said Long Spoot, rubbing his nose welcomingly on Sharpened Tooth's. 'Who's this young body?'

'Oiwa of No Words, Bear Killer, Demon Slaughterer, Goose Shaman... Potent Adventurer,' Sharpened Tooth told him.

'No? Too slight and flimsy,' Long Spoot sneered, as other craft joined them.

'I know what he's saying. I'll show him,' Oiwa said to himself. 'I'll untoggle my Albatross weather-top and pull it from my chest.'

'I don't believe it!' Long Spoot spluttered. 'A Bear Killer's necklace complete with agate ensign between the fangs. I'm sorry for mocking you, Bear Killer.'

'Yup... Thanks. The whole flotilla's cheering now. I seem to have made my mark,' Oiwa summed up, beaming with delight. 'They are wonderful canoes,' he considered as they bobbed on the strange water. 'Beautiful leather and splendid sea beasts decorating them. Their paddles are magnificent, too. Fantastically carved handles and sculpted blades, all cut from shining bone with lively engraved legend scenes. I wonder what they are?'

'Follow us, welcome visitors,' Long Spoot's echoing voice said as he leapt back into his canoe.

'Hmmm... Good, I can make his accent out,' Oiwa was pleased to note.

'That's Cove with Long Spoot,' Sharpened Tooth explained.

'Yes,' Oiwa registered. 'Their boat's crossing other coloured currents in these calmer waters. They seem to lick the small black islands of the fjord. There are houses on some. Steam's jetting from another. Long Spoot's not bothered. He's seen it before. His craft's interesting, though. Those wavy fronds that decorate it enwrap the sides. I wonder what they mean? What are those skin-roofed houses like inside? It does look peaceful here. They sing well when paddling. It sounds like a song of the deep. That's a writhing monster they mention. Could it be Ungrinn?'

'Phew, it's warm. I wish I had bare arms like them. That smell wafts about still... Rather like an Ungrinn fart. I don't expect they smell it any more. This is an ominous place, though. That Smoking Mountain far up the fjord looks threatening. The seaway is narrowing. The currents are stronger here. It's harder paddling, too.'

'Marvellous isn't it?' he heard Ugruk say.

'Yes,' Oiwa thought, 'but I feel uneasy. Aaahh!' He yelped as an immense steam jet screamed violently upwards on the skyline.

'Hear that?' Sharpened Tooth said shocked. 'I nearly dropped my paddle.'

'Cove and his band aren't bothered. It's normal to them. We'll get used to it while we're here I expect,' stated Ugruk shakily .

'It's wonderful how high it goes. Look at it change colour as the sunlight hits. There's a rainbow forming while it fades. Amazing,' Sharpened Tooth commented. 'I'd quite forgotten it. And you too, Ugruk, by looks.'

'Yes. And watch where you're not paddling. We head that way. Follow,' Ugruk urged, covering his embarrassment.

'That's Dargon's Dick charging off, Oiwa. He's meant to mate with the Great Narwhal. She refuses to go with him until the Dark

Season. Hence the horrible scream,' Sharpened Tooth said in Albatross.

'I understood every word of that. I could speak it if I could speak, so to speak,' he pondered lightly. 'Paddle on, Oiwa,' he told himself.

'The seaway is opening out again. Hot Ponds is up there,' Ugruk said, pointing. 'See the steam rising, Oiwa? Look at the warm stream running from them to vanish underground.

'Red Mud Marsh,' Sharpened Tooth announced as they passed a reedbed.

'Lava's Kiss,' Cove called from his stern before disappearing round a rugged promontory.

'Killer whales!' Ugruk warned as they rocked in their sudden wake. 'Follow Cove. Keep out of their way.'

'There's Lava's Kiss, Oiwa,' Sharpened Tooth pointed out. 'It's on that undulating pumice slope. See it dipping into the sea?'

'Yes, I see,' he answered in mind.

'The water is as clear as sky. Look down. See the rocks like waves below.'

'That's right,' Oiwa thought, peering down. 'What's that huge thing? It's not an orca. It's odd: like the decorations on Long Spoot's canoe. There goes another; now a horn blast. Bump. We are there.'

'Pull your kayak up to one of our carved nousts,' Cove called.

'Okay,' answered Ugruk.

'The rock looks sculpted with those weird curly fronds, like on Long Spoot's canoe. Lovely to be on dry land, though,' thought Oiwa.

'Welcome. Greetings,' Long Spoot said as his wives and family gathered on the slipway. 'I shall take you to Summer Fox. Follow.'

'He's still alive, then,' Sharpened Tooth remarked to Ugruk.

'Must be. Let's go.'

'My feet are sweating in these boots,' Oiwa realized as he scaled the pumice incline. 'The hammered steps grip well,' he summed up while passing the honey-scented saxifrage lining their way. Willows, covered in hoverflies, clung in fertile clefts. Bog cotton shimmered on a distant terrace.

'What's that tug?' Oiwa thought, swivelling around when excited children pulled at his clothes.

'Bear Killer. No Words. Demon Slaughterer,' they sang out, mobbing him.

'Goose Shaman, Potent Venturer,' girls screeched as he scaled the steps, to the amusement of Long Spoot's entourage. 'That's enough!' the mothers chided, 'Get off our guest.' They fell back, giggling gleefully as Oiwa straightened his necklace and smoothed his moustache, losing a bead. 'Got it,' a kid yelled, escaping with the trophy.

'This is good,' Oiwa felt, enjoying the attention. 'That must be Summer Fox,' Oiwa deduced as the trio mounted the last steps. He stood on a terrace beside the tufa jambs of his doorway. 'Are they hewn from the lava, or formed naturally?' Oiwa wondered. Summer Fox scratched his bare back on the abrasive surface.

'Welcome, brave visitors: enter,' he invited. A circle of musk ox skulls bounded his house. Sea plantains grew profusely from their eye sockets. Sedges partially obscured others. Summer Fox held out his bone and horn-bangled arms. He had short, dark hair, a thin moustache and, like many of his kin, virtually no beard. Ivory hoops swung from his leathery ears. He wore only a loin wrap of fine hide with bone-threaded tassels dangling down his thighs.

From within, his wives slowly appeared. They, too, were dressed for the heat of their house. Their long, black hair streaked over their shoulders and round their breasts.

'Welcome back, Ugruk and Sharpened Tooth,' Summer Fox greeted.

'May we present Oiwa, of the Goose Clan?' asked Sharpened Tooth.

'I'd better bow my head in respect,' he decided, whilst the youngsters recited his titles in chorus.

'Come forward, young man,' he beckoned. 'Your necklace is exceptionally fine. Does it match your deeds?' Summer Fox enquired.

Oiwa nodded once, meekly.

'Your earplugs are of fine workmanship,' he deduced. 'Come in. Duck under my portal. Eat. Tell me your news.'

'This crowded room is lined with wonderfully shining pelts,' Oiwa saw. 'They glimmer in the light through the bladder skin roof. There's inviting alcoves showing through fur hangings.'

Everyone sat cross-legged, listening to Sharpened Tooth's news. 'My parents and Clan send greetings to you all,' he said, tugging inside his tunic. 'This poorly made harpoon point is for you, Summer Fox. It is a small token of the Albatross's respect.'

'I thank you,' he respectfully remarked, admiring the symbolic ivory gift. 'It's sharp, too,' he added piercing his palm in a ritual test. 'Now, tell me of this young man called Oiwa, this youth of no words, with a hero's titles? He intrigues me,' he asked, licking the blood away.

'This gets more amazing every time I hear it,' Oiwa noticed as he crouched among the company, listening to Sharpened Tooth's version.

'Stuffed roast lemmings,' one of Summer Fox's wives announced.

'I'll pass them round,' another said. 'Bear Killer first,' she added.

'Drinking horns,' Oiwa heard, as he tasted his succulent rodent with relish.

'Plovers,' a son said as he passed the skewered birds about.

'This floor's really warm,' Oiwa noticed. 'There's no fire, just grease lamps. It's so strange to feel such heat. I'm taking my jacket off. I see Sharpened Tooth and Ugruk doffing theirs. Nobody's wearing much, anyway.'

'Now you're showing off your necklace again, Oiwa, I'll tell the tale of your bear kill. You can act it,' said Ugruk.

'Okay,' Oiwa thought in mischief, 'I'll exaggerate shitting after the battle and the pissing in its ears.'

'Show them your Albatross tattoo scars,' Sharpened Tooth suggested, after many encores. 'Only the greatest of men get them, like me and, ages past, Weir. Oiwa bred among us. Long may his line continue! May his journey be epic. May his deeds become legend.'

'Indeed,' applauded Summer Fox, to Oiwa's pleasure. 'His splendid initiation marks are like scales on the bird's leg. May he forever live up to the honour.'

To Oiwa's continued amazement, ecstatic applause, tongue clicking and whistling erupted. 'I'm lost for words,' he thought, 'Even if I could speak, I wouldn't be able. This is wonderful. I'm so happy.'

He squatted, sucking the moist flesh from the lemmings' fine bones. The plover's skeleton already lay in a neat pile beside him.

'Try this, brave Oiwa,' a voice said from behind as meat steamed on a seal's scapula. 'Musk cheeks,' she explained, 'a hero's delicacy. Eat. They are wonderful. I'm Taiga,' she told him as she crouched next to him and fingered his necklace. Her long, dark hair shone in a shaft of light from the doorway. 'We can take it outside, if you like.'

'Why not?' Oiwa indicated with pleasure, following her into the bright sunlight. Shading his eyes, he stared at Taiga as she cast his bird bones to a large furry dog. They snapped in its jaws like dead twigs. 'Here,' he beckoned, as he flung it the lemming skeleton.

'Let's sit on a musk skull,' she suggested. By the slope of pumice, tiny plants found anchorage in the minute holes. It looked busy, with hunting equipment being mended or made. Hides stretched on pegs and frames were abundant. Large whalebones lay piled, some being cut for canoe frames. The activity seemed excessive. Oiwa pointed to it all questioningly.

'We are getting ready to move,' Taiga answered, taking some meat.

'How your face glows in the sunlight. Your turned up nose is so pretty, too,' Oiwa wanted to say as he reached out and stroked it.

She laughed saying, 'The skin on your legs is remarkable,' making her own little tribal cuts dance enticingly on her cheek.

Oiwa wiggled his toes and took meat from the rounded bone.

'It didn't hurt a bit,' he would have said, but shrugged, imagining, 'Even if it was pure agony, it would have been worth it just for you to enjoy. I'll roll my thigh so she can see more of the minute cuts.'

That steaming roar startled Oiwa again. 'Dargon's Dick,' Taiga mentioned. 'It's getting more powerful. You will have noticed it as you paddled in.'

Oiwa nodded in wonder. 'I can't understand all she says, but I get the gist.'

'The elders say we have to move because of the mountain. Our grandmothers won't leave. They say that they can die here as easy or as hard as anywhere else.'

'That stinks,' Oiwa reacted, as an acrid smell drifted past when the geyser's power faded.

'There's been tremors in the ground, too: a sure sign, so Summer Fox tells us. Reeking Mountain is going to do something dangerous. Look up at its rising vapours. It's been like that all my life, but more now,' Taiga remarked.

'How long is that,' Oiwa imagined, as he watched her lips move. 'Longer or shorter than me? Maybe just a little longer?'

'But last year a fissure appeared. White-hot lava spewed rapidly down the slope. It hissed in the sea and set solid. Fish died in the bay. All the seals left. The Narwhals gathered and swam past,' she said, pointing down to the shore below. Their great long tusks stuck out of the sea. It was marvellous to watch. Here, have more meat. These cheeks from the cooking ponds are brilliant.'

'What's cooking ponds?' he wondered.

'Summer Fox says, 'If the Musk Oxen go, we go. That's his law. They really know when there will be danger.' But we should leave well before the ice and the Long Dark return, anyway.

'You look so tired, now, Oiwa. Come back inside. You can sleep. I shall show you round when you're ready,' she suggested when he yawned widely.

He finished the meat, licked his fingers and tickled her nose. She blinked and smiled, then he followed her back to Summer Fox and his companions. She showed him to a small skin drape covering an alcove. He crawled through, curled up in a heap of woolly furs and slumbered deeply.

When Oiwa woke, Taiga was next to him. Several youngsters were curled up, too. 'There's barely room to shift my arm. I need to pee,' he thought, struggling up to crawl through the floppy membrane to the main room. Ugruk was outside with Sharpened Tooth. They pointed downhill to where the ridge of pumice dropped to the sea.

'That's a toilet,' they indicated. 'You can do it over the side. There's a warm stream to wash in after.'

On Oiwa's return Summer Fox, wearing a fine jacket and leggings, came back from the hill above with Long Spoot and Cove. 'Oiwa, Bear Killer, I will speak to you of Weir,' he shouted. 'Follow us. Ugruk and Sharpened Tooth come too.' Dargon's Dick exploded again in the distance. A warm breeze blew from Reeking Mountain. The odour of a bad egg wafted past. They climbed the long pumice pathway. Eventually, they came to an extended ridge like the backbone of a great whale. From there they saw far along each coast. The fresh, pure air moved faster, being pressed over the spiny ridge. Summer Fox pointed southwest along a rugged coastline. 'That is the way you came. See again the vast swathes of pasture, lakes and marshlands. The mountains bearing snow and ice sweep down to grazing musk. Our shining river runs below to the wide ocean: Rocky islands jut, like those of Ungrinn and his fearsome pools. But that way,' he said turning and touching Oiwa's shoulder, 'is your way. You will have to go northeast for a long time.

Follow the coast. Then, if the currents are kind, you can drift across many waters to another land of ice. Beyond that, in the far distance, is the Black Isle. It sticks out high above the sea.'

Oiwa, straining his eyes to the horizon, wondered if he could look past it. 'Have I flown over it in my Goose form?' he asked himself, 'I can't quite remember.'

'That is your route if you are to follow Weir,' he explained.

'It's a horrendous distance,' he thought cringing. 'But the way I've come has already been long. So why should it matter how far a dark mark in the ocean is?' he summed up proudly.

'Black Isle is the Last Place,' Summer Fox said to Oiwa as he peered again in the direction of the invisible outcrop. 'If you go past it into the sea, only the Geese know where the end of travel is. Only the whales and auks; only the Great Albatross knows; only Long Hands of the Deep understands the distance. No man has come back from over that horizon. Not Weir: not Snaigul before him, nor Rannun, who was the very bravest of ancient adventurers.'

'Weir's name again. I feel exhilarated, but chilled by the others: the lost ones. I want to hear more of him. But all I can do is stare to the distance, wondering.'

'This way,' Summer Fox indicated, walking ahead down the spine. The rock levelled, broadening like a great head. The stone slope fell away. They stood on a promontory above a sweeping drop.

'That's Geese I hear,' thought Oiwa, cocking his ear, 'They are on the marshes below. It's like Solan's Land. It gives me strength. There's the Musk herd by the river. They taste so good. It makes me hungry again.'

'Watch this,' Summer Fox said. 'See that small hole in the rock?'

'Aye,' the trio indicated.

'Cove, put my cap over it. Now watch,' he said as Cove chanted deeply from the depths of his soul.

'The rock's trembling beneath my feet,' Oiwa felt. 'There's his hat. It's flown up into the air. It's incredible!'

'The Whale spouts,' Summer Fox announced. 'He invites us below. Follow Cove down the drop by the Whale's cheeks.' They rounded a bend on a narrow path arriving at a gaping cave. Come in; see our history carved on these whale bones.'

'There's rows of them,' Oiwa observed, 'all gleaming yellow.'

'Here are the records of our times. They are very long. They are very detailed. This is where I will stay when Reeking Mountain bursts open. By then you will all be long gone. But for now I will show you the history of Weir. Cove, bring me the rib.'

'It's beautifully polished. The whole length decorated with engraved pictures,' Oiwa and his friends saw.

'This circle of triangles is your Goose Clan's camp. Here is your river. Oiwa, trace its zigzags with your finger.'

'That's Gunnal!' Oiwa realized with a shudder. 'The Dun disappears inside that huge woman. I see it all. Between her legs are tiny images, like tattoos, but they are the cliff paintings. Inside her there are red spirals. This is where we went. And Weir too. There's the Dun gushing from Gunnal's mouth into Wolf Lake. That's a black wolf etched in the water. Further on, lands of trees. They've gone now,' he remarked to himself. 'I want to read it out loud, but I can't! My tongue's hardened. My throat is like a rock. My head reels in the cave's heat.'

Sharpened Tooth grabbed Oiwa, 'Steady now. Are you all right?'

'Yes,' Oiwa nodded and read on. 'Men's bones. That's the Bald Heads. There's Solan: he's huge. And the little skeins of stars are his kin. Here are fish, walrus, seals and sea. I was there,' he wanted to say as his companions read it.

'The yellow dots are Weir's children,' Summer Fox explained. 'It is all written in this cave.'

'That's Reeking Mountain,' Oiwa knew, 'There's three yellow dots; more of Weir's offspring. What are the two red ones?' he asked himself tugging his beard. 'Then, there's this black square with white circles and spikes around it?'

'The Black Isle,' Cove explained. 'The story goes that Weir arrived there. On that place lived a wild Hag called Skullar. She had nine ugly daughters and no sons. She ate fish and narwhals. Nobody knows how she conceived these daughters – some say it was Long Hands from the Deep.' Oiwa was intrigued, but fearful. 'Weir landed there. She wanted to mate with a human and have a boy to make her spirit line last.' Ugruk and Sharpened Tooth were all ears. 'Weir would not mate with her. He refused. Her daughters grabbed him, took him into a cave and bound him with sinews, but he sang to them and promised them many wonderful things if only they would go to sleep. As they slept, he turned himself into a goose, leaving his bindings in a heap.'

'What happened then?' Ugruk asked. 'Outside in the light he

became a man again. He had just paddled away from Skullar's island when she spotted him. In rage she hurled one of her precious narwhal tusks. It stuck in his arm. He pulled it out and hurled it back. It shattered at her feet. Then a great flock of geese flew down to him and a mist gathered around. That was the last ever seen of him. That is the story of Weir.'

Oiwa wiped his sweating brow. Cove replaced the bone next to a newly carved one and took it up. 'This is your rib, Oiwa. Look, all of you. The trail is similar. Those brown marks show where Oiwa might have successfully mated.'

'I'm blushing,' Oiwa realized as Ugruk watched his expressive face.

'We made it while you slept,' Cove said. 'Your trek was like Weir's. After the bones is Solan. See the lozenge? Your dead bear's on it, with Ziit.'

'This is where we are now,' Oiwa deciphered, 'the Musk Ox, Reeking Mountain, but who's that red Giant? Oh no! It's me. There's Ziit again and his arrows in black and my necklace in green. What's that clear dot doing at my waist?' he questioned.

50

Hot Ponds

Oiwa climbed down from the rocky heights, watching the preparations. Taiga awaited him. A new sea-going canoe was launched. Equipment was packed in neat bundles for a swift exit. Reeking Mountain had the daunting drift of vapours emitting from her top.

A pair of freshly dead goslings swung from Taiga's hands. 'Would you pluck them with me?' she asked.

'Yes,' he nodded eagerly. 'After all, they aren't actually Whale Geese. How fast they grow, after only being hatched so short ago.'

'We are going up to Hot Ponds.'

'Good,' he thought, watching her streak ahead. 'Look at her rhythm. How those goslings swing with her pace. I must catch up.'

'I love the rattle of his necklace,' Taiga thought as he strode.

'I'll carry them,' he signed when he caught up.

'It's all right, Oiwa, I go best loaded,' she remarked with a smile.

'That's so funny,' he felt, wanting to laugh.

'My feet feel good on this terrace pathway. It's the warm water oozing from the ledge at our side. How lush those ferns look growing from the crevices. That's Dargon's Dick blowing off far ahead. It doesn't seem to bother me now.'

'Nearly there,' Taiga said as she pointed to a small rounded pool. 'It's our plucking pond.'

'I wondered why we'd been so far just to pluck a couple of birds.'

'If we leave them in there for a while they'll pluck much more easily.'

'Hmmm. Yes,' Oiwa smiled, looking around. 'Indeed, there's bedraggled feathers everywhere.'

'Let's go through the bog cotton to the edge,' Taiga suggested, taking his hand. 'We can look down and maybe see the narwhals.'

'Great,' Oiwa signed. 'This warm mud between my toes feels brilliant.'

'Look at all the butterflies, Oiwa.'

'Yes,' he thought, seeing the blue hosts rising from the marsh grasses. 'There are stacks of crickets and wee grasshoppers leaping about, too.'

'I love the sound of our feet squelching,' Taiga laughed as they reached the edge. There the rock sloped upward, keeping the warm marsh in place. 'See how the red ooze seeps down. The blood of Lava's Kiss,' remarked Taiga as she bent and dipped a finger in the scarlet morass. 'Right down there is Red Mud Marsh.'

'Yes, we saw that on the way in. It looks much bigger from up here. Good hunting down there in the iris beds. Aha, there are two hunters crouching like frogs, ready to spring. And beyond, the changing colours of the calm waters. That red current?' Oiwa pointed to with a question furrowing his brow.

'That is the blood of the Great Narwhal called Sannen. She bleeds from her womb until the ice returns. That is when Dargon can dive to her depths through an ice hole, melted with his urine. Then he mates with her. In Lava's Kiss we can hear it in the darkness of No Sun,' she told him, realizing her own desire to mate with him. She turned, looked into his hazel eyes as he gazed back. She kissed him. As Oiwa pressed forward, she coyly moved back in the mire. She placed her reddened finger on to the tip of his nose, then stroked it down to his moist bottom lip and wiped it over his chin into his soft beard. 'Come on. We must pluck those goslings before they are cooked,' she said as she turned and trudged back through the muddy ooze. Oiwa, thoroughly excited, squelched behind.

'Plucking has never been so easy,' Oiwa thought as the warm water ran down his Albatross markings.

'Come Oiwa, bring your bird. We can wash all this down and mud off at Hot Ponds,' Taiga suggested, dashing off.

'How beautifully she moves,' Oiwa thought again. 'That naked gosling swinging and bouncing with her is a delight. She's vanished round the bluff. I'd better catch up.' He ran, gosling dangling, necklace beating, following the well-worn track. 'That's her muddy red footprints. They'll fade, but she'll be easy to follow. There she goes, off the track; running into the sunlight; leaping from boulder to boulder. Now she's stopped. That's a vast, steaming pool behind her. How it shines golden in the sunlight. I have to stop. I'll just look at her sheer beauty in that shining vista by the rocky cliff.

She's bending to put her gosling down. Now she's taking off her clothes. Oh, how her lovely breasts shimmer in that light. She's turned to look at me. I can't believe what I'm seeing. I want to love with her. Now she stands so tall and dives in to the misty lake. Quick, Oiwa, get there,' he yelled to himself, hearing the splash.

'Her ripples are still moving,' he spotted after hurtling rock to rock. 'I've got to get in there,' he knew desperately as he pulled his clothes away. 'There, gosling, lie with your friend. You won't be mating, though.'

'Leave your necklace on, Oiwa,' Taiga called from the rising mists, 'I want to feel it pressing on me.'

He dived, feeling the warm, deep waters engulf him. Surfacing, he spotted Taiga swimming gracefully to the pool's edge. 'The mists are parting and swirling around her. Now enfolding her as I swim. This is glorious. Now she's in bright sunshine again under the cliff.

'This is wonderful. Hot currents rise from below all around me. My skin tingles in the warmth. I'm so close. She's standing waist deep within rising vapours. I'm coming, Taiga,' he urged himself, watching her dark crotch as his feet touched the pool's smooth bed. 'I will wade now and hold her tight. What!' he gurgled, sinking suddenly as his footing dropped, 'I'm underwater. It tastes ashy, but so warm. My necklace has gone! Quick, grab it,' he screamed inside as he saw it glint, sinking in the murk. His erection, which had steered him like a prow, collapsed. 'Got it. Now surface and swim. There's Taiga, grinning. She knows these waters. Solid rock again. I will be more careful,' he stressed, putting his trophy back over his head.

Taiga ogled his silhouette, backed by the sun.

'Her laugh is lovely,' Oiwa realized while he waded the few steps to her, turning to avoid a sharp rock.

'There's his hard penis catching the light above the ripples,' Taiga noticed, as they looked at each other in the warm bliss. 'I will go to him now. Let him take me. He's holding me. I feel his tough body: Those fangs between my breasts. Now his tip inching between my legs. How he holds me as he enters: gently, slowly.'

'I can't believe this feeling,' Oiwa told himself as his penis delved through her hairs, meeting the wet warmth within her. 'Why is this so beautiful?' he wondered, as they swayed in the ripples together.

'It's as though he raises me on those hips,' Taiga felt. 'Now he's much deeper. His pressure inside lifts me.'

'My man's pushing something. Oh! It's broken. I've gone through. She's so hot around me. Deeper up I go. I'm lifting her on me as I hold her. Hold still. There's a dark sensation growling in the depths of my belly.

'I'm glowing inside,' Taiga wanted to tell him. 'He's where no other has been. Fill me with life, Oiwa,' Taiga whispered in a tremble as he leaned back, looking deeply into her eyes.

'Yes. I will. This moment. Now,' he answered within as he shook, beginning to come. They trembled together. Oiwa felt Taiga's legs gripping round his waist while she, too, moved in joy at their tryst, taking him in rapture.

'Time has stopped,' Oiwa imagined as he continued mating. He closed his eyes, feeling lost in her full embrace as his hips jerked. His hands moved instinctively, supporting Taiga's beautiful buttocks that clenched in spasms over him.

There he stood, ejaculating.

A linnet sang as Taiga moaned in ecstasy, clinging to her mute mate. Holding him. Feeling his man's work completing its task.

Oiwa felt her let go her embrace around his neck. He watched her lay back onto the water. He looked down to where his amber hairs entwined with her bright jet curls. Oiwa moved, encouraging his final beat of sperm to the buzz of a blue dragonfly among the overhanging ferns. There they remained united. Taiga's long black hair drifted in the dark, steaming water. 'He looks so beautiful,' she thought as Oiwa gazed back down at her.

Oiwa moved back slightly. He felt a new pressure on his phallus. The sensation of intense pleasure returning, he pushed forward. 'I'm overcome by this gliding movement,' he knew.

'He's mating again. It's wonderful. Do; do, do, Oiwa,' Taiga expressed as sheer ecstasy radiated from Oiwa's face. His Star shone through a glow of perspiration as he delivered his flowing seed once more. The dragonfly settled on Oiwa's shoulder and preened. Salts crystallized on his skin as Oiwa leaned looking down to where their bodies joined. Blood coloured the lapping water to disperse in eddies of a gently rising spring.

'Parting is such sweet sorrow,' Oiwa thought as he moved gracefully from their rapture. Taiga stood. They kissed lovingly as he softened in the sunlight. Time stopped. Their reflections rippled beneath midges rising in tiny spirals.

Taiga was first to move. 'Let's swim,' she suggested.

Oiwa's muscles glowed as he followed. Admiring her beauty, he shook inside, watching where he had been.

'Fuck it!' Taiga yelled from the bank, 'Blasted foxes. They've swiped the goslings. There are their footmarks. I'll skin them alive if I catch them,' she threatened.

'It was well worth it,' Oiwa wanted to console as he climbed from the pool. 'Cramp,' he suddenly experienced again, gritting his teeth as he hobbled to dress.

After some days and several matings up at Hot Ponds, Ugruk and Sharpened Tooth announced, 'We have to get the Ormer ready and return. Summer Fox is evacuating some of his people with us.'

'Be careful of Ungrinn's hungry guts,' Oiwa signed.

'First, we have farewell feast,' Sharpened Tooth said. 'Summer Fox arrange it.

At its height, Summer Fox said to Sharpened Tooth, 'Here, a special new nose-spike for you. It's notched in the middle. Push it in. The gristle will click nicely in the groove. It won't fall out so quick.'

'Marvellous,' he responded, grinning widely, snapping it in.

'For you,' Summer Fox said to Ugruk, 'Lovely obsidian from Reeking Mountain. Please press really sharp blades to slit Ungrinn's throat.'

'I'll be sad to see them go,' Oiwa knew, 'but I have my journey.'

When the flotilla of five boats disappeared from Lava's Kiss, Reeking Mountain growled.

'Come with me, Oiwa,' Taiga urged, 'I want to show you the mountain's foot.' It rumbled in the distance; increasing its reek. 'It's okay. I've been there lots in Foam Fighter,' she reassured, grabbing his hand as they ran to her canoe. 'Take this paddle,' she said flinging one at him as he clambered into the moored craft.

'Taiga is powerful,' Oiwa summed up as she pulled on her paddle. 'I'd better get into her rhythm quickly.'

'This could be my last visit,' she yelled back. 'We can see the lava kissing the water. It's marvellous.'

'What on Earth will it be like?' he asked himself as the fjord narrowed. 'There it rumbles again. I can smell the sulphur. Reeking Mountain seemed distant. Now it feels ominously close. It's pulling us nearer.'

'The valley turns further up there, Oiwa,' Taiga shouted much later, over the rumble. 'Stop paddling. Foam Fighter will glide round.'

'The sides are really steep. Like worn cliffs,' Oiwa thought as the chasm darkened. 'It resembles Gunnal's Vulva!'

'It's getting hotter,' Taiga reported. 'We'll soon see it. You wait, it's wonderful.'

'Holy Gods!' Oiwa inwardly remarked, when he saw. 'It's so high, rising from the widening waters to its distant summit. She's paddling again: slowly; carefully. So will I. It's hissing up there; now a scream and the smell of scorching rock. For Gunnal's sake! That's molten rock flowing down to the water. Taiga's going closer: please, no.'

'Don't worry, Oiwa,' she said, reading his fear, 'I know this place. See that shining pinnacle?'

Oiwa nodded in wonder at the brilliant, glassy obelisk.

'Get out your axe. Use its butt to knock a hunk off. That's our bladestone. We can take a lump with us.'

One swing knapped the top fistful free.

'Look at the hot, foamy suds floating towards us like icebergs. Stand with me. Hold me. Watch.'

'It's terrible,' Oiwa wanted to yell. 'That slick of lava is about to join the water.'

'There it goes. See it boil. The steam's hidden the lava, but still it glows pink, like pulsing flesh. Doesn't it make you want to mate?'

Oiwa nodded, his head on her shoulder, watching as the Foam Fighter bobbed on the chumbling water, thinking, 'Yes, but it's too dangerous. The lava's like a gigantic red-hot slug slewing down, shining even from below. We should go. I smell the salt, sulphur and the very air burning. It whistles and crackles as it cools then it bursts hot again. This could choke us. We mate later,' he promised himself.

'Not now, though. This is as far as we dare go,' Oiwa was pleased to hear her say. To the noise of the marine cauldron, she back-paddled from the gushing steam. The mount grumbled above. The water heaved below when she turned her canoe. 'Paddle fast, Oiwa. We must get out of here, quick! I wanted to show you the magic of our obsidian forming, but not today.'

'That's an explosion above!' Oiwa heard, quaking as they paddled.

'Hurry. Get around the bend,' Taiga yelled as the sea rose rapidly.

'That's more lava descending,' Oiwa knew from the sound.

'Faster, before that hits the water,' she commanded as the Foam Fighter's stern jerked up alarmingly.

'It's throwing us forward,' Oiwa realized as they sped awkwardly around the turn. 'She's handling her craft expertly. She's done this before,' he reckoned over the tumult of boiling ocean behind.

'Ride the wave. Ride it; ride it,' she demanded, turning to Oiwa in encouragement. 'There will be more. Hear those eruptions up there?'

'Yes, only too well,' Oiwa knew, pointing up to a tottering tooth of rock.

'It's collapsing! Paddle!' Taiga shouted as it tumbled behind them. 'Ride the new wave,' she repeated loudly when the rock disappeared below.

'Don't worry, I will,' he thought crazily as they were ejected into wider water of the opening fjord.

'Fuck! Look, Oiwa,' Taiga yelled. 'The sky's filling in. Paddle before it rains burning rocks on us.'

'I am, my dear,' he responded inside with gritted teeth.

'The water's calmer now in the broad channel. I knew it would be. That was quite something, wasn't it Oiwa?' she said glancing back into his eyes.

'Nod and smile,' he thought, 'whilst she laughs at our danger.'

'The sky's clearing. But it isn't over. Keep up the pace,' she urged, whilst grinning at his expression. 'What's up?' she demanded when his eyes suddenly bulged in horror.

'Behind you!' Oiwa pointed over her shoulder.

'Long Hands!' she screamed in awe and terror.

'It's huge. I've never seen the like. Those terrible coils, writhing in the turbulence: that vast eye focusing on us: the cruel, gnashing beak. There's its other eye, bleeding and burnt. The creature's as big as a tall pine, but pulsating, convulsing. I saw it dart beneath when we arrived. Those are the tentacles they paint on their boats, the carvings at the steps. They knew all along. Nobody said. Maybe they were too afraid. My Holy Gods! That dark liquid it jets out, fearsome, like smoke. Now its vile arms squirm in the air. Wow! It's vanished; gone. I feel sick. Where to now?'

'Long Hands is leaving!' Taiga said urgently, 'If she goes, will her children follow? Look: knots of writhing arms ahead. See, Oiwa, where the seabirds screech and circle. Did you feel that?' she asked, as the Foam Fighter lurched on something rasping beneath.

Oiwa nodded, eyes fixed on a great bulging head, like a vast inflated bladder breaking the surface ahead. Such horror he felt, as it inked the green sea black and vanished.

'They're leaving. Her whole clan's escaping,' Taiga announced powerfully. 'We must follow.'

That is when Reeking Mountain spoke. An explosion from her summit said it all. The sky darkened. Heat blasted their necks. Their canoe lurched forward. Their writhing company sped. 'Run for it!' Taiga shouted.

The water in the inlet rocked. The seismic wave forced them forward. 'Look, Oiwa. Narwhals; narwhals,' she gasped, 'See their twisted spears jutting from the billows. They are chasing the Krakens. Watch them leaping like porpoises. Paddle, paddle, paddle.'

'The whole inlet's full of escaping life,' Oiwa could see. 'There's seals, walrus, an otter. That's killer whales breaking the surface. There go the musk ox, thundering along the cliff towards Lava's Kiss. This must be the end. I can even smell them as wave upon wave of them pass.'

'The billow's slackened. Paddle more. The fjord's wider. Make speed. There's more Long Hands ahead. The sky's clearing: the wind's changed. It's being sucked to Reeking Mountain. Paddle hard against it.'

'Look,' Oiwa wanted to say, 'There are vast bubbles rising. What a stink! Now fish, belly-up on the surface. Poor sods.'

'Oiwa, there's a Long Hands. I'm sure it's dead. See, it's shrouded in strange seaweed. Mud from the bottom has floated up, too. Watch it break up and sink again.'

'Yes, the creature's beak's open. Its coloured tentacles just weave aimlessly around in the smelly morass. Paddle on,' he thought determinedly.

'There's another, Oiwa! Boiled out of its deep lair, I expect. But others will have survived. Watch. That's distant Dargon blowing off. He seems far more powerful, even from here. The wind's taking its hot spray to us; we will feel it soon,' she said as Oiwa pointed forward. 'Ah. I thought so. Everyone's leaving. Quick, Oiwa, faster if we can!' she said as another wave chased, billowing them towards the human clamour. 'Let's hurry for Lava's Kiss and get our stuff.'

'No,' Oiwa indicated. 'Leave it. It's too dangerous. We must escape.'

'Don't go ashore,' Cove shouted from his canoe. 'We have everything. Follow us.'

'One last look,' Taiga said, scanning the rising land. 'Summer Fox is going up to Whale Cave. He's not leaving, nor the elders. He's got a long bone. What's he going to carve on that?'

'Maybe the final moments of their ancestral home,' Oiwa thought.

'Raft up, Raft up,' Long Spoot commanded, uttering furiously, 'Keep together,' just before Reeking Mountain's top exploded. Blindingly hot lava skidded down from the open summit. Fissures opened. Tongues of magma swelled from gaping volcanic flues. Fire raged from the new crater. Hot rocks spewed violently up. An underwater eruption filled the arena where Oiwa and Taiga had watched earlier, forcing a boiling wave to hurtle towards them. 'Here we go!' cried out Taiga, as the swell before it lifted Foam Fighter and her clan uncontrollably. Prematurely, Dargon's Dick erupted again. Hot water fell on the escaping flotilla. The spout, higher than ever, did not cease. High on the ridge, where Oiwa and Taiga had enjoyed their mating tryst, Hot Ponds tilted. The shaken water flushed with the red mud. It slid like mashed, steaming liver down to the shaking beach.

Summer Fox never reached his whalebone cache. Nothing was glyphed on the rib. No record of Oiwa's mating. The pathway split. A newborn geyser flung the chief into boiled oblivion.

'Make for open water!' Long Spoot shouted, as Reeking Mountain spewed her hot venom on land, sea and down Long Hands' lairs. 'It's our only chance!'

51

Open Ocean

'I'm leader now,' Long Spoot told himself, 'All depends on me. I have to save us, unlike my father with his dreams and delay. The ash is filling the sky. The sucking wind has changed. Smoking Mountain's choking breath is blowing us to the open sea on this billow of speeding water. The mountain fire grows ever bigger. I daren't look back.

'Paddle. Keep on the crest. Stay together,' he shouted once more, feeling the hot breeze on his neck. 'Sail east,' he commanded.

'East,' everyone responded.

'There we have the Ice Kin to help us.'

'Are you all right, Oiwa?' Taiga asked, looking back.

'Yes,' he nodded, thinking, 'Lucky we didn't stay and mate up that creek. Later: later,' he mused as he watched Taiga working her paddle while they sped along the inlet.

'Hot stone rain,' Cove yelled. 'Cover your heads.'

'Ouch!' Taiga yelped as some hit her hand. 'Paddle faster, Oiwa,' she appealed above yelps of pain from around. 'Chase the light ahead. It's dark with cinder behind,' he heard above the hissing of the hot pellets hitting their wave.

'Keep together,' Long Spoot bellowed. 'The wave takes us. Head east when we reach the open sea.'

'Ah! That cinder got me. Quench it with the bailer,' Oiwa instantly thought. 'There's another in the boat. Drown it. Quick: splash Taiga's back to protect her. Bugger! There's another,' he cursed as he flung water in the craft.

'Keep paddling, Oiwa, we'll beat this burning rain.'

'Yes,' he thought as he watched the cooling pellets bob in the bilge. Others shot below the sea, their glow dying before floating up.

'Keep together,' Long Spoot called.

Among the clamour, Oiwa looked right from the summit of the wave, 'That's where I came from. Now I'm being ejected. Hurled out by Reeking Mountain. But I'm with Taiga. Together we'll survive. We are all chasing life and being chased. Look at the surf trails we're leaving. Bright white in this dark. This force will carry us to safety. Is that a Long Hands ahead? Where are they escaping to?'

'The wave will subside when we hit the sea,' Taiga insisted as they burst from the great inlet. 'That's better, a cold breeze,' she said to Cove's uniting horn call. 'I told you, Oiwa. Calmer, less dangerous; less exciting though.'

'No. It is exciting,' he realized, pointing with his paddle. 'Look,' he wanted to say, 'there's masses of seabirds in an arc over our wave. They are feeding on the dead fish. More are flying in. That's a flotilla of great auks surfing down the slackening wave. Now porpoises and killer whales erupt from the billow. Narwhals too,' he pointed out with his paddle, 'See their tusks sticking out like hunting spears?'

'Yes, Oiwa. The hot rain has stopped too. That's good. Do up your jacket, cover your necklace. It's getting colder,' she said to another long blast of Cove's horn and a whistle from Long Spoot. 'That's the 'Raft up' signal, Oiwa. Let's go.'

'There are lots of us. It's amazing how many. Well, there's safety in numbers,' Oiwa thought as they all nudged together, linking their paddles to each other's boats.

'We'll wait for the stragglers,' Long Spoot announced as the craft scraped together. 'Bear Killer,' he called unexpectedly, 'here's Ziit and his arrows. People, pass them to him,' he said amongst a tumult of cheering. 'Send him his parka too, he'll need it. And there's one for Taiga. We all kenned where you were when the Reeker went.

We were prepared, but you weren't. Cold and warm wind means turbulence. We must stick together, even as we are washed along by this wave. I will sound my horn three times; you all take your shell whistles and blow them thrice in response. Follow my sound. We will not lose each other if we do get separated.'

'My dog whelk's in my pouch,' Taiga said, hunting for it. 'Good, got it. I'll blow across the top. There goes. Your turn, Oiwa,' she nudged, handing it to him.

'Not easy, this,' he thought after his lips tingled with failure.

'Go on. It's simple,' she teased.

'All right,' he nodded blowing again.

'Hooray!' the Clan called at the surprisingly shrill result.

'I'm staggered,' Oiwa thought blowing it repeatedly.

'Stop now. We all know you can do it,' she teased.

'We will take it in turns to paddle on the outside of our raft,' Long Spoot instructed. 'That way, those in the middle get shelter and rest. When it is their turn, I will sound my horn twice and blow my whistle once. We must try to go east, but the strange winds may not allow that. Remember, we are safer together.'

'This wave and weather is taking us further from land,' Taiga said much later as they paddled on the outside.

'Yes,' Oiwa nodded as the breeze buffeted them. 'My star map agrees, but it is in my direction,' he knew, hearing echoing geese in his head.

* * * * *

'Utterly strange dreams,' Shala remarked, yawning after a long sleep. 'Wrasse looks much older, propped up in bed there: face drawn, thinning hair, and deeply veined hands tapping the mattress. But her eyes, flashing like wet pebbles, beckon.'

'Come, sit, Shala. Tell me those dreams.'

'He was in a dark place with a great cone of fire and a force of water. He floated with many others,' she said quietly. 'Someone gave him a long bow. He wore huge polished teeth and claws on his chest. He blew a shell whistle, then vanished.'

Wrasse studied Shala's face, trying to sit higher. 'Let me help you up and lean you on your pillows.'

Her wicker bed creaked as she asked croakily, 'Did he look at you, in this dream?' as she reached to the niche for her horn mug.

'No, Wrasse, he didn't. It's fading now. It seemed so real, yet bizarre,' she answered sadly.

'Dreams are like that,' Wrasse stated as a rumble of wind came from beneath her cover. 'Excuse me,' she said as another bout of flatulence ensued.

'Time to help Wrasse to her toilet,' Shala assessed.

'I want to gather winkles at Lille Sands this morning,' Wrasse suggested. Bees buzzed in a hive deep in the thatch. Pigeons flew noisily from their new loft as she asked, 'Before, though, I'd like cold squab with bannock and honey for breakfast.'

'Jasper's having my old house filled with midden,' she observed while squatting over a bowl under the eaves.

'Yes. It's going to be an allotment for leeks, kale, beans and the like. It's a good idea. Nice and sheltered. There goes Quernstone, with duck feathers for it.'

On the slopes to the Ancestor House, bere, barley, emmer and oats stood tall and green. The breeze waved them in a shimmer like an invisible hand. Sea grass rustled over the dune on their way to the beach.

'Those are strange high clouds. Like long fingers, Wrasse. And the air tastes dusty. Have you noticed?'

'Yes. There's an odd smell. I thought it was me.'

'No. Not now, Wrasse.'

'Something is happening in the world, Shala. I don't know what. But the peculiar clouds come from the west.'

'My amber feels hot on my skin,' she remarked, as she visualized those shining teeth moving next to another's skin, making her shiver inside.

'The lambs are fattening,' Wrasse observed as they nibbled matted sea plantains on their way. 'Do you mind if I sit and you gather, Shala? I'm not feeling so bendy now.'

'No, Wrasse. That's fine.'

'The breeze seems warmer: too warm. The smell has changed. It's like hot stones flung into water.'

'Yes. Maybe giants are bathing somewhere?'

'Ah, my favourite nook overlooking the little bay. There are a couple of trees still here. It seems like ages ago when they floated in.'

'Aye,' Shala replied. 'My redshanks love perching on them. There they go, circling over. I'll pick my way down the sheep tracks.

'She's got a few good mussels, too,' Wrasse saw as Shala shifted among the seaweed, disturbing nibbling sheep. 'Does she really understand what she will have to go through?' Wrasse considered. 'She's changed. She's becoming the young woman who one day should lead her clan and people. Her dreams and visions are true. But is she really aware of their great meaning? As I gaze to the western horizon I feel it more. If Weir had lived, I would have had to share him. She is going to have to share. She is going to have to arrange his breeding with other families to enrich their blood. She will have to make records of whom he successfully mates with. She is going to have to be strong enough to complete this task. It will go on and on. Then there will be the trouble and fights. The men won't like an intruder mating their wives. It has to be, though. It just has to be. I lost my chance. Would even I have managed to be equal to it? I don't know, but she has to be,' she pondered, sighing for herself too. 'Her heart will rend when she makes this breeding for him. She can't have him all to herself. She must mate him with others so our lines can get stronger, more successful.

'There she is, choosing the winkles. Keeping some, discarding others. Just like the females of our land that she will have to select. Pick one, reject two, choose another and cast one away. Yes, she is going to have to be so strong. She will need to deal with her own jealousy, for she will truly love this man. She will yearn for him and want to have him for herself. All this, whilst she puts him to stud among rivals for a true husband, mate and lover. And I might not even be here to guide her.'

'Was that a reflection of a huge goose on the wet sand?' Shala imagined. 'I felt a presence. My morning dream has returned clearly in my head: those fangs, his skin. Wrasse is watching. What is she thinking? This warm air flicks at her hair. How much thinner it looks. Her grass cape just droops over her shoulders. Her face, graven: gnarled like her staff. I can't lose her yet. She has to live. I need her. I need her more than Partan, more than my parents. Our eyes have met... She looks tougher than ever now: her spirit so utterly strong. May she teach me of the power that shines from her eyes!'

* * * * *

Long Spoot's horn sounded shrill. 'Storm coming. Black clouds from Reeking Mountain heading toward us.'

'It's going to rain, Oiwa. Help me with Foam Fighter's covers. Shift, please. They are rolled up in the stern.'

'Sure, Taiga,' he nodded in the darkening swell.

'Fix them at the edges with the toggles. They clip around our waists. It looks like a tempest brewing. See, black rain. It's hurtling down behind us. It will be over us imminently. Hoods up,' Taiga said as the rest of the clan finished securing theirs. Children huddled beneath in the warm along with hunting dogs. Giggles and muffled growls met his ears as the first drops hit.

'Look, Taiga,' Oiwa wanted to say, glancing at his wet hand. 'The rain's all sooty.

'Mountain's reek,' she answered. 'Those black clouds are full of it. It stinks of brimstone.'

'Keep rafted,' Long Spoot shouted urgently, after another blast. 'The sea's rising. Hang on...

Hold on together. In the roughest weather',
he sang loudly.
'*Grip our paddles tight,*
In the ocean's might.'
came the next part of their shanty,
'*Onward we go o-O,*
With the briny flow O.
O'er the next wave's crest...'
Oiwa heard them sing, when the rain lashed loudly around them, turning the black sea white with angry splashing foam.

'We are still heading my way,' Oiwa knew, 'but the distance is still so great.'

'It will be like this for days,' Taiga remarked as Long Spoot signalled a change in the outside paddlers.

'Just like us geese, as we alter order in our skeins,' Oiwa thought yearning to tell her all, while moving to the centre for rest.

Wind blew. Rain pelted. Oft, snow filled the air. Volcanic cloud darkened all.

'There's a Long Hands limb,' someone shouted as it bobbed up.

'So glad it's dead,' Cove called. 'Paddle on, leave it behind. It stinks already.'

'This seems like the Dark Season,' Taiga stated. 'There's the sun, but only a glimmer through the cloud.'

'Yes,' Oiwa thought. 'Summer's gone prematurely. Winter night is here instead. But it will surely clear.'

'Icebergs ahead, Oiwa,' Taiga pointed. 'See them glow in the dim. They will reduce the swell. If it gets really calm, we could mate under the covers,' Taiga whispered. 'I could move back and sit over your lap. Would you like that?'

'Very much,' Oiwa admitted, caressing her thighs with his booted feet.

Long Spoot's horn echoed from the masses of looming ice. 'We can unraft and fish. Keep close. Be ready to raft up as soon as I signal,' he told his company. Oiwa watched another length of dead tentacle drift close.

'Let's go behind that berg, Oiwa. It will look like we are fishing.' Taiga felt Oiwa's excited nudge in the becalmed waters. Unbelting his trousers and baring himself, he felt Taiga slip back over him. He held her shoulders, kissed her neck passionately as the suckered extremity followed in their wake.

'I feel you under me. Lie back a little. I will take you in,' she said gently as she pushed. 'Oh! You're there. This is how we make sure, Oiwa. I want my baby life from you,' she told him as she felt him moving spontaneously.

'Aaaaahh,' Oiwa wanted to say, as he heard Taiga's voice change into a high, trembling note.

'Move again: more.'

He responded, feeling his semen fly to her warm depths. She revolved gently, drawing all she could from his torso. 'She's squeezing me so blissfully. I can't believe how wonderful this is,' Oiwa wondered upon wonder. His head lolled back, rolling to one side. He gazed into the tall ice as Taiga's song of conception returned from her rippled reflection there.

The floating tentacle lengthened. The huge suckers rolled on the surface while Oiwa watched with glazed eyes.

'BLAAAAAAR!' went Long Spoot's horn from over the berg.

Up surged the Long Hand's head. Its huge, bulging eye pulsated at Oiwa. That 'dead' tentacle thrashed.

'Kraken attack!' they heard Long Spoot shout, as they were driven away by the monster's wake.

Taiga sat straight in alarm. The whirling whip of twisting limb shot past her. Oiwa watched helpless, as she whirled from his warm lap. 'Paddle!' she screamed.

'Grab the paddle! Strike!' Oiwa commanded himself. 'Where's my axe,' he thought frantically, with his left leg in cramp. The vile, gnashing beak of the risen monster clacked behind. 'Taiga! Taiga!'

he mouthed voicelessly whilst more appendages flew angrily from the sea.

Taiga's hair gyrated like those threshing arms as she paddled wildly.

'Follow!' was Oiwa's terrified instinct... 'Follow!' he repeated as their stricken flotilla came back into view.

'HELP!' cried an entwined boy from above, while his family's canoe tipped, drowning the parents' wails of horror. Their dog, barking, escaped into the foam. Oiwa saw a thin coil sweep around the hound: her barking ceased: its gnashing not: Below, in the bubbling, reddening water its fangs jagged deeply. The tentacle rose again in pain as it bit. Her premature puppies burst from her womb into the sea below.

'Paddle away. Escape!' was Long Spoot's words, recalling distant legends of these demons of the fathoms.

Cove whistled high and loudly, banging his paddle. Another Kraken rose. Cove's shape, ringed in faded sunlight, showed at his prow in the monster's pulsing eye. Like a rapid uncoiling fern, a suckered limb flashed from beneath the dark water. All witnessed the lash of hard skin whipping him round: its finely pointed end strangling his warnings as he was drawn high above, then plunged deep beneath the waves.

The kayaks dispersed in frenzy. Oiwa and Taiga paddled furiously; Oiwa struck a submerged moving obstacle. 'Long Hands,' he thought bitterly as his guts melted. 'She's pulling hard, harder... I must too,' he resolved, propelling them even faster.

'Get away!' Taiga yelled while a suckered arm flew three men's height above them. It hammered down on the surface, just missing their stern. It slewed beneath, but its momentum pushed a huge, contemptible head from below.

'Its abhorrent beak's colossal,' Oiwa took in, trembling, 'I hear its sides slicing while it gnashes in that terrible, twisting motion. Oh! NO! There's Long Spoot's stern tipping. His canoe is coiled in a crushing limb. He's being dragged below. For the Gods' sakes, it's been flung back high in the air. The twisted wreck is hitting the raging water. Long Spoot's falling. He'll hit that berg! Fuck! His head's split. There's his bleeding skull, tracing a line of bloody brain. Don't look, Taiga,' he wanted so desperately to yell as he saw him slide to a thin twist of snaking tentacle. 'It's taking Long Spoot to its pulsating beak. His skull's crushing again within the might of that mouth. Those eyes still search for further victims. This is hideous. I'm in panic. My arms won't work. Taiga is saving us. Paddle, Oiwa!' he admonished himself as a billow took them and choking cries from the drowning followed them.

'Don't look back,' Taiga shouted. 'Pull; paddle; escape.'

They sped between two shining icebergs. The water stilled. They could only see three of their flotilla. Whistles blew. Echoing voices yelled in alarm. A joint scream from a boat was suddenly cut off. The wreck of a further craft flew over a berg, banging onto the sea before them. A child emerged. Taiga paddled towards her. An unseen whip from deep below caught her ankle. She sank rapidly under, her mouth agape at her fate.

Taiga steered further into the ice floe. All became calm. Blue stripes, alternating with white and brilliant onyx, cut through the ice shapes. These layers of trapped frozen water gave signature to their birth and history. Oiwa and Taiga were not concerned about that. They paddled past the sculpted forms. Their panting breath crystallized into ice dust as they exhaled. Each breath was a cold intake, painfully wrought.

Within the towering mounts they came to a space, like a clearing in a rocky wilderness. The cries and alarm whistles of their companions dwindled.

'Keep absolutely quiet,' Taiga signalled, realizing Long Hands' powers. 'Paddle silently. There's a slanting berg ahead. We'll go gently round it. Whooosh! went the water. 'It's a whale,' she exclaimed. 'A humpback, leaping right in front.'

'The bow wave's forcing us back,' Oiwa realized as the vast animal wrestled.

'There's a Long Hands writhing over its mouth, Oiwa. It's being attacked! The tentacles are stretching down its body. It will leap again. Paddle clear.'

'There's another stricken whale churning behind now,' Oiwa signalled instantly. 'It's washing us back.'

'They aren't concentrating on us,' Taiga said as tentacles undulated over the vast victims.

'No,' Oiwa thought as they hurtled towards the striped berg's cliff.

'Push away from the ice face with the paddle, Oiwa,' Taiga told him as she paddled hard along it.

Leaping again, the whales tried bucking their sucking foes by hurling themselves at the ice as Oiwa and Taiga sped along it.

A Long Hands' twitching tentacles slithered to the humpback's vent hole. Sealed tight as a clam, the suckered limb forced its deadly entry. The whale blew water and air past the invading finger to eject it. This made it worse for the whale. The gripping spear of hard flesh delved deeply within its head. The horny mouth slanted upwards. The squid's beak dug instinctively into the whale's blubber. Its suckers and hooks anchored harder onto the cow's head.

'Paddle away,' Taiga insisted as Oiwa looked briefly, to gasp as another Kraken surfaced right in front of them. Gaping, they watched it propel to its mate who straddled her mountainous victim. The ardent squid, intent on his partner, changed colour as he moved: first, dingy brown with white undersides, then reddened. His skin quivered as his tentacles touched his intended. They slid over her clinging body. He slipped up onto her. His protracted organ entered. His skin became transparent as he gyrated. The throbbing bodies becoming as one during their mating. He turned bright yellow, his pulsating fringes, azure blue. White suckers squeezed over his dam as he pumped potent milt to mingle deep within her. Her egg shucks absorbed the sperm voraciously. Millions of ova within each pod greedily grasped their birthright.

The bull whale attacked! Its raging hulk sped across open water at the mating couple. Its racing open mouth clenched, biting the male asunder, severing the head and body. All that was left were clinging tentacles and his secreting part, still delivering life's essence. The female clung. She pulsated, ejecting blinding black ink into the clear water. The pungent mess swirled in the depths and sprayed high in the open air. She gripped her living love-bed harder, drawing the last of her widower's sperm into her egg cavity.

The cow whale raised her head, shook and opened her mouth with all the might she could muster. Her mated, sated, hanger-on split asunder. Her husband's wrenched penis died. Her egg shucks flew into mid-air to shower like those hot pumice bullets. 'They are raining on us,' Taiga exclaimed as they spewed down around them. The whale vanished then rose, sneezing. That ghastly penetrating tentacle flew like exploding lava.

'We are being washed deeper into the ice floe,' Taiga called. 'Look, Oiwa. They are all mating in a terrible frenzy over the bergs.' 'It's horrid,' Oiwa thought. 'Like draped bats they cling up there. The males squirming up to cover them. Listen to their vile sucking.' 'They are doing it below, too, Oiwa. Look in the water. Listen to the dam's beaks scraping into the ice as their suckers freeze.

'They're everywhere,' Oiwa tried to mutter, 'writhing, breeding, grinding, throbbing. Will the bergs roll over on us as they mate?' he thought, remembering their own tryst of moments before.

'That male up there's mated to death, Oiwa. Watch out. Paddle. He's slithering back. Reeking Mountain has woken them; scorched them. They have to breed and die.'

'I can't watch,' Oiwa imagined. 'They turn bright, mate over each other, fade, droop and drop. Look at that one collapse and another clamber up.'

'We must escape. Look Oiwa. Narwhals. They eat squid. We paddle to that ice cliff. Watch out for... for anything,' she instructed, as the feeding frenzy began. 'Paddle close in to the bottom.'

Oiwa's eyes bulged as he pointed, 'Taiga! There's one in front. Back-paddle!' he frantically signalled as two great probing tentacles emerged from the depths. Her beak lunged from below, cracking the ice as she dragged her terrible body up the precipice beside them. Ice splinters hailed down as she bit her sucking ascent.

'Yes, turn,' Taiga, terrified, agreed.

'NO! It's her fucking mate!' Oiwa transmitted angrily as the Foam Fighter spun.

Drawn by his beak-grinding death sentence, the Kraken advanced, pulsating.

Oiwa struck the first tentacle hitting their craft with his paddle. The Behemoth reddened, ejaculating its wretched black stain in virulent jets. 'We are drifting off,' Oiwa thought.

'Quiet,' Taiga whispered again. 'He's listening for us.'

'That terrible spreading slick's turned ominously purple,' Oiwa saw, as a deadly quivering arm emerged like a long, slippery whip. 'Duck!' he wanted to yell as he threw himself over the skin covers. The probe hurtled above. He felt its wind lashing past his cheek.

'OIWA!' Taiga screamed.

He turned. He looked. She was gone.

52

Island of the Dead

Oiwa was alone. He tried to call. He could not. He spun around and looked in horror. Taiga was nowhere.

The Kraken emerged from the water and climbed high up onto his mate. He commenced his final, deathly pleasure within her.

Deep in the blackened water Taiga's twisted body swilled. Narwhals nudged her as they assembled for their post-nuptial gorge.

Oiwa wept silently. He paddled alone into the freezing distance, lost.

'Is that a shell whistle?' he thought with faint hope. 'No, just a circling tern. I'll blow mine. No answer. They've all gone,' he moped, paddling mechanically on. 'I can't feel my star map. I can't think. All I see is Taiga's empty seat. What did she look like? I can't even remember. I can't see her in my head. I'm alive, but what is living? Why? I feel my heartbeat, but not my skin. I seem dead.

'More ice. Less ice. Who cares?' he dreamed as his paddle plied aimlessly. 'I'm neither hot nor cold sitting here, drifting,' faintly sensing the last of the gargantuan squid slipping back into the cold ocean to die. The gorging below, with the gathering narwhals, sharks and all manner of marine scavengers, went on voraciously whilst Oiwa paddled above.

Oiwa's blank mood allowed no thought. Only his muscles reacted to the dulled life force still contained within him. The prow of his sea canoe cut the water. Unconsciously, his direction was maintained.

For days, he did not know how long, he moved through the ice-ways. He did not eat. He dragged no line. He just moved, unknowingly, like a migrating bird on grim stored energy.

A heavy, snow-laden wind blew towards him. His dull instinct was to make his way to the next beckoning berg for shelter. Within the arms of an icy bay, he at last slept seated in his boat. Ziit touched his ankles below, his only comfort and solace. Oiwa's dreams were distant shadows. Mercifully, they left him undisturbed.

He wakened gradually to dull sunlight shining low across the sea. When he understood where he was, the heaviness of his situation took hold.

'The water's so calm. I'll not move,' he decided, looking at the stillness of his anchorage. 'If I do, life has to begin. If this is death, I want it to stay. But maybe it's not death? I smell that sulphur. The ash cloud follows like dreadlocks as the sun breaks obliquely through to reflect around me.

'I'm covered in dust,' he realized, looking at his own reflection. 'My beard's full of it, and my hair. My Star shines through, though and there's the blue speck. Is that a goose skein reflected behind me? It is not our time, yet. Maybe it's the Dream Geese.

'Foam Fighter's covered with grime. What stoor that cloud's made everywhere. Even the berg's covered thinly. I can't move yet. There's no need,' he yawned, falling back into a healing slumber. Beneath him, a dark shadow zigzagged in the middle depths. Gradually he began to re-awake, then something nudged the Foam Fighter. Unable still to shift far, he gazed below over the side. Clusters of elvers moved in unison, then vanished as mackerel darted to devour their oily prey.

'Something shifted? On the ice?' he wondered. 'There's that nudge again. A dark shape's darted beneath. The mackerel have vanished,' he observed, coming fully to his senses. 'Yes, I am alive. I am here, whoever that is? It's like waking from a long, bad dream. But it wasn't a dream. That's the bladestone by my ankle. Forget, Oiwa! Forget. Forget to survive. That is what I have to do: to do until when? Until then I shall merely exist,' he realized nodding back to slumber.

The splash reawakened him. 'What am I seeing?' he asked, rubbing his eyes. 'It's an auk: a great auk. It's looking right at me from my harbour. Huge runnels of water stream from its back: it's staring at me along its bright ribbed beak. Those huge white moons on the dark head shine at me. Its eyes glint like comets. The neck and magnificent breast gleam whiter than cleanest snow. Now it twists its neck and flicks the beak. What's this? A live herring, flung to me. Got it. I feel so very hungry, now. Head first. Bite. Kill. Chew. Swallow. I'm so empty inside. I don't care about the gills. It's all going down. Ah. The juicy back, that roe in the flanks. The liver. The oil. Thank... You've gone? Auk, thank you, I say.

'What's that? Did it squawk from behind? Turn, Oiwa. There you are. Another fish? Wonderful. Thank you, Auk. That hooked beak and red tongue of yours are so accurate,' he thought as the second herring hit his lap flap.

'Croak,' spoke the Auk, like a laugh.

'Bite head off. Spit it out. Eat the rest. Fling the tail,' Oiwa decided, being less starved. 'There it is... Gone again. Do come back, Auk. Please? My beard's covered in scales, so is my dusty cover. My insides seem to be working now. I'm feeling good. I'm warming. I feel energy in my blood. Life's returned: I've never been fed by a bird. Does he or she know I usually eat them? Maybe no.

'There's Auk with another fish. Catch. Got it. Thanks,' he waved, biting the neck, stopping the wriggling.

'Is my necklace on?' he wondered urgently. 'Yes,' he discovered, groping for it. 'Look for danger, Oiwa. Can't see anything, but be wary,' he summed up, as Auk flew up from below.

'Another fish, Auk. Thanks, but I'm full. Can I have it later?' he asked in his mind, as he twisted its gaping head.

'But of course,' Oiwa imagined it croak, as it wiggled its thin wings and swam around the Foam Fighter. They watched each other as Oiwa decided to have just a morsel more herring. 'Clack,' went the Auk's beak while its black feet propelled.

'More roe. Lovely,' Oiwa responded inside, as he saw Auk display its snow-white chest. Flapping its flipper wings, the undersides flashed like icicles. 'That's a wonderful bird,' he thought as it sped below again. 'Flightless above; an eagle below.

'It's surfaced already. No more fish, please,' Oiwa hinted, as it shot out spumes of guano from behind. I need to do that, too,' Oiwa suddenly realized, feeling things moving inside. 'I'd better secure Foam Fighter and clamber up before it's too late. But my trousers are already undone? Oooh, that's *so* much better,' he knew as he felt the clean snow wipe his crouching behind. 'Musk ox cheek,' he sensed in the air.

'Exercise; breathe deeply; pull myself together,' Oiwa instructed himself, watching steam rise from his coiled turd melting into the frigid surface. A yellow pool crystallized inches ahead of it.

'On we go, Oiwa,' he said to himself as he relaunched the Foam Fighter. I'm going to use Taiga's seat. Oh. Here are her leggings, and her boots. Now I know why mine were loose. Our final mating. It's all coming back. Don't let it, Oiwa. Don't let it. Kick her stuff to the prow. It's all wet, anyway. There're some of those horrid Kraken eggs. Push them aside, squash them.

'Calm down, Oiwa. Calm down. It isn't all over yet. Keep peace in your heart,' he heard inside as it thumped rapidly within his breast.

'Where did those words come from? I didn't think them? Right. I'll stop this. Get hold of the paddle, use it and go.'

'That's better, Oiwa,' came an odd answer.

'I'm going mad. Does that matter out here? I've been fed by a bird, been covered in stinking dust, mated and lost, nearly smashed by Krakens. Does life mean anything at all? Yes, but no. Carry on. Okay, mind of mine. I'll paddle. Where's that Auk? There you are. Bobbing in front. Good. Right, I'll follow you. Why not? Vanished again. Dang. No, there you are, out of the bay. Joining your flock are you? Let's see.

'This is hard, catching up. There the bugger goes. I'm meant to be following Weir, not some feathery thing. But it's fun, dare I say it. Stop hurling me fish, will you?

'No, that bird's on its own, maybe lost, like me? But I am getting out of this ice floe. Where to now? There it is, rising on that wave: paddle, paddle, paddle, Oiwa...

'Gone again. Ah well, I feel I'm going in the right direction. I could do with another fish soon, though,' he wished later. 'I should long-line with a lure. Let's rummage for the tackle. Ow! That's a mackerel hitting my nose.'

'Clack-clack,' came a noise.

'Amazing. Thank you, Auk.'

Fed, he paddled on. Auk leading.

'Guts are moving,' he felt much later. 'I'll do it in the baler. There's one of those wretched eggs inside. I'll shit on it and sling it out. Best thing. I should bale, too, but there's so little. Ah. There's Auk on another crest. I'm glad. Yes... and, far off, a berg. Paddle Auk's way, Oiwa. Gone again... Catch up. Don't think back. Go forward. Forget now, there's always later. There it goes again. Keep Great Auk in sight. I'm going to give the bird a name. Gare. There you go, Gare's your name,' he projected across the billows, 'I'll catch up.'

'If you can,' a faint answer arrived. 'I shall dive and swim under your shadow, watch your wake and look up as your paddle washes. The barnacles gather as you drive your craft. Now I see you again as the goose. I will return your star map to you, Oiwa. I like the name Gare. It is familiar to me. Yes, you're getting nervous now, as you scan the waves. I'll fly below and surface far ahead. Follow me to the berg. I will guide you. I am Queen under the sea. My beak's senses tell me where you are. I will always know. Through my bill to my wee ears, I hear all; where the whales are; where Krakens bite; the alarms of hunted fish; grinding ice and my kin, who leave me to my errand,' Gare secretly said. 'Now he cranes his Goose neck, searching again. I will gather sild for him: warm them up within me. He will enjoy them straight from my gullet.'

'There you are, Gare. Goodness! Tiny, warm fish: how did you know? Thank you, thank you,' Oiwa conveyed as he ate them from his lap leather. 'You are wonderful, Gare. I'm getting stronger. I feel at one with the sea as I ride the waves. I know we are heading in the right direction. When I feel my goose pimples, I know. I sense it even in my feet as the puddle slops round my boots. My nose kens it when I feel the cold. The grip on my paddle that won't loosen, my hood when I feel the wind behind me. Onwards Oiwa,' he bravely told himself.

'You're taking me to that huge berg, Gare. It's like a great island. I see one end, but not the other. The cliff shines so brightly. The sea lies tranquil around it. This place has such a presence. It is strange. Those wonderful green stripes rising high to the summit, shimmer in the sun, the blue ones glowing next to the amber. We must find our way on to it.

'My paddle sweeps echo as I follow Gare. How she glides through the vast caves, taking me; making me follow. The water is so clear, I can see deep below. It's as though faces look back up, but it isn't my reflection. The wonderful stripes delve deep, too. Fish nibble there, careless of Gare, who could gobble them in a trice.

'She's bobbed up again, looking at me. Yes, I'm coming. Slow down. Let me keep up. Let me see these wonders,' he appealed, almost hearing his echo.

'The cliff is getting lower as we face the sun. Now it curves. I hear my wake behind as I paddle forward. It seems so very loud. It's as though I should not be quiet, not even here, perhaps. There's Gare. Sitting on that low spur. She knows I can berth there. It's another bay, so easy to glide into. But it's so quiet now. Not a bird cry, no ripple or lap. As I move, even my wake closes behind and stops.

'Now Foam Fighter has taken me into this blue pool. How odd. The ice, rearing up in the middle, is like a huge walrus. Bands of polished green and soot-black ice lean at angles within it. We can drift to that gentle slope where Gare is waiting. I can get out and pull Foam Fighter up to safety. There's none of that dust here, either. It's pristine. It's so bright. Taiga had walrus tusk snow goggles tied to her breeks. I'm going to get them. She'd want that,' Oiwa told himself as he delved to the damp compartment. 'That's better,' he knew, as he pulled the slit ivory discs over his eyes.

'My feet have stuck. It's the wet from the boat. Pull sharply: release them. I see Gare doesn't have that problem. That's better. My soles have frosted now, so no more sticking. I'm glad my feet are so warm. Come on Foam Fighter; follow as I tow you.

'Where are you going, Gare? Slow down. Birds go faster on slippery stuff. Oh. That's magnificent,' Oiwa declared inwardly as he looked ahead to the island's ice mountain. Tiny rivulets of clear water trickled from its sheer heights.

'I can drink,' he thought bending to cup his hands. 'It tastes so of life. I don't know why, but it's wonderfully refreshing. Deathly cold but, as it warms on my tongue, it glows. Now my belly feels hot. I have never had water like this.

'That ice ahead sparkles brilliantly in so many facets. I'm truly glad of these goggles. There's Gare, still up ahead, plodding on. Yes, Gare, I'm following, but I'm having another drink, and a pee. Wait, will you?'

'Yes, I'm here. You've turned that lovely melt trickle into a steaming yellow river. Never mind. That's your life for you, Oiwa,' Gare clacked.

'Ready, Gare. Here I come. But that's queer,' he thought as he wrung his beard out. 'Something's sticking out of that projection up the precipice. Gare's waddling there: I'll adjust these lookers. I'm not used to them. That's better. I can get a grip on the fallen icy scree and clamber up. But there's some fur? Funny, it's stuck in this block. It's got a bone pin shoved in it. Who did that? I'll take it anyway. Probably useful, sometime. The fur's done, though.'

Gare croaked loudly.

From above, Oiwa thought he heard, 'You can manage up here, if I can.'

'Of course,' he thought, 'but what's that moving above?' Oiwa wondered, peering through his squints. 'It's a skua pecking at something poking out from the ice. It's hoiked a bit off and flown away. Must be wary of me? Gare's heading there, scraping over the tumble. By Gumar! It looks like a person. Yes, someone's looking down at me, a big man. Great... company. Was that skua his pet? Weird one to keep, though,' he wondered as he crawled with difficulty upwards.

'He's still there,' Oiwa panted as he arrived. 'But he's silent; staring... with only one eye. Oh horror! He's frozen. Dead. Only his head and one shoulder stick out. Here's his spear tip. It's of bladestone. Ouch! It's sharp. Why's he here? An ear has gone too. That's what that bonxie took. There it goes, up in the sky, mocking. It's sickening. Poor man. How long has he been here? Ages, by looks: I'm sure his body goes right in. Oh, his cheek's tattooed and he's a hook in his nose: red hair too. Fine stitching on his shoulder seam. Is there a white Star on his forehead? I'll scrape the frost away. Is it Weir? No,' was his answer as he peered back into the misty ice, seeing the corpse fade within.

'It's become so still again. Even that carrion has stopped,' Oiwa realized, gazing at Gare perched next to him, gurgling in her gullet. 'No, not Weir,' he heard.

'Poor frozen man,' Oiwa pitied, scraping round for his other lug. 'A greenstone plug in the lobe. How wonderful he must have looked. Will his lip move under that red moustache? Yes, just. Filed teeth, like Sharpened Tooth. His good eye; can I open it? Ah, blue with a hazel rim.

'Death comes to us all,' Oiwa thought, staring back into the melting face, touching his own, realizing the uniqueness of his own life. 'I've seen death. I've killed. too. My arrow, piercing that vile woman's guts before she fell. I've buried brothers and my friend,

Rush. I have watched ones dragged beneath the sea. Taiga, wrenched from her boat in front of me. I've eaten bits of men with the Bald Heads. I mated in a tomb and broke dried bodies, perhaps making life where there was only death. Life is hard and transient. Death is permanent, forever and always, until you change spirit. But the body stays. Who are you now, Ice Man? That scavenger, perhaps? Or will it release your next life by eating you?' He looked back to the face as though it could answer, 'When did you die? Why did you die? The cold, whistling breeze can't wake you. You could have been here since Karno's days before the ice, for all I ken about?'

Gare gurgled. Oiwa realized he was actually sobbing for him. He sniffed warm mucus back. Swallowing a smoke-tasting lump, he coughed it back to the ice where it slipped then stuck firm.

'I am going now, Ice Man. I hope your green plug chokes the skua,' he consoled, as he took a different way down under a vertical height.

'Careful, Oiwa,' he heard a lone voice advise.

'Where did that come from? There's no one else here,' he wondered, as he glanced to one side. 'There's a boot sticking out. It's too far to be part of him up there. More things? A bit of a hand coming from that hunk: fur on the wrist. It's a woman huddled within. I can just see her. There's dark hair coming from under a hood. I can make out a knife. Oh, and a child's hand on her crouched lap. Her knees in her stitched leggings are so close to the surface. Look away, Oiwa.

'You can't. We are all around you,' were the words impressing themselves inside him.

'Yes, I see,' Oiwa answered in thought, as he glared up the clear cliff face beside him. Gare gaggled. The sound echoed from on high. The bonxie circled, screeching a reply.

'I'm about to leave my mark here for these souls,' Oiwa told the precipice. 'I'm going to your foot, where your toe touches flat ice. There I'll hack my insignia deep into your face.'

He crunched his way over to the flatter terrain and removed his grey axe from his belt.

'Here goes. Hold on. No, it's just my reflection within, surely?'

He swung. His blade crunched into the hard, clear ice at the distorted forehead.

'What! Blood's running from the cut! It's on my axe? How come? I'm not bleeding,' he told himself, feeling his brow.

'Oiwa. Be careful where you swipe. Look in the ice. It's me, Rush. You took a chunk of skin with that blow. But nothing really hurts here.'

'No. It can't be,' he replied shaking in his boots, 'I was with you. You died. I helped bury you.'

'Look again, Oiwa. Take off your squints. Let my light come to you.'

'I don't believe this.'

'You don't have to. Just look.'

'Yes. It is you. Your moon face shines, but as it did in life. Not with that golden dust. You look radiant. Even my axe wound has healed.'

'I allowed you to give me that clout so you would believe.'

'There are the terrible arrows that Snaaaaar shot in you,' Oiwa said, stuttering, as Rush's image came even closer to the pitted edge. Oiwa brushed his lost friend's broad brow, feeling both ice and skin. He then felt Rush's cold hand in his palm.

'Come in. You can. Follow my grasp. Step through into our world, Oiwa. My arrows are gone now, the wounds, too. Look, Oiwa. They were there for you to see and believe.'

'I *can* move in here. But it is strange. It is as though I have to push everywhere. It's cold, but not cold.'

'Yes, Oiwa. This is our world, not yours. It will be many years before you can join us. Life is not forever. Neither is this death. I exist behind the Moon. You are here so you know we are not lost. I will always look over you. I will always be your friend. We shall meet again,' Rush said, as he turned to go deeper into the ice.

'Don't go, Rush. I can't move. The ice won't let me,' he called with a bursting heart.

'Not yet,' he heard his friend's voice call. 'Not for a long time, Oiwa,' he said turning and staring from the solidness, 'One day our spirits will meet, but not now. Not now... Not now,' Rush repeated as his voice faded.

'His words stay in my ears even though he's gone. I can just move now, but I know I can't follow. I think I see him in the far, far distance. There's a faint light glowing and movement of others deep, deep in the berg. Now I do feel the intense cold of this place against the warmth of my body. My beard tugs painfully if I shift too fast. Yes, this is their world, whoever they are. I'll go back now, if I can.

'Don't leave, Oiwa,' he heard a fondly familiar voice say.

'Who's that?' he asked, turning to face the sound. 'Bark! It's you. How your Star glistens.'

'Yes, little brother. Here I am, just as in life. Your beard has grown. Grown with you. May I touch it?'

'Of, course Bark,' Oiwa replied with tears melting the giving ice on his face.

'Your Star shines brilliantly, too. The blue speck you earned stands out well. Your journey has been long, my little brother. You have grown beyond measure. Take your life to its bounds. You have a long way to travel yet. And when you think you have arrived, your life's trek will have only just begun.'

'I have missed you terribly, Bark. It was so sudden. When we buried you, I knew your soul had gone,' Oiwa's own spirit uttered, while he dropped his axe, which drifted to hang by his fingers. 'Let me hold you, Bark,' he asked while slowly putting his arms through the ethereal ice in brotherly love.

'Of course,' Bark replied, moving towards his kin, 'hug me.'

Oiwa gradually managed the embrace, hearing ice skrink as he moved. He watched Bark's thick black fur develop. He felt it against his beard as they became utterly close. A large paw put a gentle claw through his jacket. It caught the clasp of his necklace and scratched his oily skin. 'I feel your panther-like breath, your whiskers and ear against mine,' Oiwa wanted to say while Bark's form still altered.

'You see me as I am now. We all change, following our spirit paths. When I return to the world as a human, it will be so different. I will have to learn all over again. Goodbye, Oiwa, until the end and a new beginning.'

'Don't leave. Don't go, Bark. We've only just be...' The ice clenched Oiwa's jaw, gripping his head tight as he watched the feline form take the long, slow path. He padded to the distant beings in the glimmering pool of yellow glow, sat tall and waited. 'Yes,' Oiwa then knew, 'he's now the great cat he described in Father's sweat lodge all that time ago.

'I can move now. Slowly, but it's possible. There's Gare. She's looking in. I see her coloured beak ripple in the waving ice. I know she can see me. She waits,' he thought, as hot breath went down his neck. 'What's that?' he wondered, turning to look. 'A magnificent eagle, with bright talons and a wee stick clenched in them,' he took in as the raptor's form altered in the green of the frozen waters. 'Tine. You are here. There's your Star, your little nicks on your cheeks that always reddened if you got angry. It is thee, indeed.'

'Yes, Oiwa. I'm back. Here with you. That arrow that pierced my skull began the change. Directly the water hit me, I flew over sacred groves to my mountain eerie. I made my mate's eggs fertile. She knew I would come to give lives through them, creating new souls and bringing back others. We watched you mate, too. We see it all. Spirits from before and future gather around you, like buzzing bees, for release into the world of people. There is a big crowd waiting. We see them. Make sure they are cared for, even if you never know or meet them. They will be yours, divined through you.'

'Let me hug you, Tine. I need to feel your spirit. Flesh of my kin, that I may never touch again.'

'Follow me along the icicle road a little way. Put your arm around me.'

'Yes, Tine. I see ahead. The ice feels softer, more giving. Those look like frozen watery stalactites lining the way. It weaves towards the dim glow. My boots crunch in the fine crystals covering it.'

'When *your* body dies, Oiwa, you will become the goose again, as in your dreams, just as you described in Father's sweat lodge. If ever you are in plight, even in your life, sometimes your spirit will fly to us, Solan as well. Your wings will guide you. Look into the distance. See, Oiwa? There's Fall, Rail and Marsh. That evil one put them here. Wave back to them; let them re-join their spirits. Lichen, there, will become a Caribou once more when you put your hand up... See. Now turn and give your brother a proper hug – Oiwa, my little big brother.'

'Tine, thank you,' Oiwa sobbed in joy and grief as they embraced. Then bemoaned, 'You're changing again. I feel your bones move. Your neck is in my arms and your beak flicks against my nose. Go, if you must,' he said as he watched the Eagle Spirit saunter to the distant glimmer, 'I know I can't follow. I can see my way back. There's Gare in the daylight. The sun lights up a tunnel exactly my shape. Those are goose footprints pointing towards me. I can follow them back.'

'Why do you go, Oiwa?' he heard a familiar voice ask from behind.

'Taiga. It's you,' he answered immediately as he turned.

'Yes, Oiwa. You were my great love.'

'Hold me,' he demanded, as he tried to lurch forward.

'No, Oiwa. The Long Hands tore me from you. It is forever. You have to go forward on your path. My soul is sad, but I have a journey too. I will bear your son, though. He will be born in the Spirit World to become Chief amongst the Musk Ox.

'Long Spoot bids farewell too, as does Cove, and all of us who tried to escape. You alone will live to be old. The ice will lose its grip on you only if you walk now to Gare. There is another who awaits you. Goodbye, Oiwa, think of me not.'

'You've gone. Tai...' Oiwa stopped, feeling the ice grip. 'I must turn. I must leave. But that is the smell of musk cheek from the Cooking Pond. Thank you, Taiga.

'Gare beckons. I see her watching. What spirits does she hold?' he thought as his right leg felt the fresh Arctic air.

53

Fallow Fell

'I'm knackered,' Oiwa knew, reaching the Foam Fighter. 'As I look, I see more and more bodies emerging from the ice. This place is full of them,' he thought, as he folded the hide apron on the ice. He tipped his boat over and curled up to sleep.

Gare hopped up, standing sentinel on top, enjoying her companion's snoring.

Oiwa dreamed of Rush, his kin and Taiga in the icy inner world. Other spirits came to him who dwelt, waiting. Those melting came alive and spoke of their distant lives. The skua became a vast, five-headed, soaring scavenger, gliding to people. It busily quarried their flesh to feed its young. They called from their high crag nest on a distant shore. The dream seemed endless. An ancient dog howled, and its long-dead mistress calmed it. A child's anguished cry: a parent's soothing. Long-silent fireside songs weaved gently in his sleeping mind. Slowly, slowly, the spirits would wake from their aeons of death: reborn through the gizzards of the scavenging raptor's brood; a marauding snow bear's ardour, or gendered by his own groin... somewhere?

Eventually he stirred after his warm, renewing slumber. Gare's leathery feet scraped above. Foam Fighter's bone frame vibrated as she croaked greetings.

'That was w o n d e r f u l,' he yawned, as light streaked in when the boat lifted and slewed: Gare squawked, sliding from her leathery perch.

'What a glorious day,' Oiwa signalled. 'The ice and the ocean shimmer under the clear sky. The skua screeches, but it's just doing its bidding. I feel so good after that water. I'll fill Taiga's flask. I can see her now in my mind's eye. But she is gone. She's where she is and I must travel. They are all there and I am here. That's it. Gare, we must go,' he summed up, twisting his beard, feeling life course through his veins. 'I'm alive now, I will leave death behind and meet it later... Much later.'

Gare gulped, coughing up Oiwa's breakfast.

'Thank you. Lovely sild again. Just right for the sea trek.'

Gare's feet paddled hard, piloting ahead.

Beneath the berg, a defrosting hand moved in the light current: the old body, waving farewell. A twisted string bracelet slid from its wrist to float away in the salty drift.

'There's a backing wind. My star map's returned. I'm being blown the right way. Paddling is easy. There goes Gare. She knows. And there's a length of a Long Hands floating with me. It pongs. Paddle faster, Oiwa.

'Looking back, that berg seems so distant so quickly. The swell is increasing and my sea-home is taking me. Gare's gone. No, there she is. I only have to think of her and she appears, calling me with her croak.'

Days passed as though they had neither beginning nor end. There were no more icebergs. The sea's colours changed from slate grey to green. Puffins on fishing forays flew past, as did gannets and petrels on their hunt for food.

'Well,' thought Oiwa, 'we are getting somewhere. These birds have a home. I feel it. Gare's fish is lovely, but I do need land food. My gums are sore and my teeth seem loose. I yearn for berries. I'm tiring. I can certainly go on, but I need rest soon. If I clench my eyes shut, I make out my map better. There's land to my left. Gare knows; she's just changed direction. Clever bird.

'I knew I was right!' Oiwa exclaimed inwardly, 'That has to be cliffs appearing far off. Cloud is gathering there: a good land sign. That's whittled my will. Here goes. That way, Gare,' he pointed.

'Closer now. That's a raven far off. Now a flock of terns swooping: land, land, land; coming closer. Cormorants returning. Follow them, Gare. The cliffs are clearer now, especially when I crest a wave. This is brilliant. I'm so excited. Do folk bide there?

'The sea has changed. It was light green, now black. The currents are different. The light is changing, too. Is the season altering?

'There they are, looming up high. We can't land yet, Gare. Well, you can. I will have to paddle along. Hmmm. It's becoming a little dim. The sun is lowering. It's turned the high glaciers pink. The windswept snow, too. But is that a vale far off? We should head there. Warn me if there's ice, Gare.

'It's taking so long. I seem to get somewhere, then the vale appears further. Keep paddling, we will get there. At least it is getting brighter,' he told himself as he wearied.

'The sea has changed again: clear. light blue water. It sparkles. Now we are closer, the smells have changed. Bird dung. Yes. I must have been in a trance. The valley is near. I smell fresh water running into the sea. There are rocks appearing. Cormorants are landing on them and opening their wings to dry.

'Hello, eider duck. Have you come to greet me? Careful, I could easily eat one of you. I smell volcano strongly, too. Yes, far to the east is a smoke trail. I think I will be avoiding that. For now I will just navigate through these skerries. Gare's helping. The currents are odd. It's like seaways meeting. A strange turbulence exists here. She's showing me through though. I must not damage the Foam Fighter on rocks.

'The racket those birds make, packed up there on the cliff. It's deafening, the closer I get. I'm not used to it. Their shit down the face stinks. But it feels warmer. For Spirits' sakes, I thought those were rocks. Its seals, wobbling down a beach. Here they come. Into the sea. How they change from blubber to sleek swimmers. I could eat some of that, too. Yes, there's plenty of shellfish here: limpets, winkles, mussels and whelks. But I want berries. I want meat. I need something different. That's a walrus barking. He'll do nicely. But even he's a bit beyond me just now,' he thought wisely.

Gare led on.

'Taiga's boat responds to me completely. It's like we are one, as we reach the dark sands of this beach. It's so tranquil here. The skerries shelter the bay from the turbulence. This is such a peaceful place. Even the screeching gulls seem quiet now.

'That vale past the shingle is verdant. Its steep sides wind deeply inland. Bushes and shrubs cling to its slopes. Peaty water runs into the sea from the torrent coming through it. Yes, broken reeds float by. Adolescent ducks and their brightly coloured parents nibble at them. Now they move off to the rocks for that sprouting seaweed. This place is full of life. I'm lucky; I feel as though I'm part of it.

'There's a good landing. What huge, colourfully banded cobbles. They look like giants' balls. Gare is now swimming between two great boulders. I can land there on the smooth slope of grey sand. Behind it is a thick line of driftwood. This is a great place. I want to stay. Here we go, Foam Fighter, kiss the sand. What a lovely sound that grating is. Hooray. Feet on ground,' he joyously thought, clapping his hands wildly in an ecstatic dance. 'Now I have to stretch and exercise. I'm so stiff. My neck aches and my gums are much sorer. This feeling around my teeth isn't good, either.

'Gare is back in the water. What's she doing? Never mind. I'm going to sort the boat out. That's odd. Auks don't eat seaweed. She's filling her bill with small fronds waving from the rocks. Now she's paddling to me. What is it, Gare?' he asked, when she held her bill open.

'Eat this. Men call them elks' ears,' he heard distinctly in his lugs.

'Okay, Gare. I'll take some. Thank you. Mmm... It tastes salty, of course, but there's an almost sour flavour. It's so smooth, yet thick and chewy. It's soothing. Oh, and it feels good to swallow. I like elks' ears. They make me feel clean inside too. Can I have more, please?' he asked, getting used to the strange telepathy.

Gare opened her beak while Oiwa sat on the sand. He happily supped in the slanting sunlight beaming across the wide, shining sea. 'The sun in this idyllic place is so warm, Gare. I'm breaking out in a terrible sweat in these clothes. I can already smell the reek coming up from my collar. I have to wash. I haven't had water on me since Hot Ponds. My armpits are running. Does that seaweed have anything to do with it? Probably no, but I'm taking my garb off right now and I'm jumping in the sea.

'Anorak first. The toggles are so tight. Here they come; peel away. Now my sticky felt vest. Oooh, that stinks; there it goes. The breeze in my oxters is really refreshing. Sea boots next. Loosen the laces, heave. Good. Dry inside, but sweaty feet. Eeeeeeie. Not pleasant. My toes are white and pallid. The skin is smelly and peeling. Not good. Trousers down. Ooooo: weeks of old farts escaping. Hmmm, tooth and claw indents on my chest. Well, I'm leaving my necklace on, in honour of Taiga. My feet feel good in the sharp sand. It's scraping away that rotted skin. The breeze feels refreshing, but that sweat still cascades.

'Run, Oiwa. Leap; dive. Wow! That's the stuff. Swim. Twist and turn. This is splendid after the constriction of my cockpit. Feel the deep cold depths. Let it go all round me, cleansing. The lice won't enjoy this. I'll rub myself all over, wring out my beard. Drench my hair. This cold is profound. Pretend it's only my skin that feels it. Inside I'm hot. Go underwater and swim below. There's Gare. She's joined me. She's used to it. How she flies beneath. It's misty on my eyes as she flits, but she has such grace. I feel this salt doing me good, but it is now getting exceedingly chilly. My toes are cold as quartz. My legs are shivering. My scrotum's crinkled and shrunk. I think it's enough, now that my dick's hid like a scared snail. Just a few last strokes and I'm getting out.

'But what's this?' he suddenly asked himself. 'I'm not alone. The seals are returning. They are bumping into me. How funny. My harbour's full of them. I'm staying a bit, despite the cold. But now I'm going blue,' he noticed shortly after. 'That's it. Out of here. That's nice; Gare is next to me as I wade in. The sun on my back is so good. I feel much better, though really cold.

'That's my long shadow going up the sand. Gare's head and bill cast theirs, too. I'll wave my arms and make me look even taller. See how the shadows dash across the beach. But what's that?' Oiwa asked himself, amazed. 'There's another male shadow stretching there next to mine? Look, it comes from Gare's webbed feet. There she is, but that shadow isn't hers at all. They both look like graven rock. Now a shadow hand is reaching to mine. What's happening? The head is turning from the sands to me. I don't believe this... It has a white Star on its forehead! My goose pimples have gone rock solid. I can't move. I feel the seawater run from my beard, but I'm stuck.'

'Oiwa,' he heard from the shadow-head. He scrutinized the bearded jaw moving in speech, 'I am your ancestor. I am Weir. My spirit is here, within whom you call Gare. You set out with your friends and brothers. Only you decided to follow me. You have excelled. You travelled far, Oiwa. Your spirit allies tell you that there is far to go yet, my great, great nephew. They are so right. Your journey in this life will never end. Mine did.'

'It's like I am set in that ice again,' Oiwa felt. 'I'm here naked; immovable, listening to what I do and do not wish to hear. I feel the cold lash my skin, yet the sun warms it. He for whom I have searched comes to me so unexpectedly. But he's been guiding me, feeding me. How can all this be?'

'Your Goose Spirit is with you, as it is with me, Oiwa. We hear your thoughts. Speech is a hindrance to truth. Solan watches out for you, as his ancestor did for me. Do continue to call my spirit host "Gare". The name is so pleasing.'

'Yes,' Oiwa tried to nod, but his neck remained rigid.

'Someone waits for you. She knows you are coming. My lost chance will be yours. Your seed is needed.'

'You sound so much like my father. You must be Weir. What happened to you? I have to know.'

'You have a long way to go yet,' Weir said gravely, 'I... Gare guided you. Gare will inform you. Gare will cure your scurvy.'

* * * * *

Shala went back to the Lille Sands shore. As she turned, the vision hit her. Her shoulders went cold. She watched her shadow creep up the beach. She heard voices from the far distance, not making out what was said over the sounds of the sea. Only the names Weir, Oiwa and Gare penetrated.

* * * * *

'Our shadows are fading. A dense cloud obscures the sun. I'm shivering again. There goes Gare: into the sea. I'm sure he... she will return. I'd better don that smelly clothing and get a fire going. This garb is in a state. I must do my mending. The seams are stretched, falling apart. My parka's elbows need patching; so do my knees. I'll dry Taiga's breeks. They will be useful.

'The Foam Fighter needs attention, too. A good barnacle scrape: a rub of blubber, inside and out. Her framework needs tightening. I have plenty of maintenance to do before moving from here. But first, drag her up to safety.

'Now to get a good blaze going. I hope great auks don't mind fire? Ah, here she comes. I think that's more elks' ears. Hmmm. My gums already feel better. Would Gare mind if I ate a duck?'

'Eat what you like, Oiwa. But you must have this first. Then I'm taking you to the sorrel bed up by those rocks. That's a good scurvy cure, too. And no, I don't mind a fire, as long as it's not me that's being cooked over it,' Oiwa heard in Weir's voice.

'Youch! This is sour,' Oiwa reacted when he bit into the sorrel, 'The tip of my tongue seems to have swelled as I chew. My gums feel stung and the roots of my teeth feel sensitive. I want to spit it out.'

'Eat it, Oiwa,' was all he could hear. 'It will cure you from within. Take some with you when you travel. You want to keep your teeth, don't you?'

'I'm sure this helps,' he thought after a while, 'I feel much cleansed inside. Now for that duck. I'll get Ziit oiled and ready.'

Small, bright butterflies rose from the lousewort, flowering amongst the spindly sea rocket above the beach. Eider feathers and furry down drifted among them as Oiwa plucked his bird. His fire burned nicely with a great willow stump in the middle. 'The sun's moved around the horizon and dipped closer to the sea. Summer will end here soon. I feel the stars. Shortly they will appear. I already see the Beautiful Star. She shines now. It's that easterly horizon that beckons me.'

'If you bone that duck out and stuff it with sorrel,' Oiwa heard, 'It will be even better for you. Anyway, I haven't smelled duck cooking for decades. It will be lovely. You can do it on a stone, like Rush did by the Dun. I will have to stick with fish, but that's no hardship.'

'So you watched us, Gare.'

'No. A salmon spirit told me. I followed you from Goose Landing. I knew I should care for you after the Krakens. I had to choose my moment. I heard your thoughts even then.'

'Gare, Weir, please tell me your history,' Oiwa asked as he began exposing the duck bones with his knife.

'It is long. Like yours: full of adventure, sorrow and joy. You met my children's children, born from the unity I received as I travelled.'

Oiwa sat cross-legged, listening while the boneless eider sizzled. Some places he recognized and some he did not. Tales of bravery, treachery, love and leaving unfolded, as Weir's fond memories of little North Star explained his father's yearning for news. 'He will be wanting to hear about me. Mica will have told him, by now,' Oiwa imagined.

'On my quest, following Solan's migration, I was drawn here to Fallow Fell, a holy place where only the chosen arrive: a passing place, welcoming strangers, but never allowing them to remain. People did bide here many, many times ago, before the Ice came. Only their ancient spirits remain. Their vale behind us is small, yet wonderful. It holds all that will cure; existing only for the needy, whether it be man or un-man.'

The taste of the eider made Oiwa contented and soothed. Blood coursed from his brain to his stomach linings to digest his cooking. Sleep began overtaking him while Weir's soporific spirit-voice continued like a lullaby.

'I received nurture here many, many summers ago. My way had been hard, yet good, as you have heard. Long sea journeys can make folk ill from lack of medicine foods. Here they all are, and other things too. All that is needed, whether for broken bones, a broken mind or sickness. It is here. All who deserve are given what they need. Here you will be slaked with good water and ambrose, as I was. Explore, and you will be nourished and succoured. But do not stay a moment longer than your welcome has been extended. If you do you will wither, collapsing like an ageing puffball.'

Oiwa breathed deeply in slumber, absorbing his hypnotic words.

'You will only remember parts of this epic when you need to. It will return like a clear voice. You learned things in your mother's womb, using them after you were born, not knowing from where they came. This history will be with you like that.' Weir paused, while Oiwa's slumber deepened.

'You are tracing my path. That is your destiny now. You will go much further, though. I left Fallow Fell a strong, fit man. Fluke, my sea kayak, sped across the waves. I paddled with the great auks to the last land, the Black Isle.'

Oiwa slept, curled in the sand by his glowing fire. The willow root burned endlessly. The light of the low sun flickered on the sea's ripples. It stooped, hugging the horizon. No breeze fanned the brightly glowing embers. Their warmth filled the air, cocoon-like around them.

If Oiwa had opened his eyes, he would have seen Weir in his human form, fit and well with his white Star shining, his long traveller's beard neatly groomed to a point and decorated with shell beads. He would have seen him turn a mackerel on the stone and enjoy cooked food. Instead, he slept deeply on during that private moment of Weir's hungry spirit enjoying the food of mortal man.

'I reached the towering, dark rock of the Black Isle,' Weir continued, spitting out the spine. 'Its sheer mace-stone sides lurched from the sea, as though it were thrust there from deep below by a vast sea monster. Or was it hurled there from the heavens, when the giants fought to win the stars? It was where Narwhal lived. Her daughters exist there still. She was the guardian of the sharp-nosed whales, who dine in the depths on creatures who could overwhelm the world. They eat young squid and smash the shells of Leviathan lobsters that trap and crush passing boats. But she was cruel. Her lonely life, with her ugly daughters to feed, made her bitter. She sung, luring mates to give her sons. Her voice sounded kind. I heard it as Fluke's sides scraped the smooth, shining rock where elks' ears grow. There, a great crystal band swept through the black rock right up to Narwhal's Hall.

'I took my kayak round the island to a landing place. It had been carved by many female hands and hammered out with stones. I saw the great balls of rock that Narwhal's daughters used to grind the fearsome pathway. I pulled up Fluke, securing her to an upright stone shaped like a narwhal's tusk. The rough steps were smoothed in the middle with the passage of her daughters' bare feet. At the sides, musk dung lay piled. A herd of musk ox lived there. They were wee, compared with ones on my journeys, but fierce. They had learned to attack a stranger and not run. These animals, the daughters of the Great Narwhal milked for their mother. They only killed them by stealth for special feasts. Their horns and skulls lined the stairway to Narwhal's lair.

'I heard her croon from the depths of her dark house. It sounded wonderfully dreamlike. Her daughters accompanied her melody. I smelt roasting musk ox. I ventured up her stairway and reached the portal of her basalt hall. I peered in.

'"Weir," I heard her sing, "come in and join me in my joy, for we have expected you. Come with me. Indulge in musk and all my daughters, too. For you must bear with me and send a son to my womb."

'Her voice was dreamy, languid and warm. Slowly I saw the faces of her mad daughters leering from behind a heat-wall where the musk roasted on her eternal fire. They screeched this chorus.

"Your sons in us will be our delight and we will milk you dry.
You shall eat and mate with us.
Press home your fertile thigh.'
So eat our meat and stuff thyself,
Then fill us all with your manly wealth.
Grant us this, or die."'

Weir paused in his tale to the sleeping Oiwa, recalling the peril he had placed himself in. 'I looked around, becoming accustomed to their lair's dim, demonic light. Narwhal tusks with men's skulls were arrayed in arcs and suspended from the cavernous ceiling. The backs had been chiselled away so the brains could be eaten. I saw not just the bones of musk on the cave floor. There were legs of men and ribs of men, the femurs and shins cleaved so those vultures of the black, towering rock could suck the marrow.

'The foul daughters drank from skull cups they had fashioned over the tormenting years. Small dried girl babes, lit by tallow lamps, stood in niches hewn in the cave walls behind them.

'I, Weir, took fright! I was to mate with that horror. I never placed my pin where its truth would not be cherished wholesomely. Her wretched herd of musk blocked the lair's entrance. The stench and steam from their nostrils filled the space; they, angry at the roasting in my honour.

'"Come, Weir, sit, eat then sow your seed", Narwhal commanded.

'I squatted near to her great body. Her terrible grey hair and long, curling fingernails glimmered in the firelight glow. Evil looked even more evil. I took my axe and cut a fatty hunk of meat, passing some to her in deference. As I did this, I wiped the haft in the grease that dripped slowly from the cooking carcass. I ate, too. It tasted of life and death.

'The Narwhal woman opened wide her legs, revealing her place to me. I was ushered there. Her daughters wailed in passion as I approached with my parts revealed. In place of my genital horn, I shoved my greasy axe haft up. It slid in deeply, right to the sharp blade. I pulled it back and rocked it forth. Narwhal moaned on my hot, fake phallus, not knowing that it was only my chopper. Then I withdrew, striking the first nosey daughter on her forehead. She fell dead. I leapt back. I hit the roasting spit, smashing the support with a pounding stone. The musk ox fell. Its fat blazed. I upturned the great piss pot they shared into the fire, creating a stinking fog. The women wailed as though their wicked hearts were being wrenched out.

'I hurtled for the doorway, jumping on an advancing ox. Grabbing its sharp, swooping horns, I drove it out of the stinking eerie. Kicking it and screaming in its ears, I made it run in terror with me on it. I flew down the steep steps. I leapt to the ground by Fluke. The enraged animal turned in attack. I hit the livid ox with my greasy axe. It flew from my hand, stuck in the horned skull. I ran with Fluke to the sea and paddled, possessed, from the Black Isle.

'I heard their curses, hurled from the caverns above as I paddled with all my might. Then the abuse was joined with a deadly rain. Narwhal tusks, cast with horrid force, clattered and sank before me. But one, the final one, hurled by the Great Witch herself, flew further. I saw it coming. I turned to escape. It struck as I whirled my paddle. That enchanted tusk pierced my upper arm to stick in my ribs. I wrenched the foul, poisoned weapon from my limb. I cast it as high as I could with almighty, vengeful force. Back it arched to exactly where it had come.

'Over my own agony, I heard her terrible screams. Disgusted oaths of "Bastard Fucker" hit my ears. Finally, her fatal shriek, a hideously violent yell that rent the air, making it stink like the boiling mud of Foul Fart Falls. I paddled with my good arm as vile wails of anguish from her countless fatherless daughters followed me.

'Agony paralyzed me. I collapsed in the bottom of the Fluke. I do not know when I woke. The sound of my goose friends, high in the sky, penetrated my delirium. I lay, staring above. It was dark. The sky filled with stars. I was alone on a slack sea, drifting.

'My arm and chest burned. I felt a great scab on my side. The gash in my arm oozed. I was too weak to paddle, but I could fish. The geese flew low, looking. Solan led. We had met before, just as you met his eleventh heir. Whether they took me above or no, I cannot tell. I was in a painful dream. Days passed. Nights went by. I drifted where my will wanted. My star map held. The geese flew by, low and high. But my arm festered. I tied it with whipped gut above my wound. I tried cutting it off. The pain was unbearable. I dropped my knife. I could not reach it. I fell unconscious.

'I do not know how long I drifted like that. Amongst the calling of the gathering geese and mighty swans, I was ushered eventually to a distant bay. I was virtually dead, but I knew I was being taken to a place of haven and solace. There, I was rescued and nurtured by a vision of wondrous mercy. I was taken into a majestic house and laid by a fire. Those splendid people removed my arm. But there was a special one. Wrasse. She knew I was going there. She made me stronger. Just strong enough to mate her once: it was wonderfully special. It dispelled all miseries and gave me endless hope. I traced a gander's form on her back. Then the abscess in my chest burst. My lungs flooded. That, so suddenly, killed the life in me that I could have had.

'That is my story, Oiwa, who sleeps so deeply at Fallow Fell.'

54

Lonely Departure

'Good,' Shala remarked to herself after raking at Lille Sands. 'A lovely caisie of cockles. Shoulder it up and off home.' On the familiar sheep path she noticed again how oddly long her shadow remained.

Rounding the dune, Juniper's goats bleated, following her in line to Lee Holme. Linnets flitted from the dune on that cloudless autumn afternoon.

'That was such a strange vision. I smelt burnt stone, too.'

'Lee Holme Bay is mending after the storm. The sand's creeping back. The spoots will surely return. There are still plenty of trunks above high tide. Our hometown is looking wonderful too,' she summed up, rounding the busy midden quarry.

'My back's wet,' she realized, as the grass twill stuck cold to her spine. She swung the cockle carrier off her shoulders, noisily dampening the stone path beneath the eaves.

'Milk us,' the goats bleated plaintively under the haddock drying strings.

'Yes, dears,' she answered, 'but I must see Wrasse first.'

'That's right,' Juniper shouted, 'leave your shellfish outside. I'll clean them. Don't bother to think about milking the goats. I'll do it, as usual. You go and see to your old hag,' she admonished, throwing her suede slippers at her as she climbed the log steps.

'I'll ignore that, as usual,' Shala responded, greeting Wrasse as though nothing had happened.

'Don't talk to your sister like that, Juniper,' Gull rebuked. 'We are the head family, but you are certainly not queen yet. We all have chores. Shala does her share. You milk the nannies. I'll rake the embers. I'm going to make meat-bread. Cooked venison, chopped crab apples, sloes, parasol mushrooms, salt and herbs, all mixed in the dough. That's a new recipe. It should be good,' she said aloud. 'If it works, I'll show you how. Now, go and milk.'

'Hmmph,' she growled, retrieving her footwear and stalking out.

'Another fine welcome from your dear sister,' Wrasse remarked from her straw-work seat by the open window. 'I watched you walk back. A fine raking of cockles, Shala.'

'Yes, Wrasse. I will steep them later. I had to speak to you. Are you well?'

'A little stronger, thank the Moon.'

Shala fingered Wrasse's plaited hair as she sat on a low, creaky, wicker stool. Her amber amulet swung over her chequered grass blouse. Her neck's freckles matched the pendant's hue, which stroked gently over her young breasts.

Light shone up between the narrow gaps in the rafters, crossing the angle of sunshine that flooded through Wrasse's window. Dust wafted through the beams like minute stars.

'I saw him, Wrasse,' Shala said, shivering a little. 'Well, not him, just his shadow.'

'Where?' Wrasse asked, leaning forward.

'I was raking. My shadow reached across the wet sand. Then another appeared, followed by a second. They were men shadows. One was talking. White points of light shone in their heads as he spoke. I couldn't hear properly. I'm sorry.'

'Let your mind ease, Ai... Pardon... Shala... Just close your eyes, look again quietly at the shadows. You may see more.'

'Okay, Wrasse. First I saw the shadow of a man, then a huge bird's. It could have been a great auk's. Its shadow then changed into a man's. The first one, tall and strong too, did not speak. His shadow was being told of things.' Shala opened her eyes, looking at Wrasse directly. 'I am sure the speaker said he was Weir.'

Wrasse shook. Trembling she asked, 'So that shadow came from a bird's?'

'Yes, Wrasse.'

Losing breath, her long, grey plaits fell curtain-like over her wrinkled face. 'This was your vision, not mine. It was just for you. Even if Weir was there, it still was not for me,' Wrasse mumbled soon after. 'But please tell me more, if you can.'

'Of course, Wrasse. I heard Weir speak HIS name. It came through so clearly. It is odd, though. I can hear it in my mind, but I cannot utter it. It's all vanishing now. The shadows are going. I can't hear or see anything anymore,' she said, throwing her head back and closing her eyes.

Quietly, slowly, Wrasse began from her bent pose. Outside, Juniper's goats bleated while milk was expressed into bowls. Quernstone milled. Mason's hammerstones tapped as Lee Holme hummed and Quartz fed their pigs old pea vines in their new sties.

'You saw the shadow spirit of Weir. His spirit's living host is now a bird. You saw this through the *shadow side* of the world. I do believe your man has indeed travelled far and Weir's soul has spoken with him. They are possibly in a sacred domain where spirits can be heard.' The porkers outside squealed and grunted wildly. Wrasse waited. 'Shala – What this probably means is that HE is getting closer.'

'Yes, Wrasse,' she answered, as Jasper called for a fennel tea break. 'I've been feeling a vast yearning inside. It feels like a warm mass. My throat tightens. I get goose pimples. I dream of him on the sea: sometimes in terror, others simply sleeping. What should I be doing?'

In a whisper Wrasse said, raising her head, 'I think that you should go to Skara and wait. Wait there, like I did for Weir. I understand. Nobody listened to my predictions of someone coming to Tarmin. No. Not them. Weir was coming to me. I made vigil on my own. Now it's the new Aiva's turn and duty. You must go,' Wrasse knew instinctively.

'Yes, Wrasse. I'm sure of that too. I just needed confirmation. Those goose pimples have come back, but they are hot ones. I'm shaking at the thought.'

'Yes, Aiva. The buckies in your hair rattle. Feel your amber. Is it hot?'

'It is, Wrasse, or is it just my hands?'

'No,' Wrasse answered as she reached and felt it, 'It is hot and smells of resin. It's a sign.'

'I will get ready soon. For the moment I only want to sit here with you. Talk to me. Give me strength.'

'There is much strength in silence. Be still. Meditate,' Wrasse answered with a rasp from her larynx.

'Tea break over,' Jasper called later, as Shala still pondered her past and her future. Flint dragged a reed basket brimming with fish as Sable arrived with Timber.

'He's grown,' Shala noticed. 'I see they've got mushrooms from the hill. They must have walked. Hmmm. A good collection I see from up here: ceps, sprite horns, sheep's feet, blushers and more parasols.'

'Good. Thank you,' Gull said, 'We can poach Flint's fish in Juniper's goats' milk with your mushrooms. I've got special bread baking for later. Come in.'

'We see everything from up here, don't we, Wrasse.'

'You really have to go. Skara waits.'

'I will. Very, very soon.'

* * * * *

'How long have I been sleeping?' Oiwa wondered, slowly waking from his epic dreams.

'Rousing at last,' Gare croaked from her rocky perch.

'Are you Weir or Gare this morning?'

'One of each. Now, get a move on. Rub that sleep from your eyes.'

'Yes. Somehow I seem to see a man's face and body in your beak and eyes. No. It's gone; changed. There's a woman staring. Who's she?'

Gare blinked slowly, as the image faded.

'This is an amazing bird,' Oiwa told himself. 'Surely, with us Whale Geese, Auks must be some of the Sacred Ones. Someday, at journey's end, I will venerate them. Especially Gare. They can't fly, but they're like Geese below the waves. Is that why Weir has an Auk's form?'

'Oiwa,' Gare told him, 'you should wander up Fallow Vale. Explore it like you would a favourite hunting and gathering ground. Take your time. These moments here are precious for you. You will find all you require: more, maybe. *They* will decide when it is your departure time,' he heard clearly in Weir's voice.

'For one who travelled so far, fought so hard and been so sadly killed, he has such a gentle voice. One of complete understanding, hope and guidance,' Oiwa thought as he stood, shaking the sand off.

'The fire is nearly out. I'll shove a timber on it. Funny word that, "Timber",' he wondered momentarily. 'It looks like a Wolf Lake log. I wonder? I can smell its resin so strongly, as it hits the sparkling embers.'

'No need to take Ziit,' Weir's spirit advised.

'Okay, I'll put him back with Foam Fighter. What a mess all my equipment is in. I'll sort it all out later.

'Bare feet are good: freed from boot prison. Here we splash up Fallow Burn. The water tastes splendid, too. It's like honey and elderflower. How it rushes to the broad, salty sea. There isn't exactly a path here, but wherever my feet take me, a way appears. This vale is so lush: ferns, ivies, thick dripping mosses, clumps of pink buttercups, fleshy saxifrage and sea lyme grass grows here abundantly. Each plant has its own space. None overwhelm another. Summer here has been long and blessed.

'Now for that fruit I yearn for,' he thought, gazing around. 'At home we'd pick all sorts of nuts, berries, hips haws and wonderful little plums. Maybe they grow here. That's pink flowering lousewort covered in bees. There're more bees above. Holy Varcar! Our lovely plums: they are sucking the wonderful nectar oozing from them. Excuse me, bees, but I'm climbing up there for some. Look, there're more, bursting with gorgeous flavour. Mind out, bees, my turn. They are perfect. Never mind the lichen down my back, nor the mossy bark. These are so beautiful: that dry, dusty bloom on my tongue, then the burst of flavour every time. I can barely stop. I'm keeping the stones for later. I love the kernels. Their bitter taste is amazing.

'Dang! Ripped my sleeve on a jagged stump,' he cursed, halfway up the damson tree. 'The stitching is so weakened. I will have to mend all this before moving on. Better be careful, Oiwa.

'Well. That's nearly enough,' he told himself, reaching for a final few. 'I will wander on. They'll be here on my return.

'Ah, a birch grove ahead. Their silver bark contrasts so against the green of the waving ferns. Little yellowing leaves are dropping. It is so very beautiful here,' he remarked in rapture. 'The valley sides are really steep and it's so blue above. This is such a haven. There's a hazel stand, and another. I love their nuts. The colouring leaves tell me they'll be ripe. Let me at them?' he urged himself. 'There you are, my lovely ones. Well, you certainly look bigger than those at home. You are moister, too. Oh, that milky flavour. You are the most wonderful nuts I've ever tasted. My teeth don't even move when I crack you. I'm taking some of you with me, too. Here, pockets, open wide,' he told them as he uncradled the browning harvest.

'I think I'll sit on that mossy boulder and eat a pile. I remember how we went through bags full, laughing in the woodlands. Mum dried them and crushed them for breakfast. We'd trap squirrels with them after the trees were bare. How good they tasted too. There was the clever one we never caught. I named him Nutty. I bet he bred a clever family. Yes, we made rakes to clear the ground so we could see them after we shook the trees. They will be doing that now, I suppose. Yes, it was fun catching Honey and Petal suddenly in those pelting nut showers.

'What's that above?' he asked suddenly as a shadow passed over. 'An albatross. What is he watching?' he wondered. 'But now I see mountain strawberries. They are a bit late. But they are there, tumbling out from those cracked rocks in that sunlight spot. I suppose it's their turn now. Up you get, stagger over, Oiwa. Eat your fill, "You're a growing lad", as North Star would say. Well, there are a lot of good ones left. I'll toothpick their pips. I see some have dried. I might just pocket them too. You never know, do you?

'I see Fallow Vale turns further up. When I've finished these, I think I'll move on. That water below hurtles magnificently between the worn boulders and fuchsia bushes. How their cascading flowers put honey into the air. I hear bees, even above the tumble of water. It's like music. There are dragonflies dancing to it over the pools, and damselflies. I think I'll call them damson flies from now on. I see no dragons... yet. On we go, Oiwa. Leave the strawberries now.

'Well, it looks like a huge heap of those massive beach boulders blocking the Vale. The burn runs over and through them. There are yellow flags drooping their brown seed heads into the current and wiggling. How the moss and ferns disguise the shapes. Did battling Giants cast them there, or was it angry Krakens? Even so, I can still cross the Vale here: it actually isn't slippy. My toes grip so well. The water's lovely again as I hop the boulders. From here, I can see them going deep down into the clearest waters. There are huge char rising for flies, bigger than I've ever seen. Go free, fish. I'm not hungry,' he explained as they came to his feet, taking larvae from the Giant's Causeway.

'Now I am across, I discern a faint path beneath this high crag. Oddly formed stones mark it. Shaped by whom, I wonder: the folk before the Ice? It is a wondrous place, though. There's a moss-covered boulder that looks like a breast. There's another. That one further on looks phallic. It most definitely is, as I close in on it. Why carve one here? To mate below the breasts, I suppose.

'The air is sharper up here,' he remarked much further on as he appeared above the shrub-line. It makes me feel so much fitter. I can't see the ocean, either. That, actually, is very refreshing. Just think, up above the cliffs is snow, ice and bitter cold. I saw it, paddling in. It's only here that it's so mild and protected. Or is it magic, as Weir suggested?

'There's another breast stone. I'm going to sit.' To the chirping of a wren, he dozed off, dribbling a little. Awakening, he felt refreshed. 'I've been sleeping for ages. The sun's moved round. I'm in cold shadow. It's brighter further up. I'm going there.

'It's a huge, wide ledge. I can see right down. The burn is just a thin, silver band below. Some of this ledge collapsed a short while ago. There's the fresh tumble. That's a hewn rock down there. And more still at the edge. It would have made an arc. And there's the Crescent Moon up there, huge and shining down around me from the dark blue sky. I can make out the rest of the circle. It's lighting up the whole arena. I must look at the other blocks.

'They are all sculpted Moon shapes,' he determined after his search. 'They are Her phases. This *is* a holy place. I feel it so much. But of course, Rush is looking down on me. He's there, behind the moon, his face in her shadow. I can feel the smile: his spirit in my veins, pulsing. This is indeed a unique sanctuary.

'But there, by the very precipice's edge, precariously perched, a lunar form shines in the crescent's beam. I have to touch it. Yes, this boulder has been brought here. It isn't local. Like the vast pebbles, rolled from afar, this has come a long way too.

'Yes, Moon, in the fingers of your light, I see your face.

'But I have further to climb in Fallow Vale. Under the cliff fall, the path heads up through stunted, moonlit bushes where glow worms sparkle. Excuse me, Moon effigy, I have to leave.

'Well, well, well. The path turns as the ledge widens into a disc-shaped platform ringed by menhirs. It stops at those tall, lush ferns climbing within that cleft. That's where I'm headed. Wrens fly in and out. How the fronds curl, forever unfolding. I'm sure there's a way through.

'The fern-tips are covered in pollen. It sticks as I push through. My beard's dusted with it. Warm air gently blows out from a void, like sweet breath from a sleeping partner. I'm easing myself through. It's wet and warm inside. The ferns are minute now and covered in tiny spider webs. I have to push through the gossamer. It seems hotter as it resists. Push, Oiwa. I'm in. I'm covered in hot, damp dew. It is so strange. Maybe I shouldn't be here, but I feel as though I was invited, even enticed within.

'Thin shafts of light from behind penetrate the narrow, lichen-lined passage. I can just squeeze along it. Now its soft moss presses around me. There's a faint green glow ahead in a misty cavern. It is beautifully warm now. It engulfs me. Even inside I sense its loveliness as I breathe. The shimmer brightens. That's strange, though: I hear simmering water. I'm going closer. Light shines through a drape. It looks like strands of algae. I'm parting it, entering. It smells just like Hot Ponds. I wish Taiga was here, but I mustn't. She told me to forget. It's hotter in here and far moister. Everything drips around me, sultry. I'm soaked in glorious dew.

'I see such soft stalactites dangling from above. They are of tiny matted plants that bend as I push past. How my toes love the warm, wet moss between them. I'm sure they are being cleansed and cured. That simmering comes from just ahead. On you go, Oiwa.'

'Do enter my inner cavern, Oiwa,' a deep, all-engulfing, female voice invited.

'Where did that come from?' he thought as it echoed round the hidden halls.

'Come in, Oiwa. You are most welcome,' it boomed over the rhythmic stewing sounds.

'I see no one. Who is it? I hear you breathing.'

'Do not be afraid, Oiwa,' the voice assured gently. 'I have been waiting for you. I am glad you visited my Moon observatory. Relax, young man. Don't stand there with your mouth gaping. You are hot and you are perspiring. You may remove your clothing in my presence. Just let it drop beside you. You will be a great deal more comfortable in here, naked with me.'

'It is *so* hot. The voice is right. I can hardly bear the weight of this garb.'

'Come forward from the gloom into the glimmer,' the voice asked. 'That's good, Oiwa.'

'My stomach has touched a great level rock on a roughly hewn pedestal,' his toes told him. 'Its worn edges drip gently with steaming water. It contains a pool, shallow and clear. Mist rises, condensing among the plants. I see my reflected face, wiped clean of pollen by the fine webs I pushed through. There's my blue-centred Star. My earplugs shine like the Moon outside.'

'Stop admiring yourself, Oiwa. Look up at me.'

'Oh!' he exclaimed inwardly, 'You are a giantess. I can just see parts of you through the mists. You look like graven stone. But your breasts are like great moons that loll on the other side of the basin.'

'You are most flattering, Oiwa. I read your mind. There you are before me, bare-naked with no weapon. I could crush you with one thumb if I so desired.'

'You won't. I know it. I'm not afraid. How do you know my name? Has Gare been here?' he willed her to answer.

'Yes, Oiwa, and Weir when he was Weir. But I've known you since before as a former spirit. I watched your new conception. I am Gumar, as you call me. Others name me Guman. Sometimes I live behind my Moon, where Rush bides. At others, I live in the caves of the Earth. We are in my Arctic abode where I can be closer to my Moon, touch her and see what she sees.'

Oiwa pressed himself even closer to the shallow crater, gripping it, wondering, 'Why me? What would my parents think? And Mica, would he believe?'

'Oiwa, you have been chosen. You have sought your way and destiny. Now it is discovering you. Others have been chosen before. Weir was one. He, like so many others, never quite arrived there. You may, if your wit and luck hold firm, arrive to fulfil your life. No one can tell you what that is. I know what will and will not be. I possess the knowledge of the creators who live in sacred places. This is one. You will never return here, but you will always be a part of this place if you succeed.'

'I see your face now. I dared not look earlier. You have a serene beauty. Your dark hair flows like the waters of Fallow Burn. That white streak is like the weaving band I saw from high up in Fallow Vale. You perspire, too. It runs from your shoulders to the great dish.'

'Thank you, Oiwa, for those kind thoughts. My sweat is the source of many rivers that run in the moonlight from deep caves.

'Your people, the Goose Clan, are faithful to the words of Tumar and me. You know our story. Buzzard of the Stork Clan gave you good advice about the giving of your seed. You have taken that soundly. The blood of the people of the earth must be mixed and shared to keep your races healthy.'

'Yes, I know the legends of my ancestors. I recall the Longi verses. That is what Buzzard advised, but with different words. I realize it now. That is why he allowed us to mate within his clan.'

'Oh. I'm stiffening at the very thought. He's touching the warm pedestal as he rises. The gentle plants caress me there. It is such a sweet feeling. As I push, it engrosses me. I sense those I mated with.

'

'How gracefully he moves within me,' Gumar remarked privately. 'Let my breath caress his spine as he sways in rapture while he comes. There, Oiwa. Let it go. Fertilize me as you cast your head back. How your Goose Star shines as you shake your potent pollen. Relax while I store your tiny babe. I will keep your wee one among my treasures, to be born aeons hence, when the world of Humans is in dire need.'

'All I can do is flop forward and lean here,' Oiwa found. 'My beard dips in the water. The ripples spread with my breath. I feel Gumar's waters trickle over me as I watch the reflections move. Her divine smile looks down past her huge breasts.'

'Oiwa, you have mated with the Great Gumar. Now, go yonder to multiply. Your seed is richer. It will spread far if sown well. You will be a powerful, but a wise and gentle man, should you survive your hazards.'

'Gumar's reflection fades with her voice. Now I see myriads of stars. My Star shines, too. There's the Moon with Rush's face within, but now another face. One I've only seen in dreams. How her hair moves in wonderfully fine plaits. That warm stone that matches it. Does she glance deeply into my eyes? Why do I smell resin?'

55

‘Last ‘Leg

‘I have to go,’ Shala knew. ‘I will leave my bag outside with my bow. Then I must steep my cockles in the cistern by the spring to clean. Always complete your tasks, then there’s no come back from your dear sister. Will there be geese flying there? Who knows?

‘Nothing just now,’ she thought, peering in. ‘Just cockles. No, Oh! It’s Timber,’ she exclaimed abruptly at his sudden reflection.

‘Good evening, Shala. Did I surprise you?’

‘Yes, a little,’ she answered awkwardly, rising from her knees. ‘How are things at Char?’

‘Oh, just the usual. We hunted down an auroch up on the hill, though. An extremely wild beast.’

‘Was it a raging bull?’

‘Yes: good and brave. We’ve got most of it dried and more buried in our cold place. We’ve brought some. Do you ever wear the necklace I gave you?’

‘Hmmm. Yyes, Timber. On special occasions,’ she answered, wondering if it was still in Wrasse’s keeping.

‘Will you walk with me for a while? We can watch the sun go to bed,’ Timber asked.

'That would be nice, but I do have quite a few things to do this evening. Will you be staying long?'

'A few days, if possible. Do you want any help?'

'Er... not really, Timber. But Flint would love assistance with all his fish,' Shala put in quickly. 'Let's get back to the house.'

'This isn't going well,' thought Timber.

'Timber's here, do you need help with your catch, Flint?' she asked directly they were back.

'Yes. Thanks. I need to split them for drying.'

'I have to go up to Wrasse,' Shala excused.

'Say hello to Sable, Shala,' Gull called as she dashed up the steps.

'Hello, Sable, and thanks for all those mushrooms.'

'You are welcome. Good to see you. How did your journey go?'

'Very well, Sable. We visited many villages and met many folk. It was so exciting; too exciting at times,' she answered, disappearing from the top of the stair.

'I'm leaving,' Shala whispered to Wrasse. 'I didn't want to go like this, but it's best. Can you tell them for me, please?'

'Yes. I'll explain. I'll make Gull understand. Is it Timber turning up that makes you go this way?'

'Partly. Juniper, too. I don't need her sniping just now. By the way, have you got the necklace Timber gave me?'

'Yes, it's in my things. Do you want it back?'

'No, Wrasse. Just hang it near my bed.'

'Is there anything else?'

'No. I have everything ready in my bag. I only need secrecy. I must do this on my own.'

'Quite right. I'm not fit to come. I would hold you back, anyway. My heart goes with you. We know how vital this is.'

'Privacy is the main thing. I must to do this on my own.'

'You might need your bow.'

'Yes, she's by the door, too.'

'You had better go down. Act normally. Leave after dusk. It's darker earlier now. Not so long to wait.'

'We aren't wrong about this, are we?' Shala asked with a sudden doubt.

'No. Even if we are, you have to go just to find out.'

'Okay, Wrasse.'

'I will keep hold of Weir's arm and pray for you – for you both. For us all.'

'There you are, Shala,' Timber said at the foot of the stair. 'Your mum's meat bread smells very good. It's resting by the fire.'

'Yes, none of us have tried it yet. It's for after the fish,' she answered, wishing she were somewhere else.

'Hello, Timber,' Juniper interrupted. 'Here's a bowl of haddock stew. There's smoked and fresh in it. I put the butter on top for you. I hope you like it,' she said, squeezing in between them. 'Tell me about your auroch hunt?'

'Let me look at your meat bread, Gull,' Sable asked.

'Of course. I cooked it on a hot hearth, but under a bowl, which I heaped ash over.'

'It looks wonderful. Can I taste?'

'Here, try this bit.'

'Oh, that's not bread, Gull. It's cake! I love it.'

'This is my chance. I'm going now while Jasper dishes out the beer. Good, Quernstone's turned up with ham and is asking about Mum's loaf: "cake", they are all calling it. That will keep everyone occupied. Here I go. The Moon's going down. It will be dark, but I'll see okay. I forgot. I must pull out my cockles to drain. Don't leave a job half done.

'How the stars reflect from the still, dark water there,' she noticed. 'Right, lift the caisie. Wait! There's a face. Dreamlike, bearded, hazel eyes, straw hair. He's got a bright Star with a blue speck on his forehead. He's gazing at star reflections, too, now into my eyes. Can he see me? Can he? It's like he's at the edge of the world. I can't even go back and tell Wrasse. It is he... He *will* be here. There's a strangely warm breeze blowing, like hot breath obliterating my vision. But listen... That's the first geese of autumn honking overhead. It's time. I must go. I'll pull the cockles out now. That's more geese up there.

'There you are, Juniper,' she said under her breath as she placed the caisie of cockles silently under her eaves. 'Job done. Hitch my gear and I'm off.'

* * * * *

'The stars are fading,' Oiwa noticed as he leaned, sated, onto the bowl's great rim. 'The Moon is dissipating now. But there's another face flickering under Gumar's hot breath. She looks through me. But I hear Solan honking. This is an amazing place. I'll never forget it.

'I must move. No. It still feels so glorious in there. Ohly I do think that wretched cramp's setting in. Pull out: ugh. Hop. Phew, that's staved it off.

'My feet feel wonderful on this waterworn rock. It's though it lives under my soles. Boiling sounds still echo by that dim, green light, where vapours pour from that tall rock niche. I'll push through the hanging creepers curtaining it.

'There's a great stone slab set on three of those huge pebbles in here. There's two horn beakers. One virtually empty, the other brimming with a honey-coloured liquid. It must be good. Oh, it is. It's as lovely as mating. It tastes of the scent of every flower I can think of. It's so warm as it goes down. I just absorb it: I feel it melt into that deep part of my stomach where those hot pangs pulse. I can taste every season, the parching of the sun, mouldering leaves, hard, driven snow and crocus. This has to be the ambrose that Gumar and Tumar drink. She must have drunk the other before our mating.

'I'm feeling so weary. I'll lie on the table. It looks comfortable and dry. The rock's not hard on my skin at all. Am I sleeping? I'm drifting somewhere. It's that drink. I sense invisible hands gently massaging me. I'm floating now as I feel combs in my beard. A blade shaves and shapes while my scalp is oiled. My tired dreadlocks are being eased. My hair rests over my shoulders in fine plaits like bowstrings, but I still see no hands.

'That's my calves and thighs being kneaded. All signs of cramp sink into the table with every kind move.

'I must have drifted to sleep. It seems so different here now. The water doesn't boil. The vapours have gone. I must move; find my clothing. But there it all is. Everything's been mended. Each rent patched. There's fur from the frozen graveyard for my hood-trim. The seams, newly stitched. My toggles re-strung. Everything gently oiled, like my hair to run the rain off.

'My boots look utterly different. But they are mine. They shine magnificently: no longer flabby and ragged. My necklace! It's been completely re-strung. Everything is in the same order and it is *so* radiant, even in this gloaming light. It feels splendid against me. As I dress, I'm getting stronger. Boots on over my troos, toggle up my parka and I'm ready. Thank you, Gumar. I'm going now.'

Silence answered as he made slowly for the exit.

'The spider webs I pushed through haven't been mended. Here goes, back out through the ferns. The air breathes freshly on my nose as those fronds flick shut behind me. It's so bright. It must be another day. The menhirs look even older as I take the path. It looks more defined, like I mustn't lose my way. Gumar's moonstones are overgrown, but my path goes on.

'The Giant's Causeway is dryer underfoot. The lake behind has shrunk. The char... vanished. It all looks so ordinary. The track remains. It's well tramped, by whom? Previous visitors? Past mates to Gumar? Who can tell me?

'The strawberries have vanished! There are the hazel trees, but bare, gnarled and nut-less. At least I have ones in my pockets. And the damsons: gone... stripped. I'm very glad I kept the stones.

'The trek is so much shorter coming back to the beach. That's odd, the fire must have gone out. The pine has hardly burned. But the embers glow under it. Weird. It's catching now. Was it waiting for me?

'Where's the Foam Fighter?' he asked alarmed. 'There she is. Tied to that upright. She looks new! She's scraped and oiled. That reflecting, re-stained decoration is Kraken's tentacles. What a reminder. If they weren't so frightening, they'd be beautiful.

'Where's my stuff?' he yelped inside, running to his craft. 'There it is, neatly stowed under the hide cover. There's only one hole to sit through. Taiga's has gone. It's just for me. Ziit's clipped to the side with hazel grips. There are his arrows: the flights new and clean.

'That's wonderful, and I see bags of cracked hazels and damson prunes behind my seat. Everything's provided, even a birch tyg of nut paste, honey and sorrel. That should keep the scurvy away.

'Those are Gare's webbed footprints going to the water. I hope she hasn't left me. I don't want to be alone again. That lump has returned in my throat. Shut bad thoughts away, Oiwa. It's begun to snow. Get in your boat and GO.'

* * * * *

'I'll walk up by the Ancestor House,' Shala told herself. 'I shall pick rowan berries to leave outside the tomb. From there I will go directly over the hill. I'm avoiding all towns and villages. I will have to pass through the City of Bore Brig, hopefully unnoticed.

'This is dark and wearisome,' Shala realized after some time. 'I hear the deer barking up here above the buffeting wind. The horizon keeps receding, getting further. I'll weave along this sheep path.

'There at last,' she puffed sitting on the flat rocky outcrop. 'I'll shelter below and try sleeping wrapped in my grass cape from my backpack.'

Yawning awake at dawn, she ached. 'That was a cold night. But the view is good from here. It's a wide landscape of sweeping hills down to marshlands with occasional rises to dry land. There are lochs reflecting the morning sunshine. On the hillocks I see small settlements where smoke rises from distant hearths. I do wish I had some of that cake with me,' she thought wistfully.

'Never mind cake. I am travelling to meet him, whoever he is. I just yearn for him... him alone. I don't even know him. Does he speak our language? He might have someone with him? I don't know. I just have to trust my visions. I think of him day and night. I know exactly what it all means. If he does arrive, I will have to share him. Arrange for him to breed. Record who he's successful with: plan other matings; Feed him, keep him well so he can make them pregnant. I understand this. I will make it happen, but I want him, too. Maybe I'm still too young. But if so, I wouldn't feel like this. Think on the present; pull yourself up, Shala. Get moving.'

Up she got with her rucksack and bow, making tracks through the dewy grass. As with Wrasse, she went through scrublands, woods, took marsh paths of birch branches and staves. She smelt and heard auroch. She saw deer moving through bracken, keeping their distance. Grouse flew from their vantage places in loud cackles and drumming of wings. Cappercaille called as geese flew in from the west as she progressed, possessed, thinking of him only.

'I am so glad I didn't allow the phallus stone to penetrate me in the initiation house,' she thought. 'If he is the one, then it must be him who breaks my seal. I will have no other. I don't care if I am not his first. He has come a long way. But I want him and I do so want to keep him,' she thought constantly until dusk

'I don't seem to have made any progress at all,' she thought, focusing on the horizon. 'But I must have, look how far I've come. I need somewhere to sleep. There's a sheltered copse tucked in the hillside. I'll make for that.'

The moon rose. The first stars pricked the sky through the canopy as she drank from a dripping rock. 'There's plenty of fuel for a wee fire. I have bread and dried meat. I do wish I took cake, though. It smelled so good. But I do have dried fruit and honey biscuits. I will survive, and tomorrow I can try for a grouse.' There she slept, snug in her cloak.

At Lee Holme, Wrasse heard the cockles touch the flag path. 'What shall I tell them all?' she thought, 'The truth, I suppose. There's nothing like it. Now sleep, old woman.'

The household stirred. Wrasse rose. 'Gull,' she called, 'can you and Sable come up?'

'Yes, Wrasse. Would you two like some cake?' Gull asked.

'Thank you. Is there enough?'

'Yes... No! It's gone? Who's swiped it?

'I admit. It was not me,' Jasper joked from their bed.

'Well, who then?

'Ask our greedy son.'

'Oh, bother. I'll make another then.'

'Why not two or three, if they are that popular?'

'You cut the meat and gather more parasols. The fruit's already chopped. Now I'm off upstairs to see Wrasse.'

'I bet she took it in the dead of night,' Juniper hinted.

'Sorry about the cake, here's an apple, Wrasse. Where's Shala? Have you seen her, Sable?'

'No, but her cockles are washed in her caisie outside.'

'That is why I wanted to see you up here. She's gone. Don't be shocked, Gull. Don't worry either. She's walking to Skara. She must not be followed. Shala, whom I would prefer called Aiva, hopes against hope to meet the traveller. She's sure he will land on the Dune there. I am, too. Please be patient.'

'Let me sit and take this in,' Gull asked, lowering herself into the wicker chair.

'Can I set myself on Sha... Aiva's bed?'

''Course, Sable,' Wrasse answered, chewing the stalk. 'She left last night. Stop looking so worried, Gull. She can look after herself, you know.'

'But she's my little one.'

'Nonsense. She's her own body now. She will be back. You know that. Stop fussing and listen. She has much to consider. What we have to do is prepare for her return. She will need somewhere else to live, for a start. I'm sure something can be built with all the timber around.'

'Speaking of Timber, where is he?' Gull asked.

'Never mind him. We must discuss Aiva's or Shala's, whatever she chooses, arrangements, when she brings him here. There will be a problem with Juniper. I can see that and I'm sorry. Maybe Juniper can be distracted. We discussed before how she will *have* to share him. She might not be happy about her own sister mating with him.'

'Jasper and I only want what is best for her. Shala's still very young, but after your journey she's grown in wisdom and stature. She's changed such a lot. I see it. She hides it from others, particularly Juniper. But changed she is, for the even better.'

'She's had further visions. A very striking one came to her on Lille Sands only yesterday. That is why she has left. She heard his name; spoken by the Spirit of Weir: she is sure he is now getting much closer.'

'I understand, Wrasse. But it is hard, just the same.'

'Sable, you have not had time to tell me of your trip round the townships to see the situation yet, have you?'

'I only arrived back at Char a few days ago. I needed to sort the family out. You know how things go awry when you are away.'

'Minnow? How was he?'

'He's okay, it's the menfolk, and then there's Timber. He's been like a sickening cow since he waved goodbye to Shala. That's why I had to take him here. Much against my will, I might add. He will be upset again that she's gone. I told him so, but boys just don't listen at that age.'

'They never do at any age,' Wrasse remarked. 'But do tell us about your findings?'

'Okay. Things are not good. In fact, quite bad,' she began, frowning. 'There are too many wasted pregnancies. Some of the bairns die, and others are just not viable. It is terrible to have to end their lives, but sometimes it's necessary. There are some seemingly good births, but then we do not know how they will grow up. We do have a bad breeding record. It is not any one person's fault, nor any one township's. It is just, as we all realize, the family lines are far too near. I spoke privately to women's leaders and their close sisters. They all agreed that something must be done. Men have to mate. It is their nature and desire. It is also the women's. I like it, we all do. Or did,' she slipped out, looking at Wrasse obliquely, thinking, 'It's too late for her.'

Sable continued, 'Initially, just to see how things go, the women are going to make baby stoppers for the men. We think they could work.'

'What are they?' Gull asked earnestly.

'We tried it, in fact my man and I did. It was simple, really. We used piglet guts. I had some laid by for sausages. All I did was to get a length, tie a knot in one end, and that's it! You can use a small eel skin too. It is lucky for Copse that we don't really need them. I can conceive with him at any time. You and Jasper will be the same. But families like ours are getting scarcer,' confirmed Sable. 'What we did was this; just before we were going to join up, I stretched one of the piglet skins down over Copse's Mating Rod, as he likes to call it. When he entered me, I held the skin down by his balls. He liked that, too. So did I,' she added happily. 'When he went in and out, I kept it stretched tight. He absolutely loved that, and I found the knot at the end thrilling, too. Well, when he'd finished his mating, I asked him to pull out. We had a good look at the gut and not a drop of his potency leaked. His juices were all in the baby stopper. He's going to the eel traps before I get home,' Sable laughed. 'He'd better not catch any huge ones, though, had he?'

Gull urged, 'So you think these baby stoppers will work?'

'Should do, if they are handled correctly,' Sable added, smiling.

'I think,' Wrasse put in quickly, 'that they could be an answer. If men wore them, well, with those who are too close, blood-wise, then we can gain important time.'

'Shala hopes we are planning. She will understand her duties. With this, we can help her. If her predictions are correct, then he can mate with those you select. Following a successful mating, then the man and wife can enjoy each other as before, with no risks. Well, just as long as she's milking. We just have to convince the men that it is for their good and everybody else's.'

'There will be jealousies and suspicion. Perhaps lots,' Gull intimated.

'Yes. We have to convince the men, and some women, this is our way of survival,' Sable said with deep concern, adding, 'after all, he can't get all of them full of babies. Or can he? Well, if he does, there will be inbreeding again, anyway. That won't do either. We must find others to breed with.'

'Let's worry about that later,' Wrasse advised quickly. 'Shala had a dream about that, the Goosemen dream. Remember, she told us of the forest arriving. I'm sure we can trust in her visions. I certainly do.'

56

Singing on the Sea

'I'm used to solitude, but I do so miss Gare. I know she's gone. Alone I am, again, on the vast ocean, paddling through the snow. My firelight, well behind me; gone: I know I can't go back. It is on... on. Sing a song, Oiwa.

Paddling lone on the great wide sea,
Nought but snow landing white on me.
Riding the waves to where I must go,
Where that is, I just do not know...

'But I feel I do know. Just singing those words in my head makes my star chart glow. Gare guided me when I needed her. Fallow Vale made me well. Winter is setting in. I have to flee, just as Solan does, taking his flock to his other domains. I hear them now, high over the clouds. They call me. The honks beat in my breast as their wings waft the air. My wings will work the paddle.

'"Follow, Oiwa; follow. We will guide you now", they call. I will follow, I will, Solan.

Follow us to the Rich Lands beyond the horizon.
Follow to where the Sun still lurks.
Know your way in the dark as it descends.
Look up in your head and see us as other skeins join the race.

'I feel my necklace move across my breast, like feathers, as my wings ply the salt. I've found my Goose-will. I'm strong, stronger than I have ever been.

Fly across waves on the ocean broad,
Make wake behind as I go forward.
Chase the sun to where it hides from me,
Gather its warmth in my life to be.

'It is so good what a song can do for one's spirits,' Oiwa thought, as his lifted in the backing blizzard. I am migrating, as my Sky-Clan must. Paddle, Oiwa at a steady pace: Always forward, always on. Keep that star; follow it.

'They know where they are going and they know I am also going there. Just like Weir, only, I WILL SURVIVE! Summer here turns to darkness. I must travel towards where the sun rises. Follow that course, going slightly south. My head tells me there is land there, and something between.

Beat my paddle like air-filled wings,
Ride the next wave and see what it brings.
Fly on the water like wind in the sky.
Make my way on the waves I ply.

'I hear another skein now. I'm not alone any more. The snow's ceased,' he realized later. 'The moon shines on my waves. The stars above sparkle within the rising and falling motion. Now the night is clear I see a bright glow, far to the east. Its reflection tickles the waves ominously. That smell of mountain fire touches the very air. It's something to paddle away from. Solan, don't let it scorch your feathers,' he wanted to shout. 'That is far greater than Reeking Mountain: more powerful; angrier.

'I still feel that ambrose glow in my belly. The warmth grows within and through me, from my clean toes to my plaited scalp. It gives me energy like my kin above, burning their fat in flight. The flavours of their pastures and all those good essences were in ambrose, keeping me well.'

Oiwa paddled on. Finally, he felt weariness slowly overtake him. Snow swirled in front of his prow, vanishing on the dark sea. Oiwa watched and rested, hearing the goose songs above. 'I can't see through this snow, now. But the Foam Fighter's beak points in the correct direction. I can rest and steer, maintaining my course. The waves carry me forward, as in the sea slumbers I have had before.'

He awoke to the sounds of breaching whales. 'They are sending their fountains high in the sky,' he saw, rubbing his eyes. 'They catch the starlight. There are so many. I feel their numbers all around. Up come more. Please don't tip me,' he mouthed, grabbing a handful of nuts. Keep me safe on the waves, whales. I pray we don't meet Krakens. That one's looking at me. He's so close. Their surf rushes behind, white against the dark as the moon catches their hides in yellow glory. And now, they've gone. No sight, nor sound of them. They ply the deeps below, looking up to my wake.

'Now for damson stones. There are more in my pocket than I thought. I couldn't have spat out that many. Gumar put them there. Don't eat them all, Oiwa. I will plant a grove in her name: the hazels too, even the strawberries. That's a plan. It will be a holy place. Maybe she will visit, and Tumar as well? These kernels are very fine. Crack, there goes another; each one sweeter than the one before. How can this be? It is her magic.

'Now for the hazel, honey and sorrel. It is so good with prunes, as well. Those dried damsons sparkle in my mouth, and more stones to crack. This is a lovely breakfast as dawn breaks. Follow the rising sun, Oiwa. Paddle for it, and that distant, calling skein in the brightening sky.'

* * * * *

'Got you, grouse,' Shala rejoiced, as it hit the ground with her arrow through it. 'I'll breast it, leg it and sear the flesh on my fire. Then onwards.'

'Cake?' she heard from behind, startled.

'Timber! What are you doing here?'

'Following you, of course. I noticed the smoke. I knew it would be you. Well, do you want cake or not?'

'No. I don't want your cake.'

'It's not legally mine. I stole it. But if you want none, you will just have to watch me eat it.'

'Go away. I want to be alone.'

'No. Watch. Here goes the first bite.'

'Why are you following me?'

'Simple. I love you. I want to be with you and I want you to love me. I know it's no use,' he told her, with heart thumping, 'But I'm not going to mope in a corner any more. I want you to love me, but I can see you won't. Now, do you want cake or not?'

'Yes. It's too much for you, anyway. It's best shared. You are right, Timber. I can't love you. I never will. That does not mean I don't like you. I can't stop you following me. I wish you wouldn't. I want you to go home to Char and leave me to do what I must.'

'Fine, Shala. I won't follow you anymore. But I'm certainly not going back to Char. I'll walk right by your side, wherever you are heading.'

'You can't.'

'I can. Watch. Now eat your cake. You still have a long way to go, Shala. You are avoiding people. You are not taking the most direct route to Skara.'

'How do you know I'm going there?'

'I overheard Mother. I'd partly worked it out when we looked from the tomb tower. She confirmed it when she had one of her private chats with Crill from Part Water.'

'This makes my blood boil,' Shala thought. 'But he's here. He isn't going to leave. Actually, he's changed. I quite admire that.'

'Understand this, Shala. I won't make any advances towards you. At least let me travel with you willingly. You are going to the Forgotten Place where Old Spirits lie. Where legend says the Fore Folk were drowned as the sea swallowed them. The rest fled to a distant place, to the very home they left aeons before. Those who remained alive fled there in their last boats, poor souls. Is one returning?'

'I think so, Timber,' she answered, spinning round to look at him. He saw her tears welling when she tried to continue. 'I've felt it for a long time now. Wrasse knows, so do others.'

'You have to go down to the Vales sometime. Don't you? I can do the talking for you. I can lie to others, but not to you. Everybody in Lee Holme knows that you are going to meet HIM. I can divert attention from you.'

Shala looked down to the Flow Burn below. There, small settlements and the larger farms lay. The Loch of Scap spread silvery in the valley plain. Houses on the isle at the far end had folk busy with their lives.

'You have to go near Tannus by the Marsh and then through Bore Brig. And then there's Market Ridge and Stone Road. Only past them will you get to the ocean, Shala.'

'All right, Timber. As long as you leave me when we get there. I do not want you staying a moment longer. I'm to be completely on my own. Do you understand?'

Timber's eyes blinked from his narrow forehead. His reddened eyebrows knitted together above his long, freckled nose. His new blackthorn spike tilted at an angle from his right nostril as his answer came, 'I understand perfectly, Shala. Now, have some cake.'

* * * * *

After endless hours of paddling through the darkening world, Oiwa gull-napped. He held his knees tightly against the skin sides of his sea canoe, balancing in his seat. He gripped his precious paddle like a rooted oak. He poised himself, bearded chin on his chest and slept. The moment his balance shifted, he wakened, instantly steadied himself, falling back to sleep in moments. He rested like an albatross above in the breeze.

The Arctic, snow-laden wind drove him forward again: the same current as his Geese brethren above. The flow that took the fallen trees and fetid Kraken were his too, Nature's will providing his power.

'I'm covered in snow,' Oiwa realized on waking. 'Shake it off. Get it from my apron. Shovel it with my paddle. It's weighing me down. There's still a small, sloshing pool in here. I don't want more.

'Distant dawn light shows. Paddle, Oiwa. Follow the sun's ray. There, too is a dark shape, jutting like a blackened tooth. Even from this far I hear gulls calling. I could shelter in its lee for a while. But I hear Weir's voice speaking from a dream. What is it? There's a distant rumble, too, from far behind. Even the stars in my map shake. Is that what he's warning me of?

'That tooth draws me. That great, slanting divide of shining white quartz, dashing from summit to sea, drags my prow towards it. The current swirls me along as the snow ceases. That block shines while the sun gets stronger. I'm not sure I should go near. Paddle as I might, though, I'm drawn to it. Now I hear the waves bursting at its roots, breaking like decaying gums. That rock is where grey dawn meets the night. It's surely the Last Place they spoke of: the Black Isle. It's where Weir went and was never heard of after. But he did get there. I know that somehow.'

'Go past it, Oiwa. Don't go near. Paddle away,' came Weir's dreamy voice. 'Naarwhal's daughters still work her magic. Beyond is your new world. Where the dawn shows clear; go there.'

'I'm too close already! I'm being drawn. I'm back-paddling, but the power is so great. Weir... Help! I hear them singing. I thought it was gulls. The heights are above me. The sparkling white rock, like Gumar's hair, appears to pulsate.

'The water's now calmed in its shelter. Even the waves have ceased breaking. I'm so close, far too close. But that's elks' ears waving from the pearly quartz. They look so succulent. I'll pull some to chew. The water's gone dead calm.'

'Save us! Oiwa, save us,' he heard wailed shrilly from above. 'Save us. Take us. We are lost without our mother: Weir slayed her. We are bereft. Give us sons, Oiwa.'

'That's the dream. It has all come clear. Weir told me: men's bones: dried babes, the enchanted musk oxen: the fearful Narwhal. I can't let go of the elks' ears. They are strangling my hand. 'Help us,' they still screech. My axe. Swing it. Cut the stuff. The water is shaking. That rumble from afar trembles up the quartz divide. They still scream down at me. I see them raging. The glimmering stone is cracking. The elks' ears tumble from it, pulling me out. Drag it up and over the side: I'm freed. Cut the stuff with my axe. Leave the chunks. No time... Paddle.

'The water is trembling, as the white quartz is. I see its reflection shudder. Shards of it splinter from above. Or is it those freaks hurling it at me? The water is in turmoil around me; shivering; foaming; mounting. The rock pulses and grinds like a splitting molar. I hear their agony above, but leave them. They are enchantresses, tricking me.

'I see the light ahead. I hear violent rents behind as that vile, black tooth fissures. The ocean swells. The water boils while the stack rends apart. I'm thrown forward into the light of day dawning. One glimpse back: there they are, wailing, their oxen leaping into the turmoil.

'No! Witches. No! I will not save you men-murderers, Weir killers. Stay. Sink in your disgusting caverns,' he wanted to yell as he stroked his paddle mightily. The flash of the burning mount, leagues behind, toasted Oiwa's back as the quake wave mounted. Black Isle split asunder as heaving nerves of the distant volcano cleaved the white fault. Narwhal's daughters plummeted.

'Paddle, paddle, paddle!' was all Oiwa could tell himself. 'That's drowning voices gagging. The isle has breached. The sea reddens below with escaping magma. Steam rockets, screaming skywards. Paddle against death!' he roared inside. 'Boiling musk ox and their cooking herders mix in an ocean broth. Foam Fighter, scud on the crest,' he prayed as the racing pile of displaced deeps took him. 'Steer to the light. Scalding mist pursues angrily now. I don't deserve this. Scarper on the surge, Foam Fighter. Take us away from the mayhem. Race easterly. Trace my Geese. We aren't going down. We will ride this wave. Keep at the crest. Don't allow it to break over us. Ride the driving force. Let it speed me on my path. My wake trails as I chase. Keep it up. Don't tire. Always on. Don't stop until the wave weakens, however far that may be.'

* * * * *

'There are wild auroch ahead, Shala. We should skirt them. They are not like our domestic ones.'

'Yes... They call to their brethren in those pastures below. Best not go between them. Uphill again, I think.'

'More cake, Shala?'

'It's lovely, but later, Timber. I'm worried. I felt the ground tremble. Did you?'

'No. But those geese on the loch down there have taken flight. They head back in the direction they came from. There're others doing it further off. See?'

'Yes. It's a sign. We must move quicker.'

'That's good. At least she's speaking to me. I feel so much better, having been direct. Even if it doesn't get me anywhere. Better to try and fail than not try at all,' Timber thought.

'You should have gone by boat,' he suggested on the hilltop. 'It would have been quicker if me, Flint and Dale had crewed you.'

'That is precisely why I'm walking. I wanted to be alone.'

'Well, you aren't. You've got me now.'

'Yes, Timber. But not by choice.'

'Well, we don't always get what we want in life. Do we,' he answered poignantly and walked on ahead.

'Here, Timber. Have some of this dried venison,' she called, running to catch up.

'Thank you. We can go down from here through that hazel grove.'

'There are folk there, Timber.'

'Yes. They've seen us. It would look strange if we didn't greet them. Come on.'

'Aye, what like?' The older woman asked, showing them her basket of mushrooms.

'Just grand,' Timber replied. 'Plenty of nuts too,' he commented. 'Where are you from?'

'Char,' he replied for both of them.

'Some way off. Are your grandparents buried there?'

'Aye, for a long time now.'

'What brings you to these parts?'

'Pilgrimage to Bore Brig,' he half-lied.

'You'd better get a move on before the Bore comes, then.'

'Yes, that's just what we want to see.'

'Take some nuts with you. Enjoy Bore Bridge's escaping voles,' she said.

'Thank you, we will,' he replied to the family as they made for the open slopes.

'Well. After that interview, I expect they can make up the rest.'

'Yes, Shala, and I expect it will be wonderfully exaggerated. We must press on. The land drops away further on.'

Eventually they rounded the great hill.

'Look, Timber. The landscape is like a huge bowl rimmed with undulating hills. There are the twin mounts of High Land. Some say they are the breasts of slumbering Guman and, when she wakes, all that down there will be flooded. We know that when she scratches, the Bore comes.'

'Yes, and to the north, the Harrar Hills, where the great skate from the sea's depths landed after the ebb at Skara,' Shala said as she sat on a protruding flagstone. 'You sit for a moment, Timber. Take in the view.'

'I'd rather look at you,' he mused, gazing at her fine plaits strung with cowries.

'There is Bore Brig with its tall Sentinel Stone. See the wide burn winding to it down in Harrar Vale?'

'Aye, and through the causeway's culverts. Can you make out the stone circle on the far right? See, Shala, on the ridge between two burns.'

'Yes, and there's the Seven Stones on that rise in the marsh. That's where scholars predict the tides from their House of the Moon in its centre,' Shala reminded him.

'That's right. And the winter sun hides behind Guman's Breasts then reappears, flooding the whole place with staggering light. It shines past Guman's Locket, her gift from Tuman after man first bred.'

'When I reach Skara, I feel my life-journey will only just begin, Timber. I will have so much to achieve,' she began, confiding everything in her heart. 'I'm glad you followed me now,' she concluded. 'But remember, you have to leave me before Skara. Can I trust you to do that?'

'Yes,' he answered, with bursting heart. 'I love you even more,' he so wanted to admit. 'I want to be close to her all my life. How can I bear this? But bear it I must,' he thought in a daze, screwing his blackthorn deeper within his nostril.

They sat silently. He watched mist drift over the huge oval earthwork behind the Ancestor House at Tannus, far below to the left. The small town on a knoll further in the vale lay quiet in the glow of beaming sunlight.

* * * * *

'Those are fork-tail terns,' Oiwa saw ahead. 'I've won my battle against death. They keep just ahead skimming the wave for fish. It has slackened some. I can ride the front of it and make wake down its face. The daylight is clear and up there, Solan's brethren fly, his many skeins guiding me daily.'

* * * * *

'Here's the bridge at last, Shala. There's the last folk crossing. It's amazing how tall the Sentinel is when you're standing by it. Its shadow crosses the flagstones, darkening the burn. Listen to it running under the heavy paving.'

'Yes. I feel the water rushing below. We'd better hurry past these houses. Soon this whole area will be filled with tide. Everyone's gathered on the other side, watching, waiting. Quick, let's run. Do you hear the Tannus hunting dogs baying? The folk there will see the water first as it rushes in, making them an island for a day. There are people waving from on top of their Ancestor House.'

'Yes. The Moon Henge and her Observatory will soon reflect in the flood when the sea gushes up the burn. Quick, Shala. It's coming. See the water raging?'

'Hurry,' called an onlooker. 'Come up here with us. You can see the whole land filling. Here come the geese, riding the swirling brine that sweeps over the marshes.'

'There it goes, hitting the stone causeway, Shala. What a sight. How it rushes through. It's built so well it doesn't wash away. Some say it will, one day. I don't think so. Look, here come the voles escaping from the flood. They are netting them. More folk are arriving from Market Ridge and from along Stone Road. They are catching voles, too. What a feast! I see barbeque fires up at the city. Huge, isn't it?'

'Yes, Timber, but I need to go. You can stay.'

'I'm not leaving you yet. Let's shift. Everyone's coming our way. Just smile benignly and walk on through the centre. The buildings inside are wonderful, especially the meeting house. The college is famous and so, too, the temples. The Chief's house is amazing, by all accounts. It should be: it's the centre of our civilization. Everyone's too busy to bother with us. It was the best time for you to come through.'

''Seems like it. Look, there are all the straw boats ready to launch to appease Waret. I wonder where they will end up, with their cargoes of straw animals?'

I smell the voles cooking now. We roast them on sticks at home.'

'Aye. The fur burns off and they only take moments after that. Smells, though, doesn't it. Yes, that's why they are best done outside.'

'More haste, less chat about the finer points of vole cuisine. Come on, Timber.'

'Here's the Stone Road. We go along it, below Market Ridge then past the recumbent flagstones. There's nothing happening up in the circle, anyway.'

'I feel as though I'm marching to destiny,' Shala thought passionately. 'I'm changing, altering inside. The noise of the geese on the waters is all engulfing. My visions return. I feel I'm being pulled to the horizon where the sun dips and rises again at midsummer, where the full moon kisses the ocean like a vast pearl. Where HE will come from,' she almost said aloud.

'See that distant hill, Timber? The one with the ancient pines?'

'Yes, Shala.'

'That is where the Sight Stone stands: it's within them, overlooking Skara,' she told him amid more honking geese landing on a loch to their left. 'You can come as far as that with me. No further. Can you see the red deer moving out from the copse? They sense us coming. The geese do, too. There are so many more now floating behind us over Tannus Vale.'

'This looks like an auroch path leading to the summit. Would it be the one taken at the end of the Far Folk's days? It might be.'

'Here we are at last, Timber. See how the stone leans, the edges polished by deer and auroch rubbing. The yellow lichen on top defies time. How it shines in the dipping sunlight. But down there is Skara. Ahead, the Great Dune awaits me. Look at the sea beyond.

That is my destination. I know it. You must go now,' she told him, watching skeins of geese fly out to sea, while others flew to meet them.

'So this is the Sight Stone,' Timber sighed, 'where the Winter Auk and the Auroch passed: where Gurnard and Vacar saw Skara vanish. The Sight Stone of Harrar's Top.' He drew in a long breath. 'That is your way, Shala. That, for now, is my way,' he added, pointing back to Bore Brig. 'Here,' he said, fiddling with his nose. 'This is now your blackthorn spike,' pressing it into Shala's hand.

He turned quickly on his heel and walked steadily, directly downhill to Stone Road.

57

On the Crest of a Wave

*O*iwa curled his toes in his boat, keeping his booted feet firmly forced on the bone frame. 'My paddling seems effortless,' he thought. 'Those oily sprats I caught were good. I felt like Gare as I swallowed them.

'Good, I've Fallow Burn water in Taiga's birdskin flask. There's land ahead. I sense it. That's Geese flying to me. They must have come from it.

'The wave has power to carry me, even though it's diminished. My Geese honk above, urging me: all kinds now, not just my Whale Goose brethren. I'll wave my paddle, beating it in friendship.

'Orcas, eagles of the sea, surf the wave, too. Are they guiding me? There's a great whale breeching. Have they been with me all the time? I hear them snort over the sound of the sea.

'Warm mountain breath follows, too, with its odorous, dusty wind. I can't see long-handed Krakens, thank Gumar: only dead, stinking, bits of them, still washing along.

'It's such fun riding this wave. I can do it without my paddle. Just lean this way and that and the Foam Fighter does as I wish. I can even tidy my beard and re-plait it. I'd like a fine knot in the end. The shells in it shine wonderfully.

'Now I'll pull back my parka hood. The wind feels good in my hair. I'll get my bear-tooth necklace out. I must polish my ivory ear spikes, too. I know I will see land soon. It's so thrilling after all this time.'

* * * * *

'There he goes: down the hill. I'm sorry for Timber, but he's gained my respect. Now I must make for the Great Dune. Geese are flying over it constantly. I've never seen the like. They go back and fore. Some land on the Tannus waters, then take off and return seawards. Great flocks of them rest on Skara Loch behind the dune. They make such a noise. But I've heard them like this in a dream. It is meant.

'I feel as though I'm walking into eternity as I descend Sight Hill. There's another to climb. Stone ridges, like giant's steps, go up it. Hares course over it as Geese still gaggle above the stunted, gale-blown trees. I'm certain hogs live there, too. I can smell them in the air, even though there's that dusty reek in the sky.

'Ever nearer the sea I go. The head of the Great Dune is closer. I feel like running water inside, as I follow this deer path to it. Stoor from that warm breeze has settled on the grass, turning it grey. It's all so strange.

'I wonder what Wrasse is doing and feeling right now? I feel her presence willing me onward. How alone she must have felt when her family rejected her. I'm so grateful she understands all that is going on. It gives me strength and will to go forward. How terrible Wrasse must have felt, too, finding Weir in that horrid state. This is my chance to amend all of that,' Shala thought, then worried, 'But have I imagined all of this. No! It's the Geese again. They are making such a noise. It sounds like a name they call. I can't make it out,' she thought as her bare toes touched the first sand of the Dune.

'This sea grass is rough against my straw skirt. The stunted willows bark my shins where deer simply step over them. There's the ocean. The sun glances down on it. Small islands break the surface of the sea: too small to make a home on, but the birds welcome them as a haven. The seals likely give birth there and sea otters certainly thrive on the tiny pimples. They all indicate fruitful fishing for man, beast and bird.

'I will pick my way along the Dune's spine. It slopes gradually to where Wrasse and I landed, what seems years ago. In fact it was just a matter of weeks. So much has changed for me. Is Wrasse dying? I do so hope no. Not yet, anyway. Her life seems to be fading from her, though her spirit is strong as an auroch skull. Wrasse preserved herself for her last journey. I feel so privileged to have been with her. I learned and understand so much more,' she pondered as the geese honked loudly below in the loch.

'They are making themselves into vast, arrow-shaped island on the water. There's a huge goose at the point. It leads them, paddling forward like a clan leader. It's honked once very loudly. His flocks become silent. He's trumpeting like a goat horn. They all beat their wings on the water and take flight. Up they go, away into the sky. Now they all turn and create a great fork. They circle and make for me. Why? I feel the wind from their fanning feathers: I smell their plumage. They call that name; the one I heard in the Vision of Shadows. I still can't make it out. Now they turn and fly seawards to the horizon. Others meet them. I will stay up here and watch.'

* * * * *

Oiwa looked up from his wave riding, his beard pointing out before him.

'The Goose calls are even louder. They honk and circle above. Now they swoop low and fly directly at me. Their wonderful feathery breeze fans me.

'No... No, no! It is. It's land. It's far off, but I'm nearly there. So close now to journey's end. There are two high hills. Like Gumar's breasts past some cliffs,' he made out later.

'To the south there are points of further peaks looking at me through the haze.

'Ride the wave. Ride the wave,' he yelled to himself. 'Glide across it. Turn, slew back. Watch the crest: land, land, land, I'm getting there. My heart beats so fast. There are wee islands with basking seals. Seabirds flock above and here come my Geese again. I must get my necklace out and let it shine, emblazoned on my chest.

'My Geese turn. They fly back landwards. Others follow from behind me. Paddle, Oiwa, Paddle with them.'

* * * * *

'I have never witnessed such a wondrous sight: all those geese and other birds crowding the air. Wrasse saw the like when Weir arrived. I know he's out there. The one I've dreamed of: he's somewhere on that sea. Even my redshanks fly past, twittering secretly. There they go. Down to the sand, just like when I was wee.

'Now, every goose from the flood has taken off. The sky is dark with them. They fly towards me then pass over as though heralding an approach.'

* * * * *

'My wave is breaking. I must get behind the crest now or be swamped. Turn, paddle; gain speed and *leap*. Phew! Done it. This billow's been my friend. Now it could be my murderer. It smashes over the rocky islets. It isn't taking me there.

'The sea is shallower here, so the wave breaks, foaming dangerously. Back here is safer, but at any moment that could change. I must jam my paddle in, turn the Foam Fighter against this tide and go back out to sea and slack water.

'Now I can spin her around,' he told himself later. 'I can see it break under that huge dune. It will lose power, but doubtless rush back. Be cautious.

'The Geese are calling. It has to be Solan. I want to shout back. But steady the boat, circle here and wait as the surf beats the dune.'

* * * * *

'That is a huge, tumbling wave out to sea! The foam spreads wide. I hear the rush of the surf. Is he out in that? He could sink and drown. This is terrible. Not what I'd imagined at all. Don't capsize. Keep safe. All I can do is wait here uselessly. Wait here and pray.

'But those geese still fly in a vast skein dipping low. I hear them chant. Their point has sped past something. A speck. A mere mark: it's *HIM!*' she shouted. 'It's him. I see his boat rising and falling. The geese call to him, urging him ashore.'

* * * * *

'I know that voice,' Oiwa exclaimed within, 'It is Solan! He calls from the head of his skein. He's calling my name, 'Oiwa, Oiwa, Oiwa,' he honks. They all do it in chorus now. This is wonderful. I'm elated. 'Oiwa, Oiwa, Oiwa,' they go. I will never ever forget this moment. My name is filling the sky as I paddle. Look, they fly to that dune, guiding me: follow, follow.

'The wave's last energy licks the dune. The water colours with sand as it washes back to meet me. I must turn Foam Fighter again to ride the billow out until it is starved of power. Then I can paddle ashore. Foam Fighter was well named by Taiga. How well she responds with the crests. Here it rushes. The sound is angry, but we will beat it. Up we go, rising with the buffeting billow. How it thumps as it passes under and we descend fast to the trough. The sand within sinks as the tumult slackens. I even heard the ocean bed below being scoured. My necklace bounces. My emblem hit my nose, but I'm okay. We survived that one. Now for the shore.'

* * * * *

'I'll go down to the burn,' Shala told herself, 'but the noise of that wave is overwhelming. It's power so great. I must run back up or be swept away. How it smashes the Dune in moments, taking swathes of tough grass with it. It is as though I'm on a great boat as the sea fills in the loch behind. It rushes up Auk's race, filling the loch with foaming tide, drowning the reedbeds in a swirling deluge. Now it pours, tearing away the toes of the Dune with a vengeance. The power of the sea is boundless. I only just escaped.

'Is he still afloat out there? That is my worry. No! He's gone. I don't believe it. The turbulence has taken him. He's lost. But never he is, I see the geese far out, dipping over a canoe. He's in it. Paddling proudly. He'd gone further out. Now he rides the middle of the spreading, foamy turbulence. He looks so confident.

'Now I hear that name the Geese call. The one Weir called him. It's OIWA, the call of the Geese: "Oiwa, Oiwa, Oiwa", I'm going to shout. He will hear: Louder, louder. "Oiwa, Oiwa, paddle well, land safely". "Oiwa", the Geese call back, repeating his name. I'll sing it with them.

'Now the redshanks are returning to the turmoil of churned sand on the beach. It takes me back to childhood. How far that seems. "Oiwa is coming. We told you. We told you. We said he'd be here," they pipe to me as they fly by. Yes, my friends, so he is.

'I want to run to the beach, but he rides another wave. I must stay on the Dune as it breaks, then slackens.'

'He's coming nearer, getting closer. We told you,' the redshanks called.

* * * * *

'Hold steady. Keep Foam Fighter right. Ride the wave. Scud the surf. We are going ashore,' Oiwa told himself after the crazy, turbulent ride. 'That warm wind backs me and there's a tentacle tip of a Longhands, just to remind me. Dive on it, gulls. Dive. Now the water is calm. It kisses the dune instead of tearing it. The worst is over. Redshanks fly by. They are calling my name. Even they know me. "She's waiting for you", they sing on their return.

'The wave's receding, taking me back, but it will return. Now I hear powerful wings beating behind me. It's swans. Their magnificent feathers sing in the breeze. "Paddle on with the new wave, Oiwa," they urge.

'They have flown behind the Dune. I follow. I feel myself being washed ashore gently, now the angry force is gone. That is my name again being called by my Geese. I hear Weir talking, urging me on. "I was nearly dead when I arrived. You are well, healthy and fit. Keep it that way. Have a wonderful life, Oiwa. Listen to nature calling your spirit. You have done it." I want to shout your name, Weir, but I can't. I will just beat my paddle on Foam Fighter for you, then stand holding it high.'

* * * * *

'My heart's stopped! I see him: he's paddle-waving in triumph. There's his beard pointing proudly in front. A great necklace shines on his chest. He's so strong. He's come so far, but he looks like he's only paddled from Tarmin. Now he's sitting, paddling fast in the foam to the shore. I'm going down to meet him, petrified though I am.'

* * * * *

'My Geese fly past the Dune, too. I follow them towards the cascade tumbling round the end. But someone has appeared. She's stepping from the grassy tumble. Greet her with a paddle whack. Do it, Oiwa. She's the first living soul I've seen since Taiga was wrenched from me.'

* * * * *

'He's beating his paddle again. I can't believe this. It isn't another dream? No. It is true. I want to shout, but I can't. I'm mute with emotion.'

* * * * *

'Let me show off. I'm going to snake in. Take my time. Make a twisting wake. But I feel I've seen her before. Is this another magical place of spirits? Her hands are over her mouth. She moves them. I see her face. It is she. She's waving, as though I was expected. Her fine red plaits fly in the breeze.'

* * * * *

'He's weaving closer. The outflow from the Dune slackens. It's safer. There's a great auk standing on the far side. It watches him; now me. It returns my gaze and clacks to more geese. The redshanks gather round it. That bird has a powerful spirit within. The geese fly by me and fan my hair with the wind.'

* * * * *

'He's following them towards me as I stand on the beach. He's watching me and waving. His face has a wonderful light. He moves like a bird with effortless motion, stroking the water as the skies call his name.

'He's standing again. His mouth moves to call. I hear nothing.

'I must shout as he waves his paddle high. But the geese drown my voice.'

* * * * *

'She's calling, I know, though I can't hear her over the tumult. Swans clap their wings on hidden waters. I still can't hear her.'

* * * * *

'I'm going to wade and greet him. He's so close. I can see his hazel eyes meeting mine. He's bumped the sand. A wave jerks him forward.'

* * * * *

'Now it is time: grip Foam Fighter's rope, brandish my paddle and jump out. It is my moment to wade ashore and meet this vision coming towards me,' he thought, not noticing a tiny, clinging squid releasing its suckers from his boot and jetting to freedom.

'Foam Fighter has washed in front of me between her and me. I see her green eyes staring into mine. I can't move, just twist my booted toes in the sand. I am elated again. My journey is done. Let me breathe this place in. Fill my lungs with its air and my eyes with her wonder. Weir's words run through me as I see her. I can hardly move. I hear my brothers, Buzzard, too. The sounds of those terrible arrows striking Rush; Gunnal's fearsome waters; Snaaaaar at the end, falling with my arrow in her guts after she slaughtered Tine; the bear fight; Taiga; the Island of the Dead. It is all summed up here, looking into those eyes.... There was a purpose.'

Shala pressed on the Foam Fighter's side, watching the salt in his eyebrows. 'I hear his breath panting after his exertion. His necklace rises up and down. He's pushing his boat from between us.'

'It is she who I saw in Gumar's great bowl after mating,' he realized as the tide washed between them. 'We stand before each other, she with a black spike in her ear, me with my ivory plugs. I will remove one and hand it to her.' Gare watched. The Geese flew silently.

Shala gazed into his hazel eyes as he handed her his walrus emblem. 'My name is Aiva,' she announced clearly. Her amulet glowed, swinging in the breeze, as Oiwa's hair flew forward.

'My name is Oiwa,' he exclaimed in his tongue. 'Oiwa! Oiwa! Oiwa!' he repeated, shouting in triumph as his shimmering bear-teeth rattled on his chest.

Start reading Skara ꟼꟼ...

...'We are joined,' he remarked, looking at his swinging agate tangled with her amber gem. 'I'll untie them,' he said, moving gently to do so.

'I understood that,' Aiva knew, as she gripped handfuls of sand. 'I'm going to sit and scrub his back with this as he fiddles with our amulets,' she thought. The sand stuck to his perspiration. She rubbed his weary muscles. 'Now for your chest,' Aiva suggested, as their pendants parted.

'That's splendid,' Oiwa thought as he leaned back, sitting on her shins. 'I give you two days to stop,' he said giggling.

'I didn't understand that, Oiwa' Aiva mentioned, looking confused. He tried to explain, then leaned back in delight, pointing to his stomach, nodding assent.

'I'll rub your Star, then,' she remarked, filling his navel with grits. They spilled, sticking to the blooded hairs that darkened his albatross tattoo as she massaged his tight abdomen.

'Now to bathe,' Aiva asserted, pushing him off. 'Come,' she indicated, taking his hand, making for the calming sea. There they swam, enjoying each other in the cool surf.

'I love the way the water runs from his beautiful beard, as he stands from the waves. His necklace looks so splendid. His broad grin shines from his face as his earplugs glisten in his lobes. I must keep him, even though he has to be shared,' were Aiva's inner thoughts.

'She is as lovely as Taiga,' Oiwa thought with a twinge, as he watched her. 'Maybe I will find she is more. I wonder where her people are? We seem alone. There's only the haze from our fire. No boat other than mine has crossed the sand. Even my Geese are quiet. Is this where Weir came ashore? I feel his spirit. I remember his voice from a dream, telling me.

'Here she comes: Her wet plaits dangling over her skin. How charming her breasts are. And that beautiful place where I have been. I so want us to couple again,' he thought as the ripples surrounded his tattooed shins.

'You must be so hungry, Oiwa.'

He looked confused.

'Hungry,' Aiva repeated, rubbing her stomach.

'H u n g r y.' Oiwa repeated the almost familiar word. 'Aye, I'm hungered: Most hungered,' he replied.

'I have food. Come to the fire. Get dry,' she said, taking his hand.

They gathered driftwood, feeling it scratch their skin, carrying it back in the light of the setting sun.

'Look at our long shadows,' Aiva remarked, remembering her vision.

'Like Weir?' Oiwa answered. 'I came from the sea with Gare. Our tall shadows formed. Gare's turned to Weir's and we spoke!' he rattled out.

'Weir?' Aiva challenged, dropping her wood, turning, gripping Oiwa's shoulders.

'Weir. Aye, Aiva. My ancestor,' he related again, thankful his voice had returned.

'I know of Weir. Wrasse does, too. All others called him "Sea Angel".'

'Wrasse?' Oiwa answered, dumbfounded, not understanding the rest. 'I have heard that name,' he told her slowly.

'Wrasse still lives,' she said, 'I'll take you to her,' she told him, gesturing. 'Now, come with the wood. We must eat. The air is chilling,' Aiva remarked with a shiver, watching goose pimples rise on Oiwa's arms.

By the fire they dressed and Aiva took her caisey. 'I have dried meat in here, cheese, nuts and fruit,' she mentioned, opening it. 'What?' she exclaimed. 'That's cake! Timber must have sneaked it in. How on earth did he do that?'

'"Cake?"' Oiwa queried.

'Yes, "cake", we call it. My mother baked it, a new recipe,' she said, breaking some off.

'I've never had anything like this before,' he thought. 'There's a bit of fruit and that's meat and fat of some sort. It tastes splendid. There are seeds in it, too. Well, this is grand. More?' he gestured.

'Here you are, Oiwa,' Aiva answered as the sun tipped below the horizon.

'Rush,' Oiwa said, pointing to the risen moon. 'He's behind it, watching. Soon I will tell you my whole story. I understand some of what you say, Aiva. It will just take time for me to learn. I am thrilled we have met. Why are you here when no one else is? Maybe you have a great tale, too,' he said, sitting, leaning on the Foam Fighter.

'I have been waiting for you for a long while, Oiwa,' Aiva said, resting her head on his shoulder. I have had dreams of you. Powerful visions. Even my Redshanks spoke of you. There they go along the sand, watching us. They watched us mate together. It will have made them happy,' she told him as a dozen flew right by, singing their high-pitched tunes.

'They told me of the floating forest we used to rebuild our homes after Kull's rage. Wrasse was buried, near drowned, when I found her. That is how we really met...', she told him, feeling his head droop. His breathing became steady and slow in his ever-deepening slumber, where dreams of Gumar, Weir and Gare continued. 'I'll quietly move and cover him with my ground leather. I'll make up the fire. We will keep warm now in this sheltered dip,' Aiva thought as she gently lay down beside him. As she kissed his cheek, a pair of geese flew low almost silently by.

Bibliography

Plants at The Edge: An amazing book on Arctic flora.

Arctic Clothing: This book shows the wonderful craft and artistry of clothing for survival and ritual in the Arctic.

Dawn of Civilisation: A great volume with aspects of life in the early stages of civilisation.

Many volumes of *Archaeologia Cantiana,* proceedings of the Kent Archaeological Society:

Symbols of Power: A wonderful book brought out by the National Museum of Scotland. It deals with the richness of symbolic artefacts of the time of Stonehenge.

Rising Tides: A book on Orkney's eroding shorelines showing the wonderful discoveries to be made and the irreparable damage to Orkney's archaeology.

Wilder Mann: This volume illustrates the costumes stretching back millennia that are still used in pagan rites today.

The Piercebridge Formula: Although discussing Roman waterways and canals, it has much relevance to earlier times.

The Brendan Voyage: The recreation of St Brendan's cow skin boat, in which it is thought he sailed to America.

Fauna and Flora of Canada: Invaluable information on Canadian plants and animals.

The Bog People: This is by archaeologist Peter Glob. It deals with prehistoric preserved people from Danish bogs.

And so many other books, too numerous to mention.

Biographical Note

Born 1948 in Kent, Andrew Appleby became an independent wanderer from an early age. The youngest of three brothers, he constantly lagged behind – and still does, even now, on a walk – finding clay in banks and around ponds, or searching the ground for ancient artifacts. His natural tendency towards incendiary pursuits helped fire his meagre works from the age of seven, and at eleven he was smitten with the archaeology bug. This led to discovering a Neolithic site with quantities of prehistoric pottery... his yearning to make these pots was born.

He spent most of his secondary school years in the pottery department. His father, James William Appleby, had relayed tales of Orkney in the army intelligence service during World War Two, so Andrew and his brother Malcolm hitch-hiked there from Kent. The archaeology, scenery, atmosphere and colours had a permanent effect and he next moved to the Isles permanently, setting up his pottery in an old chicken house at Fursbreck Farm in Harray. From his first weeks in residence, folk said, 'You must go and see the Harray Potter! He's just magic!', hence its trading name.

Past Chair and Vice-Chair of the Orkney Archaeology Society, Andrew has seen Orkney's archaeology scene blossom. He is currently President of the John Rae Society, the Orcadian Arctic explorer.

Besides pottery, archaeology and exploration, Andrew has a strong interest in gathering food and road kill. This has led to appearances in television programmes such as *Scotland's Larder*.

Burgess
Publishing

Map of Oiwa's Journey

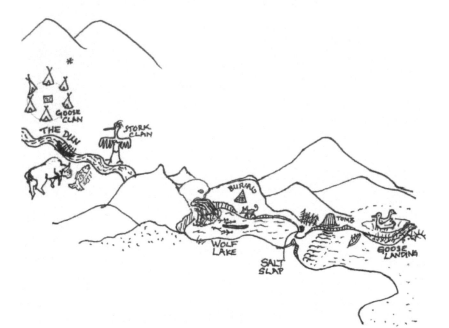

Map of Oiwa's Journey

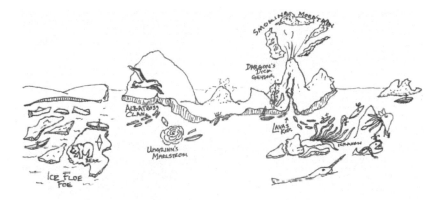

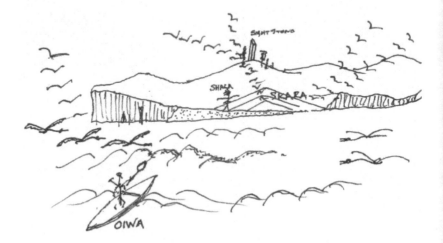

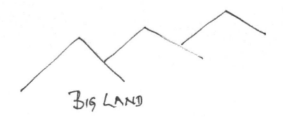